WESTERN LOVING

**It's the best loving around—
but it doesn't come easy!**

Clint's a horse trainer with a past.
He's gambling on the future.

Cole. He's a rancher and a widower with
a young son. He doesn't trust lightly.

Boyd comes from old money, but he's a
working cowboy. He doesn't have time for love.

WESTERN LOVING

They're ranchers, horse trainers, cowboys....
They're willing to risk their lives.
But are they willing to risk their hearts?

Relive the romance ...

Three complete novels by your favorite authors!

About the Authors

JoAnn Ross—Author of forty-two novels, JoAnn wrote her first story—a romance about two star-crossed mallard ducks—when she was seven years old. Now, she has more than eight million books in print and has been published in seventeen countries, including China, Hungary and Turkey. JoAnn married her high school sweetheart—twice—and makes her home near Phoenix, Arizona.

Susan Fox—This popular author's enjoyment of reading romances led to her writing them, and her books reflect her enduring interest in Westerns and cowboys. Susan's latest novel, *The Bad Penny,* was published in June 1993.

Barbara Kaye—Well-known author of over fifteen novels, Barbara's writing career actually began at age twelve, when she took it upon herself to write a weekly newsletter for her father's employees. Her latest project is the Crystal Creek series—she's written the launch title as well as two others! Barbara lives in Oklahoma with her retired air-force-colonel husband.

WESTERN LOVING

JoANN ROSS
SUSAN FOX
BARBARA KAYE

Harlequin Books

TORONTO • NEW YORK • LONDON
AMSTERDAM • PARIS • SYDNEY • HAMBURG
STOCKHOLM • ATHENS • TOKYO • MILAN
MADRID • WARSAW • BUDAPEST • AUCKLAND

HARLEQUIN BOOKS

by Request—Western Loving

Copyright © 1994 by Harlequin Enterprises B.V.

ISBN 0-373-20097-8

The publisher acknowledges the copyright holders of the individual works as follows:
RISKY PLEASURE
Copyright © 1985 by JoAnn Ross
VOWS OF THE HEART
Copyright © 1986 by Susan Fox
BY SPECIAL REQUEST
Copyright © 1987 by Barbara K. Walker

This edition published by arrangement with Harlequin Enterprises B.V.

® and TM are trademarks of the publisher. Trademarks indicated with ® are registered in the United States Patent and Trademark Office, the Canadian Trade Marks Office and in other countries.

Printed in U.S.A.

CONTENTS

"There were several things Clint Hollister would have liked to do with the beautiful new owner of Clearwater Hill Farm.

But training racehorses sure as hell wasn't one of them!"

RISKY PLEASURE

JoAnn Ross

To my niece,
Barbara Elliott, with love,
and to Star Helmer,
whose idea it was to bring Brandy and Ryan's
book to life.

Chapter One

Jason Langley was dead.

The thought struck as harshly as the intense California sun flooding Clint Hollister's bedroom. Seconds later, the dull throbbing in his head reminded him of last night. At least he'd sent the old man off in style. Squeezing his eyes shut against the blinding morning light, Clint reached out, unerringly locating the glass of bourbon resting on the bedside table. He propped himself up on one elbow and downed the fiery liquor in long, thirsty swallows.

Clint's mouth felt as if Patton's entire army had marched through it on the way to liberate Paris. Today was going to be rough enough without his having to face it with the granddaddy of all hangovers.

The ringing of the phone shattered his bleak thoughts, and he dispensed with amenities as he growled "Yeah?" into the mouthpiece.

"Hollister?" The cultured male voice on the other end displayed a moment of confusion.

Clint groaned. *When it rains, it pours.* "It's me, Blackwood," he confirmed. "What do you want now?"

"I was calling to remind you of the reading of the will this morning. You are planning to attend, aren't you?"

Clint shook his head, regretting the motion as rocks tumbled about in his brain. He flung away the sheet and swung his legs to the floor, slumping on the edge of the mattress.

"Look," he suggested, "why don't you just call me this afternoon and give me a rundown? After all, the whole deal is pretty cut-and-dried. Blair MacKenzie is the old man's only living relative. So she inherits the ranch, sells it to the highest bidder, and goes back to New York City, where she belongs."

He bent down, groping for the crumpled pack of cigarettes on the floor. He pulled out a cigarette and tapped it absently on the bedside table before sticking it between tightly set lips.

"That's a tidy little scenario you're painting, Hollister," Ramsey Blackwood allowed. "But you may be in for a surprise."

Clint lit the cigarette, inhaling the smoke deep into his lungs, willing his mind and body to forgive last night's abuse and come to life.

"No way. Jason left Clearwater Hills Farm to his granddaughter, and she's the last person in the world who'd want to hang around a horse farm."

"You seem very certain of that."

"I should be. I was with him last month when he turned down an offer to sell the place. He said he was paying off some old debts by leaving the place to our exotic Ms. Tigress Perfume . . . although what a woman like that would want with a horse farm is beyond me."

"Jason built a very profitable stable."

"It's only profitable if the owner knows what he's doing," Clint muttered. "If by any stretch of the imagination the woman did decide to stay on, she'd run the place into the ground in six months."

Jason Langley's attorney refrained from answering that accusation. "You *will* be here, won't you, Hollister? After all, you are the trainer for Clearwater Hills Farm. The old man specifically requested that you attend."

If he hadn't had enough trouble lately, Clint considered bleakly, now he was expected to spend an afternoon with Ramsey Blackwood and an empty-headed model who was about to destroy everything he'd worked for. Just what he

needed. Clint couldn't remember the last time he'd ever refused the cantankerous old man anything. Lord knew, he
was probably the closest thing to a friend that Jason Langley had ever had. But this was above and beyond the call of
friendship.

"I've still got to pack."

"You're not staying on?"

Clint ground the cigarette out in an ashtray overflowing
with butts. "Hell, no. I've worked too hard building this
place up to watch some underdressed female flush it down
the tubes."

Dispensing with politeness, he hung up the phone and
made his way into the bathroom for a well-needed shower.
He wondered idly how much Tigress perfume Jason's cover-
girl granddaughter would have to wear to overcome his
aroma of stale sweat, bourbon and cigarette smoke.

BLAIR MACKENZIE SAT ALONE in the backseat of the gray
Mercedes, lost in thought. She was vaguely aware of Marni's flirtatious chatter, designed to charm Jason Langley's
attorney, but the words were only a dull buzz in her ears.
Her gaze was directed out the tinted window, her tawny
brown eyes drinking in the vastness of the rolling grasslands. Blair was unable to believe the whole place was hers
now. She felt like pinching herself. A lifetime dream had
suddenly been dumped in her lap.

She hadn't wanted to come to the farm today; she still
didn't know why she just hadn't ignored the cable in the first
place. Blair assured herself that it had been curiosity and not
any sense of misplaced responsibility that had caused her to
arrive at Clearwater Hills Farm four days after her grandfather's heart attack. The man meant nothing to her. He'd
never seen fit to acknowledge her existence while he was
alive, and Blair was damned if she would get all misty-eyed
and pretend that she cared about his passing.

She would admit to feeling a tinge of guilt for having
wanted to dance a jig when Ramsey Blackwood had informed her that she'd inherited the farm. After all, no mat-

ter how she felt about Jason Langley personally, he *had* just died; she had no business feeling as if Christmas had arrived nine months early.

That thought brought up one nagging little problem. Clint Hollister. Her entire future lay in the hands of a man she'd never met. Blair sighed, hoping he wouldn't prove difficult. She glanced over at the rearview mirror and saw the dazed look in Ramsey Blackwood's eyes as the attorney fell predictably under Marni's seductive spell. Perhaps she should just let Marni propose the idea to Mr. Hollister, Blair mused. There wasn't a man alive who could remain impervious to her best friend's charms for very long.

As enticing an idea as that was, Blair knew she could never do it. She'd been fighting her own battles all her life, and she wasn't about to back down now. Besides, she might be borrowing trouble. There was no reason to believe that Clint Hollister wouldn't jump at her offer. Especially when she was dangling such sweet bait.

The man Blair was thinking about cursed under his breath as he viewed the cloud of dust billowing up from the road. Moments later the gunmetal gray Mercedes pulled up to a stop in front of the sprawling ranch house.

"Here, Jerry, you'd better take over," Clint said, handing the bucket of springwater laced with baby oil to the young groom standing beside him. He patted the chestnut filly's neck. "Unless my luck has changed, your new owner has just shown up," he muttered to the horse with a frustrated sigh.

Ramsey Blackwood emerged from the driver's seat of the Mercedes, his navy blue suit looking out of place in the rural surroundings. The two women also exited from the car. All three watched Clint cross the expanse of gravel to meet them.

"We missed you," the attorney began without preamble. Clint had been acquainted with Ramsey Blackwood long enough to know it was only the presence of the women that kept the man from professing his irritation in more graphic terms.

"I was busy."

"So I see. Isn't it a waste of the farm's expenses to have the trainer bathe a horse?"

"I would suppose that's up to the new owner to decide," Clint countered brusquely, his gaze moving to the two women.

He had to force himself not to stare at the lithe brunette standing next to the car. This was the Tigress perfume woman? No way. He'd checked out the advertisement again that morning, not that he didn't have the wildly erotic vision emblazoned on every memory cell of his brain.

The ad had shown her skimpily clad in a tiger-striped bikini, lounging beside a jungle pool, her parted lips moist, the open sexual invitation gleaming in her hooded, golden-brown eyes. Masses of thick dark hair had tumbled over bare shoulders, arranged in what he knew to be an exacting portrayal of casual disarray. She was the type of woman every man fantasized getting into his bed.

This woman was an impostor. Her dark hair was tucked demurely into a navy fedora. Her matching suit was relieved only by a simple white silk blouse and a triangle of crimson tucked into the breast pocket of the tailored navy jacket. Safely hidden behind his dark aviator glasses, Clint's eyes traveled down the long, slender legs, clad in dark stockings, to her pumps. If it hadn't been for those unforgettable legs, he'd have thought this woman was an associate of Ramsey's. She certainly resembled an attorney more than she did one of America's most popular models.

He forced himself to look at her companion and recognized her immediately. Long blond hair fell over deeply tanned bare, shoulders. Her body was poured into a strapless camisole and white designer jeans that looked as if they'd been spray-painted on her. Marni Roberts's face and figure were every bit as celebrated as Blair MacKenzie's, yet Clint noticed with detached interest that even though Marni was dressed in that revealing outfit, she didn't affect him with the same jolt as the Tigress Woman did. He turned his gaze back to the new owner of Clearwater Hills Farm.

As his eyes locked onto her face, Blair MacKenzie felt her breath catch in her throat. She couldn't remember ever having seen a more rawly masculine man. The effect he had on her went beyond his looks—although his thick silver hair, wide shoulders and broad chest were definitely impressive. The sleeves of his blue work shirt were rolled above his elbows, and his wet denim jeans clung to long, well-muscled legs.

His eyes were shielded by dark lenses, and Blair found herself guessing their color. A very good-looking man, she acknowledged, but in her business she knew plenty of good-looking men.

No, what this man possessed was an impression of explosive strength that boded ill for anyone who might be foolish enough to cross him. "Dangerous"—that was the only word that came to mind.

Blair nervously shifted her gaze to the rawboned chestnut horse that had surprised skeptics by sweeping the New York Racing Association's Triple Crown for fillies. "She's magnificent."

Clint took a cigarette pack from his shirt pocket, ignoring Ramsey's irritated expression as he tapped the cigarette on the roof of the car.

"I've heard a lot of descriptions of Risky Pleasure over the past three years, but that's a new one." Clint knew that most people saw only the filly's admittedly less-than-noble frame at first glance.

"I saw her run last year at the Meadowlands. Except 'run' is a poor choice of words. She flew. It was the most magnificent thing I've ever seen!"

Clint fought down the pleasure that Blair's softly issued words brought him. Shrugging with feigned disinterest, he forced his voice into a short, gruff tone as he said, "Well, she's all yours now."

"Not exactly," the dapper attorney broke in. "That's why I wanted you at my office today, Hollister. Jason Langley left Clearwater Hills Farm and all its inventory to his only living heir, Ms. MacKenzie . . . with the exception of Risky Pleasure. You both share a fifty percent interest in the filly."

"What? Jason never mentioned anything about that!"

Ramsey Blackwood cleared his throat, his pale blue eyes moving significantly from Clint to Blair and back again. His expression was definitely superior. "It isn't necessary for someone to disclose his final wishes, Hollister—especially to a hired hand."

Blair noticed that the younger man curled his hand into a fist, and she realized there was no love lost between the two. The attorney's attitude had been distinctly condescending, but after the way Clint had glared at her, she had little sympathy for him.

Ramsey cleared his throat again. "I believe I've been remiss in my duties. Ms. MacKenzie, Ms. Roberts, may I introduce Clearwater Hills Farm's manager and head trainer, Clint Hollister. Hollister, this is Jason's long-lost granddaughter, Blair MacKenzie, and her friend, Marni Roberts."

Accustomed to male scrutiny as she was, Blair was inexplicably unnerved by Clint Hollister's silent study. She nodded politely, holding out her hand. "Mr. Hollister, it's an honor to meet you. Your name is a legend in racing circles, but of course you know that already."

Clint ignored Blair's extended hand. Instead, he pulled off his sunglasses, meeting her friendly gaze with a bland look of his own. "Your reputation precedes you, too, Ms. MacKenzie. In fact, you're far from long-lost. It's impossible to pick up a magazine or turn on the television these days without seeing the Tigress Woman."

Gray, Blair considered silently, even as she fought to control her quicksilver temper at the accusing innuendo in his tone. His eyes were a rich, lustrous pewter. She forced a light laugh, dropping her hand back to her side.

"I've also portrayed a lady executive demonstrating the advantages of a computer in the marketplace. Why doesn't anyone ever remember that campaign?"

Clint's hangover made him more reckless and far more uncaring of her feelings than he otherwise might have been. "Simple," he drawled insolently. "If you want a man to concentrate on your mind, Ms. MacKenzie, you shouldn't drape yourself all over billboards in outfits that call out to his primitive instincts."

His tone flailed like a well-aimed whip. Blair stood up a little straighter, prepared to take on this male chauvinist who'd never understand how much she would have given to change places with him. Even to working with Jason Langley.

Blair had long ago decided that for Clint Hollister to have worked with her grandfather all those years, he would have had to be either a saint or every bit as cold and unfeeling as his employer. After years of speculation, the puzzle was finally solved. This man leaning against the fender of the gray Mercedes was definitely no saint.

"Well, *I* cetainly don't mind a man remembering me for my body," Marni Roberts offered, her blue eyes bright with interest. "Hello, Clint. Blair goes on and on about you all the time." Clint was not allowed to dwell on those surprising words as Marni's thick lashes fluttered exaggeratedly. "It's a pleasure to meet you…up close and personal, as they say."

Blair could cheerfully have strangled Marni for giving Clint Hollister that little bit of information. The man already had the advantage; there was no point in helping him stack the deck. Her mind went into high gear, trying to come up with a casual explanation.

"Now that the necessary introductions are over," Ramsey intervened smoothly, "I believe Ms. MacKenzie has an offer to make to you, Hollister."

Clint felt a fist twisting his stomach and knew it was more than a reaction to last night's binge. Blair's next words confirmed his gut reaction.

"I'm hoping you'll agree to stay on at Clearwater Hills Farm as trainer, Mr. Hollister."

"I'm afraid that's out of the question."

She arched a delicate eyebrow. "Oh? Won't you work with a woman?"

She said "with" and not "for", he noticed with some interest. It crossed Clint's mind that there were several things he'd like to do with the Tigress Woman. But training racehorses sure as hell wasn't one of them.

"I don't work with amateurs who consider owning a stable of racehorses a lark, along the lines of a skiing weekend at St. Moritz."

It took all of Blair's inner strength not to flinch at his gritty, censorious tone. She forced herself to appear coolly self-assured, relying on skills honed during long hours playing poker with the crew while on location. Blair MacKenzie never folded her hand this easily; she could bluff with the best of them.

"I can understand your reservations, Mr. Hollister. Suppose I assure you that I take the entire enterprise more seriously than I've taken anything in my life?"

He almost laughed at that one. What did this pampered creature know about serious enterprises? He leaned toward her, jamming his hands into the back pockets of his jeans.

"Look, lady, I'm one of the few trainers on the circuit who doesn't have an ulcer, and I don't intend to get one by having to listen to inane remarks from a woman whose only claim to fame is that she fills a bikini admirably."

Marni gasped, but Blair reminded herself that at this moment she needed Clint Hollister more than he needed her. Fortunately, her grandfather had left her one ace.

Clint unwillingly gave the woman points for composure. Only a fleeting flash of fire in those tawny brown eyes hinted at her anger.

"I see. And what do you suggest we do with Risky Pleasure?"

"Since she's half mine, I'll continue to train her."

Blair smiled sweetly, laying all her cards on the table. "I'm relieved to hear that because it would be difficult to find a trainer with your skills at this late date in the season.

And of course, since she's half mine, she'll be stabled at Clearwater Hills Farm.''

Blair paused, then folded her arms across her breasts, vowing not to falter as she watched the pewter gray of his eyes turn to cold steel. She only hoped she wasn't overplaying her hand.

"And since you'll be training Risky Pleasure," she continued silkily, "it shouldn't be that much of a burden to work once in a while with the other horses, should it?"

Damn her! Clint dragged his gaze out across the rolling grass fields ablaze with poppies and blue lupine. She'd boxed him into a very neat corner without a blink of those dark sable lashes. He recognized the technique, having seen it in action over the years. Jason Langley had been a master at the art of manipulation, so why should Clint be surprised that the old man's granddaughter seemed to have inherited the trait? Stifling a deep sigh, Clint realized he was probably about to make the worst mistake of his career.

He turned his attention back to Blair, who appeared irritatingly calm as she awaited his answer. "You really are Jason Langley's granddaughter, aren't you?" he muttered.

"So I've been told."

"I expected you to sell," he admitted.

"Ms. MacKenzie refused that suggestion immediately." While the attorney's expression gave nothing away, his clipped tones could not hide his displeasure.

"Do you actually believe you can run a racing stable without any experience?" Clint asked her.

"I've more experience than you realize, Mr. Hollister. And yes, I believe I can, with your help. After all, we both want what's best for Risky Pleasure, don't we?" she coaxed, her level gaze holding his without the slightest hint of feminine guile.

Clint folded his hand, deciding that the booze from last night must have killed every brain cell he possessed. Even attempting to work with this woman would be pure folly. Still, if that was what it would take to fulfill his plans for Risky Pleasure, he'd forge a partnership with the devil.

Blair watched Clint make his decision. She'd been waiting her entire life for the chance to work with a filly like Risky Pleasure; at this point she'd agree to sign the devil on as trainer. She put out her hand once again. "Do we have a deal?"

This time Clint couldn't refuse taking her slender hand in his. He tried not to notice how smooth her skin was or how she trembled slightly at his touch. "Just for this season," he warned. "Then we're going to have to work out a compromise concerning Risky Pleasure."

Ramsey entered the conversation. "There's always the possibility of selling the filly," he said, a hopeful ring to his voice.

"Never!"

"Not on your life!"

Blair and Clint both spoke at the same time, rejecting the attorney's suggestion instantly. They exchanged a long, appraising look.

"I suppose you want the grand tour," Clint said. It was more a reluctant statement of fact than an invitation.

"I'd love it," she agreed, her face lighting up with the first real smile she'd granted him. Clint stared, momentarily bemused by the brilliance of that smile.

"Can't we get unpacked first?" Marni complained crankily. "My clothes have been smothered in these suitcases for hours, Blair."

Blair knew that her roommate had no real interest in Clearwater Hills Farm. Marni had come along in search of greener pastures, but horses had nothing to do with it. Suffering from a disastrous end to a longtime affair, she had been uncharacteristically depressed lately. Blair had suggested that California might be a nice change for her, and from the way Marni's wide blue eyes had lit up at the sight of two eligible men in just a few short hours, Blair realized she was on the road to recovery.

"I suppose that's a good idea," Blair said with a definite lack of enthusiasm.

"Why don't I help Ms. Roberts get settled in?" Ramsey suggested smoothly. "And Hollister can show you around the farm."

Blair's questioning gaze moved to Marni, who nodded. "That's a marvelous idea," she agreed, slipping her hand through the attorney's arm. "And please, call me Marni. I have the feeling we're going to be very good friends."

Blair shook her head with resignation as she watched the two leave, hoping Marni wasn't jumping right out of the frying pan into the fire.

"Your friend doesn't waste any time," Clint offered with an extra dose of scorn.

"We all have to get over pain in our own way, Mr. Hollister."

The pounding in his head reminded him once again of last night, and although he agreed with her observation, he didn't respond to it.

"I can't take off all day," he said firmly. "There's a lot to be done around a farm, Ms. MacKenzie. It's a little different from lying around on bearskin rugs all day."

"Tiger skin," she murmured.

He arched a brow, inviting elaboration.

"The rug is tiger skin. But the bikini is one hundred percent polyester."

"Fascinating," Clint drawled sarcastically. "I can't wait to see the Tigress perfume woman mucking out a stall. We could probably sell tickets and pay the feed bill for an entire year."

Blair felt her inner tension building. "You know, Mr. Hollister, I'm going to love watching you eat those words."

"Don't hold your breath."

Despite his gritty tone, Blair experienced a rush of anticipation at his challenge. Over the years she'd proved to more than one doubting male that she was hardly an empty-headed Barbie doll. But she couldn't recall any apology for impulsive typecasting that she had savored as much as she would Clint Hollister's.

This will never work, Clint told himself as they headed toward the training barns. *Never in a million years.* The voluptuous scent of Tigress perfume filled his nostrils, and he allowed himself a brief fantasy as he imagined Blair MacKenzie's proper navy suit giving way to a tiger-skin bikini. *You're a fool even to try it,* he warned himself one last time.

This will never work, Blair told herself. In their brief acquaintance, the man had shown himself to be cold, opinionated and obviously a class A chauvinist. *You're a fool even to try it.*

THE AIR IN THE OFFICE overlooking San Diego Bay was rife with tension. The ashtray on the desk was filled with red-tipped cigarette filters, and the woman seated behind the expanse of mahogany had been tapping her fingernails impatiently on the polished surface for the last half hour.

"Well?" she asked finally. "When will we know?"

The question had been directed at the tall man gazing unseeingly out the window at the merchant ships in the harbor. "Hollister's with the MacKenzie woman now. He's supposed to call me as soon as things are settled."

"Here? Is that wise?"

"The call's being forwarded so no one will be the wiser."

"Good. I wouldn't want to take any unnecessary risks at this late date."

"I told you not to worry. It's going to be a piece of cake."

The woman lit yet another cigarette. "I hope you're right."

"I have been so far, haven't I?"

"You have," she allowed, eyeing the tense stance of the man at the window. "But don't forget, without Clearwater Hills Farm, everything we've accomplished will go right down the drain.

The man spun around, shooting a furious glare across the room. "You'll have the damn farm!"

"I hope so," she said smoothly. "Because if you end up blowing things, you'll be the one facing a homicide charge."

"I told you, it was an accident!"

She viewed him through a thin veil of blue smoke. "And such a fortuitous accident it was, darling," she purred. "I just hope you never have to convince the police of that."

The shared acrimony became a living, breathing thing, swirling about the two participants to the highly charged moment, as each tried to stare the other down. Finally, a silent truce was forged. The man threw himself into a chair, and they both returned their attention to the damnably silent telephone.

Chapter Two

Clint's head was throbbing with an unholy pain as he walked with Blair across the paddock. Already regretting his decision, he wasn't in the mood for small talk.

Blair finally broke the heavy silence. "I know you hate me, Mr. Hollister, but we are stuck with each other, whether we like it or not."

"What makes you think I hate you?" Clint glanced over at her, but she was suddenly pretending an avid interest in the rows of black Kentucky-style fences.

"Because of the will, of course," she murmured.

"The will?"

"After all, you're the one who made Clearwater Hills Farm what it is."

"Your grandfather's money is what built this farm," he corrected her brusquely. "So by rights it's yours, Ms. MacKenzie, even if you never did care enough to come home while the old man was alive."

"A lot you know about my family," she shot back.

"I know that you're just as stubborn and self-centered as your mother."

That was a low blow, even from a man who had yet to show her an ounce of welcome. Blair stiffened. "Don't you ever dare to talk that way about my mother again," she retorted in a blaze of anger, "or I'll...I'll..."

"You'll what?" he inquired dryly. "Dock my wages?"

Her tawny eyes were as hard as agates. "Just don't make cracks about a woman you never even knew."

He shrugged. "I know enough."

"Then you know that Jason Langley was a horrid man who forced his daughter to leave home so she could be with the man she loved." Blair's tone was cold with resentment.

"I know Jason didn't believe that marriage would be right for them. She was the lady of the manor, don't forget, and David MacKenzie was nothing but a hired hand. Jason was only thinking of her own good."

"Oh, he thought a great deal of her," Blair spat out sarcastically. "So much so that when I sent him a telegram informing him she had died, his only response was an expensive funeral wreath. Without any card, Mr. Hollister," Blair tacked on pointedly.

"If you're so down on the guy, why did you bother to show up today? As if I couldn't figure it out for myself."

"I've been asking myself the same question for the past two days," she admitted.

"And?"

"Curiosity," she said after a thoughtful pause. "The stables are legendary, and I guess I wanted to see everything just once. Never in my wildest imaginings did I expect to inherit the farm. It's still difficult for me to believe I own fifty percent of the best filly that's racing today."

"She's the best horse, period."

"I agree with you. But you'll never really prove that, will you?"

Clint didn't answer, feeling that this was not the time to bring up his plans for Risky Pleasure. "Your grandfather didn't want me to buy her," he said instead. "We had one helluva argument when I came home with that big-boned filly."

"My mother said he was a cruel man." Blair waited for Clint to deny the obvious question in her voice.

He only shrugged. "I can't comment on that. He was never cruel to me."

"Then you always got along with him?"

Clint exploded into harsh, unrestrained laughter. "Hell, nobody *always* got along with Jason Langley! I figured that if we had fewer than fifty arguments during a twenty-four-hour period, we were having a good day."

"Yet you stayed, when you could have worked anywhere in the world."

He nodded, his laughter stopping as abruptly as it had begun. "Yeah, I stayed."

They fell silent, and Blair looked out at the rolling hillsides abloom with fragrant color. "It's absolutely beautiful," she murmured.

"It's colorful now," he told her, "but we had a dry winter. All that color will be brown in another month."

"It'll still be lovely. I'll admit I was surprised to see so much commercial development on the drive up here from San Diego. Whoever's in charge of zoning around these parts should be horsewhipped."

That earned a laugh, and Blair fought against the way her body responded to the deep, rumbling sound.

"Yep, you are definitely Jason's granddaughter. He's been hollering about the encroaching development for the past five years."

Blair didn't miss Clint's use of the present tense when he talked about her grandfather. "You and my grandfather must have been very close."

Clint's hands tightened into fists as he reminded himself that Jason was indeed gone. He wondered how long he'd suffer this empty feeling.

"I suppose we were. As close as anyone could be to Jason Langley, anyway. He wasn't an easy man to get to know."

They reached the smaller of the two training barns. Blair inhaled the sweet, fragrant scent of hay and thought how different all this was from her apartment in Manhattan.

"We don't live a jet-set existence out here," Clint stated, as if reading her mind.

There it was again. Blair was growing extremely tired of Clint Hollister's typecasting. "I don't live a jet-set existence in New York, either."

He slanted her a disbelieving glance. "Oh, no? Swimsuit layouts in the Carribean, designer fashions in Paris, Tigress perfume ads at the Taj Mahal and in Sri Lanka—that's what you call laid back?"

"It's harder than it looks," she defended herself. "Besides, I'm not as young as I used to be. I can't be out late at night and still look presentable for a morning shoot."

She neglected to tell him that she was usually up at dawn, working at Aqueduct for Ben Winters, a trainer almost as renowned as Clint Hollister and who paid her the minimum wage. Clint would never believe it anyway. Not until she'd proved to him that she knew her way around.

"Yeah, you're absolutely ancient. Let's see, according to Jason, your mother ran off with David MacKenzie the year Moonglow won the Belmont Stakes. And you were born—"

"Six months later," Blair finished abruptly. "So not only do you know that I'll be thirty on my next birthday, but you also know that I'm what is euphemistically referred to as a 'love child.'"

He glanced over at her, unreasonably disturbed by the paling of her complexion. He wasn't usually so rough on women. Especially not on women who were capable of stimulating lustful fantasies.

"Did they?"

"Did they what?"

"Love each other?"

Her expression softened, her eyes gleaming with golden lights that had Clint thrusting his hands into his pockets. He suddenly wanted to yank that ridiculous hat off her head and let loose the Tigress Woman's flowing mane of dark chestnut hair.

"Immensely. I think that's why Mom had her heart attack six months after Daddy's accident. After twenty-five years, she didn't want to live without him."

"That's rare—a marriage lasting that long in this day and age."

Blair couldn't miss the edge to Clint's voice. "Are you married?" she asked suddenly.

His expression grew inscrutable, only the cold glitter in his gray eyes revealing any emotion. "Do I look like a married man?"

Blair turned toward him, one pink fingernail tapping on a white front tooth as she submitted him to a prolonged study. His hair was obviously prematurely gray, but it was no run-of-the-mill salt-and-pepper. Instead, it was a lush, gleaming silver. His forehead was broad and deeply tanned; his eyebrows, in a disconcerting contrast to his hair, were dark. They framed eyes that were a rich pewter gray, but she'd seen them turn just as quickly to cold steel. At the moment they held a challenging glint.

His nose was aquiline, as unforgivably sharp as a well-honed Toledo blade, directing her gaze down to his full masculine lips. His jaw was broad, and so far, she'd seen that well-cut chin directed her way far too many times already.

"Well?"

Because of his tenseness and the fact that she assumed he was in his late thirties, Blair ventured an educated guess. "You were married when you were younger. But it didn't work out."

A muscle jerked in his harsh jawline, and Blair considered once again that this man represented more danger than she'd ever faced living in New York City.

"Very good," he grated out. "What else did your crystal ball tell you about me?"

Unable to determine what she'd said wrong now, Blair decided to opt for humor and play along. "Oh, everything," she replied blithely. "Madame Tigress's crystal ball sees all, knows all. Cross my palm with silver, and we shall look far back into the murky shadows of your past," she droned in a deep, melodramatic accent.

"What the hell." He dug into a front pocket, extracting a handful of coins. Blair tried not to be affected by the way the gesture pulled the material tight against his thighs. "Here you go, Madame Tigress. Now what do you see?"

She pressed her fingertips against her temples, closing her eyes for effect. "I see a handsome young man...moderately handsome...at least not ugly enough to make babies cry," she tacked on wickedly as she caught his self-assured look through her lowered lashes.

"I preferred the 'handsome' before you added the qualifiers. So what else does the famed Madame Tigress see?"

"I see horses. Many horses. And a woman. A lovely, lonely woman who resents playing second fiddle to a stable of Thoroughbreds." It was a shot in the dark, but it was obvious she'd hit the bull's-eye.

"I think we've played this game long enough," Clint said abruptly, turning toward the door of the barn.

"I'm sorry," she said softly. "I'm divorced myself, so I know how long it can take to get over something like that."

She could also understand why the man wasn't eager to discuss his ill-fated marriage. Her own, which she'd entered into with high hopes, was certainly not her favorite topic of conversation. She'd married Keith Taylor when she was a young model just starting out and he was a struggling photographer. After her career had taken off like a sky-rocket, Keith had given up his work to act as her manager and agent.

The only problem, she thought back sadly, was that Keith had lacked self-confidence. In order to show the world that it was he, not Blair, who was responsible for her success, he'd developed an increasingly abrasive attitude that nearly ruined her career. No one in the industry wanted to work with him. Blair was eventually forced to hire another agent, but in an attempt to soften the blow to Keith's delicate ego, she kept him on as her business manager.

Five years later, when she couldn't take his abusive behavior any longer, Blair had gotten a divorce. At the same time she discovered that his foolish investments and obsessive gambling habit had left her without a cent. She had nothing to show for her five years of hard work, and her dream of purchasing a horse farm that year remained just a dream. Never one to dwell on the negative, Blair had picked herself up, dusted herself off and again started saving toward her goal.

"I'm not divorced."

"I thought you said you weren't married any longer."

His granite face could have been carved onto the side of Mount Rushmore. "You said I wasn't married any longer," he reminded her.

He was right. Blair told herself that jumping to conclusions usually made for uncomfortable landings. Before she could apologize, his words sliced through the air.

"Heather died several years ago."

"I'm sorry." Without thinking, she put her hand on his arm.

Clint stared down at the slim, feminine hand as if attempting to figure out exactly whom it belonged to. In reality, he was wondering how such a gentle touch could burn his skin, but he was damned if he'd let her in on that little secret.

It was bad enough she'd come so close in her silly guesses about Heather. Would Blair MacKenzie still want him working here—living here—if she knew the truth behind his wife's death? He was determined that she would not find out. At least not until Risky Pleasure had proved herself. Then Blair could toss him out on his ear; by that time his decision to purchase the rawboned filly would be vindicated.

"Don't worry about it," he said gruffly. "It was a long time ago."

Blair nodded, deciding that Clint Hollister must have loved his wife a great deal. That obviously explained his unwillingness to discuss the subject further. She remained silent as she followed him into the barn, her heart swelling at the realization that after all these years of working to earn enough money to buy herself a small farm, she had become—overnight—the owner of one of the top breeding and racing stables in the country.

A thrill coursed through Blair while she explored the place, reading the famous names on the door of each stall. The training barn was immaculate, not a straw askew, which told her what she had already suspected—that Clint Hollister ran a very tight operation. But one thing did surprise her, and although she knew that he would not easily take suggestions from a woman, she felt obliged to bring the matter up.'

"You store the hay in the loft?"

He arched a brow. "Something wrong with that? Historically, that's the way it's been done."

Blair's only outward sign of discomfort was that her hands suddenly brushed at nonexistent wrinkles on her skirt. Well, she'd opened Pandora's box; she might as well continue.

"In the first place, it's a lot of extra work, putting up the hay and taking it down. A separate, single-story hay shed is more desirable."

"No one around Clearwater Hills Farm has ever been afraid of a little extra work, Ms. MacKenzie."

She decided to ignore the challenge. "And dust," she went on. "Surely you've read the reports that suggest that dust in the air of barns and stables leads to heaves."

Clint remembered that he and Jason had argued about that very subject when Karma's Lady had come down with chronic obstructive pulmonary disease. While there was no hard research data to confirm that the ever-present dust from hay led to respiratory disease in horses, Clint had made his position quite clear. He wasn't quite prepared to tell this to Blair MacKenzie, however.

"I've read them," he mumbled.

Reminding herself once again how important Clint Hollister was to Clearwater Hills Farm, Blair bit her tongue. "What about fire?" she asked with feigned patience.

"The barns are made of concrete blocks," he pointed out.

"Still," she persisted, "from a purely economic aspect, if we kept the hay storage separate from the stalls, our insurance costs would be bound to be lower."

Clint understood all her arguments, having stated them himself over and over to Jason. But he was surprised to hear them come from this woman's lush red lips and wondered where she'd gotten her information.

"Is that an order?"

Blair met his challenging gaze head-on. "Merely a suggestion, Mr. Hollister."

"I'll keep it in mind," he allowed.

She nodded. "Fine."

As she toured the barn, Blair could find no other problems. The oak-wainscoted stalls were light, clean and dry, and her discerning eye recognized the cut-and-bleached rye straw used for bedding. The adjoining paddocks allowed a full acre and a half for each horse, giving them sufficient room to run.

"It's all wonderful," she murmured.

Clint shrugged. "Jason always alleged that proper management is the key to success."

Her brown eyes were admiring as she looked up at him. "And he obviously found the perfect manager. I'm glad you're staying, Mr. Hollister."

Why did her soft statement make him feel as if one of his horses had just won the Triple Crown? Clint tamped down the rush of pleasure instilled by Blair's words.

"Risky Pleasure's down here," he muttered, striding off before he succumbed to Blair's natural charms.

She shook her head with inner frustration at his remote attitude and followed him. When they arrived at Risky Pleasure's stall, she ran her palm over the white star emblazoned on the filly's forehead.

"Hello, sweetheart. How's my favorite New York Triple Crown winner?"

Clint was honestly surprised. "You really do know about her, don't you?"

She nodded. "As well as about the rest of them: Wind Song, Black Magic, Matador, all the others. You can give me a written test later if you like, Mr. Hollister. I'll bet I'd pass with flying colors."

"I think you just might. Although I'll admit to a certain curiosity as to how a model could know so much about Clearwater Hills Farm."

His tone let Blair know exactly what he thought of her profession. Previous profession, she corrected. The past few years had merely been a steppingstone on the way to a life-long goal.

"I'm surprised you're willing to stay on as trainer, since you think I'm such an empty-headed bubble brain."

"I'm Risky Pleasure's trainer," he reminded her. "It was your idea for me to continue working with the others."

Blair suddenly felt her blood turn to ice. "You will, won't you?"

His answer was a careless shrug.

"Mr. Hollister, it's only fair for you to let me in on your intentions. Are you going to train the rest of the stable or not?"

"What if I don't?" he countered, more out of curiosity than anything else."

"Then I suppose I'll have to train them myself."

"That statement demonstrates about as much intelligence as I'd expect from the Tigress Woman."

"And yours demonstrates about as much ignorance as I'd expect from a raving male chauvinist. I suppose you're one of those purists who don't believe women belong out on the track as jockeys, either."

His eyes moved with wicked insinuation over her slender curves. "Thinking about becoming a jockey, Ms. Mac-Kenzie? If you are, I feel obliged to point out that you're about seven inches too tall and twenty pounds too heavy. You'd have to ride a Clydesdale."

She glared at him. "At least all my muscle isn't between my ears."

His gaze dropped to her breasts, which were rising and falling beneath the white silk blouse as she fought to keep her temper in check. "Now, *that* I'm forced to agree with."

Blair's palm itched to slap the arrogant man's face, but she curbed the impulse with every ounce of self-restraint she possessed.

"Why don't we just wait until tomorrow morning," she suggested, folding her arms across her chest, "when you can see me ride before you make a decision as to my qualifications."

"You're not riding any of these horses tomorrow morning."

"Why not?"

"Because I don't even know if you've ever had that well-photographed fanny in a saddle."

"I ride all the time in New York."

He made a harsh, derisive sound. "These horses are a helluva lot different from lazy, old stable bums. And these hills aren't exactly Central Park, Ms. MacKenzie. No, you're sticking to motorized horsepower until I say otherwise."

"It's my farm. And they're my horses," she reminded him acidly. This man certainly knew how to bring out the worst in her.

He nodded, his expression grim. "I was waiting for that one. Do you know, in all the years I worked for him, Jason pointed that out only once?" His gaze was definitely accusing. "You can get dressed up in all the proper, ladylike outfits you want, sweetheart, but you're definitely proof that money can't buy class."

Even as he said it, Clint realized his statement was far harsher than it needed to be. But during their short acquaintance, Blair MacKenzie was proving to be the most frustrating woman he'd ever met, and he didn't see any point in retracting his rash words.

Blair had the grace to blush. He was right, she determined miserably. She was behaving like a petulant, spoiled child. She wanted to apologize, but she reminded herself that his attitude was not above reproach.

"When was that?" she asked instead.

"When was what?"

"When did he say that to you?"

There was a hint of a smile in Clint's eyes as he answered. "The day I came home from a sale with Risky Pleasure."

"You were serious about his not wanting her?" Blair wondered how a man who had the reputation for horseflesh that her grandfather had could have made such a mistake. True, the filly didn't look like anyone's idea of a winning racehorse, but she had proved a legion of doubting Thomases wrong.

"Dead serious," he acknowledged. "The old guy hit the roof and didn't come down for three days. He fired me at least a dozen times that week."

"But you didn't leave."

"I had a new horse to train," he reminded her. "Besides, Jason needed me."

So do I, she admitted inwardly, vowing not to be so quick to fight with him. If Clint Hollister packed up and left Clearwater Hills Farm before the end of the season, she might as well allow Ramsey Blackwood to bring in his real estate experts. Because then there wouldn't be anything worth salvaging. While Blair had trained long and hard, she knew her experience couldn't begin to compare to Clint's. She needed him, pure and simple. The money brought in by race winnings was nice, but the real support of the stables came from breeding fees. If a horse started losing races, its value plummeted.

"I can't believe a man with his knowledge of horses couldn't see her potential."

"Oh, he knew enough to look beyond her less-than-beautiful exterior," Clint agreed. "But he screamed bloody murder when he looked at her pasterns."

"They *are* set too high," she agreed, studying the filly's long legs. "I can see where a lot of people might worry about her going lame."

"The only thing lame was the judgment of the fools who let her go for twenty thousand dollars. They all forgot the key thing to look for in a racehorse."

"Heart," she murmured, more to herself than to him.

Clint's glance in her direction held surprise. "That's right. How the hell did you know that?"

She smiled. "Don't forget, I'm the offspring of a horse breeder's daughter and a trainer. Dad was darn good at his job, even if he never moved in the circles you do. He always told me never to bet against any horse with heart, because it would win every time."

Clint had put the sunglasses back on, and Blair couldn't read his expression as he eyed her for a long, silent time. "You may be the daughter of a damn good trainer, but I've never heard that horse sense is genetic. You're jumping in over your head, Ms. MacKenzie," he warned.

"Don't you think it's time you removed that chip from your shoulder, Mr. Hollister? If it grows any larger, you'll tip over."

She was right, but Clint was damned if he would admit it. She might be the boss on paper, but they'd have to come to an understanding about whose word was law around here. And when it came to the horses, that word was going to be his.

She'd turned away, her hand rubbing Risky Pleasure's nose while she murmured under her breath to the filly. The horse displayed instant acceptance of her new owner, nuzzling her head against the white silk blouse. Clint was suddenly and inexplicably jealous of the filly. What he wouldn't give to be able to get away with that!

"If you're going to insist on staying, you'll have to make some changes in your wardrobe," he said abruptly, his gaze raking Blair's navy blue suit. "That isn't exactly the appropriate attire to wear around a farm."

"I realize that," she responded levelly, refusing to rise to his baiting tone. "I was just anxious to meet Risky Pleasure. Why don't I change and meet you in a few minutes?"

Clint shook his head. "Mildred will have dinner ready soon."

"Mildred?"

"Jason's housekeeper. You'll probably want her to stay on." His expression indicated that he expected the total sum of Blair MacKenzie's domestic skills to be little more than the ability to boil water.

"I probably will," Blair agreed, thinking how much of her time would probably be spent in the stables. While she was an adequate cook, Marni was an absolute disaster in the kitchen. Not that her roommate ate enough to feed a dieting canary, anyway. "What time does she usually serve dinner?"

"Five o'clock. I realize that's an unfashionable hour, but we do get up before the sun around here."

"That's fine," she murmured. "I can see the rest of the farm tomorrow morning. However, after dinner I would like to sit down with you and go over the day-to-day operation."

"I'll be up to the house around six."

Her dark eyebrows rose. "Don't you live in the house?"

"No. I've got my own place here on the property."

"Oh. I thought you said dinner was served at five o'clock."

"That's right."

"But you'll be at the house at six."

"Bulls-eye. Give the lady a Kewpie doll."

"I suppose this is your way of telling me that you're not having dinner with me," she guessed correctly.

"Hired hands don't eat with the owner, ma'am," he stated in an exaggerated drawl.

"Oh, come off that hired-cowpoke routine," she snapped. "I'll bet you ate with Jason."

"Jason was my friend."

Blair nodded thoughtfully. "I see. And I am . . ."

"The boss. *La jefa*," he repeated in Spanish. "Any more questions?"

"Just one," she said, turning to walk toward the door of the barn.

"And that is?"

"As the boss, I'm entitled to set down a few rules, aren't I?"

"You are. Just as I'm entitled to ignore them." His gray eyes were as hard and unyielding as forged steel.

Blair decided they were getting nowhere this way. She softened her tone. "I'd like you to eat with me tonight, Mr. Hollister."

Clint didn't like the soft touch of her hand on his arm, just as he didn't want to hear her silky, seductive tone coaxing acquiescence. It was obvious Blair MacKenzie was a woman who was used to getting her own way with men, and from the way his body was responding instinctively to her nearness, Clint could understand why.

"I've a date for dinner this evening, Ms. MacKenzie. Even the hired hand is entitled to an evening off."

"You said you'd be up at the house at six."

"That's right. I'm a fast eater."

"What about your date?"

He shrugged. "She can amuse herself for an hour or so while I go over the books with you."

"She won't mind?"

"I'll just explain that the new boss is a dragon lady who insists on my working at all hours, day and night."

"You paint such an attractive picture," Blair murmured. "So you think that'll keep you in the lady's good graces?"

"Don't you worry about my love life, Ms. MacKenzie," he instructed brusquely, "and I won't worry about yours. Besides, I'll make it up to her after you and I finish our business."

"You've no idea how that relieves my mind, Mr. Hollister," Blair drawled on a deep, throaty tone, refusing to let him see that her exhilaration was fading fast. Even though she was admittedly a perennial optimist, Clint Hollister's attitude was less than encouraging.

As they exited the barn, Blair stopped in the doorway. "Do you wish I'd agreed to sell the farm?"

At her forthright question, Clint rubbed his jaw thoughtfully. While he'd never wanted Jason to sell out, despite Ramsey Blackwood's urgings, he didn't believe this woman could make a go of it. You had to be a combination of tough-minded pragmatist and incurable dreamer to run a Thoroughbred racing stable. Blair MacKenzie seemed to know something about horses, and he had no doubt she was a dreamer, but he didn't believe she was strong enough to pull this stunt off.

"I still think it's a dumb idea, but I'm beginning to suspect that Jason Langley's stubborn blood is definitely flowing in your veins, Ms. MacKenzie."

She grinned. "How about that? We finally agree on something."

He shook his head. "I don't know which of us is crazier, you for thinking you can run this place or for me staying on to help you."

"I'm not as inexperienced as you think."

"I don't have a single doubt about that."

Blair knew they were talking about two entirely different things, but before she could answer, Clint cursed harshly and flung her to the ground. A moment later she was pinned under him.

Blair looked up into his gray eyes, her own flare of anger extinguished as she saw his expresion of honest concern. And something else that was too expertly guarded for her to read.

"Are you all right?" he asked on a gritty tone.

"I will be as soon as you get off me," she protested, her hands pushing at his chest as she wiggled underneath him, trying to free herself.

"I was trying to save your damn neck!"

"You mean you were trying to break it," she corrected acidly. "It's amazing to what extremes some people will go to run off a new owner."

To her surprise, Clint abruptly jumped up and ran back into the barn. She heard the harsh sound of his boots as he climbed the ladder to the hayloft, letting lose a string of epithets that turned the air blue. Blair sat up, pulling her skirt back over her knees, and waited curiously for Clint Hollister to stop acting like a madman.

"Some of those horses are far too young to be hearing such language," Blair stated as Clint strode back to her.

He squatted down beside her, his strong fingers cupping her chin as he jerked her head toward the door of the barn.

"Look over there. Where you were standing a minute ago," he instructed tersely.

Blair's confused gaze swept the area. Her eyes came to rest on the pitchfork lying on the ground, and she felt the blood leave her head.

Chapter Three

"Where did that come from?"

"Obviously from overhead. And I don't think it was any accident, either."

"Because a pitchfork slips out of a bale of hay?" she argued. "That's not so unusual."

"It is in *my* training barn. Tell me, did you see one piece of straw out of place in there?"

She shook her head.

"The kids know that if they ever did a dumb stunt like leave a pitchfork where it could fall on someone, I'd can them so fast they wouldn't know what hit them."

"Perhaps someone forgot," she murmured.

"Yeah. Perhaps." His tone didn't sound convincing.

Before Blair could ask Clint what he meant by that inscrutable statement, he stood up again, towering over her.

"I've got a telephone call to make," he said, his eyes unreadable behind the dark glasses.

Blair nodded. "Fine. I'll see you at six."

"Six," he agreed curtly, turning on a booted heel and marching off.

Blair rose wearily, brushing the dust and straw off her navy skirt. Working with Clint Hollister wasn't going to be any bed of roses, she determined. Perhaps she should just come out and lay her credentials on the table and let the man see that she wasn't totally unqualified to be running Clearwater Hills Farm.

But then she'd be cheated out of watching the amazement on his face when he realized she knew a lot more than he'd given her credit for. And that, Blair considered with a small grin as she made her way back to the house, she wouldn't miss for the world.

So lost was she in her own pleasant little fantasy, Blair neglected to notice the solitary figure standing in the shadows of the barn, watching her with unwavering interest.

THE MAN CAUGHT the telephone receiver on the first ring. "I've been waiting for your call," he said as soon as the individual on the other end of the line had identified himself. "How did it go?"

The watching woman puffed nervously on her cigarette as her companion paced the floor, stopping when he ran out of telephone cord.

"She's what? You gotta be kidding!" He slumped into a chair and stretched his legs out in front of him. "Couldn't you talk her out of it?" He made a motion with his hand. The woman rose and lit a cigarette, which she then placed between the man's taut lips. "That's one hell of a surprise," he stated, once the explanations had been dispensed with. "Yeah, I'll bet it was to you, too," he agreed. "Well, good luck."

He hung up and leaned his head back against the chair, blowing a chain of smoke rings up toward the ceiling.

"Well?"

"She isn't going to sell."

The woman expelled a harsh, unfeminine oath. "That's ridiculous. She *has* to sell."

"And if she doesn't?"

"Then she'll simply have to be dealt with in some other way."

The threat in her cold voice was infinitely clear.

MARNI MET BLAIR at the front door, her blue eyes dancing with excitement.

"Blair, this place is simply incredible! Do you realize we could put our entire apartment in this room alone? My God, you must be filthy rich!"

Blair's eyes circled the living room, taking in the adobe walls, panels of carved stone and wood. A cathedral ceiling of cedar planks gave a feeling of spaciousness, while the wood contributed a warmth that was echoed in the earth tones of the furnishings.

"It *is* lovely," she said. "And large."

"Ramsey told me those sections of the walls are rare portions of old monasteries. The old man might have been a bastard, but he sure knew how to spend his money."

Blair inwardly agreed, but something else caught her attention. "Ramsey?"

Marni managed a slight smile. "You think I'm doing it again."

Blair sighed, then sat down on a leather-upholstered sofa. "What do you think?"

Her roommate wrinkled her nose. "Now you sound just like my shrink. He never answers a direct question, either."

"Don't you think Ramsey Blackwood bears a striking resemblance to Christopher Adams?"

"Of course," Marni answered promptly. "That's probably why I'm attracted to him. If it's one thing I have a knack for, it's picking out men who'll make me believe the only thing I've got going for me is great looks."

"You know you've got a lot more than that," Blair argued. "Damn it, Marni, we've been through this before. It's as if you go out of your way to find condescending men who won't accept the fact that you're also a warm, loving, intelligent woman."

"Speaking of that, how did you make out with that scowling hunk of a trainer?" Marni inquired, deftly sidetracking the conversation they'd had too many times.

"He is a hunk, isn't he?" Blair admitted. "I noticed that didn't escape your attention, despite the fact you tend more toward the stuffy, professional types."

"I'd throw myself in front of the man's horse if I thought it would get his attention." Marni grinned. "But he'd probably be so busy watching you, he'd gallop right over me."

"That's ridiculous. The man doesn't even like me."

"Oh, I think what's bothering our Mr. Macho is that he doesn't like the fact that he likes you."

Blair laughed. "Your reasoning gets more convoluted every day." She glanced over at the grandfather clock. "We're eating early tonight," she said, suddenly realizing she'd been remiss in not seeking out Jason's housekeeper immediately.

Marni looked decidedly uncomfortable. "I'm afraid I won't be eating with you tonight."

"Why not?"

"Well, in the first place, I wandered into the kitchen...and guess what the woman's cooking?"

"I give up."

"Spaghetti. And ravioli with meatballs!"

Personally, Blair thought that sounded delicious, but she knew Marni's Spartan eating habits. "So...you can pop those vitamins and keep me company while I pig out."

"Uh, there's something else."

"You're going out to dinner with Ramsey Blackwood."

Marni appeared decidedly defensive. "You're the one who's always telling me to quit moping around about Chris and go out with other men," she reminded Blair.

"I didn't mean for you to go out and find yourself a carbon copy of the guy who not so long ago had you wanting to stick your head in the oven!"

Marni managed a crooked grin. "I probably would have, but electricity doesn't have very lethal fumes. More than likely I would've ended up with split ends."

Blair rose wearily, giving up the battle. "Just be careful," she warned.

"Aren't I always?" Marni replied with false brightness.

Blair refrained from answering, but as she sought out the kitchen, it crossed her mind that Marni's romantic instincts definitely resembled the actions of a kamikaze pilot. Following the delicious aroma, Blair found the kitchen without any trouble. She was prepared to introduce herself to the woman standing at the stove, but that proved unnecessary.

"My goodness, child, you look just like your mama!"

"You knew my mother?"

"Sure did. Oh, I'm Mildred Kent, but I was Mildred Harris when Kate and I were going to school together. We were as close as sisters, inseparable. I spent more time over here with Kate and Jason than I did at my own house."

"My mother didn't talk about many good times," Blair said by way of apologizing for never having heard of Kate Langley's best friend.

The older woman shook her head, heaving a deep, regretful sigh. "I can understand that. Once Kate met David, everything just kind of went crazy.... For the first few years, she'd write every so often. Then it dwindled down to Christmas cards, and finally I just lost track of her altogether."

"We moved around a lot," Blair admitted.

"I hope she was happy."

"She was. But although she never came right out and told me, I think she missed the farm."

The auburn head laced with silver strands nodded. "I'm glad things worked out for her and David. I have to tell you, child, your grandfather sure missed her. He was really torn up when she died."

"I could tell," Blair said dryly.

Mildred shook her head and gave an unladylike snort. "Just like your mama. Really, the poor man's heart started hopping around like a Mexican jumping bean. The doctor had to put him in the hospital for observation."

"That may have explained why he didn't come to the funeral," Blair pointed out. "But he still could have called. Or sent a card."

Mildred gave her a long, pointed look. "Kate wasn't the only one who bore a grievance from those days. They were two hardheaded, foolish people. I'm guessing you've got a fair streak of stubbornness in yourself, girl, from the fact you're staying on here to try to make a go of it. But don't let that trait ruin your life. Like it did for Jason and Kate.''

With that advice she took off her apron, pulled on a bright red sweater and picked up her purse. "The ravioli is in the warming oven. I've left the spaghetti sauce on the stove. Would you mind boiling the pasta?"

"Of course not," Blair answered immediately, not used to such service in the first place.

"My youngest is playing in a high school basketball tournament over at UCSD, and I promised I'd be there to cheer him on."

"Wish him luck for me," Blair offered.

"I will. He's the last of the brood, so pretty soon I can retire my pom-poms."

"You have a large family?" Blair plopped down onto a kitchen bar stool.

The woman grinned. "Large enough. Six kids, and Jimmy's the youngest. And what a surprise he was, too, let me tell you. He was born the same day as my first grandchild."

"In the same hospital?"

"Yep. You know, I realize people are going in for smaller families these days, but myself, I kind of like the warmth you get from so many people loving one another."

"It must be nice," Blair agreed wistfully.

"See you in the morning," Mildred said, heading toward the kitchen door.

"In the morning," Blair repeated absently, her mind still on the housekeeper's words. "Good night, Mildred."

"Good night, Blair. Be sure to lock the house up after I leave."

"Out here?" Blair's Manhattan apartment boasted three sturdy locks, but there was nothing here, for miles around except rolling grasslands.

"I know it sounds overly cautious, but some weird things have been happening around here lately. If they hadn't started before Jason died, I'd think the place was haunted."

''Haunted! Surely you don't believe that, Mildred.'' Blair's tone revealed her skepticism.

The woman shrugged well-padded shoulders. ''Lock the doors,'' she ordered firmly.

''Yes, ma'am,'' Blair said with uncommon meekness, sliding off the stool to comply.

She locked the door, suddenly unnerved by the quietness of the rambling ranch house. ''This is ridiculous,'' she scolded herself, going off in search of Marni. ''You've lived in New York for years without being afraid of anything. A few minutes listening to a woman who believes in ghosts and you turn into a nervous Nellie.''

Blair found Marni preparing for her dinner date, and she settled down on the queen-size bed to watch. Her friend's black silk dress hugged her body like a second skin, the dark color a striking foil for her light complexion.

''When is Mr. Wonderful picking you up?''

''Don't be so snippy,'' Marni complained, digging through the vast depths of her jewelry box. ''What do you think?'' she asked, trying on a pair of dangling rhinestone earrings. ''I usually wear these, but perhaps they're too flamboyant for San Diego.''

''Since when do you worry about that?''

Marni ws busily rooting through the jewelry again. ''I don't want to embarrass Ramsey,'' she said under her breath.

''For Pete's sake, you're not going to eat with your fingers or tuck your napkin in your neckline or get roaring drunk,'' Blair said on an exasperated breath. ''What could you possibly do to embarrass the man? He should be damned glad you agreed to go out with him in the first place. He looks about as exciting as a slice of white bread.''

''To each her own,'' Marni murmured, giving up the search as a car horn blared outside the house. ''Gotta go.''

Blair rose instantly from the bed. ''He honked the horn for you? Like some teenager?''

Flushing, Marni hurried toward the door with Blair on her heels. ''Uh-uh. That's the taxi.''

"A taxi?" Blair's voice rose several octaves. "He's not even bothering to pick you up himself?" She couldn't believe that Marni would let her bad habits control her again so quickly.

"It's a long drive up here from the city," Marni answered defensively.

"It's a long drive for you, too."

"I've already got one mother who drives me crazy, Blair. I don't need another."

Blair gave up, knowing she was licked. "Have a good time," she offered, trying to put some enthusiasm into her voice.

Marni gave her a quick peck on the cheek. "Thanks, hon. Don't wait up." With that she was out the door, leaving a trail of Shalimar floating behind her.

Blair sighed, then decided to take a shower before dinner, hoping she would feel more enthusiastic about everything once she'd washed her hair and changed her clothes.

As her footsteps echoed loudly on the Mexican tile flooring of the hallway, the shower she'd planned seemed far less inviting.

"Don't be a ninny. You're perfectly safe," she muttered, pulling an emerald green terry-cloth robe from her closet. Feeling incredibly foolish, she locked the bathroom door before undressing.

She stood under the shower and allowed the pelting water to soothe the stiffness in her muscles that she knew was due to stress. While today would go down as one of the red-letter days of her life, it had also held a few low spots. One was her concern about Marni. And then there was Clint Hollister's attitude.

As she massaged the shampoo through her hair, with her eyes closed, she wasn't particularly surprised to find that she had no trouble conjuring up the face of the ill-mannered Thoroughbred trainer. That he did not want her at Clearwater Hills Farm was obvious. He'd let her know that as far as he was concerned, she was nothing but a member of the idle class—a lotus-eater.

Her fingers rubbed her scalp with more strength when she recalled the way he'd behaved as if she knew nothing at all about horses. He was probably safe in assuming that, she admitted, standing under the streaming warm water, and rinsing out the fragrant suds. She vowed that she'd sit down with Clint Hollister after dinner and have a serious talk about the future of the farm. At least they had that interest in common.

Just then Blair thought she heard a sound outside the bathroom door. Her hands froze at the back of her head. *Ridiculous,* she scolded herself firmly. *You've seen* Psycho *too many times, that's all. It's simply the house settling, dummy.*

Convinced, but still uncomfortable, Blair hurried through the rest of the shower, feeling unreasonably safe once she'd slipped into her robe. She ran a wide-toothed comb through her wet hair and decided she was too tired to blow it dry. Jet lag had begun to catch up with her, as well as the fact that she hadn't eaten all day. She returned to the kitchen, realizing she was absolutely starving.

Her eyes widened when she saw Clint standing at the stove. "What are you doing here?"

"Are you always this hospitable? Or do I just bring out your good side?"

"I locked that door, Mr. Hollister."

His back was to her as he lowered a handful of pasta into a kettle of steaming water. "Why don't you call me Clint? I did save your life this afternoon, remember? I'd say that puts us on a first-name basis. As for your locking the door, I have a key."

"How convenient," she said, wondering exactly how to go about asking for it back.

"I think so," he agreed.

"What are you doing here?" she asked again.

He turned toward her, his pupils flaring ever so slightly at the sight of her. God, she was lovely! Her curves were easily visible under the green robe, her hair was curling into wild waves about her oval face, and her tawny eyes dazzled with golden sparks. He still hadn't witnessed the Tigress Woman, but this one wasn't half bad.

"You're even less domestic than I would have guessed if you can't tell I'm making spaghetti."

Unnerved by the way Clint was looking at her, Blair crossed her arms firmly over her chest. "I can tell that," she snapped. "I just don't understand why you're boiling my spaghetti in my house."

"Simple. I was invited to dinner, remember?"

"I thought you had a date."

"I changed my plans. On the way over here, I ran into Mildred and she told me she was going to Jimmy's basketball game. Since even someone used to a swinging New York life-style would be slowing down after the day you've had, I thought I'd come over and give you a hand." His expression held absolutely no guile that Blair could see. "The time difference should be catching up with you about now."

She nodded, her smile of appreciation unfeigned. "It is. You'd think with all the traveling I've been doing over the years, I'd learn to conquer jet lag, wouldn't you?"

His eyes took on a hard gleam. "Ah, the painful sacrifices of the jet set," he drawled. "I can tell you're going to love getting up at three-thirty."

"I'll manage," she promised briskly, sitting down on the stool and crossing her legs in a smooth, fluid gesture that did not go unnoticed by Clint.

He turned his back on her, busying himself with the dinner preparations. Blair shifted uncomfortably. "I suppose you think I'm terrible for missing my grandfather's funeral," she said softly.

Clint took out a cigarette and tapped it on the counter. "Your grandfather didn't have a funeral."

"He didn't? But Mr. Blackwood said everything was already taken care of. I thought . . ." She tried to make some sense out of the two men's contradictory statements.

Clint lit the cigarette, taking his time to answer. "Jason was cremated yesterday without any fuss. Or without any relatives standing by to shed any false tears." He eyed her blandly. "Feeling guilty that you bothered to show up only to collect the farm, Blair?"

Why did he do this, he wondered, regretting his words as Blair shoved her slightly trembling hands into the pockets of her robe. Clint knew he kept baiting her; he just couldn't figure out why.

"I was out of the country, Mr. Hollister. It took the cable two days to catch up with me. I came as soon as I could."

"You don't have to apologize to me."

Blair didn't like the way his tone suggested just the opposite. "Well, perhaps we should have a memorial service. Could you give me a list of his friends?"

"Jason didn't have many friends."

That information didn't come as much of a surprise to her. "I see." Her smooth forehead furrowed suddenly. "Do you know what religion my grandfather was?"

"He didn't attend any church."

"Oh. Then I suppose a secular service—"

His hand sliced through the air. "No, Jason was adamant about that. No service of any kind."

Blair didn't know whether to feel relieved or distraught. After all, she hadn't even known her mother's father, and nothing she'd ever heard about the man had made her want to know him. However, he had granted Blair her most heartfelt wish, so some recognition seemed to be in order.

"I feel I should do something," she murmured, more to herself than to him.

Clint knew exactly how she felt. That was the reason for last night's drunk. It hadn't seemed right—one minute the old man was there; the next, he was gone without a trace.

"There's something you can do," he suggested, his tone softening at the sight of her beautiful, distressed features.

"What's that?" she whispered, her gaze suddenly trapped by his intense gray eyes. An odd warmth spiraled out from her innermost core, and Blair wondered what kind of woman she could possibly be to experience desire while discussing death.

Clint reminded himself that this woman represented more trouble than he wanted or needed in his life. What he had to concentrate on was Risky Pleasure—and not the luscious body of the filly's other owner. He jerked his eyes away, busying himself by setting the table.

"Clint?"

He did not miss the fact that she'd called him by his first name, and as he turned, Clint steeled himself against her confused gaze.

"What can I do? All this has happened so suddenly, I feel . . ."

"Win." He repeated it with more vigor, as if reassurring himself as well as Blair. "Win every damn race you can this season. Because that's what the old man really cared about. Winning."

The look of gratitude Blair gave him made Clint feel oddly guilty for the rough time he'd given her. "Win," she agreed slowly. "That's exactly what I intend to do. We'll make this the best season ever."

It sure won't be boring, he thought. Even dressed in those prim and proper clothes she'd worn this afternoon, Blair had struck a nerve deep within him that was a first. Not even Heather had affected him that way, and Lord knew the woman had possessed more than her share of sex appeal. And had known how to use it.

Oh, yes, Clint decided, it was not only going to be an interesting season, it was also going to be a very long one.

Chapter Four

Blair could not miss the gleam of desire in Clint Hollister's steady gaze. But what was even more unnerving was the way his warm gray eyes triggered an answering response deep inside her.

Dangerous, she reminded herself, not for the first time. She'd have to remember that.

"I'll be right back," she said suddenly, realizing that to sit in this intimate kitchen with the man, dressed as she was, was just asking for trouble.

"Running away?" he asked, his tone laced with amusement.

Blair shook her head. "I'm going to change."

His eyes took a slow, leisurely tour of her skimpily clad body. "Don't bother on my account," he drawled.

"Look," she warned, suddenly serious, "I don't know what type of arrangement you thought I was offering this afternoon, but it was strictly business, Mr. Hollister. I think we need to get that straight."

If she wanted to believe that, Clint mused, it wouldn't hurt. For now. It was going to be a long season, and he was a patient man.

"Agreed," he said simply.

Blair hesitated a moment before leaving the room, not quite trusting his easy acquiescence. Then, deciding not to push her luck, she nodded briskly and escaped to the privacy of her own room, where she changed into a pair of cream-colored jeans and a red sweater.

Clint greeted her with an admiring glance as she reentered the kitchen. "That didn't take long," he said, handing her a tall stemmed glass of burgundy. "Here. It's not champagne, but it should go nicely with spaghetti."

"Why, thank you, Mr. Hollister. That's very nice of you."

"Clint," he corrected absently, his head inside the huge refrigerator. "And I'm just trying to get in good with the boss."

He pulled out a bowl of salad and placed it on the table. Blair sipped her wine and watched him pour the dressing over the fresh greens.

"Where's your friend?" Clint asked as he took a copper colander down from a hook on the wall.

"Out." Blair's slight sigh told her feeling about that subject.

Steam rose like one of Mildred's ghosts as he emptied the pot of spaghetti into the copper strainer. "Then I guess it's just you and me tonight, huh?" He looked at Blair over his shoulder, his eyes filled with devilment.

Suddenly Blair felt as if she would have been safer if it *had* been Norman Bates of *Psycho* fame who'd come in while she was showering. She slid off the stool and refilled her wineglass.

"Don't get any ideas about this," she warned. "You're going back to your own house right after we discuss the farm."

"Wrong again."

"Exactly what does that mean?"

"In case you've forgotten, someone aimed a pitchfork at that silly little hat today. I'm moving in until I'm certain that you're safe."

"That was an accident."

"Prove it," he countered.

"I can't prove it was an accident any more than you can prove it was intentional."

"Then we'll play it my way until one of us is proved wrong. Don't worry, Blair, it's a big house. I'll be so inconspicuous you won't even know I'm around."

Suddenly too tired to argue any longer, Blair fell silent, watching as he piled the strands of pasta onto a platter that joined the salad bowl in the center of the table. She sat down in the chair Clint held out for her, but refused to allow this one gentlemanly act to make up for all the cracks he'd aimed at her that day.

He filled two plates with the homemade ravioli, meatballs and spaghetti, then offered her a thick slice of French bread. When she accepted, he appeared surprised.

"I thought all you high-fashion models lived on rabbit food," he said, his eyes skimming over her slender curves.

"This is the first thing I've eaten today," she admitted. "Besides, *this* high-fashion model is a heretic. I can resist everything except temptation," Blair added with a grin.

"I'll keep that in mind."

"Don't get any wrong ideas—we're talking about Italian food here, mister. Besides, I'm retiring. I can eat anything and everything I want."

"Retiring?"

"Retiring."

"What about the Tigress campaign?"

"I'm calling my agent Monday morning and telling him to do whatever's necessary to get me out of that contract."

"He's bound to be thrilled."

She grinned again, and Clint tried not to be affected by the way her breathtaking smile seemed to light up the room. "He'll hit the roof," she agreed happily.

"You know," Clint said thoughtfully, "it's not always wise to burn your bridges."

"It is if you're sure you're staying on the other side." Her expression turned serious. "We're going to make this work, Clint. I know we will."

"Heaven protect me from cockeyed optimists," he muttered, digging into his spaghetti. His tone, however, was not harsh, and there was a ghost of a smile at the corners of his lips.

A temporary truce settled over the kitchen as they enjoyed the excellent fare Mildred had prepared.

Blair knew the truce was too good to last. Watching her refill her glass, Clint advised, "I'd go easy on that. Considering the jet lag and that you didn't eat anything all day, the wine is bound to go right to your head."

"A few glasses are not going to make me roaring drunk."

"Too bad," he murmured. "It could only be an improvement."

"If you're hoping to take advantage of me while I'm plastered, Mr. Hollister, don't hold your breath. I'd have to be dead drunk before you got that lucky."

"You know, you remind me of that princess in the fairy tale," Clint said suddenly.

"There are a lot of princesses in a lot of fairy tales," Blair pointed out. "Which one are you talking about?"

"The beautiful one."

"I believe they're all beautiful."

He nodded. "That's true. The one I was thinking of, though, is the one with the exceptionally lovely mouth."

His eyes focused on her lips, and Blair's fingers curled tightly around her fork. If she was still capable of breathing, it would be a miracle, for such was the strength of his warm gaze.

"It's just too bad all those snakes and toads popped up every time she talked," he added, turning his attention to his ravioli.

Blair was speechless with rage, and it didn't help any when Clint glanced up and stated blandly, "Close your mouth, Ms. MacKenzie. Otherwise you'll draw flies."

She debated throwing her wine in his face, but that would have been a distinct waste of good California grapes. Instead, she took a calming slip of the excellent burgundy. While she'd never admit it to Clint, Blair realized her head was spinning just a little. The idea that he might be right about the combination of jet lag and alcohol only served to irritate her further.

Clint observed her push away the wineglass and nodded. "That's better," he stated approvingly. "Believe me, it's hell getting up at dawn and working all day with a hangover."

"I'm perfectly capable of hard work, and for your information, I've never had a hangover in my life," Blair snapped back. "I think you ought to remember who's boss around here."

Something flickered in the depths of his gray eyes, but it was gone before Blair could read it. "Such a lovely mouth," he murmured, "to be home to such a viper's tongue."

"You're pretty charming yourself," she retorted. "The way you strut that magnificent body around this place, one would think you possessed some divine right of kings."

Clint felt a burst of masculine satisfaction at her words. "Did you say what I thought you did?"

She blinked. "I don't know. What did I think you said? I mean, what did I say that you thought?" Her smooth brow puckered with labored thought. "Wait a minute," she said, holding up her hand. "I'll get it.... What did you say that I thought?"

A brilliant smile lit her face, altering her features, and Clint found himself staring, momentarily bewitched.

"Now I've forgotten."

Her look of distress was real. "Don't make me try to say that again," she begged.

He reached out, tracing the full-blown line of her lips with his fingertip. "Absolutely lovely," he murmured, his pewter eyes growing lustrous as he held her gaze. "You are the most beautiful woman I've ever seen."

"As beautiful as a woman can be with reptiles leaping out of her mouth, right?"

"I apologize for that. I should be used to it, living with your grandfather all those years." His eyes looked deep into hers, searching out a hidden message.

"I'm not my grandfather."

It was barely a whisper, but Clint heard it in the sudden stillness of the room. The only sounds were the ticking of the copper teakettle clock and the wild thudding of his heart.

"Oh, sweetheart, you don't have to point that out to me."

Pushing back his chair, he rose slowly and came around the side of the table. As he took her hands and lifted her to her feet, Blair's words of protest were suddenly lodged in her throat.

She watched the gleaming gray eyes, the strong nose, the chiseled lips approach as long as possible before allowing her eyes to drift closed. When his lips brushed hers, Blair sighed lightly, her breath mingling with his in a scented cloud. There was nothing tentative in the way Clint's mouth moved on hers, nor was it a kiss of hungry passion. His lips caressed hers in tender exploration—teasing, tantalizing, tasting—leisurely sampling what Blair was so willing to offer.

The man might drive her up a wall with his arrogant attitude, but he was one heck of a kisser, she decided as his tongue lightly stroked the flesh of her lower lip, feeling like a flickering flame against her skin.

"Mmm," he murmured, his lips plucking gently at hers. "You taste very good, Ms. MacKenzie."

Blair's body was rapidly warming to a temperature that made the California spring weather seem downright Siberian in contrast.

"So do you, Mr. Hollister. So do you."

"Clint," he corrected, his breath a gentle breeze against her flaming skin. "I saved your life, remember?"

"You and Mildred are both really paranoid, do you know that? Your wild imagination is even getting to me. When I was in the shower, I kept expecting Norman Bates to show up."

"I should have been there to protect you."

"Ah, but who would have protected me from you?"

"Would you have honestly wanted protection?"

How could she answer that truthfully, Blair agonized through her swirling senses. While that little voice of reason in the back of her mind was trying to make itself heard, her body was giving her an entirely different message.

At her silence, Clint looked down into her flushed, lovely face. No woman responded as willingly as Blair had just done without possessing some measure of trust for the man. He wondered fleetingly if, given a little time, he could convince her to sell the farm. After all, he'd only be moving the timetable up. Blair would have to sell eventually. Then, thinking he'd be damned if he would do Ramsey Blackwood's dirty work for him, Clint forced himself to back away from the all-too-tempting situation.

"No toads," he said in a voice that was still husky with unsatiated desire.

Blair struggled to return to reality. "Toads?" she whispered.

"I was wrong. Your mouth is a virtual treasure trove of sweetness. Nary a toad or a snake in residence."

She suddenly became aware that her fingers were entangled in Clint's hair, and she pulled her hands away. "That never should have happened."

"I think it was inevitable," he responded with a shrug.

"Well, it isn't going to happen again," she pledged.

He arched an argumentative brow. "Isn't it?"

"You're forgetting—"

Clint sighed. "I know—exactly who's boss. I always knew I'd hate working for a female."

"Chauvinist. May I point out that Risky Pleasure is a female?"

He began to take the dishes from the table. "You can point it out, but all that proves is that even female horses are smarter than women."

"I resent that, in the name of all of my sex!" Blair's flare of anger drained her, and she realized that the events of the day had caught up with her. She stifled a huge yawn.

"Now that's a great idea." He grinned over his shoulder at her. "Why don't you just keep that pretty little hand over that sharp little mouth for the next few months and we might just survive the season without one of us killing the other.''

"Stop teasing me," she demanded, feeling like an out-of-sorts two-year-old as she stamped her foot.

"Very good. I once saw a horse on the Carson show that could do multiplication tables. But, of course, that was a gelding. A male horse," he added, as if Blair might not know the term.

"I know that," she replied airily, tossing her head. "In fact, I'll bet I know more than you do about horses, old Clint Know-it-all Hollister."

He turned away from the sink, wiping his hands on a dish towel. "I should teach you not to make such rash statements, Ms. MacKenzie, and take you up on that bet. But there's a certain code of honor about not taking advantage of a lady when she's smashed."

"Smashed! That's ridiculous."

"Whatever you say," he agreed, spanning the distance between them in two strikes. "However, you are decidedly tipsy, lady." He put his hand on her shoulders, turning her in the direction of the kitchen door.

"What are you doing?"

"Putting you to bed before you pass out."

"I've never passed out in my life. And I've never been drunk in my life, either," she argued, nevertheless allowing him to direct her down the long hallway.

"Which room?"

"What?"

It was very difficult for her to concentrate, since his face kept going in and out of focus. Blair might not be smashed, but she had to admit she was feeling a bit tipsy, not to mention very exhausted."

"Which room are you in?"

"Oh . . . a big one. Third door on the left."

Clint flinched momentarily, remembering when he and Heather had shared that same room. After their marriage, she'd refused to live in his smaller but comfortable house, and Jason had invited them to live here. At least the room had been redecorated, expunging some of the old memories.

He sat Blair down on the bed and went over to the dresser. After opening the top drawer, he pulled out a red nightshirt that had a big orange cat covering the front of it.

"Do you actually wear this thing?" he asked.

She folded her arms over her chest. "Got something against Garfield?"

"No. I just figured you'd wear something a little . . ."

"Sexier?"

"That's it," he admitted.

She rose, swaying slightly as she held her hand out for the nightshirt. "You're stereotyping again, Mr. Hollister," she stated firmly.

"You may be right. Want some help getting into it?"

"Even if I were as dumb as you seem to think, I'd never be stupid enough to take you up on that offer." With that she marched into the bathroom and closed the door loudly behind her.

When she came out several minutes later, Clint experienced that now familiar surge of desire. "I was wrong," he said.

Her eyes widened. "Clint Hollister admitting he'd made a mistake? Did you call the papers and tell them to stop the presses? The world must be coming to an end."

He ignored her sarcasm. "You look sexy as hell in that outfit. All of a sudden I find myself envying Garfield."

She ran her hands nervously down the front of the nightshirt. "I think I should go to bed now."

Clint knew she had not been unaffected by the sensual aura suddenly surrounding them once again. "That's probably a good idea."

He'd pulled down the comforter, and as she slid between the sheets, he was treated to a flash of slender thigh. Even though he'd seen almost every inch of the Tigress Woman's body in those advertisements, Clint found himself very much wanting to see more of Blair MacKenzie. He was beginning to believe the two women were very different.

While the Tigress female inspired lust, Blair herself stimulated more protective feelings. Oh, he still wanted to make love to her, but he wanted it to be a leisurely experience; he wanted to pleasure her as no other man had ever done before.

"Good night, Ms. MacKenzie."

"Blair," she said softly. "My name is Blair."

"Good night, Blair," he repeated, loving the sound of her name on his lips. "Go to sleep," he instructed with a mock gruffness. "We've got a big day tomorrow and we start a lot earlier than you're used to."

Blair shook her head, trying to clear away the fog that made thought so difficult. "That's what you think," she murmured, burrowing into the soft down pillow. "I'm going to surprise you, Clint Hollister. Just you wait and see."

You already have, Blair MacKenzie, he answered silently. *You already have.*

HE WAS SITTING in the darkened den, smoking a cigarette, when the phone rang. Knowing instinctively who would be calling, he heaved a weary sigh as he picked up the receiver. "Hello, Blackwood."

There was a momentary silence on the other end of the line. "How did you know it was me?" the attorney inquired.

"Didn't you know? I've gotten psychic in my old age." Clint braced the receiver against his shoulder while he poured a tall glass of bourbon.

"Very funny." The dry tone indicated that Ramsey Blackwood found nothing humorous about their situation. "There was no answer at your place."

"You're an intelligent man. Obviously you figured out I wasn't home."

"What are you doing up at the house?"

"Smoking a cigarette and talking to you."

"What about later?" the attorney questioned.

"Later I'll probably get a little drunk, then go to bed. Alone," he tacked on pointedly.

"I had dinner with her friend tonight."

"I figured that much out all by myself."

"She's an amazing asset, considering how things turned out."

"Turned out?" Clint decided there was no point in making things any easier for the lawyer. He'd known Ramsey Blackwood a long time, and not one moment of that acquaintance had given Clint any pleasure.

"Well, we both expected her to sell immediately."

Clint shrugged. "Hell, she'll probably be begging to sign those papers by the end of the week, once she sees what she's gotten into."

"What do you mean by that?"

Clint didn't miss the strain in the man's usually modulated tones. "Once she disovers how much work is involved in running this place. What did you think I meant?"

"I didn't know."

"Blackwood, so help me God, if you're behind the problems I've been having, I'll break every bone in your body."

"I've already told you, Hollister, that your accusation was ridiculous the first time you brought it up, and it still is."

Clint's only response was a muffled grunt. He took a long drink of the bourbon.

"There's something about the woman we didn't know, something that might change things," the voice on the other end warned.

Clint had already discovered that for himself. He'd never expected her to be so strong, so feisty, all the while maintaining a tantalizing femininity. That morning he had dreaded Blair's arrival; tonight, sitting alone in the den, he'd been pondering how he could keep her here.

"She's been working for Ben Winters. In fact, Marni told me she'd been helping train horses since she was a kid."

Suddenly Clint understood both Blair's knowledge of his horses and her irritation at his dismissive attitude. He wondered why she hadn't just told him straight out that she'd been working for Winters. Then he realized she'd been planning to surprise him. Hell, he thought, he could go along and play her little game. What would it hurt?

"Well?" Blackwood asked.

"Well, what?"

"She might not sell so easily."

"Might not," Clint agreed, knowing that his behavior would only irritate the lawyer even more.

"You could talk her into it."

Clint decided that Ramsey Blackwood's inability to understand human nature prevented him from realizing that Clint would rather be dragged behind one of the horses than help the attorney in any way. He crushed out his cigarette in a ceramic ashtray and immediately lit another.

"What are you suggesting?"

"You're an attractive-enough man, Hollister, in an earthy sort of way. I know Heather certainly thought so, and—"

"I don't want to talk about her!"

There was a pregnant silence on the other end of the phone. "Of course," Ramsey said smoothly. "I can understand how that might be the case. Considering the way she died, and all."

Clint's jaw tensed as he fought down the anger and pain created by Ramsey Blackwood's words.

"Go to hell, Blackwood."

"We need to talk."

"I don't think so," Clint countered abruptly. "As a matter of fact, why don't you just go peddle those legal papers somewhere else?" Ignoring the man's spluttered protests, he hung up on him.

"Was that for me?" Blair stood in the doorway. She couldn't think of anyone who'd be calling her here. But it was now her phone. And her house. And her farm and stables. She'd had to pinch herself to make herself believe she wasn't dreaming.

Clint tried not to be affected by the vision she presented, her sleep-tumbled hair a dark cloud about her shoulders.

No," he replied, thinking fast. "It was simply a friend, calling to offer condolences. I'm sorry it woke you up."

"Oh." Blair stared at him for a long, silent time. His expression was shuttered, giving away nothing.

"Well, good night."

"Yes. Good night," she murmured. She'd turned away when something occurred to her. "Clint?"

"Yeah?"

"I just realized that Marni doesn't have a key."

"No problem. I'll stay up and let her in."

"She could be very late."

"I don't think so," he replied, knowing that Marni must already be on her way back to the farm. Blackwood wouldn't have taken the chance to call, otherwise.

"What gives you that idea?" Blair had lived with Marni Roberts for three years, so she knew that a date could last anywhere from an hour to a week, depending on whether Marni considered the guy a real loser or if he happened to have a Lear jet and a condo in the Bahamas. Blair had long ago given up expecting her roommate to be in at a reasonable hour.

"Hey, Madame Tigress isn't the only one around here with a crystal ball. I'll bet she's home before you get back to your dreams."

"Just make sure you get some sleep," Blair instructed briskly. "We've got a busy day tomorrow."

Clint gave her a snappy salute. "Yes, ma'am."

Blair's light laughter followed her as she headed back down the hall.

Chapter Five

It was still dark when Blair's clock radio came on. She lay in bed, listening to the unfamiliar voice, momentarily confused by her strange environment. Then it all came back to her and she stretched happily, a smile wreathing her face.

She was at Clearwater Hills Farm, and it was time to feed the horses. Her horses. Despite an uncharacteristic headache, she'd never felt better in her life. She washed her face, brushed her teeth and dressed in record time, braiding her hair as she tiptoed down the long hallway.

Marni's door was shut; Blair wondered what time her friend had gotten in. She hoped Clint hadn't had to wait up too long. She was determined to start over with her temperamental trainer, and one thing she didn't need was for him to be in a bad mood at four o'clock in the morning.

She went in search of Clint, stopping to ask a young groom where she might find him.

"He's in training barn A," the young man said, pointing toward the smaller barn that housed the fillies and geldings.

"Thanks. You're Jerry Graham, right? Risky Pleasure's groom."

"That's right," he replied, looking pleased that she knew his name.

"I'm Blair MacKenzie," she introduced herself.

"I know," he said, putting down a small plastic bucket to shake her hand. "Welcome to Clearwater Hills Farm, Ms. MacKenzie."

"Call me Blair," she said. "Tell me, Jerry, isn't it unusual for a horse to have its own groom?"

"The other grooms have three horses each," he informed her. "But Clint knows how much I love that filly, so he lets me work just with her." His blue eyes brightened. "She's the greatest horse in the whole world!"

"You won't get any argument from me on that score." Blair's gaze moved to the bucket Jerry had placed on the ground. "Is that her feed?"

"Yeah. I was just going in there."

"Would you mind very much if I fed her today?"

"Of course not, ma'am," he answered instantly. "After all, you're the boss." Despite his deferential tone, his eyes displayed concern.

Blair smiled reassuringly. "Don't worry, Jerry, I'm not going to change your assignment. I'd just like to get to know Risky Pleasure a little better, and feeding her is a good way to start, don't you think?"

"Sure," he agreed, handing her the plastic bucket.

"What's in here?"

"It's a special mix that Clint had developed by some guy up at the University of California, Davis. Bran, vitamins, trace minerals and oats. Plus an extra helping of clover hay."

Blair arched an eyebrow. "Isn't that a little fattening?"

"She seems to run it off," Jerry assured her. "There's nothing that filly likes to do better than run."

"I could tell when I saw her at the track," Blair said with a smile, turning in the direction of the training barn. "Thanks a lot, Jerry."

"You're welcome, ma'am. Uh, Blair, I mean," he corrected himself.

At the barn doorway, Blair watched Clint as he greeted each horse with a warm, individual welcome.

"Good morning!" she said cheerily, determined to start the day off on a friendly note.

Clint turned at her words, his eyes narrowing at this latest version of Blair MacKenzie. If he'd had a hard time earlier to picture her as the Tigress perfume model, now it was an impossibility.

"You look about seventeen," he responded honestly with the first thought that had entered his head.

She ran her hands self-consciously down her faded denim jeans. She always wore them when working at the track, so why did she suddenly feel like Little Orphan Annie?

"That bad, huh?"

His eyes glinted dangerously. "Turn around."

"You're making me uncomfortable," Blair complained.

"I don't know why," Clint drawled. "You've certainly displayed your body in a lot less." He gave her a devastatingly attractive smile. "Humor me," he suggested quietly.

Unwilling to admit that no one had ever caused her body to glow with such a radiant heat, Blair shrugged with what she hoped was an uncaring gesture. Holding out her arms, she turned slowly, watching Clint's reaction over her shoulder.

The tight denim jeans hugged every curve, each one more lushly rounded than he thought professional models were allowed. Her cotton shirt was open at the neck, her skin glowing in the vee framed by the madras plaid fabric. Her face was scrubbed free of makeup, but the lashes framing her dark eyes were thick and naturally dark. A high flush rose on her cheeks as his prolonged study became intensely personal. When she unconsciously licked her suddenly dry lips, Clint had to stifle a groan.

"It's your hair," he said finally.

"My hair?"

He drew nearer, picking up the thick plait and laying it across his palm, as if testing its weight. "It's a crime the way you keep tying it up. You should always wear it loose."

"Ah, yet another male seeking the Tigress Woman."

"Is that so bad?" He lifted the braid and brushed the fan of freed hair against her throat.

Her pulse leaped at the tantalizing touch, but as much as she wanted to, she couldn't move away. "Perhaps I'd like to be appreciated for myself, not for some image created by Madison Avenue."

"Oh, you're appreciated, Blair, for every little bit of yourself."

Blair backed up, her retreat stopped by the door of a stall. "I don't think we understand each other, Mr. Hollister."

"I think we understand each other perfectly, Blair." Clint held her gaze with the sheer strength of his will, daring her to deny the shared physical attraction. "The chemistry has been going crazy between us since you arrived yesterday. You can't deny that."

She couldn't. But that didn't mean she was in the habit of jumping into bed with every man she was attracted to. Not that there were that many; in her business, all the men she seemed to meet were either happily married or gay. Once in a while, she came across an interesting photographer, or a male model in some foreign, romantic locale. But all too often either the photographer was more interested in taking pictures of her or the model was unduly concerned that she might be the slightest bit more attractive than he. As it was, Blair's spare time was usually devoted to horses. At least that was one species of animal she could understand.

"I told you yesterday, our arrangement is strictly business," she protested.

"You did," he agreed amiably. "But you also have to admit you gave me just the opposite message last night."

"I said that was a mistake!" She marched over to Risky Pleasure, determined to get to work before this conversation became any more uncomfortable.

"How do you know what mix she gets?" he asked, catching up with her.

"I ran into Jerry on the way here and he gave me her feed. *He* seems to like the idea of working for a woman."

"Damn, I won't get anything out of him all day now that he's seen you."

She looked back over her shoulder, eyeing Clint questioningly.

"He's a nice kid and he adores Risky Pleasure. In fact, he insists on sleeping with her whenever she races out of town. But his hormones seem to be stuck in high. I guarantee that if we went outside right now, he'd still be standing there with a glazed look on his face."

"I wish you'd stop exaggerating," Blair complained.

"I'm not, believe me, sweetheart. If you didn't have a devastating effect on the entire male population of this place, I wouldn't be running behind schedule this morning. Mildred will have our breakfast ready before we finish feeding this crew."

"Do you personally feed all the horses?" Blair found that surprising.

"No, just the ones in training. I like to keep an eye on things."

"So you're actually up this early every day?"

"Worried about getting your money's worth?"

Blair glared at him, all her good intentions dissolving like sugar in hot tea. "Of course not. I just thought it must limit your—uh—social life."

Clint leaned back against the door of Risky Pleasure's stall, folding his arms over his chest. "Why, Blair, are you by any chance digging for personal information?"

"Not at all," Blair lied quickly. "I was just wondering how your lady friend was going to take your living under the same roof with me."

"I told you yesterday, don't worry about my love life."

Well, then, Blair thought, she wouldn't. After all, he certainly didn't seem to take it seriously. The shared kiss, which she had not been able to get out of her mind, probably hadn't meant a thing to him. She was determined not to let Clint Hollister come within kissing distance again.

They worked comfortably, Blair taking one side of the barn, Clint the other. She'd just reached Matador, a bay gelding, when Jerry burst into the training barn.

"Clint, come quick! It's Black Magic—he can't stand up!"

Hay scattered unheeded to the barn floor as Clint took off on a run in the direction of training barn B. Blair was right behind him.

She had special feelings for Black Magic, a coal black stallion that was one of the stable's home-grown prodigies. Sired by Magic Moments, the stallion was out of Illusion, both champions trained by Clint at Clearwater Hills Farm. The mare, Illusion, had been sired by Irish Rover, a Derby winner named and trained by Blair's father during his tenure at the farm.

"Oh, Lord," Clint said on a sigh.

Black Magic was lying down, his velvet brown eyes alert as Clint examined each leg. Blair squatted down beside the stallion's head, stroking his sweat-dampened neck while she crooned encouraging words in a trembling voice.

Clint moved the front leg, and the horse shuddered. "It's broken," he announced grimly. "How the hell did this happen?"

Blair had trouble forcing the words past the lump in her throat. "I don't suppose we could save him?" She was a professional herself; she knew better. But the softhearted woman in her asked the question anyway.

"It's a little difficult to keep a horse in bed while the bone heals. The pastern's shot, Blair. Even if I wanted to risk gut troubles by keeping him in a sling for several weeks, the corporation wouldn't allow it. They'd be better off collecting the insurance."

"You're thinking of this as a business decision?" Hot tears sprung to her eyes, and even though Blair knew she was being irrational, she was still furious.

"He's not my horse, honey," Clint said in a low, soothing voice. His eyes displayed his own misery at the situation.

"Well, he's mine," Blair argued.

Clint shook his head. "Your grandfather syndicated Black Magic for three million dollars after he won the Derby and the Belmont. What you and I want doesn't have a damn thing to do with it."

Blair turned her head away, unwilling to allow Clint to see her cry. In doing so, she missed seeing a similar moisture brighten his own eyes.

Clint decided to try again. "Blair, you know as well as I do that even if Black Magic could survive the weeks it would take for the bone to mend, he'd never be the same. Besides, he was born to run. He could die from inactivity."

"But surely the syndicate could recoup its racing losses with breeding fees," she countered weakly.

He took her hand in his, bringing it to the injured stallion's leg. "Feel that," he instructed gruffly. "The bone is shattered. Believe me, it'd take all the king's horses and all the king's men to put this leg together again just so he could stand. We don't have any choice."

Feeling the shattered bone under her probing fingertips, Blair realized Clint was right. She remained silent, her grief threatening to overwhelm her.

"Jerry," Clint called softly to the silent groom.

"Yes, Clint?"

"Go call the vet."

The young man left the barn, his slender shoulders drooping.

As she sat there, stroking Black Magic's sweat-drenched flanks, Blair thought back to how happy she'd been when she'd awakened that morning. That feeling certainly hadn't lasted long, she considered grimly. She wondered if anything about this enterprise would turn out the way she'd always imagined it in her daydreams.

"Blair?" Clint reached out, brushing away some errant tears with his knuckles. "I am sorry. I love this horse. I was there in the middle of the night when he came into the world. We won a lot of races together, Black Magic and I. If there was anything I could do..."

Blair put her hand over his. "I believe you, Clint," she whispered.

His bleak gaze held hers. "Truce?"

She tried a smile that failed miserably. "Truce," she agreed.

"Want to try for friends?"

Black Magic's dark eyes turned to her at that point, and it was almost as if the horse were encouraging Blair to drop her combative stance.

"I'd like that," she admitted, thinking that right now she needed all the friends she could get.

Ramsey Blackwood seemed to view the farm simply as an investment. Marni obviously considered it a resort. Only she and Clint shared a common bond—their love of horses and the thrill of watching those horses run, the wind blowing through their manes as they pounded around the track. Right now, she determined, Clint was the only friend who'd understand how much she was suffering.

She didn't know how long they sat there, trying to comfort the weak Thoroughbred. The sun was creeping above the hills when the vet walked in the barn door, carrying a black bag.

"Damn sorry about this, Clint," he said. He stopped at the stall door and looked down at Blair. "You must be Kate's daughter."

Clint introduced them. "Bill Collins, this is Blair MacKenzie, new owner of Clearwater Hills Farm. Blair, this is the best racing vet in the business."

"I should be," Collins said without a show of false modesty. "I put myself through college and vet school by working for your grandfather. He wasn't easy to work for, but I sure learned a lot."

"You must have known my mother."

"I was madly in love with the girl," he announced with a grin. "I kept thinking if I stuck it out, she'd see what she was missing. But then David showed up, and that was that."

"I'm sorry," Blair murmured, wondering why she should be apologizing because her mother fell in love with her father.

"Hey, David was a great guy. I was happy when I ran into him one day at Hialeah and found out they were happy. They were both nice people and deserved some good times."

Bill Collins's expression turned sober as he knelt beside the injured stallion, his deft fingers probing the shattered bone. "Perhaps you'd better leave now, Ms. MacKenzie," he suggested.

Blair shook her head. "I'm staying."

"I don't know if that's such a good idea."

"Blair knows what she's doing," Clint broke in, giving her a weak but encouraging smile.

She was holding Black Magic's head on her lap, and now she bent over to press a kiss against his nose, closing her eyes when she felt the man beside her insert the hypodermic needle into the stallion.

"Well, that's that," he said.

Blair rubbed her free-falling tears unselfconsciously with the back of her hands. While neither man was crying, neither looked at all comfortable with the state of affairs.

"This is one part of my job I always hate," Bill muttered. "I was hoping, after I had to put Northern Lights away, that he'd be the last one for the year."

Clint muttered an oath, banging one fist into his palm. In his despair, he'd forgotten the ill-fated Thoroughbred on the neighboring farm who'd broken a leg in much the same manner three months earlier. Perhaps it was only a coincidence. Then again, perhaps not.

"Suddenly this looks damn suspicious."

Blair reached out and put a trembling hand on his arm. "You're not suggesting..." The idea was too horrible to state aloud.

"That someone purposely broke Black Magic's leg?" Clint questioned harshly. "That's precisely what I am suggesting."

The older man's expression revealed both surprise and disbelief. "That's a strong accusation, Clint. Who'd do something like that?"

"Someone who wants to destroy Clearwater Hills Farm. It's not the first thing that's happened around here, Bill. Yesterday someone tried to deck Blair with a pitchfork."

"You've got to be mistaken!" The vet's green eyes widened. "It must have been an accident."

"That's what I tried to tell him," Blair offered, her tone not as certain as when she had said that last evening. "Besides," she continued, trying to come up with a logical reason that wasn't so distressing, "it's always possible that Black Magic was on his back and kicked out too hard. Horses have been known to jam their legs into a corner, Clint."

"If it was an isolated incident, I might tend to believe that. But I think it goes a lot deeper."

"Wait just one minute," the vet urged. "If it's somebody who wants to destroy you, why would he break Northern Lights' leg?"

"I don't know," Clint admitted. "But you can be damn sure I'm going to call Matt Bradshaw and see if we can come up with a common thread."

"I'll send someone by for the—uh—for Black Magic," Collins said, packing up his bag. Blair knew he'd edited his words for her benefit, and she tried to give him a smile to show her appreciation.

Clint's arm was around her shoulder as they stood in the doorway of the barn, watching Bill Collins drive away.

"Oh, Clint," she said sadly, "I feel as if I'm a hundred years old."

"I know. I've had to do it only a few times, but it never gets any easier." He squeezed her shoulder. "You were quite a trooper, lady. I'm impressed."

Well, Blair considered miserably, that was something. "Then you think I can make a go of it?"

"Do you still want to try? After this?" He jerked his silver head in the direction of the stall.

Blair met his questioning gaze with a level one of her own. "If it's an accident, I'll take it as such and carry on. If it was done to scare me away from Clearwater Hills Farm, it isn't going to work. I'm staying."

"Just like your grandfather," he murmured. "And I mean that in the very best way."

THE MAN SAT ALONE in the gray dawn, wondering how much bourbon he'd have to drink before reaching oblivion. The level of liquid in the bottle had lowered considerably during the past few hours, but he was still miserably aware of the pain infusing every cell of his body.

How the hell had this gotten so damn complicated? It had all seemed so easy in the beginning. But first there had been Jason Langley to contend with. And now there was his granddaughter, who was showing signs of being just as stubborn as the old man.

The phone rang and he reached for it blindly, knowing instinctively who was on the other end. Only one person would call him at this ungodly hour of the morning.

"Is it done?" the feminine voice asked.

He took a long drink of bourbon.

"Well? I'm waiting for an answer."

"Since I haven't heard otherwise, I assume everything went as planned."

"Good."

The pleasure in her voice grated on his nerves. "Don't you care about anything?" he asked brusquely.

"Of course I do. I care a great deal about money. And about you." This last was said in a silky, seductive tone that never failed to strike a responsive chord in him, despite his better judgment.

"And Black Magic?"

"He was only a horse, darling," she cooed reassuringly.

"A great horse," he muttered, tossing off the bourbon.

Her deep sigh came over the wire. "Excuse me if I can't get as excited about those dumb animals as you do, sweetheart. May I point out that they never brought you a world of wealth?"

She didn't understand, and no amount of explanation would make it any clearer. "I need some sleep," he decided. "I'll talk to you later."

"Fine," she agreed instantly. "I'll be expecting your call."

"Sure," he mumbled, "but don't worry. If this doesn't work, I've a second surprise planned that's bound to have her packing her suitcases."

"You'd better, darling," the woman warned. "Or Black Magic's little accident will look like child's play."

He stared at the telephone for a long time after hanging up. Then, heaving a weary sigh, he staggered down the hall to the bedroom, hoping the bourbon would provide sufficient anesthetization to allow him a few hours of untortured sleep.

Chapter Six

Mildred met them in the doorway, her grim expression revealing that she'd heard the news. "Jerry told me, Clint. It's a damn shame."

"Yeah."

"The coffee will be ready in a minute," she offered.

"Thanks."

"Are hotcakes okay for breakfast?"

He shrugged. "Sure."

The conversation was going nowhere. The housekeeper turned to Blair. "Good morning, dear. Don't you look nice."

"Good morning, Mildred. Thank you."

"Are hotcakes all right with you?"

"Fine, thank you."

"Is Bill coming in for breakfast?" Mildred glanced out the kitchen window, looking for the veterinarian's truck.

"He's gone," Clint answered.

Since it was obvious that no one was in a chatty mood, Mildred busied herself by mixing the batter. Clint slumped into a chair at the table. Blair took a chair across from him. Both remained silent, staring into the depths of steaming black coffee Mildred had placed in front of them.

"I'm calling Matt," Clint said abruptly, the legs of his chair scraping across the floor as he stood up.

Remembering how edgy Mildred had appeared last night, Blair followed Clint into the den, wanting to talk in private.

"Who's Matt Bradshaw?" she asked.

"He owns the neighboring farm. And he used to own Northern Lights, before the stallion had the misfortune to break his leg three months ago."

"Do you really believe Black Magic's leg was broken intentionally?"

"I do." He gave her a challenging look, as if expecting an argument.

"Why? It's such a dreadful thing for anyone to do."

"I don't know," he admitted, sitting on the edge of the desk, the telephone receiver in his hand. "When all this stuff first started happening, I thought we were simply having a rash of bad luck."

"But you've changed your mind."

"Accidents happen, even around the best-run farms. So far, taken one at a time, everything could have been a coincidence. But when you add them all up, there's a disturbing pattern."

"What's that?"

"They keep getting worse. The first few incidents weren't so bad, just irritating little aggravations. A stone in a shoe right before a race, broken fences, broken stall latches. That sort of thing."

"But nothing dangerous," she murmured, recalling yesterday's pitchfork. Her skin broke out in goose bumps as she began to wonder if Clint wasn't exaggerating the seriousness of that "accident," after all.

He shook his head. "Not really. We did have a few rough minutes last week. Do you remember Star Dancer?"

"Of course." She knew that the experts had not given the Cal-bred horse a chance against the Kentucky and Florida entries, but two years ago the roan had proved them wrong, making his Triple Crown win look easy. "I was always amazed at how calm he looked before the gate opened. Then he'd come out of that thing as if someone had shot him from a cannon.''

"He was about the most docile horse we ever had around here," Clint agreed. "Except perhaps for Irish Rover, but I wasn't around during his racing days."

No, Blair thought sadly, her father had trained Irish Rover. The horse had helped Clearwater Hills Farm become what it was today. After a long and successful career on the track, he'd been retired to stud. She'd always felt proud that many of his almost four hundred offspring had gone on to become champions. The thought of Irish Rover brought back the tragedy with Black Magic and caused her eyes to mist.

"You were telling me about Star Dancer," she said into the heavy silence.

Clint's gray eyes were the color of a stormy winter morning, proving that his thoughts were running along the same dreary lines. "Yeah, I was, wasn't I?" He raked his fingers through his hair, and it didn't escape Blair's notice that his hand was shaking.

He took out a cigarette, tapping it absently on the desk as he spoke. "Something happened when we bred him the first time. We all figured he'd be real shy, but damned if he didn't catch on right away. Since then, he's been aggressive and overly excitable if there's a mare anywhere around. We tie him up when we're breeding other horses, but he got loose a couple of weeks ago and just about tore the place apart."

"I'd never have believed that about Star Dancer!"

"You never know," Clint said, lighting the cigarette. "He turned out to be a real eager beaver, while Apache Son has to be introduced twice to a mare before he shows any interest."

"But Apache Son practically crawled out of his coat on the racetrack," she protested.

Clint shrugged, drawing on the cigarette. "As I said, you never know." He exhaled, eyeing her through a veil of blue smoke. "But the way I read things, there's a pattern to these 'accidents.' And they're getting worse every day."

"Did my grandfather have any enemies?"

His harsh laughter held no humor. "Hell, more than you could count. But most of them were horsemen who'd be incapable of doing what I believe someone did to Black Magic." He paused, his expression thoughtful. "Although there probably would have been a waiting list for the opportunity to break Jason's leg."

He began to dial Bradshaw's number.

Blair became aware that the slight headache she'd awakened with had increased, no doubt because of the morning's disaster. She left the den to search for some aspirin. Marni's door, she noticed, was still closed. After she had found the aspirin in the bathroom, she passed by the pantry on her return to the kitchen and managed a weak smile for Mildred, who was rummaging through the cans on an upper shelf.

"Matt will be over here after the morning exercise runs," Clint informed Blair as he entered the kitchen and joined her at the table.

She slowly lowered her coffee cup. "If you're right about all this, do you have any idea why these things are happening?"

"One," he muttered, thinking immediately of Jason's attorney. If Ramsey Blackwood was involved, he'd break the man's leg himself.

"Well?" she inquired finally. "Are you going to let me in on it or keep it to yourself? And whatever the reason, shouldn't we call the police?"

"No!" He punctuated his outburst with a slam of his coffee mug down onto the table.

Blair watched in wary fascination as a stream of coffee zigzagged its way along the clean surface. There had been an amazing amount of barely restrained violence in Clint's gesture, and once again it crossed her mind that he was the most potentially dangerous man she'd ever met.

"Don't look that way," he said suddenly, a shadow moving over his stormy eyes.

"What way?" she inquired on a weak thread of sound.

"As if I'm going to go berserk and kill you with my bare hands at any minute." Although his voice was low, the tone was harsh.

Her eyes widened. "I wasn't thinking that at all," she protested, telling the truth.

Actually, Blair had been considering that Clint possessed an amazing capacity for explosive passion. If she ever allowed herself to fall prey to his expert seduction techniques, she'd be a goner.

His gray eyes studied her wide golden ones, as if probing to the depths of her soul. Finally his stony epxression softened. "Truthfully, you are driving me crazy, Blair. But wringing your lovely neck is not at all what I had in mind." He put his hand over hers.

She allowed herself a fleeting moment of pleasure before tugging her hand away. "We agreed to be friends, Clint, not lovers."

"Any reason friends can't be lovers, too?"

Oh, it was so easy for him, she thought with a burst of irritation. All he had to do was turn on the charm and women fell at his feet.

"Have you ever noticed how some people seem to resemble animals?" she asked suddenly, appearing to change the subject.

"Yes," he answered instantly, thinking of the seductive Tigress Woman.

"You're beginning to remind me of Star Dancer," she murmured. "Tell me, did your wife have to tie you up to keep you from roaming into strange pastures?"

Blair was unprepared for the thundercloud that moved across Clint's face. Before she could say another word, he stormed out of the kitchen, slamming the door behind him.

"Oh, dear," Mildred sighed as she returned with a bottle of maple syrup. "And his breakfast is all ready. What on earth were you two talking about? There's only one subject I know of that could get Clint so riled up."

"I mentioned his wife," Blair admitted, not wanting to discuss the intimate nature of the conversation. Belatedly, she remembered how painful that particular subject had seemed to him yesterday. *Dummy*, she lambasted herself. *Just when it looked as if you might be able to work together*.

Mildred's harsh intake of breath caught her attention. "Oh, Blair, you didn't! And after all the time it took Clint to put that mess behind him."

"Mess?" Blair attempted to restrain her curiosity, telling herself that his marriage was none of her business. But she was becoming more and more intrigued by this complex man. Blair assured herself it was only in the interest of the farm that she wanted to understand him.

The housekeeper's face shuttered. "I'm sorry, dear. It's not for me to tell you. But I will tell you this. There's nothing you could have said that could hurt Clint more. I think you owe him an apology, even if what you said was inadvertent."

As Blair rose from the table, she wondered again if anything about Clearwater Hills Farm was as it appeared. She felt just like Alice after her passage through the looking glass.

"I'll be back."

Mildred nodded approvingly. "I'll keep both your breakfasts warm."

It didn't take Blair long to find him; he was in the training barn, brushing Risky Pleasure. As she stood in the doorway and heard him talk to the filly under his breath, she had a vague feeling that the horse was more than a source of pride for him. Risky Pleasure seemed to serve as a source of comfort as well.

"I'm sorry," she said simply, leaning her arms on the door of the stall.

He merely shrugged and continued brushing the horse's long mane.

She tried again. "You were right about the toads. Sometimes I have a tendency to talk without thinking first."

He lifted his gaze to her lips, making Blair incredibly nervous as his gray eyes studied them for a long, silent time.

"Forget it. Besides, we've already proved I was wrong about the toads, remember?"

Remember? How could she forget? Even now she felt her skin warming at the memory.

He shook his head, a faint smile on his lips. "Do you have any idea what it does to me when you look at me like that?" he inquired softly.

"Like what?" she whispered.

"As if you want me as badly as I want you."

Oh, yes, screamed her impulsive, sensual self. That woman was steamrollered over by the strict, no-nonsense side of her personality that had enabled Blair to establish her name in the modeling profession while spending every free waking hour learning how to train Thoroughbreds.

"Mildred's keeping your breakfast warm" she said, trying to drag her eyes away from his.

"I know what I'm hungry for, Blair. And it sure as hell isn't Mildred's sourdough hotcakes."

Blair knew the feeling. Very well. "Clint, we have to talk about this," she protested softly. "I'll admit I'm not nearly as self-assured as I've been trying to behave. I'm quite honestly scared to death that I don't have the knowledge to run a farm this size. And if you're right about the accidents, then I've got even more to worry about.

"I can't make a go of it without you," she admitted on a low tone, tracing circles in the dust with the toe of her boot. "But I can't work with you if I have to keep dodging these passes you're making."

"You already admitted you're attracted to me," he reminded her, putting down the currycomb. Reaching across the door of the stall, he cupped his fingers around her shoulders. Blair knew he could feel her slight tremor at his touch.

"That doesn't change things. I can't work with you all day after sharing your bed at night."

"Afraid the hired hand will refuse to take orders once he's found out how soft you really are?" he asked with a provocatively sensual smile.

Blair didn't return the smile; her expression remained grave. "You're more than a hired hand, Clint. You're what keeps Clearwater Hills Farm alive."

As soon as she heard herself say those words, Blair knew what she had to do. The idea was so obvious, she couldn't understand why she hadn't thought of it right away.

Clint wondered if, despite her words, Blair didn't honestly consider him beneath her, now that she was sole owner of the farm. After all, Jason had never apologized for his feelings about David MacKenzie and Kate Langley. He'd always believed Kate had no business marrying a mere trainer when she had every young man in San Diego County trailing after her. Rules were made to keep order, Jason had always insisted, and by eloping, Kate and David had broken those inviolate social tenets.

Clint asked himself what in the hell he was doing spending so much time worrying about this woman's feelings toward him when he had far more important things to be concerned about. He decided that Blair had a point; they couldn't go on this way.

"All right," he agreed reluctantly. "I promise to be on my best behavior. If we make love, Blair, you're going to have to ask me."

She could live with that. "I'm glad we understand each other."

"Me, too. Ready for breakfast?"

"I'm not very hungry." Black Magic's tragedy had dulled her usually strong appetite.

"Me neither," he said, leaving the stall to walk back to the house with her. "But Mildred equates food with love. It'll hurt her feelings if we don't eat her hotcakes."

Blair murmured an agreement, thinking it was sweet of him to consider the housekeeper's feelings. When Clint Hollister put his mind to it, he could be a very nice man.

Her spirits buoyed slightly by the idea that had come to her moments ago, Blair didn't want to wait for Ramsey Blackwood's office to open. He'd written his home number on the back of his business card in case she needed anything after office hours. Excusing herself, she slipped away into her bedroom to make the call.

The attorney's voice was muffled, his words coming slowly, and Blair realized she'd obviously awakened him. She could, however, hear him snapping to life when she told him what she wanted him to do.

"Ms. MacKenzie, you can't be serious!"

"Perfectly."

"Do you realize what you're giving away?"

"Not giving it away, Mr. Blackwood. I'm making an investment. If Clint Hollister owns fifty percent of Clearwater Hills Farm, he won't leave to work somewhere else. Let's face it, the man *is* the farm. Without him, I might as well close up shop."

"That's not such a bad idea," the attorney offered instantly. "I'm certain I could find a buyer who'd be willing to take the farm off your hands."

She shook her head, the gesture ineffective over the telephone line. "That's not what I want," she stated firmly. "I want to deed Clint a half interest in the farm."

"If that's what you want, Ms. MacKenzie," the attorney sighed his acquiescence, apparently recognizing the Langley stubbornness. "I'll draw up the papers and bring them out to the farm this afternoon for you to sign."

Blair smiled. "Thank you, Mr. Blackwood. I'll see you then. Oh, I'm sorry I woke you up."

"That's all right, Ms. MacKenzie," he said dryly. "In another hour or so I'll be able to watch the sun rise."

She hung up then, returning to the kitchen. Clint was busy eating. As Mildred set a plate in front of her, Blair found that her appetite was suddenly restored. She dug into her meal, ignoring Clint's amazed stare as she single-handedly made the entire stack of hotcakes, as well as two fried eggs and four pieces of bacon, disappear.

"Good Lord," he murmured after Mildred had cleared the table. "Where do you put it all?"

"Good metabolism. And daily exercise."

"That's going to be a welcome addition to the schedule around here."

"What?" She took a last sip of coffee.

"Watching you dressed in a skimpy little leotard, bending and twisting to rock music. It still isn't vintage Tigress Woman, but it'll come closer to anything else I've seen so far."

"Sorry. I'm not into aerobics," Blair stated blandly.

"Oh." His face actually fell at the news. "Swimming?" he asked hopefully.

"Nope. Sorry."

"*She's* sorry," he mumbled, thinking of the tiger-skin bikini. "What do you do to keep that dynamite shape, then?"

Blair knew he'd only laugh if she told him. "One of these days, when I can trust your discretion, I'll let you know," she promised. "Right now, don't you have morning workouts scheduled?"

"Yeah," he answered without enthusiasm, his mind on the puzzle she'd dangled in front of him. "Tennis?" he asked as they left the house.

"Uh-uh."

Jerry walked by, leading Risky Pleasure along for her workout. He kept his eyes to the ground, and his demeanor was unusually sober.

"Poor Jerry," Blair murmured. "He's taking Black Magic's accident really hard. Perhaps we should give him the rest of the day off."

It didn't miss Clint's attention that she'd said "we" and not "I." So far, except for a few instances of feminine pique, she hadn't thrown her weight around as he'd suspected she would.

"It's always hard," he agreed. "But Jerry has to learn that life does go on.... Come on," he suggested. "You're going to watch a real champion."

He put his arm around her shoulder as they walked out to the practice track, but Blair didn't feel threatened, since his touch was more a friend's than a lover's. She smiled inwardly, thinking how surprised he'd be that afternoon.

"Racquetball?" He started in on the quiz again.

"Nope."

"Surfing?"

"In Manhattan?" she asked incredulously.

He laughed. "Sorry, I forgot." His eyes held a fond message as they looked down into hers. "For a moment there, it seemed as if you'd lived here forever."

Blair had certainly dreamed of the farm enough times while she was growing up to feel the same way. "I know," she said softly, sharing a smile.

A pink glow tinted the clouds as the sun rose over the hills, bathing them in a pearly light. The meadows perfumed the cool morning air with the scents of many blossoms.

Blair joined Clint next to the fence ringing the oval exercise track. "There aren't any other horses here," she remarked with surprise.

"That's part of the reason for the early hours," he explained. "I like to get Risky Pleasure out here before any of the others."

"Why, Clint Hollister, are you by any chance showing favoritism?"

"Of course not. It's just her damn penchant for galloping. We found if there are other horses running past her, she just takes off. In fact, if you don't take a long hold on her, with that high knee action she tends to climb, and that isn't good for those pasterns."

At that moment the filly came onto the track, the exercise jockey walking her in a clockwise direction. Blair noticed that the jockey was a woman, and she felt a tinge of regret for her hastily issued words about Clint's apparent chauvinism.

"Risky Pleasure may be a terrific runner," Blair murmured, "but she's not real good at directions. Isn't she headed the wrong way?"

Jerry had just joined them, and he broke in before Clint could answer. "Clint likes to break the pattern every day," he explained, his admiration for the trainer evident. "We've found if we vary her workout, running her clockwise one day, counterclockwise the next, it keeps her guessing all the time and takes her mind off arguing with Annie and trying to run away with her."

"That's very clever," Blair acknowledged, knowing horses to be creatures of habit.

"Thank you, ma'am," Clint said with a grin. "I like to think so."

"Clint's the best," Jerry agreed, his mood seeming to pick up as he watched the big-boned filly.

Clint laughed. "If you're bucking for a raise, you're soft-soaping the wrong guy. This lady signs the paychecks now."

Blair thought she'd detected a hint of annoyance in Clint's tone, but before she could dwell on it, he'd turned the conversation back to Risky Pleasure.

"You know, she's stronger than most fillies. If she had an easier gallop, I'd let her go two miles every day. But wait until you see this up close."

Blair waited, watching as the exercise jockey jogged Risky Pleasure clockwise around the track for approximately three eighths of a mile. Even with Clint's precautions, she could tell that the young woman was having difficulty in keeping the horse from breaking into a full gallop.

Then Risky Pleasure was given her head, and Blair gasped at the sheer power the filly exhibited. The dark head was down, the ears were up. and the hooves hit the ground as if she were driving nails. She tore past, a streak of flowing mane and tail. The filly had gone a quarter of a mile before the rider could bring her to a stop.

"Well?" Clint looked at Blair, an inscrutable expression on his face.

Blair's gaze was fixed on the horse; she was stunned to see that Risky Pleasure wasn't even breathing hard. "You're right. She's not just the best filly. She's the best Thoroughbred racing today. Period."

"I'd like to prove that."

"So would I, but how on earth would you ever do it?"

"I want to race her against Cimarron."

Blair stared. "You can't be serious!"

"Of course I am. Don't you think she can win?"

Blair had seen Cimarron run only twice, the previous fall at Aqueduct. The two-year-old had shown signs of being a contender when the field of three-year-olds started narrowing for the Spring Classic—The Triple Crown. Everything she'd read about the stallion acclaimed him to be the greatest horse since Secretariat.

"Even if she could," Blair argued, "it would be too much of a risk. Don't forget what happened to Ruffian when they ran her against a stallion. She had to be destroyed, Clint."

"This horse is older than Ruffian was and has a lot more experience. Besides, as great as that filly was, I think Risky Pleasure's even greater." His expression became intense. "Blair, believe me, she's the best horse I've ever trained. They just don't come with any more natural ability."

"Or with worse pasterns," she pointed out.

Jerry seemed to sense the impending battle. "I'd better get back to work," he said quickly. Both Clint and Blair remained silent, watching him leave.

"You're against the idea," Clint said finally.

"Of course I am! My God, did my grandfather know about this crazy scheme of yours?"

"Yes."

"And?"

"He was against it," Clint admitted.

"There, you see." Blair turned away as if the matter were ended.

"I don't see anything except you're as shortsighted as he was. Don't forget, Jason Langley didn't want to spend a lousy twenty thousand bucks on a horse that earned well over half a million dollars as a three-year-old. Her earnings this year will top that easily."

"All the more reason not to risk her going lame in some stupid match race!"

"She's half my horse, Blair," he said quietly.

"And half mine," she felt the need to point out, wondering if her impulsive behavior earlier that morning had been the right thing to do. If they could argue over a single race for a single horse, how in the world could they ever hope to run the farm together?

They both fell silent, as the jockey began to jog the filly around the track once again.

"What do you suggest we do?" Clint asked.

At that moment, Risky Pleasure broke into a run, and Blair felt her breath stop in her throat at the display of raw power.

"Do you think beating Cimarron will be easy?" she asked, her gaze directed out to the five eighths of a mile practice track.

Clint tried to keep the excitement from his voice when he realized that Blair was beginning to consider the idea seriously. "No," he answered honestly. "But do you know anything in life that's easy?"

She turned, leaning against the fence and crossing her arms over her breasts. "No, I don't." She glanced back at the filly for a long, silent moment. "Let me think about it, okay?"

Clint fought to keep the breakaway grin from claiming his face. "Sure," he managed to answer casually. "Take your time."

Blair fought down her irritation as she watched the victory flags waving in his gray eyes. It was an intriguing idea, she admitted to herself. And exciting. But like so many other things around Clearwater Hills Farms, it was potentially dangerous. She remained quiet during the remainder of the workout, only responding to Clint's observations with murmured monosyllables.

FROM THE ICY atmosphere in the kitchen as Blair entered after Risky Pleasure's workout, she knew that Marni and Mildred had argued about breakfast.

"Hi," Blair greeted them, taking the fresh cup of coffee Mildred extended. "Um, nice. Thanks a lot, Mildred. You're an absolute doll."

She turned to Marni. "Hi. How was your date?"

"Okay," Marni mumbled, after swallowing her morning ration of vitamin pills. "But it's a little hard on a girl's ego when a guy takes her out and spends the entire evening talking about some other woman."

"I wouldn't think Ramsey Blackwood would be the type," Blair commented, sitting down at the table.

"You made quite an impression." Marni's voice held a sulky tone.

"Me? You talked about me?"

"All evening," Marni said. "And it got really odd, too, let me tell you. First, he told me about how hard it was to run a horse farm, and how it was no place for a novice. So I told him all about your working with Ben Winters and that you know everything in the world about horses."

"I don't know everything."

"Well, you know a lot more than I do. It's all I can do to find my way to the betting windows."

"I'm sorry you had a bad evening."

Marni shrugged. "It wasn't that bad. You should see his house, Blair. It's the most amazing thing I've ever seen! It makes this place look like a slum."

"Where did that taxi take you last night? Buckingham Palace?"

"Better." Marni leaned forward, her blue eyes sparkling like sapphires. "The house is in La Jolla, and it has an audiovisual center, two wet bars, and a two-bath master suite that takes up the entire second floor."

"Nice," Blair murmured, forcing her tone to remain neutral.

Marni bristled. "For Pete's sake, he was only showing me around. I didn't go to bed with the guy."

"I didn't say you had."

"No, but you thought it just the same."

Blair had the good grace to blush.

"Hey, I may be crazy, but I'm not dumb enough to fall in the sack with any guy who can't quit talking about my best friend," Marni assured her. "Anyway, let me tell you about his house. The lower level has a huge party room that opens onto an oceanfront dance floor. And get this—there's a pool that comes right up to the edge of the cliffside terrace. You can float in the pool and look right out over the ocean. Isn't that about the neatest thing you've ever heard of?"

"It sounds pretty marvelous," Blair admitted.

"Wait until you hear this." Marni had a smug look on her face as she got up to refill her coffee cup. "The house next door is for sale. And it's just as terrific."

"So?"

"So why don't you buy it?"

"Me? What on earth for? I've got a farm to run."

"You could always sell the farm," Marni advised casually.

"Marni! I thought you were my friend," Blair protested.

"Of course I am."

"Then how could you suggest such a thing? After all, you know how long I've dreamed about having my own stable, my own colors."

"I know." Marni observed her gravely over the top of her cup. "But it's not going to be easy Blair, running this place all alone."

"I've got Clint to help."

"That's another thing."

"What's another thing?"

Marni cast a surreptitious look at Mildred, who was cleaning off the kitchen counters. "Come with me."

Once they were behind her closed bedroom door, Marni didn't waste any time. "Ramsey's worried about your being alone all the way out here with that trainer of yours."

"I'm certainly not all alone. There are tons of people working here. Besides, what could he be worried about?"

"Your safety."

"My safety?"

Marni reached out and took Blair's hands in her own. "Honey, the man's been in prison."

The morning sun was shining through the window, but Blair heard the thunderclap just the same. "Prison?" she said, trying to keep her voice steady. "I don't believe it."

"It's true," her friend insisted. "Ramsey showed me an old newspaper story.... Blair, the man was convicted of murdering his wife."

The ominous thunderclap was followed by a bolt of lightning, and Blair closed her eyes against the pain that seared through her.

Chapter Seven

"I don't believe it," Blair stated finally.

"Ask him," Marni advised.

Blair remembered Clint's behavior earlier when she had brought up his wife. Mildred was right; the former Mrs. Hollister was definitely an off-limits subject.

"I can't do that."

"Why not?"

"It's none of my business." Blair's words sounded unconvincing, even to her own ears.

"None of your business! Honey, you're sleeping under the same roof with a convicted felon—a murderer—for God's sake!—and you claim it's none of your business?" Her blue eyes narrowed suspiciously. "Oh, shoot. You like the guy, don't you?"

"I like him," Blair agreed grimly, thinking that the word "like" didn't begin to cover the feelings she'd been experiencing.

"And I thought I was the one with masochistic romantic tendencies. Blair, we're not talking about a jaywalking ticket here. The man killed his wife."

Blair shook her head, rejecting Marni's words. "He couldn't do a thing like that," she protested, remembering the sheen of tears in his eyes as they'd tried to soothe Black Magic. "He can't even stand to see a horse in pain."

"Maybe he isn't jealous of his horses," Marni suggested.

"Exactly what is that supposed to mean?"

"A jury found him guilty of killing his wife in a jealous rage because he caught her with another man."

"Even so," Blair argued, "all he had to do was divorce her."

"Women don't usually pay alimony."

Blair was growing increasingly irritated by the way Marni was dragging out this sordid little story. "Why don't you just tell me what Ramsey Blackwood told you?"

"It wasn't only Ramsey's version. I read it in the paper, Blair. In black and white."

Blair's shoulders sank, and she felt her headache returning with a vengeance. "Marni," she pleaded, "I've been up since three-thirty and I've already had a lousy day. Can't you just spit it out?"

"All right." Marni took a deep breath. "Heather Hollister was a wealthy woman. The prosecuting attorney had witnesses who swore she and Clint argued all the time."

"Lots of husbands and wives argue," Blair pointed out. "But they don't kill each other."

"One of the more frequent arguments was over Heather's refusal to give him the money to buy Risky Pleasure from your grandfather."

"Why would he want to do that? He was already training her."

"It seems he had an obsession about the horse," Marni explained. "He and Jason Langley didn't agree on anything about her, from the day Clint brought her home. He wanted carte blanche in her training, and your grandfather refused."

Blair tried not to think of the way Clint's gray eyes turned to a polished pewter when he talked about the filly. She didn't want to remember that he himself had told her that Jason hadn't agreed with his plan to race her against Cimarron.

And when she'd asked him why he'd stayed, since her grandfather had fired him after he brought Risky Pleasure home, Clint's explanation had been simply that he had a horse to train. Not that he felt any loyalty to her grandfather. Or to the other horses. No, Blair had a feeling from the moment he'd spotted the rawboned filly, the horse had eclipsed all the others he'd ever trained.

"Blair, there's more." Marni leaned forward, placing her hand on her friend's arm. "Did you ever wonder why there wasn't any funeral for your grandfather?"

"He didn't want one."

"How do you know?"

"Clint told me."

"Just like he told you Jason wanted a quick cremation, right?"

Blair thought she knew where this conversation was going, and she rejected the idea immediately. "If you're accusing him of killing my grandfather, you're way off base. Even if he was the kind of man capable of murder—which he isn't—he had nothing to gain."

"He's already got fifty percent of his precious racehorse," Marni pointed out.

"He's going to have more than that."

Blue eyes widened. "What does that mean?"

Blair's expression warned her friend not to challenge her decision. "I called Ramsey Blackwood first thing this morning and told him I wanted to deed half my interest in Clearwater Hills Farm to Clint."

Marni stared at Blair as if she'd just grown an extra head. "What on earth for?"

"So he'll stay on here. I need him, Marni."

"As a trainer?"

"Of course. What did you think?"

"I think you're interested in the guy, Blair."

"That's ridiculous," Blair lied swiftly.

"There are other good trainers. If you really tried, with all your money you could probably hire Ben Winters away from Winterhaven Farms."

"Ben's a good trainer," Blair agreed. "But I don't want him. I want Clint Hollister."

Marni expelled a small, defeated sigh. "That's what I'm afraid of. Honey, don't you realize your life could be in danger here?"

"That's ridiculous," Blair retorted, paling as the image of that pitchfork came to mind.

"Is it?"

"Of course!"

"Then why did you look as if you'd just seen a ghost?"

Blair began to pace the floor in long, nervous strides. "I told you, I've had a bad day and not enough sleep."

"Something did happen, didn't it?"

Blair was reminded that she'd never been able to hide anything from her sharp-eyed roommate. "Nothing happened," she insisted. "Nothing at all."

"Except now you've also got yourself one dead racehorse," Marni reminded her. Mildred had filled Marni in on the tragedy.

"Accidents happen," Blair snapped.

"Sure. So do natural deaths. And we'll never know for certain about your grandfather's. But Heather Hollister was definitely killed. By her husband, the same man to whom you want to hand over half your worldly possessions." Marni's expression was atypically sober. "Blair, what if he isn't above killing you in order to get total control of Risky Pleasure? And the farm?"

Blair stared out the window, experiencing that now familiar quickening deep inside her as she watched Clint stride toward a red Blazer that had just pulled up into the driveway.

She turned, pinning a distressed Marni with a stern gaze. "Tell me this," she said tersely. "If Clint Hollister killed his wife, then why isn't he still in prison?"

Marni shrugged. "Ramsey wasn't clear on that point," she admitted. "He said it had something to do with the law. Some complex mumbo jumbo that got Clint out on a technicality." Her eyes handed Blair a warning. "But that doesn't make him less guilty."

"I don't want you to say a word to anyone about this," Blair instructed her firmly. "Not a soul. Do you hear me?"

"Who would I tell? I don't even know anyone other than Ramsey in San Diego."

For someone who professed to be a stranger, Marni had certainly tapped into a gossip line fast enough, Blair considered bleakly. She knew that whatever the explanation, Clint was innocent. He might have frustrated her in the past twenty-four hours and driven her up a wall from time to time, and he might cause her common sense to disappear whenever he looked at her with desire in those wonderful gray eyes. But she knew, without a shadow of a doubt, that the man had never tried to kill her.

Warning Marni once again to silence, she left the room and headed toward the den, drawn there by the sound of male voices.

"Blair, I was just about to send the Saint Bernards out looking for you." Clint smiled as she entered, but his eyes held little seeds of worry.

Blair couldn't quite meet his gaze. "I'm sorry. I was talking with Marni."

"I want you to meet your neighbor, Matt Bradshaw. Matt, this is Blair MacKenzie, Jason's granddaughter."

A tall blond man rose from his chair and extended his hand. "It's a pleasure, Ms. MacKenzie. Your grandfather was always talking about you."

Blair tried to focus on his words as he vigorously pumped her hand. "My grandfather talked about me?"

"All the time. He even kept a scrapbook of every magazine layout you did. In fact..." Brilliant emerald eyes scanned the room, obviously searching for something. "Hey, Clint, what happened to that photo he had framed?"

Clint refused to admit that the glossy color photo was at his house, on his bedside table. "I don't know," he replied with blatant unconcern.

"It was always my favorite thing about coming over here," Matt Bradshaw confessed with a boyishly attractive grin. "That Tigress perfume layout was really something, Ms. MacKenzie."

She managed a tight smile, willing her body to relax. But she could sense Clint's restraint and it made her even more nervous.

"Call me Blair," she suggested. "After all, we are neighbors."

"Blair," he agreed. "And I'm Matt." Then his expression grew serious. "I'm damned sorry about Black Magic, Blair."

She nodded, refusing to let herself cry over the stallion anymore. "Thank you. I'm sorry about Northern Lights, too. I think he's one horse who could have given Cimarron a run for the money at Churchill Downs this year."

Her words obviously piqued Matt's interest. "Your grandfather always said you were beautiful, but he never said anything about your following the horses."

"Blair's been working with Ben Winters," Clint offered, then suddenly remembered that he wasn't supposed to know that little fact. Blair's wide amber eyes revealed both surprise and confusion.

"Ben Winters? I'm suitably impressed." Matt's expression reinforced his words.

Clint was trying to come up with some way to sidetrack the conversation before Blair decided to pin him down on exactly where he'd received his information. He got a reprieve when Marni peeked around the corner of the door.

"Blair, there's someone here to see you."

Ramsey must have come sooner than expected with the papers, Blair thought. "Come in and keep our neighbor company," she invited.

"Marni Roberts," Matt said instantly, as she entered the room.

Marni gave him her bright, professional smile. "How nice that you recognized me," she purred, holding out a perfectly manicured hand.

"It's your eyes."

"My eyes?"

"Ever since you did that shampoo commercial, I've thought you had the most beautiful eyes I'd ever seen." Suddenly he appeared to realize that there were other people in the room. "Oh, damn. I *am* sorry, Blair. I didn't mean that yours weren't lovely. It's just that Ms. Roberts always seemed to be looking directly at me."

Matt Bradshaw groaned with embarrassment as he slumped back down into his chair, rubbing his large palm over his face. "Don't mind me, folks. I think I'll just sit here and wait for the ground to swallow me up." To Blair's amusement, a dark flush rose from the man's open collar.

"Did you really feel that way?" Marni asked.

Matt lifted distressed green eyes up to where Marni now stood in front of him. "I bet you meet a lot of jerks who say things like that."

Marni shook her head slowly. "I don't think you're a jerk at all," she protested softly. "And no, no one has ever mentioned my eyes." She allowed a little grin. "Usually they're concentrating on my body."

His gaze accepted the invitation in her tone, moving from the top of her blond head, down to the polished pink toenails peeking out of her gold sandals, then back up again.

"It's very nice, too," he offered politely.

"Thank you. Did Blair say you were her neighbor?"

"Right next door. Although, it's not as close as it would be if we lived in Manhattan. My place isn't nearly as big as Clearwater Hills Farm, but I'm getting a good stable, and I train a few horses for other owners. Do you like horses?"

His face took on an absolutely hopeful expression that had Blair cringing as she waited for Marni's answer. She'd never seen her roommate portray any enthusiasm toward the Thoroughbreds Blair had worked with over the years.

"I don't really know," Marni admitted. "I've never been around them, except when I visited Blair once in a while at Aqueduct. I'm afraid I don't know much at all about racing. But I've heard that it's always lucky to bet on the gray horse."

Matt laughed, the lines fanning outward from his eyes crinkling attractively. At the moment, he and Marni could have been the only two people in the room.

"I'll have to keep that hot tip in mind. . . . Uh, would you be interested in visiting someday?"

Marni gave his invitation some well-deserved thought. Then she said, "I'd like that."

"Terrific!" Matt rubbed his hands together. "How about tomorrow?"

"Tomorrow?"

"Oh . . . too soon, huh?"

"Actually, I was thinking about today."

"Hey, today's great," he hastened to assure her. "Why don't you drive back with me after I finish my business here?"

"That sounds nice." She nodded and smiled. "It'll give me time to change into something more suitable."

Blair idly wondered what Marni could have in all those suitcases that would be marginally suitable for exploring training barns. Suddenly she remembered her friend's reason for coming into the den in the first place.

"Excuse me. I'll see who's here and be right back."

"And I'll change," Marni said.

"What on earth do you think you're doing?" Blair asked, once they were out of hearing.

Marni shrugged. "I haven't the faintest idea. Believe me, Blair, I was as surprised as you. I heard the words and realized they were coming out of my mouth, but I sure don't know why or how."

"I thought you'd want to stick around while Ramsey's here."

"Oh, is he coming over?" Marni inquired vaguely.

"Isn't he here now?"

"No."

"Then who was at the door?"

"A delivery man. Were you expecting Ramsey?"

"He's bringing me the papers to sign, remember?"

"Oh, that. I still think you're making an enormous mistake," Marni warned her.

"I don't," Blair returned shortly. "What are you wearing over to Matt's farm? Not that I don't have a pretty good idea."

"Blair, you know I don't have anything for that kind of afternoon!"

"Only because you've never expressed an interest in the great outdoors. I still haven't figured out what you're up to now."

"Nothing. And don't forget who loaned you her Halston for that gallery opening last week. All I'm asking for is a pair of cruddy old jeans and one of those faded shirts you wear all the time. You know, the ones that have all the colors running together."

"They're supposed to bleed. They're madras. Besides, may I point out that you'd look a little silly mucking out a stall in a Halston."

Marni's smooth brow furrowed. "Mucking out a stall? Is that as gross as it sounds?"

"Worse. Take whatever you like," she offered.

Marni's grin was ecstatic. "Thanks, hon. You're a true pal." She headed toward Blair's room, humming an off-key rendition of "Camptown Racetrack" under her breath.

Blair shook her head, bemused over her roommate's uncharacteristic behavior. Then she went to the front door.

"Ms. MacKenzie?" The young man standing there had an appreciative gleam in his eyes.

"That's me," she answered briskly. "I believe you have a delivery for me?"

"That's right. I put it in training barn B, like I was told to. I just need your signature."

"What is it?" she asked, taking the plastic pen and clipboard and scribbling her name.

"Flowers," he mumbled, attempting to read upside down. "I thought it was you! Could you sign another one? For me?"

Blair shrugged, doing as requested. "Why on earth would you put flowers in the training barn?"

"I dunno. That's just what was on the delivery slip. Thanks a lot, Ms. MacKenzie."

As the delivery truck drove away, Blair debated returning directly to the den, but curiosity got the better of her. She went out the back door and cut across the paddock to the training barn, where she found the flowers. Throwing a hand over her mouth to stifle the scream that threatened to erupt, she ran back to the house as fast as she could.

"Clint!" Blair burst into the den, interrupting the two men's conversation. "You won't believe what that horrible person's done now!"

Clint felt his stomach turn over as he viewed her anguished face. "What's the matter? Are you all right?" he asked.

She nodded, unable to speak, the words frozen in her throat.

"Is it one of the crew?"

This time she shook her head in the negative.

"One of the horses?" His stomach was doing somersaults now.

"N-n-n-no," she managed to get out.

"Here, Blair." Matt shoved a glass into her hands.

"What's this?"

"Brandy."

"It's too early in the day," she protested weakly.

Clint lifted the glass to her lips. "Matt's right. Drink it, Blair. Then sit down and try to tell us what happened."

She tilted back her head gasping as the liquid heat hit her stomach. But as she drank, the alcohol spread through her system in a comforting warmth.

"It's Black Magic," she said finally.

Both men exchanged puzzled looks. "Maybe it's just sinking in," Matt suggested.

Clint studied Blair intently. "I don't think so."

She was rapidly regaining her senses. "I'll show you," she said, linking her fingers with Clint's as she led him out of the room. He had to fight down the pleasure he received from the simple gesture, reminding himself that something was very, very wrong.

Black Magic had been removed from his stall, but in the stallion's place was a horseshoe of roses, much the same as the ones that had been draped about his neck when he won the Kentucky Derby. But these roses were black and the banner read, "Black Magic—RIP."

"You were right," she said, her voice horribly flat now that her shock had passed. "It was intentional. We have to call the police."

"No!"

Clint's reaction was the same as it had been when she'd suggested that earlier, his tone just as unrelenting, and because Marni had brought home that horrible story, Blair found herself ascribing all sorts of terrible notions to his refusal.

"Why can't you call the police, Clint?" she asked quietly.

Blair hated to see how uncomfortable Clint seemed with the subject. She glanced at Matt, who didn't look too thrilled with the topic, either.

Clint took her unresisting hands in his. Blair told herself she shouldn't be allowing this, but his thumbs were making such soothing circles on the tender skin of her palms.

"Look, we've got horses we're training for other owners," he reminded her.

"And you're afraid that if the word got out that Black Magic was destroyed on purpose, those people would take their horses away from here."

"Exactly."

"That's right," Matt echoed.

"Blair, it wouldn't break you, but you'd be in danger of drowning in red ink within six weeks without the fees these horses are generating. Training fees, brood fees, stud fees . . ."

"I get the point," she muttered. "Whatever happened to the days of daddy horses and mommy horses making lots of little baby horses who won races and brought in big purses filled with money?''

"I believe that's Sunnybrook Farm you're describing," Clint offered dryly. "This farm is situated in the real world. Things are more complicated."

That's for sure, she considered bleakly.

Matt began to do his own lobbying. "You have enough of your own stock, Blair, so you'd probably survive. But I'd have to close down. If you've been working with Ben Winters, you must know how much even a single horse costs."

"That's the truth," Clint agreed grimly, his face set in harsh lines. "Especially one in training."

Blair felt a prickling of apprehension skim up her spine. Was he talking about Risky Pleasure now? He was willing to risk so much just to hang on to the farm and, by doing that, to the filly. To what lengths would the man go in order to see his dream come true? She shook her head, disallowing the vague little seed of suspicion a chance to sprout.

Marni had misunderstood the newspaper article. She'd obviously been tired last night and undoubtedly drunk some wine. And because she refused to eat any nourishing food, it was quite likely that she'd been even more tipsy than Blair. She simply had not gotten the story straight. That was the only explanation.

"All right," Blair conceded. "But we're going to have to tighten security around here."

"That's exactly what I'd planned to do," Clint said calmly. "So we agree?"

"I suppose so. But I don't particularly like the idea."

"Neither do I, Blair," Clint muttered. "But it's all we can do for now."

Her head was beginning to clear. "Perhaps we can at least check with the florist and see who sent the flowers," she suggested.

"You must have been reading my mind," he replied.

No, Blair mused as the threesome made their way to the house, she hadn't been reading Clint's mind, although she'd dearly love to possess that ability. It was impossible to discern what the man was thinking at any given moment.

"What on earth happened to you?" Marni's clear blue eyes widened as Blair entered her bedroom.

"It's a long, complicated story I'll tell you later. Right now I just want to take a shower and a long nap."

"You certainly look as if you could use both," Marni said, noting Blair's drawn face and the hay on her jeans.

Blair stuck out her tongue. "A fine friend you are." Eyeing Marni suddenly, Blair stopped in her tracks. The jeans Marni had on were looser than the tight designer ones she usually wore, but they weren't so baggy that they were in danger of falling down. She'd unbuttoned just the top buttons of the plaid shirt, the little triangle of creamy skin appearing modestly tantalizing. Her thick blond hair was tied at the nape of her neck with a yellow ribbon.

"You look terrific," Blair stated.

To her amazement, Marni actually blushed. "Thanks. You don't think I look too much like Annie Oakley, do you?"

"Not at all. Turn around."

As Marni complied, she tottered a little on a pair of Blair's wedge-heel boots.

"Those can't possibly fit. You wear a size smaller than I do. With those pointed toes, you must be dying!"

"I can handle it," Marni insisted blithely. "It's just a small matter of positive thinking."

Blair knew how ineffective it was to argue once her friend's mind was made up. Stubbornness was probably the only trait the two women shared. That and loyalty.

"Have it your own way. But don't say I didn't warn you." Blair turned in the doorway of the bathroom. "Oh, by the way, did you have anything to drink last night?"

"Only a couple of glasses of Perrier."

"Are you sure? Not even a glass or two of wine?"

"Do you know how many calories there are in a glass of wine? Eighty. Eighty horrible calories all just waiting to leap onto my hips and put me out of work."

As Marni made the suggestion sound like a Roman banquet, Blair remembered her own dinner last night and glanced down, irrationally expecting to see fat cells popping out in every direction under her snug jeans.

"Then you simply misunderstood," she concluded.

Marni folded her arms and leaned against the door frame while Blair stripped off her clothes for her shower. "We're talking about Clint Hollister now, aren't we?"

Blair reached into the shower stall, turned the water on, then adjusted it to a comfortable temperature. "We are. And I've given it a lot of thought, Marni. If you didn't misunderstand, obviously Ramsey has the story all screwed up."

"Hey, Marni! Ready to go?" Matt's voice bellowed down the hall.

"Coming," she called out gaily. Then her tone became serious. "You know, Blair, I really hate to leave you here alone."

"I'm not alone."

"I know. That's what worries me."

"Clint didn't murder his wife," Blair insisted firmly. "I told you, Ramsey's simply confused."

"I doubt he could be confused about that," Marni argued, raising her voice to be heard above the streaming water.

"If he's so perfect, why are you playing Belle Starr with Matt Bradshaw this afternoon?"

"Ramsey's far from perfect," Marni said as she left the bathroom. "But I still can't believe he'd be mistaken about this, especially since Heather Hollister's maiden name was Blackwood." Marni paused, allowing her words to sink in. "She was Ramsey's daughter, honey."

Blair stood under the shower, wondering if it was the water or her blood that had suddenly turned to ice.

Chapter Eight

Half an hour later Blair entered the sunlit kitchen to find Clint seated at the table, drinking a cup of coffee.

"You look better," he decreed, eyeing her judiciously. "But you're still a little pale."

"I feel as if I've suddenly landed in the middle of a Robert Ludlum novel," she admitted, sinking down into a chair at the table.

"I know the feeling," he said.

"Where's Mildred?"

"I sent her home. I hope you don't mind."

"Of course not," Blair answered automatically. "But why?"

He reached into his shirt pocket and took out a crumpled cigarette pack. He tapped a cigarette on the table, his forehead drawn into thoughtful lines. "I didn't think it was fair to involve her. Who knows what's going to happen next?"

Blair nodded, watching his long fingers as he struck the match. She felt a stab of desire at the memory of those beautiful hands on her body and wondered if Marni could possibly be right. Was she allowing her desire for the man to overrule her common sense?

No, she decided firmly. Even if Clint Hollister hadn't had those gorgeous gray eyes, even if his hair hadn't been the color of sterling silver, even if his body hadn't been hard and well muscled, she would still believe him innocent of Ramsey Blackwood's charges. In fact, the man could look like Quasimodo and she'd know he was incapable of cruelty.

"I've been giving the matter a lot of thought," he said slowly, his expression grim.

"And?"

"I think you should leave, too."

A traitorous little thought tried to make itself heard in the back of her mind, but she squelched it immediately. "Why?"

His attention was drawn to the smoke circles rising slowly to the ceiling, so he missed her fleeting look of distress. "Because it's too dangerous," he replied.

"I'm not afraid," she protested, trying to keep the tremor from her voice.

"Aren't you?" he challenged harshly.

"No," she lied.

His flinty gray gaze speared her. "Then you're an idiot. Because I sure as hell am." His voice softened. "I'm afraid for you, Blair. I think you ought to leave until this is settled."

Blair stood her ground. "I'm not leaving the farm, Clint. I agree with you about Mildred, but I'm not allowing anyone to chase me away. I've worked for this my entire life, and I'll be damned if I'll turn tail and run the first time I encounter some problems."

His dark brows climbed his forehead before crashing back down. "Problems? Is that what you're calling all this?"

Blair sighed. "I don't know what to call it," she admitted. "But I do know you're stuck with me for the duration." She reached out, covering his hand with hers.

Clint looked down at the fair hand and experienced a sudden urge to lift it to his lips and press kisses into the delicate center of the palm. He wondered how he could possibly be feeling desire for her when his life was ripping apart at the seams. He jerked his hand away, reminding himself that he had more important things to consider.

"Are you hungry?" he asked suddenly.

Blair allowed a slight smile. "I'm always hungry. Marni has been warning me for years that I'm going to end up looking like the Pillsbury Doughboy."

"Come on, then," he said, rising from the table. "I'm taking you to lunch."

"Are we going out?" She ran her hands down the front of her clean jeans, wondering if she was appropriately dressed.

"Uh-huh."

"Perhaps I should change my clothes."

"You're perfect," he assured her. "We're going on a picnic. Mildred fixed it before she left."

"A picnic?"

He nodded. "I thought you might like to visit Irish Rover. He's pastured a short drive from here."

Blair's shining look of pleasure gave Clint her answer. After all that had happened that day, it was so nice of him to think of the one thing that could lift her spirits.

"I'd love it," she agreed instantly. "And, Clint..."

"Yeah?"

"Thank you."

He shrugged nonchalantly. "Hey, he's your horse. It's only right I take you out to inspect all your newfound wealth."

There was a gritty tone to his voice that Blair could not decipher, but as they walked out into the bright California sunshine, she decided not to try. For the next few hours, she was going to concentrate on enjoying herself.

They remained silent on the drive to the pasture, both embroiled in their own thoughts. Blair was surprised when Clint stopped the jeep suddenly and pointed out across a grassy field.

"There he is—the horse that built Clearwater Hills Farm."

Blair was out of her seat before Clint could turn off the engine, her eyes lit with a bright, expectant glow. She looked across the pasture toward the twenty-six-year-old horse. His smooth black coat was studded with gray, and his back was a little swayed, but she knew she was looking at a true champion.

Clint came up beside her, put his fingers between his teeth and let out an earsplitting whistle.

"He's sleeping," Clint explained when the horse didn't flick an ear. "He can still see well enough, but the old guy's pretty deaf. Even whistling doesn't always work. Usually I have to go down and wake him up to call him into his paddock."

"Dear old thing." She approached the horse slowly, allowing him time to discern her presence. As the elderly stallion woke up, he observed her with large, brown eyes. Deciding he liked what he saw, he sashayed toward them.

She rubbed his neck with a long, gentle stroke. "Hello, boy," she murmured. "How's the champ?" Irish Rover snorted happily, nuzzling his nose against the soft curve of her neck. "Oh, Clint, he's so sweet."

"He always has been, to hear Jason tell it. And what a ham! People come by every day to visit him, and he'll actually stand and pose while they take his picture."

Blair's expression sobered momentarily. "I suppose we'll have to stop that for a bit, won't we?"

Clint had already considered the inadvisability of allowing the small but steady stream of Irish Rover fans onto the farm.

"I'm afraid so," he agreed.

"Poor baby," she crooned, patting the white blaze on the horse's face. "You're going to think you've been forgotten. We'll come and visit you every day, though, won't we, Clint?"

"Sure."

"And tomorrow we'll bring a camera."

"A camera? What the hell for?"

"To take his picture. You said he enjoyed that. We don't want him to get depressed because he misses posing for the photographers."

He wondered if she was speaking from personal experience. "Are you going to miss it?" he asked bluntly.

To Clint's amazement, Blair laughed, a light, silvery sound that did something funny to his heart.

"Oh, Clint, I thought you'd agreed to stop typecasting. If I never see another camera lens again, it'll be too soon."

He believed Blair was sincere, but he didn't believe she'd given enough consideration to the life she would be giving up. He'd already decided that her plan to get out of the Tigress contract was an impulsive idea. She'd probably change her mind once she got on the phone with her agent.

"You wouldn't miss the fame?"

"The fame isn't all it's cracked up to be," she said with sudden seriousness.

"At least you don't have to sit home on a Saturday night."

Blair looked up at him, her tawny eyes trying to make him understand that she hadn't found many men who were willing to get to know Blair MacKenzie. Most seemed interested only in her glamorous alter ego.

"I don't date much."

"Why not?" he inquired, even though he knew it was none of his business. But he suddenly had to learn if there was someone special in her life.

She lifted her shoulders in a graceful shrug. "It's too complicated. Besides, you really don't want to hear about my life, Clint. I promise, it would bore you to death."

He no longer could stand being that close to her without touching her. He reached out, his knuckles stroking a light path up her high cheekbones. "You could never bore me, Blair," he said on a deep, vibrant note. "I want to know everything about you. Your likes, your dislikes, where you got that little scar across the bridge of your nose, and how one of the most glamorous women in the country ended up wearing faded jeans and eating bologna sandwiches under a tree."

Blair couldn't miss the desire in Clint's tone. His voice sounded as if it were coming from the inside of a velvet-lined drum, and his fingers were creating sparks on her skin.

"Why?" she whispered.

"For the same reason you want to know everything about me," he answered. "Because you're trying to figure out why your world goes spinning a little crazily out of control every time you're in the same room with a guy who was sent away for killing his wife."

She blanched, all the color draining from her face at his words. "How did you know I had heard about that?"

"Simple. I knew last night that Ramsey wouldn't miss the opportunity to make certain you heard his side. When you came into the den after talking with Marni, you were as pale as driven snow and you wouldn't look me in the eye. Then, back in the barn, when I rejected the idea of calling the police, for an instant there you tried me and found me guilty."

"That's not true. I never believed a word of that stupid story," she protested.

"Some of it's true, Blair."

She forced herself not to flinch. "Oh?"

"Heather *was* killed. I was found guilty and spent six months in prison." The revelation came out in a low, flat voice that couldn't entirely disguise the pain he'd suffered.

"But you didn't do it."

He looked down at her, his expression giving nothing away. "You're that sure? When twelve men and women who spent sixteen long days listening to sworn testimony decided otherwise?"

Blair nodded. "I'm positive."

Clint exhaled, and she suddenly realized he'd been holding his breath. "I want to get it all out into the open, but suddenly I'm starving. How about you?"

"Famished," she agreed, letting him take her hand as they walked back up to the car to retrieve the lunch basket Mildred had packed.

Clint laid a blanket out under the spreading branches of a tree. Blair began to unpack their lunch, then started to laugh. "You said we were having bologna sandwiches."

"Aren't we?"

"All I can say is perhaps it's better that Mildred isn't around the house right now. If she keeps cooking like this, she and Marni will never get along." Blair pulled out the crisp, golden fried chicken, a bowl of marinated pasta salad, a dish of fresh vegetables, deviled eggs and thick slices of home-baked bread.

"Mildred still cooks as if she's feeding that brood of hers," Clint said, eyeing the enormous array of food.

"Oh, my God," Blair gasped, "devil's food cake! I simply cannot resist devil's food cake. I'll be as big as the Goodyear blimp before long."

"I'll make a deal with you," Clint suggested, pouring them each a glass of cold California chablis.

"What's that?"

"You eat whatever you want, sweetheart, and I promise to watch your figure for you." His gray eyes held a pleasant leer that she found unthreatening.

Her own eyes subjected him to an agonizingly slow examination, moving across his wide shoulders, down his chest, over his hips and down the long, muscled expanse of his legs.

"Only if I can watch yours for you," she returned, negotiating the bargain playfully.

"You keep looking at me that way and I'm going to forget all about lunch and start in with dessert."

"You promised," she said softly, her gaze at odds with her words.

"I'm only a man, Blair," he groaned, feeling the tightening in his loins as her eyes turned to molten gold. "I'm made of flesh and blood, not steel." Flesh that was aching for the touch of her satiny body, blood that was rapidly turning to rivers of flame.

Blair could not miss Clint's response to the silken net settling down around them even as she felt her own body warming at the idea of making love to him right now, on the plaid blanket, under the vast expanse of blue sky.

Clint knew that to make love to Blair in this sunlit meadow would be inordinately pleasing; she could thrill his senses in a way no other woman had ever done, and he had no doubt that their lovemaking would be extraordinary. But when it was over, the same problems would be there, only complicated by their sexual intimacy. It was too soon. He sighed, leaning his head back against the tree as he closed his eyes and willed his body to respond to his silent command.

"I promised to tell you about Heather," he said finally.

Blair had been lost in a sensual fantasy of her own, but his gritty tone jolted her back to reality.

"Heather," she echoed flatly. "Did you love her?"

"No."

"Then why did you marry her?"

"I thought she was carrying my baby.

"Oh."

"She miscarried."

"I'm sorry."

"So was I." His gray eyes turned to cold steel, but Blair had the feeling that his anger was directed inward. "I cried when it happened. Can you believe that?"

Yes, she answered silently, remembering his tenderness in the barn. *I can believe that.* She remained silent, though, feeling that the question was rhetorical.

Clint swallowed his wine in long, thirsty gulps, then refilled his glass. Blair shook her head when he held the bottle in her direction. She'd learned her lesson last night.

"I'll admit I never loved Heather, yet I was stunned by how much I wanted that baby. I'd never thought about being a father, but when she showed up at my house with the news, it was suddenly as if she'd given me everything I ever wanted."

"There was always the opportunity for other children," Blair pointed out softly.

Clint made a harsh, scornful sound. "No, there wasn't. Heather had the doctor make certain of that."

"Oh." What on earth could she say to that?

"We got into a hell of an argument over it, and that's when she told me it hadn't even been my child."

Blair was speechless, trying not to think how furious a man would be to hear such news.

''You're wondering if I was angry enough to kill her,'' he said with unnerving accuracy.

She shook her head, taking a sip of wine, stalling for time until she recovered her voice. ''I've already told you, Clint,'' she finally said, ''I don't believe that story.''

The harsh lines of his face softened.

''Why did she lie to you in the first place?''

Clint stared out across the flower-dotted green meadow, thinking of the many times he'd asked himself the same question. ''She was an incredibly beautiful young woman who'd learned early in life that her looks could get her anything she wanted.''

Blair was beginning to understand why Clint had resented her career. He'd been burned once by a woman with more beauty than scruples, so how could he have known that Blair was any different?

''And she wanted you.''

''Until she had me. To Heather, seduction was what kept life interesting. I knew the moment she moved into my home that it wasn't going to work, but as long as she was carrying the baby, I was determined to make a go of it. When the accommodations weren't up to what she was used to, Jason let us move into his house. That satisfied her for about two days.''

''You could have divorced her,'' Blair pointed out.

He gave a bitter laugh. ''Don't you think I suggested that? Time and time again. No, Heather may not have wanted me, but she'd be damned if she was going to let me find happiness with anyone else, either.''

''But—''

''She threatened to kill herself every time I told her I was leaving. The first few times I didn't believe her. After three trips to the hospital to pump out her stomach, I began to realize she was serious.''

''Did all this come out in the trial?''

''Of course.''

''Then surely the jury could see she was a very unstable woman,'' Blair protested.

"They could also see several reasons that would make me willing to take drastic measures to get her out of my life. Including that ridiculous charge about Risky Pleasure."

Blair hoped that she could keep her expression from revealing how that particular aspect of the problem had been hard to dispel. Obviously she failed.

"That one bothered you, didn't it?" he asked, tapping a cigarette against the face of his watch before lighting it.

Deciding that the one thing the man deserved was the truth, she nodded reluctantly.

"It obviously bothered the hell out of the jury, too. It wasn't true, Blair."

"I believe that," she said earnestly.

He exhaled the smoke on a harsh breath. "Heather was the jealous one. I knew about the other men in her life and looked the other way. She resented anything or anyone who meant more to me than she did."

"And Risky Pleasure did."

"Yeah. And Heather hated the idea. She grew more and more jealous of Risky Pleasure and started telling everyone that I was obsessed with the filly. That I wanted the horse all to myself. She'd get drunk at parties and tell anyone who'd listen that I'd threatened her in order to force her to give me the money to buy the filly from Jason."

"Oh, Clint, how horrible for you.... Let's not talk about it anymore," Blair said, hating the anguish she saw carved into his rugged face.

"I've gotten this far," he stated dully, "I may as well finish the story."

"You don't have to tell me this. I know how it must hurt."

He viewed the gentle concern in her tawny eyes and wondered how two women who'd come into the world graced with such uncommon beauty could be so different.

"It's important that I do," he insisted. "Because I don't want it hovering unanswered between us. I've learned the hard way that if you ignore a problem, it can only get worse."

He inhaled on the cigarette, closing his eyes as he breathed in the strangely calming smoke. "When Heather didn't show up for a few days, it never occurred to me to call the police. It wasn't the first time she'd taken off. To tell you the truth, I always secretly hoped she wouldn't come back."

"I can understand that," Blair murmured.

"I'm glad you can, because the police and the DA couldn't. Neither could the jury. When Heather's body was found in that motel out of town, I was the logical suspect."

"Are you telling me you were convicted on circumstantial evidence?"

He gave her a mirthless smile. "The real world isn't like Perry Mason, Blair. The culprit doesn't crack on the stand and admit his guilt. But Jason never once doubted my innocence. He had investigators out combing the country, trying to find the last man Heather had been with."

"I'm glad you weren't entirely alone," Blair said quietly, wondering if she had misjudged her grandfather. Hadn't she convicted him of being a cruel, unloving man after only listening to her mother's side of the story? David MacKenzie, oddly enough, had always defended Jason Langley whenever the subject had come up. In later years, Kate had learned to discuss the matter out of her husband's hearing.

"I'd been in prison six months when one of the investigators Jason had hired ran across an assault charge in Fresno. A woman was accusing a man she'd met in a singles bar of beating her up. When the detective went out and interviewed her, she said the man had bragged that he'd already killed one woman, so it wouldn't be that difficult to do it a second time."

This was Ramsey Blackwood's legal mumbo jumbo that got Clint out of jail? Blair thought incredulously. "I take it he turned out to be the one."

Clint nodded. "It took a while to prove the case, but finally, when faced with all the evidence, the guy confessed."

"Clint," Blair said thoughtfully, "would Ramsey have any reason to hold a grudge against you, even knowing you didn't kill his daughter?"

He ground the cigarette out on a rock before answering. "You're thinking he might be behind all this."

Blair nodded. "It's a possibility."

Clint shook his head. "I've thought the same thing over and over again. I've even confronted him with it."

"And?"

He raked his fingers through his hair. "He denies it, of course. But he wouldn't have any reason to be pulling the same stunts over at Matt's. It doesn't make sense."

They fell silent, and Blair's mind tossed the problem around like a leaf caught in a whirlpool. It circled and circled, never quite getting free.

"He could be doing it to throw you off the track," she suggested.

Clint looked at her with renewed respect. "That's not an impossible scenario," he admitted. "But why now? Why didn't all these things happen three years ago, when Heather was first killed? Or when I was released from prison?"

Blair's face fell as she attempted to think of a logical explanation and came up empty. "I don't know," she admitted. "So I suppose we're back to square one."

"It seems so," he muttered. Then he eyed the still-untouched food. "I thought you were famished."

While Blair couldn't completely put away her worries, Clint had relieved her mind a great deal by telling her about Heather. She vowed first thing to let Marni know as much of the truth as possible, without revealing the secrets of Clint's ill-fated marriage.

As if by unspoken agreement, they kept their conversation on the positive aspects of the farm, discussing the upcoming racing season.

"Ready to go back?" he asked finally, without a great deal of enthusiasm. He rose, brushing crumbs from his faded indigo jeans.

"I suppose so," she murmured, accepting his outstretched hand. Blair was no more eager than he to return to the problems they'd managed to put away as they were sharing Mildred's expertly prepared lunch. She fell silent while they packed up the basket and drove back to the house.

"We still haven't gone over this season's racing schedule," Clint reminded her as they pulled up to the house.

"Why don't we go over the list tonight after dinner?" she suggested.

His eyes flicked over her slender frame, and he grinned. Where on earth did she put it all, he wondered, remembering the Herculean lunch she'd eaten. "Sure. That is, if you're going to be ready for food again before next weekend."

Blair wrinkled her nose at him in a gesture he found ill suited for the Tigress Woman, but perfectly suited to the jeans-clad lady jumping down from the Jeep.

"I told you, I've got a fantastic metabolism," she said.

This time his gaze took a more leisurely tour of her body, and Blair felt as if his silvery eyes were probing right through to her lacy underwear. "I can see that," he murmured, his husky tone affecting her like a physical caress.

She forced a ragged laugh. "And I exercise," she reminded him.

"Ah, yes, that mysterious exercise." His eyes settled onto the soft swell of her breasts, and Blair's nipples tightened as they pressed against the cotton fabric, reaching for his touch. "Tell me, do you prefer doing it indoors or out in the exhilarating fresh air?"

From the warm look in his eyes, Blair had a funny feeling he wasn't talking about physical fitness any longer. Her heart was beating at a rate that could not possibly be normal for anyone. She was amazed he couldn't see its wild thudding under her shirt.

"Fresh air in Manhattan?" She tried to laugh as her gaze was enmeshed in molten silver pools of masculine desire.

"Inside, then," he guessed, dragging his eyes to her lips. The strawberries Mildred had included in the picnic had dyed the soft skin a deep pink. He yearned for a taste of them.

"Inside," she agreed, feeling as if she were sinking into quicksand.

Clint nodded his head, shoving his hands deep into his pockets to keep from touching her. "There's nothing wrong with indoor sports," he allowed. "But now that you live in sunny California, you should probably consider moving some of your activities outdoors. Have you ever done it at night? Bathed in the glow of a full moon?"

Although they were still ostensibly discussing exercise, his low tone painted sensual pictures in her mind. Blair envisioned Clint making love to her on that plaid blanket, lying under a black velvet canopy of diamond-bright stars, the air perfumed with the scent of California poppies and sweet lupine. She trembled slightly at the provocative image.

"How long has it been since you've seen stars?" he asked suddenly, once again giving Blair the unnerving feeling that he could read her mind.

"Why did you ask that?" she asked defensively.

He shrugged. "I thought when things settle down around here, you might like to go moonlight riding along the beach."

It sounded marvelous. It also sounded far more romantic than she was up to handling right now.

"But I thought you weren't going to let this well-photographed fanny onto one of your precious horses."

He grinned. "That was before I learned that well-shaped rear end was quite accustomed to sitting in a saddle."

Suddenly Blair remembered his words to Matt. "That's right! How did you find out about Ben Winters, anyway?"

A slight shadow came over his eyes. He busied himself by lifting the basket out of the backseat of the Jeep. "Here."

"Thanks," she murmured absently, taking the wicker picnic hamper. "Ben Winters?" she prodded him softly.

"Marni told Blackwood, who told me," he admitted, looking decidedly uncomfortable.

"But that means you've talked to him today."

She wondered if Ramsey Blackwood had called and told Clint he was receiving half the farm. Was that what had caused his change in attitude toward her?

Clint groaned inwardly, reminding himself about tangled webs of prevarication. He tapped a cigarette on the hood of the Jeep before sticking it between his lips.

Recognizing the stalling tactic, Blair merely waited.

"Last night," he admitted, deciding there had been enough half-truths between them already.

"Last night? But you were with me last night." Her smooth brow furrowed, and suddenly she remembered. "He was the one who called after I'd gone to bed, wasn't he? I asked you who it was, and you told me a friend offering condolences." Blair didn't like the way Clint's eyes shifted from her curious gaze as he inhaled on that ever-present cigarette. "Why didn't you tell me it was Ramsey?"

"He's not my favorite topic of conversation, Blair. Surely you can understand that."

She leaned against the Jeep, looking at him thoughtfully. Clint forced the muscles of his face into a casual expression.

"Of course I can. Which makes it all the more curious why in the world he'd be calling you up to tell you what he'd learned about me from Marni." Suddenly she remembered her friend's complaint that morning. "That's what last night's dinner invitation was about, wasn't it? Ramsey was pumping Marni for information."

"Blackwood doesn't keep me informed about his social calendar, Blair. I assume he invited the woman to his house because she's young, beautiful and famous." Clint suddenly spun around on a booted heel, turning in the direction of the paddock.

"So why did he spend the entire evening asking about me?" Blair challenged after him. "And how did you know they had dinner at his house?"

Then she recalled Clint's willingness to wait up for her friend. "That's how you knew when she was coming home, isn't it? He called you the minute he stuck her in that damn taxi.... Why, Clint?"

His tanned face could have been carved from granite as he looked at her over his shoulder. "I thought you trusted me."

"I do," she insisted, wishing she'd been able to put more emphasis on her declaration.

"Then why don't you start acting as if you do?" he growled before marching off again.

Furious, Blair reached down, picked up a small rock from the gravel driveway and threw it at the back of his head. It missed only by inches, and Clint skidded to a halt.

Blair held her breath, waiting for the inevitable explosion, but when he pivoted slowly around, his expression was less formidable.

"Baseball?" he inquired dryly.

She didn't know whether to laugh or cry as he turned their argument back to that ridiculous guessing game.

"If it was baseball, Mr. Hotshot Trainer, I wouldn't have missed!"

"You're angry," he diagnosed correctly.

"Furious," she admitted.

"Want to try for two out of three?" he asked, taking off his hat, baring his silvery head for a target.

"Don't tempt me," she warned.

"I could ask the same thing of you," he said huskily as he watched her breasts rise and fall under her cotton shirt.

Blair shook her head, trying not to respond to the sensual teasing in his voice. "Why don't you just get to work while I try to figure out that Chinese puzzle Jason Langley called his accounting system. The man hadn't balanced his personal checkbook for the last ten years!"

"Jason could get a little absentminded," Clint acknowledged. "He usually left the important things to his lawyer or his accountant."

"I'm not thrilled with the entries made by his accountant, either," Blair confessed. "I still haven't figured out what half of them mean.... Like 'high tower.' My grand-father never owned a horse with that name, did he?"

"Never. But it does ring a bell."

"Well, whatever it was, it didn't come cheap. He spent more than a million dollars on it last year."

Clint expelled a low whistle. "That's not chicken feed. Let me think about it, and I'll try to remember where I heard the name, okay?"

She nodded. "Okay."

"I've got to supervise the final feeding now, but I'll see you later for dinner."

Blair tried to remind herself that she was angry at Clint for not being totally open with her. Yet she was finding it so difficult to refuse the invitation in those lustrous gray eyes. She nodded her acquiescence.

"Would you like to go out? If you feel like seafood, we could always drive into the city."

"Shouldn't we stay here? To watch after things?"

"Yeah, we probably should," Clint agreed. "Since we're on our own, want to grill a couple of steaks?"

"Sounds great. I'll take two out of the freezer."

"What about your friend?"

Blair laughed, her irritation dissolving. "Marni would die before allowing all those calories to pass through her lips."

"It doesn't seem to have done you any harm." His gaze paid masculine compliments. "Gymnastics," he guessed suddenly.

"Nope."

"Too bad," he murmured, putting his hat back on and turning away again. "That one offered an intriguing realm of possibilities."

Chapter Nine

Clint couldn't get Blair out of his mind as he attended to the afternoon feeding. She was definitely not what he'd been expecting, and he was admittedly fascinated by the woman; she had far more depth than what was displayed by her advertising campaigns.

"There you are!"

When the all-too-familiar voice of Ramsey Blackwood jerked him from his thoughts, Clint muttered a low oath. The one thing he didn't need today was a visit from his former father-in-law. Especially after the way the man had made certain that Blair heard about his shoddy little story. Blackwood's side of it, at any rate.

He slowly put down the grain bucket. "Even a rattlesnake gives a warning before it attacks, Blackwood."

"Ms. MacKenzie didn't waste any time in going to you for confirmation of your past indiscretions, did she?" Ramsey said thoughtfully. "That young woman is reminding me more and more of her obstreperous old grandfather."

"May I point out that obstreperous old man kept you in Mercedes cars over the years?"

Ramsey Blackwood gave him a mirthless smile. "I earned every penny I made from that coldhearted old skinflint. And you're a fine one to talk, Hollister, since you've made out like a bandit."

Clint pulled out a cigarette, breaking his own commandment about no smoking in the barn. "I never expected Jason to will me fifty percent of Risky Pleasure."

"Oh, that was probably overly generous, but this new twist is quite a coup." The man's eyes narrowed wickedly. "As far as gigolos go, you're probably the best paid in history. When I suggested a little romance might go a long way toward convincing a woman to change her mind, I certainly didn't expect you to make it an Olympian sport."

"What the hell are you talking about?" Clint grated out between clenched teeth, his patience at a very low ebb.

"Your receiving fifty percent of Clearwater Hills Farm, of course. Tell me, Hollister, did you come right out and ask for it, or did you let the lady believe it was all her idea?"

Clint almost choked on the smoke filling his lungs as Ramsey's words sank in. "What?"

The attorney's lips pursed into a charade of a smile. "Now you're going to play it coy and tell me you didn't know."

"Not only did I not know, I don't believe it."

"Interesting," Ramsey murmured to himself. "Well, it's true. She called me before dawn this morning and instructed me to make out the papers."

"Do you have them with you?"

"Of course."

"Let me see them."

"They're not yours." At Clint's glower, Ramsey curved his fingers a bit tighter about the handle of his alligator-skin attaché case.

"Let me see them, Blackwood, or I'll break your fingers taking that case away from you."

"I'd press charges," the lawyer warned.

Clint tipped his hat back with his thumb, rocking back and forth on his heels. He dropped the cigarette to the floor of the barn, making certain he ground it out before returning his attention to Ramsey.

"You do that, counselor. It sure as hell wouldn't be the first time." He moved forward, his hand outstretched.

"I made a mistake, Hollister. I honestly thought you were guilty." The man backed away a few steps, clutching the briefcase to his chest.

"Don't give me that. You just wanted me out of here because I wouldn't encourage Jason to buy into your crazy investment schemes."

"You owed it to Heather to try. I offered you a generous commission on every one of those deals. You could have been set for life. How happy do you think she was, living here as the wife of a hired hand?" The attorney's tone was blatantly scornful. "And after the life she'd been used to."

"I'd say about as happy as she was living in that La Jolla mansion of yours. I saw the scars on her wrists. She was in trouble long before I stepped into the picture."

Ramsey waved his hand, airily dismissing his daughter. "Look, I was only trying to help. Jason Langley was a wealthy man, but except for the money he spent on these stupid nags, he might as well have kept his money in the mattress."

"These stupid nags made him all that money in the first place, because he understood them. He was smart enough to stay out of investments he didn't know anything about.... Now that we've cleared the air on that little subject, I'd like to see those papers."

Ramsey put the case down on a bale of hay, opened it and extracted a manila envelope, which he handed over to Clint. He eyed the younger man thoughtfully as Clint skimmed the pages of legalese.

"You know, Hollister, this could still work out for the best. If you've got her eating out of your hand enough to deed half this place to you in two days, you could probably talk her into selling by the end of the week. I call my buyer, you and the young lady make a tidy profit, and everyone ends up the winner."

"Including you," Clint added, "since you're holding out for a ten percent commission."

"It's a fair deal. Besides, you'd still end up with forty-five percent, which is damn good pay for a night of bedroom acrobatics."

Clint felt his fury rising and fought against the urge to rid the world of the supercilious attorney once and for all. "You're forgetting something," he said.

"And that is?"

"If Blair doesn't sell, I own fifty percent."

"She'll never make it," Ramsey blustered.

"I'm betting she will."

"Hollister, look at this reasonably. The woman can't possibly run a farm this size."

"We're going to run it together. Besides, you're not giving the lady credit. She's more than just a pretty face." Clint gave the older man a false smile. "Now why don't you go back to your office, and I'll see that Ms. MacKenzie gets these papers."

Ramsey held his hand out, shaking his head at the same time. "I don't think that's a good idea."

"You've got five minutes to get off this farm," Clint warned him in a low voice. "And if you know what's good for you, you won't show that two-sided face on the property again. Is that understood?"

"You can't fire me!"

"I wasn't talking about firing you, counselor."

There was a silky threat in Clint's voice that Ramsey appeared unwilling to challenge. He backed slowly out of the barn, climbed into his gray Mercedes and roared down the road.

Blair was on the phone when Clint entered the kitchen.

"That's okay, Marni," she was saying. "Stay as long as you like. I'm glad you're having a good time."

She hung up, a fond smile curving her lips. "Now that's a pair I'd never have in my wildest dreams imagined together. I'm amazed they're finding anything to talk about. She's not coming home for dinner, by the way."

Blair expected Clint to make some suggestive comment about the two of them having the house all to themselves, but he surprised her by shrugging carelessly and saying nothing.

"Clint, is something wrong?"

"What could be wrong?"

She didn't like the cold glitter in his eyes. "Around this place, just about anything. Has something else happened?"

He removed the papers from his back pocket. "Your attorney brought these by for you. I told him I'd see that you got them."

"Oh, damn. I wanted to surprise you!" Then her amber eyes widened. "Clint, what are you doing?"

He ripped the papers in half, then in half again, repeating the process until the confettilike pieces had drifted over the floor, resembling unmelted snow.

"I'm not for sale, Blair. At any price." He turned and walked out of the house.

She stared mutely at the scattered shreds of what had been her special surprise. Then she ran outside and grabbed him by the arm. "What did that grandstand play in there mean?"

He shrugged off her hand as easily as if she'd been a troublesome gnat. "All you rich girls seem to find it amusing sport to play with people's lives. I thought you were different, Blair, but obviously I was wrong. You're just like Heather, Kate—"

"Just one minute, mister," she interrupted, stiffening her back. "How dare you compare my mother with a woman you've already admitted had no more morals than a common alley cat!"

"Kate Langley may not have fooled around on David MacKenzie, but she sure as hell ruined his life."

"She loved him!" Blair shouted.

"Then she should have loved him enough to let him go. But no, she had to trap him into marriage and force him to give up what he probably did better than anyone before or after him."

"A lot you know." Blair tossed her head angrily. "My father was a good and sweet man, but Irish Rover was obviously a fluke, because he never trained another champion."

Clint's laugh was bitter. "Of course he didn't, you little fool. Jason wouldn't let him."

"What did my grandfather have to do with it? My father left Clearwater Hills Farm."

"Right. And Jason made certain each farm knew that if it wanted any Irish Rover or Moonglow blood in its stables, it had better not hire David MacKenzie!"

His words came at her like deadly bullets, and Blair sucked in a deep breath as they struck at the very core of her heart. She remembered her mother bitterly complaining about their small homes, their constant traveling. It had never made sense to her that Kate had placed the blame for all their misfortunes on Jason Langley, but suddenly the pieces fitted into place. She felt as if she were going to be ill.

"My father was that good?" she whispered.

Clint was not immune to the pain that his own display of exacerbation had just caused her. "He was the best."

"I'm selling the farm," she announced suddenly. "What do you want to pay for it?"

"Me?" He stared at her.

"Name a price, Clint. Any number from one to ten will do."

"Blair, be serious."

Her eyes were as hard as agates. "Oh, I'm deadly serious, Clint. And if you're not going to make an offer, I'll just have to come up with something. How does one dollar sound?"

He didn't like the way she looked. Two scarlet flags were the only color in her face, her lips were pressed into a grim line and her gaze had frozen to ice.

"Blair—"

"Sold, to the man in the gray Stetson," she announced with a smile that chilled his soul. "Stop by the house later this afternoon, cowboy, and I'll sign the place over to you and give you the key. Right now I'm going to pack.''

She spun around, making her way to the house on legs that threatened to fold at any minute. Clint caught up with her easily, one hand gripping her shoulder. ''Blair, I'm sorry. I thought you knew.''

She stared up at him. ''My God, Clint, if I'd known that Jason Langley ruined my father's chances to train champions, do you think I'd have stepped one foot on this farm? I can't accept anything from such a cruel and heartless man.''

Blair squared her shoulders. ''The only reason I got into modeling in the first place was because it paid so well. I've been saving for years to start my own stable. Oh, nothing on the grand scale of this, of course,'' she admitted, her gaze raking over the rolling fields of grassland. ''But at least I'll know I bought it with my own money—and not Jason Langley's thirty pieces of silver!''

''Jason always intended for you to have the farm, Blair,'' Clint argued. ''That's why he wouldn't sell out, even when he knew he didn't have long to live. He wanted all this to be yours.''

''What makes you think I give a damn about what Jason Langley wanted?'' she spat out.

''What about what David MacKenzie wanted?''

Blair avoided his steady gray gaze, her eyes moving rapidly over the distant fields. ''What does that mean?''

''Do you think he spent all those years training you just to have you work in second-class stables? He trained you for here, Blair. And according to Ben Winters, you're ready.''

That got her attention. ''You've talked with Ben?''

''Before lunch. He had nothing but praise for you—even if you are a woman.''

She groaned. ''I've heard that before.''

''Then you'll stay? It's what your father would have wanted.''

Blair thought back to how diligently her father had worked with her, teaching her everything he knew about Thoroughbreds. Clint was right. Her father had obviously been preparing her to train champions; to return to Clearwater Hills Farm to reclaim her birthright. If she let him down now, she'd be guilty of the same bullheaded, unbending attitude that had characterized Jason Langley. Mildred had already warned her not to allow her deep-seated trait of stubbornness to ruin any more lives. Including her own. As furious as she was about her situation, Blair couldn't let her father down.

"I'll stay," she agreed reluctantly. "How about you?"

"I don't want fifty percent of your farm, Blair."

"I need you," she protested. "I don't care what Ben says. I'm not ready to train all these horses by myself."

"Then I'll stay on for a while."

"How long?"

"As long as you need me." He turned away then, continuing toward the training barn.

That was something, Blair considered, wondering what Clint would have said if she'd told him she needed him for a lot more than to help train her horses. That confession was better kept to herself, she decided, heading back to the house.

Clint had just reached the training barn when it hit him where he'd heard the words "high tower." Jason had yelled them into the phone about two weeks before he died. It hadn't been like Jason to spend a million dollars without discussing it with Clint. And yet for a year, according to Blair, he'd done exactly that. Why?

"IT DIDN'T WORK," the man admitted, keeping his voice low as he spoke into the telephone. "She's unbelievably stubborn."

"You're an attractive enough man. Surely you can convince her it would be in her best interests to sell," the woman suggested.

"From the way she was looking at Hollister this morning, I wouldn't stand a chance."

"Clint Hollister," the woman muttered acidly. "That man has been a thorn in my side from the beginning. It'll be a pleasure taking care of him."

"I thought you said there wasn't going to be any violence."

"Unnecessary violence," she corrected. "And that's up to you."

The man heard the water in the shower being turned off. "Look, I'm not alone here. I've got to hang up," he said. "I'll see you Friday night."

"It won't be soon enough. I've missed you, darling."

The invitation in her throaty voice was unmistakable, and he felt his blood warming in response, as it always did. "Me, too."

She laughed. "I can tell. Don't let your houseguest wear you out, sweetheart. I'm expecting marvelous things from you on Friday."

He hung up just as the door to the den opened. "What kept you?" he asked with a boyishly attractive grin. "I was getting lonely."

IT WAS AS IF BOTH Clint and Blair had decided to work overtime to keep their relationship on a strictly professional level. Although their shared dinner was not without the odd moment of sensual yearning, they steadfastly ignored each one, keeping the conversation on horses, the farm and the season's racing schedule. Clearwater Hills Farm's early waking hour allowed Blair to escape to her own room soon after dinner was over, but sleep was an illusive target. Her dreams were filled with Clint Hollister, who appeared to her in a myriad of moods, like the facets of a child's kaleidoscope.

They spoke only a few words as they worked together in the predawn hours of the next day, feeding the horses in training and then watching the workouts, but each was vividly aware of the other's presence. Last night's self-restraint seemed to be eroding, like tides undermining the foundations of a sand castle, and Blair was never so glad to see anyone as she was when she walked into the kitchen and found Marni sitting at the kitchen table.

"Hi! Where's Matt?" she asked.

"He's coming. He just wanted to talk to Clint for a minute about Dancing Lady. She's run on three soft racetracks in a row back East and came home with a fungus on the heels of her foot."

Blair had been pouring herself a cup of coffee, but at Marni's matter-of-fact tone she turned to stare at her longtime friend. "Sounds as if you two found something to talk about," she finally stated noncommittally.

"All night, in fact," Marni said. "Matt was as surprised as I was to look up at the clock and see it was time for the morning feeding."

"You stayed up all night? Talking?" Blair hadn't been overly surprised when she awoke this morning to find that Marni hadn't come home. But she'd pictured quite a different scenario going on next door.

"Well, not just talking."

"I thought not," Blair murmured.

"We spend some of the time watching videotapes of races. Oh, Blair, it's such an exciting business . . . you've no idea!"

"I think I can imagine."

Marni realized what she'd said and began to laugh. "Of course you can. But I never realized there was so much more to horse racing than the betting window. Why didn't you ever tell me?"

"Perhaps my feelings don't carry as much weight as Matt Bradshaw's."

Marni's blue eyes held a faraway look, and a little smile curved her full lips. "He's a wonderful man, Blair, like no one I've ever met."

Blair sat down at the table. "This sounds serious."

Marni made a face. "I think it is. I wouldn't get blisters and saddle sores for any other man I know."

"Saddle sores? You actually rode a horse?"

"Bounced is probably a better description," she admitted, grimacing slightly in remembrance. "My rear is probably black and blue by now."

"How were the boots?"

"I've blisters over blisters. I'm going to buy a pair of my own this afternoon. Right now it's a toss-up which of us is limping worse—Dancing Lady or me."

Blair tried to picture Marni on a horse and came up blank.

"Blair, do you think it's possible to fall in love at first sight?"

"I didn't used to," she answered slowly, staring down into her coffee, as if seeking an answer in the black depths. "But I'm beginning to wonder."

Both women fell silent, content to linger in their own thoughts.

"Good morning, Blair. Boy does that coffee smell great!"

As Matt came into the kitchen, he gave Blair a wide, friendly smile. It didn't escape her notice that the smile he shared with Marni was warmer, more intimate, and sparked with a definite promise.

"Good morning. Would you like some breakfast? Clint and I ate before the workouts, but you're probably starved."

He shook his blond head. "Thanks, anyway, but Marni and I already ate. She makes a dynamite Spanish omelet."

Marni a cook? Blair wouldn't remember the last time she'd seen her eat anything that resembled a full meal. When Blair's questioning gaze caught her friend's eye, Marni only shrugged, allowing a slight, inwardly directed smile.

"How's Tidal Wave?" Clint asked Matt as he pulled up a chair and straddled it, leaning his arms along the top. "Are you going to run him in the Santa Anita Derby?"

"I think he has a good chance," Matt replied. "With Dancing Lady's problems, he's about all I've got to run these days."

"Things will pick up," Clint said reassuringly.

Matt managed a grin. "Sure they will," he agreed with false heartiness. "That thought is what's keeping me going these days."

They fell silent for a few minutes; then Matt rose from the table. "Well, we'd better be going. I promised Marni another riding lesson. She's catching on faster than anyone I've ever known."

As Marni rose to follow him, she stopped suddenly, looking back over her shoulder. "Oh, dear, we almost forgot to invite you two."

"Invite us to what?" Blair asked.

"The party Matt is throwing Friday night. He spent an hour calling people, but we almost forgot to tell the two most important guests."

"What's the party for?" Clint asked, though he was not in any mood to celebrate.

"I thought Marni might like to meet a few of the local folk," Matt said offhandedly.

"It's going to be a lot of fun," Marni coaxed prettily.

Blair knew it would hurt her friend's feelings if she failed to show up. "I'll drop in. But I can't stay long," she warned.

Marni's smile was beatific, and even Matt looked pleased. "Clint," he said. "Can we count on you?"

"Just for one quick drink. I don't want to leave the farm for long."

"Great. See you later," Matt said with hearty enthusiasm.

"Later," Blair and Clint murmured in unison as the pair left, arm in arm.

"He certainly is good-natured," Blair observed, "considering that it sounds as if he's in worse shape than we are."

"Matt's had a run of bad luck the past few years," Clint told her. "But your friend seems to have made quite a difference in his attitude."

"Marni has that effect on men," Blair allowed.

"Really?"

"Really," she said dryly. "Don't tell me you haven't noticed."

"Not really. I suppose I've been too busy watching you."

Clint's gaze bathed her face in a warm glow that went all the way to her toes. Once again a sensual net drifted over them, and without realizing that either one had moved, Blair was in his arms.

"Oh, sweetheart," he whispered, his lips against hers, so that Blair felt the words as well as heard them. "What you do to me with those huge, gold eyes."

She closed her eyes, delighting in the sound of his voice, the way his words breathed a caress on her skin, the warmth of his wide hands as his fingers splayed against her back, urging her closer still. She could feel him against her, from her breasts to her thighs, and it seemed that the heat from both their bodies was melding them into a single delicious entity.

"Is this one of those passes you didn't want to keep dodging?" he asked, his thumbs creating both ecstasy and havoc to her senses as they played lightly, tantalizingly up and down her sides, barely skimming her breasts.

"Yes." She managed to whisper her answer into his mouth, their breath mingling in a soft, scented cloud.

"Should I stop?" His lips plucked at hers, punctuating the words with little kisses.

Her fingers were toying with the hair at the back of his neck, delighting in the feel of the silky silver that curled so enticingly against his collar.

"Don't you dare," she said, tugging at a silver curl playfully. "I told you, Clint, this is one of those passes I *don't* want to dodge."

As his lips suddenly pressed against hers with an urgent, searching hunger, Blair tugged his shirt loose, her nails sinking into the muscled flesh of his back.

"That's right," he groaned, "let me feel your claws, Tigress lady. Let me know that you want me as badly as I want you."

A vague warning rippled through her as Clint's huskily muttered words sank in. He was just like the others, obviously more interested in bedding the famous Tigress Woman than making love to Blair MacKenzie.

Clint had not known he'd said the words out loud, but when her body went stiff in his arms, he realized that he'd made the primitive fantasy an obvious one.

"Blair," he muttered achingly, "you're taking it all wrong."

Her fingers left off kneading the muscles of his back and pressed against his chest as she attempted to put some space between them.

"I don't think I am," she said firmly, even now hoping that she might be wrong, that she'd overreacted to what was simply an honest slip in the heat of passion. "Admit it, Clint. You're like every other man in the country. You want to make it with the Tigress Woman!"

If she'd known that damn ad campaign was going to turn her world upside down, she would never have agreed to do it. But at the time she'd been desperate for the money offered, and there was certainly nothing obscene in the photos. The obscenities were in the minds of men like Clint Hollister.

She tried to squirm away, but Clint's superior strength held her in his arms, not hurting her, but not permitting her freedom, either.

"I'm not like every other man in the country," he rasped. "I'm not like any man you've ever been with."

"Your modesty overwhelms me," she said recklessly. "But you're right, Clint. All the men I've made love to over the years have been gentlemen."

She neglected to say that there'd been only three in all her nearly thirty years and that one had been her husband, who couldn't honestly claim that description, either. Her love life was not Clint Hollister's business—not that experimental time at twenty, when she'd been positive she was the only virgin left in New York City; not her ill-fated marriage to a young photographer who'd never forgiven her for achieving fame without him; nor the comfortable, but unexciting affair she'd shared with her accountant from Brooklyn.

Tom had been sweet, and Blair had loved him dearly, but their dreams and aspirations had been too different to make a long-lasting relationship possible.

Clint's hands locked firmly around her shoulders. "You've got the quickest tongue in the West, sweetheart. If you don't watch it, one of these days it's going to get you in a lot of trouble."

Blair trembled slightly at the cold warning in his tone, reminding herself that Clint Hollister was a man who rode his passions hard.

"In the first place, I've never claimed to be a gentleman. And in the second, of course I want to make love to the Tigress Woman."

"I knew it," Blair muttered, attempting to twist out of his arms once again.

"You're a damn fool, Blair MacKenzie," he growled, his fingers tightening even more. "I ought to beat you, but then I'd have to convince you all over again that I'm not the kind of guy who'd ever strike a woman. No matter how much she deserves it."

His tone was definitely accusatory, and Blair's eyes shot golden sparks as she glared up at him. "You're the one who admitted you only want a roll in the hay with some distorted image of me you've cooked up—some sick fantasy you've derived from what was supposed to be a simple perfume ad!"

Clint wanted to shake Blair until her lovely teeth rattled. How could she not see it? Not feel it? Before he gave into his instinct, he released her and groped for a cigarette, lighting it quickly.

Blair watched his chest rise as he inhaled, remembering how wonderful the warm skin of his back had felt to her fingertips. The sensual memory returned with devastating exactness when her gaze couldn't resist following the dark whorl of chest hair to where it disappeared beneath his belt. Her fingers almost itched with the desire to explore the intriguing path.

"What are you thinking right this minute?"

His bland voice cut through her intimate reverie, and Blair jerked her eyes back up to his face. "Nothing," she lied poorly.

He drew in on the cigarette, a vaguely amused expression on his face. "Liar. We both know exactly what you were thinking. Face it, Blair—that advertising agency picked you out of thousands of other equally beautiful women because you *are* the Tigress Woman."

"So now the man's an expert on Madison Avenue," she shot back.

"I'm an expert on *you*," he corrected smoothly. "I know that despite your attempts to remain cool and collected, you're the most passionate woman I've ever held in my arms. It doesn't do any good to deny it, Blair, because your body gives you away whenever it flames for me. I know you're feeling what I am when those beautiful eyes light up like shooting stars and those luscious lips cry out against mine."

"Your ego is honestly not to be believed," she murmured, hating the way her whole being was responding to his huskily issued accusation, warming at the words in exactly the same way it never failed to respond to his touch.

"Don't fight it, Blair," he suggested, stabbing out the cigarette in a copper ashtray. "All you're doing is postponing the inevitable.... Ready to go supervise the morning runs?"

"Of course I am," she agreed waspishly, marching out the door.

Muttering a low oath, Clint followed, thinking that Blair MacKenzie redefined "stubborn." In that respect, along with her love for the horses, she was reminding him more and more of Jason Langley.

Chapter Ten

The next three days passed without any renewed seduction attempts from Clint. Not that it would honestly be seduction, Blair told herself reluctantly. She had to admit she was becoming more and more drawn to the rugged Thoroughbred trainer.

He possessed a gentleness that she was certain very few people witnessed. It was obvious in the way he treated the horses, especially Risky Pleasure. His soft words and tender touches had her wishing fleetingly that he'd behave with such warmth toward her. Then she'd have to shake herself, remembering that she'd been the one to set the rule about their relationship remaining strictly business.

They worked well together, she acknowledged. Fortunately, they shared the same ideas about training Thoroughbreds, except for the hay storage, and she'd been waiting for the right moment to bring up the subject. Things had been going so smoothly, she wasn't looking forward to rocking the boat.

Blair reminded herself of that one morning while watching the workouts. Clint was standing next to her, one booted foot on the bottom rail of the fence surrounding the oval track. Although the morning air was brisk and cool, Blair could feel the warmth radiating from his body.

"Oh, I meant to tell you something," he said offhandedly as Matador came charging past.

"What?" she murmured, her gaze shifting down to the stopwatch she held in her hand. Blair didn't think she could ever tire of watching the glorious Thoroughbreds run.

"I'm building a single-level hay shed between the training barns."

Her eyes widened as she turned to look up at him. "Really? What made you change your mind?"

"Nothing. I always felt the same way you did," he admitted a bit sheepishly. "It was Jason who refused to consider it. He wasn't usually against new ideas, but every once in a while he'd dig his heels in, and it would take a stick of dynamite to get him to budge."

She studied Clint appraisingly, believing his statement about her grandfather. "Why didn't you tell me that when I first brought it up?"

He grinned, reaching out to tug on her thick braid. "I didn't want you to get the idea I'd let a woman walk all over me."

"Well, I certainly never thought that. You gave me some rough moments, Clint Hollister. I didn't think we'd ever be able to work together."

"Neither did I. But it looks as if we were both wrong, doesn't it? I think we make a pretty good team, Blair."

His deep voice caressed her name, and she knew her eyes were giving her away as they locked with his. "Me, too," she said softly.

"Blair..." Clint hesitated, trying to choose his words carefully. He didn't want her to run off, but he was also going crazy from wanting her. He'd thought that if he kept things casual, Blair would eventually give in to the shared desire that continued to spark between them at odd, unexpected moments. Marni had been spending almost all her time at Matt's; she'd breeze in occasionally to pick up a new change of clothes. That left the two of them alone in the house, their bedrooms just a few feet apart.

He'd been waiting for her to come to him, but so far, Blair MacKenzie was demonstrating a streak of Langley determination that made him want to wring her lissome neck.

Blair found herself trapped in a gleaming silver lair and wondered how long she could continue to fight her rebellious body. In fact, she considered with brutal self-honesty, if it were only her body that mattered, she might give in to the pleasure she knew could be found in Clint's arms. But something was happening to her heart, and that was an entirely different story.

She couldn't risk a brief, passionate affair, knowing that she'd feel miserable when it came to an end. And how could she continue to work with him then, if he shared his bed with some other warm and willing woman? The answer was that she couldn't. And since she needed his Thoroughbred expertise every bit as much as she needed him as a lover, she'd have to resist temptation.

She was trying to find the words to explain this when Matador's high whinny made her jerk her eyes back to the track. The gelding had taken off at a full gallop, as if the devil himself were after him, and Blair gasped as she saw the young girl, Annie, hanging on for her life.

"Clint!" Blair grasped his arm. "He's not slowing down at the fence!"

Matador suddenly swerved, throwing the rider against the rail. She fell to the ground, and Blair and Clint held their collective breaths, praying the wild eyed Thoroughbred wouldn't crush her.

"I'll get him," Jerry cried out suddenly, jumping onto a training horse and taking off after Matador.

"Jerry can handle Matador," Clint assured Blair as they ran toward the fallen rider. "He used to groom him. Right now Annie needs our attention."

The young girl was sitting up, holding her arm gingerly. Her face was abnormally pale, and her eyes were wide dark circles.

"I'm sorry, Ms. MacKenzie, Clint," she said immediately. "But he didn't give me any warning. One minute we were going along fine, then he took off as if he'd been stung by a hornet, or something."

"Don't worry about that," Blair said, her words seconded by Clint. "How are you?"

"I think I broke my arm," Annie said, flinching as Clint's strong fingers circled the bone.

"I think you did," he agreed. "Can you walk to the garage? We'll take you to the hospital and get your arm set."

"I can walk, but what about Matador?"

Clint's gaze cut to the far end of the track. "Jerry's got him," he assured her. "Everything's fine."

Annie's dark brown eyes suddenly filled with tears. "Not everything," she wailed. "Now I won't be able to ride Risky Pleasure against Cimarron!"

Blair shot Clint a challenging look. "Does everyone around this place know about your crazy idea?"

He shrugged. "I suppose it's been discussed."

"And I suppose they're all behind you one hundred percent," she replied archly. Glancing down into Annie's face, Blair sighed. "Stupid question. Forget I even bothered to ask."

"She's a wonderful horse, Ms. MacKenzie," Annie said fervently, momentarily seeming to forget her pain in her enthusiasm. "I know she can win." Her young face fell. "Even if I won't be riding her."

Blair knew when she was licked. "The name is Blair," she said absently. "And I've already promised Clint that I'd consider the idea.... Now, let's get you to the car."

"You won't be sorry," Annie insisted as Clint and Blair supported her on the way to the house. "She'll win. Really she will."

"That seems to be the consensus of opinion," Blair muttered, steadfastly ignoring the knowing glint in Clint's gray eyes.

CLINT AND BLAIR were directed to the waiting room by an officious admitting nurse who assured them that Annie's fracture was a simple one. Unable to sit still, Blair paced the floor, feeling inexplicably guilty.

"You didn't throw her into that fence, you know," Clint said suddenly, observing Blair's stricken expression.

She stopped in her tracks, eyeing him appraisingly across the intervening space. "How did you know what I was thinking?"

"I'm beginning to understand you."

"Oh, are you?"

He appeared unperturbed by her challenging tone. "I know that you're pacing a path in that tile trying to figure out what you could have done to prevent Annie's accident."

"Is that what you think it was? Another *accident*?"

"I don't know," he admitted. "I only know you don't have any reason to feel guilty."

Blair sank into a chair, her fingers rubbing circles on her throbbing temples. "I always thought I was so independent," she said softly. "I've spent the last eleven years with advertising people, makeup people, photographers and wardrobe personnel. Whenever I go out on a job, I'm surrounded by individuals whose job is to make me look as glamorous as possible."

He took the chair beside her, putting his arm around her slumped shoulders. "And although they always seemed to be working for you, you're beginning to think perhaps it was the other way around and that you were nothing but a pretty set decoration for them."

"Damn it, Clint, it's very disconcerting when you read my mind," she complained. "I'm supposed to be running Clearwater Hills Farm, but suddenly I'm wondering if I can do it."

"That's what they want you to be thinking," he returned grittily.

She closed her eyes momentarily, gathering strength to continue the conversation. When she opened them, she was shaken by the concern she was viewing in his dark gray eyes.

"You really don't think Matador's spooking like that was an accident, do you?"

"Do you?" he countered.

When Blair answered, she was trying to convince herself as well as Clint. "It's not impossible. I saw him race at Aqueduct and he practically bit the man's arm off at the starting gate. Let's face it, the horse doesn't exactly have the personality of Irish Rover."

"He doesn't like anyone to hold his head," Clint explained. "Once we refused to allow any help in the starting gate, we didn't have any more trouble with him. Besides, Annie's been riding him every morning for a year. He's never given her any problem."

"Oh." She fell silent for a moment. "Do you think it might have been a hornet? Or a wasp?"

"Not in that early morning air. It was too cold."

"Oh." Her flat tone echoed the depression she saw in his eyes. Before she could ask what he suggested they do next, Jerry appeared in the doorway.

"Is she all right?" His freckled young face was a mask of concern.

"She's going to be fine," Clint assured him.

Jerry looked unrelieved. "I should have done something. If only I had been riding Matador..."

"The two of you are really something," Clint said in disgust. "Will you both get it through your heads that you're not to blame?"

Blair turned her guilty gaze out the window, and Jerry appeared suitably chastised.

"The doctor should be finishing up," Clint told him. "Why don't you go retrieve Annie and we'll get out of here."

The young man's eyes lit up as he left the waiting room.

"It appears we have a case of young love on our hands," Blair murmured, a soft smile transforming the hard line of her lips.

"It used to be a problem when Annie worked for Matt," Clint allowed. "Jerry was over there as much as he was at our place."

"Annie used to work for Matt?"

"She exercised Northern Dancer."

"Oh."

"Yeah . . . Anyway, when Matt had to lay her off, Jerry convinced me she'd be an asset to have at Clearwater Hills Farm."

"You must agree, if you promised her the chance to ride Risky Pleasure against Cimarron."

"She's raced some at Santa Anita and Del Mar, so she's not without experience. Add to that fact that Risky Pleasure responds better to Annie than to any rider she's had, and I'd say going with Annie instead of a more established pro isn't such a bad idea."

"It's unorthodox."

Clint grinned. "So is the entire idea."

"You've got a point," Blair agreed with an answering smile.

At that moment Annie appeared, her forearm encased in a white plaster cast. Jerry hovered protectively beside her.

"I suppose you'll be sending me home," Annie said.

"Of course not," Blair assured her. "Clearwater Hills Farm needs you. We wouldn't let you go just because of a little thing like a broken arm."

"I can't ride," Annie pointed out.

Blair put her arm around the girl's thin shoulders. "Don't worry about that. You'll be back on the track before we know it. In the meantime, there are absolutely scads and scads of things for you to do, aren't there, Clint?"

"Scads," he repeated blankly, having no idea what Blair had in mind.

"See?" Blair's smile could have lit up San Diego County. "How about a soda before we go back to the farm?" she suggested cheerily. "I have a sudden urge for a double malted."

"THAT WAS NICE OF YOU," Clint said that evening as they sat watching television in the den, neither paying a great deal of attention to the movie.

"Nice?" she repeated.

"Keeping Annie on. You know as well as I do she's useless right now."

"That's not true at all," Blair countered. "She happens to be a whiz at figures. I've got her helping me with the books."

"You didn't know that when you assured her we had scads and scads of things for her to do." His tone was laced with affection, his smile warm.

Blair arched a challenging dark brow. "I suppose you would have sent her home?"

His grin reached his eyes, turning them to a lustrous pewter. "No. I would have lied. Just the way you did."

Blair returned his smile. "I knew it," she murmured, focusing her attention on the television screen again. She'd seen *Chinatown* so many times she could probably recite all the actors' lines verbatim, she considered, entranced as always by Jack Nicholson's performance. Then a faint idea began to flicker on the edges of her mind.

"Clint?"

"Yeah?" he asked absently.

"Have any of the farms around here sold in the last few months?"

"A few. It's getting harder and harder to make a profit these days."

"That's true," she said, remembering what Matt had told her about his economic woes. "Did they all sell to the same person?"

"I don't think so." Clint turned toward her, eyeing her interestedly. "Why?"

"I don't know," she replied cautiously, aware that she'd hate it if he laughed at her. "Perhaps it's just this movie, with Jack Nicholson tracking down all the bad guys who are buying up Los Angeles, but it suddenly occurred to me that perhaps that's what's going on here."

"Jason was approached last month, but he turned the offer down," Clint said, the wheels beginning to spin in his head. *Blackwood. It had to be.* "Want to go into town tomorrow morning?" he asked suddenly.

"Let me guess—we're visiting the county recorder's office."

He grinned. "It's amazing that you can have so many brains in that gorgeous head."

"I think I'll take that as a compliment, as backhanded as it was." Blair pointed the remote control at the television, darkening the screen. "I don't know about you, but I'm exhausted. I'm going to bed."

"Want some company?" he asked, his eyes gleaming.

Blair shook her head. "Just when I was starting to think you might be one of the good guys."

He rose from the couch, cupping her chin in his fingers as he held her smiling gaze to his. "I am," he assured her in a deep, husky voice. "Why don't you quit playing hard to get, sweetheart, and I'll show you exactly how good I can be."

Her soft smile didn't waver. "You're incorrigible."

His thumb lightly stroked her throat, causing her pulse to leap beneath his touch. "Would you have it any other way? I'd hate to think I was boring you, Blair...after all those high-powered New York men you're used to."

Blair had never known a man who could compare with Clint Hollister for raw power, but she saw no reason to let him in on that little secret.

"The one thing you never do, Clint," she professed, laughing lightly, "is bore me." She reached up and patted his cheek. "Good night."

"Aren't you going to kiss me good night?" he asked, touching her hair.

"I don't know if that's such a good idea."

"I'm only asking for a kiss, Blair, not a lifetime commitment."

Their eyes met—hers darkly gold, his brightly silvered—in a jeweled moment that was like nothing Blair had ever experienced. Her pupils widened, obscuring the brilliant irises, as she watched Clint's head come slowly, inexorably nearer.

His lips were warm, so marvelously, wonderfully warm; his touch was gentle, without being at all hesitant. Clint

Hollister was kissing her as if it was his perfect right, and as Blair's arms reached up to encircle his neck, she could not think of one logical reason why she shouldn't be doing this.

"Blair."

Her name was a sultry summer breeze against her lips, and she closed her eyes, concentrating on the sensation of pleasure that radiated outward from his touch. She had no idea how long the kiss lasted, she was floating happily on gentle tides of desire, succumbing to the sweetness of his lips. Finally, after what could have been a few moments, an hour or an eternity, they came up for air, each appearing abnormally shaken.

"Wow," he murmured, reaching out to trace her full upper lip.

"Wow," she agreed softly, trembling under his touch.

"I think we're playing with fire, Ms. MacKenzie," he stated soberly, realizing that, as much as he'd been hungering for Blair's luscious body, something else was happening. He wasn't sure he cared for it, but like everything else these days, it appeared to be out of his control.

Her confused gaze mirrored his own troubled thoughts. "I think so, too, Mr. Hollister." It was a whisper, but Clint had no trouble hearing it in the stillness of the room.

"So what do you suggest we do?"

It took every bit of willpower Blair possessed to resist the dark hunger in his eyes. "I suggest we both get a good night's sleep. Things always appear clearer in the morning."

"Are you saying I won't still want you in the morning?" His tone was incredulous.

Blair shook her head, and Clint had the feeling that her crooked smile was directed inward. "No, I'm saying that in the morning perhaps we'll both have enough sense not to do anything about it." She rose up on her toes, pressing a quick, hard kiss against his lips. "Good night, Clint," she murmured and left the room before she could change her mind.

Clint watched her go. Then, heaving a resigned sigh, he went to his own room, where he tossed and turned the rest of the night as he thought about Blair MacKenzie sleeping just down the hall.

BLAIR AND CLINT were given little time to ponder their changing relationship. They spent the next day in the basement of the county recorder's office, pouring over stacks of dusty files.

"I found another one." Blair's tone was flat, instead of exultant, as it had been at the beginning of the search through the numerous pages of real estate transactions.

"Recognize the name?"

She shook her head. "No. It's a different company from the others. Guardian Development Corporation. Does that ring any bells?"

"Not a one," he admitted. "So far we've come up with seven separate sales to seven different developers, all in the same general location. Damn, I was hoping we'd find the answer in here."

Blair wiped a dark smudge on her yellow linen dress. "All we're finding is dust. This last book even had a page missing," she complained. "Whatever happened to the computer age?"

"The clerk said they were a little behind," he reminded her, taking down another leather-bound volume. "We should actually be grateful. It might be cleaner, but can you imagine looking at this many listings on microfiche? You'd have one helluva headache before you'd gotten through the first six months."

"Speaking of that..." Blair said wearily, propping her elbows on the table as she rubbed her temples with her thumbs. "All this has happened so suddenly," she complained. "Just a few weeks ago I was sitting at my kitchen table in Manhattan with my accountant, trying to come up with the money to buy a small farm somewhere and a couple of yearlings at this year's sales. Now..." Her voice drifted off.

"Accountant," he said thoughtfully. "Let me see your list."

She handed over the piece of paper on which she written the names of the development companies in a smooth, slanting hand.

"I think we've just found a loose thread," he said, a tremor of excitement in his voice.

"What is it?"

His index finger moved down the sheet of paper, stopping in the middle of the list. "This one."

"Hanson Properties?"

"That's it."

"That's what?"

"You've been sorting through Jason's books. What's his accountant's name?"

Blair's smooth forehead wrinkled in thought. "Brian Hanson."

"Bingo!" he exclaimed with the enthusiasm one might give the winner of the sixty-four-thousand-dollar question.

Blair shook her head. "Clint, Hanson is not an uncommon name. I'll bet we could find a dozen of them in the phone book."

"I've got a better idea. We'll check the incorporation records to see who the officers of Hanson Properties are. If one of them is Brian Hanson, then at least we'll know we're on the right track."

"And if it isn't?" Blair was suddenly very tired, discouraged and hungry. At that moment the task looked about as easy as locating the proverbial needle in a haystack.

"Then it's back to the drawing board. Got any better ideas?"

She sighed. "No, not a one."

An hour later, Blair found the answer. "Well, there goes that idea," she muttered.

"Dead end?" Clint looked up from his own stack of record books.

"The Hanson of Hanson Properties isn't Brian at all," she said on an exasperated sigh. "It's Robin."

Before Clint could answer, the door to the records room opened, and an officious-looking woman filled the space. When they'd arrived hours earlier, Blair had secretly imagined the records clerk as one of those dragons in the video games, faithfully guarding the treasures of the realm. The woman had not been extremely helpful, but neither had she been impervious to Clint Hollister's personality. He'd obviously found the magic word that charmed this particular female dragon into submission, and she'd ultimately opened her precious records to them.

"I'm sorry, but you'll have to leave," she said. "We close at five o'clock."

"It can't be that late," Clint protested.

Blair could believe it. Hobgoblins of hunger had been trying to make themselves heard in her stomach for the past hour.

"I'm sorry, but it is," the woman replied. "Our clocks are very accurate. We always open at nine o'clock and close at five. On the dot."

Clint groaned. "We'll have to come back tomorrow."

Blair nodded, trying to look enthusiastic. She failed. As they walked out of the dark basement room into the bright afternoon sunshine, the thudding of her headache only increased.

"You must be starving," he said on a note of apology while he opened the car door for her. "We'll stop for something on the way home."

She nodded, still receiving a thrill whenever she thought of the farm as home.

Fifteen minutes later, although Blair realized Clint had chosen the restaurant with care, she was too tired to be aware of what she was eating. Seeming to sense her mood, he didn't try to keep a conversation going, and for that she was grateful.

Afterward, back in his car, she leaned her head against the seat and closed her eyes in exhaustion. It seemed to Blair that only a moment had passed before she felt a light, feathery touch on her cheek.

"Hey, Sleeping Beauty, it's time to wake up. Your prince has just brought you back to the castle."

Blair opened her eyes slowly and saw Clint's head incredibly close to hers.

"Want me to carry you into bed?" he asked huskily.

She was sleepy, not crazy. "No, thank you. I can manage."

He smiled. "Coward."

"You'd only be disappointed anyway," she whispered shakily. "I'm too exhausted to be much of a Tigress Woman tonight."

"Don't worry about it. Tonight you remind me of a warm, cuddly tabby cat." He ran his hand down her back. "Purr for me, pretty tabby."

"Clint, please," she murmured, her tone one of both demurral and request. She wondered when she'd become such a vacillating individual. *Kiss me, don't kiss me. Touch me, keep away. Come here, go*. She'd been giving Clint an extraordinary series of contradictory messages, and she wouldn't have blamed him if he packed up and walked out on the crazy lady who seemed incapable of making up her own mind about anything.

Clint heard the confusion in her voice and forced himself to remember that Blair needed him for far more right now than a night of lovemaking. While it would take only a few more kisses, a touch here . . . and there . . . and yes, there as well, he mused, his eyes drifting over her slender body, tomorrow morning she'd wake up and regret her momentary weakness. He'd have to bide his time until she was ready to come to him willingly, until she was as desperate for him as he was for her.

"Come on, sweetheart," he said, releasing her suddenly. "We've got an early morning tomorrow." He opened his door, climbed out of the bucket seat, then helped her out from the car, his arm around her waist to steady her as they entered the house.

"I'm going to go check on things," he said. "Why don't you go to bed?"

"This early?"

His gray eyes swept over her appraisingly. "You look beat," he observed, noting the shadows under her eyes. "You wouldn't want to disappoint everyone at Matt's party tomorrow night, would you?"

The party. It had completely slipped her mind. "I suppose we have to go," she said without a great deal of enthusiasm.

"I think we'd better. You know as well as I do that everyone will be expecting the Tigress Woman to show up," he pointed out accurately.

"I'm getting really tired of her," Blair said.

Clint's gaze was inordinately fond. "You know," he murmured, "I'm beginning to believe you about that."

"I'm glad." Her wide amber eyes held an infinite number of messages, each more enticing than the last. Clint had to shove his hands into his pockets to keep from touching her.

"I'll see you in the morning," he said gruffly, turning away from temptation. "Johnny Doyle's going to be taking Annie's place until she's able to ride again. I want to give him some instructions on how to ride Matador."

"Morning," she agreed softly, watching him leave.

As tired as she was, Blair found sleep an impossibility and decided instead to catch up on the local news. The papers had been stacking up all week, and after first allowing herself the luxury of enjoying seven straight days of comic strips, she began reading the remainder of the news.

Although not a fan of society-page gossip, Blair had spent too many years modeling not to have her eye caught by a photograph of women in expensive evening gowns, hosting a fund-raising ball for this year's "in" disease. Not knowing anyone in San Diego, she skimmed the caption, paying scant attention to the names. Then she went back to one name, captured by its familiarity. Holding her breath, she quickly scanned the accompanying article.

Blair then ran out to Johnny Doyle's room in search of Clint, only to discover he'd already left. Muttering a soft oath, she returned to the house, but it was deserted. After a cursory check in training barn B, she finally located Clint in the smaller of the two training barns, currying Risky Pleasure.

"I've been looking all over for you," she panted.

He dropped the currycomb, staring at her as he took in her flushed face and very wide, amber eyes. He had her in his arms in seconds, his worried gaze roving her face. "What's wrong? Are you all right?"

Her frantic search had left her breathless, and Clint was forced to wait until she could talk. "Look!" She shoved the newspaper page into his hands.

His gray eyes scanned the print in a cursory glance. "Dear Abby? You look as if you've just gone ten rounds with Joe Frazier, and all because you want me to read an advice column?"

She shook her head. "No. Here." She poked at the page, showing him the picture.

"'Society Ball to Benefit Less Fortunate,'" he read. "So? Don't tell me we have to go. Heather used to drag me to those things, and I really hate them, Blair."

"Damn it!" she cried. "Read the names!"

He shook his head with barely concealed impatience, but Blair watched as the idea struck home. "Robin Hanson?"

"That's not all," she said proudly. "Read the second paragraph."

"'The hostesses of the successful fund-raiser were Buffy Meredith, wife of financier Kent Meredith; Joan Palmer Thompson, wife of newly elected city councilman Steve Thompson; Robin Hanson, wife of Brian Hanson...' Brian Hanson," Clint repeated. "Damn. I should have remembered her name! Congratulations, sweetheart, you may have just found the key!"

The paper fell to the floor, and Blair found herself lifted off her feet as Clint swung her around, giving her a deep, congratulatory kiss. Blair's mouth fused to his willingly, hungrily; the entire world centered on his marvelous lips. As he lowered her slowly back to the floor, the giddy mood suddenly changed, his kiss growing more demanding even while it gave more heated pleasure.

Through the fog clouding her mind, Blair could focus only on this glorious kiss that swept the world away from under her feet and left her floating on a cloud of sheer desire. It went on and on, and even when she found herself unable to breathe, Blair hoped it would continue endlessly. Finally, Clint dragged his mouth away, pressing it into her dark chestnut hair as he held her head against his shoulder.

"Blair," he murmured, his breath a warm, welcome breeze.

"What?" she responded dazedly, her eyes still closed to the dizzy, dancing way his kiss had made her feel.

His palm stroked the back of her head. "Nothing. Just Blair."

"Oh." She looped her arms about his waist, looking up at him, her tawny eyes gleaming with unsatiated desire. "What do we do now?"

He grinned suggestively. "About what?"

"About Robin Hanson," she reminded him firmly. "That *is* why I came out here, remember?"

"Robin Hanson," he agreed without a great deal of enthusiasm. "Let's wait until tomorrow night and play the thing by ear."

"Tomorrow night?"

"Brian Hanson is also Matt's accountant," Clint told her. "They're bound to be at the party."

"I'm going to go crazy until then," she complained.

His hands tightened about her waist. "I've got a few suggestions on how to while away those hours," he said in a deep, husky voice.

Blair fought against her own desire. "I thought we'd agreed to keep this strictly business."

"We did. But I'd better warn you, cold showers are beginning to lose their effectiveness." His eyes darkened. "I want you, Blair."

"Do you always get everything you want?" she asked quietly.

His answer was succinct. "Yes."

She turned away, rubbing her temples with her fingers. "You make it sound so simple, but it isn't."

As Clint observed her standing with her head bent, he had to restrain himself from taking her into his arms again. Where she belonged.

Of course Blair was confused, he admitted reluctantly to himself. She'd come to the farm with no intention of inheriting anything. Then, just when she thought she was taking over a thriving business, she'd been flung headfirst into turmoil. Perhaps he should wait until all this was settled, and she could come to him without anything standing in their way. But God, how he wanted her!

He bent to pick up the currycomb. "I'd better get back to work."

"It's late," she reminded him needlessly.

He shrugged. "I've fallen behind by spending all day at the courthouse."

He began working with Risky Pleasure.

"Jerry could do that," she pointed out softly.

"I'd prefer to do it myself."

Blair stifled a sigh at his suddenly withdrawn attitude. "Fine. I'll see you in the morning, then."

He merely grunted a reply. The filly neighed her objection as Clint stopped to watch Blair leave. Muttering a low curse, he finished the currying with a few careless strokes. Then he left the barn and sat down on a bale of hay to smoke a cigarette and watch the deep indigo clouds play tag across the black velvet sky.

Chapter Eleven

To add to Blair's distress, Marni returned to the house the next morning, declaring her decision to move in with Matt.

"Are you sure this is what you want do do?" Blair asked as she sat down on the end of Marni's bed. Her friend was throwing things haphazardly into suitcases.

"I've never been so certain of anything in my life."

"But it's only been a week."

"That's about five days longer than I needed," Marni stated blithely. "Here." She held out her jewelry box. "You may as well keep this stuff. I can't see myself wearing rhinestones to muck out a stall, can you?"

"You actually do that, too?"

"Of course. I've discovered that I'm quite handy to have around, despite what my mother always told me."

Blair knew that Marni's mother had been partially responsible for her lack of self-esteem. According to Marni, the woman's pet phrase had always been, "I don't approve of a thing the girl does, but she *is* pretty." Marni had taken that thoughtless comment, wrapped it about her, absorbed it, and in the end, had finally come to believe that her beauty was her only value.

Blair had always known differently, but apparently it had taken Matt Bradshaw to make Marni believe otherwise. For that, Blair was glad, yet she still felt that events were happening too soon.

"I don't think you should rush into anything," she cautioned again, watching Marni pack a vast array of designer dresses, several of which she had designed herself. While Marni steadfastly insisted that she didn't have a domestic bone in her body, she did possess a unique sense of style and a flair for knowing instinctively what was flattering to her. Every so often she professed a desire to design a line of her own, but a new assignment or a new man made her forget the idea.

Blair's warning fell on deaf ears as Marni proceeded to change the subject. "So, what's happening with you and the hunk?"

Blair decided not to relate the latest bit of information concerning Robin Hanson. Even though Marni was a loyal enough friend, she never had been the soul of discretion.

"I'm still trying to break my contract," Blair said.

"Tough, huh?"

"Ironclad."

Marni eyed her thoughtfully. "I suppose you're still dead set against selling."

"Of course I am."

Marni nodded. "That's what I told Matt."

"You two were discussing me?"

Marni shrugged. "It wasn't anything personal, Blair. We were just talking about how hard it was to run a farm, and he asked if I thought you were really up to it." She grinned. "I told him it was always a mistake to underestimate you when you set your mind to something." She closed the suitcase. "Well, good luck . . . I guess I'll see you tonight."

"Tonight," Blair echoed, rising to walk Marni out to Matt's Blazer.

As Marni climbed into the driver's seat, Blair asked, "Where's Matt?"

"He had to go into the city to see about buying a stallion to replace Northern Lights," Marni said. A small frown furrowed her flawless forehead. "I hope it works out. He seemed a little edgy when he left."

"I hope *everything* works out," Blair said honestly. "For both of you."

Marni grinned. "It will," she vowed, twisting the key in the ignition. "This time I've hit the jackpot."

As Blair watched the Blazer disappear in a cloud of dust, she could only hope that this time Marni knew what she was doing.

THE MAN LAY on his back, smoking a cigarette and staring up at the ceiling. "I still don't like it," he announced.

The woman's fingers were playing in the mat of hair covering his chest. "I'm finding that a bit difficult to believe. Do you realize how many men would sell their souls to be in your position?"

He turned his head on the pillow, his eyes spearing her. "Is that what I've done?"

She laughed, sitting up in bed to light her own cigarette. "Don't go getting a conscience at this late date, darling. Besides, it's not as if you're debauching some innocent virgin. She's a grown woman. She knows what she's getting into."

He shook his head. "She thinks I love her."

Slender shoulders lifted in a careless shrug. "So? You won't have been the first man to tell a little white lie in bed."

"Or you the first woman?"

Her eyes narrowed. "What does that mean?"

He took a long drag on the cigarette, while he chose his words carefully. "Sometimes I get the feeling you're just using me—that when all this is over, you'll be on your merry way and leave me with nothing."

She arched an auburn brow. "You're calling all those millions of pretty dollars nothing?"

"Damn it, I didn't get into this for the money. I agreed to the entire deal because I love you!" he argued heatedly.

Her silvery laugh was laced with scorn. "What a selective memory you have, my sweet. What about the fact that you were on the brink of bankruptcy before we offered you a chance to bail yourself out and make a tidy profit as well?"

"You promised it'd be a piece of cake," he reminded her. "So far, it's been anything but."

"We're making progress," she assured him. "I guarantee that after tomorrow night, Clearwater Hills Farm will fall into our laps."

"And then what?" he challenged.

She looked at him curiously. "We'll all be filthy rich, of course. Just as I promised."

"And what about you and me?"

She leaned over and pressed a kiss against his firmly set mouth. "We'll continue as usual. Nothing's going to change with us."

"What about your husband? Where does he fit into this little scenario?"

"After a decent interval, I'll divorce Brian," she assured him silkily. "We don't want to rush into things—it'll look too suspicious."

The man glared up at the ceiling. "I hate this."

She plucked the cigarette from his fingers and put it out in a crystal ashtray. Her own followed. "Don't pout, darling," Robin Hanson murmured, her fingers blazing a tantalizing trail down his chest. "I can think of much better things to do than fight."

Smothering a frustrated oath, he drew her into his arms, succumbing as he always did to her expert touch.

LATER THAT EVENING Blair stood in front of her mirror, eyeing her reflection judiciously. She'd managed to cover up the purple shadows under her eyes that gave away her recent lack of sleep, but a pair of lines bracketed her lips, displaying her tension. While she was convinced that Robin Hanson somehow held the key to what was going on, she didn't have the slightest idea how she was going to go about getting the woman to admit it.

"Blair?" Clint called in to her. "Are you ready?"

"Just about," she murmured. "Come on in."

He opened the door, stopping to stare at the vision standing only a few feet away. Her hair, which she usually wore pulled back, lay loose around her shoulders in a soft, dark cloud. It was thick and wavy, gleaming in the low lamplight. She was wearing makeup, he realized, something she seldom did since her arrival. Her full lips were painted a lush red; her eyes were rimmed with slashes of dark kohl. As he approached, he inhaled the heady, evocative scent of Tigress perfume.

"Would I be hanged for a chauvinist if I admitted to a few lustful feelings right now?" he asked in a husky voice.

Holding out her arms, Blair twirled, the red chiffon swirling above her knees. The halter dress plunged to the waist in back, while the front slit allowed a tantalizing glimpse of creamy skin.

"You said they were probably expecting the Tigress Woman tonight," she reminded him. "I thought the least I could do for Matt, since Marni thinks he's the greatest thing since multi-vitamins, is oblige."

"I think I should have kept my big mouth shut," Clint muttered. "Every man in the place will be walking into walls when you show up wearing that dress."

Blair couldn't miss the irritation in his tone. She grinned. "Why, Clint Hollister, are you jealous?"

"Of course," he answered instantly. "I suppose now you're going to accuse me of being overly possessive and chauvinistic."

She shook her head. "No," she replied, thoughtfully, "I think I like it." Her brown eyes took a leisurely tour of Clint, drinking in the sight of so much man. She'd always considered him breathtakingly masculine in his working clothes, but there was something about him in evening dress that accentuated his manliness even more.

"In fact," she decided aloud, "I'm probably going to experience a little of that green-eyed monster myself. You're going to have women throwing themselves at your feet tonight, Clint Hollister."

Her softly spoken words and gleaming eyes caused his blood to surge more hotly through his veins. "I've got an idea."

Her eyes didn't move from his. "Oh?"

"Let's stay home."

Oh, how she'd like that! Blair felt her knees weaken at the look Clint was giving her. "What about Robin Hanson?"

If anyone had told Clint that he'd ever be so uninterested in Clearwater Hills Farm, he would have called that person crazy. But at this moment, he didn't give a damn about the farm, or Robin Hanson, or any of the problems he'd been having. Every nerve in his body was on red alert, wanting, needing Blair MacKenzie. Then he remembered that without the farm there'd be no reason for Blair to remain in California. She'd be back in New York, resuming her jet-set existence—and out of his life.

He raked his fingers through his hair in obvious frustration. "You're right," he agreed. "Let's go before one of us changes his mind."

The aura of sensuality that had swirled about them was not dissipated by the crisp evening air. It took all Clint's inner restraint not to turn the car around and forgo Matt's party for more pleasurable pursuits. He forced his mind on the problem at hand.

"I'll tell you what," he suggested. "When we get there, we'll split up. You see what you can get out of Brian Hanson, and I'll tackle his wife."

"That will be quite a sacrifice," she said dryly.

He gave her a questioning look. "What's that supposed to mean?"

"I saw the woman's picture in the paper, Clint," Blair reminded him. "She's beautiful."

"And about as cold as a glacier."

"I'm not even going to ask how you discovered that."

"You don't have to take a woman to bed to know that she's frigid. Or, on the flip side, to realize that some women are much warmer than they'd like to appear." He slanted her a knowing glance.

Blair steadfastly ignored the message in his silver gaze. "So, what's Brian Hanson like? Is he cold, too?"

Clint considered her words carefully. "He's good-looking enough, I suppose—in an Ivy League sort of way."

"Sounds interesting," Blair said teasingly. "Perhaps this party won't be so dull after all."

"Don't take your job too seriously, Blair. I've always thought Brian Hanson's charm was the kind that washed off in the shower. Besides, I'd hate to ruin Matt's party by having to punch out his accountant for getting too friendly with my woman."

Blair stared at him. "You can't be serious!"

"I was only speaking figuratively," Clint muttered unconvincingly, damning himself for allowing that thought to escape.

Blair looked at him for a long, silent time before turning her attention to the well of darkness outside the car window. A few minutes later they had arrived at Matt Bradshaw's farm.

As she entered Matt's house, Blair wondered if the man actually possessed so many friends, or if half of San Diego County had shown up out of simple curiosity. Before she could even make her way across the crowded living room, she had autographed seven covers of *Sports Illustrated*'s annual swimsuit issue, fielded two not-so-subtle passes, and survived the blistering glares from several women who obviously perceived Blair to be a threat.

"I'd say you're an unqualified hit," Clint murmured in her ear, grabbing two glasses of champagne from a tray held by a passing waiter.

Blair thanked him with a smile, then took a sip of the sparkling California wine. "The Tigress Woman is a hit," she corrected blandly.

"You really think of her as a separate entity, don't you?"

"Of course," Blair answered without hesitation. "You were right about one thing, Clint."

He arched an inquiring brow, inviting elaboration.

"I can't see her mucking out a stall, either," Blair admitted with a grin Clint suspected was directed at herself.

"You may have a point," he agreed, his hand cupping her elbow as they cut a swath through the throng of fashionably attired men and women. "However, I still contend that her spirit dwells inside the body of a woman who's every bit as enticing in jeans."

Blair was saved by Matt from answering this huskily stated declaration. Their host suddenly appeared in front of her, looking exceedingly handsome in his formal evening wear.

"Blair!" he welcomed her with a warm smile. "You look absolutely ravishing tonight."

"Thank you, Matt. This is quite some party. I didn't expect to see so many people."

"You and Marni proved quite a draw," he said, confirming Blair's earlier suspicion. "Speaking of which, there's someone who's been dying to meet you." His attention slid to Clint. "You won't mind if I borrow Blair for a few minutes, will you, Clint?"

"As long as you remember to bring her back," Clint drawled with a laconic air of possessiveness that should have irritated Blair but for some strange reason didn't.

"I promise not to let Brian abscond with her," Matt told him with a laugh.

At the mention of Jason Langley's accountant, Blair and Clint exchanged a quick, meaningful glance.

"Have fun," Clint advised her. Blair nodded, allowing Matt to take her hand and lead her across the room. As they approached the waiting man, Blair's heart began to pound, and she hoped that her nervousness wouldn't give her away.

"Brian," Matt exclaimed heartily, "I'm sure you recognize Blair MacKenzie. Blair, this is Brian Hanson."

The tall, urbane man's blue eyes were bright with masculine appreciation and with something else Blair couldn't quite recognize.

"Ms. MacKenzie," he said, taking the hand Matt had just abandoned, "you've no idea what a pleasure it is to meet you in person. Jason spoke very highly of you."

"It's a pleasure to meet you, Mr. Hanson," she said, restraining herself from jerking her hand away as his thumb brushed provocatively against her palm.

"Call me Brian," he suggested. "I hope we'll become very close friends." The message in his deep voice was unmistakable.

Matt cleared his throat. "Well, I'd better go check on the ice."

Brian Hanson's eyes didn't leave Blair's face. "Why don't you do that?" he agreed. "I'd like to become better acquainted with your new neighbor."

Matt looked decidedly uneasy as he nodded, then disappeared into the crowd of party guests.

"So," Blair began casually, extracting her hand from the man's increasingly familiar touch, "you were my grandfather's accountant."

"As well as his friend," Brian replied. "I still can't believe he's gone."

Blair didn't know what to say to that, so she probed a little further. "I've been having some difficulty with the farm's books. Perhaps you can explain a few of the entries to me." She gave him a coaxing, feminine smile.

"I'd be happy to discuss his accounts with you," Brian said amiably. "During business hours. After all, this *is* a party and we should be enjoying ourselves. Would you care to dance?"

"I'm a little tired," she demurred. "Why don't we go somewhere a little quieter, and you can fill me in on high tower."

There was a moment of silence, during which Blair couldn't miss the sudden narrowing of Brian Hanson's eyes as he observed her with renewed interest.

"High tower? It doesn't ring a bell."

"My grandfather spent quite a bit of money on it over the past year."

"High tower," he repeated softly, more to himself than to her. "Sorry, I can't recall any such name." He treated her to a reassuring smile. "But that doesn't really mean anything. I never was able to keep those horses' names straight."

"High tower isn't a horse."

He arched a blond brow. "Oh? Are you certain of that?"

Blair nodded, sipping on her champagne and studying him over the rim of her glass. Brian Hanson's blue eyes suddenly held a core of ice.

"Positive," she said. "Mr. Hollister assured me that there had never been a horse by that name on the farm."

"Hollister." He spat the name out as if it had a bad aftertaste. Then he put his hand on Blair's back and began to lead her abruptly from the room toward a pair of French doors.

Decidedly uneasy about the idea of being alone on the deserted terrace with Brian Hanson, she looked around for Clint but was unable to find him in the throng of people.

"What do you know about your grandfather's trainer?" Brian asked the moment they were alone.

Blair managed a casual shrug. "I know he's the best in the business."

"Do you know the man's been in prison?"

Hanson certainly didn't pull any punches, Blair considered. "Yes. I also know he was innocent." She tried not to flinch as the accountant's fingers brushed up her arm.

"I do hope you're not getting involved with the man," he said, his voice holding a definite warning. "Clint Hollister is nothing but bad news. In fact, I wouldn't be at all surprised if he had something to do with Jason Langley's death."

"If you truly believe that," she challenged softly, "why didn't you go to the authorities?"

"With Jason's history of heart trouble, it would be impossible to prove."

"Then why—"

"Jason Langley wanted to sell Clearwater Hills Farm, but Hollister fought the sale tooth and nail. He didn't want to end up out on the street."

Blair took a calming sip of champagne. "He'd hardly end up out on the street," she murmured. "I know of a number of farms that would jump at the chance to hire him."

"As a trainer," Brian agreed. "But he was far more than that to Jason. He'd infiltrated himself into the man's confidence. In fact, for the past year he had carte blanche as to the running of the place. Jason was too ill to watch over things as he should have, which gave Hollister the chance to take control. He wouldn't have been able to grasp such power anywhere else, and he knew it."

"If my grandfather wanted to sell the farm," Blair argued, "why did he leave it to me?"

"That was an old will," Brian explained. "Jason was still planning to leave everything to you. And with the profit he would have made from the sale, you would have ended up an extremely wealthy woman."

Blair ran a crimson-tinted fingernail around the rim of her glass. "My grandfather really wanted to sell the farm?"

Hanson nodded. "He did. As a matter of fact, he had an appointment with a group of prospective buyers the afternoon of his death. Unfortunately, he didn't survive to make that meeting."

His eyes glittered in the reflected glow of the landscape lights. "Now do you see why I have my own suspicions concerning Clint Hollister?"

Blair managed a slight nod, reminding herself that nothing would be accomplished by telling this man she knew he was lying. Clint might drive her up a wall sometimes; he might have a proprietary attitude toward Clearwater Hills Farm, and he admitted that he and Jason had fought continuously over management policies. But just as she'd known he had not killed his wife, she knew with an iron-clad certainty that he had had nothing to do with her grandfather's death.

"I think I need another drink," she murmured, wanting to escape the steely-eyed gaze of the man beside her.

"I'll get it for you," Brian suggested immediately, reaching for her empty glass.

Blair shook her head and gave him a crooked smile. "Thank you anyway, Mr. Hanson, but I'd like a couple of minutes alone to freshen up." She attempted a more convincing smile. "The problem with being the Tigress Woman is that everyone expects perfection."

His eyes warmed as they took a slow tour of her body. "I'd say you're managing to come very close to that ideal right now, Ms. MacKenzie," he murmured.

She forced a light, musical laugh. "Thank you, Mr. Hanson. You're very good for a woman's ego. What a shame you're married."

"Who said I'm married?" he countered.

"I saw your wife's picture in the society pages. She's a very lovely woman."

"She is," he agreed blithely. Blair had to fight from cringing as his hand once again trailed up her arm. "And we have a very good marriage. We understand each other."

His tone was unmistakable, and Blair backed away. "How nice for you both," she said, feigning ignorance of the sensual invitation in his deep voice. "Well, I've enjoyed our little chat. I suppose I'll see you later."

He nodded. "You can count on it, Ms. MacKenzie."

As she wove her way back through the crowd, Blair scanned the room for Clint. Where was he? She couldn't wait to tell him about Brian Hanson's accusations. She finally spotted him in a far corner of the room, talking with a tall, willowy redhead she recognized immediately as Robin Hanson.

Clint's silver head was inclined toward the woman, whose hands were fluttering like graceful birds as she spoke. When she laughed and placed one of those hands on his arm, Blair was stunned by the jolt of jealousy that forked through her. She was considering going over there and establishing her territorial rights when a tuxedo-clad roadblock suddenly popped up in front of her.

"Ms. MacKenzie, may I have a word with you?"

While Blair had not taken to Ramsey Blackwood from the start, knowing what he'd done to Clint certainly didn't help establish the man into her good graces.

"I'm sorry," she said, "but I promised Mr. Hollister this next dance."

Ramsey's eyes followed hers. "Your partner seems otherwise occupied," he observed blandly. "I'm sure he won't miss you."

That was what Blair was afraid of. "Can't it wait?"

"No, it can't," he said firmly.

She stifled a sigh, but followed the lawyer into Matt's deserted den. "What is it, Mr. Blackwood?" she inquired, not bothering to restrain her irritation.

He took the chair behind the wide oak desk, braced his elbows on the arms of the chair and observed her over linked fingers as he swiveled back and forth. His expression was sympathetic.

"Your grandfather and I were close friends," he began. "Therefore I feel a fatherly responsibility toward you."

She sat down opposite him, crossing her legs with a graceful, fluid gesture. The look in Ramsey Blackwood's eyes as they locked onto the fleeting flash of thigh was far from paternal.

"Now you're going to warn me against getting involved with Clint Hollister," Blair guessed.

"He's already proved fatal for one woman," Ramsey grated out with ill-concealed bitterness. "I'd hate to see you suffer the same fate."

Blair leaned forward in order to stress her point. "I'm honestly sorry about your daughter," she said. "But Clint didn't kill her."

"If you mean he didn't wield the knife, you're probably correct," Ramsey allowed. "But he drove Heather to it with his obsession about Clearwater Hills Farm. *And* that damnable horse."

"Risky Pleasure," Blair murmured.

"That's the one. He'd do anything to keep from giving up that filly, Ms. MacKenzie. Just as he'd do anything to keep from leaving Clearwater Hills Farm."

Aware of the acrimony between the two men, Blair considered the source, discounting Ramsey's harsh accusation. She was, however, curious about one thing.

"Mr. Blackwood, do you know anything about something called high tower?"

For a moment there was a flicker in the depths of his eyes, but Ramsey's expression remained inscrutably bland. "Not a thing. Why?"

"It doesn't matter," she said, instinctively understanding that for some reason Ramsey Blackwood was prepared to lie. "May I ask you one more question?"

"Of course."

"Did my grandfather intend to sell Clearwater Hills Farm?"

"That was the plan. Unfortunately, he suffered that fatal heart attack before he could finalize the deal." Ramsey's gaze narrowed. "Are you considering selling, Ms. MacKenzie?"

Blair rose. "Not at all, Mr. Blackwood," she stated firmly. "I'm here to stay." Her back was straight as she made her way to the closed door.

"Ms. MacKenzie?" Ramsey called after her.

She eyed him over her shoulder. "Yes?"

"Watch your step very carefully. Despite his charms, Clint Hollister can be a very formidable enemy."

"I wasn't aware we were enemies."

"You have something the man wants," Blackwood pointed out smoothly. "Something he's always wanted. I'd say that puts you in a decidedly perilous position.... I want you to know that you can always count on me if you need help."

"I'll keep that in mind," Blair murmured, wanting nothing more than to escape this party and go home before she had to listen to one more accusation concerning Clint.

Chapter Twelve

Blair's search for Clint was interrupted briefly by a scene she inadvertently came across as she passed one of the bedrooms. Robin Hanson and Matt were engaged in a casual conversation, although Blair wondered what they could possibly be discussing that demanded privacy. But lingering exacerbation created by her earlier confrontations kept her from dwelling on the matter.

"There you are," Clint said as she reentered the living room. "I've been looking all over for you."

"I've been looking for you, too."

"Well, you've found me," he said with a smile.

"Let's get out of here," Blair suggested suddenly.

Clint's smile faded. "Sure," he agreed, eyeing her curiously. "I'd have thought this party would be right up your alley."

Blair stopped, her eyes flashing as she looked up at him. "Don't tell me we're back to my so-called jet-set existence."

It was impossible to miss the pain in her eyes, yet Clint had the vague impression that his words were not the cause. No, something else had her inordinately disturbed, he decided, and she was simply taking out her unhappiness on him.

"Not at all," he said amiably. "I just thought every woman liked the opportunity to get dressed up and dazzle us poor, unsuspecting males."

"Well, you thought wrong," she snapped, marching toward the front door.

Stifling a weary sigh, Clint followed. Blair remained silent during the short drive back to the farm, and Clint resolved not to pressure her. He was, however, uneasy about what Ramsey Blackwood might have told her to make her that miserable. He hadn't missed seeing the two of them disappear into the den, and he had forced himself to take a long walk out to Matt's barns in order to avoid confronting her directly about her conversation with his former father-in-law.

The phone was ringing as they entered the house. "Hello," Blair snapped into the mouthpiece.

"Blair?" Marni's voice held curiosity and concern. "Is everything all right? You left before we had a chance to talk."

"Everything's fine," she lied. "I just got a blinding headache and Clint agreed to take me home."

"Oh . . . Well, I hope you feel better soon."

"I'm sure I will."

"You're still not upset about my moving in with Matt, are you?"

"Not at all. It's your life. I hope everything works out this time."

"It will," Marni professed fervently. "He says he loves me, Blair."

Blair sought an excuse to end the conversation. "Look, honey, my head is honestly killing me. Why don't we get together for lunch tomorrow?"

"That'll be fun," Marni said. "Let's go into San Diego and visit Old Town. I'd love an opportunity to do something touristy. Go to bed, now, and I'll see you tomorrow."

"Tomorrow." Blair hung up, staring for a long, silent moment at the telephone.

"Want to talk about it?" Clint asked.

She turned around, unnerved by both the gentle concern she heard in his voice and the slight hesitation that made him appear uncharacteristically vulnerable.

"Not really."

"Want a couple of aspirins?"

"No, thanks."

"I thought you had a headache."

"I just wanted to get out of there, okay?" she retorted.

He held up his hands. "Sure."

Blair settled down into a chair and picked up a novel she'd left on the table, pretending to immerse herself in the story. Following her lead, Clint took a chair across the room, waiting for Blair to give some clue as to what had gone wrong.

When she sighed for the third time, Clint looked up from the racing magazine he'd been pretending to read. "Problem?"

"The house just seems empty without Marni."

"She's probably been here only two hours since she arrived," he pointed out.

"I know. It's just that . . ."

"Jealous?" he asked casually, putting the magazine down on a table beside the chair and lighting a cigarette.

"Jealous? Why on earth would I be jealous of my best friend?"

He shrugged. "I don't know, but isn't love the ultimate female fantasy?" Blair thought she saw something flicker for a moment in his eyes, but then it was gone before she could decipher its meaning.

"Not mine."

"Ah, yes," he said, drawing on the cigarette thoughtfully, "you're one of those women who never managed to exchange your adolescent love of horses for that of a man."

"What a ridiculous thing to say," she snapped. "Although it's about as sexist a statement as I'd expect you to come up with. Using that line of reasoning, you're so in love with Risky Pleasure you wouldn't fall in love with the perfect woman if she fell stark naked into your lap."

Clint was silent as he considered that prospect. "It's an intriguing scenario," he murmured, his gray gaze moving with agonizing slowness over her taut body. "Had you been considering throwing yourself into my lap, Blair?"

"I was speaking hypothetically," she said icily, refusing to let him see how the desire gleaming in his beautiful eyes was threatening to melt her bones.

He rose wearily, grinding out the cigarette. "Of course you were," he agreed flatly. "Doing that would take more guts than you'd ever have."

He marched from the room, leaving her to stare after him. The ashtray hit the door frame after his head had already cleared the space, sending ashes scattering down onto the Mexican tile flooring.

Blair paced the room furiously, her arms wrapped around herself as if to hold in her temper. She was feeling about as explosive as Vesuvius right now, and if Clint Hollister dared to show himself again, she'd certainly tell him a thing or two. She muttered every curse word she could think of under her breath, receiving a glimmer of satisfaction as her language began to resemble that of a longshoreman.

She'd just come up with a particularly graphic expression she'd seen scrawled on a bathroom wall in a Greenwich Village bar and was repeating it over and over, preparing to fling it into Clint's dark face, when she finally realized he wasn't returning. The house had grown silent as a tomb, and she could only surmise that he'd gone to bed.

She slumped down into a chair, staring off into space, her mind churning over his accusations. Did she appear as cold and heartless as he'd so brutally stated? If so, she had definitely handled things all wrong.

CLINT LAY IN BED, his head braced by his arms. He stared up at the ceiling, wishing that he hadn't had the misfortune to fall head over heels in love with a woman as shortsighted and stubborn as Blair MacKenzie. He had just about exhausted his supply of derogatory terms when the tentative knock at the door caught his attention.

"Come in," he muttered, knowing there was only one other person in the house. He wasn't in any mood to continue that argument.

She opened the door hesitantly, her eyes blinking as she attempted to adjust to the darkness. Clint sighed and reached out to turn on the bedside lamp.

Blair was wearing a flannel robe, tied kimono-style, and suddenly he remembered the Garfield nightshirt. She sure as hell didn't dress like a high-priced fashion model at night. For one wild, fleeting moment, he had entertained the idea that she might be coming to him in a filmy, seductive nightgown, her surrender achieved. But no such luck.

"What can I do for you, Blair?" he asked, sitting up in bed and reaching for his cigarettes.

He wasn't wearing a pajama top, she noted instantly, wondering if he had anything at all on under that rumpled navy sheet. Her mind began to paint erotic pictures, and a soft shade of rose colored her cheeks.

Clint stopped in the act of tapping the cigarette against the table and watched Blair's complexion change color and the pupils of her eyes widen even further, moving like molten obsidian over the gleaming topaz. As she approached the bed, he inhaled the come-hither scent of Tigress perfume.

"Blair," he said, knowing that this time there would be no turning back if she took one step nearer, "what in the hell do you want?"

She gave him a smile like the one Eve must have given to Adam when she handed him the apple. Blair's lustrous gaze held his as she slowly untied the belt of the robe. She slid it off her shoulders, moving toward him with the sensuous glide of a jungle animal, her seductive intent gleaming in her catlike eyes. She stood inches away from the bed, clad in a sea green nightgown with lacy inserts so sheer they could have been spun from spiderwebs.

"I want to make love with you, Clint," she answered his grittily issued question calmly.

His eyes had been devouring the soft curves of her body, but now they came back to hers.

"I want you, Blair. I think I've wanted you since that first moment I saw you standing by Blackwood's car, so prim and proper in that tailored suit and silly little hat."

He swallowed, and Blair caught the movement in his throat, wondering how even that simple act could heighten the needs battering inside her.

Clint wished she wouldn't look at him that way. He had to get this said, had to explain, to allow her to understand fully. But he was rapidly losing his concentration, and when he continued speaking, his voice was only an incomprehensible buzz in his ear.

"I wanted to undress you, to peel away that false image you wore until you were in my arms, warm and willing, as if you'd waited all your life to come to me in just this way."

His voice grew more husky and it seemed as if his tenuous grasp on sanity were rapidly slipping away. "But 'willing' is the definitive word here, Blair. I don't want you to do anything you don't honestly want."

She forced herself to listen to Clint's words. He'd yet to touch her, but she was already trembling like a leaf in gale-force winds. The absolute power this man had over her was both frightening and exciting, and Blair knew they'd been moving toward this moment from the beginning.

She held out her hands. Beyond words, her gesture and the desire sparking her tawny eyes were all the answer Clint needed.

Throwing back the sheet, he left the bed, gathered her into his arms and gave her a long, lingering kiss that only had her wanting more. As her hands moved slowly across his back, exploring the muscles that went taut under her palms, Blair experienced a warm, fluttering ache to know this man totally. Her hands moved lower, and Clint groaned, pressing her against him, his flesh warming her, his desire making hers flame all the higher.

"You're wearing too many clothes," he complained, his hands caressing her body and causing it to hum under his expert touch like a live wire.

"Yes," she whispered.

His fingers slid the ribbon straps from her shoulders, and the nightgown fell to the floor in a silky puddle, allowing him a weakening gaze at her firm, uplifted breasts. "Beautiful," he murmured, stroking her satiny skin.

Blair's pulse leaped at the featherlight caress; he could feel it under his hands, and it beat against his lips as they explored her flesh. Clint imagined he could taste it as his tongue flicked across her nipple.

She moaned, arching her back, inviting him to take her more fully into his mouth, which he did, moving from breast to breast, treating each in turn to the tender torment that was driving Blair beyond reason.

"Better," he said happily, moving his lips steadily downward. His deep voice vibrated against her stomach, echoing the pulsating desire spiraling out from her innermost core.

"Better," she agreed on a gasp as his tongue made a warm, wet foray into her navel.

When he lowered her to the bed, Blair had the sensation of floating, and she wondered idly if Clint possessed the power of levitation among his vast talents. Then, as she sank into the mattress, she felt herself growing heavy, her limbs weighted, her mind languid with a thick, heavy pleasure.

"Beautiful," he murmured again, "so beautiful." He kissed her, a deep, drugging kiss that engulfed her in tides of aching warmth. He lifted his head and gazed down at her, his eyes gleaming a molten silver, his hands moving over her body in devastating trails that made her arch instinctively, seeking release.

"I've waited too long for this to rush it now," he said softly, his lips brushing lightly at her gleaming skin, tasting of her warm flesh.

Through the thick cloud fogging her mind, Blair suddenly realized that the situation had somehow reversed itself. She'd come into Clint's room to seduce him. Instead, he was the one doing all the giving.

"I wanted to make love to you," she objected on a tattered moan as his lips discovered a flash point of pleasure on her ankle.

"We've all night," he argued, his tongue tracing a damp path up her leg.

"But your pleasure—Oh!" His teeth had nipped at the delicate cord at the back of her knee.

"My pleasure comes from pleasuring you," he murmured, his mouth loitering at the silk of her inner thighs, delighting in the way she trembled when his tongue drew ever-widening circles on her skin.

Blair moaned his name, twisting to find relief; his teasing caresses were driving her to the point of despair. The deepening ache had turned into a steady, pulsating throb, moving through her body like heated honey; and when his tongue finally stabbed into the core of her, she felt something shatter within, like the finest crystal under a high note.

She cried out for him to hold her, to make her safe, and Clint obliged, taking her into his arms and murmuring soft, inarticulate words of comfort into her ear. Slowly, gradually, she stopped trembling, and lying in the circle of Clint's strong arms, Blair was shaken by a sudden renewal of desire that shot through her like a white-hot flame. Her body was acutely, fiercely, alive.

Clint was stunned by Blair's sudden change in mood as her hands, which had been gently stroking his body, turned greedy, drawing muffled groans from him as they sought to discover intimate secrets.

Blair marveled at his strength as he wondered at her softness, her fingers exploring every taut muscle, every straining sinew. She moved her fingers over him, and when that wasn't enough, her lips followed the heated path her hands had forged, tasting the intoxicating tang of his warm male flesh. Her teeth nipped at his moist skin, and when her tongue stroked away the little marks, Clint's body was wracked with a series of harsh shudders.

"Blair, I can't take much more," he warned, reaching for her in an attempt to end this tantalizing torture before he plunged over the brink of madness.

She easily avoided him, rising to her knees, her hair a dark curtain that brushed over the skin of his chest with a mind-blinding touch. Blair had never known such power, and as her avid mouth followed the dark arrow of hair downward, bliss just a moment away, she became the Tigress Woman—primitive, uninhibited, alive with savage passion.

When her lips embraced him, Blair was suddenly aware of a new sensation, that of possession. She wanted him. Not just for these few wild moments of unrestrained passion, but forever. He was hers, only hers, and the idea was so stimulating, so thrilling, that she threw her body onto his, pressing against his burning flesh, moving against him until Clint could stand no more.

He turned her over on her back, his blood transformed to flames that seared through his veins as he took her, driving her into the softness of the mattress with a hunger that transcended all bounds of time and space. Her long legs wrapped themselves about his hips and she matched his strength with hers, his soaring passion with her own, until together they crested, their exultant cries smothered by each other's lips.

Afterward, the shudders continued to course through her body. Lying passively in his arms, Blair could feel the still-wild pounding of his heart against her breasts.

Clint lifted his head and looked down at her, amusement blending with the leftover passion in his eyes. "I knew there was a tigress lurking in that beautiful body."

Smiling, Blair reached up to stroke his cheek with slightly trembling fingers. "It just took the right man to bring it out."

He pressed his lips against hers. "It's us," he murmured. "We make the magic together."

She sighed happily. "That's true. I've never known anything like it." She rained a series of light kisses across his collarbone. "Think how those photographs could have come out if you'd been in the studio with me."

Clint's body warmed anew with the memory of the brilliant passion he'd witnessed in her eyes as he'd entered her, claiming her heart and soul, as well as her body, for all time.

"They'd have been X-rated." His teeth nipped lightly at her earlobe, then lured her lips back to his.

"Mmm. But it would have made all the long hours under those hot lights a lot more fun."

"I think we can create enough of our own heat, don't you?"

She laughed, her fingers playing in his dark chest hair. "Definitely."

They fell silent, smiling at each other, lost in their own memories of what they'd just shared and in their own idyllic thoughts of the future.

"I love you."

They both said it together, as attuned in their need to state their feelings aloud as they had been in everything else. Clint looked down into her soft, loving gaze, and suddenly his mind churned up the sight of that pitchfork that had come so near to costing him everything he'd ever wanted in a woman.

"What's the matter?" she asked softly, seeing a frightening look of desperation flash into his gray eyes.

"I can't lose you, Blair."

Her expression was slightly puzzled as she framed his face with her hands. "I'm not going anywhere," she said.

Clint refused to allow himself any more thoughts of the problem that had begun with the farm and now encompassed his entire life. Nothing would happen to her, he swore. He'd see to it. They belonged together, he and Blair, and he wasn't going to allow anything to interfere.

As he stared down at her, the icy feeling of trepidation was replaced by a wild surge of need, and he took her again, desperately, urgently.

BLAIR WAS DREAMING of a stable of winning Thoroughbreds that were racing down the track, the jockeys all clad in the green-and-white silks of Clearwater Hills Farms. She and Clint were on the sidelines, cheering wildly, their arms wrapped about each other. When the entire field crossed the finish line together, they were ecstatic.

Clint kissed her thoroughly before they made their way to the winner's circle, where they were greeted with chaos. All the horses were rearing back, tossing their riders to the ground while they fought for their rightful position as victor. Their angry neighs filled the air, and their front hooves struck out at one another. As the dream grew more and more violent, the horses' screams more strident, Blair's eyes flew open.

An icy fear skimmed down her spine when she realized that the terrified screams were no dream. She pulled out of Clint's arms and ran to the bedroom window. He muttered an objection, reaching out in his sleep to the warm spot where she'd been only moments earlier.

"Oh, my God! Clint, the training barn's on fire!"

He was instantly awake and at her side. The cries of the horses filled the perfumed night air. "Damn! This has got to stop!" He tacked on a virulent series of oaths as he groped about in the dark for his clothes.

Blair turned on the lamp and found her robe under the comforter, which had slid to the floor during their lovemaking. She slipped the robe on, tying the belt while Clint struggled into a pair of jeans and his boots, forgoing socks in his haste.

Together, they ran outside, calling for water to anyone capable of hearing. Clint flung open the barn door, releasing clouds of billowing black smoke. The horses were rearing up as they had done in Blair's dreams, their hooves striking out at the smoke as if they could force it away with their efforts. Their eyes were wide and wild, their necks bathed in sweat, their mouths foaming with their instinctive fear of fire.

"Here." She shoved the sheet she'd pulled from the bed before leaving the room, into Clint's hands. "I thought this might help."

His admiring gaze normally would have given her inordinate pleasure, but there was no time for that at the moment.

"Thanks," he said, tearing the navy cloth into long strips. "You take one side and I'll take the other. Where in the hell is everyone, anyway?"

Knowing it was a rhetorical question, Blair didn't bother to answer. She grabbed a handful of the makeshift blindfolds and tied one of them around Star Dancer's wild black eyes. She stroked the stallion's soaking neck, murmuring encouraging words as she threw on his bridle and tugged hard, urging him out of the stall. The effort seemed to take hours, but finally he was outdoors, breathing in the fresh air, his chest heaving with exertion. By now the crew had arrived, and Blair handed him over to a young girl who'd recently been hired as a hot walker, the lowest rung of the ladder. It was her job to cool the horses down after exercise.

"Here," Blair said, "take him somewhere and hose him off. Then come right back."

"Yes, ma'am," the teenager answered, her own eyes wide with fright.

Blair allowed herself a backward glance, pleased to see that the girl was talking soothingly to the hysterical stallion as she led him away. Blair ran back to the barn, where three more horses were being evacuated by grooms. She did some quick calculations. They should be able to save most of the horses. She experienced an immense sense of gratitude when she spotted Annie assisting Jerry, managing incredibly well for a person with one arm in a sling.

Someone ran by, dragging a large hose into the barn and turning the stream of water in the direction of the bales of stacked hay from which was pouring forth the dense, acrid smoke.

Everyone continued to work at a frantic pace, and finally Clint led Storm Warning from the barn. Blair couldn't help crying out when she saw the stallion, whose skin was charred to a hateful black crisp. She grabbed a hose and began running cold water onto the horse's face, neck and eyes while Clint ran for ice and blankets.

As they worked feverishly, draping the horse in the wet blankets and ice-filled towels, Blair was unaware of the tears pouring down her cheeks. She couldn't remember when she'd been so glad to see anyone as she was when Bill Collins suddenly came into view.

"Jerry called me," the vet explained. He began to examine the stallion. Let's see what we have here."

"I'm not putting him away," Blair stated firmly, expecting an argument from Clint or Bill Collins.

Both men surprised her. "I'm with Blair," Clint seconded instantly.

"You might not have to," Bill said. "His heart rate isn't nearly as bad as it could be. Also, the mucous membranes are pink and normal. We might be able to save him. But it won't be easy," he added.

"We don't care," Blair and Clint said in unison. As Clint squeezed her hand reassuringly, Blair considered that just perhaps her world hadn't come to an end, after all.

They helped the vet replace the blankets and wrap the horse's legs. "We should move him to a clinic," Bill advised, "so he can get constant care."

"Blair and I will take turns," Clint said, "won't we?"

She nodded. "Around the clock."

"I can't guarantee he'll make it," Bill warned. "More than sixty percent of his body is burned, and a large part of the burns are third-degree. You know as well as I do that when an animal suffers burns over fifty percent of its body, the prognosis isn't good."

"He'll make it," Blair insisted. "I know he will."

"Then let's get started. I'll want him somewhere quiet, away from the other horses."

Clint suggested a small building that had once been used as a breeding barn. Far away from the bustle of the paddock, it should serve their purpose. Blair crooned comfortingly to Storm Warning as they led him away; she was encouraged by the way he perked up his ears in response. The attempt to save him wasn't futile. She knew it!

Blair and Clint stood by as Bill gave the stallion an injection of painkiller, as well as penicillin. With a centrifuge, the vet measured the horse's cell volume, finding him to be dehydrated. But Bill had come well prepared. Within minutes two IV's were set up, and Storm Warning was given more vitamin B to help against shock. The horse was catheterized and a tube inserted in his stomach so that additional fluids could be administered orally. When he began to swell in the early hours of the morning, he was given steroids to stabilize the swelling.

It was a long and tiring night, since more than once it looked as if they'd lose the stallion, but Blair and Clint never stopped talking to him or stroking his head or encouraging him not to give up. Storm Warning proved himself to be one plucky horse; he remained calm, responding to the three humans trying so desperately to save him. By the time the sun had risen on the eastern horizon, the swelling had gone down perceptibly and his skin was moist.

"I'm slowing the IV," Bill informed them. "For now, all we can do is keep an eye on him. He's going to need a lot of attention over the next several weeks, though."

Blair and Clint nodded wearily, Clint suddenly breaking into a deep coughing fit that had Blair worried. They'd soaked their own strips of cloth in water and covered their noses and mouths, but Clint had worked the longest without such assistance.

"Are you all right?" she asked.

He took a few deep breaths, which only brought about another bout of coughing. "Fine," he said finally as he came up for air.

"Are you sure?"

He shook his head, raking his hands through his darkened hair. "I'll be okay. I just inhaled some smoke when I first went in."

"Thank God the others are safe," she murmured.

"Thank *you*. If you hadn't wakened when you did, it could have been a real disaster."

"It was meant to be a disaster, wasn't it?" she asked softly, shivering as she considered their unseen enemy out there, lurking somewhere in the darkness.

Clint didn't answer; no answer was necessary. Seeing Blair's tremors, he asked, "Cold?"

"Frightened," she admitted, no longer hesitant to let him know her feelings after what they'd shared that evening. Had it only been that evening? It seemed like a hundred years ago.

He put his arm around her. "I know."

Before she could answer, a wide-eyed groom named Dennis Marston arrived at the door to tell them that the firemen had gone and things were under control.

"I'll stay with Storm Warning," he volunteered, "while you two get some rest."

"I don't know." Blair hesitated.

"Hey, it'll be all right," he assured her. "Storm Warning and I are old friends. Aren't we, guy?" he asked, going over to stroke what was left of the stallion's thick mane.

Storm Warning made the decision for Blair by nuzzling his head against the young man's chest. Dennis was the stallion's groom, and his love for the burned horse was evident.

"All right," she agreed. "Thank you, Dennis."

As he turned his gaze from the stallion, the young man's eyes were suspiciously moist. "Don't thank me, Ms. MacKenzie," he said huskily. "I'd never let anything happen to any of my horses."

"You've managed to hire a very loyal crew," she murmured to Clint as they walked across the yard.

"They're good kids. They love the horses like their own."

"Like you and Risky Pleasure."

He nodded. "Would you mind if I checked her before we went in?"

Blair shook her head, taking his hand in hers. "Not at

all," she said. They went over to the smaller barn that had escaped the fire.

Blair and Clint were brought up short as they reached Risky Pleasure's stall. It was empty.

Chapter Thirteen

The commotion had not gone unnoticed, and several individuals from neighboring farms had arrived on the heels of the pumper truck, ready to help. Hours later, only Matt and Marni remained. At this point, it appeared all they could offer was moral support. "Who would do such a thing?" Marni asked, handing both Blair and Clint a drink as they entered the kitchen, their faces identical masks of despair.

"I don't know," Clint muttered, before tossing off the drink. "But when I find out, I'm going to make certain the bastard pays."

Blair stared blankly at the glass her friend had pushed into her hands.

"It's brandy," Marni said. "It'll help."

Blair thought that nothing would help the way she felt right now, but at Matt's added coaxing she gave in, feeling an explosion of warmth when the alcohol hit her stomach.

"I think I'm going to be sick," she said suddenly.

Clint reached out for her, but Marni quickly stopped him. "I'll take care of her, Clint. You sit down before you drop."

Marni put her arm around Blair's shoulder and led her to the bathroom, then stood back as the combination of smoke, fear and despair made Blair ill.

"I'm sorry," she muttered, sinking down on the floor with her knees drawn up against her chest. Feeling inordinately dizzy, she lowered her forehead to her knees and drank in deep breaths of air. She could still smell the acrid smoke in her nostrils and thought she was going to be sick all over again.

"Don't be silly," Marni scolded. "You've been through a terrible ordeal. You're allowed to fall apart a little bit. You can't always be in control, Blair. The sooner you learn that, the happier you'll be."

Blair thought back to those glorious hours before her world had come apart at the seams. "You're right," she surprised her friend by saying. "Clint said almost the same thing to me."

"And?"

"And now I've got to help him find Risky Pleasure." Blair struggled to her feet.

"What you need to do is rest," Marni countered ineffectually, heaving a frustrated sigh as she followed Blair back down the hallway to the kitchen.

Clint was slumped at the table, his head in his hands.

"Feeling better?" Matt asked Blair, his green eyes solicitous.

"A little." Her voice was still not strong.

Clint lifted his head, managing a weak smile. "Shouldn't you be lying down?"

"Probably." She moved beside him, running her fingers through his smoky hair. "But so should you, and you're still up."

"I've got to wait for the police."

"It's my farm," she reminded him. "So it's my responsibility."

His arm went around her waist. "I thought we'd come to an understanding about that."

Blair viewed the weariness in his eyes and could have wept. "We did," she agreed. "We're in this together, all the way, Clint."

This time his smile was a little stronger. "That's better." He pulled her down onto his lap, and she rested her head on his shoulder.

"I can stay and give the police the report," Matt offered. "You two look beat."

"We'll be okay. Which is a helluva lot more than I can say for Risky Pleasure," Clint muttered.

"You've no idea who's doing all this?" Marni asked, her eyes shadowed with a faint fear.

"We had a couple of ideas," Clint said slowly, "but they're not panning out too well."

A gloomy silence settled over the room. Then Clint sat up suddenly, almost dumping Blair from his lap. "Jerry!"

"What?" the other three asked in unison.

Clint turned to Blair. "When we were all working to get the horses out of the training barn, did you see Jerry anywhere around?"

Blair thought back. "Yes," she said. "I saw him working with Annie when we first discovered the fire."

"Did you see him later?"

She shook her head. "Now that you mention it, I didn't.... Oh, Clint, you don't think he set that fire, do you? Jerry would never hurt any of the horses. And he'd never do anything to Risky Pleasure—you know how he adores that filly."

"I thought he did. Let's go check."

Blair struggled to keep up with Clint as they made their way across the yard to the building that housed the groom's quarters.

"Well?" Clint said, his gray eyes raking over Jerry's empty room.

Blair's bleak gaze followed his. "He's gone," she stated flatly.

"With our horse." Clint's voice trembled with pent-up rage.

Blair put a hand on his arm. "There must be a reason."

"Yeah. And when we find the kid, I'm going to beat it out of him."

She didn't answer that, knowing that Clint was speaking out of frustration. "Does he have any family around here?"

"No. They all live back East."

"Perhaps he just took her out for a while to calm her down," Blair suggested hopefully. "Maybe he doesn't have anything to do with this at all."

"Sure," Clint shot back, "why don't you tell me another fairy tale while you're at it?" A moment later he groaned, rubbing his hand over his face. When he took the hand away, his eyes revealed contrition. "I'm sorry, babe. I've no right to take this out on you."

She went up on her toes and kissed his cheek. "Don't worry about that." Then she saw the police cruiser pull into the driveway. "We'd better go talk to them," she said without a great deal of enthusiasm.

After the police had taken their report, Marni pointed out a fact that all of them, in their distress, had overlooked.

"Doesn't it seem odd to you that they'd steal Risky Pleasure?"

Clint shrugged his shoulders. "These days nothing would surprise me," he grunted.

Marni was undeterred. "But if they really were responsible for Black Magic's broken leg, then why didn't they just destroy Risky Pleasure in her stall? Why go to all the trouble of spiriting her out of here in the first place?"

"There's always the possibility of ransom," Clint mused.

"If it's simply a need for money, then why all the other incidents?" Marni argued.

The four were silent, mulling the problem over. "I'll be damned if I know," Clint muttered finally.

Blair's heart turned over at the defeat in his tone, the exhaustion etched on every hard line of his face. His silvery hair was tousled from his raking his fingers through it, and his skin was still darkened with smudges from the heavy smoke.

"Bed," Marni stated firmly. "You two need some sleep. Matt and I will try to find out if anyone else around here knows what Jerry was up to."

This time Clint didn't argue. "Just a few short hours. We still have Storm Warning to worry about."

There was never any question about Blair's going to her room and Clint to his. After that evening it seemed natural that they'd both share the bed in which only a few hours before, they'd pledged a new beginning.

It felt so right, Blair thought as she lay in Clint's strong arms. So good. Feeling safe with him beside her, she closed her eyes and allowed her exhaustion to overtake her. Soon they were both asleep.

WITH BLAIR AND CLINT safely asleep and Marni taking a nap in her old room, Matt sat alone in the den, staring into space. For the past two weeks he'd been feeling as if he were slowly, inexorably, sinking into quicksand. That morning he realized he was in danger of going in over his head.

Heaving a weary sigh, he dialed the number of Robin Hanson. "That was a lousy thing to do," he said the moment she answered the phone.

"It was a necessary thing to do," she amended. "Remember, darling, nice guys finish last. I've always thought of myself as a winner."

"What the hell did you do with the filly?" he grated out.

"Filly?"

"Risky Pleasure."

"I assume she's still in residence at the farm."

"Don't play coy with me, sweetheart. You know as well as I do she's disappeared."

There was a long, thoughtful silence on the other end of the telephone. "That's an interesting twist," Robin murmured. "But we didn't have anything to do with horse-napping the filly."

Matt suddenly felt like wringing the woman's neck. "If you're lying to me, Robin, so help me God . . ."

"Believe me, darling, I have no idea what happened to Hollister's precious horse. Although I wish I had thought of absconding with her," she added. "It's a delicious idea. He must be frantic."

"You can be a real black widow when you want to be," he muttered, unable to miss the enthusiasm in her voice.

"Flattery will get you nowhere, darling," she said silkily. "Keep me informed about the filly. I don't like the idea of someone else suddenly entering this little game we've got going for ourselves."

"Do you think Blackwood's behind it?"

"That's a possibility. Quite honestly, I wouldn't have thought the man had the guts to do anything like this, but you never know what an individual will do when several million dollars are at stake."

That's for sure, Matt considered bleakly as he hung up, wishing he'd never gotten involved in this mess to begin with. When he'd first been approached by Hightower to sell his land for the site of a new electronics factory, he'd believed it was the answer to all his prayers. A series of losing seasons had been capped off by Northern Light's accident, and he'd been on the brink of bankruptcy.

But one condition of the deal had been that he promise not to mention the sale while Hightower Development began quietly to buy up all the surrounding land. VideoTec was going to employ several thousand people, and all those new workers would need housing. While the idea of the rolling grasslands covered with rows and rows of tract housing was definitely unappealing, Matt had managed to convince himself that progress was inevitable. If he didn't cooperate, they'd simply find someone else. So he'd remained silent, watching as the bogus real estate companies began buying up the land.

He'd never expected things to get out of hand this way. Just as he'd never expected Jason Langley to have that fatal heart attack while confronting him with his suspicions. Jason had surprised everyone by his sudden insistence on reviewing all his financial records. For years he'd allowed his attorney and accountant to tend to the business end of Clearwater Hills Farm, directing his attention to the only thing that interested him: the horses.

But once Jason had accepted the fact that he didn't have long to live, he'd wanted to know exactly what he was leaving to his granddaughter. It hadn't taken him long to discover the discrepancy in the books or unearth his neighbor's part in the unusual amount of real estate transactions going on. He'd lost his temper, a not unusual occurrence, but that time it had been fatal.

Afraid that others would follow the trail, Matt had paid his own visit to the hall of records, removed the damning page that listed his sale to VideoTec, through Hightower enterprises, and burned it in his fireplace. He'd thought that would be the end of everything. But then Blair had shown up, refusing to sell, and things had turned decidedly nasty when Hanson's hired thugs had shattered Black Magic's leg.

In an effort to forestall any further tragedies, Matt had entered into the affair with Marni, hoping she could convince her friend to cut her losses and go back to New York. He felt guilty about using Marni that way. She was a nice woman and deserved better, but he'd been desperate, and at the time it seemed a viable solution.

Unfortunately, the entire idea proved a dismal failure, for Marni steadfastly insisted that Blair had a mind of her own and would listen to no one when it came to surrendering her lifelong dream.

Matt shook his head, afraid to consider what might happen next.

BILL COLLINS HAD STAYED ON catching a few hours of needed sleep. He was back tending Storm Warning when Blair and Clint showed up after their naps.

"He's holding his own," the vet assured them. "In fact, as bad as he looks, he just might be in better shape than Sun Devil."

"Sun Devil?" Blair said. "He wasn't burned."

Bill shook his head. "I know, Blair. But he inhaled a lot of smoke."

"Pneumonia," Clint muttered.

The vet shook his head. "It doesn't look good."

Clint raked his fingers through his hair. "I've seen horses through pneumonia before, and we can do it again with Sun Devil," he vowed.

"Of course we will," Blair seconded fervently. "What's your plan for Storm Warning?" she asked, stroking the stallion's head tenderly. The horse's eyes were burned so badly they were swollen shut, but that didn't stop him from responding to Blair's voice and gentle touch.

"It'll be a long process," Bill warned. "And expensive. And there are no guarantees."

"I don't care about expense," Blair said firmly.

"Our first concern is to make certain he survives his shock. We seem to be doing pretty well there," he assured Blair and Clint. "Next, we have to worry about pneumonia, so I'll be giving him penicillin for his lungs. I'm also treating him with chloramphenicol for his eyes and butazolidin for pain. We'll continue that treatment, as well as vitamin injections.

"If we manage to get through those dangers, then we still have to worry about infection. I've put a call in for some synthetic skin for grafts. We'll have to make sheet blankets to cover him during the healing process, to keep him from rubbing off the skin grafts. Silver sulfadiazine should help prevent him from wanting to scratch—it's been successful in treating burns on humans."

Bill's expression was professionally cautious. "Even if everything goes well," he concluded, "you're looking at a year at least before you'll have a healthy horse."

Blair and Clint exchanged a long look. Then Clint spoke for both of them, taking Blair's hand and giving it a tight, reassuring squeeze. "We're not going anywhere."

The following days blended together into an exhausting combination of vigil and work. Clint and Blair rotated shifts, taking turns tending to Storm Warning while the crews cleaned up the mess left behind by the fire. Neither Clint nor Blair was surprised when the fire department ruled the blaze arson; neither were they surprised when the police failed to locate Risky Pleasure. The filly seemed to have vanished into thin air.

"She has to be somewhere," Blair muttered as she exited the shower after a tiring six-hour shift of trying to keep the stallion from sloughing off his burned skin.

Clint was seated on the edge of the bed, pulling on his boots. "Now that's a brilliant observation if I've ever heard one."

Blair didn't take his gritty tone personally. He'd gotten little sleep since the fire and was obviously walking an emotional tightrope right now. The work entailed with nursing Sun Devil and Storm Warning had not allowed him the privilege of worrying about the filly during his waking hours, but Blair could see that sleep had been as difficult for him as it was for her.

"What about Annie's family?" she asked.

"I told you, they all live here in San Diego. Besides, the police checked that out already." He raked his fingers through his hair in obvious frustration. "Damn!"

"What is it?"

"There's a grandmother I forgot about. Annie's so damned Americanized, I tend to forget her family came from across the border."

"And the grandmother still lives there?"

"Tijuana, I think. But I'd better call Matt and find out exactly where."

As he rose to make his way to the phone, Blair reached out, putting her hand on his arm. "Don't do that," she advised softly.

"Why not?"

"There's something I meant to tell you about, something that happened at the party."

She told Clint about Brian Hanson's assertion that Jason had intended to sell the farm, a fact that had been seconded by Ramsey.

Clint muttered a harsh expletive, then asked, "What does that have to do with Matt?"

Blair went on to explain the scene she'd inadvertently witnessed. "I can't prove anything is going on between them, but it just didn't look right," she stated quietly.

"That's why you were in such a bad mood that night, wasn't it?" Clint sank down onto the edge of the bed.

"I was upset about the accusations against you. But yes, I was also worried about Marni," she admitted.

"Why didn't you tell me?"

"I was going to. But then we made love and I forgot. After that, there was the fire, and we've both been so busy, it slipped my mind.... What if Matt's behind all this?" she suggested softly.

"That's a harsh accusation, Blair."

"I know," she whispered. They stared at each other, their expressions bleak.

"I suppose I can find out where Annie's grandmother lives just as easily from her parents."

"I think that would be best."

Clint stood up, his eyes displaying his discomfort with this latest twist. "Matt's always been a friend," he said. "I hate what I'm thinking."

Blair's eyes were mirror images of Clint's. "Me, too." She felt like crying when he left the room, his wide shoulders slumped with the weight of suspicions.

AS THEY DROVE toward the border that afternoon, pulling an empty horse trailer in case they were lucky enough to find the pilfered filly, Blair attempted logic. Writing down all the pieces they'd found of this puzzle, she hoped to force them into a workable whole.

"That's it!" she said suddenly.

Clint glanced over at the notepad. "What's it?"

"Hightower! We've been looking at it all along and never even knew it!"

"Would you care to explain that a little further?"

She read off the list of new property owners in the area. "Hanson Properties, Ingram Property Management, Guardian Development Company, Henderson Land Company, Thompson Development, Owens Land Management, Western Corporation, Evergreen Real Estate and Randall Investments."

"So?"

"Look at the first initials," she said, tapping each letter with the point of her pencil. They're an acronym."

"I'll be damned. They spell out 'high tower.'"

"Hightower," she confirmed.

"So it *is* all one company."

"One company that seems determined to buy up every last piece of property out here. I'm surprised the zoning board has been rubber-stamping the applications for land-use change, though."

"That was undoubtedly the easy part," Clint informed her. "This is a rapidly expanding area, and the zoning board is up to its eyebrows in applications. All you need is one crooked board member to push the paper through, and unless they get a big hue and cry from the general population, the applications pass without much of a fight."

"And San Diego residents are too busy fighting beach-front development to care what happens up here," she surmised.

Clint nodded. "Got it. Jason and I went to some of the meetings. A few of the other landowners did, too, but we were like that small voice crying out in the wilderness. No one heard us."

Blair considered that idea, considered losing her beautiful farm and grew more furious by the moment. "They're not going to run me off my property," she declared fervently.

Clint chuckled in spite of his depressed mood. "Now you sound like some heroine out of a Saturday afternoon matinee."

Her eyes softened. "Then we're in great shape. Because you remind me of all those heroes I used to swoon over."

"Aren't you laying it on a little thick?"

"Not at all. I do love you, Clint." She reached out, putting her hand on his leg and stroking it lightly.

"I love you, too, sweetheart," he replied in a husky voice. "But if you don't put that cute little hand back where it belongs, I'm going to have to pull over to the side of the road."

At the way the obvious desire in Clint's voice warmed her blood, Blair regarded his suggestion as ideal. But she knew they had far more important things to do, so she did as he asked.

"Do you think Risky Pleasure will be in Tijuana, Clint?"

"I don't know," he admitted. But I can't think of anywhere else to try. It's possible Jerry is hiding her at Annie's grandmother's place."

"Is it that easy to smuggle a horse across the border?"

"If thousands of illegals can enter the country every night, it shouldn't be that difficult to move a single horse in the opposite direction."

"But why would he take her in the first place?"

Clint shook his head. "I'll be damned if I know."

As he fell silent, Blair watched the scenery flash by the truck window. They'd left the eastern grasslands and were now driving along the coast.

"Cold?" Clint observed Blair's slight tremor.

"No, but I just had a thought."

"Must not have been very pleasant."

"It wasn't. I was wondering if this could all be a trap to lure us out of the country so that we can't get any help."

Clint rubbed his jaw. "I thought of that," he told her. "In fact, I'd considered not allowing you to come along."

"Not come along?" Blair's eyes widened and her tone was incredulous. "Do you honestly think you could have kept me away?"

Clint managed a low laugh. "I said I'd *considered* it. I also dismissed the idea immediately. Keeping you out of action would probably require several lengths of strong rope, and I'm not prepared to take the inevitable consequences when I'd finally have to untie you."

Blair, too, laughed for a moment; then her expression sobered. "I know we're going to find her, Clint. I just know it."

"Ah, I forgot—Madame Tigress has a crystal ball. Did you perchance, happen to see a big-boned filly in there?"

"Of course," Blair answered promptly. "And she's beating the socks off Cimarron."

"You're agreeing to the match race?"

"Of course I'm agreeing," she said softly, leaning over to brush a light kiss against his cheek.

Clint was suddenly overcome with waves of fear like nothing he'd every known. What if he were to lose her? The thought continued to torment him as they crossed the border into Tijuana, drove past the shopping stalls, and slowed to make way for the hordes of tourists filling the narrow streets. Making a quick decision, Clint braked to a stop.

"Why are we stopping?" Blair asked, eyeing him curiously. They were outside a small café, but she knew Clint had not developed a sudden urge for a taco.

"I'm not taking you with me."

"That's ridiculous!"

"No, it's not. I've no intention of taking you into a dangerous situation like this."

"Clint..."

"Look, Blair, it might be different if I believed you'd stick to playing the maiden-in-distress part, but I've got the uneasy feeling you watched all those Saturday afternoon matinees and picked up the wrong role model. I'm only thinking of you, sweetheart."

"If you were really thinking of me," she argued, "you'd let me come with you. I can't stand the idea of your going to Annie's grandmother's all alone. I'd never forgive myself if you got hurt."

"How the hell do you think I'd feel if *you* got hurt?" he shot back.

"I promise not to do anything foolish. Besides, we don't even know if Risky Pleasure is down here. Please let me stay," she wheedled, her tawny eyes entreating him to her line of reasoning.

Clint felt as if he were drowning in deep pools of molten gold. "Damn it, Blair, this is crazy."

"Clint..."

The impatient blare of a taxi horn interrupted them, reminding Clint that he was effectively blocking the flow of traffic. He shifted into gear, cursing softly under his breath. "You are not coming with me, and that's the end of it. It's too dangerous for a woman."

Blair felt like hitting him over the top of his hard, chauvinist head. "Fine," she snapped, moving to open the truck door. "I'll just get out right here. I'm sure I'll be completely safe wandering around this place until whenever you get back. I've heard that border-town reputations are exaggerated anyway."

He grabbed her arm, yanking her back into the truck. "Damn it, you win. You're coming along."

Clint's blistering expression echoed his angry tone, but since she'd gotten her way Blair decided the prudent thing to do now would be to ignore his irritation and not flaunt her victory.

She folded her hands in her lap with all the complaisance of an obedient schoolgirl. "Thank you, Clint," she said softly. "I promise not to get in your way."

His only response was a muffled oath, but as she dared a surreptitious glance out of the corner of her eye, Blair thought she saw a ghost of a smile playing on his lips.

Chapter Fourteen

"This certainly explains all the illegal aliens," Blair murmured as they drove past the rows and rows of shanties made of tar paper and flattened oil drums. The dark gray storm clouds hovering overhead only added to the bleak scene.

"There are almost eight hundred thousand people living in Tijuana these days. They pour in from the interior, seeking higher wages and a better way of life. Unfortunately, all too many of them only end up worse off than they were in the first place. It takes more than a dream to make it, I'm afraid."

Blair remained silent, uncomfortable with the inevitable comparison in life-styles. The view became more rural, and she watched the little pastures strung with wires that housed chickens, donkeys, once in a while a cow or a swaybacked horse. Then one animal in particular caught her eye.

"Clint!" She grabbed his arm, almost causing him to steer off the dirt roadway.

"Hey!" He brought the truck to an abrupt halt. "If you don't mind, Blair, I'd like to get there all in one piece."

She ignored his gritty tone, pointing instead out the window. "Look at that horse."

At Clint's first cursory glance, he was inclined to disregard the large, rawboned filly. But as he studied her further, he felt a faint stirring of hope. "It sure as hell looks like her," he agreed. "But the star is missing. And she doesn't have the stockings."

"And the tail is the wrong color," Blair added. "But she could've been dyed, Clint. I tell you, that's Risky Pleasure."

The more he looked, the more Clint felt Blair was right. "Let's go take a closer look."

As if on cue, the storm hit the moment they exited the truck, the sky opening up as dime-size raindrops began to fall around them.

"Terrific timing," he growled, making his way through the downpour to the horse, who was standing in the middle of the field, ears up, eyeing them with curiosity.

"Wonderful timing," Blair corrected, clapping her hands. "Look at her, Clint!"

As they watched, the water running off the horse turned into dark brown rivulets, and signs of the familiar white star and stockings came into view. Clint broke into a jog with Blair on his heels, both of them calling out to the filly, who neighed happily in response.

"Shoe polish," he laughed, throwing an arm around Risky Pleasure's neck. "The kid used shoe polish for camouflage!"

"Surely he didn't expect to get away with that."

"It was just a temporary measure. In fact, I think I've finally got everything figured out."

"Well, I'm sure glad someone does," Blair muttered, "because I'm still lost."

"I'll tell you later," he promised. "First let's get Risky Pleasure out of this rain before she ends up looking like a zebra."

While they walked back to the truck, Blair talked a hundred miles an hour to the filly, who appeared to be nodding and neighing in agreement to her owner's enthusiasm. Within minutes Risky Pleasure was loaded into the horse trailer. Blair and Clint were congratulating themselves on a job well done when a dark car suddenly appeared around the curve and screeched to a stop in front of them. As two men jumped out, Blair realized she was finally face to face with the individuals responsible for all the troubles at the farm. These were the people who'd caused Black Magic's death.

At the memory of that sweet stallion, fury whipped through her. She squared her shoulders and moved toward the men, her topaz eyes shooting sparks.

"Blair!" Clint pushed her name through gritted teeth as his fingers curled around her elbow, stopping her in her tracks. One of the men had pulled out a revolver; the other man was pointing a twelve-gauge shotgun at them.

The taller of the two strangers nodded approvingly. "Very good, Hollister. If you know what's good for Miss Mac-Kenzie, you'll advise her to do as we say. Now, both of you, against the trailer."

Blair and Clint exchanged a look, then slowly did as instructed, turning their backs on the men and placing their palms against the side of the fiberglass horse trailer. If the anger directed her way from Clint's gray eyes was any indication, Blair considered for a fleeting instant that she'd be safer in the hands of these thugs.

The click of a cylinder from behind caused her blood suddenly to run cold, and she shut her eyes, seeing swirling bright spots on a background of black velvet. When the explosion sounded seconds later, she tried to scream, but only a ragged croak escaped her white lips.

As Blair slowly realized that she had not been shot, that awareness brought even a worse thought. Clint. *Dear God, these men had shot Clint!* But when she opened her eyes, he was still standing beside her, a grim expression carved onto his face.

"Dangerous country," the man with the shotgun said casually. Blair cast a wary glance over her shoulder, looking at the scattered remains of what she could only surmise had been a desert snake.

"Rattler," he informed her, seeing the direction of her gaze. "Wouldn't do to let you get bit, Miss MacKenzie.

That's a damn painful way to go. I had something a little quicker in mind myself.''

"Terrific," Clint muttered. "Now do you see why I didn't want you along?"

"We're in this together," she reminded him under her breath. "All the way. Besides, there's something I haven't told you...."

"All right, you two, knock off the chatter," the smaller man instructed, his voice sounding like a bald tire on a gravel road.

"Who are you?" Blair asked angrily. "And what do you want with us?"

"Lady, if you don't shut up, I'm going to do it for you." he advised calmly.

"And how do you suggest doing that?" she demanded, trying to judge the shorter man's weight and height. It just might work. But she'd never before used her hard-practiced skills in an actual attack. What if she failed?

"Blair, just do what they ask," Clint insisted, "before you end up getting yourself killed."

Killed? Her wide eyes returned to the barrel of the weapon pointed in her direction, and her vivid awareness of the actual danger of her situation caused her to sway slightly.

Both men shouted as Clint reached out, wrapping his arm around her waist to steady her. "She tripped, dammit! What did you think, that she was going to try to escape with those guns aimed at her back?"

"Just shut up, Hollister, and put your hands back against the trailer," the smaller man ordered. "Vince, check 'em out."

Clint complied, his eyes ordering Blair to do likewise. Vince patted them down, searching for weapons. Clint had to bite down the useless rage that surged through him as the man's hands moved along Blair's body. It wasn't the time. Not yet. He had to keep them talking.

"They're both clean, Phil." Vince returned to stand beside his partner.

"Did Blackwood set you up to this?" Clint asked conversationally.

Both men laughed harshly. "Blackwood's the next on the list. We're going to take care of him after we finish with you."

"You've got a busy day planned."

"You made it easier. It was obvious the kid had swiped the horse, but nobody at Hightower knew where he hid it. All we had to do was follow you two, and here we are."

Blair risked a glance back over her shoulder. The men were too far away. She couldn't risk it. Not yet.

"What do you want with Risky Pleasure?" she asked, stalling for time.

"Hell," Vince said, "we don't give a damn about the stupid nag. But Hanson's worried that the kid knows something. We figured if we tagged along after you and the cowboy here, we could find the kid and make sure he didn't show up later with some fool blackmail scheme."

Blair's blood ran cold as she realized they intended to kill Jerry. As well as her and Clint.

"I'm surprised Matt didn't think of Annie's grandmother," Clint remarked casually. "He is involved in all this, isn't he?"

Phil nodded. "He got a little squeamish when the job got serious. He wanted to back out after Vince here did in that stallion, but there was always that little matter of Langley's death."

"Matt killed my grandfather?" Blair gasped.

The man shrugged. "He says it was an accident. Who knows what really happened? The old bastard was dead, one way or the other."

"So Matt was stuck," Clint stated flatly, thinking how he'd always considered Matt Bradshaw his friend.

It didn't escape Clint's notice that they were telling him far too many things about the nature of the incidents at Clearwater Hills Farm. The only way they'd be so open was if they planned to kill him and Blair. He wished he could assure her that he had no intention of allowing that to happen. He could only hope she wasn't too frightened.

Meanwhile, Blair was trying to remain calm. There had to be a way out of this. She knew that whatever these Hightower people wanted with her property, they were not above killing to achieve it.

"You really are the Tigress Woman, aren't you?" Phil asked suddenly, his gaze narrowing. "I didn't see it at first. But your eyes give you away."

"Is that good or bad?" she managed to say.

"Depends on how you look at it, I suppose. Come here," he instructed, his pale blue eyes suddenly gleaming with a bright light.

Blair didn't move. The man slowly lifted his arm, aiming the revolver at Clint. "I asked you nicely to come over here, Miss MacKenzie. I don't want to have to repeat it."

"Blair..." Clint reached out, not wanting her anywhere near those thugs.

The deadly sound of the shotgun being cocked sounded like a rifle shot in the steady *plunk plunk* of the falling rain.

"You stay where you are, Hollister, or Vince will pull that trigger. This is between the little lady and me."

"Let her go," Clint said, slowly withdrawing his hand. "She doesn't have anything to do with this."

"I'm afraid she does," Phil argued. "That's right, come over here, Tigress Woman," he said, nodding his approval as Blair approached. "I think it's time we got to know each other a little better, don't you?"

Clint fought against the murderous rage that surged through him, threatening to eat away any semblance of sanity. She didn't need blind heroics now. When he made his move, he would have to be certain that he could pull it off.

"She doesn't own the farm anymore," he said. "She deeded it over to me."

"Tell me another one," Vince laughed. "You may be a helluva horse trainer, Hollister, but you're a lousy liar."

"It's true," Clint said calmly. "It's amazing what a woman will do if you tell her you love her."

At Blair's sudden intake of breath, Phil's eyes moved back and forth between the couple. The pained expression on her face made him seem more willing to accept Clint's story.

"Well, well. While this sure as hell makes everything more interesting, I'm afraid it doesn't change things. You know, all this would've been a lot easier if Vince here hadn't missed with that damn pitchfork."

"I knew it wasn't an accident," Clint muttered.

"With you out of the way, Hollister, the little lady here would have had to give up and take that cute little tail back to New York on the first plane."

"The pitchfork was meant for Clint?" Blair asked weakly, thinking how much she would have missed if these horrible men had succeeded in killing him.

"What did you think? That it was for you?" Phil asked incredulously.

Blair could only nod.

"Hell, there wasn't any reason to do away with you then," he said. "Of course, you know too much now, I'm afraid. We're going to have to do away with both of you."

His eyes gleamed as they moved down her slender frame, taking in the rain-soaked clothes that clung to her body like a second skin. The cold had hardened her nipples, and they pressed against the wet sweater, arresting Phil's heated gaze.

"Although in your case, Tigress Woman, I think we can make certain your last few hours are enjoyable."

His leer caused terror to spiral up her spine, and goose bumps rose on her skin when he reached out and dragged her back against him, his arm crushing against her breasts as his other hand still pointed the gun at Clint.

Clint was on the verge of losing control at the way Phil was looking down at Blair. Now Vince, too, seemed to be more interested in what the Tigress Woman could provide in the way of recreation. Both men were gazing at her as if she were their own personal smorgasbord and they'd been starving for months.

Knowing full well the fantasies those Tigress Woman layouts could instill, Clint forced himself to allow them their tawdry mental images for the time being. At least that activity took their attention away from him.

He slowly walked his fingers along the edge of the trailer. Out of the corner of her eye, Blair saw what he was doing. She had to keep their captors from noticing Clint's surreptitious movements.

"Can't we make some kind of deal?" she asked in a breathless little voice, her eyes wide and guileless.

"Lady, be reasonable," Vince complained, a red flush rising from his collar as he watched the rise and fall of her breasts. "You know too much."

"I won't tell," she promised, her voice half honey, half smoke as she took a chance and reached out to place a supplicating hand on his arm. By his glazed look, Blair knew that Vince was not immune to her stroking fingers. "Besides, I can pay you a lot more than Mr. Hanson is paying."

"I don't know...."

"Don't be an idiot," Phil argued. "We've got a job to do, pure and simple. Since when do you start getting all wishy-washy over a broad?"

"I just thought—"

"You're not paid to think," the smaller man, who was still holding Blair, snapped back. "You'll do whatever I tell you. And I'm telling you to take care of Hollister while I spend a little time with Miss MacKenzie."

"I take my orders from Hanson, not you," Vince said.

"Is that a fact?" Phil loosened his hold on Blair as he glared up at his partner. "May I remind you who went to college with Hanson in the first place?"

"I'm getting sick of hearing about that fancy-pants college you two went to," Vince growled.

While they'd been arguing, Clint had loosened Risky Pleasure's reins. Suddenly he slapped the horse on the rump, causing her to escape the trailer and take off at a full gallop. The commotion caught the men off guard, and with a mighty roar, Clint threw himself against them, knocking Vince to the ground. The shotgun sank ineffectually into the deep mud.

"Hold it right there," Phil ordered, flinging Blair away from him, attempting to aim the revolver at Clint, who was rolling on the ground with the larger, but less agile, Vince.

Her captor let out a loud shout as Blair suddenly grabbed his outstretched arm and flipped him onto his back. He landed on a flat rock, gasping for breath like a grounded carp. Blair picked up the gun he'd dropped, her hands trembling as she aimed it at his head.

"Blair, give it to me!"

Her attention returned to Clint, who was straddling Vince and pounding his fists into the man's doughy face. She quickly handed the revolver over, more than willing to allow Clint to take charge of the situation.

"Get some rope out of the trailer, will you, honey?" he asked calmly, covering the two men. "I think we'd better tie our friends up before they get themselves into more mischief."

Blair retrieved the length of rope quickly, relaxing only when Clint had tightly bound their hands and ankles.

"At least I've discovered the mysterious exercise program," he said with a chuckle. "My God, I could have guessed for a million years and never come up with jujitsu. Why didn't you tell me?"

Blair smiled. "I was saving it in case you ever got out of line. Then, by the time you did, I sure wasn't going to beat you up for doing what I'd wanted all along."

He pulled her into his arms, his lips bestowing hard little kisses all over her face. He'd come so close to losing her!

"There are a lot easier ways to get me on my back, sweetheart," he drawled.

Really?" Her arms looped around his waist as she smiled up at him.

"Really. All you have to do is ask."

They exchanged a long, delicious kiss, oblivious to the slanting rain pelting them.

"Hey, we're getting soaked out here!"

Clint's gaze slid to the two men lying in a pool of brackish mud. "So you are," he stated calmly. "They're getting cold," he said to Blair.

"What a pity."

"I suppose the least we can do is take them into town and have them thrown in jail."

"I suppose so."

"Hey! You can't leave us in some foreign jail. We might never get out!" Phil complained.

"He's got a point," Clint said.

"He certainly does," Blair agreed.

"Would you miss him if he never got back to the States?"

Blair shook her head. "Not me. How about you?"

"Hey, you two, quit joking around!" Phil shouted. "Mexico always waives extradition!"

Clint appeared thoughtful. "I wonder how much it would take to bribe a few government officials in order to keep good old Vince and Phil as guests here for a few years."

Blair's topaz eyes grew incredulous. "Why, Clint Hollister, are you suggesting that these two men could become lost in the system?"

"Hey, wait a minute, we've got rights, too, you know!" Vince bellowed.

"Do you hear anything?" Clint asked Blair.

"Just the rain."

"Speaking of rain, we've got a horse who's dripping shoe polish out there somewhere. I suppose we should go find her."

Blair, peering past Clint's shoulder, suddenly smiled. "That won't be necessary."

Clint turned to see Risky Pleasure walking across the field, Jerry and Annie seated on her bare back. Both their faces displayed their nervousness.

"I'm sorry," Jerry said as he slid to the ground. "I know it was a lousy thing to do. But all I could think of was getting Risky Pleasure away from the farm to where she'd be safe."

"You had us worried to death," Blair felt the need to point out, despite the young man's good intentions. "Do you have any idea what Clint's been going through? What I've been going through?"

Jerry hung his head. "I guess I didn't think it through very well," he admitted. Annie remained silent, looking as if she expected both of them to be fired at any moment.

"You certainly didn't," Blair agreed.

Clint pressed a finger against her lips. "It's all over. And despite everything, Risky Pleasure is safe and sound."

"Thank God," Blair said fervently. "We may have you two to thank for that," she told them with a slight smile.

"Come on," Clint suggested. "Let's take these thugs into town and go home."

Annie finally managed to speak. "We're not fired?"

Clint grinned. "Are you kidding? Who's going to take care of the filly if we get rid of Jerry?"

"And if we fired you, Annie," Blair added, "we'd have to start looking for someone else to ride Risky Pleasure against Cimarron."

Jerry and Annie's answering smiles threatened to banish the slate-gray rain clouds as they hurried to load the filly into the trailer.

It took the remainder of the day to get the necessary papers that would permit them to bring Risky Pleasure back across the border. But the next morning Clint and Blair were sharing breakfast in the farm's sunlit kitchen.

"All the time I thought it was Blackwood," Clint mused aloud. "I never suspected Matt."

"Well, Ramsey wasn't exactly innocent," Blair pointed out. "After all, he had gone in with Brian Hanson to skim funds from the farm and divert them to Hightower properties."

"Yeah, but he honestly thought he was doing Jason a favor," Clint said reluctantly. "The old man wouldn't agree to invest in the company, so Blackwood figured that once he could show the profit, Jason would admit he'd been wrong.... Which was a pipe dream if I ever heard one,"

Clint muttered. He knew that if Jason Langley could ever have admitted to being wrong, he would have invited Blair and her parents back to Clearwater Hills Farm years ago.

"It's interesting that Ramsey had no idea that Hightower was behind the drive to buy up all the land," Blair observed.

"It only proves there's no honor among thieves. He swears that when he was approached by Ingram Property Management and offered that commission to get Jason to sell, he planned to use his funds to pay back the money he'd embezzled. That way he could get the records in order before the old man found out what had been going on behind his back. But Jason did find out." Clint remembered that heated telephone call.

"You don't really think they killed him, do you?"

"Uh-uh." Clint patted her hand comfortingly. "I believe Matt on that one. Jason knew he only had a short time left to live. That's why he was going through his papers, in order to have everything in shape when you took over."

Clint suddenly grinned. "Oh, by the way, while Ramsey was turning everything over to the DA, an interesting little letter popped up."

"Oh?" Blair asked casually, rising from the table to get the coffee pot. She was refilling their cups when his next words almost caused her to drop the pot in surprise.

"Jason kept track of you over the years. He'd even had weekly conversations with Ben Winters."

"You've got to be kidding!"

"Seems he knew just about everything there was to know about you, sweetheart. Including the fact that you've got a stubborn streak a mile wide."

"I do not," Blair said, having the grace to flush as Clint laughed. "Well, perhaps a few feet wide," she admitted.

"That's why he left Risky Pleasure to both of us."

"I don't understand."

"He knew we were both so much alike we'd fall in love, but at the same time he figured you'd be like the irresistible force running headlong into the immovable object. So he chose the one thing neither of us could resist.''

"Risky Pleasure."

"That's it,'' Clint agreed. "He may have been an irascible old bastard, but he seemed to know people as well as he did horseflesh. He figured the filly would force us to work together until we realized we were perfect for each other."

Blair and Clint exchanged a long look, both knowing that they'd been manipulated every step of the way. But neither had a single regret.

Then she returned her mind to the subject at hand. "What's going to happen to Ramsey now? And Matt? And the men behind Hightower?"

"The Hightower people have so many counts of racketeering charges against them, they'll be lucky to get out of prison in this century. And since Matt has turned state's evidence, he's been guaranteed immunity from prosecution, although he'll have to live with what he did for the rest of his life."

"Poor Marni," Blair murmured.

"It must have been hard on her."

Blair sighed, remembering the tearful conversation she'd had with her best friend after returning home last night. "It was. But I think it did her some good. She's determined to get her life in order and stop depending on men for self-esteem."

"I hope she makes it."

"Me, too,'' Blair agreed fervently. "I hope you don't mind, Clint, but I offered to let her stay here as long as she wants."

"It's your home, Blair.

She nodded thoughtfully, determined to change that situation as soon as possible. "What about Ramsey? What's going to happen to him?"

Clint shrugged. "He'll be disbarred, but since he wasn't in on any of the other crimes, he'll probably get off with probation or a light sentence for embezzlement. The guy is like a cat with nine lives—he'll always manage to land on his feet.''

She sighed, thinking how much pain the man had caused Clint.

"Tired?"

Blair nodded, rubbing a hand against the back of her neck. "Very."

"It's been a rough few days. You should probably be in bed."

Her eyes met his, encountering an unmistakable sensual invitation. "That's not such a bad idea."

"I'm just full of great ideas."

Blair merely raised a dark brow in response.

Clint grinned and lifted her into his arms. "I've always believed actions speak louder than words," he claimed, carrying her down the long hallway.

Chapter Fifteen

As much as Blair wanted to make love to Clint, there were still some problems that had to be resolved. Lying on the bed, she did her best to ignore the gleam in his gray eyes and discuss their future.

"Clint," she murmured as he slowly undid the buttons of her blouse, "we need to talk."

"Umm. You're beautiful." He parted the material, bending his head to kiss her breasts with a lazy tenderness.

As anticipation began to build, Blair had difficulty in keeping her mind on her planned speech. "Clint," she protested softly, her voice drifting off while his lips traveled a teasing journey along her jaw. "The farm. We need to talk about the farm."

"Later." His lips moved over her face, feathering tantalizing kisses everywhere but on her lips, which hungered for his touch.

Blair raked her fingers through the lush silver waves of his hair, turning her own head in an attempt to capture those elusive lips. Finally she placed both her palms against his cheeks and held him still while she brushed her mouth over his.

"Later," she agreed, nibbling at his lips.

The kiss was cataclysmic, rocking Blair to her very core. Her eyes flew open, colliding with Clint's like a clash of cymbals. The hunger she witnessed there equaled her own, and as she clung to him, there were no more words.

CLINT WOKE to find Blair still in his arms, curled tightly at his side. Her hair was spread over the pillowcase like strands of spun silk, and he breathed in the wildflower scent of her shampoo as he pressed his lips against her head.

She sighed happily, rolling over onto her back, stretching her arms above her head.

"Gato del Sol," he murmured with a smile.

"Mmm?"

"Remember the Derby winner a few years back? He was named after a barn cat who liked to lie around, fat and sassy, in the warm afternoon sunbeams. That's what you reminded me of just now."

"Are you accusing me of being fat and sassy?"

Clint propped himself up on one elbow, tracing her slender curves with his fingertips. "Perhaps fat doesn't fit," he agreed huskily, "but if they give awards for sassy, sweetheart, you're a shoo-in for first place."

Blair laughed lightly. "I think I'll take that as a compliment."

"Good, because that's how it's meant. Most of the time," he tacked on.

"Now we're back to my stubborn streak, I suppose." She sighed dramatically.

"You are a little headstrong, darlin'."

"You're not exactly Mr. Agreeable all the time, either, Clint Hollister."

Blair's scowl only caused Clint to grin wider. "At least it'll never get boring around here."

She fought to compose her face. "Not as long as you remember who's boss."

Clint released her slowly, then sat up, resting his head against the pillow as he reached over and pulled a cigarette from the pack on the table beside the bed. Blair watched nervously as he tapped the cigarette against the wood, the sound unnaturally loud in the stifling silence that swirled between them.

"I see," he said finally, striking a match with barely controlled violence.

"I don't think you do," Blair began to argue, sitting up as well.

He lifted his hands to cut her off, then let them fall to the sheets. "Go on. I didn't mean to interrupt the boss when she was about to lay down the law." His gray eyes followed a spiral of smoke to the ceiling with apparent interest.

Blair flinched as he imbued the words with an acid scorn. She had to fight to keep her composure. "I want us to have equal say in the training of the horses," she stated firmly.

"Impossible. What happens when we disagree? You can only have one trainer, Blair. It gets too confusing for the horse otherwise."

She had already considered that aspect of the situation and was prepared for his objection. "There will be no problems with continuity in training because in cases of disagreements, your word carries the day."

"Really?" His steely eyes displayed his skepticism.

Blair nodded, clutching the sheet against her breasts. "Of course. You have more experience, so it's only right that your decision would prevail. I only ask that my ideas be considered fairly."

"I can live with that," he said. "Anything else?"

Blair suddenly realized she was holding her breath. "One more thing," she acknowledged softly. "About our uh, personal relationship..." Her voice faded as she saw the ominous hardening of his jaw.

He crushed out his cigarette. "What about it?"

"I don't think it's good for the morale of the farm if the trainer is sneaking into the owner's bedroom every night. It'll only cause gossip."

Clint pinned her with his gaze, wanting nothing more than to shake her until those gorgeous white teeth rattled. "Since when is the Tigress Woman afraid of a little gossip?"

She remained quiet for a long moment, simply looking into his darkening gray eyes. "I'm not thinking of me," she said firmly. "I'm thinking of the children."

"Children?" he reached out, taking her by her shoulders, but not to shake her. His gaze searched her solemn face.

"Children," she answered calmly.

"Blair, are you telling me you're pregnant?"

"Probably not yet, although nothing would make me happier.... I love you, Clint. I want to stay here with you and raise lots of winning horses, and beautiful children who look just like their father. But I refuse to allow people to brand our children illegitimate just because their father didn't see fit to propose to their mother properly."

"Blair, I don't think you know what you're saying," he answered unevenly.

She pressed her palm against his bare chest, feeling the rapid-fire beat of his heartbeat. "Oh, yes, I do."

Clint shook his head. "I've thought about it a lot, Blair, and I love you too much to ask you to give up your career."

"My career is here. With you." Blair's smile was so breath-takingly beautiful that Clint felt as if he were drowning in it. "If you want me to stay."

"You know I do."

"Good, because my agent called a couple of days ago. I meant to tell you, then things got a little wild around here and I forgot. They're going to let me buy out the contract." Blair grinned. "Why do you think I finally agreed to Risky Pleasure's match race? We need to make a lot of money, darling. The Tigress Woman didn't come cheap."

Clint drew her into his arms, his kiss gentle, promising. "Believe me, sweetheart," he murmured, nibbling at her lower lip, "she's worth every penny."

Blair sighed happily, settling into his arms for a long, satisfying kiss.

SIX WEEKS LATER, Blair was once again sitting on the edge of Marni's bed, watching her pack. Clint was there, his arm resting comfortingly around Blair's shoulder.

"I'm going to miss you," Blair protested softly.

"I can't believe you won't be glad to get rid of me," Marni said with a grin. "After all, how many people have their roommate living with them after they get married?"

"You'll get no complaints from this quarter," Clint stated firmly. "You're family, Marni. There'll always be a room waiting for you here."

Marni's eyes grew suspiciously moist, and she laughed shakily, then wiped at them with her knuckles. "Hey, if you two keep up like this, you're going to make me cry and ruin my mascara."

"I wish you could stay longer," Blair said, changing the subject as she felt herself near tears, as well. "It'd be nice if you could be here to cheer Risky Pleasure on."

"My God, Blair, you'd both be sick to death of me by September. And not only will I be cheering her on in spirit but, believe me, I'm placing a bundle on that filly's sweet little nose. But it really is time for me to get on with my own life. And as much as I adore this place, I really don't feel right breathing air I can't see."

"So live in L.A.," Blair argued. "It's closer than New York."

"Can't," Marni objected, carefully folding a rainbow-hued chiffon caftan. "Kyle Williams was sweet enough to pull those strings to get me into the Fashion Institute of Technology, so I'd better show up for classes."

"Sweet," Blair muttered, thinking of the brash young designer. "I'd say he owed you one. After all, you did help make him famous. I don't know how many people who can carry off his wild designs." She grinned. "I still shudder to think how many wealthy matrons purchased those outrageously expensive dresses, believing they'd help them look like you."

Marni ran her fingers over one of Williams's dresses, the brilliant purple silk shot with strands of twenty-four-karat gold. "I don't know," she said. "I like his stuff."

Blair shrugged, glancing down at her own jeans and cotton blouse. "To each his own."

Clint's hands closed over hers. "You're both knock-outs," he professed. "I've been the envy of all San Diego

County, living with two gorgeous women." He grinned wickedly. "There are rumors that I'm starting my own harem."

"Don't you dare even think about it," Blair ordered, punching her husband lightly on his arm.

They all laughed, but as Marni closed the suitcase, her expression became serious. "Honestly, I don't know what I would have done without you both. I was kind of a mess after that fiasco with Matt."

Clint heaved a sigh. "Don't feel like the Lone Ranger," he said grimly. "You know, it's ironic. I always considered Matt a pretty good friend, and look at all the grief he caused. And while Blackwood will never be one of my favorite people, it turns out that he wasn't really as rotten as I thought." He shrugged. "Just goes to show, you can never tell."

The trio fell silent for a moment; then Marni smiled. "Well, that's all behind us now," she stated brightly. "And thanks to both of you, I've had a nice, peaceful vacation and plenty of time to think. My mother was wrong, you know," she said to Blair.

"I've always told you that," Blair reminded her friend with a warm smile.

Marni nodded her blond head. "I know you have. I just never believed it before. But I'm a nifty person and I'm going to be a very successful designer someday."

"I'll buy every outfit," Blair promised.

Clint groaned good-naturedly. "I sure hope you'll give discounts to your old friends when you're rich and famous, Marni."

"Of course," Marni assured him. "Far be it from me to bankrupt this lovely farm. Where would I go on vacations to unwind?" Then she glanced down at her watch. "As much as I hate to, I'd better be getting to the airport."

Clint tucked two suitcases under one arm and grabbed the third before walking out to the car. Blair and Marni followed with a garment bag, two hatboxes and a makeup case.

"You'll come visit," Blair said later as they stood at the American Airlines departure gate.

"Of course," Marni agreed. "And you'll stay with me whenever you're in New York."

"It's a date," Clint and Blair answered in unison.

There was a great deal of heartfelt hugging and kissing. When Marni finally turned to board the plane, Blair watched her through a mist of tears.

"Come on, sweetheart," Clint murmured, putting his arm around his wife. "Let's go home."

She smiled up at him. "Do you have any idea how good that sounds?"

He dropped a quick kiss on her lips. "I never did, until I married you," he admitted. "Now I can't think of any place on earth I'd rather be."

Still holding hands, they left the airport to return to their farm.

IT WAS HARD for Blair to believe it was September. The California sun shone as brightly as it had all summer, the temperature was mild and the crowds jamming the stands at Del Mar racetrack were dressed in short sleeves, as she had been only this morning when she'd watched the Thoroughbred splash blithely along the strand.

Her heart was pounding as the recording of Bing Crosby crooning "where the turf meets the surf" signaled post time.

"There she is!" Blair jumped up, pointing at the big chestnut filly drawing cheers as she trotted past the stands.

Clint's attention was not drawn to his favorite horse, but remained on his wife instead. "Damn it, Blair, take it easy. All that jumping up and down can't be good for you!"

She tried to temper her enthusiasm, knowing Clint was only interested in her welfare. But ever since the doctor had confirmed her pregnancy, he'd been treating her like a piece of fine crystal. He supervised every bit of food that went into her mouth, insisted on her daily naps, and had steadfastly refused to allow her to ride.

"I'm fine," she insisted, waving wildly to Risky Pleasure as the filly passed their box. "Healthy as a horse."

"And as stubborn as a mule," he grunted, putting his arm about her. "You better thank your lucky stars you're so beautiful, sweetheart, or I might not keep you around."

"Speaking of round…" She patted her blossoming body, inordinately proud of her pregnancy.

"You're gorgeous. And I still love you even if you do take up more and more room in bed every night."

She laughed, punching him lightly on the shoulder. "Hey, mister, I didn't get this way by myself, you know."

Clint grinned down at her. "Don't I know it," he agreed. "Talk about your risky pleasures."

They shared a brilliant smile, then fell silent as both Risky Pleasure and Cimarron were led into the starting gates. When the loudspeaker announced the upcoming race, all eyes turned to the gate.

There was a long moment of collective silence; then a bell sounded, shattering the intense concentration of the spectators.

"They're off!"

Cimarron leaped forward the instant the gates sprang open and was a full neck in front just two jumps out of the gate. Blair's breath caught in her throat as Risky Pleasure broke indifferently, and she prayed Clint had known what he was doing by refusing to increase the filly's workouts to hype her up for the race.

She squeezed his hand, holding on for dear life as the filly strode choppily through the first hundred yards. The roar of the crowd was deafening when Cimarron raced out ahead, easily holding the lead going into the first turn.

But Annie, astride Risky Pleasure, refused to rush the horse, giving her time to make this her race. As they rounded the bend, Risky Pleasure pulled herself together, striding smoothly, ranging up to assume the lead.

Blair was screaming at the top of her lungs, and Clint gave up on keeping her calm while he added his own encouragement to the horse and rider. When they turned into the backstretch, Cimarron drew even with Risky Pleasure, getting a nose in front, but when they drove down the straightaway, the filly surged forward and regained her lead. Cimarron tried to go inside her, but she whizzed back across and shut him off.

Suddenly, as they raced that way, Risky Pleasure in front, Cimarron right behind, Annie's saddle slipped. Realizing his opportunity, Cimarron's jockey drew his stick, whipping the horse past Risky Pleasure to regain the lead.

"I can't watch." Blair buried her head into Clint's shirt, only to peek up again a moment later, her curiosity getting the better of her.

"She's going to be okay," Clint assured her, his voice harsh from yelling.

Blair breathed a silent prayer while watching the young jockey, halfway up the filly's neck. Risky Pleasure obviously hadn't given up; her ears were upright as she regained her momentum, coming within a half length of Cimarron at the far turn. The crowd was apoplectic when Annie and Risky Pleasure tucked in and made their move. The young jockey flicked her only twice, lightly, on the shoulder; from then on, the filly seemed to fly. She came charging ahead as the two horses raced past the eighth pole.

Cimarron battled back, hanging on tenaciously, but it was too late. Risky Pleasure stretched out and drove for the wire. She pulled away in the final one hundred yards to win by three-quarters of a length, creating pandemonium in the stands. Even Annie brandished her whip in the air in exultation.

Blair kissed Clint wildly, then some strangers sitting behind her, then a nonplussed photographer who dropped his Nikon in the commotion. Then she kissed Clint again. After this exchange they made their way through the congratulatory throng to the winner's circle.

Blair threw her arms around the filly's damp neck, kissing the velvety dark nose. Then she turned to Clint, her eyes sparkling like precious gems. "She won, darling! Risky Pleasure really won!"

Clint drew her into his arms, wondering if he'd ever get over his amazement that Blair MacKenzie was his wife. How could any one man be so lucky? He remembered when this race had seemed the most important thing in his life. Now it paled in significance beside Blair and the child they'd made together.

"Risky Pleasure only won a race.... We're the real winners, sweetheart," he said, brushing his knuckles against her cheek.

"Oh, Clint." She sighed blissfully, wondering if she'd ever grow accustomed to the fact that this wonderful man was her husband. How could any one woman be so fortunate?

Clint lowered his head to kiss her. Blair met his lips eagerly, oblivious to the whirring sound of camera motor drives freezing the kiss onto film.

When the tender scene graced the cover of *Sports Illustrated* the following week, Risky Pleasure appeared over their shoulders, her large teeth flashing in a broad, self-satisfied smile. There were even those readers who swore one of the filly's brown eyes was shut in a knowing wink, as if she had something to do with the lovers' happiness, but other readers insisted that idea was preposterous.

Or was it?

"Cole didn't want Veronica Spencer in his life. But his father's will made that unavoidable. Still, it was Cole who made the decisions around the ranch now.

And when he decided she would leave, she'd damned well clear out!"

VOWS OF THE HEART

Susan Fox

CHAPTER ONE

VERONICA SPENCER STEERED her rented car into a parking space for the handicapped, grateful to spot a telephone booth nearby. She switched off the engine, then rummaged in her purse for some change, which she then slipped into the pocket of her denim vest.

Slowly, giving her stiff legs a chance to adjust to movement, she opened the door and eased herself out. Once on her feet, she braced a hand on the roof of the car for support while she leaned back in and pulled her crutches from the back seat. She positioned the cushioned pads beneath her arms and let the crutches take a share of her weight before she stepped aside and pushed the door closed.

Veronica glanced around, deciding she found this particular Cheyenne street unaccountably depressing. The faint smile on her soft mouth faded slightly as a gust of warm June wind blew a wisp of brown hair across troubled violet eyes. She was nervous enough about coming here without giving in to some imagined harbinger of doom. Veronica reminded herself that the only problem she was likely to encounter was her stepbrother, Cole Chapman.

Taking the cautiously measured steps she had grown accustomed to, she moved to the pavement and headed toward the phone booth. Once inside she closed the door and took out a quarter. In moments the number was dialled, but in a fit of nervousness she hung up the phone before it could ring. The quarter dropped into the coin return, but she let it stay there.

The past six months had been a nightmare of pain and loneliness and rejection. What if Henry Chapman—Hank—

the closest she'd ever had to a real father, wasn't glad she'd come to see him? She hadn't spoken to him for several months and he hadn't answered the letters she'd sent.

The reasons she'd given herself for Hank's neglect—he hated writing letters—seemed so flimsy now. Why hadn't she thought of that before she'd travelled more than 1,700 miles?

Veronica forced herself to be calm. Surely her loving all-wise stepfather would have been able to read between the lines and discern how much she needed to see him after all that had happened.

She pressed the coin return and dug out her quarter. Yes, she finally decided, he would have seen her need. She couldn't reconcile callousness with her knowledge of Henry Chapman. After all the years of her mother's neglect and the disruption caused by her several marriages and divorces, only Hank had seen through fourteen-year-old Veronica's adolescent facade of bad behaviour. With a little patience and more loving attention than she'd known since her grandmother's death, Hank had transformed her from an obnoxious brat into someone who felt special and lovable.

The man who'd possessed such wonderful qualities of gentleness and understanding wouldn't change toward her. Not now. Her mother's divorce from Hank had wrenched them apart when she'd packed up Veronica and moved to New York. But twice a year Henry Chapman had donned his dress Stetson and city clothes and flown to New York just to see her.

The past year those visits had stopped because of his health. Veronica hadn't made it to Wyoming to see him, but they had kept in touch by phone as regularly as ever. Until six months ago. The last time she had spoken to Hank had been when he'd called to tell her he wouldn't be able to attend her wedding. The heart problem he'd had for years made the trip impossible.

After her wedding and the accident, Veronica hadn't been physically able to call Hank, and after several weeks when she was able, she didn't have the nerve. Then, a couple of months ago when she finally started to climb out of the mire of self-pity, she wrote to him. A few days later she realised that a visit to the wisest and kindest man she'd ever known might help her pick up the pieces of her shattered existence. And now she was here.

Veronica dropped the coin into the slot and dialed again. This time, she let it ring.

COLE CHAPMAN LEANED BACK in the heavy swivel chair behind his desk and ran a tanned thickly callused hand through black hair overdue for a trim. The handsome arrangement of his facial features bore the sun-browned stamp of an outdoorsman, the fine wrinkles that fanned out from cobalt-blue eyes evidence of squinting into the sun. Deep grooves on each side of the grim set of his mouth hinted at happier times. As he reached back to massage stiff neck muscles, his eyes automatically sought the digital readout of the clock on his desk. It was half past eleven, but the time didn't register as his gaze slid to the photograph of his wife.

As happened at odd times, Cole felt a fresh pang of heartache. Four years after the fatal brain aneurism that had wrenched her so permanently from his arms, he still mourned his wife, Jacqueline. So beautiful, so cheerful, so full of life, so... perfect. Suddenly impatient with himself, Cole's gaze veered to the other eight by ten inch wooden frame on his desk. As always, the picture of their son, Curtis, comforted him, swelling his heart with gratitude that Jackie had left him with a child.

The phone on the corner of the desk rang stridently in the silent room. Irritably he reached for the receiver.

"CHAPMAN RANCH."

Veronica shivered. Some things never changed. Cole Chapman's gruff voice sounded just as harsh as ever.

"Cole?" She hated the timidity in her voice, but she had long ago lost the ability to sound self-assured.

"Yes. Who's this?"

"It's Veronica." When she spoke this time, it was with a bit more confidence.

"Veronica who?" There was a long silence as Veronica tried to harden herself to her stepbrother's relentless dislike.

"Veronica Spencer."

A low sarcastic chuckle came across the line.

"So, the bad penny finally shows up. Did you decide to cash in on your gold mine?" Again he made the mirthless sound while Veronica puzzled over his remark. "I think you've waited long enough to prove to everyone you aren't the little mercenary your mother is. To everyone but me, however."

Veronica swallowed hard at the insult, but didn't respond in kind. She had no idea what Cole was talking about and no desire to get into an argument.

"I'm not interested in your money. I'm in Cheyenne and I want to see your father." Veronica clutched the phone nervously as silence stretched for several heartbeats.

"I suppose it's better late than never," Cole finally answered. "You know where you can find him."

"No, I don't know," she responded with brittle patience. "Perhaps you wouldn't mind giving me a clue. You know I haven't been home...er here, for several years."

"It's too bad you didn't stay away."

Veronica pressed a trembling hand to her forehead as she tried to hold back the resurgence of unhappy memories.

"Please, Cole," she urged. "I know how you feel about me, but I just came to see your father." Tears welled in her eyes as she waited, wondering how she could have forgotten the depth of her stepbrother's hatred.

"You remember which cemetery my mother is buried in, don't you?"

"Yes."

"That's where you'll find him."

The line went dead and Veronica hung up the phone. Of course, she remembered. Hank had taken her there several times. He frequently made short visits to Margaret Chapman's grave, making certain it was kept up.

Knowing she had to hurry or risk missing Hank, Veronica turned to leave the booth. Above all, she wouldn't go to the ranch unless Hank invited her. And when he did, Cole would have nothing to say about it.

An HOUR LATER, the black desk phone at the Chapman Ranch rang again. Irritated by the thought it might be Ronnie calling back, Cole grabbed the receiver and snapped out a hello.

"Cole?" The feminine voice at the other end of the connection was like Veronica's, but it wasn't. It was a voice that hadn't changed in eight years.

"What do you want, Miriam?" Cole asked curtly.

"Has Veronica contacted you yet?" The older woman's voice sounded anxious.

"As a matter of fact, she did call. About an hour ago."

"What did you tell her?"

"I made it plain she isn't welcome here. The same goes for you." Cole had never liked his father's second wife. After Miriam left his father for a younger richer man, he had liked her even less, although he'd always counted it a blessing that she had taken her delinquent daughter back east with her.

"Please listen to me, Cole." The feminine voice hesitated. "Veronica doesn't know about your father's death."

"What do you mean she doesn't know?" Cole's stern face went tight with anger. What were the two of them pulling?

"She doesn't know, Cole. It's a long complicated story."

"Then shorten it," he ordered impatiently. "I've got work to do."

"Oh, Cole." Miriam's voice trailed away into a seizure of sniffles and Cole muttered a curse. "About six months ago," the woman went on at last, "just the day before your father died, Veronica was involved in a very serious accident." Miriam was nearly sobbing now. "We-we didn't know for days if she'd even live, and when she did, she had so many problems that I couldn't bear—"

"When were you planning on telling her?" Cole broke in, provoked by Miriam's everlasting irresponsibility.

"She's had so many disappointments," Miriam wailed.

"And she probably deserves every one of them." Cole felt almost no sympathy for either Miriam or her daughter. "She can console herself with her share of the ranch." As much as he'd loved his father, it still galled him that Hank had willed Ronnie a one-quarter interest.

"She's been hurt so badly," Miriam blubbered on. "She can barely walk."

It took a few seconds for the nearly incoherent words to sink in. Cole's first thought was that Miriam was exaggerating.

"Veronica's only been out of the rehabilitation centre a few days," she continued. "I don't know where she got this foolish idea. I just came home and she was gone. Oh, Cole!" Miriam's voice was pleading and Cole felt his conscience being prodded.

"Give me your phone number, Miriam," he growled, hating that he suddenly felt obligated to become involved. He scrawled the hastily given area code and number on a note pad. "I'll see what I can do."

"Thank you, Cole, thank you—"

Cole dropped the phone into the cradle, torn between his anger at the mother and a reluctant twinge of compassion for the daughter.

VERONICA MOVED with care but unavoidable awkwardness, the trembling in her weak legs making her even more unsteady. She was grateful for a distraction from her grief while the owner of the motel carried her luggage into a room. She handed him a small bill and watched as he left and pulled the door closed behind him.

She couldn't cry yet. Not even the vivid memory of what she'd seen after her labour up the grassy incline to Margaret Chapman's grave released the tears. How long had she stood before the double headstone and stared at the date of death beneath Henry Chapman's name. An hour?

Veronica moved tiredly to the drawer unit along the wall and methodically unwrapped a glass from its sanitary wrapper. Her only stop between the cemetery and this motel had been a liquor store. Thanks to the man who'd carried her things from the car, the bottle of whiskey she'd purchased sat within reach along with the can of cola she'd bought from a machine in the motel office.

Veronica seemed incapable of more than fragments of thought. Her whole being was engulfed by the grief she felt for a man everyone else had mourned months ago. She hadn't made a conscious connection between the date of Hank's death and the date of her own tragedy, yet her mind was reeling with a hundred questions she couldn't seem to concentrate on. All she knew was that the person she had needed to see for so long was gone. When Hank Chapman was alive, Veronica had always felt she had someone to come back to, a home, love. Now she was truly adrift. She was both saddened and terrified.

Veronica remembered the whiskey she'd bought. She reached for the bottle, and with fingers that trembled twisted open the cap and splashed a too-generous amount of the amber liquid into the glass. Forgetting to add the cola, she raised her hand and forced herself to take the first sickening gulp, choking on the stinging bite that followed. She was not normally a drinker, but she needed desperately to dull the awful feeling that nothing good would ever happen in her life again.

COLE WALKED QUICKLY down the pavement that skirted the motel. He'd already checked out five other motels, but it was this one that had a Veronica Spencer registered. According to the clerk, she'd been there for more than two hours. Cole had made a late start from the ranch, and when he found out she'd already left the cemetery he assumed she'd be at the airport. More time had been wasted there and still more while he and one of his men made the round of motels.

When Cole reached number eight, he knocked. There was no sound from inside and no answer to his second knock. He turned the door knob on the off chance it wasn't locked, and the door swung inward. Stepping into the dimness, he waited for his eyes to adjust from the bright afternoon sunlight before he pushed the door closed, his blue gaze already fixed on the prone figure on the bed.

As Cole crossed the room, uncertainty ripped through him. The girl lay nearly face down across the bed. A half-empty bottle and tumbled glass were on the floor below fingers that hung limply over the edge of the mattress. He wondered if there had been a mixup in the room number.

The shoulder-length hair was the same mink brown as the waist-length tresses Ronnie had worn as an adolescent, but he could not be sure it was her. Miriam had warned him that Ronnie was changed, and the pair of crutches propped against the chair were what he'd been led to expect. But as he looked down at the frail, too-thin body on the bed, it amazed him to think this was Veronica.

Cole crouched low and gently brushed aside the smooth thick strands of hair that obscured the girl's face. Black streaks of mascara stained the unhealthy pallor of her cheeks, and her puffy reddened eyes were smudged with what remained of a bluish eye shadow.

Cole was astonished. It was Veronica, but her face was a pale echo of the glowing natural beauty he remembered. Carefully he eased her onto her back and straightened her legs. She weighed almost nothing. Cole sat on the bed by her hip and automatically reached for her wrist to take her pulse. It was steady, but for a fraction of a second he'd feared the worst.

Cole sat there for several moments more, staring at the physical changes eight years had wrought. He resisted the idea that Ronnie was any different from the spoiled, grasping little delinquent she had been. His dislike for her was still too intense for him to believe that.

A wave of compassion rushed at the wall of rock that was his heart. The thought of taking Ronnie to the ranch for a few days to give her time to get over the shock entered his mind. He wouldn't have sent her to that cemetery if he'd had any idea she'd never been told of his father's death. For that he was truly sorry.

But then common sense warned he would be letting himself in for endless problems if he did take her home. He had Curtis, his seven-year-old son, to consider. Helen, his sister-in-law, looked after Curtis in her home on the neighbouring ranch during the day and would probably be willing to keep him round the clock for two or three days. But did he want all their lives disrupted for Veronica? As long as she was at the ranch, he would have to give up precious time with his son. What kind of problems would he have with Ronnie? She did have a quarter interest in the ranch. What if she suddenly decided she wanted to stay and oversee that interest?

Cole's lips thinned unpleasantly. If Miriam had had any backbone at all, she would have told Veronica about Hank's death months earlier and spared them all this. But as usual Miriam had thought of little more than making things easy on herself.

Now Cole felt he was being saddled with the same problem his father had, more than ten years before. Hank had taken the impossible little Veronica on and had tried to give her the love and discipline her mother had been incapable of giving her. And not once had Hank voiced any regret. Cole had never understood that or the fact that his father had continued to think of Ronnie as a daughter, even after Miriam had divorced him and remarried.

Veronica's head moved slightly on the pillow and a small moan of pain came from her lips. Her breathing had changed and Cole started to shake her gently, but she was too deeply asleep. He picked up the half-consumed bottle and examined it with faint disgust. It would be hours before she slept it off.

Cole got up and walked into the bathroom. Taking a washcloth from the towel bar, he moistened it beneath the warm-water tap before he returned to her bedside. As gently as possible, he wiped away the dark smudges of eye makeup, then studied the pale face he'd uncovered. Suddenly he pitched the washcloth across the room in anger.

He didn't want the responsibility of Veronica Spencer. He didn't want to know her problems and he didn't want her intruding on his life. But his father's will made that unavoidable. Still, it was Cole who made the decisions around the ranch now. Veronica may have a quarter interest, but when he decided she would leave, she'd damned well clear out.

WHEN VERONICA AWOKE, it was dark. She felt ill and it was all she could do to roll to the edge of the bed. She was too sick to be startled by the barrier that stopped her before she could get one foot on the floor. Her only thought was that someone had left her hospital bed rail up. Frantically she tried to find the button to summon a nurse as she fought down a tide of nausea.

"Are you going to be sick?" asked a deep rough voice. Veronica panted her reply and was immediately pulled from the bed and carried through the darkness.

The suddenness of the bright bathroom light brought a searing pain to her head. Strong arms lowered her to her knees and held her steady over the bowl. Again and again the sickness came until she was limp and the nausea spent. Veronica heard the tap being twisted on behind her and the rush of water that followed.

The cool wet cloth that was forced into her fingers was soothing as she ran it over her face. She already felt worlds better. She didn't resist when the cloth was taken impatiently from her fingers and held beneath the cold water again. This time, the cloth was guided over her face by a surer hand than her own.

"Here." The cloth was removed and a glass of water held in front of her. "Rinse your mouth." She should have known immediately whose voice was giving the orders, but her brain was still muddled. She obeyed. The glass was taken away and the room grew still. Veronica was weak and tired but her mind was beginning to clear. She knew now who had held her steady and witnessed her sickness. She knew and was recovered enough to feel deeply ashamed.

"Thank you, Cole," she got out, wondering why he was at her motel. She was just about to ask when it dawned on her that this was her old bathroom at the ranch. "How did I get here?" She'd heard of alcoholic blackouts and was suddenly terrified she'd just had one.

"I brought you here," was the gruff reply. The note of regret in Cole's deep voice was easily detected.

"I'm sorry." She must have said that to him hundreds of times in the more than two years she'd lived here, but Cole Chapman rarely accepted her apologies. "I need to be alone in here for a few minutes," she told him quietly.

"Can you manage by yourself?" There was no concern in his voice. It was simply a question he needed to ask. Veronica nodded and was lifted to her feet. Cole was out of the bathroom and had closed the door behind him before she realised she hadn't actually seen him yet.

Veronica moved carefully into the bedroom, using the wall to steady herself. The bright bathroom light had been painful, but the soft light from the lamp Cole had left on beside the bed was soothing. Her gaze wandered lovingly around the room that had changed little in eight years.

It was still decorated in spring green and white, from the tiny white flowers and vines on the puffed green comforter to the white ruffled curtains with green tiebacks. The dark lustre of woodwork accented the wallpaper, which was a reverse of the comforter, with green flowers and vines on a white background. She remembered the horrified reaction her mother'd had when she chose this colour scheme the first month they lived on the ranch. Veronica's lips moved into a wry line. Her taste and her mother's had always clashed.

Being in this house again, this room, brought back a lot of memories. For a brief moment, Veronica was lost in the odd sensation that she'd never really left, that the eight years she'd been away had somehow been compressed into days.

But Hank wasn't here now. Remembering that brought a crush of grief so strong it forced the air from her lungs in a rush. Wearily she lowered herself onto the straight chair next to the bathroom door.

Cole watched from the hallway, reluctant to intrude. Ronnie's too-thin shoulders shook with mute sobs and her head was bowed dejectedly. He wasn't prepared for the sudden rush of compassion he felt at the sight of her grief. It reached for him, tore into the still-tender areas of his own heart. His first step toward her was hesitant.

Veronica heard Cole's soft footfalls and went rigid. She straightened self-consciously and smeared the wetness from her cheeks. She noticed then that her watch and jewellery had been removed.

"What time is it?" she asked quietly, trying unsuccessfully to hide her misery from her stepbrother.

"Midnight."

Veronica looked up at Cole for the first time. Eight years had seasoned his smooth dark handsomeness into a more appealingly rugged look. The sun had defined the lines that fanned out from dark blue eyes, while the slashing grooves on each side of his mouth boldly accented the sensuality of his firm lips. His jaw was still the strong implacable jaw she recalled, but it was rough now with whisker stubble. He was as lean and hard as ever, his body the body of an athlete, wide shouldered, narrow hipped....

Veronica's eyes shied away. She would never let Cole see her make more than a cursory assessment. She'd had a crush on him once and had been foolish enough to confess her love to him. After that, Cole rarely had anything good to say to her or about her. Those were the memories that hurt.

"H-how did Hank die?" Veronica asked, bracing herself for the answer.

"He had a heart attack," Cole began quietly. "We rushed him to the hospital, but after they got him into intensive care, he had another one and they couldn't revive him."

The huskiness in Cole's voice made her feel close to him; they had both loved Hank Chapman deeply. But after a few silent moments Veronica raised damp eyes darkening with resentment to meet the watchful depths of her stepbrother's.

"Why didn't you notify us? You knew how much I—" She bit her lip, not wanting Cole to see her cry. "And you sent me to his grave knowing what a shock it would be." Veronica's pale features flushed with the effort it took to restrain her tears. She trembled with anger, but the hurt she felt was overwhelming. Cole crossed the small space between them, then crouched down in front of her.

"I did notify your mother. She wasn't home when I called the first time, but one of her servants took the message. When I called later that day, she was still out, but her husband assured me Miriam had already been informed." Cole paused and reached out to touch the small white hand that rested on her thigh. "I wouldn't have kept my father's death a secret, Ronnie, no matter how much hostility there was between us."

The solemn expression she saw on Cole's face blurred as tears surged into her eyes. "I don't believe you," she whispered desolately. "You always resented that Hank treated me like—" Like a daughter, her heart finished for her. Cole's fingers tightened gently around hers.

"Miriam called just after you did today and she admitted she hadn't told you about Hank." Cole let Ronnie's statement pass. Maybe he had resented how quickly Ronnie and his father had taken to each other. He'd certainly never understood why.

Ronnie shook her head. "Six months? For six months she kept it from me?" Veronica was incredulous. Cole's lips twisted sarcastically.

"Miriam outdid herself this time."

Veronica threw off Cole's consoling hand.

"Don't you dare criticise her! My mother was never as bad as you always said. And you don't know anything about her now."

Cole stared. Ronnie was overwrought and surely not rational. Where was the resentment she'd always borne Miriam? Miriam had never inspired any kind of loyalty in her daughter and now she was defending her?

"Where are my car keys?" She had to get out of there. The restless sense of panic she felt demanded she do something.

"They're in my pocket," Cole answered. "You won't be going anywhere tonight." Veronica opened her mouth to protest, but Cole interrupted. "You're in no shape to be driving."

"I'm sober," she told him angrily.

"I know you are, but you aren't well." Cole stood. It was then that she noticed the row of luggage he must have carried in earlier. "Which case has your nightgown?"

Veronica didn't answer right away as she watched Cole cross to her bags, select one at random, then open it. "The small one," she was forced to say before he began rummaging on his own. Cole snapped the larger piece shut and reached for the case she'd indicated. Opening it, he also retrieved her toiletry and cosmetic bag.

In moments he'd draped her nightgown and robe across the foot of the bed. Then, he carried her cosmetic case into the bathroom and placed most of its contents on the wide counter that skirted the sink. When he finished he came back into the room and handed her the crutches.

"You'll have to dress yourself." Cole walked to the head of the bed and turned down the comforter and sheet before pushing the chair he had used earlier back into the corner.

Cole's take-charge activity had a settling effect on Veronica's nerves. She was exhausted and the inviting sight of clean sheets and a comfortable bed made her ache to lie down.

Her murmured thank-you carried a note of unconscious submission. Cole's impersonal gaze swept over her as she rose shakily from the chair.

"Sleep in as long as you need to. If you miss breakfast, there should be enough food in the refrigerator for you to help yourself."

Ronnie murmured another thanks and Cole moved toward her. She sensed his uncertainty, his reluctance, when he stopped bare inches from her. In the next moment, he wrapped her in his arms, pressing her firmly against his warm chest. Veronica stiffened. She knew that Cole's comfort was solely an observance, a hollow gesture of commiseration. The dutifully performed amenity cut her to the quick, astonishing her with the realisation that she wanted much more from him than a dutiful embrace. Awkwardly she drew away and Cole released her as if he couldn't bear to touch her any longer.

"I'll be on my way as soon as possible in the morning," she told him as she grasped the crutches and moved past him to the foot of the bed.

"There's no hurry," he said, a little surprised at his almost welcoming response.

"Isn't there?" She wanted to demand why he'd brought her to the ranch in the first place. She didn't have the physical or emotional strength to deal with both Hank's death and the problems of dragging herself and her belongings from place to place. Why hadn't Cole just left her at the motel?

"As long as you're here you might as well stay a couple of days. There are a few things we need to discuss. The sooner we have our talk, the better."

"What do we have to talk about?" Veronica reached for her nightgown, hoping Cole would just leave. Now that Hank was gone there was no one to mediate their quarrels. Veronica was not about to get into any discussions with Cole.

"You'd be surprised, Ronnie. Good night."

Veronica listened to Cole's booted stride cross the green rug, then heard the soft click of the door as he closed it behind him.

"Good night, Cole," she whispered.

VERONICA SLEPT DEEPLY, then woke to the strangeness of a new environment just after five A.M. Fixing bleary eyes on the small travel alarm on the nightstand, she decided it had been the muffled sounds of activity at the other end of the house that had awakened her. Her head pulsed with pain, but she managed the short trip from bed to bathroom to take some aspirin and have a shower.

Rapidly, with a skill born of necessity, Veronica cleaned her face in preparation for the foundation makeup that preceded the special combination of shadings, blushers and eye shadow she used to artfully conceal her pallor. She believed this restored some part of the beauty she felt she'd lost since the accident. When she had finished drying her hair, she scooped up her makeup and toiletries and put them in their case.

It took little time to pack. Making the bed was a challenge, but when she finished, the room bore no traces of her presence other than the luggage lined up by the door and the white slacks and pink blouse she'd taken out to wear. With luck, she would be on her way to the Cheyenne airport within an hour. She quickly dressed and went to the kitchen.

Savouring the delicious aroma of bacon and freshly brewed coffee, Veronica gingerly lowered herself onto a chair at the only place at the table not already set for breakfast. She watched Cole's uncommunicative back with some trepidation. Upon her entrance into the big kitchen, Cole had tossed a barely civil good-morning over his shoulder while he continued his work at the stove.

Veronica knew better than to ask Cole why he was doing the cooking, drearily remembering that he had little patience for questions before six A.M., especially hers. For now she allowed herself a few quiet moments to look around the big kitchen, marvelling again how little the Chapman ranch house had changed in eight years.

The spacious living room she'd just come through was much the same, but the traditional furnishings, which had seen better days, were now arranged more for convenience than aesthetics. Her mother had tried to make inroads into Hank's uncaring attitude toward interior decoration, but he had resisted most of the major changes. Apparently Cole's wife had not had the time or inclination to make many alterations, either.

The kitchen remained relatively unchanged, too, although a dishwasher had been installed under one section of the counter and a big microwave oven rested beneath one of the cupboards. It was amazing how much work and storage space the kitchen had. With cupboards and counters taking up nearly three walls, the room was ideal for preparing large meals for the men who worked at the ranch.

The clatter of a plastic bowl falling to the floor then wobbling hollowly in a circle drew Veronica's attention back to Cole. As he bent to retrieve it he suddenly seemed to be reminded of her presence and he scowled darkly at her. Snatching up the bowl, he turned away to toss it into the sink and get another one from the cupboard.

The grief she'd somehow managed to put aside temporarily suddenly overwhelmed her under Cole's sharp look. It was a look that seemed to blame her presence for the small calamity, and when he turned back to the stove to fish more bacon from the hot grease, Veronica rose stiffly to make a silent retreat.

Once in her room, she stretched out across the bed and lay quietly. When she heard the sound of the voices of Cole's men coming in for breakfast, she was relieved she'd fled the kitchen. She wondered if she'd know any of them now and strained to hear a familiar voice.

The good-natured ribbing Cole was getting brought a faint smile to her lips. She could hear his men bemoaning the fact that the boss still hadn't found a cook, and the complaints ranged from burnt bacon to rubbery scrambled eggs. Even Cole's not-so-good-natured reply that the next one who complained had to cook the next meal didn't subdue them, their laughter and joking continued until they evidently started to eat.

The sounds emanating from the kitchen reminded Veronica of her happier days on Chapman Ranch. But after a few moments tears again streaked from the corners of her eyes and into her hair, as she grieved for Hank and the sim-

ple happy life-style he'd once shared with her. In her two
years at the ranch, she'd been Hank's shadow, eager to go
anywhere with him. Whether she was helping with the spring
roundup and the endless summer work that followed, or
braving the frigid temperatures and deep snowfalls of winter to get hay to the cattle, or helping in the calving sheds,
she'd done it all, loved it all, because she was with Hank.

A new wave of sadness engulfed her as she was reminded
that those times were as lost to her as Hank—the man who'd
given her pleasant memories of a childhood place beyond
the home her grandmother had made for her until she was
six years old. In all her growing-up years since her grandmother's death, the Chapman ranch had been the only place
where someone had really cared for her.

The simple well-ordered life-style in which she'd received
the guidance, discipline and affection she'd needed had had
a profound effect on the young teenager, whose insolent
behaviour had been an unconscious ploy to force her mother
to notice her. Hank had been the only one of her mother's
husbands Veronica hadn't been jealous of. He was also the
only one who didn't regard her as a nuisance who needed to
be put in a boarding school and farmed out to camp for the
summer.

A sharp rap sounded at her door and Veronica hastily
reached for a tissue from the night table.

"Veronica?"

She struggled awkwardly to sit up and move to the edge
of the bed. She wasn't ready for Cole. Not yet. She'd realised that in the kitchen. Veronica couldn't take his harshness and miserably wondered if she'd be able to take any
sign of gentleness either. She was terrified at the thought of
turning into a pathetic blubbering fool if Cole said the
wrong thing to her, and her face went white with the effort
it took to lock herself into tight control.

"Come in." She wiped away the last of the wetness and
forced the hurt to subside as Cole opened the door. To her
surprise Cole was carrying a big tray laden with two steaming plates of food. He entered briskly and set the tray on the

desk near the window, then headed back to the hall. When he returned he brought another tray with a large glass of milk and juice and coffee for them both.

Veronica remained sitting on the edge of the bed while Cole cleared the desk and arranged their plates. It surprised her that he was going to so much trouble, but she was secretly thrilled that he obviously intended to eat with her. For the past six months her solitary hospital meals had been her least favourite time of the day, and so sharing a meal with anyone was a welcome treat.

"It might not be the best breakfast you've ever had, Veronica, but it's nourishing and hot." Cole was looking at her now, and at the prompting lift of his dark brows, she reached for her crutches and got to her feet. Iron-faced, Cole waited until she was seated before he sat down.

"I couldn't remember if you liked your eggs scrambled or fried," Cole began as she picked up her fork. The mere suggestion of a smile appeared at his mouth as one corner lifted fractionally. "Of course, no matter how they start out, they always manage to end up that way."

A small smile altered the set of Veronica's own mouth. "Most people don't realise how difficult it is to cook eggs properly, so don't apologise," she said, then dug into the leaden-looking curds of scrambled egg, determined to eat every bite. She never would have expected Cole to be so thoughtful and hoped in some small way that her pleasant remark had rewarded his gesture.

A quick glance at his plate revealed that her eggs looked more appetising than the ones he'd served himself. Also, the hash browns on her plate appeared more uniformly cooked and the bacon a little less crisp. That he'd provided her with the better plate of food touched her.

Yet the meal passed tensely. Veronica sensed that Cole was avoiding mention of Hank, and she barely spoke at all, uncertain of this man who'd been such a reluctant stepbrother all those years before.

When Cole's gaze drifted toward the window, she glanced at him covertly and let her eyes wander slowly over his tanned face. To her consternation, the growing light from the sunrise accentuated the small scar that interrupted the well-shaped line of his nose just below its bridge—a permanent reminder of the time she'd accidentally whacked him with a pitchfork handle. Reminded of one trespass, she automatically recalled others.

Her memories of Hank were wonderful, but the memories associated with Cole were tormenting. In her two years at the ranch she had managed to provoke Cole at every turn, earning his hostility when she secretly craved his acceptance and affection.

Her eyes started to fill with tears again and she set her fork down a bit too firmly. Cole's attention had returned to her, and her lips quirked sheepishly as she used her napkin to blot the wetness from beneath her eyelashes. To her relief, he made no comment and soon they were both eating again. By the time she finished the last of the glass of milk Cole was leaning back with his coffee.

"Thank you for breakfast, Cole." She reached for her coffee and tasted it. "I certainly didn't expect you to go to the trouble of bringing it in to me." She paused to take a nervous breath. "And thank you for joining me." Her eyes shied away from his, then warily wavered back. She felt as unsure and intimidated by him as ever, but to her immediate relief, Cole allowed himself a neutral smile.

"I notice you've packed your things. I thought we'd agreed that you would stay on a couple of days." Cole's voice was low, almost gentle, arrowing straight into her vulnerable heart. He was watching her intently now. She felt her cheeks flush and was unable to voice the polite refusal she wanted to make. Perhaps Cole was making this gesture because it was something he felt obligated to do, or maybe he still felt guilty about sending her to the cemetery. Whatever the reason, she knew that if he had a preference, it would be for her to leave.

"I can't," she finally got out, then set her coffee aside.

Cole leaned back in his chair and raised a booted foot to rest on his thigh. "My father made a bequest to you in his will, Ronnie, and it's something you and I need to discuss. Since you're here, I'd just as soon get it settled before you leave."

Veronica's eyes widened in shock at this news. Hank had left her something in his will? She felt the weight in her heart grow heavier as she thought about what Cole's reaction to that must have been. *Did you decide to cash in on your gold mine?*

"I'm sorry, Cole." Veronica flinched inwardly at the oft-repeated phrase. "I had no idea. Of course, I'll refuse to accept it, whatever it is."

"You don't even know what you've inherited." The irritation in his voice increased her unease and she fidgeted with her napkin.

"All right," she conceded quietly. "What have I inherited?"

"My father willed you a one-quarter interest of everything he owned. That includes not only the ranch, but the Montana mining interests his brother left him years ago."

Veronica shook her head slightly, unable for a moment to grasp the meaning of his words. She had expected perhaps a few thousand dollars at the most, but a one-quarter interest? Hank had never been one to flaunt his wealth, preferring a much simpler life than he could actually afford, but she was certain that because of the mining interests Hank had been a millionaire. Veronica reached for her crutches and stood wordlessly.

Finally, she managed to collect her thoughts. "Your father was always generous with his time and affection." Her voice wavered precariously on the last word. "But his money and his property really belong to you and your son." Veronica's shoulders straightened. "If you'll give me the name of your lawyer, I'll see him before I leave today and have him draw up whatever papers are necessary to see that it's all returned to you."

Veronica turned away, overwhelmed by the significance of the inheritance. A man her mother had been married to for only two years and then betrayed had not only provided her with her childhood ideal of a father, but had also left her a part of what rightfully belonged exclusively to his natural son.

Warm steady hands closed over her slim shoulders, preventing her from moving away.

"As much as I would benefit from letting you do that, Ronnie, I wouldn't feel right about taking it. I'd planned to make you an offer." Cole's thumbs began to move in slow warm circles that sent a new kind of shock through her system as she felt an answering heat pulse to life in her veins. Panicked by the sensation, Veronica shrugged off his grip, stepping away to a safe distance.

"I think I'm a little confused by all this," she said. "It's all happening so fast." She managed a thin smile as she hazarded a sideward glance. "Would you mind giving me an hour or two to pull myself together?" She was close to tears again, unable to find the strength to keep her emotions under control for very long.

"I've already offered you a couple of days, Ronnie— more if you need them." Cole's voice was gruff but not unkind.

"I know that, but I don't think I should stay." The sound she made was intended as a short laugh, but came out grimmer than she'd intended. "If I did, it wouldn't be long before I'd manage to get on your wrong side and we'd have a fight."

Cole's brow darkened ominously.

"Don't you see?" she whispered sadly. "It's happening already."

"Well, dammit, let it happen. We're both adults now and surely we can work out our differences." Cole stopped, then sighed, running a tanned hand through his thick black hair. "I'm sorry, Veronica. That came out harsher than I intended. Why don't you rest awhile, then come on into the study when you feel up to it. I'll get finished up in the kitchen and we can talk later." Cole waited for her to respond and at last, resigned, she nodded her agreement.

She had been caught off-guard by Cole's apology. True, his regretting his harshness had been a small thing, but any kind of apology from Cole was a step out of the old pattern between them.

"I think I might rest awhile, then."

"Take all the time you need. If you sleep through lunch you won't starve." The smile Cole suddenly gave her struck her emotions with the impact of a runaway freight train.

She had seen Cole charm countless other women with that smile. At sixteen she would have eagerly given her life for the privilege of being the recipient of a fraction of the charm he'd lavished on other females.

Now at twenty-four she could appreciate the irony of finally having an adolescent wish fulfilled—but only after Cole Chapman was more romantically inaccessible to her than ever.

CHAPTER TWO

VERONICA RETURNED THE PHONE to its cradle, relieved that the emotionally charged conversation with her mother was over. Miriam had been tearfully contrite about keeping Hank's death a secret, and then adamant in her appeal—no, her insistence—that Veronica return to New York as soon as possible.

Veronica leaned back comfortably in Cole's big swivel chair, a warm feeling of security enveloping her. For most of her life, she had been Miriam's little complication. In these past few months, however, the scatterbrained social butterfly who loved to play the role of enchantress seemed to have vanished, and in her place, a remarkably sensitive and compassionate parent had evolved, fretting over her only child, pampering her, loving her. When Eric, Veronica's husband, decided after the accident that he'd chained himself to a bride who was suddenly less than the physical perfection his vanity required, Miriam had consoled her, devoting hours on end to her daughter in a campaign to coax Veronica from life-threatening depression.

It had taken Veronica weeks to recover emotionally from Eric's abandonment. It was little wonder her mother had avoided adding a new shock just as Veronica had begun to cooperate with the professionals who were working to restore the use of her legs.

Too bad, Veronica mused, that Charles Whitcomb, her most recent stepfather, regarded the situation between mother and daughter with barely concealed impatience. He was the reason Veronica was in no hurry to return to New York. As much as she loved her mother now and treasured their new relationship, she didn't want to be the cause of Miriam's sacrificing the only marriage she'd ever found contentment in. Veronica hadn't made any definite plans for the future, but she was certain she had to find some gentle way of redirecting her mother's attention from her and her problems to the husband who had so jealously awaited his stepdaughter's recovery. What she needed now was some excuse to delay her return to New York. Perhaps she could do a bit of travelling, résumé in hand, or visit a few of her friends....

Her brief sense of security evaporated. It was time to come to a decision about her future. Now that she was well out of college, single once again and unemployed, she needed to make some definite plans. Veronica knew that coming back to Hank and this ranch had been an effort to delay making the decision.

The splintering crash of glassware made an almost welcome intrusion into the unpleasant turn her thoughts had taken. By the time she got to the kitchen Cole was wiping slivered pieces of glass from the sink and shaking the dishcloth of fragments over the dustbin. It was obvious from the haphazard assembly of tableware and food that he was beginning preparations for the noon meal.

"Is there anything I can help you with?" she offered hesitantly, unable to tell from Cole's granite profile whether he would tolerate her presence or not.

"Not unless you learned to cook somewhere along the line." Cole dropped the dishcloth into the dustbin, then turned on the taps to rinse any unseen bits of glass down the drain. When he finished and returned the dustbin to its customary place at the end of the counter, he turned back to her. The cynical look in his eyes told her he doubted she'd be much help. After all her mother had been nearly useless in the kitchen.

"Cooking is one of my favourite hobbies. It's something I'm good at." Veronica felt colour seep into her cheeks at her impulsive boast, then chagrin when his dark brows rose in exaggerated amusement. She didn't add that she had minored in food and nutrition at college.

Instead she felt awkward and embarrassed, certain he would decline her offer. "Of course, I haven't had much practice these past months." Now her mind was darting frantically, trying to wiggle out of her offer before Cole could refuse. "Since you'll be busy for a while, I thought I might walk down your driveway a bit—I didn't get any real exercise yesterday."

Crutches in place under her arms, Veronica started for the porch door, horribly aware that Cole's eyes followed her every move. She had just reached the door and put out her hand to open it when he spoke.

"If you could help me out, Ronnie, I'd be obliged."

Veronica's hand dropped back down to the crutch grip as she released a small pent-up breath. Trying hard to mask the pleased smile on her lips, she turned.

"What are you planning?" she asked as she made her way over to the sink to wash her hands.

"I've only got as far as thawing out four pounds of ground beef. Problem is the boys are getting tired of hamburgers."

Although Veronica cringed at the thought of the "boys" eating nothing but hamburgers, she managed to keep a neutral expression.

"If you have the right ingredients, perhaps a good meat loaf would be better. Do you mind if I look through your cupboards?"

"Go ahead," Cole invited, then began pulling open cupboard doors that held what stores of staples and foods there were. Veronica scanned the shelves, mentally listing the ingredients of one of her favourite recipes.

"I know a recipe for a cheese meat loaf with a sweet topping. If you've got some processed cheese, a couple of carrots and about three large onions, I should be able to make enough meat loaf to last you and your men through two meals." A look of real interest lit Cole's face as he reached for the refrigerator door and brought out the things she'd asked for.

"What kind of vegetables had you planned?"

After a brief discussion of the impromptu menu, Veronica set to work combining the meat loaf ingredients while Cole set the table. Soon there were three large pans of meat loaf in the oven and Veronica began making pastry for pie crusts to contain the lemon pie filling she'd found in the cupboard. For want of a more elaborate, more nutritious dessert for Cole and his men, lemon meringue pie would do.

Cole's men were coming up the path to the porch just as Veronica was cutting generous slices of the steaming meat loaf. Cole carried the vegetables she'd prepared to the table and everything was ready.

"Smells like the boss got us a cook." There was a second of silence before several pairs of heavy boots could be heard thumping up the porch steps and clumping into the kitchen. The room she had once thought so large was suddenly cramped with the entry of Cole's ranch hands.

Five sets of hungry eyes surveyed the modest bounty she'd prepared, then fastened intently on her before the brisk tide of colour surging into her cheeks had them glancing away apologetically. She'd forgotten the almost shy reserve many otherwise boisterous cowhands displayed around women. Although none of these men looked familiar to her, their quaint manner of respect and politeness was a quality she found endearing. Belatedly they swept off their hats and glanced expectantly at their boss.

Veronica chanced a look in his direction and saw the cloudy look in Cole's eyes she knew signalled a quick rise of irritation.

"Ain't you gonna make an introduction?" The oldest, shortest, most grizzled-looking cowboy she'd ever seen was the first to speak. "It ain't every day we get a spread like this one served up by a purdy young gal." Wizened brown eyes whipped over to meet Veronica's before they shot back to the boss. "Well?" There was a cantankerousness about the old cowhand that Veronica liked immediately.

"This is Veronica Spencer," Cole began. To Veronica he said, "These are the men who eat at the house every day. Shorty Blake, Ansel Edwards, Bob Brown, Teddy Ferris and Jim Fisher."

Veronica smiled silently at each man, who nodded as he was introduced. Ansel and Shorty, the hand who'd insisted on the introduction, were much older than the other three, with Bob somewhere in his late forties. Teddy and Jim, Veronica guessed, were in their late teens or early twenties.

Once the introductions were made and the men had cleaned up in the washroom just off the hall from the kitchen, they all sat down to eat. Cole seated Veronica to his right, and while the food was passed and plates loaded, the men talked about what they'd accomplished that morning and what Cole's plans for them the rest of the day entailed. Cole also had orders for Shorty to pass along to the three cowhands who had gone to their nearby homes to have lunch with their families.

"Now this is what I call cooking!"

Veronica glanced up, smiling modestly when Shorty's compliment was enthusiastically echoed by the other men around the table. The only one who didn't comment was Cole, who seemed strangely sullen. The only indication the food was to his liking was that he helped himself to generous seconds of everything.

In a surprisingly short time, the table was virtually cleared of food. Cole reached for the pieces of pie on the counter and passed them around, prompting another chorus of approval.

"I'm sure glad you've retired from the kitchen, Boss," Shorty piped up, leaning back in his chair as he patted his slightly protruding paunch with satisfaction. "I run out of Pepto Bismol just this morning." Raucous male laughter burst out, but Cole seemed unamused. "Now that you've hired yourself a good cook, I reckon I can save some money on stomach remedies."

Veronica glanced nervously at Cole. Shorty apparently thought she was their new cook and she felt her face pale.

Cole's stony demeanour warned he wasn't pleased with the assumption.

"Veronica is just visiting for a day or two, Shorty. She may only be helping out for this one meal."

Shorty's happy expression fell and he dropped the chair back down onto all four legs. "Well, shucks. D'you mean all we got to look forward to after a spread like this is more of our own cookin'?" The sour expressions on the other men's faces duplicated Shorty's dismay.

"I'm afraid so. Unless that employment agency comes up with someone real soon." Cole stood and picked up his tableware, depositing it into the dishwasher, his brisk manner effectively ending the conversation. One by one his men got up, clearing their own places and adding their dishes to the rapidly filling rack.

"That was a mighty fine meal, Miss Spencer," Shorty told her as he reached for his hat. "It's a cryin' shame you ain't plannin' to stay longer." Veronica couldn't help smiling at the earnest expression on the aging cowhand's weathered face. "A man what cooks like he does—" Shorty jerked a thumb in Cole's direction "—don't deserve to keep good men working for him long."

The solemn rancher he'd just indicated stood with his arms crossed over his broad chest, his mouth twitching with a barely concealed smile.

"I'm not worried about tomorrow, Shorty. It'll be your day to do the cooking." Cole was grinning broadly now at the sour look on Shorty's face.

"Yeah," Shorty groused. "I shoulda guessed my time'd come again before that agency could shake loose with a cook." A disgruntled Shorty ambled to the back door, shaking his head and muttering.

Ansel and Bob grabbed their hats and politely took their leave, but Teddy and Jim were slower about it. Teddy looked as if he was about to say something to her, but Cole loudly cleared his throat and the two each mumbled another bashful compliment about Veronica's cooking and disappeared out the door.

Once they were gone the kitchen took on an uneasy still-ness. Veronica was the only person sitting at the table and she rose with as much grace as she could manage, very aware that Cole hadn't taken his eyes off her.

"I think we should have that discussion you wanted so I can be on my way this afternoon." Veronica slipped the crutches beneath her arms and grasped the grips, uncon-sciously steadying herself for the unpleasantness she ex-pected. Cole said nothing and began to clear the rest of the table. "Should I wait in the den or would you rather talk here?" she prompted.

"We can start here," Cole replied as he worked. "What are your plans for the next few days?" Cole's question was not easily answered, as she hadn't really come to a decision about where she'd be going when she left the ranch. When he looked at her, she shrugged.

"I don't think I'll be going directly back to New York. Charles needs some undivided attention from Mother that he won't get if I'm around." Veronica felt her face redden when Cole's dark brows arched. "No, Charles doesn't like me much, either. Hank was the only one of Mother's hus-bands who did." She spoke frankly, since this wasn't news to Cole.

"It might be a good idea for me to look for a job until I have the strength and desire to go into business for my-self."

"What business is that?"

Veronica tried to gauge whether Cole was really inter-ested or whether he was just making small talk.

"I started an interior-design business with a friend in New York, but after my accident I let her buy me out so she could take on another partner. I'd like to try again in a few months someplace else."

"Not in New York?"

"New York doesn't have much appeal for me beyond the fact that Mother lives there."

"I heard you'd got married."

Veronica felt a tremor go through her at the abrupt turn of conversation.

"I did." The words came out surprisingly strong considering she was practically holding her breath, hoping he wouldn't pry further.

"And are you still married?"

At the dreaded question Veronica felt a sudden constriction in her throat and a fresh spasm of pain somewhere in the region of her pride. How she hated to confess even a small part of her failed marriage to Cole and risk the obvious comparison he'd make between her and her mother. Cole waited long moments for her answer, the expression on his face saying he was more than casually interested in her reply.

"No. I'm not married now."

"But you were," he stated persistently, his lips twisting.

"Yes." The admission brought a swift glimmer of hurt into her eyes before they were shielded with a defiant glare. "Go ahead. Say it, Cole," she invited bitterly. "Like mother, like daughter."

"She wasn't much of an example for you, Ronnie."

Veronica's hands clenched on the crutch grips with frustration. What could she say? It was true. Her mother hadn't been a very good influence. But she was not like her mother. Her marriage hadn't ended because of anything she could have humanly controlled. Besides, since their marriage hadn't been consummated it had never been legal anyway. The fact that her big society wedding was followed by an almost instant annulment was too humiliating an experience for her to reveal to Cole. She'd hardly been able to picture herself telling Hank about it, much less Cole with his scorn. It didn't occur to her at that moment that the brokenheartedness she'd felt the past months was now drifting closer to wounded pride.

"If we're going to come to some sort of agreement about your ranch," Veronica said at last, determined to get off the topic of her marriage, "I'd like to get it resolved quickly. The sooner I get to the airport, the sooner I can be on an outgoing flight." She didn't add that she was unaccustomed to standing on her feet in one place for so long and was battling a fatigue she hadn't expected.

At Cole's nod of agreement, she preceded him to the den, her awkward rhythm becoming less and less steady. He seemed not to notice as he gestured at the long leather couch.

Veronica sat down, grateful for the firm comfortable cushioning. Cole tossed a pillow against the end of the couch, but Veronica tried to ignore the thought of how good it would feel to lay her head on that pillow and stretch out for a few minutes. Instead she smothered a yawn behind her hand while Cole's back was still turned toward her. As Cole seated himself in a nearby wing chair the phone shrilled.

Hoping the call would not be lengthy, Veronica dropped her head back, intending to close her eyes for a few seconds. Concentrating on the warm rough sound of Cole's deep voice, she tried to follow the conversation, certain that Cole would soon finish and they could begin the talk he was so determined to have before she left.

Ronnie never knew the exact moment the low full tones of Cole's voice lulled her to sleep. She experienced a sensation of sinking, but it was pleasant, as was the layer of something that someone tucked around her. And when gentle fingers brushed her cheek, the involuntary movement of her head to prolong the contact propelled her far beyond her grasp of reality into the land of perfect dreams.

VERONICA RESISTED AWAKENING, snuggling against the pillow in an effort to cling to the last sleep-induced images: Cole so handsome when he smiled at her that way; the two of them talking long and earnestly, coming closer together; her feeling an overwhelming sense of security; then Cole taking her in his arms and holding her, no longer her adversary but instead . . .

Veronica was suddenly aware of a presence nearby. She opened her eyes to a pair of solemn grey ones that stared down at her face. Startled, disoriented, she struggled up onto one elbow, raking her fingers through her hair.

The eyes belonged to a small dark-haired boy. Their intent study of her face, coupled with a frown and a very familiar quirk of his lips, told her plainly who he was and exactly what he thought of naps.

"You must be Curtis," she said. The child was the image of his father, and Veronica marvelled at the likeness. Other than the grey eyes there was almost no resemblance to Jackie she could discern. Veronica offered Curtis a tentative smile, fully expecting the boy to react with one of his own. He did, but it was a very reserved smile, as if he hadn't quite made up his mind about her.

"My name is Veronica," she said as she sat up and began folding the afghan of granny squares that had been placed over her.

"Dad told me to come and see if you were awake." The bare smile had vanished.

"Where is your father?" she asked as she reached for her crutches and prepared to stand. A glance at her watch told her it was after five P.M. How could she have slept so long?

"He's in the kitchen." The boy stepped back and with some curiosity watched her rise before he turned and hurried away. By the time she got to the door, he'd disappeared.

She entered the kitchen moments later, interrupting the conversation Cole was having with a visitor.

"I'm sorry, Cole. I didn't mean to intrude." Veronica had started to turn away when Cole spoke.

"You remember Jackie's sister, Helen, don't you, Ronnie?"

Veronica smiled slightly and nodded, having recognised Helen instantly. She even remembered that Cole had dated the pretty, black-haired Helen for a few weeks before suddenly discovering her younger sister.

"I'd better get going, Cole," Helen said quickly. "Nice to see you again, Veronica," she added in an obvious afterthought as she hurried out the door, leaving Cole staring after her for a long moment.

"I didn't intend to sleep the afternoon away," Veronica ventured. Cole glanced at her, his eyes making a slow sweep of her too-slim frame. "If you wouldn't mind taking my luggage to the car I can be on my way."

"We still need to talk."

"There's really nothing to talk about, Cole. I'll have a lawyer draw up whatever papers are necessary to return my share of the ranch to you."

"Just like that?" The firm lips slanted cynically.

"You could pay for my legal fees," she suggested. Cole's expression turned thunderous and Veronica resisted the urge to mollify him. "I think that's only fair, Cole." She hadn't asked to be given any part of Hank's ranch, and returning it to Cole would save him a fortune. He could easily afford a modest legal fee.

Cole strode across the kitchen to her, a look of incredulous anger on his face. "I'm not going to let you just give it back to me, Ronnie. There's too much money involved!"

Veronica bristled indignantly. "I think I can guess how much money is involved here, Cole. I'm not slow-witted."

Cole raised hard rolled fists and placed them cockily on his trim hips. "All right, Ronnie. Just how much do you guess your share is worth?"

Veronica flushed, feeling like a fool. Unbidden, the memory of the perfect dream she'd had came back on a surge of sweetness that clashed bitterly with reality. She and Cole could never have an earnest talk, they would always be adversaries. The hot colour in her cheeks deepened. And Cole would never take her into his arms....

Beneath Cole's glare she suddenly felt like a sixteen-year-old again, never able to win an argument with her stepbrother. Then with astonishing clarity, the old repressed memory of the incident that had guaranteed Cole's everlasting dislike surfaced.

"I figured my share was at least worth Chapman Red," she said.

Her quiet answer wiped the irritation from Cole's strong features. Awash now in recollection, Veronica turned, moved cautiously from the kitchen and on down the hall to her room.

Chapman Red had been Colt's horse, a beautiful bay stallion with a spirit and intelligence that set him apart from the horses Hank had assigned Veronica to ride and care for. Cole had refused to let her ride Red because he believed the big quarter horse was too spirited for a young girl. Veronica had thought Cole selfish and mean, denying her out of spite the pleasure of riding the animal whose affection she coveted.

Weeks of bringing the stallion carrots and other treats and hours on end of sitting on the fence, confiding to Red all her adolescent secrets and heartaches, had forged a special relationship between girl and horse. She could still remember the way Cole used to frown when the big horse whickered a greeting at her, or when Red would trot over to her for a pat when she went near his paddock.

The day finally came when she braved Cole's wrath and took Red for a quick bareback ride just before sundown. She remembered how the pleasure and exhilaration of the ride had evaporated the instant she'd returned to the barn. Cole had come out to check on a mare with an infected cut from barbed wire, and when Veronica rode in, Cole confronted her.

Retribution had been swift, humiliating and painful. Cole had turned her across his knee and spanked her—hard. She had hated him then, hated him fiercely. But the paradox of that hatred was that she'd also desperately needed Cole's affection and admiration.

Yet her desire to ride Chapman Red was so strong that she eventually worked up the courage to defy Cole again. She took Red out for several more rides, and for a time remained undetected. The last ride had been the best. The girl and the stallion, who was so spirited, yet as gentle as a puppy with her, had covered miles, and she had carefully cooled him down on the way home. She had just finished a brisk rubdown, given Red his measure of grain and turned him into his paddock when she heard Cole and Jessie approaching.

Two years older than Veronica, Jessica Ryan lived on the next ranch, and along with half the female population in and around Cheyenne, Jessie had a crush on Cole. He knew about it, but had been unfailingly indulgent with Jessie while utterly intolerant of Veronica's infatuation.

One look at Ronnie's guilty flush had told Cole she'd been riding his horse again. After the verbal dressing down he gave her in front of Jessie, Ronnie fled to the house.

Later, the unthinkable happened.

Chapman Red had somehow escaped his paddock and raced off to challenge another stallion. One or both of the animals broke the chain on the steel gate of the second enclosure, and the stallion fight that followed left Chapman Red so severely injured he had to be destroyed.

As vehemently as she'd insisted she'd latched Red's gate properly, Cole never believed her and held her completely to blame. Over the years the deep guilt she'd felt at defying Cole by riding his horse had eaten away at her confidence until she, too, had come to believe she had somehow been responsible for the tragedy. Heartsick now at the memory, Veronica leaned against the bedroom door.

"Ronnie?"

She stiffened, then reached for the doorknob to admit Cole, her face a tranquil denial of her inner agony. "While you carry my things out, I'll make certain I haven't left anything behind." As she turned and headed for the bathroom Cole spoke.

"I've got a favour to ask."

His words stopped her and her attention snapped back to his face. Cole's expression was stern but not harsh. She'd expected him to be angry, or at least coldly aloof, but his calm visage was puzzling.

"A favour?"

Cole looked uncomfortable for a moment and she didn't miss the way his gaze dropped to her crutches then to her legs before they returned to her face.

"You don't seem to have any immediate plans," he began. "Of course, I realise you might not be physically able to take much on." Cole paused again. "But the boys were impressed with your cooking and . . ."

Veronica's eyes widened in amazement and a quick smile came and went on her lips. "You want me to cook for you and your men," she concluded, searching Cole's face for any hint that he was joking or she was mistaken.

"You mentioned that cooking was something you're good at and you demonstrated that pretty well at noon. I need someone to fill in until I can get a permanent cook." Cole halted and she sensed he was waiting for some kind of tentative reply from her.

Veronica shook her head. "Oh, Cole, you don't want me here," she scoffed. But even as she tried to get him to admit that, she wished with all her heart he really did want her to stay, if only temporarily. In many ways she was still that adolescent girl who'd craved Cole's acceptance and approval. To her knowledge there had never been anything about her Cole had much use for. But if something as simple as cooking for him while he was in a bind would lessen his hostility, she knew it was an offer she'd find hard to turn down.

"You'd only have to cook, Ronnie. No housework. We've always liked a lot of baked goods and desserts, but we'll settle for good simple meals if you aren't up to any more than that."

Veronica was silent for a few moments considering, trying to honestly gauge her physical ability. Cooking for Cole and his men would be a tiring and time-consuming job. But then, it was only temporary. . . .

"Would I have a free hand with menu planning?"

"Yes, but—" Cole was looking at her almost warily "—we need meals that will stay with us."

Veronica nodded. "I remember how hungry you can get cowboying."

"Then you'll stay on for a while?"

"How long?"

"Until I can find a good cook. And I'll pay you the same wages I'd expect to pay anyone else."

Veronica caught the almost eager sound in his voice but didn't mistake its cause being anything other than it appeared.

"When you find this new cook, will you give me a week's notice, or will you expect me to leave on the next flight to anywhere?" Veronica hadn't been able to suppress the question. She had to keep in mind that Cole had never wanted her around. She knew if he wasn't so desperate for a cook, her luggage would already be in her car and she'd be halfway to Cheyenne.

"I'll give you a week's notice." It seemed to Veronica that he made the concession grudgingly.

"Don't worry, Cole," she began caustically. "I probably won't stay the whole week. I can imagine how charming you'll be when you have no further use for me." Veronica turned away, thinking herself forty kinds of fool, but for the moment more willing to stay than leave. "One thing, though." Her back was to him now.

"What's that?" The ill temper in his voice was easily discernible.

"I don't want you to be rude to my mother if she should call me here. I know you've never liked her, but she—she's been awfully good to me these past few months. If you can't promise me you'll be a model of decorum with her I'll have to turn you down." There was a silence, as if the decision was difficult for him to make. Veronica flicked a look over her shoulder, her violet eyes sparkling with challenge. "Well?"

Cole sighed and shook his head. "I'll be so sweet to your mother she won't crave bonbons for at least a month." Cole wasn't smiling, but the glint of laughter in his eyes filled her with pleasure. The realisation that she'd so easily fallen for Cole's subtle charm made her glance nervously at her watch.

"Are leftovers from today's lunch all right with you and your men?" Veronica knew the evening meal was always served promptly at six and it was nearly five-thirty.

"I'll shoot the first one who complains."

CHAPTER THREE

VERONICA DROPPED TIREDLY onto the chair, wincing at her too-abrupt descent. Her whole body ached, and yet she hadn't felt so good about anything in months. Working for Cole the past two weeks had been hard on her, much more physically and emotionally taxing than she had imagined it would be. But she had survived and felt her stamina slowly increasing.

Despite the fact that she had conceded to his wish that she stay, Cole frequently displayed ill humour, questioning everything she did, from the rearranging of the contents of the cupboards and freezers to the lengthy grocery list she'd handed him the first day. But the fact that Cole had ultimately granted her every request indicated he had a fair amount of confidence in her judgment. She learned not to take his gruff manner too seriously.

Veronica's life on the ranch had settled into a routine. She was seeing a therapist in Cheyenne three times a week; no matter how short her stay might be, she couldn't forfeit those sessions. She also found she had more and more time on her hands. In an effort to make the most of it, she had called her mother and arranged for her favourite cookbook and some of her unfinished needlework to be sent, along with the baby quilt she'd started working on for a friend.

In the meantime the employment agency had come up with a woman who wanted to apply for cook. Cole had interviewed her over the phone, then invited her out to prepare the noon meal. At the memory of the most incredibly sloppy-looking woman she'd ever seen, Veronica sighed and shook her head. Just watching her at work in the kitchen had been enough to turn Veronica's stomach. By the time the meal was served, Veronica needed to get out and conveniently "remembered" an errand she had to run in town. She'd returned an hour or so later to find the woman gone and Cole his usual choleric self.

Prospects for the job hadn't improved since then. There had been no other applicants, and according to the woman at the agency, there were likely to be none in the near future.

Cole still refused Veronica's offer to give the ranch and mining stocks to him, and she in turn refused his every monetary counteroffer. They had clearly reached an impasse, so Cole finally let the subject drop. An undeclared truce seemed to have evolved between them and Veronica was delighted. The frequent hostilities and misunderstandings that had marred her time at the ranch years ago, were pleasantly absent now. She and Cole were far from friends, but the fact they were on speaking terms was enough for her.

The low sound of a car coming up the long drive from the highway brought Veronica to her feet. When she heard it pull up in the part of the driveway that curved around the house toward the barn she moved across the kitchen toward the window where she caught sight of a tall leggy blonde getting out of a low, fast-looking sportscar.

"Oh, no." She'd barely given Jessica Ryan a thought since she'd come to the ranch, and because Cole hadn't mentioned the woman, Veronica had just assumed she'd be spared any contact with her. Veronica watched as her childhood nemesis crossed the yard with a fluid grace that mocked her own unavoidable awkwardness.

Tall and model slim, except for her generous bust, Jessie was likely any man's fantasy in the white halter top and shorts that showed off her golden tan to perfection. Now that Cole had been a widower for some time, Veronica wondered if Jessie's old crush on him had brought them into a romantic relationship.

Jessie's perfect mouth bore a sly smirk when she walked into the kitchen as if it were her own. Although she hadn't seen Veronica for years, she made no word of greeting, no polite preamble to the direct confrontation she was apparently determined to have.

"God, Veronica." The amber eyes looked her up and down as if X-ray vision had revealed every scar, every imperfection. Jessie stared at the crutches before at last returning her gaze to Veronica's impassive expression. "No wonder Cole feels sorry for you."

Veronica braced herself against the woman's penchant for cruelty. Jessie Ryan hadn't changed a bit.

"Does he?" she challenged softly, realising that if Cole felt sorry for her, he certainly hadn't shown it.

"Of course he does. You wouldn't be here otherwise." With a dismissive wave of a manicured hand, Jessie walked to the refrigerator and helped herself to a soft drink. When she'd popped open the can with almost comical care to avoid damaging her long nails, she turned back to Veronica and took a quick sip of her drink.

"Surely you've noticed that Curtis spends very few of his waking hours at this house. He takes all his meals at Helen's, doesn't he?" The well-plucked brows arched. "And Cole hasn't left you alone with Curtis for a second," she surmised, "has he?"

Veronica frowned, unable to deny Jessica's words. Of course she'd noticed, but she'd assumed all that would change when Cole got to know her better, came to trust her fully. Yet Jessie was hammering it all home to her in a way that confirmed the situation would persist for the duration of her stay.

"I hope you haven't started thinking your little Suzy Homemaker act will convince Cole what a wonderful wife you'd make." Jessie laughed as she spoke, but her amber eyes sent quite a different message.

"Why should I?" Veronica hadn't been prepared for this verbal assault, but just as it had been when they were teenagers Jessie always managed to get the upper hand and have the last word.

"Take my advice and forget it. Cole will never trust you alone with Curtis. I'll just bet he'll see to it you two don't even become friendly." Jessie paused for effect. "And Cole would never consider becoming romantically involved with a woman who can't be trusted with his precious son."

Veronica felt her heart constrict as the truth hit home. But before Jessie could claim a sure victory, she rallied. "Jackie's been dead for four years, Jessie, so I guess you'd know better than anyone why Cole hasn't remarried."

There was dead silence. Jessie's flawless features contorted and her cheeks flushed with anger. Veronica remembered well all the many times Jessie had twisted her words, taking malicious delight in the misunderstandings that had been created, especially between Veronica and Cole. It was wickedly satisfying to be able to turn one of Jessie's cruel barbs against her for a change—but Veronica's satisfaction was short-lived.

"You'd better hope Cole finds a permanent cook soon, Ronnie," Jessie warned. "History has a nasty habit of repeating itself." Jessie smiled at the stunned look on Veronica's face. Her good humour once again restored at Veronica's expense, Jessie disappeared out the back door with her can of soda.

Veronica moved out of the kitchen, her weariness forgotten. The mere suggestion that history could somehow be repeated and that she might once again be held responsible for a tragedy terrified her. Without consciously directing her steps, she found herself just outside Hank's bedroom. Assuming Cole would not object if she spent a few minutes inside, Veronica went in.

The room was austere, with its simple functional furniture. Austere, but at the same time warm and comforting, the much-washed wedding-ring quilt that Margaret Chapman had made when she was a teenager enhancing the country charm of the antique bed. A thick layer of dust covered the surfaces of the once lustrous furniture, but Veronica resisted the urge to brush it away. Old habits die hard, and the old habit of never daring to touch without an invitation was deeply ingrained. If only she had stuck to that habit with Chapman Red!

Locked into the bitter memory, her mind automatically went over every detail. As always, Veronica was sure the gate had been latched, the security chain in place. But later, there had been no evidence that the stallion had somehow broken out. Red had never been one of those animals who challenged a gate, so Cole had concluded that Veronica had been careless.

"Damn you!" he had bellowed at her, fury and torment on his face. She could still see the big horse writhing on the ground, sucking in every painful breath.

Veronica squeezed her eyes closed, forcing the recollection to subside. Hank had never believed her negligent. He had told Cole so, and his unshakable belief in her innocence had sparked numerous arguments and brooding silences between father and son. How she'd loved Hank for believing in her!

Veronica wandered around the room looking, resisting the urge to touch the small mementos or tiny gilt-framed photographs on the tall chest. The trunk at the foot of his bed, she knew, held a lifetime of treasures and souvenirs. Hank had let her go through it once, and Veronica's thoughts turned to that happier memory.

"Ronnie!"

Veronica started guiltily at the sound of Cole's voice, then moved quickly to the hall. She had just closed Hank's door when Cole emerged from the kitchen.

"Could you help me with this?" he asked, walking briskly toward her. Veronica's gaze dropped to the hand he extended just before he reached her. Its work-toughened palm, which she assumed had calluses too thick to penetrate, was peppered with scores of splinters that ran across the heel toward the more vulnerable flesh of his wrist. The fact that it was his right hand and Cole was right-handed made her assistance necessary.

"Of course." Veronica followed Cole into his room. When she saw the sewing-machine cabinet sitting in front of the double windows on the outer wall, she was reminded that it had also been the room he'd shared with Jackie. The frilly tieback curtains adorning the windows matched the pastel tones of the ruffles and lace bedspread and canopy, all evidence Cole had changed nothing of the decorating so obviously done by his late wife.

On top of the dresser was a framed photograph of Jackie, side by side with one of Curtis, and Veronica knew without looking that Jackie's clothing would still be hanging in the huge wardrobe that held Cole's clothes, that her personal things probably still took up several drawers. It dawned on her that just as Hank's room was a kind of shrine, Cole's bedroom was a shrine to Jackie.

Strange how she'd never imagined him capable of real love—the sort he'd evidently had for Jackie and the sort he must have for his son. Now she realised she was wrong. And until that conversation with Jessie, she'd assumed Cole was keeping his son from having any close contact with her because of sheer possessiveness rather than the protectiveness shown by a loving father.

Jessie's remark about Cole's precious son had been accurate. Just as Jackie had been precious and much loved by this harsh rancher who could summon so little affection for Veronica, young Curtis was likely loved to distraction. Veronica felt guilty that her presence here was costing Cole time with the boy. At Curtis's age, that time was far too valuable to miss.

Veronica watched as Cole whipped off his hat and began rummaging in the medicine cabinet for tweezers and peroxide. A quick scan of the large bathroom told her that only Cole's things were scattered around the somewhat untidy interior. When her eyes came back to his, he was watching her with a shrewdness that made her gaze shy away. It was as if he'd been aware of her observation and wondered what she thought. *That's ridiculous,* she chided herself. *Cole doesn't care what I think.*

"Where would be most comfortable for you to work?" he asked, and she glanced around the room for a well-lit spot. Instead of waiting for her decision, Cole was already clearing a space on the counter top next to the sink. "Sit here."

Veronica eyed the counter with some misgiving, then decided it was the best place for light. She set her crutches aside and had just turned her back to the counter to use her arms to lever herself up when Cole's big hands spanned her small waist.

"Cole—your hand!" She reached to gently push it away so that the wood slivers wouldn't become more deeply imbedded.

"Never mind. I can do this." With far more ease than she could have managed alone, Cole lifted her onto the counter. Then bracing a lean hip against the counter top by her knee, he held his injured hand over her lap.

The instant her fingers came into contact with Cole's warmth, a tremor of sensation sped up her arm. Her worried gaze shot up to meet the dark glimmers in Cole's cobalt-blue eyes. Cole stared back, seemingly oblivious to the warm shock she'd just experienced. Instead, his gaze dropped to her barely parted lips. Flustered, Veronica returned her attention to his hand and carefully inspected the wood slivers, some of them driven in so deeply they had drawn blood.

"How did you do this?" Veronica asked, reaching for the tweezers to begin plucking out the largest of the fragments.

"The colt I was working with this afternoon decided he'd like me a whole lot better if I was on the other side of the fence. Damn near threw me over the top rail." Visibly alarmed, Veronica glanced up, only to meet Cole's grin. "I grabbed the fence post and broke my fall, but I ended up with a hand full of splinters."

Veronica felt a smile tug at her mouth. Cole and his father always made the worst spills sound like high comedy.

"Next time, I'll wear my gloves."

Veronica stared a moment more, realising how powerful her attraction to Cole really was. Uneasy with the thought, she lowered her head and got back to work.

Taking out one of the larger splinters, she glanced around for someplace to deposit it. Cole reached for the small towel that hung on the rack by her shoulder, and laid it across her lap, indicating she could use that. Veronica worked on in silence, intent on what she was doing. Occasionally she angled Cole's big hand so that the light hit it more directly, but she worked steadily.

Yet for all her outward competence and seeming concentration, her senses were awash with the man. The press of his hip against her knee, the warm hard feel of his hand, the dizzying nearness when his head brushed hers while they both watched her work. Then there was the tantalising male scent of him, something that after-shave and soap only heightened. With every breath her senses became heightened, and for the first time in her life, she considered initiating a kiss.

The instant the thought came to mind she almost groaned. She would be out of this house in ten minutes, cook or no, if Cole even suspected what was going on in her mind. How he'd hated her infatuation with him all those years ago! Now that she had grown up, he would appreciate it even less.

"What are you thinking?"

Veronica jerked, unintentionally driving one of the larger splinters deeper.

"I'm sorry, Cole—you startled me." It was half the truth anyway. Yet Cole hadn't pulled his hand away or lost his temper. Instead he was being more than patient with her as he continued to let his hand rest lightly in the palm of hers. Veronica forced her attention back to her work.

"Are you going to let my question pass?"

Veronica glanced up, surprised that he was pursuing a conversation with her. She paused and considered for a moment. Perhaps this was a good time to broach the subject of his son. While she went back to pulling out splinters, she tried to assess the best way of bringing the subject up, then resolved to be direct.

"I was just thinking that you've sacrificed a lot of time with your son since I've been here." Cole's hand tensed slightly, but didn't withdraw. "Children grow so fast, Cole, and Curtis is still at an age neither of you can afford to miss."

"So?" It wasn't the belligerent comeback she'd half expected, but it betrayed annoyance nonetheless.

"So, I thought you might think about having Curtis home more while I'm here, if I promise to keep my distance from him." There was no change this time in the tension of Cole's hand and no verbal indication that he'd even heard what she'd said. "I think I can be a friendly presence in his home without courting his friendship," she went on. "Besides, if you're together as much as you both need to be, Curtis won't even notice I'm anything more important than an appliance or a piece of furniture."

"That's enough!" Cole's voice was a gritty hiss. Violet eyes, wide with apprehension, shot up to stormy blue ones. Cole was angry now. Intuition told her he was angry because she'd voiced aloud the very conditions he would have dictated himself if he hadn't thought he'd feel so guilty doing it. She opened her mouth to brazenly suggest just that, but his free hand came up to touch her cheek and a thumb pressed gently over her soft lips. Its hard pad rested partially on her teeth, setting off a primitive reaction deep inside her. Not even Eric's passionate kisses had produced such a deeply thrilling response in her. Yet Cole had breeched her reserve with a mere touch. Frightened at what that might mean, Veronica pushed his hand away.

"Do you want me to finish this or not?" she demanded. Now she was the one who was irritable.

"I'd appreciate it," came the reply. "Please, Veronica."

Those last words invaded her confused irritation and warmed her all the way to her heart. She set to work again, searching out the remainder of the splinters, then wiping the tweezers clean on the towel. Her stirred-up feelings settled finally, but her acute awareness of Cole didn't subside.

Cole's awareness of her hadn't abated, either. She had no way of knowing that the gruff rancher was just noticing the subtle red glints in her dark hair and letting his gaze wander at will over her classically shaped features. Persistently the cobalt-blue eyes were attracted to her lips, watching her moisten them occasionally. He had been just as surprised as she at his own reaction to the feel of her soft lips and the smooth surface of her teeth beneath his thumb. He couldn't remember a time in the four years since his wife's death when he wanted to taste a woman the way he wanted to taste Veronica. The urge to do so was increasing with every passing moment.

Veronica finished with the tedious removals, then tenderly rechecked for any she might have missed. Satisfied she'd got every one, she reached for a gauze pad from the box Cole had set out and moistened it with peroxide. Again and again she wiped the treated gauze over the tiny slits, watching them turn white with cleansing bubbles before she smeared on an antibiotic cream. When she finished, she taped a fresh gauze pad over the area to keep out the dirt.

Cole didn't step away, maintaining contact with her knee while she twisted the caps back on the peroxide bottle and cream tube and closed the box of gauze pads. She'd inched her leg away from his hip and started to ease herself off the edge of the counter when Cole's hand shot out to stop her.

"Thank you, Ronnie."

Veronica looked up in time to see his dark head already making a slow descent, closing the few inches between their lips. At the last second, she somehow found the strength to turn her face away. The kiss caught the corner of her mouth and lingered.

"I thought you'd welcome this," he murmured, his lips grazing her cheek. Veronica was unable to formulate a believable denial. A leaden sensation was invading every muscle and her thoughts were evaporating.

"But you don't even—" *like me,* she tried to get out, but the belated attempt was a waste as Cole's mouth settled over her lips, catching them parted. Emotion flooded her heart and shot its fluid heat to the very depths of her femininity. It was as if a flash fire was bursting inside her and she was helpless to stop herself from wrapping her arms around

Cole's neck and kissing him back. Nothing in her entire experience had prepared her for this. Eric's kisses had been dull by comparison, and the imagination of her teen years hadn't had the sophistication to conjure up more than a fraction of this reality. If she had been rational, she could have reminded herself that even as an adult, she hadn't acquired the kind of experience necessary to foresee this.

Cole made a husky sound deep in his throat and his lips slipped off hers to glide enticingly toward her ear. Playful nips elicited an unwilling sigh of pleasurable torment.

"Has it been a while, Ronnie?" asked Cole, as his warm breath caressed her ear.

The sigh of delight caught in her throat. Another tender love nip distracted her briefly as he went on, "It's been a long time for me, too."

Inexperienced though she was, Veronica suddenly knew exactly what Cole was asking and she went rigid in his arms. To discourage the resistance he sensed, Cole's lips found hers again.

Neither of them heard the soft footfalls coming through Cole's bedroom or the shocked gasp that came from the doorway. "I think I'd better come back later."

Cole's lips didn't abruptly abandon hers, but Veronica felt his passion die as embarrassment overcame hers. Keeping her in his arms, Cole glanced over his shoulder at his sister-in-law.

"Afternoon, Helen." Cole eased Veronica off the counter before he turned fully to the brunette whose dark eyes shifted from Veronica's pink-tinged cheeks to Cole's expressionless face. "Hello, Jessie."

Veronica's discomfort increased as Jessie stepped into view.

"I was just coming over to ask a favour of Veronica when Jessie came up from the barn saying she'd heard you'd been hurt." The confused concern on Helen's face gave way to disapproval when her dark eyes skittered toward Veronica.

"Yes, darling." Jessie crowded her way past the brunette. "It's not serious, is it?" Her amber eyes were all over

Cole before they shot directly to Veronica's slightly puffy lips.

"Ronnie has taken care of it."

"I can see she has." Jessie's husky voice was just a tone above a growl, but she turned her sweetest smile on Cole as she reached to take him by the arm, effectively separating Veronica from him as she wedged her long perfect body between them. "Now that your injury is tended to, how about showing me that filly you promised?" How quickly the cattiness had changed to something more like baby talk. Veronica was sickened.

"Excuse me." Veronica inched toward the door and Helen stepped aside to give easier passage. Self-consciously Veronica moved through the bedroom to the hall, then made for the kitchen.

Once there, she could no longer hear Jessie's cooing voice. There was a faint murmur of conversation, but Veronica managed to block out even that sound as she briskly unloaded the dishwasher and tried to distract her mind and her body from the aftereffects of Cole's kiss.

Only now was she fully aware of how unexpected that kiss had been. Never in a million years would she have believed it could happen. Not with Cole. Not with any man, she reminded herself. When Eric abandoned her, he'd stripped her of any confidence she might have possessed about her sexual attractiveness. For what man could ever find her scarred body desirable?

"I'll be down at the barn, Ronnie." Cole came through the kitchen, his dusty black Stetson firmly in place. Veronica felt herself impaled by his riveting blue eyes, which told her nothing of his thoughts before they swung away. Jessie dogged his steps, her bow-shaped mouth pursed in annoyance at the pace Cole set. Helen followed the pair in, but when Cole and Jessie went out the back door, she stayed behind.

"You had a favour to ask?" Veronica invited the woman to speak, hoping Helen wouldn't mention anything about seeing her and Cole kissing. Veronica remembered Helen, who was nearly Cole's thirty-four years, as being cool but polite. Neither Helen nor Jackie had ever had much time for her. It wasn't that they'd slighted her, but both of them had been older and much more housebound than she. For most of her two years on the ranch Veronica had been an unabashed tomboy, and she'd had little in common with the sisters.

"I was wondering if you'd make a couple of the dishes I've planned for the barbecue I'm having tomorrow night." Helen was smiling pleasantly. "Cole mentioned what a good cook you are and suggested you might consider helping me out if you're up to it." Veronica felt herself relax, absurdly pleased that Cole had complimented her to someone. "Jackie and I used to do this every year and, well, after she passed away, Hank's cook always helped out. You don't need to feel obligated, Veronica, but I could sure use your help."

"I'll be glad to help, Helen. Just tell me what you want and I'll make it."

"Good. Thank you. I'll send home the food and recipes with Cole when he comes for Curtis." Helen paused, and the pleasant smile turned cool. "And there's something else I'd like to ask."

Veronica waited, not smiling either. She could guess what was coming, and she fervently wished Helen would just let the incident pass without comment. "What's that?"

"I think perhaps you should talk to Cole about moving you into that small vacant house between here and the highway, the one that's usually assigned to the ranch's cook. I don't think it's good for Curtis to live in a house where there are two single adults sleeping within a few feet of each other." Helen at least had the grace to blush. "And after what I just saw, I think it's even more imperative."

Veronica stared, knowing Helen was overreacting but that her firm tone signaled she would tolerate no dissent. Until now Veronica hadn't really given much thought to the propriety of living under the same roof as Cole. She wasn't too concerned about her reputation or Cole's, either, since nothing was going on between them.

Interpreting Veronica's initial silence as resistance, Helen went on, "I know Cole is a very attractive man, Ronnie, so maybe he's a lot of temptation for you—you had such a crush on him once." Helen smiled tolerantly at the tides of colour that washed into Veronica's cheeks. "Sometimes those lovesick feelings resurrect themselves at awkward times when we grow older. But once you get settled someplace where you're not in such close contact with Cole, I'm certain you'll regain some perspective."

Veronica nearly choked with outrage. She stood quietly for a few moments before she trusted herself to speak, her hands clenched so tightly on the crutch grips they tingled.

Veronica tried valiantly to match Helen's cool. "Cole would be the first to remind you that what goes on in his home is his business," she said. "But if you feel so strongly about my presence here, then by all means speak to Cole about it. I'll abide by any decision he makes."

Helen looked a bit dismayed before she recovered. "But you should be the one to speak to Cole."

"There's nothing between Cole and me, Helen, and I'm not about to suggest to him that I think there is by asking him to move me out of this house." Veronica was trembling, hating the angry humiliation she felt. "Now if that's all, I've got a lot to do before the evening meal."

Helen left without another word. Veronica turned back to the cupboard, distressed that she'd just made another enemy.

And for what? One silly, impossibly thrilling kiss? Veronica sighed. Despite what Helen and probably Jessie had seen and despite what she'd felt in those brief moments of ecstasy, there had been no indication from Cole that his kiss had been anything more for him than a mere sensual impulse.

CHAPTER FOUR

AFTER SUPPER, when Cole came home with Curtis and the food and recipes from Helen, Veronica managed to be conveniently absent from the house. She was in the side yard out of sight of the driveway, carefully poking about the ill-tended flowerbeds to see if any perennial blooms had managed to survive the weeds. When Cole and Curtis went inside, she moved around to the front of the house, then decided to make her way down a portion of the long driveway that wandered in a lazy arc to the highway more than a mile away.

The warm evening air was laden with dust from the recent passing of Cole's car, but Veronica cared little that it settled over her clothing or found beads of perspiration to cling to. She was thinking about the awful tension at supper more than an hour earlier. Cole had been terse with his men to the point of rudeness, and he'd barely acknowledged Veronica's presence. There could have been no clearer indication of how much he regretted his impulse that afternoon, or how anxious he was to disabuse her of any notion that it had meant anything to him. His aloofness reminded her of his initial attempts to ignore her infatuation with him years ago.

Veronica cringed at the memory of the time she'd so foolishly confessed her love to Cole. He had not taken to a brotherly role, the fifteen-year-old Veronica had reasoned, so perhaps he didn't think of her that way. And when Cole looked at her—as he had occasionally—with neither irritation nor dislike, she'd begun to think he'd secretly found himself liking her as a woman. That was all the encourage-

ment Cole's adoring little stepsister had needed to try out
her newly discovered feminine wiles.

Incautious and inexperienced, the young Veronica began
to flirt with Cole when they were alone. Cole ignored her
amateur attempts to imitate what she'd seen her mother do
so often, until he finally got tired of having Veronica constantly under foot.

"But I love you, Cole," she declared, with all the melodramatic intensity only a lovesick adolescent can portray.
But he just laughed at her and told her she had a particularly bad case of puppy love. The scorn in his laughter hurt
deeply. He didn't even like her enough to rebuff her in a way
that left her with any self-respect. In daring retaliation,
knowing that Cole had no use for her as a sister or a lover,
she had ridden Chapman Red for the first time.

Preoccupied with her memories, Veronica made a mis-
step but deftly regained her balance. She'd already managed the prescribed half-mile daily walk, and the physical
therapist had cautioned her not to push herself and risk the
possibility of a setback. Since the last operation, she'd had
fewer and fewer muscle spasms and she certainly didn't want
to spoil her record. Reluctantly she turned toward the house
and started making her way back, curious about what recipes Helen had sent over for her to prepare.

JUST AFTER BREAKFAST the next day, Veronica started to
clean and prepare the enormous amount of fresh vegetables Helen intended to serve with the four sour-cream based
dips Veronica had mixed the night before. The three-dozen
eggs that had been boiled lay chilling in the refrigerator,
waiting to be devilled. Veronica was disappointed that there
was little to be done that challenged her cooking skills.

"Helen didn't give you much more than busy work to do,
did she?" Cole whipped off his hat and tossed it carelessly
toward the coat tree in the corner as he came in the porch
door. Veronica noticed that he'd discarded the bandage on
his hand.

"There's a lot of busy work involved when you cook for a crowd," Veronica replied noncommittally. "I don't mind." Cole crossed the room to the coffee pot.

"Is this my coffee or yours?" he asked, referring to the expensive decaffeinated brand Veronica preferred.

"Yours," Veronica said, trying not to let Cole's presence in the kitchen throw her off balance. It was the first time since yesterday afternoon that they had been alone together and Veronica was battling an impossible longing for his nearness.

With a small shock, she realised that her feelings for Cole weren't motivated as much by the leftovers of her adolescent crush on him as by the much more complicated, full-blown longings of a woman who wanted the companionship and intimacy of a special man. That realisation sent her gaze skittering in his direction. Cole had poured himself some coffee and was sipping it, the hint of a satisfied smile on his mouth as he tasted the rich dark brew.

Those were the same firm sensual lips that had so thoroughly possessed hers less than twenty-four hours ago. The long tanned fingers that dwarfed the coffee cup were the ones that had reached for her and combed through her hair with gentle ferocity. Helplessly her eyes traced the snug fit of his chambray work shirt and worn denim jeans, overwhelmed by the sudden memory of what that lean hard body had felt like beneath her hands.

Veronica had to look away. This intense physical longing was something she'd never experienced, and that Cole had so quickly brought it to the surface signalled the potential for a far more devastating hurt than the one Eric had inflicted on her.

"You haven't heard a word I've said." Cole's deep rough voice intruded on her troubled thoughts in gentle accusation.

"What?"

"I asked if you wanted to ride over to Helen's with Curtis and me this evening." Veronica's knife halted in midair, then came down on a helpless stalk of celery with finality.

"No, thank you." Veronica didn't mention that Helen had neglected to invite her. Until she did, Veronica would take nothing for granted.

"Good coffee, Ronnie." Cole strode from the kitchen, leaving Veronica with an irrational wish that he'd found some reason to stay longer.

"VERONICA!"

Cole's thundering voice from the front yard brought her quickly from the kitchen just as she slid the cake she'd just mixed into the oven. A delivery truck was parked out front. Veronica thought she'd heard an engine earlier, but she'd been running the mixer off and on and hadn't paid much attention.

"Oh good." Veronica smiled at the large box that had been left on the porch. The delivery man had just climbed back into his truck and was driving away. "I didn't expect this until sometime next week," she explained hastily to her iron-faced stepbrother as she went through the screen door onto the porch.

"Would you mind carrying this box to the kitchen for me?" she asked as she stepped aside and held the porch door open expectantly. Cole didn't move and his stern expression didn't alter a whit. Veronica's smile thinned to a slight line.

"What's in it?" Cole eyed her curiously, but Veronica missed the gentle look that had come over his face at the defensive stiffening of her thin shoulders.

"Just a cookbook and some needlework," she told him, forcing herself to look at him. "And before you jump to any conclusions, that doesn't mean I'm planning to move in permanently."

Veronica turned awkwardly and went back inside. Cole followed a few steps behind her, his booted feet the only other sound in the house as she moved stiffly into the kitchen.

"Where do you want this?" came the gruff question and Veronica relaxed, recognising the hint of gentleness that softened his deep voice.

"On the table," she answered, then cautioned, "but be careful, I've got a cake in the oven." In no time, Cole had the taped seam sliced open, and Veronica began unpacking the box, looking for the cookbook.

"What's that?" Cole's attention was fixed on the large plastic bag of hexagon quilt patches that Veronica had lifted out of the box.

"A baby quilt." Cole's eyes jumped up to meet hers, his gaze intense. "It's for a friend of mine whose baby is due in another month," she explained. "I thought I'd work on it while I'm here."

"Does that go with it?" Cole gestured toward the huge wooden quilting hoop she was taking out and Veronica nodded. He watched as she pulled out quilt bat and fabrics, a couple of partially completed needlework projects and sewing supplies before she came to the large, loose-leaf cookbook she was after.

"Do you know what to do with all that?"

Veronica was irritated by the faint incredulity in Cole's voice. "That's right. Astonishing, isn't it?" Veronica turned toward the cupboard and placed her cookbook next to the meagre collection at the back of the counter.

"Discounting the fact that your mother couldn't teach you things like this, I'd say you have a few old-fashioned hobbies for a woman of the eighties. Aren't you one of those liberated females who wants a career and a sophisticated life-style—husband and children be damned?"

"Careful, Cole. Your chauvinism is showing." But the look she flashed over her shoulder was indulgent. Cole was an old-fashioned male, but from what Hank had told her, she'd got the impression that Cole had always encouraged Jackie to use her talents and be all she was capable of being.

Veronica turned back toward the box, noticing uneasily that Cole was waiting for her to answer his question. Flustered, she began putting all the sewing supplies back in the box while she considered her reply. A quick glance upward caught Cole's speculative gaze.

"After so many years of not having a family or any real home, having a husband and children and making a good home is more important to me than having an outside career." Veronica shrugged as if the disclosure was not the deep confession it really was. Suddenly overcome with heartache, she looked down at the box. She had thought she'd have all that with Eric Marshall. "And you can find classes that teach you to do just about anything these days," she added airily. Veronica forced a smile onto her lips and met Cole's ever-watching eyes. "What would you like for supper?"

"You've got tonight off." Cole's stern visage relaxed.

"That's right. I guess I forgot." Veronica paused, then decided to ask Cole about something while they were getting along. "I was wondering if you'd mind letting me use Jackie's sewing machine." His gaze darted from hers and Veronica instantly regretted asking.

"That's all right," she assured him hastily. "I can piece the quilt by hand. In fact, it might be easier to work with if I did. Besides, that overstuffed chair by the lamp in the living room is far more comfortable than a straight chair."

Cole's eyes turned a stormy blue. "Stop walking on eggshells around me, Ronnie."

Veronica's mouth fell open at the gruff order.

"And don't look so surprised. Hell, you'd think I was some kind of tyrant the way you act," he grumbled.

"Don't swear."

"It's my house and my temper. I'll swear if I want to," he thundered, but the suggestion of a smile had reached his lips, a companion to the sparkle of laughter in his eyes. The world had brightened considerably. "The instruction book for the sewing machine is in one of the drawers," he said, his voice lowering. "You're welcome to it any time as long as I'm not sleeping. And watch where you drop your pins. I'm still finding Jackie's."

Veronica smiled at Cole's false ferocity, marvelling at the friendliness between them and loving it. "Thank you, Cole."

"You might not be thanking me if you suddenly find yourself stuck with the mending," he warned.

"Oh, no, I won't," Veronica teased. "You promised me I was only hired to cook, nothing else."

Cole growled good-naturedly, then said, "I was a desperate man then. I hadn't had a decent home-cooked meal for weeks and I was probably delirious." He grinned at Veronica's sceptical smirk. "If you'll let me renegotiate our agreement to include mending, I promise to come up with a bribe you'll like better than a raise—not that you can't have a raise instead," he added quickly. "The boys already think I got the better part of our first deal," he told her. "Will you think about it?" Veronica giggled at Cole's earnest expression.

"As long as you don't deluge me with mending, I'll do it in return for the use of the sewing machine. Forget about any deals or bribes."

"You're really quite a pleasant surprise, Veronica." Cole's low rough voice warmed her and she felt her emotions scramble to harden themselves against the appeal of Cole's long-awaited approval. The small-scale inner war she'd been waging against allowing the compellingly deep feelings she had for Cole to blossom naturally into love suffered a severe setback at the affection behind his words.

She made some inane comment about flattery then that casually brushed off Cole's remark. She couldn't even remember what it was the moment after she'd said it, but was just grateful when she could finally retreat to the quiet sanctuary of her room.

THE PHONE RANG STRIDENTLY in the quiet house and Veronica rose from the sewing machine without her crutches and with stiff caution covered the few feet to the telephone extension on Cole's night table.

"Chapman Ranch."

"Are you all right, Ronnie?" Cole's voice betrayed a concern that threw her for a moment.

"Of course I'm all right," she assured him. "What could be wrong?"

"I was afraid you'd had car trouble or something. What's taking you so long to get here?"

Confused and surprised by Cole's impatient tone, she was slow to answer.

"I'm not coming to Helen's," she said quietly.

"What did you say?" The sound of the party came clearly over the connection.

"I'm not coming," she repeated.

"What do you mean, you're not coming?"

"I wasn't invited," she told him truthfully, her fingers twisting the phone cord.

"Maybe Helen didn't send you an engraved invitation but you were invited," Cole stated confidently.

"When?" Veronica released the phone cord to massage her forehead wearily.

"When she spoke to you about helping her out, I suppose."

Veronica's mouth twisted in grim amusement.

"Has she asked you where I am tonight?" she challenged. There was a second's silence.

"Well, no. But she's been busy," he hastened to add. "I'll be there in ten minutes to pick you up. Be ready."

"Don't, Cole," she warned. "It will be a wasted trip. I'm not about to go to Helen's." Veronica took a deep breath. "I wouldn't come to Helen's even if I had been invited."

"Why not?" Cole was angry now.

Veronica frantically tried to think of some reason that would not put him at odds with his sister-in-law. She hadn't mentioned the confrontation she'd had with Helen the day before. Veronica squeezed her eyes closed.

"You know me," she began, letting just the right touch of snobbery affect her soft voice. "I'm afraid Helen's little get-together is just a little too down-home for my uptown taste." Veronica winced at the lie. "But you and Curtis have a good time," she enthused before she dropped the phone into its cradle, not wanting to hear Cole's temper explode.

Veronica made her way back to the sewing machine and methodically picked up the quilt pieces and sewing supplies. She folded the machine into its cabinet and prepared to take her things back to her room. A good long bath and an early night would shorten the lonely evening considerably.

CHAPTER FIVE

VERONICA TOOK HER WALK early the next morning, and feeling fit and increasingly stronger, she decided to double the prescribed distance. Cole and Curtis would probably spend the day at Helen's, she thought, and Cole's men didn't come to the house for meals on Sundays. It was supposed to be her day off, but she planned to spend the afternoon baking. Although the weather forecasters were predicting a hot day, the central air conditioning in the house would enable her to work comfortably.

Her walk completed, Veronica was just stepping onto the porch when Curtis burst out the back door, brushing past her in a flurry of motion that had her turning to watch his strong young legs carry him swiftly toward the barns. She had just turned back toward the door when the soft smile evaporated from her lips. Cole was staring at her stonily from beneath the black brim of his Stetson.

"Good morning, Cole."

"Good morning, Miss Uptown," he mocked. Veronica couldn't maintain contact with the harshness in Cole's gaze and she glanced away. She had started to step aside for Cole to pass when he reached for her chin and lifted her face to his scrutiny.

"I've got a pretty good idea that you and Helen haven't exactly hit it off," he growled. "But if you ever tell a wild tale like you did last night about being too uptown, I'm going to turn you across my Neanderthal knee and warm your backside." Veronica was unprepared for the brief hard kiss that followed his warning. Cole's lips released hers and he bounded down the stairs to catch up with his son, leaving Veronica in an emotional whirlwind of pleasure and relief.

Later that day, just as she removed the last of the chocolate-chip cookies from the oven, Veronica heard the muffled jangle of spurs and the harsh snort of a spirited horse out back. When she heard Cole come up the porch steps, she hurriedly slipped the last of the cookies onto the cooling rack and switched off the oven. Cole was just coming through the door as she turned to put the mixing bowls and utensils into the dishwasher.

"Are you finished in here for a while?" he asked, then spied the cookies. Veronica caught the look and smiled.

"Help yourself."

"Mmmm." Cole's eyes were lit with appreciation as he savoured the taste of a warm cookie. "Wait till Curtis gets wind of these."

"There might not be any left," Veronica laughed as Cole wrapped a couple of cookies in a napkin and put them into his shirt pocket.

"Come on outside with me. I have a surprise for you." He crossed to the porch door and held it open for her. Veronica reached for her crutches and readily complied. She was well onto the porch when her heart seemed to come to a stop. Cole strode past her, descended the stairs and picked up the trailing reins of a horse.

The sight of the big bay stallion struck at her heart with the force of a physical blow. Instantly eight years dropped away and she was once again the stepsister, the intruder who'd coveted everything Cole Chapman loved, particularly the big stallion with hide the colour of blood.

"Are you coming?"

Cole's voice snapped her back to the present and she felt her balance waver.

"What?"

Cole studied her with a frown, tipped his hat back, then repositioned it and tugged the brim lower.

"I promised to bribe you into doing the mending. Of course, another benefit of getting you on a horse again is that riding will help strengthen your legs. Spending more time in the fresh air should bring some colour back into those cheeks and help out that puny appetite of yours."

Veronica felt the lump in her throat thicken. She suddenly felt weak and leaned most of her weight on her crutches. A tremor started in her knees and worked its way into every joint until she feared she'd collapse.

"I don't . . . ride anymore."

"I talked to your mother about it earlier this morning and she said your therapist back in New York had recommended horseback riding." Veronica was too stunned to take in that Cole had consulted her mother about anything.

"I haven't ridden a horse in years and I—I'm not interested anymore," she managed, nearly strangling with unshed tears. "I've got work to do inside." Ronnie's haste made her feel more awkward than usual as she turned to make a quick retreat.

"Ronnie?" The pulsing roar of blood in her ears obscured the concern in Cole's voice.

"I'm going in," she choked out, then tugged sharply on the screen door. She didn't return to her baking. Instead, she moved as quickly as she could to the hall, anxious to get to her room.

Once there, she closed the door and leaned a shoulder against it. The tears had started, but when she heard her name being called from the kitchen she wiped them away impatiently with the back of her hand. She then crossed the room to the bath and through the window caught sight of the bay horse standing riderless with his reins wrapped around a porch pillar. In moments, she had jerked the shades closed.

"Ronnie?" Cole had come into her room.

"Get out!" Veronica began shaking, unable to comprehend the reason Cole was inflicting this punishment on her. She edged toward the bathroom door, wanting only to escape Cole's astonished expression.

Cole was striding boldly closer, reaching for Veronica when she pressed herself against the wall in an effort to

avoid his touch. One of her crutches clattered to the floor
when she tried to shake off his gentle grip.

"Come for a ride. Just down to the barn. I'll walk beside
you." Cole's voice had an eerie stillness to it.

"I don't ride anymore. I told you that." Veronica's other
crutch fell to the floor as she gripped Cole's wrist in self-
protection. His expression softened.

"How long has it been, Ronnie? How long have you
stayed away from horses?" Cole paused when he saw tears
streak down her flushed cheeks. "Your mother seemed to
think that you haven't gone near a horse since you lived
here." Cole's voice was a husky rasp. "Is that true?"

Veronica felt her body wilt and she sagged miserably
against the wall. She couldn't look at him.

"The half-wild little tomboy I knew ate, slept and
dreamed horses," Cole kidded gently. "She didn't swear off
them, did she?"

Veronica's eyes squeezed closed and she nodded, missing
the bleak look that came into Cole's eyes.

"Why?" he rasped. Veronica shook her head, her delicate features crumpling. It was a long moment before she
could speak.

"I was so sure I'd fastened that gate. I could have
sworn..." Veronica's soft voice lapsed into a childlike sob
and Cole drew her into his strong arms.

"Have you been punishing yourself all these years?" Cole
demanded in a gruff whisper. "Hmm?" His arms tightened promptingly.

"I was untrustworthy...careless," she mumbled disconsolately into Cole's warm shirt front.

He gripped her chin and forced her to look up at him.
"You said at the time you could have sworn you'd fastened
the gate—that you clearly remembered latching it and fas-
tening the security chain," he reminded her.

"And I believed it, Cole. I believed it with all my heart."
The tortured violet eyes fluttered closed in anguish. "But I
must have been wrong. Red died and I was the last one with

him." Cole pulled her against himself again and she heard him curse softly.

"Listen to me, Ronnie." The sternness in his voice insured her full attention. "You weren't the only person around the barn that day. Anyone could have forgotten to make sure that gate was properly latched." Cole held her away from his chest to see her face, but her eyes shied away. "I never should have accused you like I did," he grumbled. "And I never wanted to deprive you of the pleasure of horses." Fresh tears slid down her damp cheeks and Cole's voice softened.

"I'm sorry, Ronnie. You were just a kid and I was too hard on you. You loved that horse even more than I did, didn't you?" Veronica nodded and gave a half sob of agreement. Cole cuddled her against his broad chest and rested his chin on top of her head. "Angry as I was then, I never once thought you'd punish yourself this way."

When Veronica pressed her hands against Cole's chest and tried to push away, he let her. "Why are you being so nice, Cole?" Veronica's spine stiffened. "Do you feel sorry for me?" She didn't want his apology if he did. Veronica studied Cole's face while he seemed to consider her question.

"No. I don't feel sorry for you, Ronnie," he said at last. "But I've come to regret a lot of things that happened between you and me back then. Looking back on those two years, I realise now that I never really gave you a chance." Cole repositioned his hat in a betrayal of his unease. "I guess in that way I do feel sorry for you," he admitted. "Is it too late for us to be friends?"

Veronica could scarcely believe what she was hearing.

"If that's what you want," she answered unsteadily.

"Is it what you want?" he countered, a half smile lifting the corners of his mouth.

"Yes," she admitted shyly and her gaze wavered. She didn't want Cole to see the joy in her eyes that might have revealed how much she'd always wanted the two of them to be friends, more than friends....

"Then come on," he urged. Veronica started to comply by putting her hand into the strong tanned one he held out for her, but then she hesitated, remembering the crutches that lay on the floor at their feet. Cole's gaze followed hers and he leaned down to pick them up before she could.

"Uh-oh." Belatedly Cole tried to catch the small crumbs of cookie that slipped out of his shirt pocket. When he straightened, his lips formed a wry line as he slipped his fingers into the pocket and felt the crumbled remains. The solemnity of the past few minutes was lifted. Veronica started to grin, then found herself laughing with Cole.

"Wait a minute." Cole handed her the crutches and moved into the bathroom. She listened to the sound of running water before he came back with a warm wet washcloth, which he used to tenderly brush the dark half circles of mascara from beneath her eyes and smooth away the grey tear trails from her cheeks. He gave the washcloth a quick toss through the bathroom door and watched it land on the side of the sink.

Satisfied, he asked, "Think you're ready to go out and meet Red's most promising grandson?"

"Grandson?"

He nodded. "You'll be amazed at the temperament of Red's Early Riser, Ronnie. You've never seen two animals more alike. Of course, Riser has a few personality quirks Red didn't have, but the resemblance is striking."

Veronica smiled. Cole trusted her enough to offer her a ride on the grandson of Chapman Red. How could she refuse? And he was speaking to her as if they shared something much more basic than a mutual love of horses. As Cole continued to extol Riser's virtues, she marvelled at the warm sense of companionship developing between them.

"A short ride can't hurt," she said confidently. "Let's go."

The sun was bright and hot on her face, the light breeze teasing her hair into tangles as Cole lifted her on Early Riser's saddle and handed her the reins. Veronica felt sixteen again, healthy and whole, every part of her aching to dig in her heels and let the big horse run.

But the dull twinge of discomfort radiating up through both her thighs warned her to be cautious, reminding her she had neither the strength nor the agility to tolerate more than a few minutes in the saddle.

The stallion tossed his head and Veronica reached down to give his sleek red neck a loving pat. Riser moved off at a walk, then pranced sideways, as if impatient with the gentle, yet authoritative hands on the reins.

"Let me know if he's too much for you," Cole called as he walked a few feet to Veronica's left, carrying her crutches, watching for any sign of a problem.

"He's all right," Veronica called back nonchalantly, enjoying the splendid feel of the powerful horse beneath her, savouring the mobility she hadn't felt in the months of lying in bed, limited by weakness and pain. But more than that, riding again—especially the grandson of Chapman Red—gave her a feeling of happiness and contentment deeper than any she'd known for years.

Sensing the short ride to the barn would not be enough for her, Cole walked the horse slowly around the huge two-level barn, then suggested that Veronica ride on her own around one of the smaller paddocks. She gladly consented, but Cole allowed her to complete only two laps in the enclosure before calling her over to him.

"Don't overdo it, Ronnie," he cautioned as she brought the stallion to a halt a few feet from where he stood. He entered the paddock and in seconds had lifted Veronica to the ground, leaving her disappointedly earthbound once again as he handed her the crutches. After removing Riser's saddle and bridle, he ushered Veronica out of the paddock and into the stable. In a few minutes they were walking side by side down the wide aisle of the stable, Cole moving with loose-jointed ease while Veronica made short stilted steps with legs that were only slightly stiffer after her brief ride. But if Veronica was feeling any discomfort from the unaccustomed exercise, her smiling face gave no indication.

Cole was amazed at the transformation in her. Within the past hour, the pale withdrawn young woman with her aura of loneliness had vanished. In her place was a more youthful, animated young woman whose wide smile, healthy flush and sparkling eyes gave her a beautiful warmth and radiance.

She was chattering delightedly to him now, and Cole smiled, suddenly struck by the thought that forgiving Veronica after all these years had liberated this charming young woman. He felt a run of guilt for his harshness eight years before. He couldn't wait to see how she'd react to the second part of his surprise. Touching her arm, he directed her across the aisle to a side door that opened onto another paddock.

Veronica gasped with pleasure when she looked outside, "She's beautiful, Cole," she said as a young sorrel mare trotted over and nudged Cole's arm amicably. He reached up and rubbed the animal's cheek as she automatically nosed Veronica's shoulder then curiously inspected her crutches. "She's not spooked a bit by these."

"Honey Lamb is one of the sweetest-tempered horses I own," Cole explained, then grinned. "We own," he corrected. "She's a little too inquisitive at times, but she's smooth gaited and gentle enough for you to ride until you regain the strength to really handle a spirited horse."

"Oh, Cole." Her bright smile wavered and tears began to flood into her eyes.

"Hey," Cole chided gruffly as he slipped a strong arm around her waist. "If you're going to turn on the sprinklers over every little thing, how am I going to know when I've done something right?" Veronica sniffed back her tears and looked up at him.

"Honey Lamb?"

Cole laughed and his arm tightened briefly. "Jackie named her favourite animals the damnedest things." The wistful look came and went so quickly in Cole's eyes that she almost missed it. Cole glanced down into Veronica's face, his smile coaxing a return of her own. They turned to reenter the barn and were almost to the wide main aisle when Veronica spoke.

"Cole?" The big rancher stopped and cobalt-blue eyes slanted down to meet hers. She was somehow on the verge of both tears and laughter. "Cole, I . . ." A mere thank-you seemed such an inadequate expression for the gratitude she felt. As foolish and impulsive as her next action was, she reached up and placed both hands behind his neck, heedless of the crutches that fell to the floor. Cole allowed his head to be drawn downward by the gentle pressure on his neck, and his hands naturally fell to her waist as he accepted the quick touch of her lips to his.

"Thank you so much, Cole." The kiss had been too light, too gentle. "I can't tell you how much all this means to me." Veronica had unclasped her hands from his neck and they were dropping away when Cole's renewed grip on her waist brought her against him. Veronica's happy smile was startled from her lips as her hands landed gently on his shoulders.

Cole didn't wait to hear the half-formed question on her lips. His mouth descended swiftly, yet settled like a whisper on hers. What started as a simple need for a more satisfying kiss sent a jolt of heat rocketing through his system, surprising him with the unexpected stirring of a depth of passion he'd known only with his wife. But that was long ago, so long ago, Cole realised, and as he took Ronnie's soft mouth more vigorously, his desire for the woman in his arms became all consuming.

Veronica's had been a child's kiss, a simple sweet expression of gratitude, but the firm pressure of Cole's mouth was mature male. There was an element of wildness in Cole's kiss that she'd never experienced with Eric, a spontaneity that alarmed, yet fascinated.

Before she quite realised it, Veronica was matching Cole's wildness with her own mouth in a fevered attempt to give him a measure of the sensual excitement he was lavishing on her. Somehow she was slipping past rational thought into an unknown area nearing total surrender.

Cole's lips were becoming more insistent, but Veronica was oblivious to the fact that he had lost control or that he was lowering them both onto a bale of hay. His embrace tightened once she was on his lap, and Veronica felt the involuntary melting of her small frame into the hardness of his.

The last remnants of reason called to her, warning her love-drugged mind that something of her essence was being drawn away. The overpowering need to merge with Cole warred against the frightening notion that he was stealing into her very being and extracting the untapped wellspring of love in her heart....

"Dad?"

Veronica floated closer to sanity at the sound of the childish voice. Cole's arms slackened, but he was slow to break off the kiss.

"Dad." Curtis was clearly annoyed.

Sensitive to the impatience a child often feels in the presence of adults who are kissing and embracing, Veronica tried to draw away, embarrassed that Cole kept her firmly in his arms.

"What is it, Curtis?" he asked sternly.

The small boy looked as if he'd forgotten what he'd been about to say. Cole watched his son's obvious discomfort with amused indulgence, but Veronica didn't like the resentment building in those large grey eyes. She liked it even less when his gaze moved over her and noted that she was sitting on his father's lap, held there securely in his father's oaklike arms. There was no mistaking the tiny glimmers of anger that darted into those solemn grey eyes, or the companion tightening of the small mouth.

"You promised to take me for ice cream," he said sulkily, his tone of voice bringing a frown of displeasure to his father's face.

"I said I might," Cole corrected patiently. "Your timing leaves something to be desired, son. Haven't we talked about interrupting?"

Curtis blushed, embarrassed. "You weren't talking to her," Curtis told his father reasonably.

Veronica might have found Curtis's reply amusing, but the hurt in the boy's expression tugged at her heart. The slim fingers that rested behind Cole's head jerked warningly on a thick black lock. In response, a wide smile spread across Cole's face. Curtis seemed to relax at the sight.

"You've got me there, Curt," Cole admitted. "What do you say the three of us climb into the pickup and go for ice cream? I heard they're having a special on hot-fudge sundaes." Curtis's quick grin dissolved. Instantly, Veronica sensed she was the reason.

"What do you say we leave me at home?" Veronica suggested, allowing her tiredness to show. "I'm afraid I've overdone things a little today. Would you mind handing me my crutches, Curtis?"

The boy was quick to comply, but the unfriendly look in his eyes told her clearly that his eagerness had more to do with getting her away from his father than giving his assistance. Veronica thanked Curtis and he ran out to the truck.

"Are you really tired, or are you trying to do an imitation of a small kitchen appliance?" Cole's question referred to her offer not to court Curtis's friendship if Cole kept him home more, assuring him Curtis would likely pay her no more notice than he would an appliance or a piece of furniture.

"Both." Veronica got to her feet. Now that she wasn't touching Cole, now that the delayed sense of weariness was asserting itself on her tired body, Veronica was sobering rapidly from the euphoria of the afternoon. One glance at Cole's iron expression as he fell into step beside her thrust her back into all the old familiar insecurities. So he had forgiven her, taken her riding, then offered her the use of a lovely mare. And her foolish little kiss had triggered his sensual appetite. He'd said before that it had been a while since he'd been with a woman....

A cold sick feeling of shame and fear rushed up inside her. She remembered how she'd felt after the kiss she and Cole had shared when she'd bandaged his hand. She couldn't be intimate with a man—ever. The scars from her accident were too repulsive.

Veronica glanced at Cole again. What a superb virile male specimen he was, with a sexual confidence and experience that warned her he was accustomed to much more from a woman than kisses.

"I hope the ride won't make you too sore," Cole said. "Should I get out the liniment later and give you a rubdown after Curtis and I get back?" His intimate tone as they reached the porch steps sent a jolt of apprehension through her—magnifying her fear of what such physical closeness would reveal to him. No man could stand the sight of her scars—Eric's abandonment was proof of that.

Veronica stepped onto the porch, then turned to face Cole. "Look. I think it would be wise to keep our relationship with each other as businesslike as possible while I'm here. I'm not going to be here long, so there's no sense in flirting with complications." A wry smile twisted her lips, stilling their trembling. "We've shared a couple of hot little kisses, but I think we both recognise a mistake when we see one."

Cole's expression grew so thunderous she almost faltered.

"And poor Curtis!" She went on. "We've managed to make him feel threatened and unhappy."

Cole's jaw muscles flexed ominously and Veronica took that as her cue to be silent. "Have fun at the Dairy Queen." Veronica turned and moved through the porch door, leaving Cole staring after her for a moment before he turned to join his son.

CHAPTER SIX

"WHAT'S THAT STUFF?"

Veronica smiled tolerantly at the boy who stood by her elbow. Now that Curtis was eating breakfast and supper at the house and generally spending much more time at home, the relative calm of her first weeks at the ranch had vanished. Veronica didn't mind Curtis's rambunctiousness, but the fact that he seemed determined to make things harder on her had proved to be more emotionally wearing than she'd have thought possible. It gave her a whole new perspective on the problems she had caused her mother's suitors.

"It's called Christmas Stew."

His nose wrinkled into an expression of disgust that was becoming all too familiar to her. "Christmas Stew! I hate stew."

"You might like this stew. Can you guess why it's called Christmas Stew?" Her smile was open, friendly.

"I don't know." And the scowl on his handsome little face told her he didn't care to know. Patiently Veronica continued talking.

"It's called Christmas Stew because most of the ingredients are either red or green, like Christmas decorations."

"That part ain't," he challenged as he pointed to a piece of meat. Veronica glanced down at the triumphant look on his face and knew Curtis was only interested in the stew now because he'd found something to be disagreeable about.

She resisted the temptation to correct his grammar and said, "There's one other ingredient in there that's not red or green." She wondered if he'd spied the diced onion that had been cooked almost transparent.

"Where?"

Veronica lifted the wide wooden spoon from the rim of the simmering pot and deftly skimmed off a few bits for Curtis to see.

"What's that?" he asked suspiciously.

"Onion."

"I hate onion, too."

Veronica laughed. "You're going to be in sad shape come supper," she kidded. "But you'll at least give the stew a fair tasting, won't you?" Curtis's expression was pure mutiny.

"I don't like that rule," he scowled, referring to Veronica's requirement that he at least taste a new food before he rejected it.

"I'm sorry, Curtis, but the only way you can find out what you like or don't like is by tasting," she told him patiently.

"If you were as good a cook as my Aunt Helen, I'd like everything you cook." Veronica refused to be either surprised or rankled by the childish jibe. With a thoughtful expression on her face, she glanced down at Curtis's glum face.

"Would you like me to ask Helen for some of your favourite recipes? There's no reason I can't make some of the foods you like best." Veronica's smile was meant to be encouraging, but Curtis only managed to look more annoyed.

"I don't like the way you cook." And with that final pronouncement disappeared out through the porch door.

Veronica pondered for a moment, then checked her watch before crossing the floor to another cupboard. Opening the door, she selected enough boxes of chocolate instant pudding to fill eight parfait glasses.

"He'll probably find something wrong with that idea, too." Cole's voice startled her. Guiltily she glanced over her shoulder at him, then disheartened, she started to put the boxes away.

"Go ahead and make some up if you want to, Ronnie. If he complains, I'll split his share with you." Cole walked to the refrigerator for a glass of iced tea.

Both Chapman males had been hard to get along with all week. Since Sunday, Cole had been cool and uncommunicative. Veronica had spent nearly every moment she wasn't preparing meals, or taking her daily exercise, working on the small baby quilt she'd started—contributing her part to the distancing between them by avoiding Cole altogether. She had begun riding Honey Lamb every day, but Cole didn't once offer to go with her, instead leaving the task of saddling the mare or accompanying her to Shorty or one of the other men.

"I'm giving you the day off tomorrow, Veronica."

Veronica looked at Cole, who was leaning against the counter nearby while he drank his tea.

"There's a woman coming out in the morning to cook breakfast and I thought she might as well give us a full day. Her references indicate she's pretty good in the kitchen, so she could be the one to replace you." Cole's face was absolutely unreadable, his eyes betraying nothing but a casual interest in her reaction.

Veronica summoned up a smile from the surprise she felt, then turned back to the mixing bowl and began tearing open pudding boxes. "I wish you luck," she told him, moving toward the refrigerator for milk. Stronger now, she managed very well on one crutch while she carried the milk jug to where she was working.

"Which day will we count as the first in the week's notice you're giving me? Tomorrow?" Veronica measured out the milk while she talked.

"I haven't hired her yet," Cole reminded her gruffly.

"Oh, you will," she said, then smiled, certain Cole wouldn't know that her amused expression hid the hurt she felt. "Curtis is getting pretty tired of corn flakes and peanut-butter sandwiches." Veronica switched on the mixer to discourage further conversation.

With the end of her stay in sight, she felt nothing but disappointment. As Cole left the room she chided herself. Things between her and Cole had improved more than she'd ever imagined they would. Just because they were avoiding each other now was no reason to feel disappointed. They would part on friendly terms and Cole would surely remember her the way she was now—older, more mature, useful. At least if they happened to meet in the future, there would be no hostile exchanges like the ones they'd had when she first came back to Wyoming.

Yet when Veronica poured the thickening pudding into the parfait glasses, she felt a prickle of tears. Scolding herself for being such a sentimental sap, she finished up in the kitchen and left the house for a walk.

THE EVENING HAD BEEN LONELY. Veronica had gone to her room after cleaning up the supper dishes. She'd spent a long time soaking in the tub before she put on her nightgown. She had just finished drying her hair when she heard a knock, then Cole's voice at her door. Hastily grabbing her robe, she belted it around herself and called for him to come in.

Veronica was seated before the dresser mirror brushing out tangles as he crossed the room and stood behind her. Their eyes met in the glass with an impact that brought a rush of excitement into her system. Even now that she was sure her stay was limited only to a few more days, she couldn't help the secret longing she felt—a longing more than just to stay.

Yet that longing was as futile as it was unwelcome. She had looked at Jackie's picture only the day before and had been reminded of what a beautiful woman she had been. After being married to someone like Jackie, Cole would never be content with anyone less, and certainly not his former stepsister. Although the past had been virtually resolved between them, Veronica felt herself no match for the sweet memories Cole would certainly have of the mother of his only child—a child who resented Veronica's presence.

"There are one or two things I'd like to take up with you, Veronica." Cole had her instant attention when he spoke to her in that tone, dropping the use of the nickname his father had bestowed upon her. Veronica waited, expecting him to go on, but he merely stood there, silent.

"Well?" she prompted, uncomfortable with the way his eyes were starting to stray over her reflection. The obvious preoccupation he seemed to have with the way her light robe was draped over her small breasts signalled her to beware. Had her earlier fears been correct? Had Cole been without a woman for so long that he'd developed an interest in her because she was convenient?

Fully aware of how vulnerable she was to any demonstration of affection from Cole, she was anxious for him to say what he had in mind and leave her room.

"Since I gave you tomorrow off, I was wondering if you'd have dinner with me tomorrow night." Cole's deep voice was like rough silk, a caress of her senses. Resisting its drawling persuasion was almost a physical pain, but Veronica didn't hesitate.

"No, I don't think so, Cole. Besides, don't you want to taste the new woman's cooking?

"I'll be there to sample breakfast and lunch. The boys will give me a report on dinner. After all, it's them she's cooking for."

She ran the brush briskly through her thick brown hair for several strokes before finding her hand captured in the firm warmth of Cole's. Violet eyes found his again in the mirror.

"So why not come?" His look was shrewd, almost calculating. Veronica tugged her hand free.

"Don't tell me you're so accustomed to having women fall all over you for a dinner date that you give the third degree to the rare one who declines," she kidded, hoping to deflect his question. One corner of Cole's mouth lifted in mild amusement.

"I think I know what you're trying to do, Ronnie."

"I'm relieved," she parried, smiling brightly to cover the trapped feeling that engulfed her suddenly. "I was beginning to think you weren't going to take no for an answer." Veronica started to rise when Cole's hands settled over her shoulders, their pressure just enough to keep her seated.

"You're tense, Ronnie," he said, as his fingers began probing her taut muscles. The warmth of his touch was sending an almost unendurable heat through her system.

"Thanks, Cole," she said hurriedly, raising her hands to brush away his gentle grip. "It's much better now."

Stubbornly he maintained his hold.

"The country air has done you good, Ronnie." Cole's husky voice was a sensual accompaniment to the feel of his hands and the heat that radiated from the strong muscular body just behind her. "I can't get over the change in you in only three weeks."

Veronica felt a rush of panic. Cole had asked her once before if it had been a long time since she'd been with a man. It was clear to her from his invitation to dinner, his flattery, and his seductive ministrations, that he was about to hint at the mutual release he thought they were both seeking. The fact that she'd likely be leaving very soon permitted Cole to indulge in an affair that would be brief and remain discreet.

"Relax," he coaxed softly as his hands worked a bit harder to disburse the increasing tension in her shoulders, his eyes never leaving her face. "And say yes about tomorrow night."

"Why?" she challenged, determined to resist the slow seduction of her will. Cole's brows rose at her tone.

"I'd like to be with you in a relaxed atmosphere where we're served good food that you don't have to tire yourself preparing." Cole's hands worked toward her neck, then paused to comb tenderly through her silken hair. "And I'd like to get to know you better."

The hot and cold shivers of pleasure caused by the teasing involvement of his fingers in her hair changed into a blazing resentment that brought her to her feet with surprising speed.

"What a clever line," she snapped, rounding on him. "Now that I'll be leaving soon, you suddenly want to get to know me better. I suppose you think I'll be so flattered I won't remember how determined you've been to avoid me all week. I might be a little susceptible to a man who knows how to push all the right buttons," she ranted, unable to hold back the anger that had simmered in the months since Eric's departure, "but experience has destroyed any illusions I might have had about men and what really motivates their interest in me." Veronica halted, then rushed on recklessly.

"If you're looking for some desperate female to relieve your male frustrations, you'd better look someplace else. You're about six months too late with this one." Cole's eyes narrowed and Veronica suddenly realised her uncontrollable outburst had revealed too much.

"Careful," Cole cautioned as he braved the temper in her violet eyes. "I think you're jumping to conclusions." Heat shot into her cheeks as her anger faltered and chagrin mingled painfully with her roiling emotions. "Just because your divorce has left you feeling wary of men, don't assume that every man who finds himself attracted to you is only looking for a release of sexual tension." Cole paused. "And I'm not in the habit of bestowing my attentions on a woman because of a warped sense of generosity. I don't feel sorry enough for any woman to take her to bed." Silence fell and left a painful awkwardness between them.

"And while we're on the subject, how long did it take for this prize-winning husband of yours to leave you with such dismal expectations of men and their motives?"

Veronica couldn't look at Cole. Fumbling fingers reached for the crutches leaning against the wall. "I don't want to talk about it," she murmured as she moved past him in as much of a retreat as she could manage.

"Maybe you'd be better off if you did," Cole suggested, his tone mellowing from harshness to a velvet rasp.

Veronica didn't comment; she'd said too much already. Strange how until her angry outburst a few moments earlier she'd only been able to feel hurt and humiliation over Eric's defection. But however strong her delayed anger had been, her charge hadn't been fair to Cole.

"I'm sorry about that little tirade, Cole. It was uncalled for. I guess I have developed a pretty negative attitude in some areas."

"You could take the first dose of cure for that negative attitude by changing your mind about tomorrow night." Cole moved closer, but didn't touch her. He didn't have to. His gentle tenacity was persuading her.

"All right," she murmured, sadly realising she wasn't strong enough to resist what could be one of her few opportunities to be with Cole before she walked out of his life forever. "I'll go with you tomorrow night."

DESPITE ALL HER BEST EFFORTS, Veronica was behaving like a teenager on her first date. She fussed over her appearance for almost two hours before she was satisfied with her makeup and her shoulder-length page-boy hairstyle. She used gold combs to draw the hair on each side of her head into soft upsweeps that accented her high cheekbones.

She found the ride into Cheyenne slightly unnerving, as she recalled being in the passenger seat with Eric driving and the awful results. Yet as if Cole was aware of her silent torment, he did his best to distract her with conversation.

Of course, Cole was a powerful distraction, and no more so than tonight in the navy slacks that encased his lean hips and muscular thighs, and the sky-blue silk shirt with the elaborately embroidered yoke that intensified the blue of his eyes. The western-cut jacket and the black dress Stetson completed the casual look of a rancher going to town on a Saturday night.

Veronica nervously adjusted a lapel of her ivory jacket, which matched her linen slacks. She'd chosen the indigo blouse beneath the jacket for the way its colour flattered her violet eyes, not realising until she'd seen Cole what a pleasing harmony of colour the two of them created with their choices of blue and ivory.

Once they were seated next to each other in the lounge of the newly opened Western Club, Veronica enjoyed the warm ambience. The booth Cole had chosen for them while they waited for a table in the dining room was upholstered in a saddle-blanket weave with carved leather insets that continued the western theme of the restaurant and lounge.

"Are you as nervous a driver as you seem to be a passenger?" Cole asked her after he'd ordered drinks. The question reminded her that she'd always found some excuse to drive herself into town, even when she and Cole were going to buy groceries together.

"No. I guess it still bothers me to ride in the passenger seat," she answered without thinking. "I had to keep reminding myself that you were so—" Veronica's face paled at what she'd almost said. Sober. Cole was sober, she'd reminded herself over and over. Eric had been drunk.

"Your mother said your accident was caused by a drunk driver," Cole probed, and Veronica was uncomfortable with the sudden interest in his eyes. The waitress came and smilingly placed their drinks in front of them, but she departed too quickly for Veronica to manage a smooth change of subject.

With a sigh she said frankly, "I was involved in one of the most preventable of drunk-driver accidents—if there is such a thing. I was sober, but I let a drunk climb behind the wheel and drive because I..." Veronica hesitated, knowing her confession would take Cole a step closer to knowing what really happened to her marriage. "Because I didn't want to risk an argument." Perhaps it was time to allow her humiliation to be aired. She had carried it so long now that she was growing more and more weary of trying to conceal it from those who didn't already know about it. Besides, all of her friends and half of New York knew the story.

Yet still she held back the entire truth. "We'd just been to a beautiful wedding and then attended the reception. It had been a perfect day I didn't want to provoke a scene," Veronica explained, listening to the recounting of the story as if it were being told by someone else. "All our friends were there, all Eric's relatives, even the press. I can remember thinking that it was only a few blocks to our hotel and the traffic was about as slow as it was going to get for New York. I made the near-fatal mistake of assuming that accidents only happen to other people. Thank God it was a one-car accident and no pedestrians were involved!"

"What happened to the driver?" Cole asked when she paused for several moments.

Veronica forced her eyes to meet Cole's as she continued, "He passed out before impact and bruised his forehead on the steering wheel. My corner of the car hit a brick building and I didn't fare nearly as well," she admitted in an attempt at light understatement. In fact she'd almost bled to death before rescue workers could free her from the wreckage.

"This driver," Cole persisted, his expression changing from repressed anger to a look of dawning realisation, "was he your husband?"

Veronica's gaze lowered to the glass she'd been twisting nervously on the cocktail napkin. "Yes." She still found herself unable to tell Cole that the wedding they'd just come from had been her wedding. Or that Eric had been shocked and sickened by the swollen black-and-blue mask that had once been his bride's face, and the battered broken body swathed in plaster and bandages. So much so that when the doctors gave Eric their initial grim prognosis for her recovery, he'd fled from the hospital—and by the time she had regained consciousness several days later, he'd fled from her life. She learned from her mother later that he'd already consulted a lawyer about an annulment.

A strong tanned hand reached for the slim one in her lap and gave it a consoling squeeze. Veronica forced a smile and looked up into the eyes of the man who sat next to her in the booth. She saw sympathy there, but not pity. Thank God she didn't see pity. That she couldn't have stood. Still, she wasn't ready to tell Cole the rest of it. Not yet. Besides, what she'd told him already threatened to put a pall of gloom over the entire evening and she didn't want that. Not with Cole.

"What about the new cook, Mrs. Engstrom?" Veronica asked, changing the unhappy direction the conversation had taken. "Do you think you're going to hire her?" The thought of the cook's eccentricities made Veronica's eyes twinkle with amusement, and she had to bite her lip to keep from smiling.

Cole's brows went up as he shook his head. "I've rarely heard a man cuss the way that woman did today. She was a good cook, but I heard words come out of that mouth that'd scald the hair off a dog. It's a wonder the smoke detectors didn't go off."

Veronica wasn't able to hold back any longer, and she dissolved into laughter, "I thought Teddy and Jim were going to faint from embarrassment," she gasped when she was able to control her mirth. "And Shorty! His face went so red it was nearly purple!"

"It was probably all that blue air that made it look purple," Cole added, joining Veronica in her laughter. Their joking went on for several minutes—until the moment Cole happened to glance toward the door. The change that came over his happy relaxed expression prompted Veronica to look in the same direction.

Helen and her husband, Bob, stood in the doorway to the lounge with Jessica Ryan and a man Veronica recognized as Wylie Edwards, a local rancher. Helen and Jessie seemed to spy Cole and Veronica at the same time, and there was no mistaking the subject of the conspiratorial whispering between the two women. Helen guided Bob in their direction just long enough for him to see Cole and think it was his idea to stop by their table to say hello.

Veronica glanced sideways at Cole to see if he had interpreted Helen's manoeuvering the way she had, but he seemed to be taking a lot of belated interest in his drink.

When Veronica looked again at the approaching couples and saw the possessive way Wylie Edwards had hooked his arm around Jessie's waist, she realised what had prompted Cole's quick change. He was jealous.

CHAPTER SEVEN

"BY GOLLY, COLE," Bob was saying in his typical fashion as he grasped Cole's hand and pumped it firmly. "What are you doin' in a place like this when you got Veronica cookin' for you at home?" Veronica blushed at the compliment from one of her most recent admirers. Bob had been over at noon one day and had left raving about the delicious casserole she'd prepared.

"If I don't give her a night off once in a while, I might find myself doing my own cooking again," Cole joked back before he greeted Helen and Jessie. His nod to Wylie was cool.

"Say, it isn't often we're all together like this," Helen piped up, beaming at the group. "Do you mind if we join you?"

Put that way, how could she and Cole refuse, Veronica thought sourly. Both couples slid into the horseshoe-shaped booth, crowding Veronica and Cole closer together physically, but driving them apart in every other way, as the conversation around the table centred on topics that excluded Veronica. They'd been sitting there only a few moments before Helen made a second suggestion—that they all change their table reservations in the dining room to avoid dividing the happy group.

Jessie echoed Helen's suggestion, and in an instant Veronica and Cole had become part of a party of six. Veronica felt much of the evening's pleasure fade. Even if Cole had wanted to, there was no polite way for him to refuse.

It was clear to Veronica that happy-go-lucky Bob was oblivious to his wife's impromptu scheme. Besides, he seemed to thoroughly enjoy the fun and companionship of a group, the bigger the better. Poor Wylie was looking at Jessie as if he'd walk over hot coals for her, while Cole, sipping his drink, appeared to have temporarily withdrawn into himself. Veronica became convinced that he wished he'd asked Jessie out instead.

So she kept a polite silence, toying with the swizzle stick in her drink, listening to the happy conversation, yet feeling as distinctly separate from this group of old friends as if she'd been seated at the next table. And when they were ushered into the dining room, Veronica felt even more dismal when Jessie was seated on the other side of Cole.

Despite what Veronica expected, Cole made certain she was included, deliberately drawing her into the conversation. Their decision to order the dinner for two—they both found the roast tenderloin of beef with Madeira sauce appealing—enabled them to be involved with each other much more closely than if they'd each chosen something different.

And from the dagger looks Jessie gave her, Veronica was certain neither she nor Helen cared for the fact that for dessert Cole ordered one piece of the disgustingly rich chocolate fudge cheesecake with the understanding that Veronica share it with him.

"I admire a man who knows when to pull away from the table," Bob commented, a mischievous twinkle in his eyes. "Since you and Veronica have been dividin' everything tonight, I reckon you've noticed her cookin' is startin' to put a little weather boarding around your middle." Cole looked anything but amused as he drew open his jacket to glance at his stomach. When he looked up, his sheepish grin brought a chorus of laughter.

"Speaking of cooking," Helen put in, "when does that woman you had come in today start working for you, Cole?"

Cole grimaced and Veronica watched his profile with amusement as he explained Mrs. Engstrom's colourful dialect. Neither Helen nor Jessie concealed their disappointment very successfully when Cole told them in no uncertain terms that he wouldn't consider hiring the woman.

"If I could clone Ronnie, I'd have just what I'm looking for," Cole told his friends, and Veronica flushed with pleasure at his outspoken praise. Cole raised his arm then and settled it warmly over her shoulders. He didn't remove it until dessert arrived.

After dinner the group migrated back to a table in the bar that looked out over the dance floor. Jessie and Helen excused themselves and went off in search of the ladies room. A few moments later, Veronica decided to follow, making her way carefully with her crutches through the evening crowd. The door to the ladies room had just swished closed behind her when she heard Helen's voice.

"I certainly wouldn't let it upset me, Jess," she was saying. "Besides, you can't possibly think that Cole honestly prefers Veronica to you. Look at her."

Veronica had heard enough. She had just turned to make a quiet retreat when Jessie spoke.

"So you think this is just a mercy date?" Jessie asked.

"What else could it be? About all she can really do is cook. She doesn't even have much of a personality."

Stunned at the cruel words, Veronica stepped into the small sitting room area just outside. Was she really only a "mercy date"? Getting a firm grip on herself, she re-entered the room noisily, making sure her presence was noticed. There was absolute silence as she repaired her makeup and ran a brush quickly through her hair. After Helen and Jessie left, Veronica waited a few moments before heading back, determined to forget what she'd just heard.

"Come on, Cole." Jessie was saying, her perfect lips set in an appealing pout as she tugged on Cole's arm. "Dance with me. You know how I love to dance to fast numbers."

Bob and Helen were already on the dance floor, and Bob was swinging Helen around with more enthusiasm than grace. Wylie danced only to slow music, and this gave Jessie the opportunity to pursue Cole.

"Go ahead," Veronica said at his questioning glance, forcing a smile to let him know she didn't mind. But she did. It had been a long time since she'd danced and she suddenly wanted more than anything to have the grace and freedom to be able to get on a dance floor. She wanted to dance even more as she watched Cole go off with Jessie, joining the thickening crowd of dancers.

Sullen and in obvious bad temper, Wylie ordered a double vodka, which he drank broodingly as he watched his date dance with Cole. When Jessie persuaded Cole to stay with her for a second number, Wylie moved into the chair next to Veronica.

"Now that she's got him, this is what it will be like the rest of the night," he predicted glumly.

"Surely not," Veronica said with far more confidence than she felt. Although she knew that Cole wouldn't abandon her for the evening, she couldn't say the same for Jessie's sense of fairness. There was no doubt in her mind that Jessie could easily arrive with one man and spend all her time with another without feeling the slightest twinge of conscience.

"Damn!" Wylie's voice could be heard in the lull between songs. When the band started a new number, a slow one this time, Wylie grew even angrier. "Look at them," he said, nodding toward Cole and Jessie. "They aren't going to stop till morning." Wylie downed the rest of his drink in one gulp and motioned to the waitress to bring another.

Veronica knew that with Wylie it was the booze talking, but as she watched Cole and Jessie together on the dance floor, she had difficulty fighting her own jealousy. They looked perfect together. Jessie's voluptuous body was pressed sensually against the lean hardness of Cole's, her blonde cover-girl looks providing the perfect complement to Cole's rugged dark handsomeness.

Suddenly, Veronica found herself wishing Cole would hire Mrs. Engstrom. If he did, she'd be leaving in a day or so, before these hopeless feelings grew into something with a far greater potential to destroy her. *I barely survived what Eric did,* she thought, *and if I fall in love with Cole, how will I recover from that?* It came as a shock to realise that the emotion Cole aroused in her was far more intense than what she'd felt for Eric. But her shock was even greater as she realised she was already deeply in love with Cole.

How had it happened? How could she have blundered into something as dangerous as falling in love with Cole after the way she'd been hurt by Eric?

"Nothing keeps that woman from chasing Cole," she heard Wylie grouse. "If she ever got any real competition for him, she might get discouraged and give up." Wylie took another drink. "Hell." Wylie's glass hit the table top with a thud. "I'm not gonna just sit here like some mongrel dog and wait for her to come back to the table. I spent too damned much money on her tonight to put up with this." Wylie turned his head and stared at Veronica with drunken intensity for a moment. "You want me to drive you home?"

The colour fled from her cheeks at the very thought of getting into a car with anyone in Wylie's condition.

"They've only danced a couple of dances together," she said reasonably. "Let's give them a little more time." Wylie lurched back in his chair and his anger seemed to subside, but Veronica realised his dark mood was affecting her. She was beginning to feel as jilted and unwelcome as he did, perhaps more.

As she studied Wylie's profile, she decided that this hazel-eyed young man with sun-streaked brown hair was more than marginally attractive. He and Jessie would make a nice-looking couple, but it was plain that Wylie felt far more for the beautiful Jessie than she felt for him. Veronica understood his hurt and disappointment all too well.

When the song ended, Cole and Jessie made their way back to the table while Bob and Helen remained on the dance floor for the slow tune that followed. Jessie took her seat next to Wylie, a sense of obligation in her sulking manner. Veronica watched her and Wylie together, amazed at how their less-than-cheerful dispositions made them well suited to each other.

As Veronica sipped her drink, she felt awkward knowing that Cole had probably returned to the table out of consideration for her and Wylie rather than out of genuine desire to be with her. He and Jessie had surely been having a much better time with each other than they could expect to have with their respective dates.

Cole was still standing. He touched Veronica's shoulder, and she turned her head, her gaze travelling up his long lean body to the darkly handsome face smiling down at her. The evening was over. The thought had her fumbling for her bag.

"You don't need your bag to dance," Cole said as he removed the purse strap from her fingers.

"But I can't dance," she said.

"Yes you can," he said smiling. "I'll help you."

Feeling uncoordinated and more than a little embarrassed, she reached for her crutches.

"You don't need them," he said as he helped her up and assisted her to the edge of the dance floor. Moments later, she was in his arms, moving stiffly in contrast to his masculine grace. Cole led with a small stepping pattern to accommodate her, and even though their embrace gave her legs all the support she needed, Veronica was all too aware of her awkwardness.

"Relax," Cole growled. "Don't worry about winning any dance contests. Just listen to the music and let your body do what it feels." Veronica looked up into his face and was drawn to the intensity of his gaze. Violet eyes registered the unmistakable change that came into Cole's as the darker blue deepened, their pupils widening until only a tiny rim of colour surrounded the blackness.

She was dimly aware of the softness and gradual pliancy of her body against Cole's hard thighs. The strength of the large frame she was pressed ever tighter against sent her into a near-hypnotic state of arousal. Cole moved to the rhythm of the music whether she faltered or not and the very constancy of his movements suffused her body with sensual heat and made her weak with wanting. She hardly noticed when one slow song melded into the next. She was aware only of the power and male vigour of the body that guided her, supported her and subtly brought her femininity to life.

Cole's arms tightened until she was against him fully, her cheek pressed against his broad chest. Her eyes were just drifting closed blissfully, inhaling Cole's warmth and scent of after-shave, when she caught sight of Wylie and Jessie on the dance floor.

The venomous look Jessie gave her over Wylie's shoulder was chilling, sobering, snapping Veronica from her daze of sensuality. For Jessie's displeasure, Veronica knew, could have unpleasant consequences. More than once in the time Veronica had spent at the ranch years earlier, she had unwittingly been manoeuvered and victimised by Jessie's vengeance. Jessie and Wylie disappeared from view when Cole angled their steps in a new direction.

"You and Jessie still have it in for each other, don't you?" Cole's question was more a statement of fact than a question, and Veronica pulled away slightly to look up into his frowning expression.

"I don't have it in for Jessie," Veronica said.

Cole's face hardened and his eyes shifted away from hers. "Jessie denied it, too."

"Well, Jessie is—" Veronica stopped her angry exclamation, frustrated that she couldn't be candid about Jessie without sounding vindictive.

"Lying?" Cole supplied for her, the smirk on his lips conveying his scepticism.

Just like before, Veronica thought, astonished at the old feeling of helplessness. Cole had never been able to see through Jessie's perfidy. Veronica abruptly stopped dancing, and made a move to leave the floor.

Cole's hands clamped like steel around her narrow waist. "You're really worked up, aren't you?" His eyes narrowed with faint incredulity on Veronica's flushed face. Violet eyes that sparkled with anger stared back steadily, defiantly.

"Yes, I'm angry," she said as calmly as her quivering voice would allow. "Jessie could tell you the earth was flat and you'd believe it." Veronica was unaware of the sudden glint of perception in Cole's expression. Her eyes shied guiltily from his and her slim fingers tightened on the thickly muscled forearms beneath her hands.

"I'm sorry," she murmured contritely. "You love Jessie and I shouldn't have said anything against her. Please don't let anything I've said colour your relationship with her." Veronica again tried to move away, her eyes veering apprehensively to his when he didn't release her.

"Would you stay and dance with me some more?" Cole asked as the band began another slow tune. The inviting smile on his face brought an uncertain curve to her lips.

"You aren't angry with me?" Now it was Veronica's turn to look surprised.

"I wasn't angry in the first place," Cole rumbled softly, as he pulled her close and began to lead her gently in the dance.

But as Veronica relaxed in his arms and felt her senses succumb to Cole's nearness, she knew they were both less than pleased with the way the evening had turned out.

CHAPTER EIGHT

"YOU DON'T WANT CURTIS to have any fun, do you?" Jessie hissed at Veronica, berating her for her cautiousness.

The two young women were standing in the yard between the house and the driveway, one wearing soiled garden gloves and old clothes with grass stains on the knees, the other dressed in a bright red halter top and designer jeans, her sunglasses parked on top of her lush golden head. Curtis stood in the back of Jessie's green pickup watching the two argue, the mutiny on his young face a clear indication of who championed his cause.

"I mean it, Jessie," Veronica insisted. "I won't let you take Curtis without Cole's permission, and even with it he'd have to be buckled into a seat belt inside the cab of that pickup."

"What gives you the right to say what Curtis does or doesn't do?" the blonde challenged.

"Cole left Curtis with me for the morning. He's not going anywhere without Cole's permission, and when he gives it I'm going to suggest that allowing you to give Curtis a wild ride into town in the back of that truck is dangerous."

"My God, Veronica. Curtis has ridden all over this ranch in the back of pickups from the time he could walk." Jessie's arm swung in a belligerent arc.

"That may be, Jessie, but I doubt very much that anyone around here pulls stunts like you did just coming in here. If you had wanted to convince me that you're a responsible driver, you shouldn't have fishtailed the last quarter mile then slammed on the brakes just in time to miss my car by a hair's breadth."

"I know what I'm doing, Ronnie," Jessie insisted. "I'm in control of that truck every moment."

"And that's what makes you such a dangerous driver—you think you're in control. You've been trusting a lot to luck and I won't let you take chances with the boy's life." Veronica was immovable on the subject. She had spent enough time in hospitals and rehabilitation centres to have seen and heard several horror stories, most of the heartbreakingly tragic ones concerning children who had become tiny projectiles in relatively minor accidents because they were not properly restrained in car safety seats or seat belts.

"Oh, I get it." Now the amber eyes were narrowed, speculative. "You really are after Cole, aren't you? You must think that keeping Curtis from spending time with me will cut me off from both of them."

Veronica was distressed at Jessie's words. Furthermore she was sure that Curtis could hear every word—whatever Jessie's faults, Veronica knew the boy idolised the woman.

"I am not 'after' Cole," Veronica said quietly, struggling to keep her agitation under control. "And I have no objection to you taking Curtis anywhere—if you get Cole's permission first and see that Curtis wears a seat belt while he's in the truck with you."

"But I've had Curtis ride with me a hundred times and he's never got so much as a scratch," Jessie said dismissively. "All you have to do is tell Cole when he comes to the house that I've taken Curtis into Cheyenne for the day. He won't mind." Jessie turned away and strode toward her truck. Curtis's face broke into a big smile as he obviously assumed Jessie had got her way.

"Jessie!" Veronica moved swiftly on her crutches after her, desperate to keep Jessie from undermining her authority and endangering Curtis. *If anything happens to that boy while he is in my care...* Veronica was terrified at the thought. "Wait Jessie! You can't just drive off with the boy."

But Jessie ignored her and was striding around the truck to the driver's side when Veronica reached the passenger door. Quickened by frustration and concern, Veronica jerked the door open and climbed in far enough to pull the keys from the ignition. She had just closed the door and slipped the keys into her jeans pocket when Jessie came around the truck to confront her.

"That was a childish thing to do, Veronica!"

"Childish or not, you're going to get Cole's permission first." Veronica's eyes shifted from Jessie's furious face to Curtis's scowl. "Come on, Curtis. Let's go find your father." Veronica turned to head in the direction of the barns, then froze when she saw Cole's iron expression as he stood watching from the corner of the house.

"What's going on here?" Cole's gaze slid from Jessie to Veronica, his look seeming to lay the blame equally between them. "You can give Jessie back her keys."

Veronica felt her face warm as she realised Cole had seen how she'd come to have Jessie's keys in her pocket. Removing her glove, she dug into her jeans and handed them to a triumphant Jessie.

"I told you, didn't I?" Jessie said to Veronica, giving Cole a knowing look that made Veronica feel small.

"Come down out of the truck, Curtis," Cole said. "You're not going anywhere."

Suddenly Jessie didn't look so triumphant as Curtis reluctantly obeyed, but began whining to know why.

"Go to your room, son. I'll be in to explain why in a little while." Curtis's lower lip was trembling and Veronica's heart went out to him. When Curtis went inside, Cole moved closer to Veronica and Jessie.

"I don't want Curtis witnessing anything like this again." Cole's stern look included them both. "Jessie, Curtis was Veronica's responsibility, and from now on I expect you to abide by her decisions without passing judgment on them in front of Curtis. And I don't want you to make any remarks to him later, either," Cole added before his voice went less stern. "I'd appreciate it if you'd forget about taking Curtis today. Maybe one day next week you can stop by."

Jessie looked stricken. "But Cole—"

"Please, Jessie." Cole's voice was gentle, regretful, and Jessie seemed to brighten. Flashing Veronica a satisfied look, Jessie strode off with her usual easy grace and climbed into the pickup. The smirk that marred her perfect mouth told Veronica whom the woman believed would bear the brunt of Cole's displeasure. When the green pickup roared out of earshot, Veronica faced Cole.

"I'm not sorry, Cole," she told him firmly. "And I was going to insist that you not allow Curtis to go with her even if she did agree to buckle him in a seat belt. She's just too reckless."

"I saw the way she drove up," Cole said grimly, his eyes running over Veronica's defiant look.

"I think it would be a good idea if you kept Curtis with you when he's home," she said. "I can't guarantee he won't be in the middle of something just as unpleasant in the future." She took a steadying breath. "And I just don't want the responsibility of taking care of him." Besides, she thought bleakly, Curtis resented her presence and would barely heed anything she said.

"If that's the way you feel." Cole let his voice trail off, his jaw flexing with what she thought was ill-concealed displeasure. "But I think you ought to know that there's no doubt in my mind that you have Curtis's safety and best interests at heart. After what I just saw, I trust you completely with my son."

Veronica frowned in confusion. "But I handled it all wrong." She was thinking of the way she'd grabbed Jessie's keys and stuffed them into her pocket when she couldn't think of a more mature way to handle the situation.

"Jessie didn't exactly leave you with many polite options," Cole acknowledged, then paused. "I'm sorry, Ronnie. I didn't realise how spiteful Jessie could be with you when she thinks no one else is around."

Veronica found herself smiling.

"And I can tell by the look on your face that I'm several years late with that observation." Cole was restlessly slapping the work gloves he had in one hand into the palm of the other.

"Better late than never," Veronica hazarded as she tugged the soiled garden glove back on her hand. The action drew Cole's gaze downward. He glanced toward the flower bed where she'd been working, and Veronica watched him closely for any sign of disapproval.

She hadn't asked permission to weed the overgrown beds. The bright Sunday morning air had enticed her out and since it was her regular day off, she'd planned to spend the day recovering some of the straggly perennials from the weeds. Cole turned and walked toward the house, wordlessly surveying the garbage bag of weeds and debris she'd gleaned and the extra bag she hadn't opened yet. The dark earth around each little plant she'd saved had been tilled with a hand rake, then carefully watered.

"I hope you don't mind." She spoke to Cole's uncommunicative back. He didn't answer right away. Instead he crouched down and tenderly ran a finger beneath a mum leaf.

"It's a wonder any of these have survived." Cole spoke so softly that Veronica almost thought he was talking to himself. "For quite a while after Jackie died, I had someone keep these up. I guess I haven't thought too much about them lately." Cole was quiet and Veronica sensed he was remembering.

Suddenly the tragedy of Jackie's death and how hard Cole must have taken it brought a wave of sadness over her. It was apparent that Cole had been very much in love with Jackie, and in his letters to Veronica, Hank had always said that if it hadn't been for Curtis, Cole might not have recovered.

How different Cole was from the way she remembered him. And now that she was getting to know him, she found him to be the reverse of the harsh unfriendly stepbrother she could never please as an adolescent.

Her gentle heart suddenly constricted with sadness and compassion, and Veronica felt, to her consternation, the welling of tears in her eyes. Cole stood up, and self-consciously, she tried to blink the tears away before they could fall, but Cole had already seen. He stepped closer.

"I'm such a sentimental sap," she kidded, smiling sheepishly. A warm callus-toughened palm came up to cup her cheek. Her eyes had cleared now and were fixed on the compelling blue of Cole's. Veronica's senses began to reel as Cole's lips came over hers in a tender chaste kiss.

In the next moment, his other hand circled her waist and pressed her almost fiercely against the hard thrust of his hips. The tenderness vanished at the burst of raw hunger in his kiss. Her mouth opened, craving more, and Cole needed no clearer invitation. She fairly melted in his arms as his tongue did things to hers that left her trembling, her insides like warm butter.

"I want you, Ronnie," he murmured against her lips. "I think I'd do just about anything to keep you here with me."

Reality whirled away into the distance, and Veronica wondered if she'd just imagined Cole's words. He moved his lips to the soft flesh of her throat, then nibbled a path to her ear.

"Will you stay?" his warm mouth whispered. "It will be good between us, Ronnie."

Veronica's heart thrilled to the velvet edge of his gruff voice, to the sensual promise of more of this taste of heaven. At first she resisted the weak intrusion of sanity, as her slumberous eyes opened to the passion-blackened depths of his.

"What I feel for you just won't go away," he was saying. Veronica was too lovestruck to recognise the difference between what she'd longed to hear from Cole and what he'd actually said. Joy welled up inside and Veronica pulled his mouth back to hers, taking her turn at loving aggression. Cole's ragged breathing mingled with hers, his arms tightening almost painfully around her slenderness. Now she recognised the difference between the love she'd thought she'd felt for Eric and the blinding intensity of the love she now had for Cole.

"If we don't stop this…" he murmured. "Just stand still for a moment." Veronica was only too happy to comply, delighted that Cole was struggling to restrain his arousal—his arousal for her. He released her slowly.

"Curtis will think I've forgotten about him." Cole's lips quirked before they came down on hers for a last brief kiss. Then he was leaning down for her fallen crutches. "We'll take up where we left off after Curtis goes to bed tonight," he promised in a rough whisper.

Veronica was helpless to keep her eyes from following Cole as he started to walk away from her toward the back of the house. He turned momentarily, his eyes still burning as they raked over her in a promise of possession that sent a fresh flood of weakness through her system. Then he disappeared around the corner of the house and went inside.

SANITY DIDN'T RETURN IMMEDIATELY, and Veronica had finished her work in the flowerbed before niggling little doubts began to creep in. Facing Cole over the kitchen table at lunch with a sullen little Curtis between them had brought what was really happening into clearer focus. By supper that evening, Veronica's feet had finally touched earth.

I want you, Ronnie… it will be good between us… I'm afraid I won't be able to wait… again and again Cole's words paraded through her mind. *We'll take up where we left off after Curtis goes to bed tonight,* he had said.

Cole was offering her an affair.

Veronica squeezed her eyes closed and felt like an idiot. How had she let her love for Cole get so out of hand that she'd been unable to understand what he had so clearly said? If she'd doubted her sanity after Eric deserted her, she was certain she was more than a little crazy now. And when Cole came to her room as he seemed to have every intention of doing, how would he react when he saw her scars and found out the truth about her marriage to Eric?

Heartsick, Veronica realised she had to seek him out—talk to him, make some excuse. Perhaps she could defuse the whole situation before it blew up in her face.

Veronica moved nervously into the hall, then stopped. She was as close now as she was going to come to telling Cole everything about her marriage to Eric. *Would that be so bad,* she asked herself.

Before she'd come back to Wyoming, she'd dreaded Cole's finding out about her marriage to Eric because of her fear that he'd either make the obvious comparison between her and her mother, or worse, tell her outright he wasn't surprised that Eric had wised up and dumped her before he'd consummated the marriage. Getting to know Cole better had slowly eroded those fears, but what would Cole say if she admitted her lack of experience and told him she wouldn't, couldn't, let their relationship go any further? Forcing herself to get it over with, Veronica moved down the hall to the den.

Cole looked up when she stepped into the doorway. Seeing her, he leaned back in the big chair behind his desk, his gaze lazily appraising her slender body. For the umpteenth time that day, Veronica was reminded of the ugliness he'd see if he saw her unclothed.

Funny how she'd consoled herself with the psychologist's assurances that the man who truly fell in love with her would not mind the scars. Now that she'd come this close to intimacy with Cole, she realised she hadn't really believed those assurances.

"I'd like to talk to you, Cole." Veronica suddenly had trouble maintaining eye contact with the roving gaze that had returned to rest on her flushed face.

"I was just finishing up in here," Cole said, his look gently chiding her for what he must have assumed was impatience.

"What we need to talk about has to be discussed before then," she said, her voice as firm and as determined as she could manage.

"Having second thoughts?" There was only a touch of sternness in Cole's voice. From the almost indulgent smile on his face Veronica knew he was confident that a few kisses would remove any reservations she might have acquired since late morning. It also confirmed that Cole did indeed intend for them to make love.

Veronica was extremely apprehensive and her hands clenched and unclenched on the crutch grips. "I misled you this morning, Cole," she began, watching the slight narrowing of his eyes. "Not intentionally," she hurried to add, "but I just got...carried away. I know it was unfair of me to allow you to think I would be willing to..." She paused nervously. "I guess I wasn't...thinking clearly." Her stumbling speech must have sounded absurd. "I'm sorry."

Cole's expression turned flintlike before he glanced away from her, a crease forming slowly between his dark brows. When his eyes came back to hers, she could discern nothing of what he was thinking other than he must be angry with her.

"Do you want something a little more permanent than what you thought I was offering this morning?" Cole's gaze was intent, and probing.

"I don't want you to misunderstand me," she said, her voice sounding abysmally virginal. "I realise you can't offer me a permanent relationship—not that I'm trying to pressure or coerce you into one," she assured him hastily, her mouth going dry. "But I can't have an affair with you." Cole stared at her steadily, unnerving her with his ongoing silence.

"Do you want some kind of commitment from me?" A speculative gleam darkened his eyes.

"I'm not asking for one, Cole."

"But there can be nothing more between us if I don't make one," he surmised grimly, yet without anger.

"That's right," Veronica murmured, suddenly unable to think of anything but the promise of heaven she was forcing herself to give up.

"Then I guess I'll see you at breakfast." Cole's total attention returned to what he'd been working on when she'd interrupted. Veronica accepted the aloof dismissal and retreated dismally to her room.

CHAPTER NINE

FOR THE NEXT TWO WEEKS, Veronica's life settled into a pattern of work and exercise. She walked a mile a day and took Honey Lamb out regularly, riding the gentle mare around a small pasture near one of the barns where the gregarious Shorty was within shouting distance.

The increase in exercise had been hard on her, but in the past day or so her body seemed to have adjusted and her physical therapist was pleased with her progress. She would be trading in her crutches for a walking cane any time now and she was eager for the change.

She saw Cole only at mealtimes, unless he was in the house doing paperwork. Even then, if she wasn't preparing a meal or cleaning up after one, she slipped outside for a walk or to work in the flower beds.

Curtis was home a lot more, but he was with Cole, except when Cole went out for the evening. Then Shorty or Teddy's teenaged sister, Brenda, would come in.

Veronica had a lot of early nights, partly because she was worn out by seven-thirty, but more because she didn't want to know when Cole came home. She'd heard enough speculation from Shorty to guess that on most evenings Cole was with Jessie.

It hurt that Cole could so quickly and completely turn to pursuing Jessie. But it was just as well, she told herself, that she'd seen how easily the shallow interest Cole had shown in her could be switched to someone else. If Veronica had entertained any fairy-tale notions about Cole being the man of her dreams, they were gone now.

Cole's remoteness made Veronica feel they were no longer even friends. She could see that soon she would find living in the same house with Cole and his recalcitrant son intolerable.

"YOUR MOTHER CALLED while you were in town," Cole said as he came into the kitchen for a glass of iced tea. Veronica had just returned from a session with the physical therapist and was tiredly contemplating a nap before she started dinner preparations.

"I'll call her later," Veronica replied as she tossed her car keys onto their usual spot beside the sugar canister.

"She sounded upset," Cole added, and Veronica allowed herself to look at Cole for the first time since he'd come into the room.

Unfair! her heart cried when she was suddenly weakened by the sight of Cole leaning against the counter, sipping his tea, his indolent pose reminding Veronica what it felt like to be pressed against the length of his solidly male form. Unaware that Cole had seen both the slow sweep of her violet eyes and the tinge of colour that had come into her cheeks, Veronica tried to bring her attention back to what he had just said.

"What did she want?" Veronica was too tired to waste any of her available rest time on the phone for a false alarm. Sometimes her mother tended to exaggerate.

"She was upset with me," Cole said, the quirk of his lips telling her what he thought of that.

"It seems to me we agreed you would be polite to my mother," she reminded him, a touch of anger coming into eyes that had seemed almost spiritless to Cole for the past two weeks.

"I was the perfect gentleman," he assured her. "Even when she jumped all over me for taking advantage of you."

A frown crossed Veronica's face. "Where did she get an idea like that?" She could think of nothing she'd said that would have given her mother that impression.

"She doesn't like the idea of your working for me. She says I've taken advantage of your generosity long enough."

"Mother said that?" Veronica couldn't imagine her mother standing up to Cole or challenging him in any way. Men like Cole had always cowed her.

"That, and more." Cole sipped his drink, watching her over the top of the glass.

"More?"

"She's afraid you're going to fall in love with me." High colour stung her cheeks at Cole's words. "She's afraid you're too vulnerable after what Eric did to you."

Veronica was mortified. What else had her mother told him?

"I apologise. I'm sorry Mother jumped to such awkward conclusions." Veronica hastened across the room toward the phone extension. "I guess this is one call that shouldn't wait." Veronica hoped her brisk manner would assure Cole that her mother's fears were unfounded. She couldn't let either of them know that it was a little late for motherly concern.

She had just begun to dial the number when Cole came up behind her and slipped his arms around her waist. Enveloped in the electric warmth that pressed against the entire length of her body, Veronica misdialled. Surprise brought her head around just in time for her lips to brush Cole's. But before she could succumb to their firm sensuality she turned her face away again, then silently endured a further shock to her system when Cole nudged aside her shoulder-length hair and began placing slow lingering kisses on her neck just beneath her ear.

Lethargy spread through her system, clouding rational thought. She opened her mouth to voice some false words of vague outrage and heard herself give a melting sigh. Cole evidently took that for encouragement and nuzzled against her ear before he traced the delicate shell with his tongue and nibbled the sensitive lobe.

"Now," Cole whispered with husky satisfaction when he felt her go slack in his arms. "Now you can tell your mother

all about how living with me hasn't affected you much one
way or the other.''

It took a few seconds for Cole's gently mocking words to
penetrate the seductive haze. When they did, Veronica made
a movement of protest and Cole released her to accommodate her step away from him.

She had just turned toward him, her face awash in embarrassed colour, when he picked up his glass of iced tea and left
the kitchen. Veronica put down the telephone receiver, then
picked it up again and shakily redialled, hoping her mother
would not detect the tremor in her voice or the confusion in
her less-than-honest denials.

"ARE YOU CERTAIN this is what you want to do?" Helen's
voice, coming from the hall outside Cole's bedroom,
reached Veronica's ears.

Her fitful nap was due to be over soon, but the sounds of
activity in the house had awakened her a few minutes earlier than she had planned. She stepped into the bathroom
and ran a brush through her hair hoping to give Helen a
chance to go back into the main part of the house. Evidently she had arrived with Curtis.

But when Veronica went out into the hall, she heard Helen in Cole's bedroom. As she reached the doorway, she
could see Helen and Cole standing in front of the large
wardrobe, boxes littering the floor nearby. Cole happened
to glance Veronica's way and she allowed his gaze to hold
hers only momentarily before she continued past the door
on her way to the kitchen.

"Hello, Curtis," Veronica called cheerfully as she entered the kitchen. Curtis mumbled a response but didn't favour her with a look. Standing on the counter top in his
dusty sneakers, he was busy going through one of the upper cupboards.

"What are you looking for?" Veronica hoped to find
some way of getting his dirty shoes off the counter without
directly asking the boy to get down.

"I'm hungry," Curtis announced.

"There's some fruit in the refrigerator, but if you'd rather have something else, the cookie jar is full. Just be sure you put the milk away if you get it out." Veronica made her way to the sink and washed her hands while she waited for Curtis to get down. But when she turned around again, he was digging into another shelf.

"Why don't you get down from the counter, Curtis? There's nothing up there but canned goods and baking supplies."

"No."

"Come on, Curtis," Veronica prompted, pasting a neutral smile on her face as she crossed to the boy and touched his arm. Curtis jerked away as if her fingers had burned him, but Veronica gave every impression of not noticing. "You get out the milk and I'll put some cookies on a plate."

Her suggestion was ignored. Curtis continued to shove canned goods around, making chaos of the precise placement Veronica made in order to keep better track of what to buy on her weekly grocery trips to town. She and Cole had spent a lot of time organising what Curtis was so pointlessly disrupting.

"Can you read the labels on those cans?" she asked as he moved to a lower shelf and continued to rummage.

"I can read," he answered sulkily, and Veronica felt her irritation rising at the boy's continual show of defiance.

"Good," she said. "Then when you've finished looking for something that's not up there, you can go back and put every can and box back exactly the way you found it." That earned her Curtis's complete, although hostile, attention.

"That's your job." Those words had become Curtis's pet refrain.

"Normally it is," Veronica agreed, her patient-sounding voice and manner worthy of an award. "But when you come along and make a mess of my work, I think it's only fair that you fix it. It's a good way to make certain you don't make the same mistake again."

"This is my house—mine and my dad's," Curtis corrected. "You just work here." Curtis returned to what he was doing, obviously satisfied that the matter had been dealt with.

"I hope you aren't this rude to everyone, Curtis," Veronica commented before she braced herself for more unpleasantness. "You can begin with the top shelf."

There was complete silence for a fraction of a second before Curtis gave the canned goods on the lower shelf a parting shove. The cupboard door banged shut and Curtis started to get down. Veronica stepped deliberately into his path.

"I don't have to do what you want." Curtis's sassy look was far removed from the solemn-eyed reserve she'd once found so adorable.

She was suddenly reminded of how she'd felt when a new man began making inroads into her mother's life. After Jessie's comment that day two weeks ago, Curtis likely believed her presence threatened Jessie's relationship with his father. Despite her momentary irritation with the boy, Veronica felt compassion for him, concerned about the needless worry he was being put through. Nevertheless she didn't intend to allow Curtis to bully her.

"I'm afraid you do this time, Curtis," she said firmly. "I need to start working on your supper." They stared at each other for a moment, defiance sparkling in his grey eyes before they wavered toward a movement in the doorway to the hall. Instantly his little lip thrust out endearingly and his grey eyes went tragically woebegone.

"What's going on, Veronica?" Helen demanded as she bustled across the room and reached to cuddle Curtis protectively in her arms.

"Curtis just made a shambles of this cupboard and I told him he had to straighten it up," Veronica told her.

"Oh, for heaven's sake!" Helen scolded as she pulled Curtis down from the cupboard, forcing Veronica to move aside quickly or collide with the boy's body. "This kitchen is your responsibility, not Curtis's." Helen gave Curtis a nudge toward the porch door. "Go on outside and play until supper." Curtis hurried out, his face the picture of childish glee.

Veronica was trembling with anger. "Please don't ever interfere like that again," she told Helen once Curtis was safely out of earshot. "I'm having enough problems with him without you rushing in to take his side and cast me in the role of villain."

"Someone needed to take the boy's side just now and I intend to speak to Cole about what just happened," Helen said huffily.

"Go ahead," Veronica invited, keeping her voice even. "But be sure to tell him all of it. Cole can come in and see for himself what has become of the cupboards we spent all that time organising."

Helen looked a bit disconcerted at that, but Veronica didn't give her a chance to say more. She moved aside to another section of cupboards and noisily began taking out the things she needed to start supper. Wordlessly Helen left, easing the angry tension in the room.

"WHAT'S COLE DOIN'?" Shorty asked as he started laying out the Scrabble game he was so fond of playing. "I seen all them boxes he hauled outta here and put in Helen's car." Veronica smiled at Shorty's avid hunger for gossip. It was something he didn't even pretend to suppress.

"I think they were Jackie's things, but he didn't say," she replied as she set the controls on the dishwasher and started it.

"You didn't ask?" Shorty would have, but Veronica was not quite so bold, especially since she was almost certain she was right. Cole would probably not appreciate any questions from her about Jackie. Veronica shook her head and Shorty grunted.

"I noticed Curtis's got his ma's picture on his lamp table. It was the one that was in Cole's den from the looks of the frame." Shorty's voice lowered. "Once I seen that, I noticed Jackie's wedding keepsakes were gone out of the china cabinet in the dining room."

"Shorty!" Veronica scolded. "You are without a doubt the most..." She hesitated, a teasing grin on her face. "Let's just say you're observant."

"Observant?" Shorty looked somewhat offended.

"I'm too polite to tell you I think you're nosy. Observant sounded much more tactful," Veronica said, then giggled when Shorty pointed at her waggishly.

"You'd better watch that, gal," he threatened. "T-a-c-t don't get as many points in Scrabble as n-o-s-y does," he said, referring to the point values the game gave each letter.

"Is that so?" Veronica challenged as she stationed herself across the table from the weathered old cowhand. "You're going to have to think of some more clever uses for any high-value letters you happen to draw tonight," she warned him playfully. "I plan to give you a little stronger competition than I did last time."

Veronica was a bit embarrassed to admit it, but when she and Shorty first started playing Scrabble together, she hadn't expected him to be so good at a vocabulary game. Her rather low expectations had left her unprepared for her repeated losses to him. Shorty might have been one of the most casual speakers she'd ever known, but his reading vocabulary was really quite vast.

"It looks to me like the boss is fixin' to pop the question on someone about any time now," Shorty piped up later as he carefully laid out the right combination of letters on high-value spaces to earn himself twenty-seven points. Veronica added the total to Shorty's rapidly climbing score, his statement bringing a pain she could barely conceal from her pale features.

"Do you think he's really ready to remarry?" she managed in her best casual manner, shocked at the realisation that she found the thought of Cole's remarrying intolerable.

"Yep, I do."

Veronica laid out the letters for her next word and silently counted up the pitifully low number of points it gained her. Suddenly she just wanted to finish the game—

anything to hasten the end of this distressing turn of conversation.

"Course, at this point, it's mighty hard to tell which one the boss'll choose," Shorty jabbered on.

"What do you mean, which one?" Veronica couldn't help asking. Was there someone besides Jessie? "I thought you said Cole was seeing Jessie nearly every evening."

"I didn't say that," Shorty corrected as he rearranged the letters on his rack. "He mighta gone over to see her once or twice, but he had some business with her daddy. Besides, I got my own private thoughts as to where he's been takin' hisself off to."

With that, Shorty fell maddeningly silent and Veronica tried to focus on the game. She chanced a look up every now and then, as if she could tell from Shorty's weathered face what thoughts he was keeping to himself. But all she could detect was the same unwavering concentration that would likely make tonight's game another one of his triumphs.

Veronica rested her chin on her hand and continued to stare unseeingly at the letters she'd drawn. Her thoughts moved back into the same track they'd followed for hours, trying to find the logic in Cole's sensual assault that afternoon.

The only conclusion that made any sense was that he'd been irritated by her mother's call and had taken some kind of perverse pleasure in making certain Veronica would have a problem convincing her mother she had been unaffected by him. In her romantic heart of hearts, she hoped he'd done it because he really did feel something for her and didn't want her to deny there was nothing between them. But, Veronica reminded herself, those kind of romantic fairy-tales happened only to others.

"There's a lot of that goin' around," Shorty said. Veronica had only half heard Shorty's comment.

"Hmm?"

Shorty pointed to the word he'd just laid out.

"D-a-y-d-r-e-a-m," Shorty spelled aloud, then chuckled. "Seems to be affectin' two-thirds of the people who live in this house."

Veronica's gaze turned away from the teasing in Shorty's dark eyes as a heavy blush settled on her cheeks. She quickly tallied the score he'd managed to get by adding the word "dream" to the "day" she'd put down. The fact that the "m" covered the triple-word space set his score even further ahead of hers.

The little lacklustre word Veronica put down next failed to get her any substantial point count, but it forced Shorty to return to contemplating the five letters he'd just drawn and kept him from making any more observations about her and Cole. At least she assumed Shorty had meant her and Cole. He certainly hadn't been talking about Curtis.

Veronica's attention was drawn to the sound of Cole's pickup coming up the driveway. She'd hoped to finish this game long before Cole returned, and now she fidgeted impatiently with her letter tiles while she waited for Shorty to play.

Cole's booted feet clunked up the porch steps and into the kitchen almost before she could adjust to his unexpected return. The black Stetson made its usual twirling arc toward the coat tree in the corner and managed to catch the same hook it always did. A wide grin split the usual sternness of Cole's demeanor as his eyes flicked from Shorty and lingered warmly on Veronica.

"Is Curtis in bed?" he asked as he turned a kitchen chair backward and sat astride it, his thickly muscled forearms resting on the chair back as he watched the game that was clearly in its last moments.

"Yep." Shorty was too intent on the letters in his rack to say more.

Veronica was trying to summon at least a pretence of interest in the game she'd already lost, but the steady look Cole was giving her made it hard to concentrate. Poor Shorty. Her preoccupation hadn't made the game much of a challenge for him.

"How did that talk with your mother go, Ronnie?"

Fresh colour flooded Veronica's cheeks. She glanced in Cole's direction and encountered the same knowing glimmer in his eyes that had mocked her response to him that afternoon.

"Just as you planned it to," she answered, a trace of irritation in her soft reply as she pointlessly rearranged the letters in her rack.

Shorty chuckled as he laid out his remaining letters, again using a word she'd just put on the board to add another thirty points to his score. And just when Veronica thought the old cowhand had been concentrating too hard on the game to pay attention to the veiled conversation between her and Cole, she saw him give them both a sly wink.

Veronica couldn't see any way to use her last three letters to tie Shorty's score, much less win the game. Besides, now that Cole was home, she was especially eager to end the game.

"You win again," she conceded good-naturedly, then helped Shorty clear the board and put the game away. Shorty stood up, stretched, then walked to the coat tree for his hat before he turned back toward Veronica.

"Don't forget," he cautioned, pointing at her just as she was rising from her chair. "Playin' at Scrabble is a lot like what some say about playin' at cards."

Veronica was focused so intently on escaping Cole's presence that Shorty's words didn't make much sense at first.

"What?"

"You think on it," he advised with a wink. "It'll come to you in a second." With that, the old man was out the porch door, whistling a merry tune.

"What he means is 'Lucky at cards, unlucky in love,'" Cole recounted, then chuckled. Veronica's gaze continued to shy from his.

"I don't put a lot of faith in old saw," she told him as she grasped her crutches and turned to leave the kitchen.

"What about the one, 'The way to a man's heart is through his stomach'?" Cole rose from his chair and turned it around to slide it under the table. Veronica forced a laugh to cover her inner reaction to that particular saying.

"If that was true, Mrs. Engstrom would still be here, colourful dialect and all," she joked, then started for her room as Cole crossed the stretch of floor between them. "Good night."

Cole caught her arm, stopping her before she could take another step.

"I'm tired, Cole," she said quickly, frightened by the wave of sensation that rocked her slim frame and sent a burst of heat into the deepest part of her. Veronica was unaware of the hunted look in the violet depths of her eyes, which had flown to his, unable to avoid their determined cobalt glints. They stood staring at each other for a long moment before Cole stepped close and lifted her chin with the side of a lean finger.

"Don't," she whispered as his lips lowered to hers. Cole allowed her to turn her face away slightly, but the light touch of his finger slid upward to trace a pattern of sensation on her flushed cheek.

"Would it help to apologise for the other night?" he asked huskily as the fingers of his other hand slid along the line of her jaw and combed gently into her hair.

"An apology won't change anything," she said, her eyes sparkling with resentment when they shot back to his—resentment that he thought an apology would get her into bed with him!

"Oh, but it will," he rasped confidently, his voice going softer.

"But I wo—"

Cole's finger tapped silencingly on her lips. "I don't expect you to," he assured her, smiling gently. "Friends again?" His dark brows arched and Veronica felt herself unfairly swayed by what she must have been mistaking for anxiety in his eyes.

"All right," she said at last.

Cole's mouth settled tenderly on hers before he drew away, his lips stretched in a satisfied smile.

"Then good night, Ronnie," he whispered.

Veronica stared up into his eyes for a confused moment before she turned and headed to her room.

CHAPTER TEN

COLE WAS IMMEDIATELY AWARE that something had happened the moment Veronica entered the den.

Her cheeks were burning with anger and humiliation, and her eyes held glimmers of hurt. The way she tossed the set of keys onto the desk in front of him betrayed more than average irritation, and Cole rose swiftly to his feet.

"What is it, Ronnie?" he demanded gently.

"You'll have to go pick up Curtis from Helen's yourself," she said, and he sensed rather than saw that she was about to burst into tears.

"Why? What's wrong?"

Her battle to control her hurt and anger was nearly lost when she tried to explain. The memory of Curtis's frightened grey eyes cut into her heart afresh. She had no explanation for the boy's sudden inexplicable fear of her and it hurt unbearably to think of it, much less tell Cole.

"Curtis didn't want to get into the car with me," she managed, her voice wavering. Cole came around the desk, his iron visage mildly alarming. "Curtis—" Veronica took a deep breath to steady herself "—Curtis was frightened of me and . . ." Veronica's throat closed up in a spasm of hurt.

"And what?" Cole caught her upper arms gently and bent slightly to look closely into her tear-stung eyes.

What could Veronica tell him? Helen was Jackie's sister. How could she tell him about the humiliating way Helen had taken Curtis aside and hugged him protectively while she coldly ordered Veronica off her front porch? Helen had seemed glad of both Curtis's reluctance to go with her and the opportunity to send Veronica home to Cole without his son.

"Helen didn't think it was a good idea to send Curtis home with me," she told him, struggling to remind herself that Helen had been sensible not to send the boy with someone he mistrusted.

"The hell you say!" Cole burst out. Veronica tried to shrink out of his grip, and instantly his harshness softened. "I'm not angry with you, Ronnie," he assured her, but when he started to pull her into his arms, she put up a firm hand to deny herself the comfort of his broad chest.

How it had hurt to see another display of Curtis's inability to tolerate her! And now something had made him mistrustful—and worse—frightened of her. But what?

"Let's go get this straightened out." Cole hadn't commented on Veronica's sudden resistance to his nearness, but when he sensed she was doing so to withdraw from him emotionally, he pulled her closer. "Whatever this is between you and Curtis is going to change," he promised. "I'll see to it."

Veronica shook her head. "You can't force the boy to like me, Cole. Besides," she reasoned, "it's not as if I'm going to be living here indefinitely. Let's just leave him alone." Cole's grip on her arms tightened.

"I won't have my son behave this way without provocation," he said gruffly.

"How do you know I haven't done something to cause all this?" she challenged. Cole's gaze never wavered.

"Because I know you," he said quietly.

Veronica was instantly angry.

"Because you think you know me," she corrected. "What do you really know about me?" Her demand hung heavily between them. "I could tell you a few stories about men my mother thought she knew. I used to cause a lot of problems for her with each new suitor, but at least when I was frightened of one, she'd give credence to what I told her. How can you do less?"

Cole's mouth tightened grimly. "The fact that you're taking the boy's side against yourself only reinforces my trust in you, Ronnie," he told her stubbornly. "But I intend to get to the bottom of this." Cole's sombre countenance was intimidating. "Let's go." He had started to guide her to the door when she pulled back.

"This should just be between you and your family. My presence might colour any explanations you get." Veronica was barely aware of the way her hands were twisting on the crutch grips.

Cole seemed to accept her refusal, but before he turned to go and pick up Curtis from Helen's, he bent to place a quick kiss on the unrelaxed line of her lips, leaving a warmth that lingered long after he turned away. Veronica listened to his booted stride continue through the silent house until the porch door closed. It was then that the brimming wetness in her eyes coursed disconsolately down her cheeks.

COLE SIGHED HEAVILY as he leaned back in the porch swing where Veronica had spent a good share of the evening alone.

"He won't talk to me." Cole's deep voice was husky with frustration as he automatically set the wide swing in motion with the rhythmic bunch and release of his powerful thigh muscles. Veronica relaxed and allowed Cole's easy strength to rock her as she inhaled the warm night air and caught a whiff of the masculine scent of soap and aftershave she associated exclusively with Cole.

"Where is he now?" It distressed her that her presence had divided father and son.

"He's confined to his room for the rest of the evening." Cole's irritable tone betrayed his hurt. He was just as bewildered as she by Curtis's behaviour.

"Please don't be impatient with him," she urged. "And don't treat him harshly. He'll not only blame me, but your relationship with him is too precious to risk for the sake of an outsider."

Cole cursed roundly and turned toward her in the swing, his abrupt movement destroying the rhythm and bringing the swing to a lurching halt.

"You're no outsider," he growled as he pulled her roughly to himself. "You're—" The grooves on each side of his well-carved mouth deepened in exasperation when he couldn't seem to finish the sentence. Veronica was pressing against his chest trying to separate them before the raw sensuality she sensed in Cole was released. But it was too late.

Cole's lips captured hers as he crushed her to him. All thoughts of resistance vanished beneath the insistent pressure of the hard mouth that mastered hers and drew her into the emotional whirlwind that claimed them both. She had no thought of refusal when Cole's hand came between them to unfasten a few buttons of her blouse before his vanquishing lips wandered lower.

Fierce, possessive, drugging. Cole's mouth set every nerve ending writhing in sensuous torture as he kissed a trail to the shadowy cleavage of her breasts. Veronica was breathless when she felt the front of her bra being unclasped. Then a sharp intrusion of fear suddenly had her clutching at her blouse, struggling to cover herself. But the lean fingers that restrained hers were stronger.

"Please don't." The anguish in her voice stopped him. Cole placed a couple of coaxing kisses on each corner of her love-swollen lips, but at last her resistance made him stop.

"What's wrong?"

Veronica felt her reserve weaken at the tenderness in Cole's voice. He wasn't angry, only perplexed. One look at the concern in the darkened depths of his eyes was almost too persuasive for her to resist.

"I'm...I'm..." Veronica paused, licking her dry lips. "There was a lot of twisted metal in the accident." Her voice wavered hoping Cole would take the hint without her having to explain further, but he didn't seem to understand. "I've got a lot of ugly scars," she whispered, her gaze dropping to his collar. She couldn't bear to watch the revulsion that would surely come next.

The large hand that had caught her small frantic ones pulled her slim fingers away from the front of her blouse. Panicked eyes shot back to his face. In spite of what she'd just told him, she read the determination on his iron features and went still in his arms. Her dark-lashed lids drifted closed at the tender intrusion of his fingers into the V of her clothing, then crept open, unable to keep her eyes from his face. A part of her sensed Cole would not react in a hurtful way, and that sudden bit of intuition enabled her to endure the next few seconds.

Cole released her hands. Slowly he parted the front facings of her blouse, then gently pushed away the concealing lace of one side of her bra. Veronica trembled as her unscarred breast was bared to his gaze. Tides of embarrassed colour came into her face as Cole's breath started coming unsteadily.

Without prolonging her discomfort more than necessary, Cole uncovered her other breast. Blue eyes that missed nothing followed the still-vivid scarring along her shoulder that dwindled to a jagged red seam that slashed over the outer curve of her right breast to just below the nipple. The natural symmetry of the silken mound had been altered only slightly. Cole gently traced his thumb over the breast section of the scar before he abruptly lowered his dark head.

"No!"

The strong fingers that had just touched her breast intercepted the hand she put up to keep him away, his firm grip making resistance impossible. Veronica gasped in pleasure as his teeth closed tenderly around the dusky tip, his tongue teasing the nipple to full hardness. Veronica had to bite her lip to keep from crying out. All her fear vanished in the flash fire of sensation Cole kindled in her. Her hand was released and Veronica clutched at his shoulders, her head slowly dropping back in sensual surrender as his mouth journeyed to her other breast for a few bone-melting moments. By the time his mouth made an unhurried ascent to her lips she was liquid in his arms.

"Sometimes it amazes me how worked up women get about such damned trivial things as scars," he growled against her mouth, then took her lower lip between his teeth and gave it a reproving tug. "There are other qualities more important to me than physical perfection, Veronica, and I think it's about time you realised it."

The stern angles of Cole's face had softened, and the deep blue of his eyes revealed tender sincerity. Veronica felt soul-liberating relief. Cole hadn't found her repulsive. His unexpected acceptance of her body restored much of the self-esteem she'd struggled for months to regain.

For the first time since the accident Veronica realised that the consequences of that tragic ride were not quite as final as she'd first believed. It was gradually dawning on her that she really would recover fully, that her life could be salvaged, her personal goals resurrected.

Cole brought his hands around to her blouse front, one corner of his mouth curved in self-directed mockery. "There's nothing like getting carried away on a porch swing with the audience potential this one has," he said as he nodded toward the barn and outbuildings that included the bunkhouse. Capable fingers fastened her bra and slowly re-buttoned her blouse. Then he was kissing her again and the tremor that went through her echoed in Cole's large frame.

"This has to stop," he rasped between kisses, but he was pulling her even harder against himself, making the extent of his arousal clear. Reluctantly Veronica summoned what was left of her modesty, striving to remind herself that any of Cole's men could look toward the house and see them.

Veronica pulled her arms from around his neck and slipped her hands between herself and Cole. He accepted the wordless signal, but Veronica sensed the effort it cost him to relax. Even when she decided he had there was a tenseness about him that indicated he could easily become aroused again.

"Do you mind if I ask what Helen had to say about this afternoon?" she ventured, hoping her question would distract them both. Cole loosened his embrace. "Has she had any insight at all into what caused Curtis to be frightened of me?''

Cole shifted on the swing, then stretched his long legs out in front of him. Keeping her against his side, his arm resting more casually around her shoulders, Cole sighed and set the swing in motion again.

''Helen can't figure it out, either,'' he said, ''but she insisted she was right not to send Curtis with you.'' The frustration had come back into his voice, and Veronica again regretted that her presence was causing problems.

''I think she was right, too.'' Veronica meant what she said, no matter how angry Helen had made her or how hurt she'd been at Curtis's refusal. However, she wasn't ready to believe that Helen didn't know why Curtis was frightened of her. Other than Cole, Helen was the one person who spent hours at a time with the boy. It didn't take much to conclude that Helen's disapproval and dislike of her had been picked up by Curtis. Veronica tried not to think about the possibility that the boy had actually been encouraged not to like her.

''I didn't come out here to talk about Helen,'' Cole said gruffly, as his gaze turned from staring into the distance to find her face in the slowly dwindling light. ''I've started making plans for a camping trip this weekend.'' Cole's voice had lowered, implying that his plan included her.

Deliberately misunderstanding, Veronica smiled and said, ''That sounds like fun, Cole. Curtis will love having you to himself for an entire weekend. Maybe a couple of days together will make up for the problems my being here has caused you both.'' Her eyes shied away from the instant exasperation on Cole's face.

''But you're the most important part of my plan, Ronnie,'' he said. ''Did you ever learn to fish?'' Cole gave her a reassuring squeeze.

''This isn't a good idea,'' Veronica insisted, shaking her head. She had to look away from the glimmer of purpose in Cole's eyes as she searched for some way to discourage him. ''I can't go, Cole. What about the sleeping arrangements?

What will Curtis think about the three of us going off to the
woods together?''

"I've thought of all that. You'll have your own tent and
Curtis and I will bunk together in the bigger one. Besides,
this will give you two an opportunity to spend some time
together away from the ranch. I want him to get used to us
being together."

Veronica tried not to think about Cole's last remark and
her excuses continued. Cole merely smiled at her hasty attempts to dissuade him, patiently listening to every point she
made before firmly rejecting each one. His mind was made
up. Nothing would disrupt his weekend plans for three.

"TIRED?" Cole grinned down at Veronica as he pulled up
the tent stake she'd just started to pound into the ground.
She watched as he stretched the tent rope and repositioned
the stake several inches beyond where she had struggled to
place it. With a wry twist to her lips, she followed on her
hands and knees.

"Here's the hammer," Veronica said, offering it to Cole,
but he shook his head, his hand gripping the tent stake.

"Go ahead. I trust you."

Veronica raised the mallet, then glanced up at his smiling
face. "Are you sure?"

"The longer you hesitate, the less sure I get. If you miss
and smash my hand instead, at least it's the last stake." His
smile widened to a grin.

Veronica grinned back, then fixed her eyes on the head of
the stake and carefully pounded it into the ground. When
she finished, Cole took the hammer and helped her to her
feet.

"Come on, Curtis," Cole yelled toward the truck. "Let's
get that gear over here." While she and Cole were putting up
the tents, Curtis was supposed to be unloading the truck so
they could set up their campsite. But so far he'd managed
only a few things and these he'd placed near the ring of
smoke-blackened rocks left by a previous camper.

Veronica glanced around the campsite, which stood in a small clearing surrounded by dense forest, and took a savouring breath of the clean pine-scented air. So far, the day had been ideal. After a quick breakfast at the ranch, Cole had loaded the truck and they had set off for the Laramie Mountains, leaving Shorty and the other men to fend for themselves for the weekend. Cole had offered to share cooking duties with Veronica on the trip, and since Curtis had been a model of good behaviour, Veronica was beginning to feel more optimistic about their two days and one night together.

Cole went over to hurry Curtis along and Veronica unzipped the flaps of the tents, which were set up side by side, to begin tossing their bedrolls and extra blankets inside. The last things she threw in were the small duffle bags that held their clothing. By the time she'd finished, Cole had deposited the canvas bag of towels and cooking utensils on the small wooden table he'd carried from the truck. Once the campsite was put in order, Cole got out the fishing poles and tackle. Curtis held a Styrofoam cup of worms they'd purchased on the way, avidly interested in the live lures that squirmed in the dirt.

"Let's go get supper." Cole led the way down the slow incline to the small lake, which wasn't visible from their campsite. Veronica followed, carefully using her crutches to negotiate the rocky dirt path that curved haphazardly to the lakeside. Tree roots ribbed the path in spots, making an occasional natural step that levelled out the path slightly before it started downward again. Veronica made her way down with much more ease than she anticipated for the return trip, but she was ecstatic.

Although she'd spent a lot of summers at camp, she never fished, preferring to spend her time swimming or horseback riding. Hank used to promise to take her one day, but he'd never found the time. And as Veronica grew older, she didn't think much about it, adapting to the more ladylike pastimes of her friends.

"How are you doing?" Cole asked as she reached the bank and watched him search through his tackle box for hooks. Curtis was already threading his onto the end of his line like a pro, his young face intent on his work.

"Just great," she returned as Cole unfolded his lean length from a crouch. Veronica paid close attention as he put hooks on her line and his, then gave each pole a quick check. The plaid shirt he wore stretched appealingly over his broad chest and back, emphasising the effortless play of hard muscle, she noticed, while the comfortably faded jeans he had on clung to his every move, reminding her how it felt to be pressed against the unyielding contours of that length.

"May I try?"

Cole had started to bait her hook when her question stopped him. He grinned, his look telling her he expected her to change her mind. Curtis was suddenly right beside her, holding his Styrofoam cup of bait practically under her nose, his face a picture of glee.

Without missing a beat, Veronica dug into the pungent, earthy-smelling container and pulled out a long fat worm. As she held it at eye level, she glanced down at the small face that was watching for her to make some delicate expression of revulsion. Instead, Veronica smiled.

"I have a recipe somewhere for earthworm cookies. I've always wondered what they'd taste like." Veronica pretended to give the worm a considering look.

"Yuk!" Curtis's face was screwing up disdainfully as Cole started chuckling. Curtis realised then that Veronica was joking and his disdain turned to a childish giggle, then to impish delight. "Hey, how about making some of those cookies for Shorty?"

"What?" Curtis's question caught her off-guard, but she suppressed a smile at the boy's uninhibited sense of mischief.

"Shorty is always talking about the weird things his mother made him eat when he was a kid," Curtis explained. "We can see if he recognises the taste." Curtis was turning the cup this way and that as if counting the number of worms they had left.

"Let's just feed the worms to the fish and forget about earthworm cookies," Cole suggested to his son with mock sternness as he exchanged a sparkling look with Veronica. "Why don't you go ahead and get your line in." Curtis seemed only mildly aware that his father had nixed the idea. Eagerly he skipped off to the water's edge and swung his pole in a near-expert arc.

"I might regret getting the two of you together," Cole told her after Curtis was out of earshot. "I can see now that it might turn out to be a case of what one won't think of, the other one will."

Veronica's gaze shifted from Cole's grinning expression to the sight of the small boy fishing on the bank. She was unaware of the look of faint longing in her eyes.

"Am I going to stick this poor helpless worm, or not?" she asked him suddenly. The wistful look had disappeared. Cole stared at her for a few uncomfortable moments before he answered.

"You've got too much worm there, Ronnie. You'll have to break him in half."

Veronica's face was incredulous. "Do you mean I'll have to...?"

"'Fraid so," Cole answered. Then holding out his hand, he said, "I'll do it."

"I'll do it myself," she replied. "You and Curtis came up here to enjoy fishing, not bait hooks for a squeamish female." She gritted her teeth and performed the unpleasant but necessary task.

Cole chuckled. "I'm glad to see that little tomboy is still in there somewhere underneath that quiet reserve of yours, Veronica." His low rough voice brought her attention back to his face. "It would be a real shame if she couldn't come out and play with the boys once in a while." Cole's kiss was swift and set his hat askew. He just barely caught it before it fell to the ground.

Moments later, Cole was giving Veronica a few pointers about fishing, teaching her how to cast hook and bait into a deeper part of the lake.

"Dad always says that a good fisherman cleans his own fish." Curtis giggled.

"Someone should have mentioned that earlier," Veronica commented wryly as she glanced across the large flat rock into Cole's laughing eyes. The three of them were sharing the same rock, and soon each was busily cleaning and scaling their catch. The elation Veronica had felt at catching four fish to Cole's and Curtis's two had definitely tapered off now that she struggled with the task of cleaning what she'd caught.

It wasn't so bad, really, she'd decided, but she hoped her appetite for fried fish wouldn't be unduly affected.

Once she had finished the task Cole expertly filleted the fish. Before they left for the campsite, he deposited the scraps in a shallow hole he'd had Curtis dig earlier.

Curtis gathered up their poles and the tackle box, carefully stowing the cup of worms inside the box before he started up the trail ahead of Cole and Veronica. Veronica had all she could manage with her crutches and Cole followed her with the large plastic freezer bag of fillets, giving her an occasional hand up over a steep spot on the trail.

The afternoon had been idyllic. The three of them had fished companionably the entire time, with Curtis jabbering to them both despite Cole's chuckling reminders that he would scare off the fish. Veronica was thrilled that the boy spoke to her nearly as often as he did to his father. There had been no trace of inhibition or inkling of the reason for his mistrust and fear of her the other day.

At Veronica's insistence, Cole had agreed to stop questioning his son about the incident at Helen's. Apparently, if today was any indication, it had been the right thing to do and Veronica felt untold satisfaction. They were almost at the campsite when they heard Curtis's whoop of excitement.

"Uncle Bob!"

Veronica heard Cole growl something under his breath, and they both increased their pace as the path grew level. Now they could hear the sound of tent stakes being driven into the hard ground. Cole and Veronica stepped into the clearing just in time to see Curtis launch himself into Jessica Ryan's welcoming arms.

CHAPTER ELEVEN

"HEY, DAD! Look who's here!"

Curtis was behaving as if he hadn't seen Jessie and his aunt and uncle for months instead of just the day before. Bob and Wylie, who'd come along too, were nearly finished setting up one of their tents, and Helen and Jessie had already unfolded a large camping table and carried most of their gear to the campsite across the stone ring from Cole's tent.

"What is all this, Helen?" Cole's voice was deceptively soft, but Veronica could almost feel its underlying hardness.

"We were coming up the trail on our way to that site north of here—you know the one—" Helen explained, as if she hadn't noticed her brother-in-law's annoyance. "Well, we saw your truck and decided to join you and Curtis. We didn't think you'd mind." Helen managed to look just worried enough about Cole's reception of their intrusion to bring a resigned twist to his lips, then a more sociable smile.

"Ronnie and I were about to start supper."

It was only then that Helen's eyes moved from Cole to Veronica.

"And you have Veronica with you." Helen's pleased expression rang false to Veronica, and from the look Cole shot her, it had to him, too. "Well . . ." Helen glanced around to catch her husband's attention. "Bob? Maybe you won't need to set up the tent. You men can bunk in with Cole and Curtis, and the girls and I will use our tent."

"No. Put up the other tent, Bob," Cole called, his cool gaze never leaving Helen's. "Ronnie and I already have all the chaperoning we need," Cole responded casually as he set the bag of fish on the small table he'd brought, then went off to the truck for the other food. Veronica managed a polite smile at the interlopers, hoping their arrival didn't signal a premature end to the happy relaxed atmosphere of the camping trip.

CURTIS HAD BEEN ASLEEP for at least an hour and Veronica had gone to her tent soon after, changing out of her clothing and shrugging into a thigh-length T-shirt nightie. She was still uncomfortable with the tension that had all but ruined the evening for her, and she lay awake listening to the sounds outside. The others hadn't gone to bed yet, but the talk around the fire dwindled to near silence when Cole decided to retire for the night. She noticed through the small nylon mesh window that the light in Cole's neighbouring tent was now off. She could hear the others bidding good night to each other, and then, almost suddenly, all was quiet.

Just as Veronica was drifting off to sleep, a shuffling sound outside her tent summoned her back to complete consciousness. She could hear the low buzzing sound of the double zipper at the door flap and sensed Cole's presence in the darkness even before he leaned over to crawl inside her tent, zipping the flap closed behind him. She felt a thrill of excitement when he gently touched her shoulder.

"Ronnie, are you awake?" he whispered, crouching beside her.

"Yes," she whispered back. "What are you doing here, Cole? What will the others think . . . and Curtis?"

"Shh." He placed a finger gently over her lips, his eyes now nearly adjusted to the blackness. "Curtis is sound asleep. If there's a problem, we're right next door, and I'll be back there before he's awake. As for the others, I don't care what they think."

"Cole, I—"

"Ronnie, I'd just like to lie close to you for a while." The words wrapped irresistibly around her heart and she whispered her consent. Cole eased himself onto the edge of Veronica's bedroll, sliding beneath the blankets to stretch his length alongside hers.

"I'm sorry about tonight, Ronnie. I had no idea Helen and Jessie would pull something like this." Cole's whisper was harsh.

"You don't need to apologise," Veronica whispered back. She wanted to end the conversation there. She didn't think she could keep from commenting on several barbed remarks Jessie had made that evening, or the way Helen never missed an opportunity to link Cole's name with Jessie's. Wylie had been short-tempered—and with cause, Veronica thought sympathetically. He had apparently been counting on a cosy little trip with Jessie, but Jessie had obviously used him so she would have someone to toss in Veronica's direction while she went after Cole.

Veronica felt the subtle tension next to her escalate just before she heard a stirring of movement as Cole reached for her in the darkness. She didn't resist when he drew her close and rearranged the blankets until they were sharing one another's warmth.

Slowly, hesitantly, as if giving her a chance to refuse, Cole's lips found the shell of her ear. The hard arm that encircled her waist began to move upward as his gentle fingers found the neckline of her nightie and tugged it aside to bare her shoulder to his kiss. With a distinct absence of haste, Cole slipped his other hand beneath her head, pillowing her on his forearm as he turned her onto her back and found her lips. As she felt herself begin to melt, Veronica's arms went around Cole's neck in unreserved invitation.

A tremor shot through her when Cole thrust his tongue forcefully into her mouth while his hand found the hem of her night shirt. With a riveting mixture of laziness and determination, Cole stroked her thigh, then let his hand wander up to her hip and across her flat stomach before moving higher. In moments, Veronica was feverishly returning Cole's kiss, going breathless when he slipped a jeans-clad leg between her thighs and shifted more and more of his weight onto her smallness.

Her night shirt slid higher as Cole's warm sure fingers toyed enticingly with her breast. The heat beneath the blankets became sweltering as Cole's lips left hers to burrow beneath the ripple of clothing and find the small hardened peak.

Suddenly there was a cry from Curtis's tent.

"Look at this fish, Dad," the childish voice called out.

Cole went as still as if he'd heard a shot, and Veronica's pleasure-tormented gasp died in her throat. The only sound for startled moments was the rapid staccato of two racing hearts as they listened for more.

"See him?" they heard Curtis say.

Cole carefully smoothed Veronica's night shirt down over her hips.

"What'd I tell ya?" the happy little voice chattered, and Veronica began to shake with silent laughter.

"Talking in his sleep," Cole whispered unnecessarily before he, too, started to chuckle. "Let me make a quick check on him. I'll be right back."

He rose and moved toward the tent entrance, then exited and looked in on his son. After watching him roll over and lie in silence for a few minutes, Cole decided the sleep chatter must be finished.

"I guess we couldn't ask for a better chaperon than a seven-year-old boy," Cole said as he made his way back into Veronica's tent. He started planting skin-branding kisses on her neck, but Veronica sensed his self-control was back in place.

Suddenly Cole said, "I think I'm falling for you, Veronica."

Veronica's rapidly beating heart skidded to a halt at the unexpected words. A warmth came into her, a free-flowing, heart-bursting heat that crested deep inside, yet left her with a bittersweet ache.

Careful, her mind cautioned. Cole's very choice of words was a clear intimation that he was still unsure of what he really felt. He *thought* he was falling for her, she reminded herself. That was still eons away from a simple heartfelt "I love you, Veronica."

"I care for you, too, Cole," she heard herself say, desperate to sound casual and unaffected. "But I'm really tired. I'd like to get some sleep now." She started to roll out of Cole's arms and pull away from him when his arms tightened almost fiercely around her.

"You can't just turn over and go to sleep!" Cole's whispered rasp was incredulous.

Veronica kept silent, staring up into the shadow of Cole's face. She couldn't see him clearly, but she could almost feel the harsh line of his mouth. In another moment Cole relaxed his hold and Veronica took the opportunity to turn away from him.

Although she was reluctant to abandon the whipcord length that warmed her back, she managed to summon the strength to shift away from Cole to the far edge of the rumpled bedroll.

"You don't have to go, Ronnie," came the near-silent whisper. Veronica paused, feeling the emotional tentacles of his words wrap around her and tug at her resistance. Her mind raced frantically for a way to escape Cole's persuasion.

"Playing around with you like this can only lead to one thing," she whispered irritably. Veronica drew the blankets to her chin as she lay on her side and stared at the blackened tent side.

"So?"

Veronica sighed then pulled her knees up to lie in a defensive curl, wondering what she should say. What *could* she say? Was it time to tell Cole everything about her marriage to Eric? Or would there ever be an appropriate time? Did Cole even care to know? Maybe, she thought, there was really no reason to tell him anything. Veronica squeezed her eyes shut, electing to sleep and say nothing.

"It's your husband, isn't it?" Veronica's eyes popped open. "Or rather, ex-husband."

The silence of the night had grown unbearably loud. The sounds of the forest around them had paused, as if waiting for her to respond. Suddenly, it all seemed a secret not worth keeping. The months since the accident felt like years, the agony of Eric's abandonment no longer the raw wound it had been.

"I don't still love him, if that's what you mean," she said quietly.

"Is that why you divorced him?" came the inevitable question.

Veronica made a restless movement. "Is this just idle curiosity, or do you really want to know about my marriage to Eric?" Cole didn't hesitate.

"There are things you do, things you've said, that raise a lot of questions, Ronnie. So yes, I'd really like to know about your marriage."

Veronica started slowly, telling Cole only a few things at first about her relationship with Eric—the wedding, the accident, but including enough so he'd know that her sexual inexperience was total.

Veronica was able to relax then and found herself confiding her heartache that after his first visit, Eric had never been back to the hospital to see her and that he'd had their marriage annulled soon after. She even mentioned the personally unattractive part about sinking into depression for weeks, resisting anyone who tried to help her.

When she finished, Veronica lay quietly, her heart emptied of emotion, cleansed of the fear of humiliation that had lingered inside her for months.

"I survived," she whispered, aware of the awkwardness Cole must be feeling.

There was a rustling movement and Cole was suddenly propped on an elbow. Veronica turned her head and stared up at the breathing shadow that hovered over her and waited. She felt Cole's warm breath on her face the instant before his lips settled on hers. There was no passion in his kiss, only a gentle, compassionate, coaxing kind of contact.

"I'm sorry, baby," came the velvet whisper. Veronica didn't resist as Cole turned her to face him, then drew her close.

This time, she lay facing him, cradled against his lean length by strong arms. Neither spoke as Veronica snuggled deeper into Cole's embrace, feeling at peace with herself. The warmth and strength Cole's body offered was like heaven, the broad, hair-roughened chest she was cuddled against tantalisingly male. With the warm wonderful scent of him in her nostrils, Veronica gradually found sleep, comforted by the complete trust she now felt toward him.

FOR THE TENTH TIME in the past half hour Veronica glanced out the kitchen window, checking to see where Curtis was. Something about the way he was acting today distressed her. He had been sullen and uncommunicative since the day after they'd returned from the camping trip, but Veronica was hard put to pinpoint the reason.

The camping trip itself had turned out a success. After a very early quick breakfast that Helen and Jessie had insisted on preparing, the two women packed a huge lunch for the hike they assumed Bob and Wylie were taking on their own. Minutes after the lunches were loaded into backpacks, Helen and Jessie found, to their dismay, that they were expected to go along. Cole's frosty demeanour discouraged either of them from finding excuses to stay behind.

With the two women thwarted for the remainder of the day, Cole and Veronica had spent most of their time fishing with Curtis. At first, Veronica was uncomfortable when Cole used every opportunity to touch her, regardless of whether Curtis was watching or not. But gradually, Curtis stopped making faces of revulsion every time he saw his father kiss her. He even parked himself and his fishing pole next to them on the bank while Veronica sat on the ground in front of Cole, leaning back companionably against his chest.

By the time they packed up their tent and camping supplies to head for home, anyone seeing the three of them together might have assumed they were a family. That was probably the reason, when Helen and Jessie trudged back to the campsite behind Bob and Wylie, that the two footsore, whining women's every look indicated they would surely set another plan in action to disrupt the newly bonded threesome. Now that plan, if one did exist, seemed to be working.

Veronica pushed the door open and walked out onto the porch, aided by the walking cane that the therapist had recommended she begin using after her last visit. Unable to see Curtis anywhere out back, she carefully descended the porch steps and headed toward the side of the house. Just as she rounded the end of the porch, the charred smell of burning paper assailed her nostrils.

"What are you doing, Curtis?" Veronica bent at the waist, her hand braced on the porch rail for balance, to peer under the porch. Her quiet approach had been missed by the boy who was scrambling to toss clumps of earth on the tiny pile of shredded newsprint he'd just touched a match to. "Come out from under there."

Round-eyed, Curtis obeyed the calm order without question.

"Give me the matches." Veronica put out her hand, silently debating the best way to handle the situation. Cole wouldn't be home for at least a couple of hours, and Veronica was still uncertain how far he expected her to go in disciplining the boy. Curtis's face was filled with mutiny as he dropped a single matchbook into her outstretched palm. "Is that all of them?"

A dusty sneaker speared the sod. "Yep."

"I'm surprised at this, Curtis," Veronica began, feeling her way with the boy, not liking that she had to further risk his resentment. "You know how dangerous fires can be."

The sneakered toe twisted. "You gonna tell my dad?" Curtis's small chin came up at a defiant angle.

"I think one of us should tell him, don't you?" Curtis's lower lip quivered and Veronica had to harden herself to the boy's distress. "Why don't you run into the house and get a pitcher of water? The plastic one on the counter next to the sink will do fine."

"Why?" Again that challenging lift of chin.

"I want you to make sure that the fire is properly doused," Veronica explained patiently.

"It was just some paper," Curtis protested, and Veronica saw definite signs of Jessie in his shrugging, faintly ridiculing attitude.

"Are you going to mind me, or do you want to spend the afternoon in your room?" Veronica uttered the ultimatum with unwavering calm, trying to remember what she'd read about offering children options like that. The experts often disagreed, so Veronica had little to draw on but her own childhood experience. Unfortunately, as she recalled a bit belatedly, the problem adults had usually run into with her was that she almost always chose the punishment.

"Oh, all right," Curtis grumbled, then reached for the porch rail to climb onto the end of the porch like the half boy, half monkey he was. In a few minutes, he was carrying the pitcher out the back door, choosing the more conventional stairs before he came around the porch toward her. Veronica leaned down and watched as Curtis spilled the water over the powder-fine remains before he crawled back out.

"Thank you, Curtis." Veronica took the pitcher. "I've been baking cookies this afternoon," she said in a brighter tone. "How would you like to sample some?" She was grateful to be able to have something to offer that would let Curtis know she was still willing to be friendly despite the problems.

"I saw 'em. I even tasted one," he replied, almost as if he were daring her to tell him he shouldn't have.

"That's all right," she assured him. "Why not come in and have a big glass of milk with some more?" Veronica took heart at the sudden waver in the boy's defiant expression.

"Because I didn't like 'em," he burst out, then raced past her toward the trees at the edge of the yard. Veronica watched him go, hurt by his refusal.

"Your father wants you to stay in the yard," she called after him, then, disheartened, started for the porch steps.

The tentative acceptance Curtis had shown on their trip had vanished. If anything, the boy seemed more intolerant of her than ever. He'd spent Monday and Tuesday at Helen's, but Cole had kept him home the rest of the week, asking Veronica if she minded keeping an eye on him the few times he couldn't take Curtis with him around the ranch.

Yet in spite of Cole's almost too-obvious machinations to give her and Curtis more opportunity to get to know each other, Curtis remained withdrawn from her, unless he found something to criticise.

That had led her to suspect that Helen had possibly had a hand in the boy's sudden reversal. Things had been fine between Veronica and Curtis until he'd come home Tuesday afternoon, and there hadn't been a truly relaxed moment with him since. It upset Veronica that Helen could be so vindictive.

And really there was little point in Helen's being so, for Cole's interest in Veronica was just a passing thing, she was sure. She had likely come along at the time when Cole was finally ready to stop mourning Jackie and think about a new relationship. Even though Veronica was head over heels in love with Cole, she didn't delude herself into thinking his feelings matched the intensity of hers. It hurt to remind herself that every look, every touch, every kiss and every confidence they shared would eventually come to nothing. Veronica had no illusions about her ability to sustain Cole's romantic interest. She only hoped that when that interest did wane, she could anticipate it and take the initiative to end their relationship by quietly slipping out of Cole's life.

With these depressing thoughts on her mind, Veronica made her way to the freezer to choose what meat to set out to thaw for the next day. She was just about to remove a roast of beef when she heard a scream from the back yard.

Grabbing her cane, Veronica turned and rushed awkwardly outside, hitting the porch door and sending it banging against the house as she did so. The horror that met her eyes when her frantic gaze found Curtis next to the barbecue grill made her grab the throw rug that lay across the porch rail. Fear propelled her still weak and unsteady legs rapidly down the steps, and she was heedless of the jarring pain that rocketed through her limbs to her hips and backbone.

In moments she reached Curtis. He was doing a wild kicking dance that served only to spread the hungry blaze of fire from his right sneaker to the ankle of his jeans. Veronica half lunged and half fell to drag the boy to the ground, smothering the flames with the small rug. Curtis writhed with pain as she tried to gauge the extent and severity of the burns that had eaten away at the top of his shoe and crept up past the hem of his jeans.

"Shorty!" Veronica's yell was directed toward the barns where Shorty usually spent a good part of the afternoon. She held Curtis tightly, her heart wrenching at the sight of his small tearless face, pale as he stared up at her in a mute plea for reassurance.

"You'll be all right, sweetheart," she crooned. "We'll get you to the doctor right away. Shorty!"

"I want my dad," Curtis whispered, and Veronica hugged him even closer.

"We'll get him. Don't worry." Veronica didn't have time to wonder how they would reach Cole. Shorty raced over from the barn, his weathered face whitening at the sight of Veronica on the ground, cradling Curtis.

"Lord a mercy! What'd he do, get hisself burnt?" Shorty was already swooping down to whisk the boy into his arms.

"Get him to the car and see if you can get his shoe off. Then elevate his foot, Shorty," Veronica ordered. "Can we take the station wagon?" She reached for her cane and rose painfully to her feet. Teddy, who'd just arrived on the scene, came close to steady her. "Teddy?" She barely noticed that the small fire was licking across the dry grass of the yard or that Jim Fisher was running from the barn with a feed sack to beat it out. "Get three of those bags of ice out of the freezer and grab a sheet out of the linen closet."

"Can you make it to the car okay?" Teddy's gentle brown eyes were worried.

"Yes. I'm fine. Please hurry." Reluctantly he released her and ran to the house. Veronica forced her aching legs toward the old station wagon where Shorty had deposited Curtis. Just as she reached the wagon, Teddy emerged from the house with the bags of ice and the sheet. Hampered by leg cramps that threatened to draw her thigh muscles into knots, Veronica climbed into the rear of the wagon. She partially unfolded the sheet and slid it beneath Curtis's injured foot, which Shorty had managed to free from the burned shoe and rest on a tool box. Frantic fingers tore open the plastic ice bags, gently packing the ice on and around the boy's foot and ankle before she wrapped the soothing cold securely with the sheet. Curtis whimpered during her ministrations but didn't pull away, and in moments Teddy had climbed behind the wheel of the car and got it started.

"I'll see if'n I can raise Cole on the CB," Shorty said, poking his head into the wagon. "If'n I can't, I'll go find him."

"Good. But call Helen first and ask her to come to the hospital. Curtis may feel better if she's there. Then call the hospital to let them know we're coming." Veronica was unaware that her hands were trembling.

"Will do. You two take care." Shorty smiled encouragingly at the small boy who managed a quirk of lips before the old cowhand closed the tailgate securely.

Teddy gunned the engine and they shot down the driveway while Veronica held Curtis's hand. The boy clung to her, bravely trying to hold back tears.

OUTSIDE THE TRAUMA ROOM at the hospital, Veronica waited nervously, her lower body enveloped in a relentless ache. But the ache in her heart was far greater. She had let Cole down, violated the trust he'd put in her. And now Curtis lay in pain just beyond that door because of her negligence.

Veronica doubted she'd ever forget the anguish and fear in those so solemn little eyes, a look that had gripped her soul and brought every mothering instinct she possessed to the surface. During the ride to the hospital she had held Curtis's hand, stroked his forehead, and spoken reassuringly to him, frustrated that she could do no more to comfort him or take away his pain.

But the instant Helen had come through the trauma-room door, Curtis had shrugged off Veronica's touch and reached for his aunt. Helen had hugged the boy, her curt "You can go back to the ranch, Veronica—I'm here now" effectively dismissing Veronica from the room.

Veronica remained in the hall, leaning against the wall to take some stress off her legs. She waited almost fearfully for Cole to arrive. Teddy had gone back to the ranch when a quick call home told him that Shorty still hadn't been able to track down Cole. Veronica had no way of getting back to the ranch, but even if she had, she wouldn't think of leaving. Not until she was certain Curtis would be all right.

Veronica's stomach twisted with guilt, her mind incapable of formulating thoughts that didn't begin with "If only..." If only she'd watched Curtis more closely. If only she'd paid more attention when he'd come into the kitchen that last time. If only she'd noticed he'd taken the can of charcoal lighter fluid from beneath the sink when she'd pulled out a new garbage bag. If only...

"What's happened to Curtis?"

Veronica turned, startled by the angry demand in Jessica Ryan's voice.

"He was playing with matches and had some charcoal lighter fluid out by the grill. He must have spilled some on his foot and it ignited when he struck a match."

"How bad is he?"

"He's burned his foot and ankle, but I'm not certain how badly. The doctor is in there now and Helen is with him," Veronica answered, brushing the dampness from her pale cheek. "Shorty hasn't been able to reach Cole yet." Jessie's cloudy look darkened.

"Well, you've done it this time," Jessie jeered, a slim hand waving in the air in an I-told-you-so gesture. "Cole should have known better than to let you look after Curtis." Jessie rearranged the angry lines of her face into a satisfied smile. "If I were you, I think I'd be getting out of town on the next bus, train, or plane going anyplace far, far from here. I don't think I'd even go back to the ranch for my toothbrush."

Veronica looked away guiltily, only able to think about the obvious parallel between Curtis's accident and Chapman Red's all those years ago. She'd been at least indirectly at fault both times, the blame resting on her irresponsible behaviour.

"I warned you about history repeating itself, didn't I?" Jessie needled.

Veronica felt cold and sick, smothered by the escalation of the guilt she'd already assigned herself. She was terrified of facing Cole now, but face him she must. She deserved everything he'd have to say to the person who had violated his trust and allowed his only child to come to harm.

"I can't leave, Jessie," she murmured, then turned away from the lovely blonde whose perfect face tightened unpleasantly.

"You can't be thinking to talk your way out of this, are you?" Jessie's voice was filled with scorn. Neither of them noticed the trauma-room door opening only to be pushed almost—but not quite—closed again.

"Do you honestly think," Jessie went on, "that just because Cole seems to have developed some kind of passing interest in you that he'll overlook your negligence?" She laughed. "Not a chance, Veronica. He'll be out for blood, and this time Hank won't be around to protect you. Cole will hang you out to dry."

Veronica took a quick breath.

"Then I guess that's the way it will be," she whispered, feeling as if she deserved to be hung out to dry.

"Look, Veronica," Jessie persisted, "this is not at all like what happened to Red. Oh, I suppose in some ways it is," she conceded when Veronica glanced back at her. "But you and I both know you didn't forget to properly secure that damned horse," she said with a toss of her head. "This time, Curtis was in your care and you failed to keep an eye on him." Veronica turned then, unable to put her finger on what Jessie was saying, but alert to it. "You really are a naive little sap, aren't you?"

"What?"

"You're a naive little sap," Jessie repeated as if she enjoyed saying it.

"No. The other. About you and I both knowing I didn't forget to secure Chapman Red." Veronica's eyes narrowed. "You were the one who reminded Cole that the two of you had just seen me coming from Red's paddock. I always thought you believed I was at fault."

In fact, Veronica recalled, Jessie had been the one who had incited Cole's volatile temper and goaded him on, feeding the fire of his anger toward Veronica. It came as a shock to hear that Jessie had actually believed, *known*, otherwise. Why hadn't she said so at the time?

"I knew you weren't," Jessie dismissed with a flourish of her hand.

"Then why didn't you say so?"

"Are you really so dense, Veronica? Why should I have? After I went to all the trouble of turning Red out myself, why shouldn't I have made certain you were blamed?" Jessie was untroubled by Veronica's gasp. "I was hoping for better results, though. Especially after that stupid horse had to be put down. I'd hoped old Hank would turn against you then, too, so I wouldn't have to worry about him throwing you at Cole one day. He was always so damned determined for Cole to like you."

Jessie smirked as Veronica's jaw dropped in astonishment.

"You did it deliberately, then blamed me?" Veronica was trembling. "You let me think all these years that I'd..." Veronica stared, incredulous. "My God, Jessie. How could you have destroyed a valuable animal like that? Cole loved that horse."

"Cole could have any horse he wanted. What was the loss of one horse when I had such a great opportunity to ruin your chances with Cole forever?"

"But I was sixteen years old, Jessie. I wasn't any threat to you, and Cole couldn't even stand to have me around. Besides, he was in love with Jackie."

"You're right about that," Jessie admitted ruefully. "Jackie could do no wrong as far as Cole was concerned. I never could think of a way to come between them before they were married. But when Jackie died so conveniently, I promised myself that no other woman was going to be the next Mrs. Cole Chapman but me. That's why I've got so close to Curtis," she went on. "I have him wrapped so tightly around my little finger that I almost have him believing you're a two-headed monster from the nether world." Jessie's laughter was cold.

"You used the boy?" Veronica felt sick. No wonder Curtis had been so hostile and frightened of her.

"Of course," Jessie readily confessed. "Remember the day Curtis refused to ride home in the car with you from Helen's?" Jessie chuckled at Veronica's look of confusion. "I told Curtis you were the one driving six months ago when you had your accident. I said you were a very bad driver."

"But that's not true," Veronica cried.

"Curtis thinks so," Jessie reminded her. "And the fact that Curtis and I are buddies made it easy for me to persuade him to keep quiet and not tell Cole." Jessie's smile was almost sinister. "And now, thanks to Curtis's timely little accident, I'm going to be able to keep that promise to myself after all, since you'll be out of the way." A smug look crossed her face. "I still can't figure out what Cole sees in you."

With these words Jessie turned away and walked toward the elevator bank, leaving Veronica in a daze. So Chapman Red's death had been caused by Jessie. The knowledge of the woman's premeditated evil shocked her and forestalled any relief she might have felt at the revelation. And then to hear that Jessie had been manipulating Curtis! No wonder Veronica was having problems with the boy.

Yet how ironic it was that Jessie was accepted and championed by Cole's unsuspecting sister-in-law. At least Veronica assumed Helen didn't know—not when Jessie's admission showed such contempt for Jackie and such deliberate exploitation of little Curtis.

Veronica stared at the leggy blonde who was preening before her reflection in the glass of a wall-mounted floor directory near the elevators. Her thoughts were disrupted by the cautious opening of the trauma-room door as Helen stepped into the hall.

"Veronica?" The concerned look Helen was giving her sent a jolt of fear through her, obliterating any thought beyond Curtis's condition.

"How is he, Helen?" Veronica's eyes were haunted, her heart wrenched with anxiety. From the look on Helen's face, Curtis's burns must have been much worse than the doctor had initially thought. *If only I'd watched him more closely,* she again cried to herself.

"Curtis will be all right," Helen said, but the odd look she was giving Veronica indicated differently.

"Are you certain?" Tears of relief coursed down Veronica's pale cheeks and she clumsily reached to dash them away. Helen put out her hand and Veronica flinched, unprepared for Helen's gentle touch of consolation.

Helen started to speak, but just as she did, Veronica was drawn to a flurry of movement down the hall. Cole had burst through the double doors into the emergency entrance. He paused momentarily, his granite expression forbidding, his blue eyes like polished steel as his gaze skipped over Jessica and riveted on Veronica.

Long purposeful strides brought Cole quickly down the hall, and Veronica felt herself begin to tremble. He looked lean and tough, his dusty battered Stetson resting at a dangerous angle over his glittering eyes. Cole reached for her, his iron fingers seizing her upper arms just as her knees threatened to buckle.

CHAPTER TWELVE

VERONICA DREW BACK, throwing her hands up against Cole's chest in self-protection. Then the gentleness of his grip registered. He was leaning down, his raking gaze missing nothing as he searched her pale features.

"Are you all right, Ronnie?" he rasped with concern as he tugged her closer. Veronica nodded, unable to suppress a tiny sob.

"I wouldn't waste my precious time coddling her if it was my son lying in that trauma room suffering." Jessie had followed along the hall and now her icy voice brought his head around. "All that talk that day about Curtis's being safe in the pickup truck meant nothing more to her than a way to keep me from your son. I told you that, Cole. Curtis's safety didn't mean a whole hell of a lot when she couldn't be bothered to notice he was playing with charcoal lighter and matches."

Jessie was the picture of outraged femininity, her face flushed, her eyes accusing, her manicured hands balled into dainty fists that rested on her shapely hips. She fully looked the part of an angry concerned mother—just the image she wanted to project, Veronica realised helplessly.

"Are you Mr. Chapman?" An authoritative male voice cut between them and Cole released Veronica to thrust out his hand to shake the doctor's.

"How's my son?"

"He's a very lucky little boy," the sandy-haired emergency-room doctor declared. Veronica hung on every word as he informed Cole that Curtis's burns were mostly second degree, that the thickness of his socks and sneakers had kept the fire from burning more quickly through to his skin. Then he praised Veronica for applying the ice, because it had alleviated much of Curtis's discomfort. Also, he said, her quick action in smothering the fire had prevented Curtis from getting extensive third-degree burns.

Although relieved that Curtis's condition was not serious and that the doctor had commended her, Veronica's sense of doom increased. Cole had physically withdrawn from her, leaving her to lean exhaustedly on her cane.

He blamed her, she was certain, unable to argue with that because she blamed herself. Veronica experienced a brief spurt of encouragement when Cole turned again to face her, asking her once more if she was all right. Thanking her, he followed the doctor back into the trauma room.

"Why don't we go and sit down?" Helen offered, taking Veronica's arm to coax her to the tiny waiting area nearby. Veronica shook her head and turned away, but not before she caught sight of the smug look on Jessie's face. "Please, Veronica," Helen urged.

Why was Helen being so kind, Veronica wondered, her eyes drawn from Jessie back to Helen.

"Maybe later," she said. "But you go ahead," she hastened to add, then moved unsteadily to a spot where she was within sight of the trauma-room door, but out of the way.

Jessie lost no time in stepping next to Helen, leaning over to whisper conspiratorially when Veronica glanced their way. To her surprise, and evidently to Jessie's by the look on her face, Helen walked away from the blonde woman in midsentence. Jessie stood open-mouthed for a second, then hurried after her friend.

Veronica continued to watch only because this was a clear departure from the norm in Helen and Jessie's relationship. She could have sworn the two women were close friends, but Helen's expression was closed, her whole manner discouraging further talk on Jessie's part.

Veronica looked away, forcing herself to watch the activity in the hall, wishing she had a more absorbing distraction from the guilt and apprehension she felt. Mercifully she wasn't kept in suspense much longer.

The trauma-room door swung open wide and Cole emerged, followed by the doctor. After a brief leave-taking and another handshake, Cole's gaze sped to Veronica. She tried to discern what would happen next as she watched him move toward her in his loose-jointed cowboy walk. Visibly shaken, Cole stopped and let his eyes sweep over her.

The time that passed while Veronica waited for Cole's ashen expression to switch to rage seemed frightfully long to her, but was only the blink of an eyelash to anyone else. Any moment he would explode the way he had eight years earlier. Knowing now that Red's death hadn't been her fault did nothing to dim the memory, and Veronica stood bravely, waiting for the inevitable.

Suddenly she was in Cole's arms, his lips moving over her cheek as he placed possessive kisses on her pale skin.

"I'm so sorry, Cole," Veronica murmured. "It was all my fault. I thought I'd gotten all the matches—" Veronica's voice broke on a sob, heartsick that Curtis was hurting. The steellike arms tightened, pulling her small body even more firmly against him.

"It's not your fault, dammit," he growled into her ear, then planted a kiss on her wet cheek. He straightened slightly, pinning her weeping gaze with the anguished blue of his own. "But you expected me to jump all over you, that right?" Cole's expression revealed that her fear and uncertainty of him had hurt. "Damn." He hugged her fiercely. "I trust you completely, Ronnie, especially with my son. The way you handled this whole crisis only reinforces my faith in you."

Veronica's heart leaped into a joyous rapid cadence as Cole continued to hold her.

"Mr. Chapman?" The nurse stood a couple feet away from where they stood in each other's arms, but Cole only loosened his embrace enough to turn his head toward the white-clad woman. "You can go back in with Curtis now," she said. "It will be a few minutes before he's ready to go upstairs."

"Thank you, nurse." Cole faced Veronica again, releasing her slowly. "Did you hurt yourself?" he asked, looking at her legs.

"A little," Veronica admitted. "But it's nothing that some liniment and a couple of heating pads won't cure. Don't worry about me." Veronica wanted him to hurry in to his son and not waste time with her. Curtis needed his father.

"Come on." Cole stepped back only enough to signal that she was to precede him. "Curtis was asking to see you." Veronica hesitated, surprised. "Come on," Cole repeated and Veronica brushed away any lingering dampness from her cheeks, glancing up at Cole in silent question. Grinning, Cole reached into his hip pocket and brought out a garish red handkerchief, which he used to tenderly wipe the wet wedges of mascara from beneath her lashes. They were nearly to the trauma-room door when Jessie stepped into their path.

"Excuse us, Jessie." Cole's hard arm brusquely swept the blonde woman aside without giving her a chance to speak. "Ronnie's going in to see Curtis." The door swished closed behind Veronica, muffling the sound of Jessie's instant objection.

Veronica stared at the small sheet-covered form on the gurney, smiling when Curtis's solemn grey eyes found hers. She started across the tiled floor hesitantly.

"You hurt your legs." The child's words were more a statement than a question.

Veronica shrugged. "I just overworked a couple of muscles. No damage done. How are you feeling?" Veronica stopped at Curtis's side, glancing at the nurse who hovered nearby taking the boy's blood pressure.

Curtis didn't look too comfortable and Veronica reached for the small hand that rested on the side rail, curling her fingers consolingly around it.

"I hurt a little," he admitted, and Veronica hoped they had given him something for the pain he must have surely felt. "I just wish I didn't do what I done."

"I guess you learned an awfully hard lesson," she whispered, nearly overcome with compassion. Not only had he been hurt, he'd probably been scared to death. "I'm sorry I didn't catch you before you lit the match."

Curtis's eyes fled from contact with hers. "You weren't supposed to catch me. I snuck the lighter fluid out when you went into the bathroom." Curtis's eyes brimmed with tears. "But I'll never do it again. Fire hurts." Veronica gripped the side rail and snapped it down, leaning over to give Curtis a hug.

"Oh, sweetheart, I'm so sorry you're hurting." To her surprise and heart-bursting pleasure, Curtis's arms hooked around her neck and pulled her closer. She held on to him until he loosened his arms and withdrew.

"Dad said I should tell you I'm sorry." Curtis's words revealed that what had just happened between them had been unintentional on his part and he wasn't quite comfortable about it.

"I'll accept your apology, Curtis, on the promise you'll do everything the doctors and nurses tell you so you can hurry home. It's going to be hard on your father for the two of you to be apart too long." The boy seemed to brighten a bit at that. "We're all going to miss you," she added sincerely.

"Okay," Curtis readily agreed.

Veronica glanced at the nurse who nodded in response to her unspoken question. "I guess I've got to go now, Curtis. Is there anything we can bring from home for you?"

"Dad and Aunt Helen know already."

"All right. I'll see you after you get up to your room." She smiled down at him, then started to turn away.

"Veronica?"

Veronica turned back to the boy, who looked so small and vulnerable.

"If you wouldn't mind, I'd like some of those cookies you baked." Curtis blushed, then glanced at the nurse to see if she was listening, but she seemed totally absorbed in making notations on his chart. "I only pretended not to like them," he confessed. "Would you?"

"Of course I will." Veronica's smile broadened. "You concentrate on getting well, okay?"

Curtis's little mouth curved. "Okay."

Elated, Veronica went back out into the hall.

"I'm not going to argue with you about it, Jess," Cole was saying. "Maybe it's time you made an attempt to make up to Veronica. This feud between the two of you has lasted long enough."

"You can't be serious, Cole," Jessie scoffed. "How can you even suggest that when you know what she's like? If the incident with Chapman Red wasn't bad enough, then surely what happened to Curtis today should have convinced you. You can't mean to keep her around."

Veronica stared at Jessie, frozen, chilled by Jessie's unrelenting determination to drive a wedge between her and Cole. Veronica suddenly knew she couldn't listen to any more of Jessie's vindictiveness. She was about to edge away when Helen stepped close, her slim brunette form positioned between her brother-in-law and her best friend.

"There are a few things you ought to know, Cole," Helen began, and Veronica glanced away from the look Helen tossed in her direction, certain she was about to lend her influence to the unpleasant discussion.

"First of all, it was Jessie who was responsible for Chapman Red's injury, not Veronica." Jessie's mouth dropped open, her eyes widening on the woman she thought was her closest ally. Cole's gaze had narrowed on both women while Veronica just stared, incredulous. "From what I overheard just a little while ago, I'm afraid it was premeditated, Cole. Jessie apparently planned for Veronica to be blamed."

Helen paused, then looked directly at Jessie. "I also understand that Jessie has been manipulating Curtis, persuading him into disliking, even being frightened of

Veronica." The look Helen was giving Jessie was one of contempt. "There are a few other details—" her gaze flicked back to Cole "—but I think you've heard enough for now."

"How dare you?" Jessie challenged, her fingers curving like claws, as if she was seriously contemplating scratching out Helen's eyes.

"Is what Helen's saying true?" Cole's jaw was like iron, his eyes diamond hard. Veronica shuddered, knowing all too well how frightening it was to have that near-wild look focused on her.

"I love you, Cole," Jessie stated simply, as if that explained and excused everything. "I'd do anything for you, you know that. But there have been times when you've been...distracted. I had to do something to get you back on the right path again. If I can keep you from making another mistake like Jackie, I will." The delicately pointed chin came up in defiance.

"Mistake?" Cole's voice was deceptively quiet.

"Jackie was all wrong for you, Cole." Jessie laid a proprietorial hand on his thickly muscled forearm. "She had too many ambitions that had nothing to do with you or the ranch. I on the other hand am perfectly willing to devote myself to you. I think I've more than proved that."

Veronica felt a surge of pity for Jessie. She didn't seem to see that what she'd done eight years ago and what she'd tried to pull with Curtis was more than marginally wrong. To her, the end justified the means. Indeed, in Jessie's mind the lengths she had gone to merely proved her love for Cole.

Veronica's eyes shifted from Jessie to Helen then to Cole. Neither Helen nor Cole seemed to be feeling a particle of the pity she felt for the misguided Jessica.

"What kind of woman are you?" Cole breathed. Fear flashed across Jessie's worried expression.

"Jessie was only eighteen at the time, Cole," Veronica put in, instinctively wanting him to treat Jessie gently. Obviously the woman was deranged.

"The thought that an eighteen-year-old is capable of what you did, Jessie, sickens me." Cole's lip curled faintly.

"Aside from your callous disregard for the pain and suffering of an animal, you made Veronica suffer damage to her reputation and untold emotional distress." Cole angrily shook off the manicured hand that had started to clutch at his arm.

"And you would have let all of us go on thinking that Veronica was responsible, wouldn't you? If Ronnie hadn't come back..." Cole took a deep breath. "And then using my son.... I trusted you with him." Cole's brow furrowed deeply as Jessie's face drew into an unattractive scowl. "And you aren't sorry, are you?" he stated with dawning perception.

Jessie started to agree, but clamped her mouth shut. The only indication that Cole was right was the unconscious dip of her chin.

Cole's expression suddenly turned to flint, his jaw set. "Curtis and I won't be wanting any more to do with you, Jessie, and I'd appreciate it if you didn't test me on that."

"But, Cole—"

"I mean it, Jessie. I can't speak for Helen, but if I ever catch you on my ranch or within shouting distance of Curtis or Veronica again..." Cole's jaw flexed, hardened to the frantic look on Jessie's face as she burst into incredulous tears.

"But, Cole..."

He turned to Veronica, his gentle touch on her elbow signalling her to leave with him.

"Cole?" The blonde seized his arm but Cole brushed her hand away as he would have a pesky fly. "Veronica isn't right for you, Cole," Jessie called after them, desperation giving her voice a high keening quality.

Veronica shot a worried sideways look at Cole, but the glitter of rage in his eyes forestalled any thought of persuading him to be a bit more merciful to Jessie. In spite of what Jessie had done, Veronica felt sorry for her. When Helen fell into step on the other side of Cole, Veronica realised that she was wasting no sorrow on her former friend, either.

IT WAS LATER, after they'd grabbed a cup of coffee in the cafeteria, then gone upstairs to make certain Curtis was settled in his room for the night, that the three of them left the hospital. They were in the parking lot beside Helen's car when Helen spoke.

"I can't begin to tell you how sorry I am for the way I've treated you, Veronica. I guess I've been suffering from a particularly bad case of stupidity."

"I understand, Helen," Veronica said sincerely. "It's all right."

"No, it's not all right," the brunette said vehemently. "I've been unforgivably rude and ungracious to you."

"It's all right—really," Veronica assured her. "I'd feel more comfortable if we'd both just forget about it." Veronica had no problem managing a smile, pleased when Helen's worried look slackened and she allowed herself to smile back.

"Thank you, Veronica," Helen said, then hesitated. "I'd really like it if we could be friends. I have a feeling we're going to be neighbours." Helen's dark eyes slanted up to meet Cole's. "At least if Cole gets his way."

Veronica felt colour tinge her cheeks, but she gave no other indication of the thrill of hope that surged inside her, showering her heart with joy.

"I'll call you tomorrow, Helen," Cole said to his sister-in-law. "Either that or I'll see you here at the hospital. Thanks again."

Cole and Veronica walked the rest of the way to his truck in silence. The sun had gone down, the dark-blue sky overhead deepening rapidly to diamond-studded blackness.

The ride home was quiet, as if both were too preoccupied with thoughts that couldn't be discussed yet. But when Cole pulled off the highway onto the ranch road, he took the left fork that led north of the house and deep into the rolling grazing land that stretched for miles beneath the night sky. He braked the truck to a halt on the crest of a hill and switched off the engine.

They sat in silence several moments, Cole's wrists draped over the top of the steering wheel as he stared into the darkness. Uncertain, Veronica tried to avoid the feeling that the next minute would be the most important of her life.

Sensing Cole was about to speak, she glanced in his direction. He leaned back, pulling his wrists from the steering wheel, and removed his Stetson. Lean tanned fingers pinched the crease of the hat as he looked down at it thoughtfully. Then he hung it on the rifle rack behind his head and turned to her, the lights from the dash illuminating the gentle loving look on his face and highlighting the vulnerability on hers.

Cole shook his head, his mouth tightening. "I'm sorry, Veronica. You deserve a more romantic setting than this."

Veronica's heart seemed to slam against her breastbone. Cole turned toward her fully, reaching to pull her into his arms. Veronica's hands slipped around his neck as his lips swooped down and took hers. When he deepened the kiss, Veronica felt the heated languor spread until she was thrall to the sensations his lips called forth.

"I love you, Veronica," Cole rasped. "And I'm going to be a miserable man if all you can say this time is that you 'care' for me." He didn't give her a chance to speak before his lips met hers with renewed vigour, releasing her mouth only when she was breathing as unsteadily as he. "Well?"

"Are you certain you want my love?" Veronica stalled, and Cole pressed a tender kiss on her mouth.

"You're scared to admit it, aren't you?" he asked, his eyes narrowing perceptively. "But you aren't a sixteen-year-old child experiencing her first crush, Ronnie. You're a woman," Cole said, then waited for her to speak.

"I love you, Cole," she finally whispered. "I loved you eight years ago, but what I felt at sixteen was only a childish version of what I feel now." Veronica turned her face slightly, deflecting another of Cole's kisses as she released a nervous breath. "I don't think you're going to be able to get rid of me very easily. I'm afraid I love you too much to leave you now."

Cole chuckled at Veronica's confession and she watched him almost worriedly.

"That's awfully damned convenient, Ronnie," he growled, "because once we stand up before the preacher, you're stuck with me for life, for better or worse, in sickness and in health. And I'm not some faint-hearted pantywaist who's going to take back my vow or break it over every little thing that comes along." Cole's expression relaxed. "So unless you're planning to marry me and stay married, you'd be wise to choose your next words with care."

"Wait, Cole." Veronica pressed her fingers gently over his mouth, her eyes glazing when Cole took a fingertip between his teeth and wrapped his lips seductively around it. Veronica stared, mesmerised by the sight, paralysed by the molten pleasure that radiated in wave after delicious wave through her slim body. "S-stop." Cole grinned at the small stutter, the satisfied look in his warm gaze telling her he enjoyed arousing her. "We need to... talk."

Veronica barely had enough sanity to get the words out before she dazedly wondered what there was left to say. Cole reached up and took her hand away, but not before he turned it over and placed a kiss in its sensitive palm. Rational thought returned in slow degrees as violet eyes stayed fixed to much darker blue ones.

"Will you marry me, Veronica?"

"Oh, Cole, I..." The joy she felt tumbled over her, sending her blood pulsing through her veins in a frenzied staccato of exhilaration. "I want to marry you very much," she said. "But what about Curtis?" She had been a reluctant stepchild too many times for her to be insensitive to the boy's feelings.

"Curtis is coming around, sweetheart. Now that we know the reason for your problems with him and got rid of the source, he'll accept you. There's no doubt in my mind that he'll come to love you like a mother." Cole pressed his forehead to hers, the tips of their noses touching.

"And that brings me to the next problem," she whispered, running a gentle hand along Cole's whisker-roughened cheek. "I'll never be able to replace Jackie." Veronica caught back a small sob, amazed at the heartache she felt at the forlorn words.

Cole's fingers threaded into her hair and tugged her head back as he brought his lips down forcefully on hers. Veronica welcomed the ferocity of his mouth, opening her own to the onslaught, encouraging the raw passion of it as she combed her fingers into his hair, pressing him even closer. At last Cole withdrew, his fingers tightening in her hair to keep her mouth from reclaiming his. He saw the tears that glittered in the depths of her eyes.

"I stopped looking for a replacement for Jackie a long time ago," he told her. "And now that I've come to love you, Veronica, I know it's not only possible for that kind of love to happen twice—" Cole's husky voice dropped to a whisper "—but it can run deeper and sweeter the second time around."

Veronica was nearly overcome with emotion. Cole held her close again, the way he clung to her underscoring his every word, leaving her with no doubt about his love for her.

"If you'd rather have a more romantic setting for this marriage proposal, I'm willing to take you someplace else." Cole drew back, gazing down into the violet eyes that shimmered in the faint light from the dashboard. "Just as long as you say yes."

"I've already had all the romantic trappings," Veronica whispered. "And that's all they turned out to be—trappings. But you've provided the most romantic part of any marriage proposal—your love."

Veronica kissed him sweetly and said, "Yes. I'll marry you, Cole. But for nothing less than you threatened," she added, smiling happily. "For better or worse, in sickness and in health," she repeated, secure in the knowledge that whatever the future held for them, their vows of the heart were eternal.

"By now he should have known far more about her than he did. He knew nothing, and he obviously wasn't going to get anywhere by calling upon his well-practised masculine charm.

She intrigued him, she worried him, she fascinated him. And he was going to find out what made her tick. Sooner or later he would find out all there was to know about Audrey Hamilton."

BY SPECIAL REQUEST

Barbara Kaye

PROLOGUE

BENEATH A CLEAR TEXAS SKY the blackland prairie stretched ahead for seemingly endless miles, fresh and emerald-green even in the heat of July. Generous rains had fallen all spring and early summer, and the pastures were in excellent condition. Jesse Murdoch nudged his horse across a rise and down into a small creek's grassy valley, oblivious to the beauty of the landscape. He rode for perhaps half a mile. Then reining in his horse and squinting under the big brim of his black Stetson, he gazed down the creek bank toward a stand of post oak. When he spied the slim figure of a young woman lounging against a tree trunk, her pinto mare tethered nearby, a grin spread across his face and excitement pumped through his veins. Audrey was waiting for him, just as she'd promised. Setting his horse at a gentle canter, he closed the space between them.

Audrey Hamilton straightened when she heard the approaching horse. Nervously she wiped her hands on her jeans; her fingers felt stiff and cold. She found it hard to believe that only a few hours ago she had been filled with happy anticipation. Now she was sure she had never been angrier in all the twenty-two years of her life. Her nerves were stretched to the snapping point, and she prayed she would get through this encounter with Jesse without completely losing her composure.

She studied the man on horseback. His ever-present black hat was shaped in the distinctive style known as a "Montana peak," and he sat tall and straight in his saddle. As he came nearer, she could see that charming boyish grin on his rugged tanned face, and she seethed inside. Lord, he was a handsome one! He oozed effortless charm and confidence.

For months she had been so sure that she was, at last, deeply in love. Now her only conscious emotion was shame at having been taken in by such an unprincipled, deceitful bastard!

Unaware of the dark thoughts spinning inside Audrey's head, Jesse rode to within a few yards of her, swung out of the saddle and tethered his horse to a tree. Then he sauntered toward her, his arms outstretched. "Hi, honey. Been waiting long?"

Audrey stepped back, avoiding his intended embrace. The grim expression on her face stopped Jesse in his tracks, and warning bells began clanging in his head. *Something's wrong,* he thought. For the first time it occurred to him that Audrey's father might not have welcomed her alliance with a common cowboy as readily as she had assumed he would. If so, Jesse had no idea what his next move would be. "Well, did you talk to your dad?" he asked warily.

"No." The word was precise, clipped.

"You . . . said you were going to."

Audrey took a deep breath. "I won't be talking to Dad about us, Jesse. I talked, or rather listened to Sam Graves instead."

Jesse frowned. "Who the devil is Sam Graves?"

"Dad's friend, the one you saw yesterday. He's visiting from Wyoming." She placed some emphasis on "Wyoming" and waited to gauge his reaction.

"Oh?" Now a very real fear swept through Jesse.

"Yes." Audrey folded her arms across her chest, turned and walked away a few steps, then turned back. "He saw you and asked me what your name was. I told him, and . . . it seems he knows you."

Jesse attempted a smile. "Sorry, hon, your friend's mistaken. I never met anyone named Sam Graves."

"Oh, he doesn't know you personally. But he sure knows of you. You see, he's very well acquainted with a family named Revis. Maybe the name Janet Revis rings a bell."

The color drained from Jesse's face. Judas, talk about the bad-luck kid! How many miles could the Revis ranch be from the blackland prairie of Texas? A thousand-plus? Not in his wildest dreams would he have imagined that the Hamiltons would ever hear of the Revises. For the first time in his adult life, Jesse Murdoch was at a loss for words. He could feel his great dreams crumbling like clay at his feet.

Audrey never took her eyes off him. Somewhere in the back of her foolish romantic mind she had harbored the hope that Sam would turn out to be wrong about Jesse, but one look at Jesse's face banished that hope. She felt sick inside. Dear God, she had come within a whisker of being the biggest fool ever.

Poor Janet, she thought, recalling the story Sam had told her. The unsuspecting woman in Wyoming had honestly thought Jesse was sincere, right up until the minute he rode off into the sunset. Jesse had come very close to his goal that time, but he hadn't counted on Janet's father's chauvinistic attitude. Once Jesse discovered that Janet would never own the ranch, that it would go to her uncle in the event of her father's death, he had packed up and left, without so much as a goodbye to the young woman he'd assiduously courted for six months. According to Sam, Janet had had a hard time getting over it.

Audrey's chest heaved in agitation. Maliciously, she was enjoying every second of Jesse's discomfort. "And Janet wasn't the first, was she, Jesse? Sam also told me about the woman in Montana. But she was only eighteen, and her father saw through you right away. Oh, you have quite a reputation out west! You're a good cowhand, so you can always find work, but you have this peculiar fondness for working on ranches whose owners have single daughters. You make me sick!"

Regret, despair and grudging resignation settled over Jesse. He wasn't the least remorseful over having wooed Audrey with avarice in his soul. He was only sorry that another goose that could lay his golden egg had escaped his clutches. He supposed he could try turning supplicant, vow to the heavens that his feelings for Audrey were completely different from anything he'd felt for Janet, but he didn't think Audrey would buy that for a second. That had always bothered him; Audrey was a helluva lot smarter than Janet had been. Damn!

Jesse wanted to shake his fist at whatever fate had sent Sam Graves to the Hamilton ranch. Audrey had been the perfect "catch"—young, beautiful and the only heir to the various Hamilton enterprises, which were considerable. Besides the ranch, the old man owned a company in Dallas and a splendid home there, along with another on the Gulf Coast. Compared to the Hamiltons, the Revises had been strictly potato patch.

Jesse had envisioned a life far beyond his most optimistic expectations. His sojourns in Montana, Wyoming and Texas had taken a precious three years out of his life. He was nearing thirty and anxious to secure his future. Long ago he had decided that the best way to do that wasn't by hard work but by taking advantage of his attractiveness to women.

Desperation overtook him when he saw Audrey turn toward her horse. He had to do something. He couldn't let Audrey walk out of his life. Grabbing her by the arm, he spun her around to face him. "Audrey, honey, you're overreacting to an old man's gossip. I really am fond of you, and we make a good pair."

She laughed harshly in disbelief. "Save it, Jesse. You are incredible! I'm going back to the house and tell Dad to send you packing."

"I wouldn't do that, if I were you. Guess I oughta warn you of something. I can ruin your daddy if I set my mind to it."

"You're also crazy! *You* ruin my father, one of the most important men in this state. You overestimate yourself."

An indolent smile matched the tone of Jesse's voice. "I'm not sure I do. I've been on this ranch some time now, and I've heard things I wasn't supposed to hear, mainly because I keep my eyes and ears open. One word from me, and the high and mighty Hamiltons will be in the pits."

"I don't have any idea what you're talking about."

"I'm sure you don't, but if you're as smart as I think you are, you'll take my word for it. I can ruin your daddy. I promise, marrying me will be the lesser of two evils. You might even learn to like it.''

Angrily Audrey disengaged herself from his grasp, ran to her horse and mounted. As she galloped away, tears of fury stung her eyes, and a despondent sense of failure and inadequacy overtook her. All of her life she had heard people tell her how fortunate she was. "You have everything, Audrey," they would say. "Looks, money, wit, intelligence."

But the one precious commodity called love, the thing that other women seemed to find so easily, had eluded her completely. Until Jesse. How could she have fallen for that kind of man? Was there some kind of flaw in her psyche? She felt embarrassed, humiliated.

At that moment Audrey was sure she would never regret anything as much as the minutes she had spent in Jesse Murdoch's arms. She had no way of knowing how much more there would be to regret.

CHAPTER ONE

Phoenix, Arizona
Five Years Later

"CAREFUL, AUDREY," Helen Drake warned as she strolled into the office and took a seat behind her desk. "The boss is in a very peculiar mood this morning."

Audrey had been deeply engrossed in the new brochures the graphics company had sent over that morning, but Helen's remark brought her head up. "Peter? I wonder what's wrong."

"Don't ask me." Helen shrugged as she whipped the cover off her typewriter. "He got a phone call a few minutes ago, and it really played heck with his sweet disposition. He didn't even finish his dictation, and he wants you to get in there right away."

"Of course," Audrey said, getting to her feet immediately and leaving the office.

"In there" was the office only a few yards down the mezzanine corridor from Audrey's own. She lightly tapped on the door marked Manager, then pushed it open and stepped inside.

Peter Sorenson was standing with his back to her, hands clasped behind him, staring out the window that overlooked the sixteenth fairway. He turned slowly and faced her with a dark, worried expression. A scowling Peter was an unusual sight. Audrey had often thought he had the most placid disposition of anyone she'd ever known.

"Yes, Peter?" She approached his desk.

"Sit down, Audrey."

Not even his customary "good morning." Puzzled, Audrey sank into one of the leather chairs facing the desk, crossed her long shapely legs and watched her employer slip into his swivel chair. He picked up a pencil and began drumming it on the desk. "I've just had a call from the Benedicts," Peter told her.

"Oh?" That got Audrey's attention. The Benedicts were the wealthy family who owned the Greenspoint, the posh resort hotel near Phoenix where Peter was manager and Audrey his assistant. She knew very little about the prominent family, but if one could believe rumors, the Benedicts owned half of Arizona.

"It seems one of them is paying us a visit this afternoon. Why, do you suppose?"

Audrey uttered a little laugh. "You're asking me? I have no idea. I've never so much as set eyes on any of the illustrious clan."

"It's been years since I have. They never stay here, or in any public place for that matter. They have a house in Paradise Valley, and that's home when they're in Phoenix. All our dealings with them are through lawyers, although I'm sure they have some of their spies check us out from time to time. But the Benedicts never show up, so why this unexpected visit?"

"I'm sorry, Peter, I don't have the foggiest idea."

"The old patriarch died last week. A shake-up maybe?"

Audrey could only shrug. How was she to know why people like the Benedicts did anything?

"You know, Audrey, scuttlebutt has it that the Melton chain has made an offer for a Phoenix hotel." Peter's tone was ominous. "So far it's all very hush-hush, but what if that hotel is the Greenspoint?"

She looked at him blankly. "What if?"

"You and I might be out of work, that's 'what if.' The Melton bunch likes to bring in their own people." He paused to let her digest that. "Now, just suppose the Benedicts have received an offer and are sending one of their own here to look us over, to decide if we're worth keeping."

Audrey did her best to appear concerned, but she couldn't understand why an impending visit from one of the owners was such a big deal. Surely Peter wasn't worried about the impression the hotel would make. The Greenspoint was the grande dame of Arizona resorts. The hotel had played host to heads of state, deposed royalty and spoiled movie queens, always to raves. The Benedicts couldn't possibly be any more particular or demanding than some of the celebrity guests they had dealt with in the past.

"Strictly conjecture, Peter," she said.

"Maybe. It just seems damned funny to me that one of 'em is showing up, out of the blue, with no warning, no explanation. Well, something's up, you can bet on it." Peter picked up a notepad and read from it. "Boyd Benedict, that's the one who'll be here. I'm not sure if he's a son, a nephew or what, but he's a Benedict, so he has clout." He looked squarely at Audrey and spoke earnestly. "Let's give him a hotel stay he won't soon forget. And if he wants the grand tour, I'll expect you to handle it with aplomb. We'll put him in the Durango Suite."

Audrey nodded.

"Now, I want you to get up there and make sure it's ready."

"You know it's ready, Peter."

He went on as if she hadn't spoken. "Get in touch with housekeeping. Then spread the word among the staff. I want everyone to drown the man in contentment. I'm sure I don't have to stress the need for making his visit a perfect one."

"Of course not. I'll get right on it." She stood up. "Mr. Benedict won't have any complaints, you can be sure of that. The President was lavish in his praise."

"The President of the United States doesn't own the Greenspoint. The Benedicts do!"

"True," Audrey conceded.

"And you might tell everyone that if I hear any complaints from the man, some heads are going to roll!"

Audrey looked down at him, horrified. "Oh, I'll do no such thing! This is a seasoned staff, but you'll have everyone so uptight they won't be able to do their jobs. I'll simply tell them to be on their toes and to proceed in their usual efficient manner. That should impress Mr. Benedict more than anything." Pivoting, she left Peter's office and returned to her own.

"So, what's up?" Helen demanded as Audrey stepped into the room.

Audrey crossed the carpet and sank into the swivel chair behind her desk. Succinctly she told her secretary about the impending arrival of one of the owners. "It's certainly gotten a rise out of Peter. Helen, what do you know about the Benedicts? I've never even seen any of them."

"I don't think any of us have," Helen said. "I've seen some pictures in the newspapers, but that's about it. They're powerful, influential, and they keep a low profile. They've been around for...oh, I don't know...forever! If you were a native you couldn't avoid hearing about them. They're sort of Arizona's answer to the Kennedys. There are Benedict Memorial this-and-thats all over the place. I think they first made their money in ranching, but I'm sure no one really knows what all they're involved in now. They don't give out interviews, and they stay strictly to themselves."

"Well, let's just hope Boyd Benedict turns out to be a man who appreciates class when he sees it."

Helen uttered a little gasp, and her eyes widened. "Is it Boyd Benedict who's coming?" she asked breathlessly.

Audrey nodded. "Why?"

"He used to cut a pretty wide swath through Arizona society. Made all the gossip columns frequently, but I haven't heard much about him lately. He's probably married and settled down by now. Ooh, I'm anxious to get a good look at him. I hear he's really something."

Audrey smiled. She, like everyone else at the Greenspoint, was well aware of Helen's penchant for the opposite sex. "Helen, you'll think he's 'something' if he's breathing."

"Probably," Helen said and laughed wickedly.

A FEW MINUTES LATER Audrey stepped out of her office into the mezzanine's carpeted corridor. Turning right, she walked toward the stairs that led to the main lobby. As she passed one of the hotel's ballrooms, she paused for a moment and watched a group of waiters putting the finishing touches on a dozen or so banquet tables. A professional organization was holding its annual awards dinner at the hotel that evening, and the ballroom glittered with crystal, silver, white linen and fresh flowers. No one, she thought, did this sort of thing quite as well as the Greenspoint.

Continuing on, she smiled and spoke to two young bellboys who were passing by, but she didn't slow her pace and was oblivious to the frankly admiring stares that followed her. What the two young men stared at was her shapely figure—slender, leggy and full-breasted. Her carriage was erect, and she moved with ease and grace. Her ash-brown hair was thick and glistened with health. When worn down it fell to her shoulders in a waving cascade and framed an oval face with delicate features that were memorably attractive. What most people remembered longest, however, were her eyes—large, expressive, straightforward and of a lovely shade of brown flecked with golden glints.

At the head of the stairs she paused, and those unusual eyes took in the scene below. There was an amazing lack of hustle and bustle in the lobby, even though the hotel was booked almost to capacity. Guests who checked into the resort expected serenity, impeccable service and a gracious atmosphere, and they received it. The lobby of the Greenspoint exuded an air of elegance and charm, of quiet opulence. The overall ambience was one of stepping back in time to a less frantic era. Audrey never tired of it.

But even if she had hated it she would have stayed. For three years the Greenspoint had been her haven of peace and protection. Here she felt safe. Here she could forget the past and not worry about the future. She still found it hard to believe that with only high school typing, some shorthand and eighteen months' experience with an advertising agency in Dallas she had fallen into such a marvellous job.

"You're a natural, Audrey," Peter had told her when he made her his assistant. "You know how to meet people, and you know how to pamper them. That's what this job is all about, and you don't learn it in a classroom."

Audrey had learned the social graces from her socialite mother, a woman of flawless good taste. She called upon the lessons learned at Constance Hamilton's knee almost every day. Whenever a guest was difficult or displeased, she always asked herself, "How would Mom expect to be treated? What would impress her?" It worked every time.

She began a slow descent of the winding stairway, her alert eyes taking in everything at once. Several middle-aged matrons sat engrossed in needlepoint and magazines. Teenagers in tennis togs crossed the lobby carrying racquets. Golfers came and went. Laughing children in swimsuits dashed through the glass doors leading to the loggia surrounding the pool.

At some tables by the tall front windows, groups of elderly men sat engaged in card games. Intently Audrey searched their faces, looking for one in particular. Not finding it, she crossed the lobby and went out onto the long covered veranda that ran the entire length of the front of the building. Most of the rocking chairs were occupied, but, again, she didn't find the face she was seeking.

Just then Craig Smith, a young college student who worked part-time at the hotel, bounded up the steps and onto the porch. Audrey halted him.

"Craig, have you seen Bert?"

"Who?"

"My friend, Bert Lincoln. You remember."

"Oh, you mean the old guy with the beard and shaggy white hair? No, come to think of it, I haven't seen him in weeks."

"Four weeks, to be exact." Audrey frowned and bit her lip. "And I didn't particularly like the way he looked last time he was here. Kind of... tired and pale. I do hope nothing's happened to him."

Craig fell in step beside her as she reversed her direction. Opening the door to the lobby for her, he said, "You've become real fond of that old gentleman, haven't you, Audrey?"

"Oh, he's such a sweet guy, and so lonesome. I guess I feel sorry for him. He must not have a family. I can't imagine a family letting him roam around alone at his age."

"How long's he been coming here?"

"I first noticed him about nine months ago. He'd show up every day and sit on the veranda, sometimes all day long. He seemed to enjoy just watching people come and go. He intrigued me, so I started talking to him, and first thing I knew we were friends. I don't have any idea where he lives or what he used to do for a living, but you're right, I've become awfully attached to him. I always worry about him when I don't see him for a while."

Craig flashed her a boyish grin. "Well, I wouldn't worry about him too much, Audrey. He seems to come and go like a phantom. He'll show up again one of these days."

"I hope so, Craig. I hope so." She smiled sheepishly. "I also hope I haven't been taken in by a pair of old, sad eyes. The last time he was here I loaned him fifty dollars—money I could ill afford, I might add."

"Boy, are you easy!"

"Probably. Well, if you see him, come and get me, okay?"

"Sure."

"See you around, Craig."

"Take care, Audrey."

Audrey waved a greeting to the desk clerk as she swept through the lobby, past the cocktail lounge, the gift shop and the beauty parlor, to enter the Gold Circle Room, the most opulent of the Greenspoint's three restaurants. In the gleaming stainless-steel kitchen she found the young chef, Jacky Jordan, backing out of the industrial-size refrigerator.

"Good morning, Jacky."

"Hi, Audrey. You look like a breath of spring. What brings you down so early in the day?"

"I'm here, like Paul Revere, to sound the alarm. The Benedicts are coming."

"The Benedicts?"

"The people who own these hallowed halls. And actually there'll only be one."

"They're ranchers, right? He probably eats well-done prime rib and drinks black coffee with his meals." A contemptuous look crossed Jacky's face.

Audrey laughed. "Just tell everyone to be on their toes. You may have dealings with the man, and you may not."

"They're always on their toes, but I'll give them a pep talk."

"Thanks, Jacky. By the way, you know Mrs. Marsten in two-twelve, don't you? Today's her birthday."

"Gotcha. One cake, coming up."

From the dining room Audrey made her way to the lounge for a short talk with the bartender, then one by one she conversed with the desk clerk, the people in the coffee shop, the bell captain and the housekeeping staff. Once she was sure that everyone had been contacted, she stepped into the elevator and went up to the third floor and the Durango Suite.

The suite was the Greenspoint at its grandest. Consisting of a parlor, two bedrooms and two baths, it was a study in subdued elegance and supreme comfort, designed for guests who were accustomed to the finest of everything. Not a luxurious detail had been overlooked. And, as Audrey had expected, it was spotless, at the ready, although the Durango was not heavily booked. Not many people, even wealthy ones, cared to fork over the astronomical sum the suite commanded.

Audrey made a slow, painstaking inspection of the place, noting with satisfaction the thick, oversize towels in both baths, the imported castile soap, the luxurious gold fixtures, the gleaming tile on the floors and around the sunken tubs. Back in the parlor she made a mental note to have the florist deliver fresh flowers right after lunch. And, of course Mr. Benedict would receive complimentary hors d'oeuvres and a bottle of wine in late afternoon, then fruit, croissants and coffee in the morning. She checked the sideboard in the dining room to make sure it was stocked with liquor and mixes. It was ironic, she thought, that the guests who could afford anything got all the free goodies.

Satisfied that not even a Benedict could find fault with these accommodations, she left and took the elevator down to the mezzanine and Peter's office. His expression still was as dark and gloomy as an approaching desert thunderstorm.

"Everything's ready, boss," she announced brightly.

"It had better be," Peter replied tersely, without glancing up from his desk.

IT WAS MIDAFTERNOON when word reached the executive offices that Mr. Benedict had arrived and was checking in. Peter, who had been waiting anxiously in Audrey's office, jumped to his feet and hurried to the door.

"Wait here!" he commanded over his shoulder as he disappeared into the corridor.

"I don't think I've ever seen Peter so uptight," Helen commented when he was gone. "Is this really that big a deal?"

"Who knows? Peter sure seems to think it is." Audrey continued checking the inventory one of the housekeepers had given her. She fully expected Peter to be tied up with their VIP guest for some time, so she was surprised when he returned to her office in less than twenty minutes. She could see that his meeting with Mr. Benedict hadn't done anything to brighten his mood. His brow was deeply furrowed.

"Well?" she demanded impatiently when Peter merely stood in front of her desk, silent and scowling. "Is our guest satisfied with the suite?"

"I have no idea. He didn't say a word about it."

Audrey shrugged. Perhaps to a Benedict the Durango Suite wasn't all that impressive. "Did he say anything about selling the hotel?"

"No."

Why was he being so confoundedly mysterious? "Peter, why are you making me drag this out of you? Did he give you any idea why he's here?"

Peter tugged on his chin and eyed her intently. "Yes, he did. That's what's so peculiar."

"Peculiar? If you ask me, you're the one who's acting peculiar. Why is the man here?"

"He wants to see you."

Audrey's eyes widened. "M-me?"

He nodded. "You."

"Peter, is this some kind of joke?"

"No joke. As a matter of fact, I got the distinct impression that the man's chief reason for being here is to see you."

"That's absurd. Why on earth would one of the Benedicts come here to see me?"

"I can't imagine. We shook hands, introduced ourselves, then right off the bat he asked me if my assistant's name was Audrey Hamilton. When I said yes, he asked if you were here. I told him you were, and he asked me to send you up right away."

Audrey glanced at Helen, whose eyes were wide with bewilderment, then back at Peter, who was staring at her in the strangest way. "That's all? He didn't say why he wants to see me?"

Peter shook his head. "What have you been up to, Audrey?"

"Nothing!" She affected a nonchalance she certainly didn't feel. "You know there's a reasonable explanation for this. Maybe he just wants to meet all the key staff. I've done nothing to make him single me out."

"You'd better get on up there," Peter said.

"Yes, of course," she mumbled. Squaring her shoulders and trying to ignore her suddenly nervous stomach, she hurriedly left the office and took an elevator to the third floor.

CHAPTER TWO

AUDREY'S FIRST IMPRESSION of the man who answered her knock was of height. She was five-six and wearing two-inch heels, yet he still towered over her, so she had to assume he was six feet or more. Then her dark eyes met his smoky gray ones, moved downward, and her next impression was of startlingly white teeth that contrasted sharply with tanned skin. When her gaze took in the entire countenance of craggy male features, her interest quickened into something that went far beyond normal curiosity.

Somehow she found her professional welcoming voice. "Mr. Benedict?" she inquired politely.

"I'm Boyd Benedict, yes."

He fit none of her preconceived notions about him. For one thing, since Helen had told her Boyd Benedict used to cut a wide social swath, Audrey had been expecting someone a bit older, someone approaching middle age. But this man was, she guessed, no more than six or seven years older than she and was undeniably handsome in a rugged sort of way.

A shock of dark brown, almost black hair topped his head, and his skin was very tanned. It was not the sort of tan that came from long hours by the pool, but rather the tan acquired from years of being in the outdoors. That was another surprise. Considering all the Benedicts' various enterprises, she had fully expected a businessman, but this man simply didn't look the part of an executive.

Laugh lines splayed out from the corners of his mouth and eyes. His features were sharply defined—piercing eyes, prominent nose, strong mouth, a slight cleft in the chin—and his physique was admirable—broad shoulders, trim waist and hips. He was wearing a cream-colored shirt, sleeves rolled to the elbows, and dark tan slacks that hugged well-shaped thighs. Both were of Western-cut. "Vital" and "virile" were the words that immediately popped into her head. Even without money and influence, Boyd Benedict would have attracted attention, especially female attention, wherever he went.

"I hear he's really something," Helen had said. She had heard right. Suddenly Audrey was very conscious of the way she herself looked. The tailored peach blouse and the simple off-white skirt had seemed quite all right when she had dressed that morning. Her hair had been swirled into a French twist, a hairdo she felt made her appear older, less ingenuous. Neat, feminine, businesslike—the image she tried to project on the job. Only now she felt like a drab wren and was absurdly wishing she looked more alluring.

Collecting her wits, she extended her hand and flashed her brightest smile. "I'm Audrey Hamilton, the assistant manager, Mr. Benedict. Did you want to see me?"

Then the most peculiar thing happened; Audrey was at a loss to explain it. The smile on his face faded abruptly, and his expression changed from one of idle curiosity to one of startled confusion. He glanced down at her outstretched hand, then took it briefly, furtively.

Boyd Benedict's eyes raked over her in a way that made her cringe inside. Men normally weren't indifferent to her, but Audrey didn't think she had ever been so thoroughly scrutinized. Nor did she think she had ever had a man react to her in such an odd way. His eyes asked questions she couldn't interpret. Suddenly her face felt very warm, her mouth dry, and she experienced a brief wild urge to run from him. Inexplicably, she felt threatened.

But her years at the Greenspoint, dealing with the public and disguising her reactions to unpredictable human behavior, had instilled in her a poise that never completely abandoned her. "You wanted to see me, Mr. Benedict?" she inquired again.

He brought himself up to his full height. "Oh, yes, I did. Forgive my rudeness. I was staring, wasn't I? It's just that you're something of a surprise."

Audrey's heart lurched as the mystery deepened. He had known her name and her position at the hotel, but he easily could have acquired that information. The question was, why would he? And why had he, too, formed some preconceived notions? Why on earth would the prominent Mr. Benedict have given her a moment's thought?

Stepping back, Boyd made a wide sweep with his arm. "Yes, Miss Hamilton, I wanted to see you. Please come in."

Automatically, Audrey moved forward to stand in the center of the room, although some strange instinct was demanding she leave. She could feel the man's gray eyes beating through the back of her head. Her own eyes darted about, making observations and seeking a safe place to rest.

The suite was decked out for a celebrity's arrival, and she supposed the man behind her fit into that category. The bouquet the florist had sent was extravagant, to say the least. A bottle of fine California Cabernet Sauvignon stood next to it. Inhaling deeply, Audrey slowly turned around to once again face Boyd Benedict's unsettling stare.

"What did you wish to see me about, Mr. Benedict? Are your accommodations satisfactory?"

"They're fine, just fine," he said in a way that suggested he'd barely noticed his elegant surroundings. "Please have a seat, Miss Hamilton." His voice was rich and low and carried authority.

Audrey would have preferred to remain standing, for she felt that being seated would somehow put her at a disadvantage. Nevertheless, she stiffly crossed the room and took a seat on the sofa, crossing her ankles and primly folding her hands in her lap. She swallowed rapidly several times, hating the way he made her feel. The poise she believed would never abandon her was dangerously close to doing just that.

I'm going to be fired, was her immediate thought. But that was ridiculous, and she knew it. One of the Benedicts wouldn't show up in person to fire an assistant manager. She waited with suspended breath.

Boyd walked purposefully to the dining table and opened a briefcase that was lying there. Withdrawing some papers, he propped a hip against the table and studied them for what seemed forever. The room was so quiet Audrey could hear the thump-thumping of her own heartbeat. Finally he looked up.

"How old are you, Miss Hamilton?"

"Twenty-seven."

"It is Miss, isn't it? You aren't wearing a ring, although not all women do."

"Yes, it's Miss." What on earth was all this?

"Have you ever been married?"

"No."

"How long have you been working here at the Greenspoint?"

"Three years." Audrey thought if he didn't get to the point of all this she might actually scream.

One dark eyebrow arched slightly. "And you're already the assistant manager?" His tone implied that she couldn't possibly have come by the position honestly.

Audrey clinched her teeth. "I...I have a friend who knows Peter. Three years ago he was looking for someone to fill in for his secretary, who was on maternity leave, and my friend recommended me. It was supposed to be a temporary job, but the secretary never returned, and Peter and I had discovered we worked well together. He eventually hired Helen Drake and promoted me."

Boyd digested that and seemed to accept it. "And before that?"

Audrey's heart constricted. Dear God, was that what this was about—her past? How could Boyd Benedict know anything about that? "I spent a year and a half with an advertising agency," she said simply and prayed that would satisfy him.

Apparently it did. "All right, Miss Hamilton, now I'll tell you why I wanted to see you. I'm afraid I'm going to have to ask you a very personal question, and I expect a direct answer."

The first bristle of indignation struck Audrey. The man was unbelievably abrasive. Being a Benedict didn't give him that right. "Very well," she said stiffly and braced herself for whatever was coming.

"What exactly was your relationship with Bertram B. Benedict?"

Audrey blinked. "Who?"

"Bertram B. Benedict. I'm sure the name is familiar to you."

"No, Mr. Benedict, it isn't. I've never heard of the man." Relief engulfed her. This wasn't what she had feared at all.

"Come, come, Miss Hamilton, I was hoping you would be completely honest with me. It's vitally important that I know the exact nature of your relationship. Nothing can be served by lying to me."

Audrey's face flushed crimson, but she forced herself to remain calm. "I'm not lying, Mr. Benedict. I don't know anyone by that name. I would tell you if I did."

Boyd uttered an impatient sound and slammed the papers down on the table. Glaring at her, he barked, "Let's not play games! I'll find out the truth sooner or later."

His tone was insufferable. Audrey didn't care who he was or how important his family was. She didn't even care that he could have her job in an instant. "I'm not playing games!" she exclaimed angrily. "I don't know anyone named Bertram B. Benedict."

"Miss Hamilton, I'm a very busy man. Coming here to see you has taken time I really couldn't afford, and I'm anxious to finish this business so I can go home. Now, please tell me what I want to know, and we can get this over and done with...."

"Get what over and done with?" Audrey's temples began to throb. "I don't have the slightest idea what you're talking about."

Boyd glowered at her. "I'm going to insist that you cooperate with me. It's imperative that I know all about your relationship with the man."

Audrey took a deep breath. There was plenty she would have liked to say to him, such as what he could do with his insistence, but yelling back and forth would accomplish nothing. He was being rude and overbearing, but she wasn't going to lose her composure. Boyd Benedict obviously had mistaken her for someone else, thank God, and she was certain they'd get the whole thing straightened out in a minute.

"You must have me confused with someone else, Mr. Benedict. Another Audrey Hamilton. It can't be an unusual name. I told you, I've never met Bertram B. Benedict. I'm sure I would remember if I had. Why would I lie to you?"

"I can't imagine," Boyd said tersely.

Audrey was becoming curious about Bertram. Who could he be? Probably a brother, cousin, nephew who'd gotten himself mixed up with a woman, a woman the lofty Benedicts didn't approve of. Seeing the grim expression on Boyd Benedict's face, she was relieved that she wasn't the Audrey Hamilton in question. She had a feeling that life could be unpleasant for anyone who got crosswise with the powerful family.

Boyd picked up the papers and brandished them at her. "Then possibly you can explain why a man you say you've never met would choose to mention you in his will."

Audrey's mouth dropped, and her eyes widened. "Will?" she asked incredulously. "Well, I...can't imagine. I'm sure there's been a mistake. It simply can't be me."

Boyd read from the paper. "Audrey Hamilton, currently employed as assistant manager, Greenspoint Hotel, Phoenix." He lifted his eyes. "Does that sound as though there's been a mistake?"

"No, I..." Audrey was certain she'd never been so confused. Her mind reeled and stumbled, but it was useless to try to sort and analyze what she had just heard. None of it made any sense. "I can't explain any of this, but you must believe me, I've never met anyone by that name. I would know, wouldn't I? Was he..." She faltered. "He must have been a relative of yours."

Boyd's eyes moved over her. Audrey clearly saw the suspicion in them and was at a loss to understand why he wouldn't believe her. Did she just look suspicious? He waited a moment before saying, "Yes, he was my grandfather."

"Oh, yes...I remember that a member of your family passed away recently. I sent flowers from the staff. There was a picture in the papers, but it certainly wasn't of anyone I've ever known."

"That photograph was taken fifteen years ago when my grandfather was still a very active, vigorous man. It bore little resemblance to the man he had become." Slowly, deliberately, Boyd placed the papers back on the table, folded his arms across his chest and leveled a look at her. Audrey stifled the urge to cringe. Instead, she met his gaze steadfastly.

"Let me tell you some things about my grandfather, Miss Hamilton. They just might jog your faulty memory." The bite of sarcasm was unmistakable. "He was eighty-one, was rather stooped and had thick white hair that he was careless about having cut. He often wore a beard. He had a gift of gab second to none, and his proudest possession was a railroad watch his father had given him—"

"Bert!" Audrey cried. The description fit her elderly friend to a T.

"So!" Boyd said with satisfaction. "You admit knowing him. Perhaps now you'll tell me the nature of the relationship."

"I...I know a man named Bert who fits that description. He comes to sit in a rocking chair on the veranda, and we talk. I've always felt sorry for him because he seems so lonely. I thought...honestly I thought he didn't have a family."

Abruptly she stopped as the full realization hit her. "Oh, if Bert's your grandfather...he's dead!" She placed her hand on her forehead. "For days now I've wondered what had happened to him. He'd stayed away so long this time."

"He'd lived with a bad heart for years."

"I...didn't know that." Her eyes grew misty. "He didn't talk about the present. He liked to reminisce about the way things were when he was young."

Boyd stared down at her bent head. "Are you asking me to believe that you didn't know who he was?"

"Yes, because it's true! How was I to know? He told me his name was Bert Lincoln, and I didn't question that any more than I question that you're Boyd Benedict." The man could go to hell! All Audrey could think of was her old friend, the sweet, lonely man who was dead.

"He was called Bert, all right, but Lincoln was my grandmother's maiden name."

Boyd stepped back, shaken by the young woman's distress. Shoving his hands in his pockets, he walked to the window. None of this was working out the way he had envisioned. Audrey Hamilton had turned out to be a surprise, and that was an understatement. Ever since the reading of the will, a document that had been drafted less than a week before his grandfather's death, Boyd and his father had speculated on what the Hamilton woman would be like. Buck Benedict, in his characteristically cynical fashion, had expected a worldly sophisticate with a dollar sign for a heart. Boyd, on the other hand, had imagined an empty-headed bit of fluff whose feminine wiles had captivated the old man.

Well, they both had been wrong, and that put Boyd at a disadvantage. He thought he would have known how to deal with a gold digger or a flirt, but he wasn't prepared to deal with a lovely young woman who had genuinely cared for her friend Bert. She wasn't faking her grief. He'd never seen anyone more sincere. So now what did he do?

Sighing, Boyd took a moment to wish he weren't the one his father always sent to "put out fires." Why not Brent once in a while? His brother was all business. Brent could have dealt with Audrey Hamilton dispassionately.

He turned around to see Audrey flicking at her tears with a forefinger. From his hip pocket he removed a handkerchief, crossed the room and handed it to her.

"Th-thank you," she whispered.

Boyd cleared his throat. "How long had you known my grandfather?" he asked. Now his own curiosity was sharpened.

Audrey alertly noticed that the imperiousness had vanished from his voice, replaced by a husky, uncertain quality. "Less than a year," she said. "He simply showed up one day and sat on the veranda for hours, watching people come and go. Then the next day he was back, and the next. Finally I spoke to him, and we had a nice long chat. After that, I kept my eye out for him. Little by little we became friends. He seemed to be interested in my job, how I liked working here."

"And you never inquired about his background or his family?"

She shook her head, dabbing at her eyes. "I was content to just listen to him. He told me anecdotes about 'old' Arizona. And he liked to talk about his wife. Her name was Margaret. But, of course, you know that."

"Yes. My grandmother died two years ago. Granddad never got over it. He'd begun spending most of his time at our house in Paradise Valley, rather than at the ranch where the rest of the family lives. Too many memories, I guess."

"Weren't you worried about him, an old man living all alone like that?" Audrey asked with censure.

"Miss Hamilton, the Paradise Valley house is staffed by a full complement of servants who took care of my grandfather's every need and whim, and they included a chauffeur who was his constant companion. I'm positive that when Granddad was here at the hotel, Clarence wasn't far away. Besides, no one, I mean no one, told Bertram Benedict what he could and couldn't do. He must have taken to spending time here at the Greenspoint and, for reasons known only to him, chose not to tell anyone who he was. It wouldn't have been difficult for him to remain anonymous. It had been years since he'd appeared in public. He had lost quite a bit of weight, and that scruffy beard was an effective disguise."

Audrey looked up at him through misty eyes. "Then you believe me? Honestly, I had no idea who he was. I thought he was just a lonely, impoverished old man."

"My grandfather was quite possibly the wealthiest man in Arizona."

Audrey shook her head, trying to equate the elderly man she had befriended with the patriarch of the state's most prominent family. But it was impossible. Bert had been such an unassuming person. "The last time I saw him I loaned him fifty dollars. I was afraid he wasn't eating right, and he never had any money on him."

Boyd had to smile at that. It sounded like the old man. His grandfather, for all his wealth, simply never had thought to tuck twenty dollars into his wallet. He hadn't even carried a wallet. In fact, there had been a standing joke among Bert's acquaintances: "If Bert asks you to lunch, be prepared to pick up the check."

"When I told him to spend it wisely because it was all I could afford to give him, he—" Audrey's voice broke with emotion "—he said it would be returned to me tenfold. I assumed he meant in God's blessings or something like that."

Boyd turned his head for a moment. *Great, just great!* he thought. *I really needed this.*

Silence descended. Then Audrey inquired, "May I ask about the bequest? Did Bert happen to leave that railroad watch to me?"

"As a matter of fact, he did."

She smiled sadly. "I admired it once, and he said he would leave it to me someday. Imagine his actually remembering to do it."

Then something occurred to her. If Boyd Benedict had taken the time and trouble to come to see her because of the bequest, the watch must have some family significance. "If the watch is valuable, a family heirloom or something of that nature, I'll understand, of course. I wouldn't dream of accepting it under those circumstances."

"No, the watch is yours."

Audrey's shoulders rose and fell. She understood none of this. Earlier he had been so furious, so accusing. There was more to all this, she was sure of it. "It was awfully nice of you to come here to tell me about this in person, but you're a very busy man, as you pointed out. Couldn't you have informed me of this by telephone?"

"Miss Hamilton, I'm here because my grandfather also bequeathed you something else."

"Oh? What was it?"

Boyd inhaled deeply. He picked up the papers. Slowly his eyes skimmed over them. Then he read aloud the pertinent passages. "To my friend, Audrey Hamilton...I'm sure she'll know why...the sum of one hundred thousand dollars." Boyd quickly looked up at her. He wanted to monitor her reaction to the news.

CHAPTER THREE

FOR A MOMENT Audrey could only stare at him in stunned disbelief. She couldn't have heard correctly. Even if she had, it no doubt was some kind of joke, and a poor one at that. "Wh-what did you say?" she gasped.

Boyd relaxed. She had passed with flying colors. No actress, no matter how accomplished, could have played the scene with such sincerity. And he was at a loss to explain why that pleased him so much. It struck him suddenly that he must have been hoping she would turn out to be the real McCoy, and he didn't understand that, either. "You heard correctly. One hundred thousand dollars. Nice little sum, wouldn't you say?"

"You can't be serious!"

"Oh, I'm completely serious, I assure you. You'll be receiving official notification from our lawyers any day."

Audrey couldn't think. Her mind whirled with stupefaction. There was such an air of unreality to all this. "Well, I...I don't know what to say. I'm...just having such a hard time believing any of this. Why would Bert do such a thing?"

"Apparently he thought you would know why, and I was hoping you might be able to enlighten me."

Her hands nervously twisted the handkerchief. "I've told you everything I know. I felt sorry for him. He'd just sit there, like he didn't have a soul in the world."

"I'm surprised someone didn't ask him to leave. This hotel is a pretty classy place. Why let a scruffy old man loiter around?"

"Someone mentioned it to Peter once, but I intervened. After all, Bert did no harm."

"I can't help wondering why you singled him out, one old man among many."

Audrey's head jerked up, and she looked at him with cold unflinching eyes. He was still suspicious, damn him. "Not one among many, Mr. Benedict," she snapped. "The only one on the veranda who was all alone. That's why I singled him out."

To Boyd her explanation was like a slap in the face. Unnerved by her cold regard, he walked to the window, paused a moment, then turned suddenly and said, "Miss Hamilton, I have to make a phone call. I'd like you to wait right here while I go in the bedroom and place it. Will you do that for me?"

Why should I? was her first thought, but she was weary of their sparring, and there was still so much to be cleared up. "All right," she mumbled.

"Thanks. This shouldn't take but a few minutes."

Audrey stared after his retreating figure, certain she knew the reason for the call. He would be checking in with the rest of his family, waiting for further instructions. She imagined that all really prominent families operated that way. She further suspected that the Benedicts didn't like outsiders, even innocent, unwilling ones, intruding into their lives. What must they have thought when they learned that Bert had left an unknown woman such an incredible sum?

Although the bedroom door was closed, she could hear the sound of Boyd's voice. She couldn't make out any of the words, but her ears burned anyway. Oh, Lord, the last thing she wanted was trouble—she'd had enough of that, thank you—and somehow she felt that getting involved with the Benedicts would lead to trouble beyond her wildest imagination.

INSIDE THE BEDROOM, Boyd sat on the edge of the bed, phone to his ear, and listened to his father.

"What's the woman like?" Buck Benedict demanded.

"Young, pretty, intelligent. Not at all what we were expecting."

"God a'mighty, what was Dad thinking of? What was the relationship?"

"Friends. Just friends."

Buck scoffed. "The hell!"

"No, Dad, I believe her. She's the genuine article. She didn't have any idea who Granddad was, and she's thunderstruck over the inheritance."

"Just how pretty is this woman anyway?"

Boyd swallowed his irritation. "I haven't been taken in by a lovely charmer, if that's what you're thinking. The Hamilton woman thought he was just a lonely old man."

"How the hell did she meet him?"

"Get this—he used to show up here at the hotel and rock on the veranda all day."

"Dad?"

"Uh-huh. She befriended him. She—" Boyd paused to chuckle "—she once loaned him fifty dollars. You know how that would have touched Granddad."

"Damned if she didn't get a good return on her money!"

"Whatever his reason for leaving her all that money, he apparently wanted her to have it."

"It's not the money," Buck growled. "I don't give a damn about the money! Hell, Dad left ten thousand to that bellhop in Flagstaff. But a hundred grand? The newspapers are going to have a field day with this."

Boyd rubbed his chin thoughtfully. "I don't suppose there's any way of keeping it quiet."

"No, there isn't. We don't need this kind of notoriety! Lonely old man wiling away his dotage on a hotel veranda, grateful for the kind attentions of a sweet young thing, leaves her a bundle. Everyone will think we neglected him, or that Dad had become senile. Dammit, he was a force to be reckoned with in this state for half a century, and that's the way I want him to be remembered." A pause followed, then Buck spoke urgently. "Listen to me, Boyd, I don't want that woman talking to reporters or anyone else, do you hear me?"

Boyd frowned. "And just how am I supposed to prevent it?"

"Don't let her out of your sight. I mean it. Don't let her talk to anyone, not anyone. And first thing in the morning you bring her down here where we can keep an eye on her. I want her under this roof until the threat of scandal blows over."

"Come on, Dad, this isn't a good time to have to play watchdog. Roundup starts next week, and we're all going to be busy as hell."

"I don't care. I want her here."

Boyd's breath made a whistling sound through his teeth. "Dad, you're not dealing with a docile child. Audrey Hamilton is a grown woman, and I don't think she's going to take kindly to being ordered around. I can't bind and gag her and drag her to the Triple B."

"You can if that's the only way to get her here," Buck bellowed. "She'll damned well come. You might remind her that she's going to be pretty well off thanks to this family, so she owes us something. I don't care how you get her here, just do it!"

Boyd knew better than anyone how useless it was to argue with Buck Benedict. "I'll see what I can do," he said resignedly.

"Find out about her family. With our lousy luck she'll have kinfolks in every nook and cranny of the state, and they'll all show up with their hands out. Get her here, Boyd! And remember, don't let her out of your sight until you do."

"Am I supposed to sleep with her?" Boyd asked facetiously.

"If you have to." And there wasn't a trace of facetiousness in Buck's voice.

AUDREY LOOKED UP when the door to the bedroom opened and Boyd reappeared. His mouth was set determinedly, but otherwise she couldn't read anything in his expression. During his absence she had thought and thought about the situation and had decided the money wasn't worth a big flap. That was the last thing she wanted. If it came down to a court battle... She shuddered just thinking about it. So when he stepped into the room she took the initiative.

"Mr. Benedict, I can well understand that your family wouldn't want me to have that money, and I can't really blame them. If you're worried that I'll cause trouble over it..."

Boyd silenced her with a wave of his hand. "The money was my grandfather's to do with as he pleased. Take it and have a good time."

A good time? She would have money again, be financially secure... again! But now she really was perplexed. "Then I don't understand why you're here. Couldn't your lawyers have handled all this?"

In an instant Boyd decided how he would deal with Audrey Hamilton—with the truth, not only the truth about what he wanted her to do but why he wanted her to do it. Gut instinct told him it was the best way. He was a good judge of people, and she was no fool.

He crossed the room and took a seat beside her. Gently touching her on the arm, he said, "Miss Hamilton... ah, may I call you Audrey?"

Audrey stiffened. The touch of his hand sent a sensation like an electric shock through her. He was so close she could feel warmth emanating from his body, and her nostrils were assailed by the citrus tang of his after-shave. His head bent closer to her, and she set herself on guard. "I... wish you would."

"Audrey," he began earnestly, his voice turning warm and confidential. "It's imperative that you tell no one about this inheritance."

"All right, I won't."

"So imperative, in fact, that my father wants you to come to our ranch with me and remain there until this blows over."

"What?" she cried incredulously. "That's ridiculous! I can't do it. I have my job, and—"

"I'm sure that once I explain this to Peter he'll be more than happy to give you the time off."

Oh, Audrey was sure of it, too. Peter would go along with anything the Benedicts wanted. "Aren't you making too much of this? I promise I won't say anything to anyone. I'm a very private person, and I don't do much socializing. I'd rather not go.''

"Our ranch is a delightful place, Audrey, but it's remote and the one place where we can regulate who comes and goes. Actually, I'd think you would welcome the chance to get away from here. Confronting those vultures from the press can be a grueling ordeal for the uninitiated.''

Audrey almost choked. "The press?" she asked, horrified.

He nodded solemnly. "Once the news of this inheritance hits the newspapers, as it will any moment, everyone will want a statement from you. Unfortunately, we Benedicts are the source of endless gossip. This bequest is going to make colorful copy. You'll be bombarded day and night.''

A sinking sensation hit Audrey's stomach. Oh, God—the chaos, the notoriety, the cameras and reporters. Hopefully he was exaggerating. "Is Bert's will really that newsworthy?"

"A dozen or so years ago my grandfather was listed as one of the three most newsworthy men in Arizona. The other two, as I recall, were the governor and Barry Goldwater.''

"Just leave me alone," she implored, her voice almost a whisper. "I won't say anything to anyone.''

"I'm sure you mean that, Audrey, but a skilled reporter could force you to say things you had no intention of saying.''

She was such a spirited filly that Boyd was expecting a flat refusal, but he alertly noticed that his last remark had struck some kind of responsive chord, so he quickly pressed his advantage. "And it won't only be the press who'll hound you. Long-lost friends will pop out of the woodwork. Every imaginable investment scheme will be offered to you. You'll be besieged with requests for donations.''

Nothing he could have said would have made a greater impact on Audrey. How on earth had she gotten involved in this? Why hadn't Bert considered all the ramifications when he wrote that will? But, of course, he hadn't known anything about her life before she'd come to the Greenspoint.

Once again she felt herself being swept into a tangle of circumstances she couldn't control. "How . . . how long would I have to stay at your ranch?" she inquired hesitantly.

Boyd smiled. That had been incredibly easy. "It's hard to say at this point. A week or two. The public's attention span tends to be short. This won't be news long."

"But I can't leave my job for two weeks! There's a big convention coming up, and it's my responsibility."

"You might want to give some fresh thought to your job's importance in your life. Thanks to my grandfather, you'll soon be financially comfortable."

"I . . . I guess I will," she said vaguely. "It's all so unreal."

Boyd pressed on. "I dislike putting it this way, but I think you owe us one small favor. All we're asking is that you enjoy our hospitality for a short time, then you can be on your way with the means to do whatever you want."

Audrey sighed. She wanted to refuse to go along with the Benedicts and be done with it. She had become accustomed to controlling her life. For three years now she had been the one in charge, the one who had made decisions, and she cherished her independence and freedom more than anything. They had been hard-won.

On the other hand, she needed the sanctuary the Benedicts were affording her. She wanted all this to pass over as quickly and quietly as possible. She didn't want to cause the family any problems, for Bert's sake, and she certainly didn't want media attention focused on her.

Besides, in a more pragmatic vein, she had a feeling Boyd wouldn't leave the Greenspoint without her. "All right, Mr. Benedict. Provided it won't jeopardize my job here in any way, I'll go to your ranch with you."

Boyd got to his feet, rubbing his hands together with satisfaction. "Good! We'll leave first thing in the morning. It's too far to turn around and drive back now. Is there anyone who'll be worried about you if you're gone for a week or two?"

She shook her head.

"No parents?"

"No."

"Brothers, sisters, aunts, cousins?"

"No."

"Almost everyone has someone," he persisted.

"I don't." No one but Aunt Martha in Houston, and she'd prefer cuddling up with a colony of lepers to admitting she was kin to a Hamilton.

"A man then?"

"No."

"That seems unusual. A woman your age who looks like you do would reasonably be expected to have a man in her life."

Audrey accepted that as a compliment. "Naturally I date several men, but none is special. And even if one of them calls for me, he won't think it the least unusual for me not to be here. I sometimes work odd hours, and I travel around the state on occasion."

Boyd could hardly believe their good fortune. She was as unattached as it was possible for a person to be. "All right now, Audrey, I'll have to fill Peter in on all this. He'll have to know where you'll be, but he's the only one who will. Then we'll go to your place so you can pack. No need to make a production of that. If you find you want or need something you don't have with you, someone will be glad to go into town and get it for you."

Audrey was quick to note he didn't say *she* could go into town and get it. Apparently she was going to be held under close surveillance. They would be surprised to discover how cooperative she was going to be. "Can't I pack tonight, since we aren't leaving until morning?"

"No, you'll pack and come back here with me. You'll be staying here tonight."

"You mean here in the hotel?"

"I mean here in this suite with me."

Audrey gasped. "Oh, really! I can't stay here with you."

He silenced her with an inscrutable look. "You can and will. This suite has two bedrooms, Audrey. I assure you I have nothing improper in mind. My father's instructions were not to let you out of my sight until I've deposited you safely at the Triple B, and that's the way it's going to be."

"Do you always do exactly what your father wants?"

"Just about. Do you live far from here?"

Resigned to the incredible turn of events, Audrey acquiesced quietly. "No, not far at all."

"Good. Can we take your car? I flew to Phoenix and am without transportation."

"Of course. Will we be taking my car to the ranch?"

"I hadn't thought about it. Do you want to?"

"It might be a good idea. That way, when it's time for me to come back, I can just leave, without troubling anyone for a ride."

"I don't see anything wrong with that." Boyd went to the telephone and dialed an in-house number. A few seconds passed, then he said, "Peter, this is Boyd Benedict. Can you come up to my suite right away? There's something important I need to discuss with you. Yes, right away. Thanks."

He replaced the receiver and turned to Audrey with the air of a man whose mission had been accomplished. "Wipe that worried frown off your face, Audrey. Fate seems to have thrown us together for a while, so we might as well become friends and enjoy it. Won't you please call me Boyd?"

Enjoy it? Warning lights were flashing in her head. Five years ago, when her serene, comfortable life had started coming apart at the seams, she had somehow coped. Now, however, a nagging inner sensation told her that this startling involvement with the Benedicts was going to tax her ability to cope to the limit.

CHAPTER FOUR

TWO HOURS LATER Audrey was edgy and restless, ready to jump out of her skin. She often had yearned to stay in the Durango Suite, to be surrounded by its luxury and remember what it felt like to belong in such a place. Now she realized it could be just as boring as any other hotel room if you were stuck in it.

And stuck she was. Boyd didn't intend letting her out of his sight, and he had work to do. The moment they had returned from her apartment he had opened his briefcase, spread papers all over the dining table, placed a calculator beside his right hand and set the telephone nearby. And his head had been bent in concentration ever since.

Audrey had learned to enjoy solitude, and welcomed it most of the time, but this enforced confinement had her feeling jittery. She wandered from room to room, then kicked off her shoes, stretched out on the sofa and tried to lose herself in the paperback novel she had grabbed as they left her apartment. Twenty minutes later she gave up and put it aside. Settling back against the sofa cushions, she kicked off her shoes, tucked her feet under her and gave in to her thoughts.

Peter had been just as cooperative as she'd known he would be. He was stunned to hear of her inheritance but relieved that the hotel wasn't changing hands. Naturally he'd insisted that Audrey do whatever the Benedicts wanted. Sworn to secrecy, he had been instructed to tell anyone who asked for her that she was on vacation and couldn't be reached. Helen would know better, of course, and Audrey wondered if Peter would confide in the secretary. Probably not, she decided. Helen had an incurably loose tongue, and Peter was aware of it.

Her eyes strayed across the room to Boyd, seated at the dining table. Now that the day's shocks had subsided somewhat, Audrey was concentrating more of her interest on the man who had entered her life so abruptly and dramatically. Even though he had accompanied her to and from her apartment, she knew very little about him. His conversation had focused entirely on the weather and how Phoenix had grown. He was, she noticed, marvelously adept at not talking about himself.

She wondered if he was married. Probably. He was, roughly, thirty-four or -five, and most men that age were married. Of course, he might be divorced.

A woman couldn't fail to notice him. He was splendidly male and not nearly as formidable as he had seemed at first. He was also brimful of self-confidence, but she supposed that went with the territory. A member of the illustrious Benedict clan would hardly be shy and unassuming.

She wondered if he had any children.

She had made a few close-up observations of him. His eyes were very expressive and candid, without deviousness. She usually admired people whose emotions were open. Plus, Boyd Benedict was one fine-looking man, and she was no more immune to that than any other woman. She'd be willing to wager every cent in her savings account that he knew exactly how attractive he was and wasn't above using it to his advantage.

Thinking of her meager savings account brought money to mind, which in turn reminded her of her changed circumstances. It wasn't entirely real to her, not yet, but little by little it was dawning on her that life, if she so desired, could be very different from now on. She, who for three years had existed from paycheck to paycheck, could once again buy all sorts of luxuries. No, it wasn't real. Not yet.

She glanced at her watch, then back to Boyd, who was still working. Didn't he know what time it was? Her stomach was reminding her that it had been a long time since lunch, and the salad she had eaten. Slipping on her shoes, she got to her feet, walked to the window and looked down. Waiters were setting up trestle tables on the loggia beside the pool, and some delicious aromas were beginning to waft upward as trays of food were brought out. Audrey swallowed and ran her tongue across her lips.

Just then Boyd laid down his pencil, rubbed his eyes tiredly and stretched his arms high above his head, flexing his shoulder muscles. Audrey turned at the sound of rustling movements. "All finished?" she asked hopefully.

He swiveled his head. "Um-hmm. Sorry it took so long."

"What are you doing?"

"Paperwork. There's an astonishing amount of it associated with running a ranch the size of the Triple B."

"Triple B," she mused. "I have to assume that has something to do with the family name."

"Right. The first Benedict to move out to public lands was Bernard B. Benedict of Pennsylvania. The offspring have had triple-B names hung on them ever since. Corny as hell, right?"

"I guess most family traditions are sort of corny, in a nice way. So, you're Boyd B. Benedict."

"Yep."

"What does the B stand for?"

"Nothing. None of the middle B's stands for anything."

She indicated all the papers spread out on the table. "Why don't you get a computer?"

"Oh, we have several of them, but I don't happen to have one with me." He looked at his watch. "I had no idea it was so late. Bored?"

"A little," she admitted.

"I haven't been very good company."

"I didn't expect you to keep me entertained. As you pointed out, you had to take time you could ill afford."

Boyd winced. "I guess I said that. Pompous ass, huh? Tell you what, Audrey. I'll clear away this mess, take a shower, then we'll have a few drinks, and I'll have dinner sent up. How does that sound?"

"Must we stay cooped up in here? There's a Polynesian buffet on the loggia tonight. Can't we go down to it?"

He gave it some consideration. "Nope," he finally said. "Better not. Dad wants you kept under lock and key."

On second thought, Audrey decided that being kept under lock and key was safer.

"If it's the buffet you want, I'll call downstairs and have them send up enough for two," Boyd offered. "How's that?"

Audrey turned from the window, shrugging nonchalantly. "If it eases your mind, have dinner sent up. I'm going to take a bath."

Boyd wrapped an arm around the back of the chair, propped his chin on it and watched her leave the room. With masculine approval, he noticed the movement of her trim hips beneath the off-white skirt, the scissoring motions of her shapely legs. He liked the proud, erect way she held her head. In fact, he admitted there was a great deal about Audrey he liked.

Yet there was something about her, something he couldn't quite put his finger on. She'd seemed nervous from the beginning, which wasn't surprising, but her nervousness had intensified when he'd begun asking questions about her past. He'd dropped the questioning, since what she'd done before coming to the Greenspoint wasn't pertinent. Still, it made him wonder.

And she'd been totally against going to the ranch with him until he'd mentioned newspapers, reporters, the media. Then she'd grabbed the idea like a lifeline. But there wasn't anything particularly suspicious about that. Media attention scared the dickens out of most people, and Audrey had described herself as a private person.

His mind exploded with questions about her, and he hoped they would be answered before the evening was over. Normally he was pretty good at gleaning a lot of information from a person's face and mannerisms, but he hadn't figured out Audrey. Nor had he figured out why she unsettled him so. From the moment she'd first stepped into the suite, his equilibrium had been in a curiously unbalanced state, and he was filled with a knifelike awareness of her every second she was near. He was quite certain nothing remotely like this had ever happened to him before.

It was strange. He'd been every bit as annoyed as the others over his grandfather's will, a fact that had nothing to do with the money. Rather, it was a disturbance, and the Benedicts didn't kindly tolerate disturbances in their lives.

He had been even more annoyed when his father had summoned him into his august presence and ordered him to "get to Phoenix, find that Hamilton woman and get to the bottom of this." It had seemed to Boyd that the platoon of fancy lawyers they kept on the payroll should have handled it. There were dozens of things he would have preferred doing.

But now he was glad he had come. Audrey bothered him, but she intrigued him more. He didn't entirely trust her, though she had passed all the tests. There was an air of mystery about her, and he usually didn't like mysterious women. Still, he was filled with the sure knowledge that meeting Audrey Hamilton wasn't something he soon would forget.

AUDREY SANK DEEPER into the warm comfort of the perfumed bathwater and reflected on how easily one could adapt to luxury. It was adapting to a lower standard of living that tested a person's mettle.

She could hear the sound of the shower in the bathroom next door and Boyd's slightly off-key baritone rising above it. That created an air of intimacy that she found nerve-racking, though she smiled as she listened. He was no great shakes as a singer, but his voice was strong, lusty and confident, like the man himself. What was there about the sound of rushing water that made a man want to burst into song? She recalled that all her father had to do was step under a shower's spray to turn into a poor man's Pavarotti.

She gave herself a shake. She wanted no memories of her father.

The shower next door stopped and so did the singing. Audrey envisioned Boyd reaching for a towel, pulling it back and forth over those admirable shoulders, then down his back to his attractive male derriere. His chest, she decided, would be smooth and as bronze as his arms. There might be a few tufts of dark chest hair that would taper in a thin line down to his waist and below.

Warmth diffused Audrey's face. She reached for a washcloth, soaped it and scrubbed vigorously. The action effectively dispelled the appalling stirrings inside her. How could she spend even a minute thinking of Boyd Benedict as a desirable man? Their paths were destined to cross only briefly, and she suspected that any woman who had the bad sense to get emotional about him would live to regret it.

Good Lord, I don't even know if he's single!

She stayed in the tub until the water cooled. After drying, she wrapped the towel around her sarong-fashion, applied her makeup and went into the bathroom to dress. She reached for a rose-colored sundress. It was an exquisite garment with a halter top, obi sash and full skirt, a dress she hadn't worn in years. Swirling her hair up again, she slipped her feet into low-heeled sandals and gave her reflection in the mirror a cursory glance. Then she left the bedroom and returned to the parlor.

During her absence one of the night staff had brought a tray of fruit and cheese and placed it on the dining table. She was nibbling on a slice of kiwi when she became aware of the heady masculine aroma she was beginning to associate with Boyd. Turning, she discovered she was staring at the broad expanse of his chest. The two-inch heels she had worn earlier made quite a difference; now she felt dwarfed by him.

"Don't you look nice," he said. "That color's great on you."

"Thanks."

"Shall we have a drink?"

"I guess so. Some of the wine would be nice."

"Only wine? Wouldn't you like something stronger? There's an impressive array of complimentary booze in the sideboard."

"No, thanks. Wine is fine. I'm not accustomed to much alcohol."

While Boyd poured their drinks, Audrey took a seat on the sofa and studied him at leisure. He was wearing a pearl-gray shirt, open at the throat and tucked into the waistband of darker gray slacks. He wore his clothes well, she noted, and the color of the clothing emphasized the smoky hue of his eyes. His hair was still damp from the shower, its curl more pronounced, especially at the back of his neck. In all her life Audrey didn't think she had seen a more attractive man.

He brought their drinks and took a seat beside her on the sofa. "Do you have medical or moral objections to alcohol?" he asked.

"Not at all. Wine is also alcohol. I guess I drank my share of liquor in college, beer busts and all. But frankly, it's expensive, and we working women have to watch those hard-earned dollars."

Boyd sipped his drink and tried to study her without being too obvious. She somehow didn't fit his image of a penny-pinching working woman. The dress she was wearing, for instance. It looked expensive, and it didn't seem to him that a working woman who wouldn't spend money on alcohol would fork over eighty or ninety dollars for a dress like that. Working women bought sensible clothes that could do double duty, didn't they?

You're a suspicious bastard, Benedict, he thought. That dress would look perfect at a Polynesian buffet on the loggia. Maybe she needed things like that to wear to some of the hotel's activities. Her clothing requirements probably differed from those of a secretary or accountant.

"Well, you're probably fortunate not to get tied up with the stuff," he said. "During my late teens and early twenties, alcohol was far too closely associated with recreation."

"How's that?"

"During those years I worked on the ranch when I wasn't in school, and more than anything I wanted to be accepted by the real cowboys, the pros. So that meant going into town on weekends, getting tanked up on beer and winding up in . . . er, altercations."

"Fistfights? Good heavens, why?"

"Beats me," he said with a lazy chuckle. "I guess we thought we were supposed to, that it was expected of us. It was part of the mystique of being a cowboy. It also was exhausting."

"But... who did you fight?"

He grinned charmingly. "Anybody we didn't know."

Audrey laughed. Boyd took a hefty swallow of his drink while she sipped daintily at her wine. Then he turned and lavished a smile on her that could have melted an igloo. "I don't want to talk about me. Let's talk about you. I don't know much about your background. You're twenty-seven, never been married, have no family. Where's home originally?"

"Texas," she said.

He noticed she averted her eyes briefly. "That takes in a lot of territory. Where in Texas?"

"Dallas."

Maybe, he thought. Maybe not. Dallas was a convenient answer. But she had come up with it quickly, so it probably was true. Why did suspicions persist that had nothing whatsoever to do with his grandfather? Audrey was one of the loveliest women he had ever met. Why not enjoy that, come on to her strong and see what happened? "Nice place. Ever go to the Astrodome?"

She leveled a tolerant look on him. "The Astrodome's in Houston, as I'm sure you know. Yes, I've been there many times, but more frequently to places like Texas Stadium, Reunion Tower and the State Fairgrounds, which are in Dallas."

Again she had given him an answer that made him feel apologetic. "Sorry, Audrey, I get Dallas and Houston confused. And I have this affliction: I'm terribly curious about people, so I ask a lot of questions. Sometimes I come across like an investigative reporter."

"Or a district attorney," she added and immediately wanted to bite her tongue. Her insides churned with agitation. That dumb question about the Astrodome—why? Why was he testing her? He didn't seem to have any qualms about the inheritance; that and their employer-employee relationship were their only common denominators. He was looking at her in the strangest way, peering deeply inside her—too deeply.

"What brought you to Phoenix in the first place?"

"An invitation from a friend, the friend who knows Peter. Once the job here came along, I stayed."

"You never went back to Dallas?"

"No."

"That seems odd."

"Does it? There simply was nothing left for me in Dallas, that's all."

"Is your friend still here in Phoenix?"

"No, her husband was transferred. They live in Seattle now." *So there's no one here in Phoenix who can tell you a thing about my past,* she thought with relieved satisfaction. It was time to get off the subject. "Tell me about your family, Boyd," she urged. "They're into things other than ranching, right?"

He took the hint. The lady didn't like talking about the past. But she had no family, so perhaps there was some tragedy in her background, something too painful to recall. "Yes," he said, "and sometimes all those other things overshadow the ranching. My dad considers himself first and foremost a businessman, and he's been chiefly responsible for our diversification. Granddad, on the other hand, called himself a cowboy and professed to have no interest in the other things. My brother Brent is a businessman, too. He runs the office in Tucson."

"And what are you?" she probed. "Cowboy or businessman?"

"A little of both, I guess. But given the choice, both Betty and I would ranch exclusively."

"Betty?"

"My sister, the best cowhand the Triple B has. She majored in animal science at Arizona State, and she knows those cows inside and out."

Audrey raised her glass to her lips, took a sip of wine and then asked the question she'd been itching to ask. "Are you married?"

"No."

"Ever been married?"

"No. And that probably was the only real disappointment in Granddad's life. He thought I should have married years ago. I suffered through several of his clumsy attempts at matchmaking before he gave up on me."

"He was a darling man," Audrey mused.

"He was a firebrand in his heyday. But, of course, you wouldn't have seen that side of him. I was terrified of him when I was a kid. Later, he became my hero."

They sipped their drinks in silence for a moment, then Audrey asked, "Why haven't you been to the Greenspoint before?"

"As long as things are running smoothly, why interfere? We have plenty of problem spots that require constant attention."

"Peter does a good job."

"I admire loyalty to the boss."

"I'm completely sincere."

"I'm sure you are. Do you enjoy your work?"

"Yes, I do. Every day."

"Why?"

She gave some thought to her answer. "For one thing, this hotel feels aristocratic. Staying here is rather like visiting a wealthy relative who, for one reason or another, wants to pamper you outrageously. I don't mean just in this suite, but in every one of the rooms. We like to give our guests little extras... like turning down their beds at night, setting out candy and fresh flowers. Things like that pay off in return visits."

"Whose idea was that... the 'little extras'?"

"Peter's. Well...maybe one or two were mine. Like I said, we work well together."

Boyd drained his glass and got to his feet. "More wine?"

"No, thanks."

"Then I'll order dinner." He sauntered to the phone and placed the order, then walked to the sideboard and mixed himself another drink. "What are your plans now?"

"Plans?"

"You'll soon have enough money to do anything you want. What are you going to do?"

"I don't know. I really haven't had time to think about it. I might not 'do' anything, just stay here and enjoy my job."

She heard the plop-plop of ice cubes, then he was walking toward her, sitting down beside her, again too close. The scent of him was wonderful. "Now, that surprises me. It seems to me that anyone who'd just received an unexpected windfall would have dozens of things to spend it on—travel, a new car, something."

Audrey stared down into the almost empty goblet. Funny, last week she'd been fretting because her Datsun needed new tires. Now she could buy a new car, but why do that when the Datsun only had twenty thousand miles on it? She'd pay it off and live a payment-free life for a couple of years. She could get a larger apartment or make a down payment on a small condo, but she loved her little apartment. She'd simply fix it up. She could take a trip to someplace she'd never been, but there were few appealing places she hadn't been. She'd become so sensible and frugal in three years, and that pleased her. Learning to make ends meet had given her more self-confidence than anything she'd done in her life. "Oh," she said lightly, "I'm sure I'll find something to do with it."

"Yeah, money's easy to get rid of."

"I don't intend getting rid of it, not at all."

"Investments?"

"I'm too conservative for that. I'll put it in the bank and draw the interest."

"There are better returns on your money. You could build a hundred thousand into a tidy sum."

"I don't want a lot of money."

"You really are a different one, then. How do you know you don't want a lot of money?"

Audrey ignored her stomach's flip-flop. She mustered a smile. "I just know, that's all. I don't want anything that will complicate my life."

"And you think money would complicate it?"

"It might. You've seen my car and my apartment. Why would I want more than that?"

Boyd recalled her apartment—small, impeccably neat, very feminine and furnished with an eye for detail, though nothing in it looked expensive. While she packed he'd wandered around the living room and kitchen, looking for anything—photographs or something—that would give him further insight into the woman. There was nothing, not even a magazine addressed to her. "Then Granddad seems to have wasted the bequest."

She looked at him askance. "I beg your pardon."

"I'll bet he expected you to take the money and have a ball with it."

"I don't think so. I'll bet he wanted that money to take me into my old age."

"Why would a twenty-seven-year-old woman even think of her old age?"

A knock on the door heralded the arrival of their dinner and effectively terminated the conversation, much to Audrey's relief. He was trying so hard to get her to open up and tell him the story of her life. He wouldn't succeed. There wasn't a soul left on the face of the earth who really knew Audrey Hamilton. She allowed no one to get close to her.

Boyd got to his feet, started for the door, then stopped and looked back at Audrey. "Maybe you'd better go powder your nose or something."

Cocking her head, Audrey quizzed him with her eyes. "Our waiter might know you," he said, explaining his request. "Probably no harm in that, but we might as well play it safe. I'd prefer that no one sees us together."

"You don't overlook details, do you?"

"Hopefully, never."

Audrey rolled her eyes toward the ceiling, but nevertheless she went into her bedroom and stayed there until she heard Boyd call her name. When she returned to the parlor, he was inspecting the food-laden cart.

"You may have to help me with some of this stuff. My idea of food is beef and more beef."

Audrey would have bet on it. "Let's see . . . roast pork, yams, fried shrimp. And this is salmon marinated in lime juice, these are scallops, and those little crispy things are curry puffs. Everything's delicious, I promise." And in the end, she noticed, he sampled a little bit of everything.

Boyd was easy to talk to, so dinner passed pleasantly. She listened to him and watched him intently throughout the meal, putting in a word now and then and wondering what it was about him that inspired her usual interest. Oh, there was an attraction, all right, and it was based on more than his good looks. She'd met dozens of attractive men since coming to Arizona. The Greenspoint drew them like flies, all those suntanned Greek gods who played golf and tennis and lazed around the pool. Not one of them had aroused more than a brief flurry of interest in her. There was something distinctive about Boyd. The moment she'd laid eyes on him, before he'd given her that incredible news, she'd felt some sort of inner stirring, and she simply didn't react to strangers that way. It alarmed her that she had this time.

Boyd was asking her a question. "Pardon? I'm sorry, Boyd, what did you say?"

"I asked if you wanted more of the pork or shrimp or anything. They sent up enough food for six people."

Audrey glanced down at her plate. She had cleaned it but could scarcely remember actually eating. "Oh, no, thanks. I'm stuffed. Did you enjoy it?"

"Yes, I did. It was a nice change of pace."

"Jacky, he's our chef, does wonderfully authentic Polynesian dishes."

"Well, I'll take your word for that, since I wouldn't know the authentic from the bogus." Boyd pushed his plate away and got to his feet. "I'll just wheel all this out into the hall, and then we can get some fresh air on the terrace."

The suite's small terrace overlooked the pool below. It was later than Audrey had realized. The pool's lights had been extinguished, and the waiters were stripping the buffet tables. The hotel's grounds were as quiet as they ever got. From the terrace, they could look on beyond to the lights of nighttime Phoenix, a city that was growing, spreading, splitting its seams.

"I liked her better when I was a kid, some twenty years ago, before the snowbirds discovered her," Boyd commented.

"Then you've spent a lot of time in Phoenix?"

He nodded. "And in Flagstaff, and in Tucson, and in Prescott. We have interests all over."

This was said without a trace of conceit, nor was it said to impress her, Audrey instinctively knew. He'd merely made a statement of fact. Considering who he was, who his family was, Boyd was surprisingly unpretentious. She stood at the railing and felt him behind her. He casually placed a hand at the small of her back as he moved to stand beside her. It was a simple gesture that meant nothing, but some queer trick of nature was playing havoc with her erotic senses. Her pulses were pounding.

Then, in a surprising move, Boyd's hand moved from her waist to her nape. "Your hair's coming down," he drawled.

Audrey's fingers flew to her neck to touch the wayward tendrils. "Oh, when it's this clean I can never do anything with it." She could feel the hairdo slipping, so she reached up and deftly removed all the pins, and her hair fell to her shoulders.

"You should never wear it up," Boyd said huskily. "Hair like that should never be confined." He experienced an absurd urge to tell her she was the most beautiful woman he'd ever seen.

"I'm going to take that as a compliment."

"Good, because it was meant to be one."

"Thanks, then."

"You're welcome."

Somewhere in the back of Audrey's sensible mind lay the thought that the entire day had been a wonder. The man standing beside her—a man she hadn't known when she'd crawled out of bed that morning—was gazing at her in a most seductive way, with an air of familiarity that certainly didn't exist. A little thrill of excitement raced through her, and she had to look away.

This couldn't be. She wouldn't allow herself to be drawn to Boyd in any romantic sense. He was probably only having a little flirtatious fun with her anyway, or putting on an act designed to weaken her defenses and let him inside her head. It wouldn't work. There was a time in her life when she had taken people at face value, but her father and Jesse Murdoch had cured her of that. Now she was cautious, and she was going to put an end to this mood of near intimacy Boyd was trying to create.

She stepped back from the railing, away from him slightly, and clasped her hands in front of her. "I think I'll say good-night now, Boyd. It's been a long day."

An odd little half smile crossed his face. "So soon?"

"Yes, I...I've been up since six, and I'm really very tired."

"All right, Audrey. I don't see any need for an early departure tomorrow. It might be nice to sleep in for a change. Let's plan to make it to Tucson in time for lunch. That'll get us to the ranch by early afternoon. Are you sure you don't mind taking your car?"

"Not at all. See you in the morning."

"I'll have breakfast sent up. Good night, Audrey."

"Good night."

Boyd watched her leave and shook his head in bafflement. He, too, had sensed the intimate mood, but it was nothing he'd deliberately created. It was just there, an almost tangible presence between them.

By now he should have known far more about her than he did. He knew nothing, and he obviously wasn't going to get anywhere with Audrey by calling upon his well-practised masculine charm. She intrigued him, she worried him, she fascinated him. And he was going to find out what made her tick. Sooner or later he would find out all there was to know about Audrey Hamilton.

CHAPTER FIVE

AN HOUR OR SO down the highway that stretched from Tucson to the Mexican border, the Santa Cruz Valley dozed in the afternoon sun. Audrey had expected desert; instead she discovered a lovely grassy valley some four thousand feet above sea level. The brilliant sun splashed pink and purple shadows over the jagged mountains that rimmed the horizon. The heady fragrance of mesquite wood fires perfumed the air. The space and silence were awesome. She felt worlds removed from the bustling sunbelt cities to the north. Here roadrunners and deer darted undisturbed, cattle ambled lazily and horses grazed peacefully. The valley, she decided, would be the perfect place to hold the world at bay until Bert's will became stale news.

Audrey stole a sidelong glance at her traveling companion. Boyd had insisted on doing the driving, which had suited her fine. The trip had passed uneventfully, broken only by their stop for lunch in Tucson. She had spent more uninterrupted time with him during the past twenty-four hours than she had with anyone else in the past five years. Yet still he baffled her.

Yesterday he had been full of curiosity about her, but today he had been casual, disinterested, even remote. Not once during the trip had the conversation strayed toward the personal. She thought about last night's mood of intimacy and decided it had been a product of her imagination. The mood today had been anything but intimate. She was relieved, of course, but it was unexpected.

She studied him covertly. That morning when she'd emerged from her room, the sight of him had taken her by surprise. His expensive tailored clothes had been replaced by a faded blue shirt, scuffed boots and the most disreputable pair of jeans she had ever seen. They were worn almost white at the knees. When she had commented on the clothes, he had grinned and said, "This is the real me. Yesterday I was traveling incognito." Now he had added a battered straw cowboy hat that was in almost as bad condition as the jeans. He could have passed for any fifty-dollar-a-day cowboy she had ever known. Except Boyd was undeniably more attractive than most, and the scruffy clothes only enhanced his rugged good looks. She forcibly tore her gaze away from him and returned it to the landscape whizzing past the window.

Abruptly Boyd braked, slowed and turned off the highway onto a country road. A few miles down the deserted stretch he made another turn, driving over a cattle guard and under an iron arch whose lettering announced that this was the Triple B Land and Cattle Company. Audrey's attention was drawn to the sights ahead of her. The ranch headquarters was a cluster of buildings on the west side of the road. There were barns and corrals and sheds and all the other trappings of a modern cattle operation. The ranch house itself was a sprawling whitewashed adobe hacienda situated in a grove of trees.

"Why, it's absolutely beautiful!" she exclaimed.

"Thanks," Boyd said, "but you sound surprised."

"Not all ranches are pretty." Then, remembering that she wasn't supposed to be knowledgeable about ranches, she added, "I used to visit a dude ranch when I was a kid. It was beautiful, too, but that was all for show."

"Not here. This is a hardworking ranch, no frills. We like to do things the old-fashioned way: cowboys on horseback herding cows. I keep hearing that cattle raising is all specialized now, that the old traditions are gone and cowboying is a dying art. But the Triple B has been running cattle for a hundred years, and I can't see that changing anytime soon. The altitude, the climate, the soil—everything makes this part of the state ideal for cattle. And as for cowhands, there still are a few left, and some of them find their way here every year at roundup or branding time. Some of the same faces show up year after year."

"How big is the ranch?"

"Not as big as it used to be, but it's still respectable. About forty thousand acres—the biggest privately owned spread in these parts. The government owns about eighty-five percent of Arizona, you know, but my family has managed to hang onto this land since Geronimo's last stand. There's an Apache graveyard in the southern quadrant of the ranch."

Boyd swung the car into the circular driveway fronting the house. In the center of the yard a fountain bubbled cheerfully; beneath it stood huge pots filled with red and white geraniums. A pair of barking dogs heralded their arrival. Boyd parked alongside a tan pickup, just as a man in soiled khakis appeared and called to him in Spanish. Boyd answered in the same language, and Audrey noticed that his accent sounded perfect. "Jorge will see to your luggage," he said, turning to her. "Let's go inside and find Mom."

The interior of the Benedict house was a surprise. Audrey didn't know what she had expected, perhaps something more like the old ranch house in Texas—sturdy masculine furniture, steer heads and gun racks on the walls. This place was entirely different, as elegant in its way as the Greenspoint. There were arches and curved wood doors that emphasized the hacienda look, but Audrey took note of the magnificent Baccarat chandelier in the dining room to her left. And the living room on her right was furnished with splendid antiques.

Boyd motioned her to follow as he led the way down a hall to a capacious, sun-drenched room with floor-to-ceiling windows and chintz-covered furniture. Here the colors were bold and vivid; plants of every description abounded. Unlike the front rooms, the sun room had a beckoning warmth that proclaimed, "This is home!"

A woman was seated on the sofa in front of one of the windows, and she stood when they entered the room. Slender and silver-haired, she exuded an air of ultrafemininity, although she was dressed in tailored slacks and a plain white shirt. In some ways she reminded Audrey of her patrician mother. Without a doubt, this woman was responsible for the elegant decor. "Hello, darling, I'm glad you're back," she greeted Boyd.

"Mom, I'd like you to meet Audrey Hamilton. Audrey, this is my mother, Elizabeth Benedict."

"How do you do, Audrey. Welcome to our home."

"Thank you, Mrs. Benedict. It's such a lovely place."

"How nice of you to say so, my dear." Elizabeth then turned to her son. "Your father is at the Summerfield camp and left instructions for you to join him the minute you arrived."

Boyd nodded. "Just let me get Audrey settled in."

"Perhaps you should go now," Elizabeth said firmly. "You know how your father is. I can see Audrey settled into the guest room."

"Well . . . maybe you're right." Boyd glanced at Audrey apologetically. "I hate like the devil to run off and leave you."

"It doesn't matter," she said, though it did. "You just go do whatever it is you have to do."

"Have you had lunch?" Elizabeth inquired.

"Um-hmm. We stopped in Tucson. I'd best get moving if Dad wants me." He touched Audrey on the arm. "See you later."

He left the room. The heels of his boots beat out a staccato rhythm as he walked back down the hall, across the foyer and out the door. Foolishly, Audrey felt abandoned. Facing Boyd's mother, she managed a credible smile.

"Come, Audrey," Elizabeth said. "I'll show you to the guest room." And Audrey fell into step behind her.

The house was large and built in a U-shape around a central brick courtyard. All of the bedrooms opened onto it. As she followed Elizabeth down a long hall, Audrey paused to admire a group of portraits hanging on the wall. Seeing her interest, Elizabeth stopped to explain. "This is my husband, this is Bert, and the other is Bert's father. Pity we don't have one of the original Arizona Benedict. Someday Brent's and Boyd's portraits will hang here. Traditionally,

the Benedict men have their portraits painted on their fifti-
eth birthday."

Audrey wondered why there were no portraits of the
Benedict women but didn't ask. "Bert was such a distin-
guished-looking man," she commented, studying the picture of her friend. It bore little resemblance to the man she
had known.

"Yes, he was in younger years. Formidable, too. I was
frightened to death of him when I first came here as a bride.
How long had you known him?"

"A little less than a year."

"Strange," Elizabeth murmured obscurely. "But then,
Bert had become very unpredictable. We never knew what
to expect from him. He changed a lot after Margaret died."

"I wish I could have known her. Bert talked about her
constantly."

"She was a lovely woman, so gentle and refined. She and
Bert presented quite a contrast. This way, Audrey."

She led the way to a room two doors down the hall. A
four-poster bed dominated the guest room; over it hung a
distinctive Navaho tapestry. A large brass urn holding a
dried flower arrangement stood on the floor beside an upholstered wing chair, and several pieces of Native American pottery sat on top of the polished walnut dresser. The
room, above all, looked comfortable and inviting.

"How charming!" Audrey exclaimed.

"I think you'll be comfortable in it," Elizabeth said.
"There's a private bath over there."

"It's very nice. I hope I won't be imposing on your hospitality for long, Mrs. Benedict."

Elizabeth faced her squarely. "I suppose the length of
your stay will depend on Buck. He's very adamant about
this. We've all been instructed to say nothing to anyone
about Bert's will. Sara and I thought it best to cancel several upcoming social engagements in order to avoid a barrage of questions."

"Sara?"

"My daughter-in-law, Brent's wife. You'll meet everyone tonight."

Audrey was acutely conscious of her awkward position in the household and felt she should apologize. "I'm awfully sorry for any inconvenience I've caused you."

Elizabeth brushed her comment aside with a wave of her delicate hand. "Don't fret over that, my dear. The important thing is to let Buck handle it as he sees fit. He'll take care of everything; he always does. Now, I'm afraid I'm going to have to leave you. I have an appointment at the hairdresser's in Agua Linda, and I'll have to rush to make it. I'm sure Betty will be along the minute she hears you've arrived. It's going to be nice for her to have a woman to talk to. She and Sara have so little in common." Boyd's mother then gave Audrey an appraising glance. "I wonder why my daughter doesn't look as feminine in jeans as you do. Betty's really an attractive girl and has a nice figure, but she always manages to look like she just slid off a horse. I suppose that's because she usually has. Well, Audrey, please make yourself at home. Maria and Tina are always around, so if there's anything you want, feel free to ask one of them for it."

Audrey assumed that Maria and Tina were household domestics. "I'll be fine, Mrs. Benedict. Thank you for being so kind."

Elizabeth cast her eyes around the room before leaving and closing the door behind her. Audrey stared at the door a minute, then sank into the wing chair by the window. *Well, here I am,* she thought. *What now?* Elizabeth's gracious welcome hadn't eased her sense of discomfort. She felt like an intruder and fully expected the Benedicts to consider her one. There was no way she would feel at home in this house, and she prayed her stay would be of short duration. What in the world was she going to do for the remainder of the day? What about tomorrow and the day after that? The entire situation was ludicrous.

As she sat pondering her preposterous exile, there was a knock at the door. "Come in," Audrey called, and the door opened to admit two people. One was the man in khakis whom Boyd had referred to as Jorge. He carried her luggage. Setting the suitcases on the floor at the foot of the bed, he gave her a shy smile, mumbled something in Spanish, then hurried out of the room. The other was a young woman whom Audrey guessed to be in her early twenties. She was tanned, wholesomely pretty and wore her jeans and cowboy boots as though born to them.

"Hi, Audrey, I'm Betty Benedict."

Audrey brightened. "Boyd's sister."

"Ah, yes. Boyd's sister, Brent's sister, Buck's daughter. The story of my life." She crossed the room and sat on the edge of the bed, facing Audrey. "Mom's afraid you might be shy about asking for what you want at first. Don't be. This is a very informal household."

"Thanks, but I feel strange about being here, considering the circumstances."

"Yeah, I can imagine, but you'll get over that, I hope." Betty leaned back and propped herself on one elbow. Audrey noticed how much she favored Boyd. She was tall and slender and shared her brother's dark hair and smoke-colored eyes. And, also like Boyd, she had that easy friendliness that seemed inherent in people who live in open spaces and sunny climates. So far, the Benedicts she had met had been amazingly unpretentious, and she wondered if the rest of the clan would prove to be the same. If so, this stay might turn out to be a pleasant one.

"Frankly," Betty went on, "this whole business has been the most exciting thing that's happened around here in ages. How did you meet Granddad?"

Audrey's succinct account of her friendship with Bert amused Betty, who chortled delightedly. "Oh, can you beat that? I'll bet he got the biggest kick out of not letting anyone know who he was. There was a fey side to his sense of humor. He was my favorite person on earth. Granddad sometimes worked hard on that gruff exterior of his, but his heart was made of marshmallows." She looked at Audrey thoughtfully. "What did you think of Boyd?"

"Well . . . he's . . . nice."

"Really? If that's true, I'm glad. Sometimes he tends to come on like barbed wire, but that's because he has to work so hard at being a Benedict. And sometimes it is work, believe me. If the truth were known, Boyd would be happy spending the rest of his life right here and leaving all the other stuff to Dad and Brent, who seem to like the business and high finance end of it." Betty paused to chuckle. "Boyd was mad as the devil when Dad sent him to Phoenix to find you and 'get to the bottom of this!' I'll bet he changed his mind fast when he saw you, though. Both of my brothers have always had an eye for pretty women."

Audrey smiled, not only at the compliment but at Betty's frankness. "Is Sara pretty?"

"Yeah, in a cool sort of way. She's from one of Tucson's toniest families, but, dear God, she loves being a Benedict! You'll see what I mean when you meet her. Sara's nice enough, but she's so upper crust she always makes me feel like a peasant. More my fault than hers, though. Well, Audrey, I can imagine you're not exactly thrilled over being here, so I guess it's up to me to see that you aren't bored to death. The Triple B is pretty much a man's world, so there's not a whole lot to do if you aren't involved with the cattle. That's one reason Mom and Sara are such social butterflies. Let's see . . . I could give you a tour of the ranch. That ought to kill some time."

"That sounds great. But I don't want to keep you from anything you have to do."

"You won't. There's nothing that absolutely, positively has to be done this afternoon. Do you ride?"

"I do, but I haven't in some time."

Betty glanced at her watch. "Well, maybe we ought to drive. We can cover more territory in less time."

"My car's here. You're welcome to use it."

However, when Betty saw the Datsun she frowned and said, "Some of these roads are pretty rough. We'd better take something a little sturdier."

The chosen vehicle was a midnight-blue Cadillac that Betty drove at a heart-stopping rate of speed. Audrey was thankful that her little car had been spared such punishing treatment. The ranch was crisscrossed by a network of roads, some hard-surfaced, some little more than dirt paths.

To Audrey's horror, there was no perceptible difference in Betty's speed, regardless of the condition of the road.

The sights, sounds and smells of the ranch brought back both painful and happy memories. Though the Texas ranch had been mostly a hobby for her father, Audrey had loved it there. It was the aspect of her former life that she missed most of all. And the Triple B was no ordinary ranch; its sheer size was unbelievable. The Hamilton ranch had been perhaps a third as big, small enough that there had been landmarks everywhere. To Audrey's eyes, everything here looked like more and more of the same. "Do you ever get lost?" she asked.

"Shoot, no!" Betty replied. "I know every square foot of this ranch. I've never lived anywhere else, unless you count the dorm in college. Even then, I came home most weekends. I've just never been able to stay away for long."

"Is that why you're still here? I mean, most women your age would have left home by now, to get married, to get a job in the city or something."

"Ranching's the only thing I've ever done or wanted to do," Betty said simply. "I studied animal science at Arizona State."

"I know. Boyd told me."

"Did he now? What else did my brother tell you about me?"

"He said you're the best cowhand the Triple B has."

Betty looked enormously pleased, leading Audrey to suspect that what Boyd thought of her was important to the young woman. "Well, I'll be! He'd cut out his tongue before he'd tell me that. But he's right. I can work circles around any man on this place, and most of 'em know it. I can't imagine living any way but the way I live, and I can't stand a city for more than a day or two. I start feeling all closed in."

"Do you intend staying here forever? I thought you said the Triple B is pretty much a man's world."

"That's okay. I can handle myself in a man's world. At least I can in this man's world. I don't know what I'll do, Audrey. Most of the time I don't think about it one way or another. I've been mildly content since leaving college, and I just take it one day at a time.''

Mildly content? Audrey tried to remember the last time she had met someone who was satisfied with being mildly content. Everyone these days, it seemed to her, was searching for absolute, complete happiness. She and Betty had that in common—she, too, chose to take life one day at a time and not make too many plans for the future.

The road they were traveling on ended abruptly. Instead of turning around, Betty stopped the car and switched off the engine. Audrey glanced around, thinking perhaps Betty wanted to show her something, but she couldn't imagine what it would be. For as far as the eye could see there was nothing but grass and sky and the mountains in the background. She quizzically glanced at the woman behind the wheel.

"Do you mind?" Betty asked. "I'm supposed to meet someone here."

Audrey shrugged. "Fine with me," she said, thinking that the far-out spot was an unlikely place for a meeting.

Betty gestured with one hand. "Here he comes now."

Audrey looked in the direction Betty indicated. Over a rise of ground a lone rider appeared. For a moment she watched absently, but as the rider drew nearer, she froze with shock. Surely her mind was playing tricks on her. She couldn't be seeing what she thought she was. It was impossible!

Then another minute passed, and she knew what she saw was no trick of the mind, no apparition. She wasn't going to need an introduction to the man on horseback; she recognized him immediately. If the black cowboy hat shaped into a Montana peak hadn't been enough of a giveaway, the way he sat in the saddle would have been. Jesse Murdoch!

Audrey's stomach twisted into a tight knot. Years ago she had fled her past, put it firmly behind her. Through great force of will she had reached the point where she rarely thought about it. Now, out of the blue, a very big part of that past rode toward her on a bay stallion. What cruel twist of fate had placed them in the same place at the same time?

This can't be happening, she thought wildly. *The past can't resurrect itself without warning.*

Then Jesse was upon them and she knew it could. A moment or two passed before he saw her, and Audrey took advantage of that to scrutinize him carefully. He hadn't changed much; maybe he seemed a little older, but that was about it. He still was a devilishly, dangerously handsome man. What a shame that such an unprincipled bastard was so physically attractive.

Jesse finally saw her. His eyes widened in disbelief as the color drained from his face. Reigning in his horse, he stared at her, absolutely thunderstruck. Audrey was sure the only thing that got her through the startling encounter was seeing Jesse's stupefied expression. He looked as though he had been kicked in the stomach. *He must think he is the unluckiest so-and-so on the face of the earth,* she thought with malicious satisfaction.

Betty had opened the door and gotten out of the car. "Come on, Audrey," she called over her shoulder. Jesse slowly dismounted, but his eyes remained riveted on Audrey, who also was getting out of the car.

The strange tension that filled the air went unnoticed by Betty. The young woman's eyes shone as she slipped a possessive arm around Jesse's waist and stared up at him adoringly. "Jesse, I want you to meet my new friend. She's going to be staying with us awhile, so I want you two to be friends, too. This is Audrey Hamilton. Audrey, this is Jesse Murdoch."

Audrey stopped some distance from Betty and Jesse, and a contemptuous smile curved her mouth. "How do you do," she said stiffly.

Jesse managed to lift his hand and touch the brim of his hat with a forefinger. "Hello." His voice was none too steady.

"Audrey's from Phoenix," Betty explained. "She works at the hotel the family has there. She's here because...well, it's a long story. I'll tell you about it later. Like I said, she's going to be here awhile, so I guess it'll be up to you and me to see she has a good time."

"Of course," Jesse muttered, finally tearing his stunned gaze away from Audrey to attempt a smile at Betty. "Been here long?"

"No, we just got here. I've been showing Audrey around. How was your day?"

"Busy, as usual. Listen, Betts, I hate running off, but a couple of the boys found some calves that need some doctoring. They've taken 'em down to the infirmary, and I'd better go supervise. I'm not sure those boys know what they're doing."

"Do you want me to meet you there? I'm the best amateur vet on the ranch."

"Oh, I don't think that's necessary. I wouldn't want you to leave your...friend."

Betty stepped back. She looked terribly disappointed. "Well, I guess Audrey and I really should be getting back to the house anyway. We'll be expected to put in an appearance at the cocktail hour. Will I see you tonight?"

"I'll do my best."

"Ten-ish?"

"Fine." Jesse glanced in Audrey's direction without making eye contact. "Nice...er, meeting you. Be seein' you around."

She nodded curtly but said nothing. She hadn't recovered from the startling encounter as nicely as Jesse had, but, then, she wasn't as adept at deceit as he was.

Giving Betty an affectionate pat on the shoulder, Jesse mounted and rode away swiftly. Sighing, Betty turned to Audrey apologetically. "I did so want you to get to know him. Any other time I'm sure he would have stuck around to visit with us, but he's very busy. I'm afraid everyone around here has come to depend on him. Boyd says Jesse's the best cowhand he's come across in years. You just don't run into his kind much anymore."

Fortunately, Audrey thought caustically. So charming, handsome, dangerous Jesse was up to his old tricks! How she wanted to warn Betty about the clever, devious fortune hunter, but she couldn't very well do that without revealing things about her past that were no one else's business. And, too, if the starry-eyed expression on Betty's face was any indication, the woman was already totally smitten. She probably wouldn't have believed anything Audrey had to say. How did that man so easily ingratiate himself? Then she recalled her own starry-eyed self five years ago and had her answer.

In spite of herself, Audrey was curious about the circumstances that had brought Jesse to the Triple B. As she and Betty returned to the car she questioned the young woman. "If his kind are so hard to come by, how did you find him?"

"We didn't. He found us. Jesse used to work on a spread in Texas, but its owner got into some kind of trouble with the government, and the operation shut down. So, in tried-and-true cowboy tradition, Jesse started moving west, working here and there, searching for a ranch that still did things the old-fashioned way."

No, he was searching for a ranch whose owner had an eligible daughter, Audrey reflected. Jesse was a clever one, but not clever enough to change his method of operation. Dismayed, she slid into the passenger seat and closed the door. Another ranch, another daughter, another love-struck female. She hadn't known Betty but a few hours, yet she already liked her. Betty didn't deserve Jesse; no woman did. Audrey wouldn't have wished Jesse on her worst enemy.

But there was nothing she could do about it. Whatever happened to any of the Benedicts wasn't her concern, and Betty, after all, was a grown woman who could take care of herself. Audrey was somewhat consoled by the knowledge that Jesse would have to be one worried man about now, wondering if she was going to blow the whistle on him, the way Sam Graves had all those years ago. The thought of him "stewing" in his own caldron was so pleasant that Audrey almost smiled.

"Is it serious between you and Jesse?" she asked off-handedly.

Betty started the car and reversed direction. "Not as serious as I hope it's going to be," she said with a grin. "Of course, there are a few problems. A certain caste system exists on a ranch, so that puts Jesse and me at opposite ends of the social structure. And, as Benedicts, Boyd and I are supposed to marry well, the way Brent did. But I'm hoping the fact that everyone thinks so highly of Jesse will count for something.''

''What does Boyd think of him?''

''Boyd? Well . . . I doubt he thinks of him at all, except as an unusually good cowhand. In time I'm hoping to enlist Boyd as an ally in this, though. Dad listens to my brothers more than he lets on.'' Betty sobered and cast an anxious glance Audrey's way. ''I don't know why I'm trusting you with all this. You see, no one knows about me and Jesse— not yet. I'd like to keep it that way.''

Audrey stared vacantly through the windshield. Betty had no way of knowing what a trustworthy confidante she had chosen. ''Don't worry, Betty. You can count on me. I wouldn't dream of saying a word to anyone.''

CHAPTER SIX

THE OUTING had taken up more of the afternoon than either woman realized. When they returned to the house Betty glanced at her watch. "It's later than I thought. We're going to have to get a move on, friend. Dad expects everyone to gather in the sun room at six-thirty sharp."

What would happen if someone was late, Audrey wondered, recalling how Boyd had hopped to earlier that afternoon. Apparently no one kept Buck Benedict waiting. "No problem. I'll be ready."

"I don't envy you, Audrey. You're going to be on display tonight, no getting around it."

Audrey smiled nervously. "I hope I don't disappoint them."

"I'll tap on your door when I'm ready, and we'll go in together. Now, don't let Dad intimidate you. He's really a nice person, but he plays the role of head of the family to the hilt. He's like a traffic cop when we all get together—you come here, you go there, you stay here. Even men who've worked for him twenty years or more stand a little in awe of him. Granddad was the only person who ever had any real influence with Dad, and those two used to have some arguments that rocked these walls."

Wonderful, Audrey thought as she ducked into the guest room. Just wonderful! She was beginning to wish she could forgo the "pleasure" of meeting Buck B. Benedict. Frankly, she was tired of adjusting to one startling development after another.

Someone had considerately unpacked her suitcase and put everything away. The few dresses she had brought had been pressed and hung in the closet. After a moment's deliberation, she decided on the sundress she had worn the night before. She took fresh underwear and panty hose out of the dresser, then laid it all across the bed. In the bathroom she took a quick shower and shampooed her hair. Towelling dry, she slipped on a knee-length terry cloth robe, cinched it around her waist and stepped back into the bedroom just as a knock sounded at the door.

It would have to be Betty or one of the servants. "Come in," she called, and the door opened. Boyd entered the room. He was freshly showered and had changed from jeans and boots to dark blue slacks and a white shirt. He looked, in a word, marvelous.

"Oh, I . . . I thought you were Betty."

"I just stopped by to see how you're getting along, if you need anything. I can come back later." But he made no attempt to leave, and his eyes boldly moved over her damp, tousled hair, her scrubbed face, her shapely legs beneath the robe's hem.

"No . . . that's all right. Have a seat. It will just take me a minute to get dressed." She scooped her clothes off the bed and carried them into the bathroom. Once there, however, she couldn't find her bra. She would have sworn she had gotten one out of the dresser, but it wasn't there. With a disgusted sigh, she opened the door and saw Boyd sitting on the edge of the bed. One strap of the wispy undergarment was draped over his forefinger, and he was studying the bra as though it were the most fascinating thing he'd ever seen. When the door opened he glanced up.

"You dropped something," he said with a grin.

"So . . . I did." Flushing slightly, she walked to the bed, all but snatched the bra out of his hand and returned to the bathroom. She was almost certain she heard him chuckling as she closed the door.

While Boyd waited, he recalled his afternoon with his father. Naturally, Buck had been curious about Audrey and wanted a full report. Boyd had given a lot of thought to what he said. "There's not much I can tell you about her, Dad, since she's not one for talking about herself. She used to live in Texas. Her parents are gone, and she seems to have no other family. She came to Arizona to visit a friend about four years ago and ended up staying when a part-time job at the hotel came along. She's...I guess 'reserved' is the word I'm looking for. She's obviously intelligent, poised, attractive. From what I've been able to gather, her job demands it. I'm convinced she had no idea who Granddad was. She thought he was 'sweet.' That's about it."

"How does she feel about being brought here?" Buck had wanted to know.

"She seems to realize it's best for everyone concerned. No one likes dealing with the press."

Boyd had been relieved that his father accepted the report without more questions. For reasons he didn't fully understand he'd decided not to voice any of his reservations or suspicions about Audrey. Maybe he hoped they would prove to be unfounded.

The door to the bathroom opened, and she emerged, looking fresh, energetic and very beautiful. The dress she was wearing was the same one she'd had on last night. Boyd was aware of a peculiar stirring in the region of his heart, and it appalled him. There was no place in his life for an attraction to a woman he had doubts about. His eyes remained on her as she walked to the dressing table, sat down and flipped open her makeup case.

"So, how was your afternoon?" he asked.

"Enjoyable," Audrey replied. "I spent it with Betty. I really like her."

"That's good. I think Betty could use a woman friend. She works almost exclusively with men, and she and Sara are too different to be really close. What did the two of you do?"

"Oh, she showed me around the ranch, and...she introduced me to a man named Jesse."

Boyd nodded. "Jesse Murdoch. Good man. We're thinking of making him foreman. I guess Betty can keep you busy while you're here. God knows, she always seems to find something to do. Maybe you won't be too bored."

"I doubt I'll be bored at all," she lied. "And I'll try to stay out of the way."

"You won't be in anyone's way." He watched as, stroke by practiced stroke, she applied her makeup, then brushed her hair. His reflection in the mirror seemed to be making her nervous—he could tell by her somewhat jerky movements—but he didn't want to take his eyes off her. When she finished, she stood up and turned to face him. Boyd shoved himself off the bed and went to stand in front of her. "Lovely," he said matter-of-factly, but his gaze was like a physical caress. "A true work of art."

"Well...thank you." The compliment came as a surprise. Audrey's breath caught somewhere between her lungs and her throat. He was standing very close, and she loved the smell of that after-shave. She would have liked to tell him how nice he looked, too. But she was sure he knew how handsome he was, just as she was sure she was reading more into his expression than he intended.

There was a chameleon-like quality to him. Earlier that day, during the drive from Phoenix, he had been thoroughly remote. Now potent, sensuous energy seemed to radiate from him. Unwillingly, she stared up at him, her mouth slightly parted in fascination.

Boyd frowned slightly. He didn't recall that either of them had said or done a thing out of the ordinary, yet the atmosphere in the room had changed dramatically. He experienced an absurd urge to reach out and finger a few strands of her silky hair.

At that moment Betty rushed into the room. "Hey, Audrey, you ready? Ooops..."

Audrey could visualize the picture she and Boyd must have presented, standing so close and gazing deeply into each other's eyes. Giving herself an imperceptible shake, she quickly stepped back to put some distance between them.

Betty looked at Audrey, then at her brother, a mixture of surprise and amusement on her face. "When did you say you two met each other?" she asked, stifling a bubble of laughter.

Boyd collected himself, took both women by the arm and propelled them out the door. "Come on," he said gruffly. "Let's not keep the others waiting."

WHEN THE THREE OF THEM entered the sun room, four pairs of eyes turned toward them. For a moment, Audrey had the distinct sensation of being under a microscope. Then Elizabeth rose and rushed forward.

"Audrey, dear, how nice you look."

"Thank you, Mrs. Benedict. How was your afternoon?"

"Rather hectic. I barely made my appointment. I do hope you were able to amuse yourself."

"Yes, I had a delightful time. Betty took me on a tour of the ranch. It's impressive, I must say."

"Good. Boyd, why don't you introduce Audrey around."

"Of course." Placing a hand on the small of her back, he guided Audrey toward a blond woman who was stylishly dressed in a soft shade of blue. "Audrey, this is my sister-in-law, Sara."

"How do you do, Sara."

"It's nice to meet you, Audrey." Sara's lips barely moved when she spoke, and she had the iciest blue eyes Audrey had ever seen. Her beauty was of the Dresden-doll type, and she projected the image of the quintessential socialite. Not an easy person to get to know was Audrey's immediate impression.

Boyd then turned to the tall, slender man at Sara's side. Audrey would have known the man was related to Boyd no matter where she had encountered him. The physical resemblance was remarkable, though the rugged handsomeness she associated with Boyd was less pronounced in his brother, possibly because of his more pallid complexion.

"Audrey, this is my brother, Brent," Boyd intoned.

"How do you do, Brent."

"Welcome to the Triple B, Audrey."

Boyd applied a bit of firm pressure on Audrey's waist as he guided her toward a man who had been standing aloof from the rest of them. "And, Audrey, I'd like you to meet my father. Dad, this is Audrey Hamilton."

Buck B. Benedict was bigger-boned than either of his sons. The Arizona sun had burned a permanent layer of bronze in his skin, and his hair was more salt than pepper.

Tall and straight-shouldered, only slightly soft in the middle, he was distinguished and maturely attractive. He greatly resembled the portrait of Bert that hung in the hall.

But it wasn't Buck Benedict's looks that arrested Audrey's attention as much as the aura surrounding him. He was a commanding presence, a figure of authority. Here was a man of importance, his manner said, a man in charge of himself and all he surveyed. He was so unlike Bert, who had been such a simple man. But then Audrey was reminded that she had known Bert in the twilight of his life. Apparently her old friend had been just as authoritarian as his son in earlier days.

Would Boyd be the same fifteen or twenty years down the road? She wondered why that question had even crossed her mind.

She studied the man who now was the patriarch of the family. She found Buck more interesting than intimidating, but, after all, she had been raised in a household where prominent people had often been guests, and during her years at the Greenspoint she had shaken hands with presidents, prime ministers and princes. It would take more than Buck Benedict to intimidate her.

"How do you do, Mr. Benedict," she said politely, extending her hand.

Buck took it and shook it firmly. "Welcome to my home, Audrey. I trust you are being looked after properly."

"Yes, I am. Your wife and daughter have been most gracious."

"Good, good. I apologize for any inconvenience we might have caused you, but it was necessary. Now, please sit down and have a drink with us."

The male hand at her waist dropped, and Boyd said, "I'll get it. Audrey prefers to drink wine. What'll you have, Betty?"

"Get me a beer," his sister said and motioned for Audrey to join her on the sofa.

Elizabeth, Brent and Sara took seats around the room, while Buck moved to the far end to sit in a huge high-backed rattan chair behind a long table that served as a desk. This

had the immediate effect of directing all eyes to him, something Audrey suspected the desk's location was meant to do.

Boyd brought drinks to Audrey and his sister, then went
to stand in front of the big windows, slightly apart from the
mainstream. He sipped absently on his drink and focused
his attention on his father, who, as usual, was "holding
court." Buck, he noticed, was playing it low-keyed tonight.
Normally these predinner gatherings took on the air of a
business meeting, with everyone reporting on the day's
events. Tonight, however, his father kept the mood more
amiable and social.

Within minutes Boyd's attention strayed to Audrey. His
dad didn't seem to faze her a bit, and that was unusual, since
Buck intimidated just about everyone at first. She was as
calm and collected as if she had known the family her entire life. What kind of background had instilled such poise
in her? Somehow he didn't think it came solely from greeting the famous and near-famous at the Greenspoint for three
years.

Alertly, he listened to the conversation flowing around the
room. Everyone was bombarding Audrey with questions,
but Boyd noticed how adroitly she evaded any that were
personal. Instead she launched into a series of anecdotes
about some of the celebrities who had stayed at the Greenspoint, which made for amusing entertainment but wasn't
very enlightening. Why he was obsessed with knowing more
about her he couldn't imagine—yet he was.

She's such a lovely charmer, he thought with a sigh. *I just
wish she rang true.*

Audrey wasn't accustomed to being the center of attention, and she was uncomfortable having all eyes trained on
her. Moreover, she was acutely aware of Boyd standing off
to the side, studying her intently. She could feel his eyes
beating down on her, so she carefully avoided looking directly at him. A strange feeling persisted—that he was just
waiting for her to make a slip of the tongue. Damn him. The
others seemed to have no trouble accepting her at face value.
Why was he so suspicious?

She more or less had braced herself for the first questions concerning her relationship with Bert, but no one said a word. In fact, everyone was exceedingly courteous. The reason for her impromptu "visit" to the Triple B was not mentioned. Still, Audrey was on edge, and she felt a great surge of relief when the plump woman named Maria appeared to announce dinner.

The evening meal in the Benedict house, Audrey was soon to learn, was an unhurried affair meant to last an hour or more, and nothing was allowed to interfere with it. The food, which was served in courses by Maria and Tina, was hearty and laden with calories. First came a spicy soup. It was followed by a rice dish laden with chili peppers and onions. The main course was steak strips rolled in flour tortillas and accompanied by beans, avocado slices and the Mexican tomato relish curiously named *pico de gallo*, or "rooster's beak." Just in case anyone still had room, the meal was topped off with sherbet, almond cookies and strong coffee laced with chocolate.

Audrey's appetite was completely satisfied after the rice, but as a guest she felt obligated to eat a respectable amount of everything. She noticed that none of the Benedicts had the slightest trouble putting away the food. She wondered if the altitude had something to do with their robust appetites, since she herself had consumed more at this one meal than she normally did during an entire day. She also wondered how the women kept their svelte figures if this was their typical fare.

Buck and Elizabeth sat at opposite ends of the table, with Boyd and Audrey on one side, Betty, Brent and Sara across from them. Conversation throughout the meal was dominated by the men, whose interests were many and varied. Buck and his sons hopped from the weather and pasture conditions to state and national politics, Wall Street and the cattle market. The family, Audrey soon surmised, was very active politically. Elizabeth's and Sara's lone contribution to the talk concerned a luncheon they were planning for the wife of a state senator. Betty kept silent except when the conversation turned to cattle. As for Audrey, she said virtually nothing at all.

Dinner finally ended, and Buck got to his feet. As if on signal, the others also stood and began filing out of the dining room. Betty lingered to speak to Audrey. "Everyone else will watch TV for a while, but I'm in the middle of a great book, so if you don't mind, I think I'll go to my room."

"Of course I don't mind, Betty. Please don't think you have to stay by my side every minute. I want to turn in early, too."

"Okay, see you in the morning. We'll find something to do tomorrow."

Audrey smiled. "Good night. Thanks for everything."

Betty left, and Audrey turned to push her chair into place. She discovered Boyd standing behind her. He took the chair and slid it up to the table. "Did you enjoy your dinner?" he asked.

"Very much. It was delicious."

"You didn't eat much."

"I ate far more than I usually do."

"Were you serious about turning in early?"

"I thought I would."

"Then I'd better warn you of something. Dad has it on good authority that the terms of Granddad's will are going to break in the morning papers. He wants all of us to stay fairly close to home for the next few days."

"Where else would I go?" Audrey inquired sensibly.

"Where else indeed?"

At that moment Maria and Tina appeared to clear the table. Boyd fell into step beside Audrey, and they went into the foyer. "Of course," he said, "I'm beginning to think we could have let you talk to the press all you wanted, and there'd be no harm done."

She stopped and eyed him quizzically. "I beg your pardon?"

"You're amazingly adept at talking without saying anything. You've been with us all evening, and still we know almost nothing about you."

Audrey tensed slightly. "You know everything that's important."

"Really? I wonder."

"Tell me, Boyd, are you always this vastly curious about people you've just met?"

"Only when they make me so. Only when they withhold the most basic information about themselves. Where were you born?"

An amused glint came into her eyes. "Guthrie, Oklahoma."

"I thought you were a Texan."

"I was born in Guthrie because my folks were returning from a trip to Kansas when I put in an unexpected appearance. You see, I was premature... almost six weeks premature, to be exact. My mother had to remain in Guthrie a month before they'd let her take me home. Isn't that fascinating?"

Her sarcasm didn't dissuade him. "What did your dad do for a living?"

"He owned his own business."

"Were you very young when he died?"

Audrey's mouth set in a tight line. "He died five years ago. My mother died a few weeks earlier."

Boyd felt a rush of color diffuse his face. "Good Lord, Audrey... I'm sorry. I..."

Audrey stepped back from him. "Now, if you'll excuse me, I must tell everyone good-night."

Boyd watched her walk away and chastised himself severely. He'd come across like an insensitive clod. Why couldn't he have left well enough alone? She was being cooperative as hell, and the rest of the family seemed to harbor no suspicions. Why did he? Why was he so damned interested in her past? It had no bearing on anything.

He was still standing in the foyer, lost in his thoughts, when he heard Audrey return from the sun room. She paused a moment, and he searched his brain for something to say. Before he could, however, she turned and disappeared down the hallway. He heard the door to the guest

room open and close behind her. He felt terrible. Had it
been physically possible, he would have kicked his own butt.

I HOPE HE'S damned well satisfied, Audrey thought as she
closed the door. She had rather enjoyed that embarrassed
look on Boyd's face. Maybe now he would leave her alone.
Everything she had told him was the unvarnished truth, yet
it had revealed nothing important.

The room was completely dark. She reached for the light
switch on the wall, then saw that the door to the veranda
was standing slightly ajar. Not wanting to lure a swarm of
insects with the light, she crossed the room to close the door.
As her hand closed around the knob, however, she caught a
whiff of the clean, fresh scent of night air. It was irresistible. Stepping out onto the veranda, she gazed up. With no
nearby city lights to obscure its beauty, the sky was like
black velvet studded with a million diamonds. At this ele-
vation, the stars seemed close enough to reach out and
touch. Drawn by nature's spectacle, she crossed the veranda and walked out onto the lawn. There, not even the
few lights from the house detracted from the breathtaking
view. How long had it been since she'd really seen a night
sky? It was back on the ranch in Texas, and that seemed a
lifetime ago.

Mesmerized by the night, Audrey at first didn't see the
shadowy outline of a man's shape moving toward her. He
was almost upon her before some movement caught her eye.
Startled, she opened her mouth, but a rough hand closed
over it, silencing her. Wide-eyed, she looked up into the face
of Jesse Murdoch.

"Hush," he growled. "Don't make a sound. Understand?"

Mutely she nodded. Jesse studied her uncertainly for a
moment. Then, apparently satisfied she wouldn't cry out,
he dropped his hand and clutched her upper arm. "Small
world, isn't it, Audrey?"

Angrily, she flung his hand away. "What are you doing
here?"

"I work here, and I'm simply taking my customary nightly stroll. I might ask you the same question."

"I'm getting some fresh air, and I want to be alone."

"I don't mean what are you doing outside," Jesse said. "I mean, what are you doing here at the Triple B? I damned near fell dead when I saw you this afternoon."

"I can imagine," Audrey countered acidly. "Knowing that made my day."

"Repeat, what are you doing here?"

"I don't consider that any of your business."

An unpleasant smile crossed Jesse's face. "Still sore after all these years, huh? I only did my civic duty, Audrey. Your daddy was a crook."

"Oh, come off it, Jesse! I know you, remember? My father did a dreadful thing, and he deserved to pay for it, but I question your motives for turning state's evidence. I don't think your 'civic duty' came into play for an instant."

"You do me an injustice. I've always been a law-abiding citizen."

"That's right. There's no law against what you do, not one on the books, anyway. And since you have the moral fiber of a mountain goat—"

"Betty said you work for the Benedicts?" Jesse interrupted brusquely. "How well do you know them?"

"Again, that's none of your business." Audrey took a deep breath. "Leave Betty alone."

"Hey, the woman's crazy about me. I'd break her heart if I left her alone. I'm not going to do anything to hurt Betty. I'll make her happy. If I feather my own nest into the bargain, what's the harm in that?"

"You know something . . . the awful part is, I think you really believe that. Do something decent for once in your life, Jesse, and leave her alone."

He grabbed her arm again, this time clutching it with painful tightness. "Now you listen to me. When I saw you this afternoon, my first thought was that you'd throw a monkey wrench in all my plans. But the more I thought about it, the more I realized you weren't going to say a word, not one damned word. If you were going to say something to the Benedicts about me, you'd have done it by now, and I'd know about it.''

His grip on her arm relaxed, and his ugly smile returned. ''I don't know what your business with the Benedicts is, and I don't care, as long as you don't interfere. If you know them at all, then you know what upstanding citizens they are. Hell, they practically own this state, and they have some pretty high-and-mighty friends. I don't think they'd want to have much to do with a gal whose daddy was sentenced to a federal pen. So you keep your mouth shut about me, and I'll keep mine shut about your daddy's shenanigans. Everybody will live happily ever after, and that includes your friend, Betty. Deal?''

Uttering a sound of contempt, Audrey shoved him away. ''I don't deal with scum!'' she hissed. She turned on her heel and marched back across the patio and into her room. But before she could close the door, she heard another one open. That was followed by the sound of footsteps hurrying across the patio. Turning, she peered into the darkness in time to see Betty step out onto the lawn. Going to meet Jesse, Audrey guessed. Obviously he'd been waiting for her when he'd seen Audrey.

Closing the door, she leaned against it a moment, her chest heaving in agitation. *Oh, Audrey,* her inner voice said in despair, *you know you should blow the whistle on Jesse! Betty's such a nice person.*

I know, I know, she responded tiredly, *but I can't. It would require spilling too many things that I've kept bottled up for years. Why should I chance throwing my own life into turmoil again? Betty isn't my responsibility.*

Jesse infuriated her to the point of making her sick to her stomach, but he'd been very right about her. If she had been going to say anything about him to the Benedicts, or at least to Betty, she would have done so by now. And that was the worst of it. Knowing she probably could send Jesse out of Betty's life with only a few words, and having no intention of doing so... well, that really made her sick!

CHAPTER SEVEN

THE SUN HAD BARELY PEEPED over the horizon the following morning when Buck and his three offspring gathered for breakfast in the dining room. They helped themselves to the food from several chafing dishes on the sideboard, then took their customary places. In the center of the table was the usual pile of newspapers that were delivered to the ranch every morning from the nearby town of Agua Linda. The pile contained the morning editions of the major state papers, along with a day-late *Wall Street Journal*. This morning the *Journal* was neglected. The Benedicts were interested in only one story.

They ate in silence until Buck, having thumbed through most of the newspapers, murmured, "Well, it's not too bad. Just straight news stories so far. But there's a lot of human interest stuff here, so I fully expect the phone to start ringing off the wall any minute. May I remind all of you that I'll be the one to handle all calls." He folded a paper, placed it beside his plate and looked at Brent. "Are you sure you want to go to the office today?"

Brent nodded. "Might as well. I'll just pass the word that I'm not seeing anyone or taking any calls. No problem."

Buck shifted his attention to Boyd. "What about you, son?"

"I'll spend most of the day hiring the extra hands we need for roundup. A couple showed up yesterday, so the word's gotten around. I expect more today."

Buck nodded. "You know, this isolation is hard on your mother and Sara, so they've decided to go to Los Angeles for a few days of shopping." He turned to his daughter. "Guess looking after our guest will be up to you, Betty."

"Suits me. I really like Audrey." Betty's eyes darted to Boyd. "That doesn't mean I have to miss roundup, does it?"

"Sorry, love," Boyd said sympathetically. "We can't very well go off and leave Audrey alone. That wouldn't be fair."

"I know, but I haven't missed a roundup in five years." Then Betty had an idea. "Boyd, Audrey says she can ride a horse. I thought I'd take her on my rounds today. If she proves she can handle herself..."

"Oh, hey, come on." Boyd chuckled. "Surely you're not thinking of asking a greenhorn to tag along. You know how the men feel about women on roundup. It goes against the grain."

"I'm a woman, or hadn't you noticed?"

"That's different."

"Give me a little credit, brother dear. I wouldn't dream of bringing her along if I didn't think she could handle it."

"It's not a good idea," he said stubbornly.

"Think about it," Betty persisted just as stubbornly.

"Talk to me tonight, but I'm afraid the answer is going to have to be no."

AUDREY AWAKENED EARLY, disturbed by some unfamiliar sounds. Then she realized it was the lack of sounds that disturbed her. Her apartment in Phoenix was in a large complex located just off a busy thoroughfare. The area began teeming with activity and noise at a very early hour. Now she turned her head on the pillow and listened. Muted voices came from somewhere. The kitchen, she guessed, for she could smell the delicious aroma of freshly brewed coffee. And from outside, in the far, far distance, came the lowing of cows and the bawling of calves. Otherwise, all was quiet.

Sitting up, Audrey hugged her knees to her breasts and yawned. She had slept fairly well once she'd finally fallen asleep, but the combination of the strange house, strange bed, Boyd's questioning and the disturbing encounter with Jesse had kept her awake an hour or more after she'd gone to bed.

At some point before succumbing to sleep she had conveniently absolved herself of any responsibility for warning Betty about the unscrupulous man. Now, in the light of morning, her damnable conscience began nagging her again. She liked Betty a lot. Given the time, Audrey thought the two of them could become close friends. And the Benedicts, after all, were Bert's family. She certainly owed her old friend plenty.

A moment later, however, she successfully shook off her guilt feelings. Whatever happened in this house was not her concern. Once she went back to the Greenspoint, she more than likely would never see any of them again. And since no one seemed to begrudge her the inheritance, none of them would ever again give her another thought.

Besides, she thought confidently, something might happen to thwart Jesse's big plans. Betty was no dummy; she might see through him eventually.

You were no dummy either, Audrey, that nagging inner voice reminded her, *but what if Sam Graves hadn't happened along when he did?* She shuddered just thinking about it.

She suddenly realized that she was hungry, and she wondered if breakfast was being served. After last night's gigantic dinner she had planned to forgo breakfast altogether, but coffee, juice and perhaps some toast wouldn't play too much havoc with her weight. Flinging aside the covers, she padded into the bathroom, took care of her morning routine, then dressed hurriedly and followed her nose to the dining room.

Betty, her father and both brothers were seated around the table. "Good morning," Audrey said brightly, and every head turned in her direction. She had the distinct feeling she had interrupted a conversation that had concerned her. When she noticed all the newspapers spread out on the table she was sure of it.

"Hi," Betty replied cheerfully. "Sleep well?"

"Yes, thanks."

The Benedict men mumbled greetings and started to rise, but Audrey raised her hand in a staying gesture. "Please, don't get up."

Buck and Brent paused and sat back down, but Boyd got to his feet. "Let me get you some breakfast," he offered, pulling out the chair next to his.

"I can get it," Audrey protested.

"Please, let me."

She slid into the chair. "Thanks. Just juice and coffee."

"Oh, you'd better eat more than that," Betty advised. "I thought I'd take you on my rounds, and that means a lot of riding. Lunch will be whatever we can carry in our saddlebags."

Audrey hungrily eyed the sausage, eggs and hash browns on Betty's plate. "Well, maybe a little food, but very little, please."

"I'll fix you up," Boyd said, moving toward the sideboard where several covered chafing dishes stood, along with the coffeepot and a decanter of juice. "How do you like your coffee?"

"With a touch of cream." She watched him as he took a plate and heaped it with too much food. He certainly was playing the part of the solicitous host this morning. Atoning for his previous sins, she thought with some satisfaction.

Boyd placed her food in front of her and took his seat again just as Buck got to his feet. "Have a good day, all of you. I'll see you tonight." With that he left the room.

Brent wasn't far behind. Standing up, he said, "I'll be off to the mill. Keep the home fires burning." He nodded politely to Audrey and walked out.

Boyd got up and carried his coffee cup to the sideboard for a refill. "Either of you two ladies need more coffee?" he asked. When both Audrey and Betty shook their heads, he filled his cup, downed the contents in a few gulps and set it on the sideboard. "Guess I'd better get rolling," he announced and made for the door.

But as he passed Audrey's chair, in a surprising move, he reached out and gave her shoulder a reassuring pat. The gesture, performed casually, and so quickly he barely broke stride, brought her head up with a jerk. He seemed to be trying to make her feel better. Better about what? Then her eyes fell on the newspapers, and she thought she had her answer.

Now that they were alone, Audrey turned to Betty. "The papers . . . is it bad?"

"No. I don't see what all the commotion is about," Betty said. "Granddad left a bunch of money to a bunch of people. So what?"

"Did he leave anyone else a hundred thousand dollars?"

"Well, no, but . . . Forget it, Audrey. You just had the bad luck to get tangled up with a family that seems to fascinate the media. Damned if I know why. Frankly, I think we're a pretty uninteresting lot."

Audrey sighed. "I wouldn't blame any of you for feeling resentful. No one likes having a complete stranger show up and throw everything out of kilter." She reached across the table and picked up the newspaper Buck had been reading. She saw it was the state edition of a Phoenix paper. Scanning the page, she noticed a headline in the lower right-hand corner: Phoenix Woman Beneficiary of Benedict Estate. She set the paper down, deciding she didn't want to read the article. "How do you manage to get these papers so early when you live way out here?" she asked.

"Some newsdealer in Agua Linda gets them from a dealer in Tucson who carries a big selection of out-of-town papers. Dad reads most of the state papers and the *Wall Street Journal* every day. I'm sure he pays handsomely for them, but he can't do without his papers. Listen, Audrey, the whole business will blow over in a few days."

"I hope so."

"You and I are going to be busy, so the time will pass like that." Betty snapped her fingers.

"Betty, please . . . I told you, I don't want you to feel you have to keep me entertained."

"I don't. You're going to keep me entertained. I'm riding fence today, and I could use the company. You'll enjoy your stay here so much more if you ride, because a lot of the ranch can only be reached on horseback. I'll pick your mount for you.''

Audrey knew exactly what riding fence entailed, and the thought of riding again appealed to her. Once, she had been completely at home in the saddle. "If you don't mind riding herd on a greenhorn, I'd love to go along.''

"Do you have boots?''

"No, sorry.''

"What size do you wear?''

"Seven, seven-and-a-half, depends on the shoe.''

"I have a pair that are a bit small for me. You can wear those. And you'll need a hat or that sun will kill you. No problem. I have plenty of hats.'' Betty pushed herself away from the table and stood up. "It's time for my weekly business conference with Dad, so I'll give you a holler when I'm ready. Okay?''

"Fine. Betty, do you suppose anyone would mind if I call my office? I'll make it collect, of course.''

Betty thought about it, then shrugged. "Has Dad told you not to make any calls?''

"No, it hasn't been mentioned.''

"Then I don't see anything wrong with it. The phones in the bedrooms are a different number from the one in Dad's study, so you won't be interfering with business calls.''

"Thanks. See you later.'' Audrey left her half-eaten breakfast and went back to her room to place a call to the Greenspoint. It seemed much longer than twenty-four hours ago that she had left Phoenix.

Helen screeched when she discovered who was on the line. "Audrey!''

"Hi, Helen. What's going on?''

"Are you kidding? I'll tell you what's going on. It's hit the fan, that's what's going on! Where are you?''

"In exile.''

"Jeez, you wouldn't believe this place. Our nice laid-back little office is about as laid-back as Mission Control at T-minus-ten-and-counting.''

Audrey's stomach made a sickening revolution. "Can I talk to Peter?''

"Yeah, guess so. Every light on this phone is lit up. Hold on."

Peter came on the line almost immediately. "Audrey?"

"Helen tells me confusion reigns. I'm sorry, Peter. Wish I were there."

"No, you don't. I've spent the past hour with the phone stuck in my ear. And some guy got past the security people downstairs and found his way up here. I thought I was going to have to throw him out bodily. He wanted to talk to you about some land in Colorado. So far three insurance salesmen have called, to say nothing of every newspaper in the state. Seems everyone wants to know the real story behind your relationship with Bertram B. Benedict."

Audrey groaned. "And to think I had hoped all this would pass quickly and I could come home."

"If you're smart you'll stay right where you are. If these people can't find you, they'll lose interest after a while. Be grateful that the Benedicts were thoughtful enough to protect you from all this. You'd hate it."

He was right. Dear God, that she of all people had gotten involved in something like this! Wasn't once in anyone's lifetime enough?

BOYD CAME out of the stables just as Betty and Audrey were preparing to ride off for the day. He approached them, his eyes all for Audrey, who looked downright fetching in boots and a cowboy hat. He took note of the mount Betty had chosen for her—a gentle cutting horse named Ranger—and he approved. You could turn a child loose on Ranger.

"You don't need to worry," he said, coming up to her. "Ranger's as gentle as they come."

"I'm not worried."

"Betty tells me you've ridden before."

"Yes, but it's been years."

"Was that back in Texas?"

"Um-hmm."

In a fluid motion, Betty swung up on her own horse. "Ready?" she asked Audrey.

"Yes."

Boyd stepped forward to give Audrey a leg up, but she didn't seem to need his help. Effortlessly, she swung herself up in the saddle, gently nudged Ranger and trotted off beside Betty. Boyd hooked his thumbs in the pocket of his jeans and stared after them. In particular he noticed the easy way Audrey sat in the saddle. Most true greenhorns approached a horse, even a gentle one, timidly. She didn't. To his knowledge she was a city slicker, yet she sat a horse as though born to it. That was one more interesting piece of information about a woman who intrigued him in ways he didn't fully understand. He was still trying to come to grips with his strong attraction to her.

AUDREY THOROUGHLY enjoyed the day out on the open range. She and Betty rode the entire length of the fence on the western boundary of the ranch, stopping often for Betty to dismount and repair breaks in the barbed wire. At midday they sat beneath the shade of an ancient tree and ate the lunch Maria had provided for them. Audrey listened while Betty gossiped about her family, something she loved to do.

"Boyd once commented that the Benedict clan is organized along military lines, and I guess he's right. Dad's definitely the colonel of the regiment, and Granddad was sort of a commanding general. We all have jobs to do, and it's been that way as long as I can remember. Brent oversees the banking and real estate from the Tucson office. Boyd's the troubleshooter and PR man. He runs around smoothing ruffled feathers. He also sets overall policy for the ranch, and I carry it out."

"What about your mother and Sara?" Audrey asked. So far it seemed to her that Elizabeth and Sara's main task was to look beautiful at all times.

"They spend most of their time entertaining and being entertained by wives of people Dad considers important. They're pretty good at it, too. And they spare me from having to do much of it, thank God."

"How long have Sara and Brent been married?"

"Seven years. And no kids. They were supposed to have kids. All of us are supposed to have kids, but you gotta figure Brent and Sara might never have them, not after seven years. Sad, really. I know Sara feels...inadequate. Now, since any kids I have won't carry the name, I guess it's up to Boyd to give the world a new generation of Benedicts."

Audrey strove for casualness as she asked, "Any prime candidates for a wife?"

"Nope, not one. Sometimes Dad acts like that's a personal affront. Boyd was supposed to marry a woman named Linda Ames, but it never happened."

"Supposed to?"

Betty nodded. "Yeah, Linda's father was a state senator and a drinking buddy of Dad's. The two of them thought that marriage would be perfect. It was really funny the way they tried to throw Boyd and Linda together. Trouble is, neither of them cooperated. Shoot, they'd known each other since they were in grade school. Oh, they went through the motions of dating for a while, but then Linda went off to college and married some starving medical student. Now the man's a big-shot radiologist in Los Angeles, and Linda has three kids, all boys. Dad all but cries when he thinks about it." Betty paused to chuckle. "I feel sorry for the woman who finally snares my younger brother. I'm afraid Dad will look on her as a brood mare. He might insist she have a gynecological checkup before the wedding, like Princess Di."

"What about you, Betty? I believe you said you're expected to marry well, too."

Betty's face clouded. "Yeah, and that presents problems, real problems. I've had plenty of 'suitable' men paraded by me. Dad's about as subtle as a meat cleaver when it comes to matchmaking. But ever since I was old enough to think about such things, I've dreamed of a man exactly like Jesse, a cowboy who loves this life the way I do and doesn't yearn for more."

Oh, Betty, Audrey wanted to wail, *Jesse isn't what he appears to be at all. His real yearnings would stagger you.* "Could you defy your father?" she asked.

"I don't know. I've never had to. None of us have. I wonder if either Boyd or I could just dig in our heels, stick out our chins and say, 'No, that's not what I want.' I wonder.''

Audrey's heart sank, but then, almost immediately, a ray of hope stirred inside her. Buck B. Benedict might belong in another century, but that could prove to be a blessing in disguise for Betty, though she wouldn't think so at the time. Buck just might thwart Betty's romance with Jesse for good. It was a comforting thought.

Off and on for the remainder of the afternoon she pondered the things Betty had told her about the family structure. It was a bit archaic, to say the least. Peculiar that a dynamic man like Boyd would go along with all that dynasty nonsense. But then she was reminded of how little she actually knew about him ... and how little his private life meant to her.

BY DINNERTIME that evening, Audrey was beginning to be painfully aware of every minute she had spent on Ranger. There wasn't a muscle in her body that didn't ache. She and Betty returned to the house late, so there was only time for a hasty shower instead of the hot bath she wanted. Audrey would have liked nothing better than to miss the dinner hour completely, but she was ravenously hungry after all the fresh air and exercise. So she suffered through another sumptuous, leisurely meal and excused herself as soon as she decently could.

"I hope you don't mind," she said as the family began filing out of the dining room, "but I seem to have overdone it today. I think I'll soak in a hot bath and fall into bed."

Betty looked at her apologetically. "I should have known better than to keep you out so long."

"I'm sure I'll feel better in the morning."

Actually, Audrey suspected the others were relieved to see her go. They would have plenty to talk about but couldn't, or wouldn't, as long as she was around. She said good-night and went to her bedroom. Once there, she filled the tub with steaming water, shed her clothes and climbed in, stretching out full length. The liquid heat worked wonders, soothing the soreness. She stayed in the tub until the water cooled, then briskly rubbed herself dry. Now she thought she could sleep.

Slipping into the knee-length terry cloth robe, she walked into the bedroom and turned down the bed covers. A bed had never looked so inviting. But before she could take off the robe and put on her gown there was a knock at the door. Opening it, she was astonished to see Boyd standing in the hall.

"You weren't already in bed, were you?"

"No, I just got out of the tub." Audrey then noticed he held a bottle in each hand. One he thrust toward her.

"Aspirin," he said.

"Thanks. That might help."

He held up the other bottle. "Liniment. Tonight you looked as though every step was an effort."

She smiled ruefully. "I'm afraid it was."

"Tomorrow will be worse if you don't use this stuff." Over her shoulder he glanced at the bed. "A good rubdown will work miracles. I'm something of an expert, since I've rubbed down many a sore horse in my day. If you want to go over there and lie on your stomach, I'll see what I can do for those legs of yours."

"Well, I..." She had the worst feeling that her cheeks had just turned a flaming vermilion.

"You'll thank me for it in the morning, I promise."

"I, ah..." She opened the door wider and stepped back to allow him to enter. "I guess... you'll probably do a better job than I can."

"On your tummy, please."

Self-consciously, Audrey complied, stretching out across the bed and pillowing her head on her arms. She tried to relax but felt herself tense as the mattress sagged when Boyd sat down. Beginning at her feet, he slowly worked the liniment into her legs. The sensation was indescribably pleasant, and Audrey found it impossible to remain tense under the onslaught of his soothing touch. She swore she could feel the soreness abating, though her mind was focused more on Boyd's strong, sure fingers than on her sore muscles.

"Was today very bad?" she finally asked, feeling the need for some conversation. "I mean, with the newspapers and all."

"Not really."

"Were there a lot of calls?"

"Quite a few, but nothing Dad couldn't handle."

"What did he tell them?"

"The party line is that the family isn't personally acquainted with any of these people mentioned in Grand-dad's will. If we don't know them, we can't very well give out any information about them, right?"

"And they buy that?" From her experience Audrey knew that a reporter would stop at nothing to get a story he or she really wanted.

"Probably not, but what can they do? Dad did get a little steamed over one call, though. Ever hear of Jerome Jordan?"

Audrey frowned in thought. "Seems I have, but I can't remember who he is."

"Gossip columnist. Arizona's self-appointed chronicler of the rich and famous."

"Oh, yes. The man who uses all the exclamation points. I've read his column a few times and always felt sorry for the people he writes about. I wonder how he gets by with all that stuff."

"You've read him, all right. He loves taking potshots at any Benedict. He called Dad this morning and suggested— I'm not making this up—that you might have been Grand-dad's illegitimate daughter."

Audrey raised up on her elbows and looked over her shoulder in wide-eyed disbelief. "That's despicable!"

"But very like Jerome Jordan. Lie down and relax. Anyway, that was about the worst of it. Dad handled it with aplomb, and not even Jerome would dare print such nonsense. But that should tell you the kind of thing you would have had to deal with if you'd stayed at the hotel."

Audrey settled her head back on her arm. "I...guess I should thank you, all of you, for asking me to stay here."

"You're welcome," he murmured dryly. Discreetly, he inched the hem of her robe to midthigh as his practiced hands continued their soothing ministrations. Audrey felt her face growing warmer. His tactile touch elicited a sharp sensation in the pit of her stomach.

Boyd worked slowly, kneading and stroking, until his fingers encountered the hem of her robe and decency demanded he stop. Abruptly he pulled the garment down to its original length, screwed the cap on the liniment bottle and set it on the bedside table. Getting to his feet, he said, "Your bottom will be sorest, but I guess I'll let you take care of that."

Audrey shoved herself to a sitting position. "Th-thanks."

"Don't mention it," he replied with a grin. "My pleasure. Feel better?"

"I . . . think so."

"Good. Now, take a couple of those aspirin, and you'll feel almost brand-new in the morning."

"All right."

"Night. Sleep well."

"Good night."

Boyd walked to the door, then turned back to look at her. "Don't go to sleep without taking care of the derriere, or you'll be sorry tomorrow." And he left, closing the door behind him.

Audrey's heart was beating so rapidly she thought it would jump out of her chest. With some difficulty, she got up and reached for the bottle of liniment. Shrugging off the robe, she poured the liquid into her hands and massaged it into her buttocks, imitating Boyd's sure strokes. Then she gulped down two aspirin before putting on her gown and sliding between the cool sheets.

Plumping her pillow viciously, she made a conscious effort to empty her mind. She wasn't going to think about Boyd. He was nothing to her, nothing! In a week or so she would be back at the Greenspoint, back to the life she had so painstakingly made for herself, and the Benedicts once again would be nothing more than the wealthy family who owned the hotel where she worked.

Still, just before succumbing to her weariness, she thought of his strong, sure hands kneading and coaxing the soreness out of her legs. She hadn't wanted him to stop. A delicious tingling sensation spiraled up her spine. She fell asleep with a smile on her lips.

SLEEP DID NOT COME so easily for Boyd. He prowled his room restlessly before undressing and sliding into bed nude. Then he rested his head on his folded arms and stared at the ceiling.

He recalled his conversation with Betty after Audrey had gone to her room. His sister seemed to think Audrey could handle a horse and herself and would be no problem on roundup. Still, he'd refused, though he hated making Betty miss the adventure. Fall roundup was the high point of a ranch's year, the final accounting. Betty, of all people, deserved to be in on it since she worked as hard as anyone on the Triple B.

His sister had been disappointed by his refusal but magnanimous about it. Betty agreed that leaving Audrey at the ranch, especially with Elizabeth and Sara gone, not only would be unfair but would border on rudeness. After all, Audrey hadn't asked to come here. So that was that, the end of the matter.

What Boyd didn't understand was his lingering regret. Being honest with himself, he admitted he wanted Audrey along, and that wasn't sensible. Traditionally, the men disliked having women on roundup. They tolerated Betty because she had proved herself, but Audrey was a different matter entirely. Still, he wished she could go, and that didn't make any sense.

He sighed. A mixture of resignation and self-disgust overtook him. He had a problem, and his problem was lying in bed in the guest room. Try as he might, he couldn't be indifferent to Audrey. He had told himself time and time again to stay away from her, yet he gravitated to her like a fly to honey. And when he was alone with her she made him feel vulnerable, a feeling he despised above all others. Still he found excuses to seek her out.

From the beginning he had suspected that falling head over heels for her would be the easiest thing in the world. He didn't want to think it might already have happened.

CHAPTER EIGHT

AUDREY STROLLED from the house in the general direction of the stables, searching for Boyd. She was very upset over the conversation she'd had with Betty at breakfast, and though she doubted talking to Boyd would do any good, she had to try.

The ranch grounds teemed with activity and with more people than Audrey had previously seen milling about. She knew that the ranch had hired on extra men to help with the roundup, and she spotted three of the newcomers perched on the top railing of the corral fence. All three of the men were young, lean, wore black cowboy hats and sported facial hair. Looking at them, one was reminded of a Wanted poster. She was familiar with the type—itinerant drifters who followed the flow, hiring on wherever and whenever a ranch needed extra help, willing to sacrifice anything for this archaic way of life. Her father once had referred to them as "the infatuated few."

Audrey had almost reached the stables when Boyd came riding up on the beautiful horse he called Rocky. She saw that he had a young calf draped across his saddle. The poor animal had a bleeding tear in his cinnamon-colored hide, and his small white face was as frightened as a hurt child's.

"Oh!" she cried in dismay. "What happened?"

"The little guy strayed from his mama and got tangled up with a barbed-wire fence." Boyd dismounted and gently removed his hog-tied passenger, cradling him in his arms like a baby. "He needs some attention."

"Do you want help?" Audrey asked, falling in step beside him as he headed for the barn.

"I don't think you want to watch this, Audrey."

"I guess you'll have to cauterize the wound, right?"

"Right. He's gonna bawl his head off."

"You might need someone to help you hold him."

"All right. If you're sure you want to, come along."

One section of the barn had been partitioned off and was used as an emergency first-aid station for the ranch animals. A long stainless steel table stood in the center of the area, and a glass-fronted cabinet contained medical supplies. The place was as clean and sanitary as was possible under the circumstances. Boyd nodded toward the cabinet. "There's a blue spray bottle and some gauze pads in there. Would you mind swabbing down the table? I seem to have my hands full at the moment."

Audrey quickly performed the chore, then Boyd placed the calf on the disinfected table where it lay helplessly bawling for its mother. Audrey did the best she could to comfort the animal, soothing and petting it while Boyd cleaned and disinfected the wound. All went well until he applied the caustic solution. The calf thrashed and bellowed in protest, forcing Audrey to tighten her hold on him. "Come on, darling," she cooed, "it's going to be all right. Just calm down. You're going to feel lots better in a few minutes."

The pain did subside gradually, and Boyd released the rope binding the calf. Setting the animal on its feet, he pushed open a door that led to an isolation pen outside. "Sure sorry you had to learn about barbed wire the hard way, little feller." Smiling, he turned to Audrey. "They're curious as little kids. Thanks for your help."

"You're welcome, but I didn't do much."

"That's not true. You were a big help. It's hard to hold an animal and doctor it at the same time. The veterinary work didn't seem to bother you."

"No."

"Unusual."

"Guess I'm tougher than I look."

"Guess so. You don't look tough at all." They left the barn and walked as far as a Jeep parked at the side of the house. "How are the muscles this morning?" Boyd asked.

"Pretty good. Just a little sore."

"Didn't I tell you? Missed you at breakfast. I thought you might still be suffering some."

"No, but I'm afraid I overslept. Betty was the only one left in the dining room when I got there." Audrey stared at the ground a minute, then lifted her eyes. "Boyd, she tells me she asked if I could go along on roundup but you refused."

"Not a good idea," he remarked tersely. "The men don't like it."

"But if I weren't here, Betty would be going."

"Right, but Betty's a cowhand. You aren't."

"I can handle myself. I wouldn't be in the way. No one would have cause to complain. I promise. I wish you'd let me go."

"'Fraid not."

"Then I insist that you let Betty go. I can tell she wants to very badly."

Boyd shook his head. "Mom and Sara left for L.A. this morning. You'd be alone."

"I don't need a keeper." Audrey fought to keep the exasperation out of her voice. "Are you worried I'll run away? I promise I'll stay here like a good girl until I'm officially released."

"I'd hate to think you feel imprisoned," he said with a frown.

"Oh, of course I don't, but I wish you would try to understand how awful I feel about keeping Betty from something she obviously wants to do."

"She'll survive and live to see another roundup."

Audrey could see she was getting nowhere fast. Boyd, she was discovering, could be a maddeningly stubborn man. She decided to drop the subject for the time being, though she certainly planned to mention it again . . . and again.

Glancing around, she spied a pile of supplies on the ground beside the Jeep. There were cans of motor oil and large containers of gasoline. Boyd began loading them into the back of the Jeep. "What are you doing?" she asked.

"Gotta hook up a couple of windmills to gasoline engines. Summer rainy season's over and the wind's died."

"Why on earth would you do a job like that?"

"I wouldn't ask any man on this ranch to do something I don't do myself." Then impulsively, he added, "Want to come along? You seem to want a taste of ranch life."

"I really don't mind spending the day alone," she hedged.

"Are you sure? There's not much for you to do around here. Look at that gorgeous sky and tell me you want to spend the day thumbing through magazines. Windmilling's not my favorite chore, but at least it keeps me outside, and I sure could use some company."

Audrey hesitated. Common sense told her to steer clear of Boyd. He was far too curious about her, and keeping her guard up constantly was tiring. Besides, she seriously doubted he really wanted her company. It occurred to her that, save for the hours she'd spent sleeping, she hadn't been out of the sight of a Benedict since she had arrived at the Triple B. She wondered if that was a coincidence or by design. Perhaps Buck wanted someone to keep an eye on her at all times. Perhaps that was why Boyd insisted Betty miss roundup. If that was true, it rankled.

Still, there was something enormously appealing about the prospect of spending the day with Boyd. A perverse part of Audrey's nature was curious about him, too. "Well, if you really want some company..."

Boyd grinned. "I'll ask Maria to pack a lunch for two. Meet me here in about twenty minutes."

AN HOUR LATER, somewhere out in the vast grasslands of the ranch, Audrey perched on the hood of the parked Jeep and watched Boyd as he wrestled with a contrary pump jack. This engine apparently was giving him some trouble, and his mouth worked as busily as his hands. A muttered "goddammit" reached her ears.

She thought it unusual that Boyd, who easily could have been a rich man's spoiled son, seemed to enjoy the physical labor as much as he did. He worked efficiently, with economy of movement. He actually wasn't at all like the impeccable gentleman she had first encountered in the Durango Suite.

Minutes passed, then he returned to the Jeep. Hopping down from her perch, Audrey climbed back into the vehicle. "Did you get it fixed?" she asked.

"Sure," he replied. "I know all the right cuss words. Are you bored?"

"Not at all. This is nice."

He chuckled. "If windmilling appeals to you, you'll like anything."

"Oh, it's not that. It's everything...the weather, the wide open spaces..."

"The company?" he prodded playfully.

"Of course," she said with a smile. "That, too."

Boyd shifted into gear. With a lurch the Jeep moved forward, and they drove to the next windmill. By the time he'd finished with that one it was one o'clock, so he suggested they stop for lunch. He knew the perfect place, a grassy meadow at the foot of the Santa Rita Mountains. He parked near a spot where water tumbled down from the crags and crevices to form a slow-moving stream. "There's a blanket in back," he told Audrey. "Spread it out and I'll get the food."

Maria had packed cold fried chicken, bread, butter, a plastic container filled with raw vegetables, another with fruit, and a thermos of iced tea. They sat cross-legged on the blanket, and while they ate they talked.

"Have you always lived here, Boyd?" Audrey asked.

"Yep, I was born here. So was Dad. So was Granddad. When my great-great-grandfather left Pennsylvania, he went to Texas, bought two hundred head of longhorns and moved them onto the public domain in 1879, though he didn't get a clear title to the place until the Apaches were routed. The original deed is hanging in Dad's study. It was signed by President Grover Cleveland in 1895. The Benedicts have been here ever since."

Audrey shook her head in wonder. "That kind of family continuity is almost unbelievable. What was it like, growing up surrounded by all that tradition?"

It was a simple question but hard to answer. Boyd found it almost impossible to explain what it was like growing up as a Benedict in the valley, the source of the local citizens' pride and gossip, with so much to live up to. "Oh, not so bad, I guess," he said offhandedly. "But I'll confess something to you—when I was younger I hated seeing my name in the newspapers. I think that was the worst of it, knowing I couldn't indulge in normal teenage mischief for fear of landing on the front page. There have been many times when I wished my last name was Smith."

Audrey could understand that. To a lesser degree, bearing the name Hamilton in Dallas had sometimes been a burden. She guided her questioning along another path. "I think you said the ranch used to be bigger. How much bigger?"

"About a hundred thousand acres at one time, but as the family's business interests grew, we sold off some. Dad and Granddad used to argue about that a lot, along with other things."

Betty had mentioned Bert and Buck's arguments. Audrey slowly was piecing together a new picture of her elderly friend. More and more in her mind, Bert was becoming the "firebrand" Boyd had described that night at the hotel. "Betty told me that Bert and your father used to argue a lot. What did they argue about, other than selling your land."

"Politics, mainly. Granddad had the old-time cowman's inherent distrust of anything done or said in Washington, D.C. Occasionally he would tolerate 'interference' from Phoenix but never from the federal boys. Dad, on the other hand, is fascinated by politics and politicians. He always wanted Brent to run for office, but my brother just doesn't have the charisma for it. Don't get me wrong—Brent's a good guy and has a great head for business, but..." He shrugged and let the sentence die.

He didn't need to explain. Audrey had noticed how reserved Boyd's brother was. On a scale of one to ten, she felt Brent's personality rated a four or five, at best. She couldn't imagine the man hitting the campaign trail, pumping hands and hugging babies. And Sara wasn't much in the warmth department, either. Brent's wife was beautiful and gracious but terribly aloof. "What interests you, Boyd?" she asked. "Over and above work, I mean. I really don't know much about you."

He gave it some thought. "Oh, ordinary things. I like country music, football, baseball. Guess I'm Joe Average."

"No hobbies, no passions? Does anything unusual fascinate you?"

He regarded her over a drumstick. "Yep. You fascinate me."

It was, to say the least, an unexpected answer. "I do?"

"You do."

"In what way?"

"In many ways. You say you don't know much about me, but I know even less about you."

Audrey tensed, a reflex action. Every time she began to feel comfortable and at ease around him, his inquisitiveness reared its head. It was a shame that she had to keep so much of herself locked inside. That tended to place boundaries to her life and make attachments difficult to form. Boyd was the first man in years who had interested her beyond idle curiosity. *If things were different,* she reflected, *I believe I could feel some honest emotion for him.*

The thought alone was exciting. For some time now Audrey had been aware of a vague restlessness growing inside her. Basically she had been alone for five years, and an intrinsic part of her longed to savor romantic love. Occasionally she had reevaluated her priorities. Was it really so vital to keep her past a secret? After all, she'd done nothing wrong, and any man worthy of her time and interest surely would realize that. But always she would quickly recall those awful days after her father's trial when she'd been a victim of "guilt by association." No one would ever know how difficult it had been to start a new life. So everything would be locked away again.

Boyd saw her troubled expression and thought of all the questions he wanted to ask. *Where did you learn to ride a horse? How come you weren't the least bit squeamish about handling a wounded animal? What makes you think you'd last fifteen minutes on a roundup?* They would have to remain unasked. He'd never find out anything about her if he kept her wary. The last thing he wanted was an aloof Audrey. He enjoyed being with her too much. "The chicken's good, isn't it?" he commented casually.

Audrey released her pent-up breath. Maybe she'd been wrong; maybe he hadn't been going to pry, after all. She had become too touchy, and that, she realized, only added to her air of mystery. "It was delicious."

"Are you finished?"

"Lord, yes. I'm stuffed. I'm going to have to do something about this voracious appetite I seem to have acquired. When I get back home I'll have to go on a diet, and I despise dieting. It makes me crotchety."

"Surely you don't have weight problems." Boyd thought she was as trim and sleek as a colt.

"I do if I don't watch it." Audrey wiped her hands and mouth with a napkin, then waited for him to finish eating. When he did, she began clearing away the debris. Repacking everything in the hamper, she brushed aside Boyd's offers of help. "You've been working hard, and I need to move around. Just relax and digest your food. I'll do this."

She smoothed out the blanket, then carried the hamper and thermos to the Jeep. When she returned to their picnic spot, she found Boyd stretched out full length on his back, eyes closed, as blissfully relaxed as a baby. A soft smile curved her mouth. She stood over him for a moment. He was, she decided, the picture of masculine perfection, and she marveled at the pleasure she derived merely from looking at him. In repose his face was very somber. Audrey rubbed her hands on her jeans, dismayed at the crazy emotions and unmanageable thoughts he aroused in her.

Apparently he was asleep; his chest rose and fell in even, shallow breathing. She sank to her knees beside him, thinking she might get in a nap herself. The combination of sun and food had made her drowsy. She raised her face to the sun and closed her eyes. Then she reopened them and glanced down to find Boyd staring at her.

It seemed to Audrey that he was focused squarely on her mouth. His gaze lingered there before moving down to her breasts, and he made no effort to pretend he was looking elsewhere. The expression on his face sent her heart knocking against her ribs.

"I'm . . . sorry," she stammered. "Did I awaken you?"

"No, I wasn't asleep. I was watching you watch me."

"You just looked so peaceful. What were you thinking?"

"Oh, nothing much." Boyd pushed himself to a sitting position, brought his knees up and folded his arms across them. "No, that's not true. I was thinking how nice this is. Like you said earlier, the sun, the sky, the wide-open spaces. The company, of course. Just the two of us. Not another soul around." He smiled lazily. "If I had come out here alone I would have hurried through and gotten back home as soon as possible, but I wouldn't mind if this afternoon went on and on, would you?"

Audrey studied him quizzically. Some sort of change had come over him, something she couldn't give a name to at first. His eyelids drooped slightly, sensuously, and his lazy smile altered. Something told her he hadn't been thinking about the sun and sky at all. "That might be nice, but we, or rather you still have work to do."

"Yes. Duty calls, but who says I have to answer immediately? I don't suppose the world would stop if the other windmill had to wait until tomorrow." Boyd reached out and took her hand in his, encasing it warmly.

Suddenly, and without too much surprise, Audrey realized what the change in him signified. He was slipping into the role of desirable male. Some men did it so effortlessly, and apparently Boyd was one of them. Now, what brought this on, she wondered. Does he think I expect it?

Fascinated, she watched like a detached spectator as he inched closer to her and cupped her face with his free hand. "You have the most beautiful eyes I've ever seen," he said huskily.

The trite line didn't seem so trite when he said it. "Thanks."

"What color are they?"

"Brown."

"Come on, Audrey, that sounds ordinary, and your eyes are far from ordinary. They have funny little gold glints in them."

"Then I guess they're brown with funny little gold glints in them." Her voice sounded odd, curiously tremulous.

Boyd's hand dropped to her waist. There was a good solid feel to Audrey, he noticed. The sun had heated her skin, and its fragrance enticed him. He hadn't planned this romantic overture; it had just happened naturally. All of a sudden it had occurred to him that she was the most interesting woman who'd ever come into his life. Then one thing had led to another.

He intended moving cautiously, however. If she rebuffed him—and the chances were pretty good she would—they still would have to see a lot of each other in the coming days. He didn't want her suffering any embarrassment or bitterness. Slowly he brought his face closer to hers.

Audrey was as still as a statue. She couldn't have moved if her life had depended on it. Her heartbeat accelerated dramatically. She thought she was pretty well insulated against this sort of thing, but within seconds she learned how vulnerable she was to this very effective act of his. She knew she could jump to her feet, break the spell, and Boyd probably wouldn't persist. What she didn't know was why she didn't do just that. Maybe because this was fun, an exciting part of an age-old game. Basically it was harmless as long as she was aware of what was going on and kept it in proper perspective.

As Boyd's face came closer, she instinctively closed her eyes and parted her lips. His mouth touched hers tentatively, with scarcely any pressure at first, as though he was testing her reaction before proceeding further. She liked that. Meeting no resistance, he increased the pressure. Tilting her head slightly, Audrey leaned into the kiss. Thus encouraged, Boyd delicately penetrated her mouth with his tongue.

The slow spreading warmth was delightfully languorous as it crept into her pores. Audrey simply gave in to the sensation of being female and desired. A number of years had passed since she last had experienced such a thrilling kiss, and she wasn't a bit shy about thoroughly enjoying this one.

Boyd wrapped his arms around her, and hers crawled up his chest to lock behind his neck. Finally breaking the kiss, he nuzzled the gentle curve of her shoulder, then gathered her close and laid his cheek on top of her head. Audrey realized she had all but forgotten the sensation of being close to a man. It felt good. She pressed her face against his chest, heard the steady thump-thumping of his heartbeat and wondered what it would be like to make love with him. She imagined he would be a magnificent lover. Perhaps it was because Boyd seemed the type who would take time to please a woman.

One of his hands began stroking her back. It was hypnotizing, eliciting a spontaneous sigh from Audrey. There they were, out in the middle of nowhere without another person for miles. A few more minutes of kissing and stroking, then he would start murmuring all the erotic nonsense designed to lull her into a state of well-being. A knot formed in the pit of her stomach. It might be nice . . .

Perhaps, but thinking about it was ridiculous. She didn't know Boyd well enough for making love to even cross her mind. On top of that, this entire episode might be nothing but a ploy on his part, something he hoped would break down her defenses and cause her to tell him more than she wanted him to know.

Moving away from him slightly, she let her arms fall to her sides. "We really should be going, or we'll never get back to the house before dark."

Boyd's hand stopped its sensuous maneuvers. He raised his head and looked at her, puzzled. What had happened? One minute she had been so pliant in his arms, soft and warm; the next minute she was pulling away. He'd thought everything had been going just fine. Naturally he hadn't

expected to go much beyond a kiss, but it had seemed the
start of something wonderful. What had happened?

Oh, what the hell! What difference did it make? He told
himself he wasn't really disappointed. The pass probably
had been a dumb move to begin with. Wrong time, wrong
place, wrong woman.

"Yeah, I guess you're right," he muttered and rolled
away from her. Standing up, he brushed at the seat of his
pants. Then he turned to give her a hand, but she was already on her feet and moving toward the Jeep.

BOYD STUCK STRICTLY to business the rest of the afternoon. He and Audrey were friendly but impersonal, though
occasionally he caught himself stealing quick glances in her
direction. Each time he was aware of a catch in the region
of his heart. It was easy to say that one little kiss had meant
nothing; believing it was something else.

The last windmill was located some distance from ranch
headquarters, so the sun was quite low in the western sky by
the time they returned to the house. Audrey carried the
hamper and thermos inside, while Boyd unloaded the Jeep.
That done, he walked toward the bunkhouse, which stood
just beyond the corrals. The long wooden building was almost deserted, but he found two of the hands seated at a
card table in a far corner, playing gin rummy. They looked
up when he entered.

"Hi 'ya, Boyd," one of the cowboys greeted him. "What
can we do for you?"

"Have either of you seen Skeet?"

The other man jerked his head toward a side door. "Saw
him go outside a few minutes ago."

"Thanks," Boyd said and walked through the door the
cowboy had indicated.

The object of his search was standing at the corral fence,
one booted foot propped on the first rail, puffing on a cigarette. Skeet Drummond was sixty-five, weather-worn, gray-
haired and something of a fixture around the Triple B. He'd
been "out to pasture" for a number of years, the victim of
age and arthritis. Now he was reduced to doing odd jobs

around the ranch and taking charge of the chuck wagon during roundup, but in his heyday he had worked most of the big ranches throughout the West. A cowboy for forty-seven years, Skeet considered himself a historian of sorts. He either personally knew or knew of everyone who was anyone in the ranching business, and it was the man's vast storehouse of knowledge that sent Boyd in search of him now.

"'Evenin', Boyd," Skeet drawled. "How's it goin'?"

"Pretty good, Skeet. How's it with you?"

"Can't complain." Skeet pushed his battered Stetson farther back on his head. "Ain't this weather somethin'?"

"That it is."

"Hear it's s'posed to hold clear through roundup. Good omen if you believe in omens."

Boyd draped one arm over the fence and watched as the ranch's newest filly guzzled dinner from her mother's underbelly. "Pretty one, isn't she?" he commented idly.

"Sure is," Skeet agreed. "You folks jus' might have yourselves a cham-peen in that one."

The two men contemplated mother and daughter for a few wordless minutes. Then Boyd got to business. "Tell me, Skeet, have you ever heard of anyone named Hamilton who ranched in Texas, probably somewhere within a reasonable distance of Dallas?"

Skeet squinted his eyes in thought. "Hamilton. Let's see.... Now, myself, I never worked that far east, but I did hire on at the J.A. for a while. That's in West Texas, though. Hamilton. You know, that name sounds familiar, but I can't rightly recall where I heard it."

"Sure would appreciate anything you come up with. It's pretty important."

"Oh, I'll remember directly. Almost always do. Jus' give me a few days of ponderin'."

"If you come up with something, don't mention it to anyone else, okay? Come and see me personally. Like I said, it's pretty important, and I'd just as soon no one knows I asked questions."

Skeet shrugged. "Whatever you say, Boyd."

"Much obliged, Skeet. Be talking to you."

"Sure. Take care."

Boyd walked back to the house, deep in thought. He re
alized he was clutching at straws. It was highly unlikely tha
Skeet would know anything about Audrey's family, sinc
they might not have been ranchers at all. Still, Boyd couldn'
shake the belief that the Triple B wasn't the first ranch Au
drey had been on, and he was obsessed with the need to
know why she chose to keep that a secret.

He had no conscionable right to pry into her past. Nor
mally he wouldn't dream of doing such a thing, but this wa
no normal situation. He had to own up to the fact that Au
drey was special to him. He might not want her to be, bu
she was. He wanted to get inside her head and heart and fin
out what made her tick.

His thoughts were still whirling when he opened the fron
door and crossed the foyer. Tomorrow he, the regulars, an
the extra hands would ride out to set up camp; the next da
roundup would begin. He might be gone three days or h
might be gone a week. He couldn't be sure Audrey woul
still be at the ranch when he returned. One word from hi
father and she'd hop in her Datsun and be gone like a shot
Of course, the Greenspoint wasn't that far away, but hi
work didn't require his being in Phoenix all that often. Th
opportunity to really get to know her might escape him al
together.

Then, for some unfathomable reason, his mind took
different turn. If his suspicions about Audrey's back
ground were right, she was probably no stranger to the out
door life. She seemed damned confident she could take car
of herself on the open range, and he thought a real tender
foot would have some doubts. But then again, she just migh
not have any idea what roundup entailed.

The last thing a man needed during roundup was some
one who required a nursemaid. Why was he even consider
ing taking her along? Giving himself a shake, he turne
down the hall and headed for his room. When he passe
Audrey's door, however, he stopped and tugged on his chi
thoughtfully.

Well, what the hell? If she couldn't hack it, the world wouldn't come to an end. He could just dispatch one of the hands to see her safely back to the house. No harm done to anything but Audrey's pride. Raising a hand, he hesitated. When his dad heard about this, he was probably going to think his younger son had lost his mind. Boyd wasn't too sure he wouldn't be right. He knocked twice.

The door opened and she stood before him, dressed in a bright yellow jumpsuit. A towel was wrapped turban-style around her head. A sweet, clean scent overpowered his senses. She obviously was just out of the shower. "Hi," she said, cocking her head and eyeing him questioningly.

"Hi. I, ah...you know, it can get damned cold out on the range at night this time of year."

She stared at him blankly. "Oh?"

"Yeah. It's the altitude."

"Well, I..." She didn't have any idea what he was getting at. "I imagine so."

Boyd shoved his hands into his pockets. "Then it can turn around and be hotter'n hell the next afternoon. What I'm trying to tell you is, life on the range isn't comfortable. You sleep in a bedroll on the ground. If it rains, your only shelter is a tent, and I've yet to see one that didn't leak."

Audrey's eyes lit up. Suddenly it dawned on her what he was offering. "Discomfort doesn't throw me, Boyd. I'm not a hothouse plant."

"You won't receive any special concessions or privileges because of your sex."

"I expect none. I don't want any." Did she really seem that fragile and delicate to him?

"Then if you're damned sure you want to come along, I'll have Betty outfit you. But I want you to promise me something in return."

"What is it?"

"No suffering in silence. If you don't feel well, I want you to let me know."

Audrey smiled radiantly. "Agreed, but I think I'll surprise you. Betty will be so pleased. Thank you."

"Yeah, you're welcome. Well, see you at dinner."

He ambled away, leaving Audrey to stare after him. He certainly didn't seem overjoyed by the prospect of having her along, so why had he acquiesced? What in the world had happened to change his mind? She guessed she could add "complicated" and "unpredictable" to the growing list of adjectives that came to mind when she thought of Boyd.

A feeling of accomplishment and anticipation overcame her, and it had nothing to do with the pleasure of knowing she wouldn't make Betty miss roundup. Rather, she was excited by the prospect of spending days in Boyd's company. She didn't particularly want the excitement, but it existed nevertheless.

CHAPTER NINE

THE MOOD around the dinner table that night was light-hearted, almost festive. Betty, especially, was in unusually high spirits as a result of Boyd's decision to allow Audrey to join the roundup crew. Buck looked slightly askance when the announcement was made, but after a minute's consideration he said, "Good idea." Audrey supposed it would be a relief for him to have her safely unreachable for a few days. She had no idea if he was still having to field phone calls from the press, since that was never discussed in front of her, but she hardly expected the notoriety to have died down so soon.

Once the meal was over, the three Benedict men headed for Buck's study, and Betty turned to Audrey with shining eyes. "How in the world did you ever convince my brother to let you come along?"

"I don't have the slightest idea. I would have sworn it was a closed issue, but he changed his mind for some reason."

"Strange. Once Boyd makes up his mind about something, it usually stays made. Well, whatever you did, I thank you for it. Lord, it's going to be fun having another woman along. After four or five days, that all-male atmosphere begins to get on my nerves. Come on, let's get our stuff together. You'll need a bedroll and the right kind of clothes."

Betty led the way to a part of the house Audrey hadn't seen before, a large storage room beyond the kitchen. There she gathered up two bedrolls, a duffel bag, a couple of canteens and a first-aid kit. "The men won't carry canteens or medical supplies," she told Audrey. "They claim they're sissy, but you and I, thank God, don't have to prove how tough we are."

They carried the gear to Betty's bedroom, where she be
gan rummaging around in dresser drawers. "I'll take ever
pair of warm socks I own, and you'll need a heavy jacket
You never know what the weather will do this time of year
For sure you'll need a jacket when you crawl out of tha
warm bedroll every morning. I hope you realize you'll b
living in and sleeping in the same clothes for days. Fastidi
ousness falls by the wayside on roundup, but when we mov
the herd to Summerfield camp, there's a permanent bunk
house where we'll be able to clean up and change. It alway
feels like heaven."

For the next ten minutes or so the two women concen
trated on the task of packing what little clothing and toilet
ries they would take with them into a small duffel bag. Th
bag and their bedrolls, Betty explained, would be carried i
one of the two trucks that would accompany the crew. Th
trucks were the lone concession to modern civilization
Otherwise, the annual roundup ritual had not significantl
changed since the 1890s.

Just as they finished packing, Brent appeared in th
doorway. "Betty, Dad wants to see you as soon as you ca
get free."

Betty nodded in acknowledgment, and Brent walke
away. The young woman glanced at her watch. "Damn,"
she muttered under her breath.

"Something wrong?" Audrey asked.

Betty cast an anxious glance toward the open door an
lowered her voice. "I'm supposed to meet Jesse out back i
a few minutes. Audrey, do me a favor. Go find him and tel
him I'll be late."

The last thing Audrey wanted to do was talk to Jesse. Sh
couldn't very well refuse, however; Betty would think tha
awfully strange. "Sure," she agreed.

"I think we're finished here," Betty said. "I'll put ou
bedrolls and the bag out in the hall, and Boyd will get then
in the morning. Remember to set your alarm tonight. Now
I guess I'd better go see what Dad wants. Good night."

"Good night, Betty."

In her own room, Audrey opened the veranda door and stepped outside. There was a definite chill in the air. At this altitude the temperature difference between day and night could be dramatic, and she knew it would seem even more marked out on the open range. Hugging herself and rubbing her arms briskly, she hurried across the patio and onto the lawn. She assumed Jesse would be out there somewhere watching the house.

He was. He emerged from the shadows, looking somewhat surprised. "Well, well, if it isn't the heiress."

The mere sound of his voice irritated Audrey. Stiffening as he approached her, she said, "Betty's father wanted to see her. She'll be out as soon as she can get away." With that she reversed direction and started back to the house.

"Whoa!" Jesse ordered, quickly moving in front of her. "Aren't you going to stay here and keep me company until Betty comes?"

"No," she replied icily. "I told Betty I would deliver her message. It's delivered. Good night."

"Come on, Audrey, stay and talk to me. I'm itching to find out all about your inheritance, all about you and the old man. I'll bet it's an interesting story."

"Get out of my way, Jesse."

"Talk about feathering your nest! Must be nice to have money again. How'd you butter up the old codger?"

Audrey seethed inside. "Assuming I intended discussing it with anyone, which I don't, it certainly wouldn't be with the likes of you. Now get out of my way!"

Grinning sardonically, Jesse stepped aside, and Audrey brushed past him. As she crossed the patio and headed for her room, something unpleasant crossed her mind. So far she had successfully managed to stay away from Jesse, but now she would be seeing him every day. He galled her to the point of fury, and she wasn't a very good actress. She just prayed she'd be able to hold her tongue in check and keep her real feelings hidden. No one would be able to understand why she despised someone she wasn't supposed to know.

THE ALARM next to Audrey's bed went off at five o'clock the next morning. Groaning, she reached out to silence it and scrunch back under the covers. Then she remembered what day it was. For a moment the idea of going on roundup wasn't quite as appealing as it had been. In fact, it sounded downright grim. But having Boyd allow her to go was a big concession on his part and a victory of sorts for her. Flinging off her misgivings, she crawled out of bed and went into the bathroom to splash cold water on her face and brush her teeth.

Back in the bedroom she dressed in the sturdiest pair of jeans she owned and a long-sleeved shirt, heavy socks and the borrowed boots. From force of habit she walked to the dressing table to begin putting on makeup. But she realized she would be going without makeup for quite some time, so she made do with lotion and a swipe of lip balm, then brushed her hair and secured it at the nape of her neck with a scarf. She knew it probably was a bit chilly outside, so she slipped on the jacket and set a hat on her head. Her reflection in the mirror was anything but the loveliest sight she'd ever seen, but she'd look a lot worse before she set foot in this room again. Psyching herself for the adventure, she turned off the light and went into the hall.

The house was absolutely quiet. Betty's door was open, but the room was dark and empty. As Audrey walked toward the front of the house she saw that Boyd's room was the same. It couldn't possibly be much past five-thirty, but apparently she was the straggler.

The dining room was deserted, and no sounds came from the kitchen. Surely they weren't going to ride out without breakfast. Moving quietly, Audrey let herself out the front door, crossed the long porch and went around the side of the house. Lights shone from the bunkhouse in the distance, and a large group of people were gathered around one of the pickups. The smell of coffee and food permeated the fresh morning air.

Audrey suddenly was overcome by a feeling of shyness, of being someplace she shouldn't be, and she was hesitant about joining the gathering. This was an all-male inner sanctum, save for Betty, and she was about to invade it. Not only was she a female, she was a rank outsider without credentials, and she knew with certainty there were plenty of men in the group who were going to resent her presence. Not openly, of course, since she was here by Boyd's invitation, and cowboys never questioned the boss. The resentment would be there, nevertheless, and she found that hard to take.

Then a figure moved away from the crowd and walked in her direction. It was Betty, though at first Audrey didn't recognize her. Betty blended in with the group as she herself never could. "Good morning," her friend said brightly. "I was afraid you might miss breakfast."

"Am I that late?"

"Actually you're right on time. I guess the rest of us are early. Everyone's itching to go. Come on and get some coffee. There are biscuits and sausage, too. Eat as much as you can. It'll be a long time before you'll eat again."

As if on signal, the men clustered around the truck moved back to make a path for her. Audrey imagined all eyes were disapproving, but in truth, the men accepted her with equanimity. A few even touched the brims of their hats in silent greeting.

Skeet Drummond was serving chuck off the truck's tailgate. Once breakfast was over, the elderly cowboy would drive the truck containing his equipment and supplies to the campsite. There he would prepare all the meals for nineteen hungry people for as many days as it took to gather the herd, and he would do it superbly. The food served by the Triple B was one of the things that brought the same cowboys back to the ranch year after year at roundup time.

"'Mornin', ma'am," Skeet said cheerfully. "Coffee?"

"Yes, please."

The cook poured the strong black brew into a heavy mug and handed it to her. Then from a large pan he scooped up the biggest biscuit Audrey had ever seen, deftly pulled it apart and shoved a thick sausage patty between the halves. "Eat hearty. There's more where that came from."

The biscuit was almost too hot to hold, but napkins apparently weren't standard chuck wagon niceties. Audrey was certain nothing had ever tasted as good as that crude breakfast served in the morning air just as the first sign of daybreak crept over the horizon. Leaning against the side of the truck, she drank and ate and surveyed the busy scene before her.

Most of the men had finished eating and had gone to their horses to check saddles and gear. There wasn't much conversation since they weren't a talkative bunch. They never used words when a grunt or a nod of the head would do. To a man they were the sort who could spend a winter alone in a line shack with only a horse for company and think it was the greatest life on earth.

As Audrey ate she found herself searching the crowd for Boyd. Finally she spotted him standing away from the mainstream, studying something on a clipboard he was holding. Pettishly she wondered why he didn't come over and say good-morning or something. She finished the biscuit, drained the coffee cup and declined Skeet's offers of more. She would regret that before the day was over, but for the moment she felt completely satisfied and fortified.

The tempo of activity around the corrals picked up, but there didn't seem to be anything for her to do. Wanting to stay out of everyone's way as much as possible, she strolled to the spot where Ranger was tethered and checked the saddle rigging.

"I saddled him myself, so everything's perfect." Boyd's voice came from behind her.

She turned. "Thanks, but I could have done it."

"Really? I wasn't sure." His eyes raked her from head to toe. "You look dressed properly. We ride in ten minutes. Are you ready?"

"Yes."

"Stick close to Betty or me on the way. It's hard enough to find a lost calf out on the range, much less a person."

His attitude made her bristle. "Do you think I'm completely stupid? I don't intend getting lost."

"No one ever does." He walked away, the clipboard under his arm.

Since most of the others were mounting, Audrey did likewise. Ranger took a few sideways steps as his burden settled in the saddle. Almost immediately Betty rode up beside her and slung something over her saddle horn. Audrey saw it was one of the canteens. Nudging her horse, Betty motioned for her to follow. "We might as well ride out. No need to wait for the others. I could find Number Five camp blindfolded."

The sun had cleared the horizon and was playing hide-and-seek with streaky gray clouds that would burn off by midmorning. Audrey turned in her saddle in time to see the two trucks veer off to the east, following a ranch road. Then the rest of the riders began heading their way. It was a spectacular sight. The scene reminded her of an old John Wayne movie and was something she was sure she wouldn't soon forget. Nobody was in a hurry; today would be an easy one, when all they had to do was set up camp. Tomorrow was what would test her mettle.

Still, they spent long hours in the saddle, and once they'd reached camp—which proved to be nothing more than some pens out in the middle of nowhere—there was work to do. Horses had to be unsaddled, rubbed down, fed, watered and corralled. By the time that was finished it was nearing four o'clock. The day had turned warm, so Audrey shed her jacket and tossed it aside, knowing she would need it again once the sun got low in the sky. It occurred to her that none of them had had anything to eat for ten hours. Furthermore, it looked as if it might be some time before food was forthcoming. Skeet and the truck containing the chuck wagon, having had to take a roundabout route, hadn't yet reached camp. But she seemed to be the only one who found that a dismal prospect. Sighing wearily, she sat on the ground, propped an elbow on a knee, rested her chin in her hand and tried to ignore her weary bones and empty stomach.

If the others were tired or hungry, they showed no signs of it. Now that they had reached camp, the cowboys seemed to come alive. They stood around laughing and swapping stories. A few practiced rope tricks. Betty strolled away to find Jesse. Audrey was too tired and too hungry to move. When she saw Boyd walking her way, she barely managed a wan smile.

He squatted on the ground beside her. "A far cry from the Greenspoint, isn't it?" he said with a lazy smile.

She shrugged. "A bit."

"You must be tired."

"Oh . . . a little."

"Liar."

"I'll get used to it."

"Yeah, reckon you will, but you can always go back to the house if it gets to be too much for you."

Audrey gave him an implacable look. "It's not going to be too much for me, Boyd. Why don't you wait and see how I handle myself before assuming I'm going to fold?" The only way she would leave camp, she decided, was on a stretcher . . . and at the moment that didn't seem too remote a possibility. However, she'd die before she let Boyd know that.

"I just don't want you getting sick."

Audrey was sensitive to every nuance of his voice, maybe too sensitive. He sounded sincerely concerned about her welfare. On the other hand, his manner indicated that he expected her to be nothing but trouble. "I have to get my sea legs, that's all. I'll be fine. You don't need to worry about me."

Boyd stared at her a minute. He was worried about her, dammit, because he cared for her far more than he wanted to. He knew he'd never forgive himself if she got hurt or sick or whatever. He couldn't imagine what had possessed him to ask her along.

That wasn't exactly the truth, and he knew it. He'd simply wanted her close by, so if anything happened to her the blame would rest squarely with him. Getting to his feet, he said, "All right, but you promised me you wouldn't suffer in silence. I'm holding you to it." With that, he walked away, although he wanted to stay, to sit beside Audrey, talk to her, be with her. But he didn't want to give the men something to speculate on. As it was, a couple of the younger cowboys were watching him with knowing looks.

At that moment Skeet and the chuck wagon came lumbering into camp, eliciting whoops and shouts from the crew. Not far behind came the other truck carrying the tents and bedrolls. While the cook went about setting up his "kitchen" and beginning dinner, some of the hands put up their tents, though most elected to sleep under the stars. Audrey and Betty put theirs some distance from the main gathering, near a thick stand of trees, scrub bushes and knee-high grass that would serve as their bathroom, as much privacy as the two women would have for some time.

As the sun slipped lower in the western sky, everyone once again bundled up in their jackets. When Skeet bellowed "Chuck!" a beeline was made to the camp fire. Audrey's plate was piled high with steak, fried potatoes, bread and cherry cobbler. Vegetables were nonexistent; the cowboys on roundup ate carbohydrates and protein and lots of both. She ate like a starving field hand and so, she noticed, did Betty. Since mealtimes in the great outdoors were serious affairs, talk was held to a minimum, but once stomachs were full, the conversation picked up. Surprisingly, the men seldom used profanity, and that had nothing to do with women being present. They hardly ever used it. There was a certain courtliness to their style that a lot of swearing would have spoiled. An occasional "damn" or "hell" was about as lurid as it got. In fact, "dadblamed" seemed to be the favorite expletive.

And they were unfailingly polite to each other. There was a respect among them that Audrey rarely had seen displayed in the business world. They joked back and forth, and while their jokes were sexist, they weren't sexual. The homespun humor concerned women drivers, lazy wives and that sort of thing. A few of the cornier ones caused Audrey and Betty to exchange wryly amused glances, but nothing was said around the camp fire that night that couldn't safely and without embarrassment have been said in front of an eighty-year-old woman or an eight-year-old child.

Once everyone had finished eating, the cowboys went back to their amusements, practicing roping and pitching horseshoes. When it got too dark for horseshoes, some gathered around the fire to play cards, others just sat drinking coffee and telling anecdotes about other round-ups. Audrey lasted as long as she could, but it had been dark less than an hour when she slipped into the tent and crawled into her bedroll. The subdued horseplay around the fire went on for some time, and just before everyone retired, one of the men brought out a harmonica and led a spirited sing-along. Audrey didn't hear a sound.

SHE AWOKE BEFORE DAWN, scooted out of the tent feet first and made for the thick brush. Returning to camp, she saw that Skeet was the only other person stirring. Audrey had feared she would be in agony after all that riding the day before, but the stiffness lasted only a few minutes. This morning she was imbued with a strange kind of energy, almost uncontainable. She went to the chuck wagon, where she and Skeet conversed in whispers while he put on the coffee and made pancake batter. She stood huddled in her jacket, watching the sun come up and marveling at the cook's efficiency with a minimum of equipment. Breakfast was pancakes, bacon, eggs and, of course, gallons of scalding black coffee, all cooked over an open fire.

An hour later all of them had saddled, mounted and sat astride their horses in a semicircle facing Boyd. He was dividing the riders into four groups, each headed by a Triple B regular. Audrey noticed that Betty didn't wait for instructions from her brother; instead she joined Jesse's group, and Boyd didn't protest.

When everyone but Audrey had been assigned to a group, Boyd rode up to her. "You'll ride with me. Stay close."

The groups fanned out in separate directions, making a wide circle through the easternmost quadrant of the ranch, gathering cattle where they found them. Following orders, Audrey stayed close to Boyd as they rode slowly through heavy brush and across endless meadows. Though they could see for miles in all directions, they didn't spot a single cow for almost an hour. Suddenly one of the riders in their group spurred his horse forward to chase seven or eight calves that had seemingly appeared from nowhere.

"I'm going down to help head them off and turn 'em toward camp," Boyd said. "You stay right here and look for strays."

Audrey interpreted that to mean "Stay the hell out of the way," so she did. She sat there for more than an hour, watching as Boyd and two other cowboys worked the brush, dredging up cattle the way a magician pulls rabbits out of his hat. Finally, having gathered a hundred head or so, the cowboys expertly turned the herd toward camp, and Boyd motioned to Audrey to follow.

The cattle formed a long tight oval and lumbered across the grasslands, stirring up a cloud of dust. One cowboy rode point in front; Boyd rode left flank, another cowboy rode right. Whether by accident or design, Audrey found herself riding drag. Occasionally one of the men would encounter a stray, and with sure, easy motions he would soon have the animal moving with the herd. It was an amazing ritual, fascinating in its repetition.

Audrey was congratulating herself on having come this far without committing one goof or getting in anyone's way when a slobbering old bull with a mind of his own suddenly turned from the herd and reversed his direction. Immediately Ranger wheeled around and started after him.

Had anyone warned her that Ranger had been trained as a cutting horse, she wouldn't have been startled. As it was, she experienced a horrifying moment of panic, fearing her mount had been spooked, and she frantically tried to rein him in. It took her only a second or two, however, to realize the kind of horse Ranger was. The summer she was sixteen she had won first place in the junior division of a cutting horse competition. Instinctively she loosened her grip on the reins and relaxed in the saddle, giving the horse his head. Almost before she knew what had happened, Ranger had overtaken the bull and nudged him back into the herd. Audrey hoped her grin didn't look as foolish as it felt.

Boyd rode up to her; the expression on his face was that of a man recovering from shock. "You all right?" he asked anxiously.

"Sure," she said matter-of-factly.

"You handled that pretty well."

"Ranger did it all."

"I know, but I'm wondering how you knew he would." His eyes still speculative, he retook his position on the left flank.

There was no stopping for lunch. As they slowly moved toward the camp they, one by one, were joined by the other groups, and the size of the herd doubled, tripled, quadrupled. Audrey continued to ride drag, partly because she now knew she and Ranger could take care of any stragglers, mostly because no one had told her to do otherwise. At one point during the long monotonous drive, a young cowboy rode up beside her and shyly handed her a strip of beef jerky. "Sure helps to stave off the hunger pangs, ma'am," he drawled.

"Thanks," Audrey said. It had been years since she'd chewed on a piece of the hard, salty stuff. She wished she could remember the young man's name, but with their black hats and handlebar mustaches so many of the cowboys looked alike.

"Joel Garrett. Idaho," he offered.

"Thanks, Joel. This is going to taste wonderful."

Touching the brim of his hat with a forefinger, he rode off.

At a spot near a water tank, the hands circled and held the herd while Boyd, Jesse Murdoch and another cowboy cut out the steer calves and their mothers, separating them from the cows with heifer calves and the young calves that had been born since last spring's branding. The heifers and young calves and most of the mothers would be turned out to pasture to rebuild the herd. The steer calves would be shipped to feedlots for further fattening before going to market. In the grisly cycle of the cattle business, the mothers of the steers would lead their babies to the cattle trucks, then go back to pasture to breed again. When the mothers reached the bovine menopause, they too would go to slaughter to be turned into "cheap cuts."

It was late afternoon before the riders returned to camp and drove the cattle into the waiting pens. Audrey calculated she had ridden maybe twelve to fifteen miles that day, but with all the scurrying to and fro chasing cattle, the others had ridden perhaps twice that far. She was covered with dust, but so was everyone else. She was tired, but tonight the fatigue felt good. The worst was over; she had earned a stripe, maybe two. From now on, as her confidence grew, each day would get easier.

After tending to Ranger, she squatted on the ground in front of the tent, removed the big hat, untied the scarf at her nape and let her hair fall free. She shook her head, massaged her scalp a couple of times, then retied the scarf. At that moment Skeet bellowed "Chuck!" Audrey was beginning to think that was the sweetest word in the English language.

She ate two bowls of the chili Colorado that Skeet dished out so lavishly, and lost track of how many flour tortillas she dipped into the spicy stuff. Afterward, using her saddle as a backrest, she stretched out her legs, sipped coffee and contemplated the Arizona sky. Out here she could see the Milky Way as clearly as she could see the ceiling in her apartment. Lost in a lazy languor, she vaguely wondered how things were going at the Greenspoint...but only vaguely. This was light-years removed from that elegance, but oddly, at the moment she didn't want to be anywhere else on earth.

Her eyes roamed over the camp scene. Boyd didn't do much sitting. He moved through camp constantly, keeping an eye on everything. Like a dorm housemother, Audrey thought in amusement. She caught sight of Betty and Jesse, sitting apart from the mainstream, and thought it strange that no one seemed to notice how close the two of them were. But then everyone treated Betty like one of the boys. Audrey herself was shown a little more deference, something that didn't particularly please her.

Lost in a private reverie, she didn't see Boyd coming toward her until he sat on the ground next to her. "Not quite as glamorous as you thought it would be, right?"

"I didn't think for a minute it would be glamorous. But there's a kind of grandeur to it."

"I know."

"Out here you get an insight into why some people love this life so much. And it's easy to see why the valley itself holds such appeal."

"Yeah. Granddad loved it in a way that's hard to describe. He liked talking about the old days, the 'old days' being the forties and fifties. The place was known as the 'Santa Booze Valley' then, because a bunch of rich New Yorkers moved in and threw round-the-clock parties. Then Hollywood started making movies here. John Wayne was an old drinking buddy of Granddad's. Guess it was pretty wild for a while. Things have quietened down, though."

Glancing toward the cowboys near the camp fire, Audrey remarked, "They're all peas out of the same pod."

"Mostly. Better educated than the old-time cowboys but cut of the same cloth."

"Are any of them married?"

"A few of the regulars are. Their wives and kids live in Agua Linda. Most of the drifters were married at one time, too, but cowboying takes its toll on a marriage. Now they just roam from place to place, carrying everything they own with 'em."

Audrey twisted her head to look at him. "Did you ever yearn for that kind of life?"

"Yeah, when I was a kid. But I also wanted to be an astronaut and to play shortstop for the Dodgers. Hard to work those three careers into one lifetime." He grinned, and she grinned back. "You impressed me today, Audrey, you really did."

"Hate to say I told you so," she said smugly and took a sip of coffee.

"I damned near had a heart attack when I saw Ranger take off," he confessed. "If you could have seen the look on your face..."

"It just took me a minute to figure out what was happening, that's all. No one told me Ranger was a cutter. I thought he'd been spooked."

Boyd sipped from his own cup and thought about what she'd said. Not only did she know what a cutting horse was, she'd instinctively known to relax, almost go limp and turn the job over to her mount. That wasn't something a person learned in a day or two. She'd been trained; he'd bet on it. If so, he could stop worrying about her. She wouldn't be a hindrance. In fact, she and Ranger could earn their keep, if Audrey was willing to admit she was no novice. Damn, he wished she would talk to him.

The cowboy with the harmonica had struck up a tune, which drew most of the others around the camp fire and left Audrey and Boyd alone on the periphery. Someone burst into song; everyone else soon joined in. "More coffee?" Boyd asked.

"No thanks. I wouldn't want it to keep me awake." Audrey laughed lightly. Nothing short of an earthquake would keep her awake tonight.

Boyd took her empty cup out of her hand. "I'll give these to Skeet." Getting to his feet, he walked over to the chuck wagon. Audrey saw him exchange a few words with Skeet. She assumed he would join the group around the camp fire. However, when he turned away from the chuck wagon he came back to sit beside her, this time very close. He stretched his long legs beside hers and slid an arm around her shoulders. Audrey felt her pulse quicken; with some effort she kept her eyes straight ahead. She pretended to be watching the music makers around the fire, but she saw nothing. All her senses were attuned to Boyd's closeness. She thought of what she must look like and was glad there was no mirror handy to confirm her suspicions. Surely she was at her unlovely worst. Of course, Boyd's clothes were as rumpled and dust-covered as her own, but none of that detracted from his attractiveness. Whenever she was near him she was reminded of the vital something missing from her life.

There were rustling sounds around the camp fire as some of the cowboys got up and made for their bedrolls. As bone-tired as she was, Audrey wished the day didn't have to end. The soft, sensuous beauty of the night and the comforting feel of Boyd's arm around her seduced her. The hand that had been resting lightly on her shoulder moved to the nape of her neck, and he untied the scarf that held her hair. She felt it fall to her shoulders.

"I told you . . . hair like that should never be confined," he murmured softly.

"It's a mess," she objected shakily. "It's filthy."

"Looks beautiful to me." His fingers played with a few strands. She was covered from throat to feet in plain, un-feminine clothes, yet that seemed to make him even more aware of the feminine body beneath the masculine clothes. A stirring began in his loins. Of all the times for a man's thoughts to turn to sex, tonight was the least likely, but that was exactly what he was thinking about. She drove him crazy. He couldn't recall a single woman who'd had such a stunning effect on him, and he wondered what he should or could do about it.

The tension that had formed between them was like a third presence. Audrey shivered. Slowly she turned her head and met his gaze. In that instant it was as though a camera had been clicked, a picture taken, one that would be around forever. Audrey finally recognized him for who he was, the other part of herself. She felt the chemistry, a hackneyed word but the only one that described the profound physical attraction between them. She felt it, and if she could trust what she thought she read in his eyes, he felt it, too.

She watched in fascination as his head bent toward hers. Like the last time, she simply gave in to the kiss and re-turned it, nestling into the curve of his arm, mildly sur-prised that his beard didn't scratch any more than it did.

Just then there was a burst of laughter around the camp fire. Audrey broke the kiss quickly and straightened, re-membering where they were. Her heart was racing at breakneck speed. She felt as foolish and as furtive as a teenager smooching in the back seat of a car. Then, thankfully, she saw that no one was looking in their direction. Apparently someone in the group had botched the words to a song or told a joke.

Beside her, Boyd shifted restlessly, and she heard him sigh. "I doubt that anyone would be scandalized if we were caught kissing," he muttered.

"I don't think you want a lot of camp gossip floating around any more than I do."

She was right, though he didn't tell her that. The others were beginning to accept Audrey to a degree he wouldn't have dared hope for, but if they suspected she was important to the boss in a personal way, resentment might flare up. So romance would have to wait for a place more conducive to privacy. But he wanted her to know how he felt. Maybe then she'd tell him how she felt. Two measly kisses did not a romance make. "If I were better with words, I could keep you here an hour telling you all the things I do want." His voice was low, husky and confidential.

Audrey swallowed hard. He was taking her breath away. "Do you realize how long we've known each other?"

He pretended to give it serious thought. "Well, let's see now. We spent the first night together in the hotel suite...."

"Oh, good grief! Keep your voice down."

"Then we came to the ranch. The next night I gave you the rubdown in your bedroom. There was our picnic, and we've been on the drive two days. Gosh, Audrey, I've known you almost a week!"

"Exactly. Almost a week."

"Seems longer."

"What's that supposed to mean?"

"Just that I've thought about you for a long time. Now that you've finally shown up...it just seems I've known you a lot longer than a week, that's all."

Audrey placed her hand on her forehead and uttered a light laugh. "Do you have any idea how much it astonishes me to hear you say something like that?"

"Really? Why?"

"Well, it's brash for one thing, and I never figured you for brashness."

"This is more like it. Give me a peek at the thoughts inside your head. How did you have me figured?"

Audrey was spared having to answer that one. The crowd around the camp fire was dispersing, and Betty was heading their way. "Hi," she called. "How come you didn't join us? What have you been so deep in conversation about?"

"Oh, the nature of life and love and the mysteries of the universe," Boyd said blithely.

"All that, huh?" Betty yawned. "Sounds fascinating. If you come up with any sound conclusions, clue me in, will you? Night." Lifting the tent flap, she ducked inside.

"Good night," Audrey and Boyd chorused. A long wordless moment passed before Audrey said, "I guess I'd better turn in, too."

"Yeah," Boyd agreed resignedly. "I guess so." He got to his feet and held his hand down toward her. She took it. With one strong tug he pulled her to her feet directly in front of him. They were standing so close Audrey could feel his breath fanning the hair at her temple. For a moment they simply stared at each other, recognizing the currents of sensuality passing between them.

"You're cold," Boyd said finally.

"Not really."

"Yes, you are. You're shivering."

"Well, maybe, a little."

"You'd better . . . get to bed."

She nodded. "Good night, Boyd."

"Good night, Audrey. Sweet dreams."

Lifting the flap, she disappeared inside the tent, leaving him overwhelmed by the sensation of being on the verge of something wonderful, the something he had been so sure would elude him forever.

Good Lord! Could it be, was it even possible that he was, at long last, in love?

CHAPTER TEN

BY NINE O'CLOCK the camp had quietened considerably. The few who weren't already asleep were bedding down. Boyd and Skeet Drummond squatted by the dying camp fire, talking in hushed tones. "You said you remembered something, Skeet?"

"I think so. There was a fella named Hamilton . . . Jack, I think it was . . . who had a spread in North Texas. He was a big businessman in Dallas and ranched as a hobby. Does that sound like the man you're looking for?"

"Might be." Boyd's interest was piqued. "To tell you the truth, I'm not sure what I'm looking for. What happened to Hamilton?"

Skeet scratched the stubble on his chin. "My head's hit the pillow a lotta times since I heard the story, so I'm kinda fuzzy on the details. Hamilton got in some kind of trouble with the federal government, and his operation shut down."

"You don't remember the nature of the trouble?"

"Damned if I can. I do remember one thing, though. It was one of his own men who turned him in to the feds. That always stuck with me. It's one sorry so-and-so who ain't loyal to his boss. Either stick by him or quit him, I always say."

"Agreed, Skeet. Now go on."

"Hamilton stood trial and was convicted, but for the life of me I can't remember what the charge was."

"Is Hamilton in prison now?"

"Nope. Now this part I remember good. He died before he served a day."

"Did he have a family?"

"Seems like there was one, but then again I might have this mixed up with someone else."

"When did all this happen?"

"Well...must'a been about five years ago. I heard about it when that drifter from Texas hired on at roundup four years ago, and it was all over by then."

Boyd digested what Skeet had told him. Audrey had said her father died five years ago, but that was pretty thin evidence. He reminded himself that she might not have been even remotely connected with Jack Hamilton, but if she was, his heart went out to her. A father who was a convicted felon wasn't something anyone would find easy to live with, much less someone like Audrey. That would explain so much about her—the reluctance to discuss her past and her decision to stay in Phoenix. If her father had been a big Dallas businessman, she probably had been to the manor born, so that would explain her poise and obvious class. And if he'd owned a ranch, she might have grown up on horseback. Plus, the time frame fit. The indictment, a trial, Audrey's decision to leave Dallas and her stay with the friend in Phoenix easily could have consumed the lion's share of two years, and she'd been at the Greenspoint three.

"Thanks, Skeet."

"Hope it helped. Say... isn't the little lady's name Hamilton?" The cook inclined his head toward the tent where Audrey and Betty slept.

"Remember, Skeet, this is just between you and me," Boyd cautioned.

"Mum's the word, boss. You can count on it."

Preoccupied, Boyd restlessly prowled the outskirts of the campsite for half an hour or so before bedding down. The information wasn't something he could quiz Audrey about; it was much too sensitive. He wondered if she would ever trust him enough to tell him the story herself.

As tired as Boyd was, sleep was some time coming. He couldn't get his mind off Audrey. He was irresistibly drawn to her, and he no longer considered that a disturbing weakness. Rather, he welcomed the new dimension to his life.

He'd waited a long while to find a woman like her. And she was attracted to him, too, or would be if she'd let herself.

How could he make her believe he didn't care about her past without saying it in so many words? What had gone before meant nothing... unless it jeopardized the future. Just before dropping off to sleep, for reasons that escaped him completely, he thought of his father.

THE FOLLOWING DAY was a repeat of the previous one, except they worked the northern pastures and rounded up more than five hundred head. Audrey was beginning to feel like a veteran hand, and she thought she could sense a subtle change in the cowboys' attitude toward her. When Boyd asked her to spell him during the cutting process, she and Ranger performed admirably.

Boyd rode up beside her as they drove the herd back to camp. "This job pays fifty dollars a day, plus chuck and all the tobacco you want," he said with a grin.

She laughed. "Even for a greenhorn?"

"Yeah, if the greenhorn works as hard as you do."

"So you're not sorry you brought me along?"

"I've never been sorry about that, Audrey. Never."

"Liar."

"Concerned for a while, maybe, but never sorry. And I'm not concerned anymore."

That moment of acceptance was memorable and created a kind of euphoria in Audrey. She felt wonderful. On top of everything, tomorrow they would be taking the herd to a place called Summerfield camp, where everyone who wanted to would be able to clean up and change clothes. That was something she really was looking forward to. The lack of bathing facilities was the only truly uncomfortable thing about this adventure. Once they reached the camp, two of the hands were dispatched ahead to get Summerfield ready for habitation.

Much to Audrey's regret, she and Boyd weren't alone for even a few minutes that night. The next morning the crew broke camp at dawn and moved the herd to higher ground nearer headquarters. Audrey wasn't sure what she had ex-

pected Summerfield camp to be like, but after three days at
Number Five, the place was a real touch of civilization.

Situated by a clear stream, the camp consisted of a large
weather-beaten bunkhouse, some horse corrals, a maze of
holding pens and a windmill and water tank. Once, when the
Triple B had been much larger, Summerfield had served as
year-round quarters for six cowboys, so some basic modern
amenities had been added—a septic tank, water well and
electric generator.

The roundup crew reached the camp around four o'clock
that afternoon. After the cattle had been herded into the
pens and the horses taken care of, the hands began setting
up camp while Boyd, Betty and Audrey went inside to inspect the building.

There was one room austerely furnished with bunks, a
long table, some chairs and a potbellied stove. A lone light
bulb hung from a crudely wired socket in the ceiling. They
actually would have electric light! But the camp's most
welcome feature was an honest-to-goodness bathroom with
a shower stall. When Audrey spied the water heater standing in the corner she realized they also would have hot water. At the moment, that seemed an almost sybaritic luxury.

"We'll be working out of here until we move the herd to
headquarters," Boyd explained for her benefit. "So you two
ladies can bunk in here."

"No concessions to sex, remember," Audrey admonished.

"Well, maybe one or two."

"Don't knock it, Audrey," Betty said with a grin as she
stretched out on one of the bunks. "Besides, the guys would
rather be outside. Sleeping on the ground is part of the
mystique."

"If the weather turns bad you might have a lot of company in here," Boyd added. "But I see no signs of that, so
you should have all the privacy in the world." He clomped
across the bare plank floor, heading toward the door. But as
he reached for the knob, he paused. "To tell you the truth,
I wouldn't mind shaving and washing off some of this

grime. When you two are finished with the bathroom, how about giving me a holler."

"Sure," his sister agreed, stretching languidly.

He shot Audrey a faintly mysterious half smile, then left. She crossed the room and flopped down on one of the other bunks. "Oh, I hate admitting how good this feels!"

"Yeah, I know." Betty chuckled. "The hardest thing about being a woman on roundup is pretending you don't miss the comforts of home."

"I thought you loved it."

"I love the work. I don't love being without a bathroom. I'll arm-wrestle you to see who gets to shower first."

"Be my guest. That'll give me more time to lie here thinking about how wonderful it's going to feel."

Rolling over, Betty propped herself on one elbow. "Audrey, will you do me a favor?"

"Of course."

"Do you think you can make yourself scarce for a little while tonight? I'd like to entertain a gentleman caller."

Audrey faced the wall to hide her look of disgust from the other woman. If only she could think of a way to dilute Betty's infatuation with Jesse, short of coming right out and telling her he wasn't the man she thought he was. "Aren't you afraid there'll be talk that will get back to your father?"

"Naw, as far as everyone's concerned, Jesse and I are just buddies. And none of the men would go to Buck Benedict with the time of day unless Dad asked for it."

"What about Boyd?"

"If Boyd had questions, he'd ask them of me." Betty paused, then said. "He likes you...a lot. I know my brother. He looks at you like he's starving to death and you're a hot fudge sundae."

Audrey thought a minute before saying, "I like him, too."

"Well, I'll be damned! And he was so sure this wouldn't happen to him. He thought that if he'd been going to fall in love he would have long before now. I told him that was dumb, that it could happen anytime, but he really believed it never would."

"It's pretty farfetched to mention 'love' in conjunction with our relationship, Betty. Nothing's happened. Or almost nothing." And most likely nothing ever would, she could have added. She couldn't shake the notion that a real romance with Boyd belonged in the pie-in-the-sky category.

"I'll bet something will happen if Boyd wants it bad enough," Betty confided. "He won't give up. Bullheadedness is my brother's middle name."

Audrey grinned. "And he told me the middle B doesn't stand for anything."

AFTER SHOWERING, shampooing her hair and brushing her teeth, Audrey felt like a new person. It was wonderful to wash away three days' accumulation of grime. From Betty's duffel bag she took out clean jeans, socks and a long-sleeved velour pullover. They didn't have much in the way of cosmetics with them, but there was lotion and lipstick. She felt human again.

She and Betty were sitting on the bunks, fluffing their wet hair in an attempt at drying it, when Boyd knocked on the door. "Are you decent?" he called.

"Come on in," Betty yelled.

He was carrying a shaving kit and some clean clothes under his arm. As he stepped into the room, his eyes fastened on Audrey, and he felt a flush creep up his neck. "Don't you look nice."

"Thanks. Quite an improvement, huh?"

He opened his mouth to say something else, then noticed his sister's amused expression and decided against it. "Hope you saved me some hot water. And if I were you two, I'd stay inside for a bit. Most of the hands are bathing in the creek, and modesty isn't in their vocabulary."

The bathroom door closed behind him. Audrey heard some rustling movements, then the sound of the shower. It occurred to her that this was the second time in the short space of eight days she had listened to Boyd take a shower. When he emerged from the bathroom a scant twenty minutes later, he was dressed in different clothes, was clean-shaven, and he looked marvelous. Suddenly she wished it were she and Boyd who would have the bunkhouse all to themselves that night instead of Betty and Jesse, and it had nothing to do with her concern over Betty's relationship with the disgusting man.

"Ah, that feels good," Boyd said. "Can I toss these dirty things in with yours?"

"Sure," Betty replied and indicated the duffel bag on the floor by the bunk where Audrey sat. "Over there."

Picking up the bag, he stuffed his clothes in it, then turned to Audrey. "Want to go for a ride?" he asked tersely.

"A ride?" The thought of climbing up on Ranger again wasn't the most appealing prospect in the world, but getting away with Boyd was.

"Actually, a drive in the truck. There's something I'd like to show you."

Audrey glanced at Betty, who encouraged her with her eyes, then back at Boyd. "We'll miss supper."

"No, we won't."

She assumed that meant they wouldn't be gone long, and that disappointed her. "All right," she agreed.

"Better bring your jacket."

Driving off into the fading daylight, they chugged and bumped along a rutted road that seemed to lead to nowhere. Then they topped a rise and Audrey saw what must have been their destination—an earth-colored adobe cottage that blended in with the terrain so well it virtually was camouflaged. The truck rumbled to a halt in front of the house. It was neat and well-kept, Audrey observed. Then she noticed some evidence of construction work, so perhaps it had been restored, for the house obviously was not new. She turned to Boyd with a questioning expression.

"This is where my grandparents began their married life," he explained.

Audrey looked at the structure again. "This was Bert and Margaret's house?"

"Yep. I'm in the process of renovating it. One of these days it's going to be my house. I want you to see inside, but first there's something else I want to show you while it's still light."

They got out of the truck. Boyd took Audrey's hand and led her to a spot some distance from the adobe house, to a small cemetery enclosed within a picket fence. "I thought you might like to see this. It's our family plot. Every Benedict since Bernard B. has been buried here. There's Granddad's grave."

Bert's headstone was simple, as were all the others. Audrey shoved her hands into her jacket pockets and stared at the headstone, overcome with emotion. A lump formed in her throat as she thought of the changes the elderly man had wrought in her own life. The money, of course, but more than that. Bert had inadvertently introduced her to Boyd, and while she had yet to decide if that was a blessing or a pity, she had to admit he was an exciting addition to a life that had been lonely and barren too long.

A couple of minutes passed before Boyd said, "It's getting dark. Ready to go?"

She nodded. "Yes."

Turning away, the two of them walked toward the adobe structure just as the last rays of daylight slipped below the horizon. The house, Boyd explained as he ushered Audrey through the front door, had no electricity at present, but it was stocked with kerosene lamps. He walked through the rooms, lighting the lamps, while Audrey followed. The walls had been painted recently, and the bathroom fixtures seemed new. It was a small place—living room, kitchen, two bedrooms and a bath—but it had charm. The tile floors were magnificent and would be horrendously expensive in today's market. When she commented on them, Boyd told her the tiles had been brought up from Mexico in a horse-drawn wagon in 1928 when there hadn't been a paved road or a telephone in the entire valley.

Furniture almost was nonexistent. There was a single bed in one of the bedrooms and a sofa in the living room. The main room also had a pueblo-style beehive fireplace and the exposed wooden beams called *vigas*. The kitchen still had an old-fashioned pump at the sink and an ancient cast-iron woodburning stove. "You're going to live here?" Audrey asked incredulously. As charming and picturesque as the cottage was, it was a bit on the primitive side.

"Sure am," Boyd replied proudly. Picking up one of the lamps, he motioned for her to follow him out the back door. They stepped onto a long back porch, a third of which had been enclosed to make a storeroom. Opening the door to it, he pointed to several large cartons that contained new appliances. "I've already bought almost everything I need to modernize. Winter's the slowest time around the ranch, so a couple of the men have offered to help me with the place after Christmas. There's a lot of work to be done, but I hope to be in here next summer. I need some space of my own. Living in the main house suits Brent fine, but it doesn't suit me."

"Well, it certainly is... private," Audrey affirmed, although she thought "isolated" might have been a better word.

Boyd led the way back into the house and set the lamp on a small kitchen table. "You're thinking it's in the back of beyond, but it's not nearly as remote as it seems. That road outside leads directly to headquarters, and it takes maybe ten minutes to drive there. Sit down and I'll rustle us up something to eat."

"We're having supper here."

He nodded. "I stock quite a larder. Sometimes when I'm working on the place I spend several days at a time here. I have plenty of kerosene and there's running water. Admittedly, when I want to bathe I have to heat the water, but I've never minded that. I probably could live here with the place the way it is... plus electricity, of course. I won't, but I probably could."

Audrey thought it amazing that a man like Boyd, who was accustomed to the very finest of everything, would enjoy such a back-to-basics existence. She seemed to be learning something new about him every day. She sat down at the little table and eyed the monstrous stove, which was an ornate relic of a bygone era. "Do you know how to use that thing?"

"The stove? As a matter of fact, I do, but you can't turn a wood stove on and off the way you can an electric or gas one. It takes some time and patience, and it gets hotter'n blazes. To my grandmother, 'slaving over a hot stove' had real meaning." He indicated a propane-fueled countertop cooking unit, the kind used by campers and other outdoor types. "I use that most of the time. I don't cook gourmet meals here."

Opening a cabinet door, he removed a coffeepot and filled it with water from the pump. Audrey was certain that once she left the Triple B she would either be hopelessly addicted to strong black coffee or never want another cup of the stuff as long as she lived.

She found it fascinating to watch Boyd work. While waiting for the water to boil, he studied the array of canned goods in the cabinet, chose three and expertly opened them with his pocket knife. When the coffee was set aside to steep, he dumped the contents of two cans in one pan, the contents of the third can in another and set them on the stove. "Dinner in five minutes," he said, "and it's the specialty of the house."

The "specialty" turned out to be nothing more than canned Spanish rice to which chunks of Vienna sausages had been added. The concoction was served on paper plates, and Audrey couldn't believe how good it tasted. But the highlight of the meal, as far as she was concerned, were the green beans he had heated up. They were the first vegetable she had tasted in four days.

"How is it?" he asked after a few bites.

"Delicious."

"You're not just saying that?"

She shook her head. "No, it's really very good." She didn't add that at the moment she could have eaten dog food if that had been all that was available. "It's an unusual combination. I never would have thought of it. How did you?"

"Necessity. I was working here late one night last summer and was hungry. This was all I had. Turned out to be not half-bad."

"Do you spend a lot of time here?"

"Haven't been able to lately, but once roundup is over I'll be able to tackle the place in earnest."

"How long have you been working on it?"

"Off and on for two years. It was a mess when I started. Granddad built it in 1926, and this was really out in the boondocks then. When he and my grandmother moved into the main house, this was abandoned for years. One of our foremen lived here some time ago, but he was single and didn't do a thing to it."

"Thanks for showing it to me. In some odd way it suits you."

"I wonder if it would suit someone else."

"Someone else?"

"I don't intend spending the rest of my life alone, Audrey. I wonder if a woman could live here and be happy. You, for instance. Do you think you could?"

Audrey had raised her coffee cup to her lips. Now she set it down without taking so much as a sip. Staring at the black liquid, she strove for nonchalance. "Oh...I suppose I could...given the right circumstances."

Across the table, Boyd's eyes impaled her. "And what would those 'right' circumstances be?"

"I'd have to live in a place like this—or anywhere on earth, for that matter—with the right man. That's all most women want."

"Oh? Describe this right man to me."

"That's impossible."

"Why? Haven't you met him yet?"

Audrey opened her mouth, then quickly closed it again. Her fingers tightened around her cup, and she clutched it so hard she wouldn't have been surprised if it had shattered in her hand. Sucking in her breath, she held it for several heartbeats. They were very far removed from the rest of the world, and considering all the unmanageable emotions he aroused in her, that probably wasn't a good idea. She had longed to be alone with him, but now that she was, she felt as awkward as a young girl on her first date.

Boyd never took his eyes off her. She was as disturbed by his proximity as he was by hers, and that knowledge sent the blood coursing hotly through his veins. With great deliberation, he reached across the small table and pried her fingers from her cup. Encasing her hand, he tugged slightly, then more insistently. Audrey's luminous eyes widened as he, seemingly without effort, pulled her from the chair, around the table, and settled her in his lap, wrapping his arms around her. He pressed her against his chest and placed his lips at the hollow of her throat. "The truth of the matter is," he murmured, fanning her skin with his warm breath, "you have met him. 'Fess up.''

"Boyd," she whispered in a voice that didn't sound like hers, "this is crazy. We barely know each other."

"Oh, Audrey, spare me that old chestnut. How long does it take two reasonably intelligent adults to know they were meant for each other?"

"I . . . don't know. Longer than a week."

"Eight days," he corrected.

"That's . . . not very much time. Boyd . . . please . . . don't . . ."

Beginning with a shower of quick, light kisses on her throat and the underside of her chin, he assaulted her senses. One of his hands strayed from her back to the side of her breast, paused enticingly, then moved to her waist, along the curve of her hip and came to rest on her thigh. His mouth traced her jawline, nibbled on her earlobe, kissed her cheek, then captured her mouth.

Audrey thought she was strangling. Every fiber of her being sprang to life when his lips closed over hers, and she didn't want to think about problems or consequences or anything pertinent and important. For years, ever since the embarrassing fiasco with Jesse, she had been cautious in relationships with men, so cautious that her heart had remained untouched. Now she realized how much she had longed for something, someone who would make her feel alive and feminine and desirable. Boyd's touch lit a spark, then fanned it into a roaring blaze. Just thinking about the pleasure he promised made her giddy and weak. She ached for emotional release, and he could deliver it. Was there anything wrong with that? Both of them were adults, single... and very, very willing. Where was the harm?

As his kiss grew more insistent, Audrey responded to every pressure of his lips, his hands, his body beneath hers. She trailed her fingers sensually along the back of his neck, hearing him groan, feeling him shift impatiently in the chair. His hand left her thigh and brushed across her breast, as lightly as the touch of a butterfly's wings. The gentleness was more exquisitely tormenting than more overt fondling could have ever been. An involuntary sound escaped her throat.

The moment the sound was uttered, Boyd's hand closed over her breast and he raised his head slightly. "Audrey, I swear to God I think I'm in love for the first time in my life. I want you, and I have from the moment I saw you that day in the hotel."

Audrey fought to regain her breath. "That's probably your imagination."

One corner of his mouth lifted in a half smile. "You've turned my life upside down, inside out. That's not my imagination." Holding her tightly, he pressed her more insistently against his lap, giving her proof of his arousal. "And neither is that."

She started to remind him that he was talking about sex, but she checked herself. Of course he was talking about sex, and she was thinking about it. She was very close to wanton abandon in her desire for him. "Oh, Boyd," she breathed. "This has just happened too fast. It's impulsive, and I've never been impulsive. I really don't trust anything I'm feeling."

"Funny. I trust what I'm feeling. I think it's more honest than anything I've ever felt in my life."

He kissed her again. This time the kiss was a long, drugging one that stripped her of what little restraint she had left. He was masterful at the art of seduction, leading her to wonder vaguely how many other women had been treated to his expert onslaught of sensuality. Not that it mattered. She was on the receiving end now, so she was going to relax and enjoy it. Her insides had turned to liquid, and the feeling was wonderful. It had been a long time coming.

Then reality set in, as it invariably did with Audrey. She wasn't going to have sex with this man whom she scarcely knew. It was unthinkable. A man could enjoy a woman, then forget her, but a woman—most at any rate—got emotionally involved. Audrey didn't think she was willing to risk that. One of her first impressions of him was of a man who would be hard to forget. She didn't need that complication, thanks. Loosening her grip on him, she all but jumped to her feet.

Caught off guard, Boyd was stunned. "Hey..."

"Let's clean up this mess. We really should be getting back to camp."

He couldn't believe it. "Audrey, what in hell happened?"

She gathered up the paper plates and cups, moving in jerky little motions. "What do you do with the trash?"

Boyd reached for her. "Sweetheart, come here."

Audrey faced him squarely. "Oh, Boyd, I'm not your sweetheart! How could I be? When roundup is over, and from talk around camp I gather that will be in two more days, we'll go back to the ranch house, and no doubt I'll be leaving. Our relationship is...transient." Her eyes begged him to understand. "Look, I know there are women who take lovers whose names they don't even know...."

"You know my name."

"...men they know nothing about, but I'm not one of them. Sorry."

"Seems to me I recall telling you that I think I'm in love."

"You can't possibly know that. Don't you see?"

"Maybe I'm dense, but no..." Then he saw Audrey's implacable expression and decided he was wasting his breath. "Son of a bitch!" he muttered under his breath.

"But it's really been...fun," she offered.

"Fun?" he cried incredulously.

"An adventure. I'll never forget my time here, never."

Boyd rolled his eyes toward the ceiling. "An adventure yet! That doesn't do much for my masculine ego." Placing his hands on his thighs, he shoved himself out of the chair.

Audrey couldn't determine if he was angry, disgusted, disappointed or what. Her insides fluttered like a covey of quail on the wing. "What . . . do you do with the trash?"

He threw open a drawer and produced a brown grocery sack, which he unfolded and held open. His eyes never left her as she threw the plates, cups and empty cans into it. "Lady," he said, "you sure know how to spoil an evening."

The drive back to camp was accomplished in almost total silence. Audrey slumped in the passenger seat, while Boyd stared resolutely through the windshield at the clear, black night. Thoughts spun inside both their heads.

Audrey kept reminding herself that calling a halt to the sexual encounter had been the sensible thing to do. Nothing had happened to indicate that more than the desire of the moment had been involved. She and Boyd hadn't known each other long enough to have established any kind of solid relationship. She didn't care if he was angry; she had been right.

Boyd's thoughts were more complex. He probably hadn't handled tonight so well. As powerful as his desire for Audrey was—and it *was* powerful—he wanted more than just her body. It still astonished him that he'd finally found someone he wanted to build something enduring with. No, he probably hadn't handled tonight so well.

But tomorrow would be different.

CHAPTER ELEVEN

AUDREY DIDN'T SEE Boyd at breakfast the next morning. It occurred to her that he might very well have been avoiding her, which was just as well. She felt terrible about last night but had managed to convince herself that she definitely hadn't teased or led him on. And she was more certain than ever that getting sexually involved with him was just asking for trouble.

Later, however, all her sensible inner resolve melted like ice on an August day. When the riders had mounted and stood waiting in a semicircle, it was Jesse, not Boyd, who rode before them and gave out orders for the day.

"Where's Boyd?" Betty asked with a frown.

"He said we'd have to do without him today," Jesse explained. "Said he had some things to take care of. Okay, let's ride."

Peculiar what a difference his absence made. Although the now familiar work went smoothly and quickly, Audrey thought the day would never end. She missed having Boyd ride along beside her from time to time, missed simply knowing he was nearby. When the crew returned to camp that evening she was in miserable spirits for no reason at all. As soon as she'd tended to Ranger she made straight for the old bunkhouse without taking part in any of the camp camaraderie. She thought she felt a headache coming on.

Later, after she and Betty had showered, they sat on their bunks and waited for Skeet to announce supper. "Do you suppose you'll be going back to Phoenix when this is over, Audrey?"

"I guess so. I've been gone quite awhile. I really should get back."

"You're going to stay over the weekend, aren't you?"

"Weekend? I hadn't thought about it. Why?"

"You mean, no one's mentioned Tri-County to you?"

"No. What is it?"

"Tri-County Fair and Rodeo. It's held at the end of roundup every year and is the biggest event in these parts, for sure. All the ranches in the valley compete for everything from best chili cook to best guitar picker. The Triple B's won the majority of the events three years running."

"What do you win?"

Betty grinned. "Braggin' rights for another year. But the rodeo's the best part. Ever been to one?"

Only hundreds. "I went to the Parada del Sol in Scottsdale last year," she evaded.

"Well, Tri-County's nothing like that. It's strictly amateur, but exciting, since you know all the contestants. Oh, Audrey, you have to stay for it!"

It sounded like fun, but Audrey seriously doubted that Boyd would want her prolonging her stay. "Well, Betty... we'll see."

At that moment there was a loud rap on the door. "Come in," Betty called, and Boyd stepped into the room. Audrey's heart leaped straight up into her throat and stayed there. Her almost-headache magically vanished.

"Well, well," Betty said sarcastically, "look who's showed up now that all the work's been done."

Boyd barely acknowledged his sister's presence. His eyes were riveted on Audrey. "Will you come with me?"

Audrey started to ask, "Where?" Then she decided she didn't care. "Yes," she replied simply and reached for her jacket.

"Don't hurry," Betty called after them.

There wasn't much mystery about their destination, but she asked anyway. "Where are we going?"

He kept his eyes on the road. "I'm taking you to dinner."

"At your house?"

"Um-hmm."

"Boyd, about last night... I..."

Still without looking at her, he reached for her hand and raised it to his lips. "Hush, Audrey."

As the pickup rumbled down the road toward the adobe house, Audrey reflected on her perverse nature. All day long, when she hadn't been too busy to think, she'd congratulated herself on her good sense where Boyd was concerned. No deep involvement. That was the bottom line. Yet he'd shown up, done little more than crook his finger, and here she was.

Sighing, she glanced at him surreptitiously, enjoying the view of his attractive profile. Apparently he held no grudges about last night. In fact, he seemed to be in a pretty good mood. Even as she watched, he puckered his lips and began to whistle.

The minute Audrey entered the house all her questions about his activities that day were answered. A cheerful fire blazed in the beehive fireplace. A colorful area rug was on the floor in front of it, and the sofa had been moved in closer. The aroma of something wonderful permeated the rooms. Drawn to take a peek at what it was, Audrey gasped when she entered the kitchen. The little table had been set with a cloth, china, silverware and candles. A bottle of wine rested in a bucket of ice.

Turning to a grinning Boyd, she folded her arms across her chest and eyed him warily. "This is what you were doing while the rest of us were out in the sun and dust working our buns off?"

"Um-hmm."

"What are you up to? Did you bring me here to seduce me?"

He feigned hurt. "I brought you here to woo you. There's a difference." Gesturing toward the living room, he said, "Please have a seat, and I'll get you a glass of wine."

Trying desperately to hide a smile, Audrey reversed direction. "Plying me with liquor won't work," she threw over her shoulder.

She didn't distinctly hear what his comment to that was, but it sounded suspiciously like, "We'll see."

AUDREY WAS PREPARED to call it the most glorious evening
of her life. Boyd, it seemed, had spent all day scurrying back
and forth from the ranch house to the adobe one, procur-
ing whatever was needed for this cozy setup. He'd brought
a portable cassette player so Merle Haggard could serenade
them while they sipped wine in front of the fire. Later, he
served dinner with an exaggerated flourish, and the food,
prepared and packed by Maria, was fantastic. There even
was a salad. After days of chuck wagon fare, that salad was
quite possibly the best thing she'd ever eaten. Audrey was
sure no one had ever gone to so much trouble for her. Boyd
was pure delight.

They finished the meal, then washed and repacked everything. Wiping his hands on a dish towel, Boyd refilled
their wineglasses, and they returned to the living room and
sat on the sofa in front of the fire. "How am I doing?" he
asked seductively.

"You must be doing all right. My head is spinning, and I
don't think the wine's responsible."

"Good. Drink up."

"I really don't think I need any more."

"Whatever you say." He took the glass from her hand, set
it on the floor out of the way and placed his beside it. Settling back on the sofa, he pulled her into a tight embrace,
and the sensual assault began. He held her face against his
chest, and the smell of her freshly shampooed hair filled his
nostrils. He thought how clean she always smelled, even after a day on horseback. Odd how simply holding Audrey
brought him such pleasure. He wasn't sure he had ever experienced a thrill from just holding a woman. He felt her
arms slowly go around him, her palms flatten against his
back, and he wanted the moment to go on forever.

Audrey was thinking the same thing. Resting her head
against his chest, she listened to the rhythm of his heartbeat and thought how wonderfully warm he felt. The evening had been pure delight from the beginning. He had
successfully created the atmosphere he'd intended. She felt
safe, comfortable and content, locked in an impregnable
capsule with Boyd, far away from the rest of the world.

Sighing, she melted against him, became as pliable as putty and waited for his next move.

He curved a forefinger under her chin and tilted her face to receive his kiss. Mouths fused, tongues touched, arms tightened. As the kiss deepened, his hand moved to the front of her shirt, flicked at a button and slipped inside to cup a full breast that felt like a velvet pillow. His thumb made circular motions, teasing the nipple to erect hardness. All he wanted was to make Audrey feel good; hearing her low moan he guessed he was succeeding. His kisses became fierce and hungry.

Audrey didn't feel good; her insides felt like the belly of a volcano on the brink of eruption. A hot dizziness whirled inside her head, overcoming all rational thought. She felt a tingling warmth between her legs and a tightening of her womb. Her body yearned, almost cried out for fulfillment, and there didn't seem to be a thing she could do about it.

Boyd lifted his head and looked into those incredible eyes, now glazed with desire. "I'm waiting," he said huskily.

"For...what?"

"To hear that song and dance about what a short time we've known each other."

"Oh, that. Well, I...I guess that doesn't seem so important to me anymore."

"God, Audrey, all I do anymore is think about you. Please...put me out of my misery."

His entire body seemed to encase hers. Audrey arched into it, clutching him. "Yes," she whispered. "Yes, yes."

With some difficulty Boyd got to his feet and pulled her with him. He would have liked to scoop her up into his arms and dramatically carry her to the bedroom, but in his present condition there was some doubt in his mind that his weakened legs would even carry him. He held her tightly against him, and together they somehow negotiated the width of the living room and the length of the small hallway.

During his fit of housekeeping that afternoon he had changed the sheets. Audrey stared at the bed as though she'd never seen one before. Boyd came up behind her, slipped his arm around her waist and kissed the back of her head. Slowly she turned in his arms and slid hers around him. For a long wordless moment they simply stood locked together, lost in erotic sweetness. Then she raised her face, and the look he gave her seemed to melt her bones. It was absolutely insane to feel so much for a man she'd known such a short time, but there it was, real and insistent and undeniable. It shook her down to her toes.

Smiling, she closed her eyes and settled into the niche of his hips. Boyd's hands wandered over her back and down her arms. They drove her wild with desire, and with the passion came the first persistent stirrings of another emotion. Audrey wasn't prepared to call it love yet, but it was a caring tenderness she'd never experienced before. She knew that making love with him was going to intensify the feeling. She wouldn't be the same again. Boyd had played havoc with her senses from the beginning. What was left of her rational mind wondered if this had been inevitable from the moment she'd stepped through the door of the Durango Suite.

Then he broke the embrace slightly, stepping back to tug her shirt free of the jeans and fumble with its buttons.

"Boots first," she managed to say.

He mumbled something, and she stepped back to sit on the edge of the bed and offer him a leg. Tugging, he removed one boot, then the other. When he sat down beside her, she returned the favor. Then with shaking fingers they divested themselves of their clothes. Somehow the task was accomplished, and they were under the covers of the small bed, clinging to each other.

Boyd's stomach muscles were so tight they hurt, and the pounding of his heartbeat drowned out all other sounds. His mind and body were poised toward one goal, to make Audrey want him as much as he wanted her, not just tonight but again and again, for every night they could manage to be together. How to excite her the way she excited him? With no knowledge of her pleasure points, he moved cautiously. His hands sought and touched, rubbed and petted, while he muttered incoherent, guttural sounds from deep in his throat.

Audrey squirmed. "I can't hear you. What are you saying?"

"Nothing, nothing," he whispered. "You're on fire."

"Yes. Oh, Boyd..."

"I've been on fire for days." Boyd curved her against him, and the sensation of her warm flesh against his sent a thousand sparks shooting through him. Restlessly his hands explored, touching. The body he'd admired so often was as perfect as he'd expected it to be. His arousal complete, he ached to take her, yet sensed the need for restraint. He'd pushed her awfully far awfully fast. One insensitive move and he risked putting an end to something that had just begun. And he wanted her to remember this forever.

Taking his time, he nuzzled her neck, licked a nipple grown hard with desire, then buried his face in the valley between her breasts. Audrey arched against him, moaning softly. The fire burned out of control. Finally there was nothing to do but give in to it. Deftly he maneuvered her beneath him. Poised above her, he looked down into her heavy-lidded eyes, thrilled by the desire he saw on her face. Audrey felt his hard, throbbing maleness pressed against her stomach, and her arms tugged at him impatiently.

"Boyd...please..."

He filled her with as much gentleness as could reasonably be summoned at a time like this. The gentleness overwhelmed her. It was she who became reckless and abandoned, binding him with her legs and arms, wanting him as she had never wanted a man, moving against him again and again, faster and faster. Her inherent sexuality, so long held dormant, flowered and bloomed. Pure pleasure held her in its grip. Wishing the ecstasy could go on and on, she nevertheless drove toward the climax, caught in a whirlpool of passion. Her fingernails bit into his shoulders as she cried his name. He tensed, then shuddered and collapsed on top of her.

It was some time before either of them stirred. Boyd moved first, rolling off her, then bringing her close. "Audrey..."

"Mmm..."

"You...stunned me."

"To tell the truth, I stunned myself."

"I have the worst feeling I'm never going to be able to do without you."

Audrey couldn't help wondering if either or both of them had left themselves wide open to heartache because of this. It was a sobering thought and unworthy of the moment. What was that damnable trait of hers that prevented her from simply letting life happen? Why did she always have to think, ponder and analyze? "Don't say too much," she said.

Her remark brought a frown to Boyd's face. Propping himself on one elbow, he stared down at her. "You're not sorry. Tell me you're not."

Tracing the shape of his mouth with her forefinger, she said, "I'm not sorry. It was wonderful. You were magnificent. I wouldn't have dreamed I could be so...uninhibited."

He chuckled. "You were pretty magnificent, too."

"Really?" Not once in her life had she ever wondered what kind of lover she'd make. Did women think of such things?

"Really."

"What makes a woman good in bed?"

"Good God, what a question!"

"That's no answer."

"Well...I don't know, Audrey. A lot of things, and none of them have anything to do with...er, prowess or technique. I guess so much depends on how the man in question feels about her. If he cares, then she's...wonderful."

"That's nice," she said, sighing.

Boyd grew solemn, thinking of so many things. The tragedy in her past, for one thing, if indeed it had been her father Skeet had told him about. And, too, something about her involvement with him troubled her, which in turn troubled him. Did she fear complications? He would have liked to tell her how he felt, that this was so right for both of them, but she might not believe words uttered in the aftermath of passion.

Oddly, Audrey wasn't apprehensive in the least. She had no regrets. She felt relaxed, sated, filled and at peace. Even if this proved to be the only time she and Boyd ever had together, she wouldn't regret it. But she didn't want him making promises he couldn't fulfill. Something Betty had told her came back to her now: "As Benedicts, Boyd and I are supposed to marry well, the way Brent did." In other words, Audrey Hamilton might be acceptable for an affair but not for anything more permanent.

Oh, what a time for that! Pushing aside all thoughts of the future, of anything but the moment, she settled against him. "We should get back to camp."

"I know."

"Do you suppose there's been talk about us?"

"I don't know, and frankly, I couldn't care less."

"Everyone seems to think we'll finish up tomorrow. Do you?"

"Yeah, probably." He looked at her. "Then the next day, home."

Neither of them had to voice their thoughts. They both knew they were thinking the same thing. The end of roundup meant the end of this idyll. Then it was back to reality and the workaday world. Back to the Greenspoint.

"Boyd?"

"Hmm?"

"Can we come back here tomorrow night?"

He kissed her shoulder. "It's a date."

THEY DIDN'T LEAVE CAMP until after supper was served the following night, and it was very late when they returned. Lost in the sensual discovery of each other, Audrey and Boyd had tarried in the adobe house, loath to leave, each wondering when they would be in it together again...if ever. Their lovemaking had been even more intense than before, increasing their need for each other.

On the way back to camp, Boyd was swamped by sadness and worry. He didn't think he could bear to say goodbye to her. His spirits were somewhat restored, however, when Audrey said, "Betty has asked me to stay through the weekend for the fair and rodeo."

It was hard to believe he'd been so preoccupied that he'd completely forgotten Tri-County, the celebration of the end of roundup. "Are you going to?" he asked expectantly.

"I'd like to."

He breathed a little easier. That would give them an extra day or two. It wasn't much, but he accepted it with gratitude. For now it would have to be enough.

CHAPTER TWELVE

"Well, son, what's the tally?" Buck stood on the back porch of the ranch house and watched the milling herd being driven into the pens.

"Fifteen hundred head, I figure," Boyd answered. "Murdoch came up with the same number."

"Not bad. Respectable. Any problems?"

"Not a one."

At that moment Audrey and Betty rode up to the corral, dismounted and began unsaddling their horses. "How did she do?"

"Audrey? She did fine."

"Surprising."

"She's . . . ah, quite a woman." He noticed how his voice took on a peculiar quality when he spoke of Audrey, even casually. She had become everything to him, and the knowledge still shook him a bit. He wondered about his father's reaction to the news that he was head over heels in love with a woman he'd met less than two weeks ago. His grandfather might have understood; his father never would. Benedict men, so tradition had it, did not act impulsively when it came to affairs of the heart. They gave the same care to choosing their women that they gave to choosing breeding stock. In Buck's eyes particularly, the two weren't all that dissimilar, and there was no question in Boyd's mind that his father was going to consider this latest development impulsive.

But it's the sanest thing I've ever done, he thought confidently. It felt wonderfully liberating to, for once, do something not rooted in careful thought.

Buck didn't seem to notice any peculiar inflection in his son's voice. The two men stood and watched as the young women walked toward the house. "Welcome home," Buck said, obviously addressing his daughter.

"Thanks, Dad." Betty gave him a perfunctory hug when she stepped up on the porch.

Audrey stood to the side, taking care not to look directly at Boyd. She was too afraid her heart would be in her eyes. Then Buck turned his attention to her. "How was it?"

"I enjoyed every minute of it, Mr. Benedict."

"Good, good. Well, Audrey, I think I have some good news for you."

"Oh?"

"It seems some Phoenix socialite shot her husband last night. Not fatally, fortunately for the gentleman in question, but it's had the effect of making Dad's will yesterday's news. I thought you'd be pleased."

Audrey tensed. She didn't know what to say. Was she being dismissed? Overcome by a terrible letdown, she felt like Cinderella at five minutes past midnight. Chancing a sidelong glance at Boyd, she saw his startled expression. Her gaze flew back to Buck. "Oh, well, I..."

Betty came to her rescue. "Dad, Audrey's promised to stay through Tri-County. She worked hard on roundup, and she should be able to enjoy the celebration."

"Well, of course," Buck said, shrugging. "I certainly didn't mean to imply that you should leave, my dear. You'll be missed. I just wanted you to know that there's no objection when you want to leave."

"Thank you, Mr. Benedict. I really would like to stay for the rodeo, but then I must get back to my job. Has my office called by any chance?"

"Peter did telephone day before yesterday. He seemed rather surprised when I told him you couldn't be reached."

"I'll bet. I suppose I should check in with him."

That small exchange took Boyd aback somewhat. For three days he had been living in something of a dreamworld, but now reality came crashing down on him. Audrey would be leaving soon, perhaps within a few days. It was going to be hard to find time alone with her now that they were back at the house, but they needed to talk, to make some plans. And before too many more days had passed, he was going to have to sit down and have a talk with his father. Buck would need some time to get used to the idea of Audrey as a big part of Boyd's life.

He stared after her as she and Betty went into the house, aching to follow, to go to her room with her, talk to her. This was going to be damned difficult. After a week of being with her all day, riding with her, eating with her, making love to her, he resented every minute he had to be away from her. But Buck was speaking to him, so he regretfully gave his father his attention.

Inside the house, Audrey went straight to her room, though it crossed her mind that she should look up Elizabeth and say hello to her. She didn't act on impulse, however. Elizabeth was seldom home in the afternoon, for one thing, and she was too tired and dirty for another.

The first thing she did was call Peter, who sounded impatient. "When in the devil are you coming back, Audrey?"

"In a few days. The Benedicts have asked me to stay and attend some sort of celebration this weekend, and since they've been so nice, I hated to say no." And that was only a tiny fib.

"Have you forgotten the United Hardware Dealers?"

Audrey put a hand to her mouth. She had. After spending months luring the organization's annual convention to the Greenspoint, she had forgotten about it completely. "Of course not."

"They'll be here Tuesday, two hundred strong, and I expect you to be here, too."

"Then I will be. Don't worry, Peter. The groundwork's been done. Everything will go smooth as glass."

They said goodbye. Then Audrey stripped off her clothes and headed for the shower, where she gave her hair a good scrubbing and used a conditioner. Afterward, she wallowed in the luxury of once again having at hand all the things she had always taken for granted—a blow dryer, a curling iron and a full array of cosmetics. And once her hair and face had been done, she put on panty hose, slip, skirt, blouse and low-heeled pumps. The transformation felt fabulous.

When she had finished, she checked the time and discovered it was a bit early to go to the sun room. Propping her elbows on the dressing table and resting her chin in her hands, she wondered what Boyd was doing. Showering and getting dressed for dinner, too, probably. She felt oddly bereft at being deprived of his company for even a short time. How could she possibly have grown so used to him in a week? She'd been so immersed in him she'd forgotten the convention, and two weeks ago it had occupied huge chunks of her time and thoughts. She didn't know how she was going to do without him once she got back to Phoenix. Life had such a way of sneaking up on you when your back was turned. After all those years of working hard to keep her life uncomplicated, he had shown up out of nowhere and complicated it good.

THE FOOD THAT NIGHT tasted wonderful but still, dinner was a palpitating ordeal. Seated on Boyd's right at the table, Audrey felt the strain of being so close to him without being able to touch him. And from his uncharacteristic silence and tight-lipped expression, she suspected he felt it, too. They didn't dare look at each other, and the steady stream of banter that was floating around the table just served to make her more uncomfortable. She was glad she wasn't expected to contribute much to the conversation. Save for a few light comments about her experiences as a "tenderfoot cowhand," she remained silent.

Audrey had never been so glad to see a meal come to an end. She tried to think of a good excuse for not joining the family in the sun room for their customary postprandial session, but a headache was the only thing that came to mind, and that sounded pretty lame for someone who had just come from a week of roughing it in the great outdoors. Gamely, she followed the others as they filed en masse out of the dining room.

Lagging behind, Audrey was crossing the foyer when a strong arm went around her waist and spun her around. Startled, she gasped his name. "Boyd! You scared me to death."

He placed a finger on his lips to silence her, then took her hand and pulled her to the front door.

"Where are we going?" she whispered.

"Hush. You'll see."

"Won't the others wonder where we are?"

"Let 'em."

Grasping her hand firmly, he led her out onto the front porch, sprinted its length and loped across the side yard toward the barn. Audrey's feet all but left the ground as she frantically tried to keep up with him. He didn't slow his pace until they had gone some distance from the house. Audrey's chest heaved as she fought to catch her breath. "I repeat, where are we going?"

"And I repeat, you'll see."

Clutching her hand tightly, Boyd led her around the corral to a secluded area behind the barn where an enormous stack of hay stood. Scooping her up into his arms, he tossed her onto the hay, then fell on top of her.

Laughing lightly, she slipped her arms around his neck. "Lord, Boyd, what's gotten into you?"

"God a'mighty, you look gorgeous tonight. It was all I could do to keep my hands off you during dinner. I kept wanting to reach over and..."

Audrey wiggled against him and held him tight. "That might have raised a few eyebrows."

"I imagine so." Bending his head, he kissed her soundly. "Hmm. Twenty-four hours without that is about as long as I can stand."

"What are you going to do when I leave?"

"I don't even want to think about it." He kissed her again, crushing her farther into the hay. This time when he raised his head, she was covered with the prickly grass.

With one hand, Audrey brushed it away from her face. "Oh, this stuff is awful, coarse and scratchy. How in the world did a 'roll in the hay' ever come to stand for..."

"For what?"

"You know."

"Tell me." His hand went to the hem of her skirt, slipped under and moved upward, stroking and petting until it found its destination. Her panty hose were only a slight hindrance.

His hands tugged, and Audrey gasped, even as the first thrill of desire rippled through her. "Lord, no! You wouldn't, not here!"

"Why not?"

"Someone might see us. Boyd, please . . ."

"No one's going to come out here."

"How . . . can you be sure?"

"Twenty-seven people could walk by this haystack right now and never know we're here. At least they wouldn't if you'd be quiet."

"Boyd . . ."

"Hush." He effectively silenced her with his mouth. His lips were soft, coaxing, demanding. Their persuasive power stripped away her resistance. She felt herself relax to allow his wandering hands free access to her pliant body. They petted and stroked her with sure yet tantalizing touches. Her heartbeat accelerated, then hammered inside her chest. Beneath her skin an undeniable glow crept through her body. It amazed her and would always amaze her how easily and masterfully he could arouse her. There was such a delicious thrill associated with Boyd's touch.

With a feeling of pure satisfaction Boyd sensed her growing ardor and sought to intensify it. His mouth left hers, and his tongue made an impatient foray across her cheek and down the smooth column of her throat. With his hands he nudged her legs apart, then settled his hips between them, claiming the secret niche he now thought of as his.

"This . . . really is indecent," she whispered.

"Hush."

"In our clothes and . . ."

That was the last thing Audrey was able to say for a very long time. His body probed hers, and she became its welcoming sheath. Soon they both were moving to pleasure's rhythm, satisfying a desperate longing.

SOME TIME LATER they strolled arm in arm across the moonlit grounds, lost in the wonder of what had transpired between them. Neither of them saw the man who lounged against a tree trunk in the distance, but he saw them. He watched intently as the couple stopped in the shadows and shared a kiss before continuing on toward the house. He alertly noticed how their arms dropped when they reached the front porch, and how they separated before going through the front door.

Jesse smiled. So Audrey had a thing going with Boyd. Good! To Jesse's mind it was his ace in the hole. Throughout roundup he'd stayed as far away from her as he could. She despised him and wasn't very good at concealing the fact. Not wanting to arouse suspicions, he had prudently given her a wide berth. Though he no longer worried that Audrey might influence Betty against him—Betty was too besotted to believe anything Audrey might say—he'd still been afraid she might squelch his plans in ways he couldn't foresee.

Now he could stop worrying. If Audrey had the means to ruin his plans, he now had the means to do the same to her, and she would know it. One peep out of her, and he'd run to Boyd and his old man as fast as his legs would carry him. Things couldn't have been working out better.

THE POPULATION of the peaceful little village of Agua Linda tripled for one day every year. Some of the local merchants declared that they usually made more money during Tri-County Fair and Rodeo then they did at Christmas. By the time the Benedict clan arrived on Saturday morning, the main street of the town was teeming with activity. Buck, Elizabeth, Sara and Brent rode in the blue Cadillac, while Boyd drove Audrey and Betty in one of the ranch's pickups. They parked at the fairgrounds on the outskirts of the community, then strolled around to take in the sights. Dozens of judgings were taking place, of everything from livestock to sweet pepper relish, and at noon a chili cook-off was held. Audrey was just as proud as the rest of the Triple B hands when Skeet Drummond won first place.

Betty didn't linger long with the family. She soon left them with a promise to join Audrey and Boyd at the rodeo that evening. Ostensibly she was joining some friends, but Audrey correctly guessed that the "friend" was Jesse. She and her conscience waged a constant war over Betty's infatuation with the man, but Audrey knew that if she couldn't bring herself to tell even Boyd about her past, and she couldn't, she wasn't apt to reveal it to any of the other Benedicts.

The family was well-known, she noticed. No one passed without speaking. Audrey was not yet aware of the fact that her old friend, Bert, had been the virtual patron of Agua Linda, and the mantle had been passed to Buck. Almost every institution in town was owned or controlled or heavily endowed by the Benedicts, and that included the bank, the newspaper, the cattle association and a nearby private school. Audrey was introduced to more people than she ever could remember. More than a few of them obviously recognized her name as that of the woman who'd inherited all that money, but no one would have dreamed of asking pointed questions.

The day passed lazily. By midafternoon it was obvious that Elizabeth and Sara had had about all of the festivities they could take. Not long afterward, Buck and Brent and their wives returned to the ranch, leaving Audrey and Boyd to enjoy the rest of the day by themselves.

And they well might have been alone instead of among thousands of people. They had eyes only for each other and kept to themselves as much as possible. Away from the restrictive influence of his family, Boyd's entire manner changed. He knew he was wearing his heart in his eyes, but he didn't care. He was wildly in love with the beautiful woman at his side. There were problems, of course, but he'd deal with them when the time came. His immediate worry was that Audrey might slip out of his life as quickly as she had come into it. He suspected he was going to be a very busy man in the upcoming months, tending to business as usual while hurrying to Phoenix often enough to keep the flame burning.

He wondered how long it would take to convince Audrey to marry him, while smiling at the thought. How strange to know with absolute certainty that he wanted to marry her. Two weeks ago he hadn't known she existed.

The day wound down to evening. Audrey and Boyd sat in the pickup, eating hot dogs, drinking beer and waiting for the rodeo to begin. Audrey sighed contentedly and rested her head on the back of the seat. "It's been a glorious day. It's going to be awfully hard to climb in my car and drive back to Phoenix Monday."

Boyd's hand went to her nape and massaged gently. "I'll drive you. I don't like your being on the highway alone."

They exchanged knowing smiles. "A lame excuse is better than no excuse at all, I suppose. Will you really go with me?"

He nodded. "And once I deliver you safe and sound, I might have to stay a few days. I think it's time the family took more of an active interest in the Greenspoint, don't you?"

"Oh, indeed. Much more active." Audrey was flooded with happiness. She still wasn't prepared to say where all this was going to lead. It seemed highly unlikely that she and Boyd were going to walk arm and arm into the sunset to live happily ever after, so she didn't think about it much. She was seizing the moment and tomorrow be damned, something she hadn't done in her entire life. The inner loosening that brought on was wonderful.

They finished their food, crammed the napkins and cans into a paper sack, and Boyd left the truck to go in search of a trash bin. Audrey waited and scanned the scene through the windshield. Dusk had fallen. More and more vehicles were arriving by the minute, and the stands were beginning to fill up. Boyd finally returned to the truck, but just as he opened the door on the driver's side he was accosted by three cowboys. Audrey recognized them as Triple B regulars.

"Hey, Boyd, got a minute?" one of them called.

Boyd closed the door and turned in their direction. "Sure, Joe. What can I do for you?"

The men approached, and the man named Joe spoke up. "We're wonderin' if we can talk you into signin' up for the bronc ridin'."

Boyd laughed. "Afraid not, fellas."

"Aw, come on, Boyd," another man cajoled. "You were the best dadblamed bronc rider in the valley."

"That was some time ago. I'd better pass. But thanks for asking." He reached for the door handle, but Joe put a detaining hand on his arm.

"Hey, listen . . . there's no way the Triple B is gonna win this thing if we don't win the bronc ridin'. The Bar H bunch is probably gonna take the ropin' event, so we need to throw our best in the bronc ridin'."

"Well, now, boys, I'm flattered as all get out, but I haven't ridden in five or six years."

"Come on, Boyd. If Lefty Jarrell can ride a bronc, you can, too."

Boyd paused and frowned. "Lefty Jarrell? Is Lefty riding tonight?"

"Yep, and the money's on him."

"The hell it is! Lefty's as old as I am."

"Older," Joe said, pressing his advantage. "And he never was half as good as you were."

Audrey could see Boyd vacillating, and a sudden fear clutched at her. Surely he wasn't seriously considering such a foolhardy stunt. A wild horse was the meanest animal on earth, one who had soured under the saddle and would rather be shot than ridden. Bronc riding was terribly dangerous, and it definitely was a young man's sport. Bronc riders "retired" before thirty, if they lasted that long.

Her worst fears were realized when she heard Boyd say, "Okay, Joe, go sign me up. I'll get Audrey settled and meet you back in the chutes."

The three men hurried away to carry the news to the other Triple B hands, and Boyd walked around the truck to open Audrey's door. "Boyd, please don't do this," she beseeched.

But the adrenaline was flowing, and his eyes were bright with the challenge. "Don't worry about me, honey. I grew up riding broncs."

"It's dangerous, and you know it! Please, for me, don't."

He paid no attention. He merely shoved his hand into his hip pocket. "Here, you'd better hold these for me," he said, handing her his wallet and the truck's keys.

"Boyd, please . . ."

"Don't worry about me, Audrey. I know what I'm doing. Let's go find Betty."

As they crossed the parking lot, Audrey continued protesting, but then they were joined by some of the other cowboys, so she had no choice but to keep quiet. Once they spied Betty in the stands, Boyd patted Audrey on the shoulder, said he'd see her later, then walked away with the men. Filled with apprehension, she climbed the steps and took the seat Betty had been holding for her.

"Where've you been?" Betty wanted to know. "We've looked all over for you. Where's Boyd?"

Audrey saw that Jesse was sitting on Betty's right. She acknowledged him with a curt nod, then sat down on Betty's left. With a jerk of her head in the direction of the chutes at one end of the arena, she said, "He's entering the bronc riding."

Betty's mouth dropped. "He's what?"

"You heard me. Some of the men talked him into it."

"Oh, God, Jesse," Betty moaned. "Did you hear that? Go down there and put a stop to this!"

Jesse snorted derisively. "Are you kidding? Do you honestly think I'm going down there in front of the other guys and tell Boyd not to ride a bronc? He'd fire me on the spot. No way!"

Audrey's fear intensified when she saw the horrified look on Betty's face. It became almost paralyzing when Betty cried, "He must be crazy! He hasn't ridden a bronc in five or six years. Has he been drinking?"

"A couple of beers, that's it."

"Well, we've got to do something." Betty got to her feet. "Come on, Audrey..."

But Jesse grabbed her arm and pulled her down. "Don't make an ass of yourself, sweetheart," he muttered. "Boyd's a big boy. He'll be furious if you go down there and make a scene in front of everyone. I'm bettin' he can go the full eight seconds and then some."

Resigned, Betty turned to Audrey. "He's right, you know. There's nothing we can do, except cross our fingers and pray my dumb brother doesn't get his fool neck broken." She bit her lip. "Besides, he once was the very best amateur I ever saw."

Audrey noticed the lack of conviction in Betty's voice. The evening that had promised to be so fun-filled turned into an endurance run. Everyone around her, with the possible exception of Betty, was having a grand time, but she sat woodenly through the barrel races, the clowns' antics, the calf roping, and the bulldogging events, barely seeing anything. Had she been granted one wish, it would have been that the bronc riding would have been canceled altogether.

Naturally, the wish wasn't granted. An eternity later, the loudspeaker announced the bronc riding event. Audrey forced herself to watch the first four riders, which wasn't too difficult since they were strangers to her. One young cowboy barely cleared the chute before he landed rump first on the ground. The fourth contestant was the man named Lefty Jarrell, whom she had heard mentioned in the parking lot. To loud applause, he stayed on six and a half seconds. Then she heard Boyd's name come over the speaker, and a great roar went up from the crowd.

Fear-induced nausea rose up in her throat. "I... don't think I can watch," she told Betty.

Betty's mouth set in a grim line. "If my brother lives through this, I might personally try to blister his butt."

Audrey was certain she'd never be able to watch, but seemingly hypnotized, she discovered she couldn't take her eyes off the arena. Had it been anyone but Boyd out there, she might have thought it a spectacular sight. With a rolling motion as powerful as dynamite and as unpredictable as lightning, horse and rider came out of the chute. While the crowd roared and whistled its approval, the horse pulled every trick he knew in an attempt to dislodge his hated burden. Boyd rolled with him, hanging onto the rigging with one hand while the other arm flailed about freely. Most of the spectators were on their feet, and Audrey learned that night just what an eternity eight seconds could be.

"God, what a ride!" a man behind them exclaimed. "Benedict always was one ridin' machine!"

Then the eight-second buzzer sounded, and the crowd's applause became deafening. Audrey almost collapsed with relief. It was over. *When I get him alone, I'm going to kill him for putting me through this!*

The thought had no sooner formed, however, than the noise around her changed from unrestrained cheering to a collective gasp from hundreds of throats. Audrey thought she heard Betty scream. Her eyes flew to the arena where Boyd and the horse still flailed around. *What is he doing? Why is he still on that horse? Why the devil doesn't he dismount?* A split second passed before she realized what was happening.

Dear God, he was hung up, caught in the rigging and couldn't dismount! Audrey's hand went to her throat. If she thought she'd been afraid before, it was nothing compared to the stark terror that now raced through her. That horse was going to beat him to a pulp!

CHAPTER THIRTEEN

BOYD DIDN'T PANIC. He had been hung up before, and he knew there wasn't anything he could do but ride with the flow. Instinctively, he stopped using his spurs. Freed of that irritant, even the cussedest horse eventually would slow down enough to allow its rider to work free and get off. But an eight-second ride on a bucking bronc was grueling enough; getting beat around the arena for three or four minutes was a severe jolt to the system.

By now the horse was wild with fury. The frustrated animal kept banging his body against the fence, so Boyd knew his right leg was going to take a beating. At this point, since he couldn't work himself free, the one thing he didn't want was to be thrown and dragged on the ground. He'd once seen a young cowboy killed that way. It was fast becoming a catch-22 situation. The horse's wild antics were scrambling his insides, but he had to stay on until he could get free of the rigging.

It was amazing how many things a person could think about while being tossed in the air. It occurred to him that Audrey was watching all this. He was dimly aware of the clowns who were frantically trying to distract the horse. Two cowboys had jumped the fence and were attempting to help. Not too smart of them, but Boyd fervently hoped they would succeed. He'd drawn one goddanged mean horse, so maybe he'd win the dumb event after all.

By the time he had finally worked free and hit the ground, he knew there wasn't an inch of him that wouldn't be black and blue by morning. His head had struck something during the fall, and it was exploding. He vaguely wondered if he had any broken bones, and he hoped there was a doctor in the crowd. He had a moment to be grateful for two pairs of strong arms lifting him before he closed his eyes and slipped into unconsciousness.

Since accidents weren't uncommon at rodeos, a make-shift infirmary had been set up behind the chutes. It was nothing more than a tent with a few cots in it, and the physician on hand was a local doctor who always attended Tri-County Rodeo to take care of just such situations. Audrey, Betty and Jesse had hurried out of the stands and were waiting near the tent. When Audrey saw the unconscious Boyd being carried by two cowboys, she thought she would faint. His mouth was slack; his arms dangled. Blood spurted from the cut over his eye. He looked so awful she was sure he was dead. As her vision blurred sickeningly, she felt Betty's arm go around her shoulders. "He's going to be all right, Audrey. I just know he is," she said, but her voice didn't carry the conviction Audrey would have liked.

She didn't know how long they stood outside the tent, waiting. Probably not as long as it seemed. They had been joined by several Triple B men who, along with Jesse, congregated in a tight circle apart from the two women. Their murmuring, concerned voices reached Audrey's ears. *They think he's dead, too,* she thought, and tears welled in her eyes. *How could I have let this happen? I should have stopped him. I've never even told him I love him.*

At long last the doctor emerged from the tent. He scanned the anxious faces, recognized Betty and smiled. "He's all right. A bit battered, but nothing's broken. He's just going to have to rest and let everything mend. But I think I should warn you—he's going to feel like walking death tomorrow."

The cowboys broke into happy whoops, while Audrey all but collapsed with relief and gratitude. Betty hugged her impulsively. "Go on in and see him, Audrey. We're going to have to take him home. I'll bring the truck around. Are the keys in it?"

Distractedly, Audrey reached in her jeans pocket, withdrew the keys and handed them to Betty. Then, as the young woman walked away, she went in to see Boyd.

A kerosene lantern illuminated the inside of the tent. The air was heavy with the smell of disinfectant. Boyd was lying on one of the small cots, his hands folded on his chest. Fearfully, Audrey moved toward him, and when she peered down at his prone figure she uttered a choked gasp. She didn't think she'd ever seen anyone who looked so terrible. The gash over his eye had stopped bleeding and was beginning to swell. His right pant leg had been slit to the thigh, revealing angry red skin and dried blood. The knuckles of the hand that had been caught in the rigging were scraped raw. He was so still it frightened her. Placing a hand on his shoulder, she whispered, "Boyd?" When there was no response, she shook him gently. "Boyd?"

His eyelids fluttered. He coughed and opened his eyes. "Hi, hon," he murmured, then groaned. "God, do I have a granddaddy of a headache!"

"Headache?" she cried. "You're lucky that's all you have. I . . . thought you were dead."

"Well, I'm not. Messed up a little, I guess, but quite alive. At least, I think I'm alive."

"Ohh!" Audrey sank to the ground and placed her head on his chest. Fairly controlled until now, she began to cry. "Oh, God, I thought you were dead!"

"Don't cry. I'm all right."

"You're not all right! You'll probably be dead by morning. Anyone who'd do something so stupid ought to be dead."

As rotten as he felt, Boyd managed a small smile. "You should have been a nurse, Audrey. You have the most soothing bedside manner."

"How could you possibly do something so incredibly dumb?"

"Hey, I made a good ride. Getting hung up is just something that happens every once in awhile. Don't cry. Calm down and help me up."

Audrey's head came up with a jerk. "Boyd, I think you need to go to a hospital."

"I'm not going to a hospital. The doctor says I haven't broken anything."

"How can he possibly know that? I don't see any X-ray machines. You should go to a hospital and let someone check you over good. There might be internal injuries. I really think—"

"Dammit, honey, don't think. Just help me up and take me home."

THERE WERE SEVERAL unfamiliar cars parked in front of the ranch house when the pickup arrived, and the house was ablaze with lights. Boyd groaned. "I guess the folks have a house full of company. They usually do on the night of Tri-County. I don't want to have to answer a lot of damned fool questions. Betty, go in and see what's going on."

Betty, who had driven the truck home, switched off the engine and opened the door. "Right. I'll be back in a jiffy."

The trip from Agua Linda had seemed to take forever. Audrey knew Boyd was in more pain than he would admit. She had seen him wince at every bump in the road. But he was adamant about not going to the hospital, so she just prayed that that doctor at the rodeo had known what he was doing.

"I wish there was something I could do," she said lamely. "I know you're hurting, and I feel so helpless."

"Just stay close by. Oh, and you might give me a kiss. Isn't that supposed to cure everything?"

Smiling, she kissed him tenderly. "Promise me you'll admit it if you start feeling really bad. No suffering in silence."

"Promise."

Betty returned and opened the door on the passenger side. "Everyone's in the sun room, so I think we can get the patient in his room without anyone seeing us."

The two women gave Boyd a hand and helped him into the house. The threesome had crossed the foyer when Elizabeth came out of the sun room carrying an empty tray. At the sight of her son she let out a startled cry and almost dropped the tray. "Boyd! Good heavens, what happened to you?"

"The idiot forgot he isn't twenty anymore," Betty scoffed.

"It's nothing, Mom, really," Boyd hastened to assure her. "Just a little accident. I'm fine."

"How can you be fine when you look so dreadful? Do you need medical attention?" Elizabeth looked from her daughter to Audrey. "Isn't anyone going to tell me what happened?"

"Betty will fill you in," Boyd muttered. "Don't worry, Mom. I've seen a doctor, but I've got to get off this leg."

Betty stayed behind to explain everything to a clearly unappeased Elizabeth, and Audrey let Boyd lean on her while she helped him to his room. Once there she hurried to turn down the bed. "In you go."

"I don't want to go to bed," he protested. "I want a drink and a shower."

"Oh, Boyd, the shower can wait. I'll get you a drink if you want it, but you really should be in bed."

"I'm not getting in that bed without a shower. I'm too filthy."

She frowned thoughtfully. "Well, I guess you probably will rest better if you're clean. But you won't be able to stand in the shower. I'm afraid you might fall. Let me run a bath for you."

"I hate taking baths," he grumbled.

"If you insist on getting cleaned up, you'll simply have to take a bath."

"Whatever you say, dear," he said with a grin and sank to the edge of the bed. The grin faded immediately as he held his injured leg rigidly in front of him. "You're going to have to help me with my boots. This son of a bitch leg is throbbing like crazy."

Audrey looked at him sympathetically. "You're really going to have something to moan about when that water hits it. Maybe you should reconsider that bath."

"Don't worry, I'm tough. Get these boots, will you?"

Audrey straddled his leg, presenting him with her backside. She held his leg between her knees, tugged on the boot, and it thudded to the floor. She repeated with the other, and that boot joined its mate on the floor.

Boyd's hands wandered seductively over her buttocks. "You have the cutest rump I've ever seen. Why don't you take a bath with me?"

Audrey straightened, moved away and shot him a disgusted look. "In this house? Don't be ridiculous."

"We'll lock the door."

"And, of course, no one would wonder why the door was locked."

At that moment Buck charged into the room, concern written all over his face. "You okay, son?" he asked anxiously.

"Yeah, Dad, fine."

"You look like hell."

"So everyone tells me."

"Betty told us what happened. Your mother's plenty worried about you." Buck crossed the room and leveled a stern look on his son. "Have you lost your mind? Don't you know bronc bustin's for kids?"

Boyd grinned. "Reckon my memory was refreshed tonight."

Buck turned to Audrey for the first time since entering the room. "A doctor saw him?"

She nodded. "He said nothing's broken, but Boyd's supposed to get a lot of rest."

"Mmm." Buck's gaze returned to his son. "Maybe having to spend a few days in bed will teach you a lesson. Maybe next time you'll think twice before you climb up on one of those fool things. You sure you're all right?"

"Fine, Dad."

Buck appeared to have his doubts. "Let someone know if you need anything. Now, I've got to get back to our guests. I'll swear to God, I thought you, of all people, had better sense than to do something that crazy." With that he left the room.

Audrey breathed a sigh of relief. What there was about Boyd's father that kept her on edge she didn't know, but she never fully relaxed around the man.

Boyd muttered disgustedly, "Lord, you'd think I was the only guy who'd ever gotten bunged up in a rodeo. Close the door, hon, will you? I want to get undressed."

Audrey closed the door, then crossed to the bathroom. "I'll go draw the water."

Boyd's very masculine private bathroom was much larger than the one in the guest room. Audrey turned on the tub's faucet full force, checked the water temperature, then returned to the bedroom. Boyd had shed his shirt and was struggling out of his jeans and undershorts. He chuckled dryly when he saw the rise of color in her cheeks. "Nothing you haven't seen before. Why are you blushing?"

"I don't know. I...oh, Boyd...how awful!" If the sight of his magnificent nude body was unnerving, its condition was alarming. His bronze skin had turned black and blue in an astonishing number of places. "You must feel dreadful. Are you sure you want to get in that water?"

"It looks worse than it is, Audrey, and I definitely want some soap and water. I told you, I'm tough."

"You'll put something on those cuts when you get out of the tub, won't you?"

"Yes, yes. You're going to make a nagging wife. I can already see signs of it. You'd better go turn off that water before you flood the place."

Audrey turned and went back into the bathroom to shut off the faucet. Boyd came in behind her and grabbed a nearby towel rack. She held his other arm tightly as he eased down into the warm liquid. The first stinging drops elicited a violent oath. Then as he settled down, he murmured a satisfied "Ahhh!"

"You all right?" she inquired with concern. When he nodded, she released his arm and said, "Now I'll go get you that drink. But don't try to get up until I get back."

The party was still going on in the sun room. Audrey realized that the bar was in there, and she didn't particularly want to barge in on Buck and Elizabeth and their guests. Standing unnoticed at the door, she managed to catch Betty's eyes and mouth "Boyd wants a drink." Betty nodded in acknowledgment and walked to the bar, while Audrey waited in the hall.

"How's the patient?" Betty asked when she brought the drink.

"Mildly cooperative. I know he's in terrible pain, but—" she winked "—he's tough."

Betty snorted. "Yeah, aren't they all? Come and get me if you need help with him. Otherwise, I'll see you in the morning."

Returning to Boyd's room, Audrey walked to the bathroom door and listened. She heard nothing. "Are you still there?" she called.

"I'm here, and my skin's getting wrinkled. I waited in case you wanted to dry me."

"Funny man. Can you get out by yourself?"

"I'm not crippled."

"Don't forget to put something on those cuts. Can I get your pajamas for you?"

"I sleep in the raw, Audrey."

She couldn't help smiling at the growled masculine curses coming from the other side of the door. She waited until it opened. Boyd stood before her with a towel wrapped around his waist, scowling at a bottle of antiseptic in his hand. "This damned stuff hurts!"

"Poor thing. I thought you were tough."

He handed her the bottle and a wad of cotton. "You do it for me."

"All right. Go sit on the bed."

First she gingerly dabbed the gash over his eye with the medicine, then blew on it. Inching the towel up past his knee, she knelt at his feet and carefully treated his wounded leg. "I hate hurting you," she said as she heard him suck in his breath. "Believe me, it hurts me worse."

Even though absorbed in the nursing task, Audrey was acutely aware of the way he looked, of the strength in his legs, of the dark hair covering them. Without realizing she was doing it, she stroked his powerful calf muscles with her free hand. As for Boyd, he hardly noticed the antiseptic's sting, for he was intent only on the lovely woman at his feet and her gentle touch.

When Audrey was certain she had tended to all his cuts, she pressed her face into the side of his leg and kissed it. A tender fire was burning in his eyes when she recapped the bottle and glanced up. Their eyes locked together in silent communication. His gaze never wavered as he took the bottle and cotton from her and laid them on the bedside table. Placing his hands under her arms, he lifted her to sit beside him. Audrey sighed contentedly as his arms encircled her.

"Kiss me," he commanded.

She complied with sweet insistence. Their mouths fused together. The kiss was a deep, draining one, and when they parted, Audrey's mind reeled with the wonder of his power over her. All he had to do was touch her.

Boyd's hand hovered near her breasts, then closed over one and felt her expected response. Through the fabric of her shirt his fingertips molded the hardened bud. "Do you think we know each other well enough by now?"

She moaned softly. "Awfully pleased with yourself, aren't you?"

"What do you think?" His crooked smile was delightfully wicked.

"You're really terrible. Here you are, practically at death's door, and you're thinking about sex."

"You're damned right I am. Aren't you?"

"We aren't alone. I shouldn't be in here with you as it is."

"In an hour or so everyone will be asleep, and it's just a short walk from your room to mine."

"I couldn't do that, not even if we were alone. You need to rest. I might hurt you."

"I'll risk it."

Audrey's arms crept up the wall of his chest, and her hands locked behind his neck. "Boyd, promise me you'll never do anything as stupid as getting on that horse again. You could have been killed."

"You were worried."

"Of course I was worried! I was frantic."

"Good. That means you care a lot more than you want me to think you do."

She kissed him tenderly, then gazed at him with luminous eyes. "How could you doubt I care after what's happened between us?"

Cupping her face in his hands, he looked at her adoringly. "Audrey, love... this wasn't supposed to happen to me. I thought I was immune. But now that it has happened, I'm not going to waste a lot of time denying it."

Lost in each other, neither of them heard the door open. Buck's voice shattered the sweet eloquence of the moment. "Boyd, I'd..." He stopped short when he saw the couple seated on the bed. "Oh, excuse me...."

Audrey disentangled herself from Boyd's embrace and jumped to her feet so quickly she nearly lost her balance. Straightening, she stood some distance from the bed with her hands clasped tightly in front of her.

Buck looked at his son, then at Audrey and back to Boyd. "The guests have left, and your mother and I are going to bed. I thought I'd best check on you before calling it a day."

"Thanks, Dad. I'm fine."

A heavy silence fell over the room. Buck made no move to leave. Audrey didn't know why she felt so embarrassed, but she did. Something in the man's expression made her heart sink. Instinctively she realized that Buck wasn't going to leave until she did. Not knowing what else to do, she walked to the dresser and picked up the drink, then placed it on the nightstand. "I'm going to bed now, Boyd," she said stiffly. "Drink that, then be a good boy and get some rest." With as much poise as she could muster, she sailed past Buck and offered him a small smile. "Good night, Mr. Benedict."

"Good night, Audrey."

Out in the hall she put her hand to her racing heart. *That man doesn't approve of me,* she thought with certainty and dismay. *I don't know why, but he doesn't. Well, I'm not too sure I approve of him, either. So where does that leave Boyd and me?*

Unfortunately, she feared she knew the answer to that one.

CHAPTER FOURTEEN

LONG AFTER ELIZABETH had fallen asleep, Buck stood at the window of their bedroom, deep in thought. He had been surprised, to say the least, over barging in on Audrey and Boyd during what obviously had been a tender moment, and Buck wasn't fond of surprises where the family was concerned.

Contrary to what Audrey believed, however, he wasn't particularly alarmed or displeased. Now that he'd had time to think it over, he realized that the young woman from Phoenix passed all his rather rigorous criteria. She was pretty, educated, poised and charming. Elizabeth spoke highly of her, and Buck had learned to trust his wife's first impressions of people. Added to that was the fact that his own father had held Audrey in high esteem. All in all, Boyd might have made an excellent choice.

But Buck didn't like something going on that he wasn't right on top of. If his son was seriously interested in Audrey, he needed to know more about her. Perhaps a phone call to Peter Sorenson was in order. And it might be wise to have a heart-to-heart talk with Audrey herself before this thing went any further. It was imperative that she knew exactly what would be expected of her. Then Buck would decide whether to bestow his blessings on the relationship or stop it dead in its tracks.

The future, in his estimation, was much too important to be entrusted to the willy-nilly ways of young people who thought they were in love.

WHILE AUDREY was getting dressed the following morning there was a knock on her door. "Come in," she called. The door opened and Maria entered the room.

"Pardon, *señorita*," the housekeeper said shyly.

"Yes, Maria, what is it?"

"The *señor* would like to see you in his study as soon as you've had breakfast."

Although three men lived in the house, when Maria said "the *señor*" there was no question in anyone's mind to whom she referred. A tremor of trepidation swept through Audrey. A private conference with Buck Benedict was not her idea of a good way to start the day, and she didn't have to spend any time wondering what the subject under discussion would be.

However, she had anticipated something like this. Not for a minute had she thought Buck would let the cozy little scene he had stumbled upon last night go uncommented on. "Thank you, Maria," she replied calmly. "Tell Mr. Benedict I'll be along as soon as I finish dressing. I'm not really hungry this morning."

"*Sí*, very good." Maria said as she backed out of the room.

In spite of her apprehension, or possibly because of it, Audrey didn't hurry. She finished dressing and applying her makeup, then took the time to check on Boyd, who, thankfully, was dead to the world. Standing over him, her heart constricted sharply. In sleep, he looked peaceful, almost boyish, and she longed to crawl into the bed with him, to wrap her arms around him and take comfort from the feel of his body. How incredible it was to have grown so fond of him in such a short time. She had expected love, if it came to her at all, would develop gradually over months or years. Yet, for better or worse, Boyd had changed her life dramatically in two weeks. Giving herself a shake, she quietly left the room and went to Buck's study.

The door was closed. She tapped lightly, heard his summons and entered the room. The study was unlike any other room in the house. It was a cozy, completely masculine re-

treat furnished with sturdy, leather-upholstered furniture
and dominated by a massive mahogany desk. Dozens of
framed photographs and official documents lined the pan-
eled walls. Buck sat behind the desk in a chair that faced the
door. Seeing Audrey, he got to his feet and smiled. "Come
in, my dear, and have a seat. Maria tells me you haven't had
breakfast. Please, at least have some coffee and one of these
cinnamon rolls. They're very good."

A coffee service had been set up on a small table in front
of one of the windows. The smell of coffee and freshly
baked cinnamon rolls was irresistible. "Thank you," Audrey said. "That sounds wonderful."

She walked to the table, but Buck was there first, pouring coffee and putting a roll on a small plate. "The rest of
the family has brunch later on Sunday morning, but I've
never been able to sleep in, no matter what the day. I've
noticed that you're an early riser, too. I like that. Morning's the most productive part of the day."

Then, instead of motioning her to a chair, Buck slipped a
hand under Audrey's elbow and guided her around the
room, pointing out and explaining the various mementos on
the wall. "We haven't had much of a chance to visit while
you've been here, Audrey, and I regret that. I always like my
guests to leave the Triple B knowing something of its history. I'm not exaggerating when I say that the history of this
ranch parallels the history of Arizona. Here, for instance,
is the original deed to the ranch. You'll notice the date...."

Most of what he told her she already had learned from
Boyd. Still, it was interesting and the photographs were
fascinating. The Benedicts had been or were acquainted with
a lot of famous people. There were pictures of one Benedict or another with every President since Harry Truman.
Audrey made appropriate comments when they seemed
called for, but her mind was on something else altogether.
Buck appeared to be going out of his way to put her at ease.
Why?

When they had covered the room, Buck asked her to be
seated. Then he sat behind the desk once more, folded his

hands and regarded her intently. "Audrey, I hope you'll forgive my being blunt, but I'm not accustomed to small talk or beating around the bush. Unless I'm mistaken, and I don't think I am, you and my son seem to have become rather fond of each other."

Audrey had to give him credit for his direct approach. "Yes, we have. We . . . er, get along well."

"He must have been taken with you from the first."

At this Audrey had to smile. "As a matter of fact, our initial meeting was a bit on the testy side. But you can understand that, considering the circumstances that brought us together."

"Yes." Buck pursed his lips thoughtfully. "Dad's will was something of a shock to all of us, but I want you to know that no one in this family begrudges you your inheritance."

"Thank you, Mr. Benedict."

"Do you mind my asking if you and Boyd have discussed any future plans?"

"We've only known each other a couple of weeks, Mr. Benedict. I assure you things have not gone that far."

"Yes, but I know my son. I've been waiting a good dozen years—a bit impatiently, I might add—for Boyd to show some kind of unusual interest in a woman. Now he has. I don't think he's going to let any grass grow under his feet. You know, Audrey, I'm fond of thinking I'm aware of everything that goes on in this family, but this came like a bolt out of the blue. Are you certain you don't find my questioning offensive?"

"No, not at all," she said decisively, which was only a tiny white lie. Vaguely she wondered why Buck was talking to her instead of to Boyd. She also wondered what Boyd would think about this little tête-à-tête.

As if reading her mind, Buck explained, "I'm having this little chat with you, my dear, because, while Boyd is fully aware of the family structure and what is expected of him, you probably aren't. The woman my son marries will immediately take on certain obligations."

"Most wives do."

"Yes, of course, but I'm speaking of special obligations. Before I tell you what they are, I want to assure you that I have nothing against you. On the contrary, I find you a charming young woman, and you certainly are adaptable. That's very important. Also, my father obviously thought highly of you, and I trusted Dad's judgment. So if you're thinking I don't approve of your relationship with Boyd, forget it. This has nothing to do with that."

Audrey didn't understand why Buck's words had the effect of making her feel even more tense and edgy. She couldn't imagine what all this was leading to, but she was beginning to be very curious about those "special obligations." There was more to this conference than simply getting acquainted, she was sure. "Thank you," she said and waited with suspended breath.

"Like all fathers, I suppose, I have had some grand plans for my children. Parents seem to do that sort of thing in spite of better intentions. Not all of my plans have been realized. I'll confess to having been disappointed in the past. There's the matter of grandchildren, for one thing. There have been Benedicts in Arizona, in this house, for a very long time, and I'm anxious for the line to continue. Do you have any objections to motherhood?"

Good Lord, Audrey thought, *this really is a bit much!* "Not at all. I think I would love being a mother."

"Good, good. One never knows about modern young women. And, of course, Boyd's wife would be expected to do a certain amount of important entertaining, but given the job you do for us at the Greenspoint, I doubt you would find that distasteful. Peter Sorenson tells me you're a natural at that sort of thing."

Audrey's eyes widened slightly. "You've spoken to Peter about me?"

"I telephoned the hotel this morning on the chance he would be there. He was. Do you mind my asking Peter about you?"

Would it make any difference if I did? "You own the hotel, Mr. Benedict, and I work there. You have every right to
ask about my performance."

"You might enjoy knowing your employer was effusive
in his praise."

"It's not difficult to do a good job when you like your
work as much as I do."

"Indeed. But I'm wondering how the prospect of public
life would appeal to you."

"Public life?" Audrey didn't understand.

"Yes. I'd like to see Boyd go into politics."

"Does he know that?" Never once had Audrey heard
Boyd say anything to indicate he wanted to do something
other than what he was doing now.

"Well, we haven't discussed it in so many words, if that's
what you mean," Buck admitted, "but when the time
comes, I don't expect him to resist. The family has always
functioned as a single unit. What's good for one is good for
all, that sort of thing. Brent and I agree that Boyd is a natural for politics. He can charm the birds out of the trees if
he sets his mind to it. Naturally, he'll need the right kind of
wife at his side. But again, you have beauty and poise, and
you know how to deal with important people. I'm not worried on that score."

To Audrey, the term "public life" brought one thing to
mind: notoriety. She felt an unpleasant shiver race up her
spine.

"Right now," Buck went on, his eyes alive with anticipation, "I'm planning to launch Boyd's political career in
a couple of years or so. Some state office, I'm not sure
which one, but something with high visibility. We have party
connections, and his name is well-known, so I don't expect
problems. From there it should be a cakewalk to the governor's mansion."

Audrey couldn't believe it. "Mr. Benedict, are you telling me that if your plans work out, Boyd will someday
be . . . Governor of Arizona?"

Buck smiled and nodded. "Why not? And I'll confess something else to you—that's only the beginning. The next logical step is the U.S. Senate, and after that... Why not reach for the sky? Audrey, if these plans work out, someday Boyd might very well be President."

Audrey gasped. "President? You mean... of the United States?"

Buck nodded. "Again, why not? It will take some time, of course. The groundwork has to be laid. But the year 2004 will be an election year. Boyd will only be fifty-two and will have put in a goodly number of years in public service. By then his name should be a household word. Yes, I'm thinking 2004 might be the perfect time."

The revelation was so astonishing that Audrey was speechless for a minute. Then she said, "Isn't that terribly ambitious?"

"Of course it is, but it's no pipe dream. It could happen. So now you understand why I'm so interested in the young woman my son marries. The right kind of wife can be a tremendous asset to a man with political ambitions."

Or a horrible liability, Audrey thought and had not the slightest doubt into which column she belonged. "Mr. Benedict, are you...absolutely sure Boyd will want all the things you want?"

"It's more or less assumed that my offspring will follow my wishes. They never disappoint me. Or at least, almost never."

Audrey guessed the last remark was prompted by Boyd's failure to marry Linda Ames. If he had "disappointed" his father once, he might be willing to again. That hope stirred briefly. "I was led to believe you Benedicts shunned publicity."

"It's more accurate to say we like to control what's written about us. I have no objection to publicity if it's the right kind. I trust you realize the sort of life Boyd's wife would be forced to lead. Virtually every move she makes will be duly noted and commented on. Every aspect of her life will come under close scrutiny. Rarely will she awaken to a day she can completely call her own. Some women hate that sort of existence; some thrive on it. Tell me, Audrey, do you think you could cheerfully live in the goldfish bowl we tend to put our First Ladies in?''

The hope died. Whom was she kidding? She'd seen nothing to indicate that Boyd wouldn't go along with anything the family, meaning Buck, wanted him to do. If his father wanted him to be the governor or a senator or the President, he would give it his best shot. A hopeless despair washed over her for a minute, the feeling of being forced to give up something wonderful she had just found. It would have been nice, she thought, if it actually had worked out. Boyd, this house, this family. They really were a nice group of people, even the man sitting before her. Buck no longer seemed the formidable figure of authority he once had; he was just a man who took his responsibilities seriously. I could have fit in. Boyd's father and I might even have become friends.

The despair was quickly replaced by resignation, however. If nothing else, she was a practical person who accepted the inevitable.

''Well, my dear?'' Buck prompted.

Sighing, Audrey leaned forward and placed her cup and plate on the desk. Then she got to her feet. ''I'm going to be completely honest with you, Mr. Benedict. I could never live that kind of life. Not in a million years.''

Buck sat back, slightly startled. He would have understood had she expressed uncertainty; in fact, he would have been wary if she hadn't. But the last thing he had expected was a flatly negative answer. In a curious way he was disappointed. Audrey had seemed to him the kind of woman who could field whatever life threw her. ''You seem awfully sure of that.''

''I am, believe me, I am. I know my own nature. Thank you for the coffee and roll, Mr. Benedict. I really enjoyed our visit. Now, if you'll please excuse me, I . . . think I'll be leaving before the day is over. That way I can be ready for work bright and early tomorrow morning.''

"I've upset you."

"No, not really. Just brought me back to reality. It's all right if I leave, isn't it?"

"If that's what you want, Audrey, I have no objection." Buck glanced at his hands a moment, then back at her. "I'm sorry. I didn't mean to be discouraging. I simply thought it fair to warn you of what lies ahead."

"Yes, and I do appreciate it, Mr. Benedict. You'll never know how much. I'll see you again before I go."

Leaving the study, she hurried back to her room and closed the door. Squeezing her eyes shut, she fought back tears. She'd been a fool to fall for Boyd. Hadn't she always suspected it would be an unwise thing to do? One of these days she was going to have to trust her gut instincts. She'd always known that a woman with her past couldn't fit in with such a prominent family. She was certain that Buck's "controlled publicity" did not include a woman whose father had been sentenced to a federal penitentiary.

Sadly, she had to put an end to her involvement with Boyd, and it was going to be the hardest thing she'd ever done. Audrey sat on the edge of the bed, thinking and planning her next move. She couldn't tell Boyd she'd simply decided she didn't care for him. He'd never believe that.

She had to get back to the Greenspoint immediately, to put some distance between them. Oh, Boyd would follow when he was able, she was sure of it, so the break wouldn't be quick and easy. But he was a busy man and could spend only so much time in Phoenix. As the days and months passed, the visits would become fewer and farther between. Love couldn't flourish without nourishment. The thing would die a natural death.

Now, the immediate problem was telling Boyd she was leaving.

"WHAT?" BOYD ROARED, sitting up straight in bed. "Audrey, how can you even think of leaving? Look at me. I'm a beaten and broken man!"

Audrey stood by the edge of his bed, looking at his shocked face. She was determined to keep the mood light-hearted. Under no circumstances must Boyd suspect she meant this to be the beginning of a permanent break. He would get suspicious and start asking questions she dare not answer. "You just got through telling me you feel fine."

"I lied. I feel terrible. How can you desert me when I'm in this condition?"

"You wouldn't be in that condition if you hadn't been showing off."

"You have a cruel, mean streak that hasn't surfaced before."

"Look, Boyd, I'm simply going back to work, that's all. You've always known I'd have to one of these days."

"But not now. You have to stay here and nurse me back to robust health. I'll call Peter...."

"Please, don't. I've already talked to him, and he needs me. There's a big convention coming up... hardware dealers. I worked for nine months to convince them to hold their meeting at the Greenspoint, and Peter's going to expect me to be there to run the show."

"Oh, forget that damned job! You don't need it."

"Yes, I do, Boyd, but even if I didn't, I owe it to Peter to be there to run the show this week. It's not as if I'm leaving the country. I'll be three hours away."

Boyd flung back the covers, forgetting he was stark naked. "I'm going with you. Get me some clothes." But when he moved his injured leg, he groaned and fell back against the pillow.

"Don't be ridiculous," she chided, discreetly covering him again. "The doctor said you were going to feel terrible today, and you have to worry about infections and things like that. You're going to stay here and recuperate. Besides, I'm going to be so busy the next few days I wouldn't be able to spend much time with you. Please cooperate, love, and get well. I've got to go pack."

"That's it, huh? Just like that. You're sailing out of my life...."

Audrey rolled her eyes toward the ceiling. "Spare me the melodrama. I'll be back in a few minutes."

It took her less than thirty minutes to get ready to leave. She merely tossed her things into her suitcases, then sought out the rest of the family members, as well as Maria and Tina, to say goodbye and thank them for their many kindnesses. Finally she returned to Boyd's room.

He had put on a robe but still was propped in bed, and he wasn't alone. Betty was at his bedside, but the moment she realized Audrey had come to say goodbye, she hurried out of the room and shut the door. Audrey wished she hadn't. Leaving was difficult enough; she didn't want it to become emotional.

She walked to the bed, hating that subdued solemn look on Boyd's face. She held out her hand to him. He took it, but neither of them said a word for several uncomfortably long minutes.

"Ready?" he finally muttered inanely.

"Yes."

"I'd ask you to stay, but we've been through that."

"Like I said, I'm only hours away. You can telephone me anytime."

"Phone calls are highly unsatisfactory."

"I know. Please take care of yourself and get well."

He grunted. "I guess I'll have to if I'm going to be shuttling back and forth to Phoenix." He gave her hand a tug. She bent and accepted the melting kiss he placed on her mouth. "Remember that."

Audrey had to get out of there fast. "Oh, Boyd, you can be very sure I'll do that."

His eyes impaled her. "Be careful on the highway and call me the minute you get home so I'll know you arrived safe and sound."

She was getting too choked up to speak. Nodding silently, she gave his hand a squeeze, then turned and hurried out of the room.

Betty was waiting in the hall and walked her to the car. "I'm going to miss you. It's been fun, almost like having a sister. And from the look on Boyd's face a minute ago, that might come to pass one of these days."

"I wouldn't count on that, Betty. And I'm going to miss you, too. Come to Phoenix and see me one of these days."

"I just might do that."

"I'll show you the sights, we'll eat out and go shopping, all that stuff."

"Sounds like fun."

Again Audrey grappled with her conscience, thinking about Jesse, but in the end she drove away without a word, trusting that Buck's considerable influence would keep Betty out of the unscrupulous man's clutches. It was the best she could do.

CHAPTER FIFTEEN

THREE DAYS LATER Boyd sat in his bedroom brooding. He was in a rotten mood and had been ever since Audrey left. The slightest thing seemed to tee him off, something Betty had mentioned to him several times. He thought it damned peculiar that he'd never noticed what a humdrum existence he had led before Audrey came along.

He had called her every night, which probably wasn't a good idea. Hearing her voice only served to make him feel more alone and bereft. For two weeks he had been with her almost constantly; then in the blink of an eye she was gone. Of course he'd known he would miss her, but he hadn't known just how much. He reminded himself of a simmering kettle of water that had almost reached the boiling point.

From their phone conversations he'd gathered that Audrey was completely tied up with that damned convention. It was always late when he reached her at home, and she usually sounded bone-tired. He envied her the activity. His own enforced idleness coupled with her absence had him as restless and edgy as a caged tiger.

That was going to change. Today he felt much better. The swelling had gone down over his eye, the cuts were healing nicely, and the bruises would fade with time. His mind was focused on the upcoming weekend. He ought to be almost as good as new by then, and the convention would break up Friday afternoon. He was going to be in Phoenix this weekend if he had to be carried there, and he and Audrey were going to talk seriously about the future. Maybe he was rushing things, but being without her for three days had convinced him he didn't want to contemplate a life that didn't include her.

He lounged in the easy chair in his bedroom. He had done more walking today than he had since the accident, and he was genuinely tired. Deep in thought, he at first didn't notice when Betty walked into his room. Then she made some sort of noise, and he looked up. "Hi," he said.

"Hi. You're feeling better, aren't you?"

"Much."

"That's good. Got a minute?" Betty asked crisply.

"I seem to have plenty of them. What's up?"

Betty closed the door and went to sit at the foot of the bed, facing him. It was then that Boyd noticed the expression on his sister's face. She obviously was upset, and that surprised him. Betty, without a doubt, was the most serene individual he'd ever known. "Something wrong?"

"Plenty." Betty's mouth set in a tight line. "Dad and I just had 'words.' "

Boyd chuckled sympathetically. "Ah, well, you know Dad. What unpardonable goof did you commit?" He naturally assumed it had to do with the running of the ranch. To his knowledge, that was all Betty ever thought about. She'd probably made a decision Buck didn't agree with.

Betty heaved an agitated sigh. "Somehow Dad found out I've been seeing Jesse privately, and he doesn't like it a bit."

Boyd frowned. "Murdoch? How long's this been going on?"

"Months. Almost from the time he first came here."

"Well, I'll be damned! I never noticed."

"You wouldn't. You don't think of me as a woman. And for the past two weeks you haven't noticed much of anything but Audrey. Have you talked to her?"

"Every night."

"You've really fallen for her, haven't you?"

Boyd grinned. "Like the proverbial ton of bricks."

"I hope you remember who told you it would happen one of these days. That's why I thought I could talk to you, Boyd. Maybe you'll understand how I feel." Betty got to her feet and began pacing around the room. "Dad's ordered me to stay away from Jesse. No daughter of his is going to get involved with a common cowhand, not when there are so many fine, upstanding young men from good families out there. Dad wants to know why I gravitate toward the ordinary." Betty uttered a derisive snort. "I don't think I can stay away from him, Boyd. And why should I have to? Jesse wants me to marry him."

Boyd let out a low whistle. "That serious, huh?"

"Yes, that serious."

"Did you tell Dad that?"

"No, the coward in me surfaced, just like it always does when Dad gives me one of his lectures. I don't know what I'm going to do. If I keep on seeing Jesse, I'll be openly defying Dad, something I've never done. Oh, I think it's so unfair of him to put me in this position. Lord, I'm twenty-three and still under his thumb."

"To some extent we all are. That's the way things have always been done in this family."

"Tell me about it." Betty stopped pacing and went to stand in front of her brother, her eyes bright and earnest. "What . . . what do you think would happen if Jesse and I married against Dad's wishes?"

Boyd had some ideas, none of them particularly pleasant. "I'm not sure," he said carefully. Like his sister, he often thought their father sometimes put them in untenable positions, and he, too, felt that was unfair.

"I just might do it," Betty said defiantly. "I just might."

"I'd think long and hard about taking such a drastic step, if I were you. Try to be patient. I can't say I've ever regretted being patient when dealing with Dad. Sometimes he talks first and thinks later. He might come around in time."

But Betty was in no mood for patience. "Wait and see, you mean. That's so easy for you to say. Tell me, dear brother—if Dad disapproved of Audrey, if he ordered you to stay away from her, would you be willing to 'wait and see'?"

The question brought Boyd up short and made him think again of the things Skeet had told him that night at camp. He had no idea if the man named Jack Hamilton was Audrey's father, but suppose he was? What would Buck have to say about that? Boyd was only too aware of his father's preoccupation with "good" marriages for his children, and Buck had some pretty straitlaced, old-fashioned notions about what constituted "good." To date, none of his notions nor his authority had been challenged, but Boyd wondered what would happen if they were.

"Well," Betty challenged. "Would you?"

"I'm not sure. No, that's not being honest. I don't think I would wait, Betty. I'm not saying that would be the smart thing to do. I'm only saying, I don't think I could stay away from her."

"Then you must understand what I'm going through. That's the way I feel about Jesse. Dad doesn't have the right to keep us apart."

"I'm sorry, sis, I really am. I wish I could be more help to you," Boyd said, feeling terribly inadequate. Yet, he couldn't come right out and advise Betty to defy their father. "This is one time I'm not going to give you any advice. This is something you're going to have to work out for yourself, because you're the one who'll have to live with your decision."

"Yeah." Betty sighed again. "I didn't really expect you to solve the dilemma. Guess I just wanted someone to talk to. I wish Audrey was here."

"So do I."

"I'll bet you do, but I wish she was here for a much different reason. Right from the start, I could talk to her, like I'd known her for years, almost like she was a sister. Strange, huh?"

"No," Boyd replied, "not so strange. I know the feeling."

THE HARDWARE dealers' convention had been a resounding success. At the closing meeting a motion was made and passed to make the Greenspoint a yearly tradition. Audrey couldn't have been more pleased, but the work it had entailed had taken its toll on her. Not only had she had to oversee the arrangements for all the meetings and luncheons and the closing night's banquet, she had had to orchestrate the outside activities for the accompanying spouses. She had put in four straight thirteen-hour days, and she couldn't say she was sorry to see the affair wind to a close.

Late Friday afternoon, when the last of the conventioneers had checked out, she went into her office, sank wearily into the chair behind her desk and kicked off her shoes. "I feel like I could sleep for a week."

Helen was closing up for the day. "Yeah, I can imagine. You've been so busy I've hardly had a chance to talk to you. I'm dying to know about everything. In fact, I'm about to burst with curiosity. I'll buy you a drink before I go home, and we can talk."

Audrey didn't have to wonder what the "everything" Helen wanted to talk about was, and she was no more willing to talk about her inheritance now than she'd been three weeks ago. "Thanks, Helen, but will you give me a rain check? I'm pooped."

"Sure. You working this weekend?"

"No."

"Got big plans?"

"I'm not sure. Maybe." Boyd had called every night since she'd been back, and he'd vowed he would be in Phoenix by Saturday. However, she hadn't heard from him today, and something could always happen to keep him from making the trip. She had mixed emotions over the prospect of seeing him again. She missed him twice as much as she'd thought she would, and the nightly phone calls were an exquisite torment. Then she would be reminded of the necessity for making a permanent break with him and would start hoping something would prevent him from coming to Phoenix. The more time that elapsed between visits, went her theory, the easier the final break would be.

But the theory was full of holes. It would never be easy. From the phone calls she could tell that Boyd thought things were just beginning, and she suspected he would be a persistent suitor. How would she ever muster the courage to call it off? The thought of hurting him was more than she could bear, just as the thought of all that loneliness stretching before her filled her with a kind of emptying despair.

What a mess you got me in, Bert. She imagined her old friend had thought that bequest would make life easier for her. He could never have guessed it would bring on problems and complications galore.

"How about you, Helen? What's on tap for your weekend?"

The secretary shrugged. "Not much. I'll take my mom shopping tomorrow, which is always an ordeal, since she finds it so hard to part with a dollar. Then . . ."

At that moment the telephone at Helen's elbow jangled; she lifted the receiver to her ear. "Manager's office . . . Yes, sir . . . No, Mr. Sorenson has gone for the weekend. Yes, sir . . . Well, I'm very sorry, but perhaps in the meantime you could take a shower. . . . Yes, sir, right away." Replacing the receiver, Helen shot Audrey a disgusted look. "Some guy in the Durango Suite is pitching a walleyed fit and wants to see the manager this minute! He says the stopper in one of the bathtubs doesn't work."

Audrey groaned. "Oh, for Pete's sake!"

"You heard me suggest he take a shower. He said he always takes a shower, but when he pays two hundred and fifty bucks a night for a room he expects everything to work, and he's pretty steamed that it doesn't."

"One of those, huh? Takes all kinds to fill up a world."

"You look so tired. Why don't you scoot out of here? I'll sic the night manager on our disgruntled guest."

Audrey stuffed her feet into her shoes and stood up. "I'm going to take you up on that. Good night, Helen. Give Maintenance a call before you leave and have a good weekend."

"You, too, Audrey."

Halfway home Audrey remembered the depleted state of her refrigerator, so, as tired as she was, she suffered through the usual Friday night mob at the supermarket. It was after seven when she finally unlocked her apartment door. Just as she pushed it open, a figure stepped out of the shadows in the hallway, startling her so much she almost dropped the sack of groceries. Wide-eyed with fright, she whirled around and found herself staring into a pair of familiar smoke-colored eyes. "Boyd!"

"Hello, love. Allow me." Relieving her of the groceries, he pushed her inside, kicked the door shut and set the sack on the nearest table. Then in a fluid motion he pulled her into a strong embrace. After giving him a long, thorough kiss that took her breath away, he held her at arm's length, his eyes sweeping her from head to toe. "Let me look at you. I'll swear you've gotten more beautiful."

"Oh, Boyd," she breathed in a shaky voice, "you said Saturday. Why didn't you let me know you were coming?"

"I suddenly decided about three hours ago that I couldn't wait until tomorrow, and I knew the chances of reaching you by phone were slim. So I just got in the car and headed this way." He paused and the smile on his face faded. "It's all right, isn't it? You said the convention would be over. You don't have plans for tonight, do you?"

"No, no." She touched the cut over his eye. It had just about healed. "How are you? You said you were doing fine, but I don't trust you to tell me the truth."

"Honest, I'm fine." He executed a little dance step. "See, almost as good as new. Miss me?"

"Yes," she admitted truthfully. "Very much." At that moment Audrey conveniently decided the break would have to be a gradual thing...very gradual. Going back into his arms, she kissed him tenderly and settled pliantly against him. "I'm so glad you're here."

"I'm glad I'm here, too. For five days I've been a man with a problem. All the time I was sailing down that high-way I was making plans. I intend being here for breakfast in the morning." His eyes smoldered. "How does that sound?"

"Do you have to ask?" Audrey pushed all problems to the back of her mind. Their hips locked together, and her memories stirred. The familiar scent of his after-shave filled her nostrils. She laid her cheek against the smooth fabric of his shirt and smiled like a contented child. "You feel so-o-o good."

His hands moved downward to cup her buttocks and pull her up to meet him. "Yes, I definitely have a problem, and I think we'd better go into the bedroom and solve it right away."

Audrey's breath escaped in a part moan, part sigh. "That seems like the only sensible thing to do." Reluctantly she stepped back. "But first, those groceries have to go in the refrigerator."

The task was accomplished quickly. When Boyd closed the refrigerator door after the last of the food had been stored, he turned to her, and she glided back into his arms. "Now, where were we?" he asked.

"On the way to the bedroom, as I recall."

"Lead the way. I'm right behind you."

Boyd had to make a conscious effort to calm himself. If he didn't, what would follow would come close to ravishment. His fingers shook as he unbuttoned his shirt and unzipped his pants. The sound of Audrey's clothes being discarded intensified his desire. He supposed he should go to her and undress her slowly, layer by layer, but neither of them needed foreplay. Five days apart had been all the enticement they needed.

Somehow they both were naked and under the covers. As wonderful as Boyd's lovemaking had been before, Audrey thought it even more so that night. Tender at first, and so beautiful she wanted to cry, it grew strong and urgent, the great, hungry rhythms driving them with mind-boggling passion. The mutual climax was explosive, shattering, indescribable ecstasy. Mutual. That's the wonder of it, she thought as she lay weak and numb in his arms. Her mind drifted somewhere between dreams and reality, and she clung to him with what little strength she had left, dreading the moment when she would have to release her hold on him.

How on earth am I ever going to end it? He's everything I ever dreamed of, longed for. It isn't fair.

"Are you asleep?" Boyd's quiet voice penetrated the sensuous fog.

"No."

"You were so quiet."

She shifted, seeking a more comfortable position. "I was thinking."

"About what?"

"Oh . . . everything and nothing."

Rolling over, he propped on his elbow and looked down at her. "I've hated every damned minute of this week. Audrey, we have to talk."

"Not now."

"Yes, now. Listen, hon, I know you have qualms about this, and I think I understand. It's happened pretty fast. But I don't have any doubts at all, none. I'm awfully old to be falling in love for the first time, but I'm so sure this is right for both of us."

Audrey closed her eyes for a moment, then opened them and gazed at him lovingly. "Maybe that's what bothers me. Most men your age have been in and out of love half a dozen times. How can you trust that what you feel for me is really love? You don't have anything to compare it with."

"I don't know. I just do. There's been a good, sound reason for just about everything I've done in my life, and when you think about it, that's pretty damned dull. Maybe the fact that I fell head over heels in love with you practically at first sight is precisely why I trust this. I didn't think love was ever going to happen to me. Now that it has, I'm impatient."

Audrey traced the outline of his mouth with the tip of her forefinger. "And that's a mistake."

Boyd's head went back to the pillow. He drew her into the circle of his arm, but his mind whirled with a jumble of thoughts. Something was wrong or, at least, not quite right, but he couldn't pinpoint what it was exactly. He was pretty confident that Audrey cared for him as deeply as he cared for her, but for some reason she was reluctant to give in to her feelings completely. He didn't know what was bothering her, but he did know that something pretty complicated was going on in that head of hers.

But he would try to get to the bottom of it later. Right now he was a very contented man. Feeling her stretched out beside him erased the emptiness of the past week and left him sated with happiness. Brushing her temple with his lips, he asked, "Hungry?"

"Um-hmm. I was too busy to do more than grab a milk shake at lunch. I could eat a horse." Sitting up, Audrey hugged the sheet around her breasts. "However, I'm afraid we'll have to settle for the deli stuff I got at the store."

Throwing the covers aside, Boyd swung his legs off the bed, stepped into his trousers and slipped on his shirt without bothering with shoes and underwear. "Sounds fine to me. Now that I think about it, I'm close to starving myself."

AN HOUR OR SO LATER they had finished dinner and were sitting on the sofa, sipping the last of their wine, when Audrey thought to inquire about the rest of the family. "How are your folks?"

"Fine."

"And Betty? I miss her."

Boyd turned serious. "Betty's not so fine, I'm sorry to say."

"Oh? What's wrong?"

"It seems my sister has gone and gotten involved with one of the ranch hands. You remember Jesse Murdoch, don't you? Somehow word got around to Dad, as it usually does. He's not happy about the relationship, and that's putting it mildly. Things have been a little touchy around the house for the past few days.''

Audrey raised her glass to her lips, and her heart skipped a beat. This was exactly what she had hoped.

"I don't know what's going to come of all this. Apparently Betty and Dad had another row last night. She came to my room in tears . . . first time I've seen her cry since she was a kid. She swears she's going to marry the man, no matter what. Once they're married, goes her theory, what can Dad do?''

"What does your mother think of all this?''

Boyd chuckled. "Whatever Dad does. I'm trying to stay the hell out of it, but I've never seen my sister so determined. She just might marry Jesse, who knows?''

Dismayed, Audrey set her glass on the coffee table and stared across the room for a minute. Betty was just too nice a person; Audrey's conscience finally won the battle. "Don't let her, Boyd.''

"What?''

"Betty thinks the world of you and really cares what you think of her. Maybe she'll listen to you. Don't let her marry the man. It would be the worst mistake of her life.''

He stared at her, deeply puzzled. "Hon, why would you say that? You don't know a thing about Jesse.''

"Yes, I do. I knew him years ago.''

"Years ago? You knew him in Texas?''

"Yes. He . . . used to work for my father. Please take my word for it and don't ask too many questions. Jesse Murdoch is a scoundrel.''

"He must have recognized you.''

"Oh, he did.''

"Yet neither of you gave the slightest inclination you'd known each other before.''

"No, which makes me only a bit less of a scoundrel than Jesse. You see, I've known about Betty's involvement with him since my first day at the ranch, and I chose to say nothing. I could tell you I did that because Betty swore me to secrecy, but . . . that wouldn't be the truth.''

Boyd felt his muscles tighten. He noticed the way Audrey's eyes shifted away from him, the firm set to her mouth. Something about this turn of conversation disturbed her. It wasn't much, but it was his first glimpse into her past, and though she'd asked him not to question her, he had to. He set his glass beside hers on the coffee table, then turned and took her hands in his. "Audrey, I wish you would tell me about your life before you came to Phoenix. I've always known there was something you wanted to keep hidden, but I love you, and I think I have the right to know all about you."

Audrey looked down at their entwined hands, studied the crisp dark hairs on the back of his. It was a comforting sight. She thought of walking hand in hand through life with him, and her heart ached. Words wouldn't come.

"Audrey?"

"Yes."

"I wish you would trust me enough to talk to me. Whatever it is can't be that bad."

Confusion assailed her. How little he knew. Once he heard the truth, he'd realize, as she did, that they couldn't have a future together. That was what made it so damned hard to tell him. It would have been nice to make the magic last a little longer.

But that was selfish and dishonest. Boyd deserved to hear the story. Then he would know the inevitable split had nothing to do with her feelings for him, and she at least could prevent Betty from making a disastrous mistake.

However, she wondered if she actually could get it out. Everything had been bottled up for so long, and it wasn't the kind of thing anyone would relish telling.

"I . . . don't know where to start."

"The beginning's always a good place," Boyd said gently.

Audrey settled back against the cushions, tucked her feet under her and began talking. Surprisingly, once she began, she couldn't stop. It all tumbled out, and with the telling came a great loosening within, the releasing of a burden. Her voice was flat and monotonous, and she felt as though she was relating a story she had seen on television or read in a magazine, something that had nothing to do with her.

CHAPTER SIXTEEN

"I WAS BORN with the proverbial silver spoon in my mouth," she began.

"I would have bet on it," Boyd said.

"It was my paternal grandfather who started it all. He owned a company that manufactured aircraft parts, and he made a fortune during World War Two. He died at a relatively young age, and that made my father a very young millionaire. Then, not long after I was born, the company came up with a gadget that could sense the temperature of fuel. They called it FP44, patented it and sold it to the air force and navy to use on their jet airplanes. Since the company was the only source for the device, the income from FP44 was enormous."

"I can imagine," Boyd murmured.

"I led an idyllic life. We had a beautiful home in Dallas, another one on the Gulf Coast and a ranch. It wasn't anything like the Triple B, of course, but it was a working ranch, a basic cow-calf operation. That ranch was my favorite place on earth. I could ride a horse long before I could ride a bicycle."

"I would have bet on that, too. From the beginning I suspected that you had either lived on a ranch or spent a lot of time on one."

Audrey looked at him in mild surprise. "Really?"

"Really. You ride too well, for one thing. And you never asked enough questions. Most real greenhorns are curious as hell when they get on a ranch for the first time. And there was the time you handled the wounded calf without flinching. Just a lot of things made me think ranch life wasn't entirely foreign to you."

She nodded and sighed. "My mother hated the tomboy in me. She worked so hard to turn me into a lady. I was sent to the finest schools. She took me all over Europe and the Far East and taught me all the social graces. I guess I was something of a pampered princess, and I might very well have grown up to be a real snob if it hadn't been for the down-to-earth influence of the ranch. If there are disadvantages to growing up with a lot of money, I didn't know about any of them."

"That kind of life is pretty far removed from being the assistant manager of a hotel," Boyd commented, alive with interest. "Even a hotel as classy as the Greenspoint."

"I know. Sometimes it amazes me that I was able to make the transition at all. It wasn't easy at first."

"What happened, hon?"

Audrey struggled with her memories. "It was about five years ago when everything started coming apart. One day, out of the blue, some FBI agents showed up in Dad's office with a search warrant. Someone had called over the Fraud, Waste and Abuse Hotline. Dad was accused of fraud on the FP44 contract. The informant claimed he was keeping two sets of books and charging the government far more than the actual cost of manufacturing the gadget. Naturally, Dad pleaded innocent. He acted downright indignant, in fact, but after an investigation that went on for months, the federal attorney took the case to the grand jury and got an indictment. The trial lasted two months and was a nightmare for Mom and me."

She faltered at this point, and it was on the tip of Boyd's tongue to tell her to forget it since the revelation obviously was so painful for her. He couldn't, though; he was too fascinated.

Taking a deep breath, Audrey continued. "The defense based its case on Dad's reputation and character, on his wealth and 'good works.' Why, our attorney kept asking the court, would a man of Jack Hamilton's stature steal from the government and jeopardize a contract that brought his company millions of dollars a year? There simply was no motive. Dad could have conducted business like a straight-arrow saint and made more money than he ever could spend.''

"I was thinking the same thing," Boyd said.

"So did everyone else at first. Public sentiment ran strongly in Dad's favor for a long time. Then the federal attorney dropped his bombshell. The government's investigation revealed that years before, unknown to anyone, especially Mom and me, Dad's business had been on the verge of bankruptcy due to some bad debts and unfulfilled contracts. He had gotten overextended at the bank, and he had poured money into the ranch. In turn, it made almost nothing. Meanwhile, Mom and I were living like the millionaires we thought we were. I can't even imagine how much money it must have taken to keep up that life-style.''

Audrey paused and frowned. "I also can't imagine why Dad didn't tell us. Maybe he thought his financial troubles would diminish him in our eyes, but he should have told us. We could have tightened our belts and maybe none of it ever would have happened. It was all so useless.''

Her voice trailed off. Boyd patted her hand in a sympathetic gesture; she collected herself and went on. "Anyway, Dad miraculously had come up with a great deal of money to plow back into the business until it was financially solvent again. This was just about the time the alleged fraud began taking place. The evidence against him just mounted and mounted. In the meantime, a government audit of the company had been going on, and its figures indicated that Dad had been defrauding the government out of approximately a million dollars a year for ten years.''

Boyd expelled a ragged breath. "Ten million?''

"Yes, ten million. Then the prosecution produced a surprise witness, Dad's comptroller. As it turned out, he had been in on the scheme. He was terrified of going to jail, and he confessed everything, even turned over the second set of books in return for immunity from prosecution. That pretty well iced the cake. The fraud had been so skillful, so clever, it might never have been discovered if it hadn't been for the informant. The verdict, of course, was guilty.''

Boyd was silent and tense. So Skeet's information had been correct. He'd always harbored the suspicion it would be. He couldn't take his eyes off Audrey. In one way he was sorry he had asked about her past. None of this was any of his business, nor did it have any bearing on the future and what they'd found together.

However, he had asked, and now that she'd begun talking, it was as though a dam had burst to let the river flow through. Boyd didn't dare speak for fear the river would dry up. Apparently Audrey needed to talk about it.

"The whole thing was awful, and it killed my mother," she said stoically. "She had been an absolute rock throughout the trial. No one had been more confident of acquittal than she, but when the comptroller confessed, she broke down. Mom had had high blood pressure for years. She had a stroke the night the guilty verdict came in and died a few days later." Her voice turned wistful. "She was the gentlest person I've ever known, a lady down to her fingertips. I don't think she ever did an ungracious thing in her life. Your mother reminds me of her.''

If Boyd remembered right, Skeet had told him that Jack Hamilton never made it to prison. He'd never felt so much for anyone as he felt for Audrey at that moment, but he seemed to be held in the grip of a morbid fascination. He had to know everything, whether he had the right to or not. "Your father, hon . . . did he go to prison?''

Audrey wiped at her eyes, but when she removed her hands her eyes still were dry. "He was sentenced, but he never got there. He had some sleeping pills the doctor had given him while the investigation was going on. He . . . took a handful of them and died of heart failure.''

Boyd was astonished that she could talk about it at all, much less talk about it in that unemotional monotone. "Audrey, what about you? What was happening to you all this time?''

"You can imagine the notoriety," she said dully. "Back
i Texas my father was almost as well-known as yours is
ere. The press hounded us for months. My mother's fu-
eral was turned into a circus. The day Dad killed himself,
couple of reporters tried to force their way into the house.
he servants and I were literally prisoners. The cook
ouldn't go to the grocery store, and I couldn't go to work.
Iy boss was wonderful about it at first, but finally, out of
airness to him, I quit... over the phone. I didn't even go
ack to clean out my desk. One of the women in the office
ailed my personal things to me."

"No wonder you reacted the way you did when I men-
oned the media."

Audrey nodded. "We finally had to have police protec-
on, and one of the policemen did our shopping for us. On
op of everything, none of our lifelong 'friends' came
round."

"But why?" Boyd exclaimed. "You hadn't done any-
ing."

She turned to him with the saddest pair of eyes he had
ver seen. "Boyd, I'm glad you've never been in a position
o learn how people can behave when the chips are down.
ou'd be surprised how many of them honestly believe that
ie apple doesn't fall far from the tree."

He shook his head slowly. He couldn't even imagine the
normity of all she'd been through. He doubted he would
ave survived it as well as she had. Now he could add tre-
iendous admiration to his love for her. "So you left Dal-
s then?"

"No, not right away. The furor eventually died down, and
began hoping I could return to some sort of normal exis-
nce. But there was another shock in store—the small mat-
r of income tax evasion. Dad had made roughly ten
illion dollars more than he'd reported. His estate
wed... oh, I can't remember, some enormous sum, far
tore than was available, since the legal fees were astro-
omical. Part of the sentence had been to prohibit the com-
any from ever doing business with the government again,

so that put it under. The ranch was confiscated, then th[e]
houses, just about everything I thought was mine.''

"By that time I was numb. I began having terrible head[-]
aches and stomach upsets. My whole system just went ou[t]
of kilter. What was worse was my mental state. I began t[o]
despise the father I'd always loved so much. Our famil[y]
doctor feared I was on the verge of a nervous breakdown[,]
and he urged me to go away and start over again some[-]
where else. But I didn't have the slightest idea how to g[o]
about doing that. I was twenty-three and had never had t[o]
hang up my own clothes or boil water. Suddenly I had n[o]
one, and very little money, just a small savings account Da[d]
had opened for me when I was in school. To this day I don'[t]
know what I would have done if my friend's phone ca[ll]
hadn't come when it did.''

"The friend in Phoenix?''

She nodded. "I guess she was too far removed from th[e]
scene to feel 'tainted' by our friendship. She asked me t[o]
stay with her until I could get my head on straight. It was [a]
godsend. After a few months in Phoenix my health re[-]
turned, I took the temporary job at the hotel, and the res[t]
you know.'' She sighed, emotionally drained. "For some[-]
one who'd never given a dollar a thought, I did pretty well[.]
I learned to take care of myself, to pinch pennies and mak[e]
do or do without. I discovered there's a great deal of per[-]
sonal satisfaction in becoming self-sufficient. My life wa[s]
wonderfully uneventful until the day you showed up wit[h]
that incredible news about Bert's will.''

Boyd felt almost as drained by the account as she was. H[e]
put his arms around her and hugged her tenderly, momen[-]
tarily too overcome to speak. Then he remembered what ha[d]
gotten this conversation started in the first place. "Audre[y,]
what did Jesse Murdoch have to do with all this?''

"He was the FBI informant.''

"Jesse?''

"Yes, Jesse,'' she said bitterly. "He worked on our ranc[h]
as I told you. It seems Dad and his comptroller held the[ir]
secret planning sessions there, in a small office located a[t]

one end of the bunkhouse. That was where the second set of books was kept. That was how cleverly they covered their bases. If anything happened, there was no evidence in Dad's offices or in any of our houses, and who would think to look in the bunkhouse? Anyway, Jesse accidentally overheard part of a conversation between Dad and the comptroller, just enough to arouse his curiosity. Being the kind of man he is, he nosed around until he found those books. They didn't mean much to him, but he suspected something shady was going on. From that time on he merely kept his eyes and ears open. He'd known about the double-dealing for a long time before he went to the law."

"What made him finally decide to do it?" Boyd asked.

Audrey averted her eyes for a moment. This was going to be the hardest part of the whole ordeal, telling Boyd she'd once had the bad sense to think she was in love with Jesse. It was like owning up to some terrible weakness of character, and Boyd's opinion of her had become the most important thing in the world.

Still she had come this far; she really had no choice but to go on. Somehow she managed to tell him everything she knew about Jesse, concluding with, "He turned my father in out of spite, nothing else. Dad fired him at my request, and Jesse's parting shot was a visit to the authorities. I'm not saying Dad shouldn't have been punished, but Jesse's motives were something less than admirable."

It came as something of a shock to Boyd to hear Audrey say she once had been in love with the man his sister wanted to marry. The shock passed quickly, however. That had all happened so long ago, and it was to Audrey's credit that she had sent him packing the moment she'd learned his true colors.

"You can't let Betty marry him, Boyd, you just can't!" Audrey exclaimed fervently. "Please call her and tell her not to do anything foolish."

Boyd agreed that Betty would be making a terrible mistake if she married Jesse, but how was he going to prevent it? He certainly wasn't going to be the one to repeat Audrey's story; that would be betraying a confidence. But without that story, his pleas to his sister would fall on deaf ears. Betty would simply think he was acting on their father's behalf.

Getting to his feet, he shoved his hands into his pockets and walked to the terrace door, deep in thought. Suddenly he turned to Audrey. "I'm not sure she'll listen to me, Audrey. She's got her heart and mind set on marrying the man. But I'll bet she'd believe you if you told her everything you've just told me."

Twisting around, Audrey fastened pleading eyes on him. "Do you have any idea how difficult that would be for me? Can you imagine what your father would think?"

Boyd returned to sit beside her. "Tell Betty in confidence. No one else has to know about this."

Audrey rubbed her temples and thought carefully before speaking. "The story might help Betty, but it won't do a thing for us."

"What are you talking about?"

"Boyd, listen to me. I know you want to believe that you and I have a future together, but now that you know the whole story, I'm sure you realize it's impossible."

Boyd sat back and eyed her quizzically. "No, I don't realize that at all! What are you saying, Audrey? Surely you don't think I feel any less for you because of something your father did. No one else has to know a thing about any of this...no one but Betty, of course, and she'd never tell anyone."

"You're not thinking straight, my love. What about all your father's plans for you? People in the public eye can't afford family skeletons. It would all come out, believe me. I'd be nothing but an embarrassment to you when you run for governor."

He looked at her as though she was speaking a foreign language. "When I do what?"

"Your father and I had a long private talk the day I left the ranch."

"Oh? This is news to me. Suppose you tell me what the talk was about."

"You, mostly. You and your future. You see, he was beginning to suspect there was something going on between us. After that scene he stumbled onto in your room the night of your accident, I'd think it strange if he didn't suspect it. He wanted me to know what I was getting into."

Boyd's eyes narrowed. So this was the complicated something going on in Audrey's head. What the devil had his old man said to her? It galled him no end that his dad had talked to Audrey. Buck B. Benedict was not yet in charge of the world, in spite of what the man himself thought. He doubted that the private talk had been pleasant for Audrey. Talks with his father seldom were.

"This is very interesting. Suppose you tell me what you'd be 'getting into,' other than the love affair of the century."

"Please, be serious. Your father told me about his plans for you—first a high-visibility state office, then governor, maybe the U.S. Senate . . . and eventually the presidency."

Boyd almost choked. "Presidency!" he roared. "Are you talking about . . . the White House, Washington, D.C.?"

Audrey nodded solemnly. "In 2004, I think he said. Boyd, a woman with my background cannot be First Lady of the land!"

He stared at her for a split second, disbelieving. Then when he saw that she was completely serious, that she was indeed relating something his father had actually said, he fell into a fit of convulsive laughter. Audrey had never seen Boyd really amused, and the sight was something to behold. The laughter began deep in his chest, rumbled up and spilled out. He fell back against the sofa's cushions and laughed so hard his entire body shook. Twice he tried to collect himself, only to begin laughing again. Audrey thought it would never end.

Finally he was able to compose himself enough to speak. "God a'mighty, I've got to hand it to Dad. When he dreams he doesn't waste time on the penny-ante stuff. The presidency yet!" Then something occurred to him. "Audrey, was Dad the reason for your hasty departure last Sunday?"

"Yes. He was very nice, but once he told me about his political plans for you, I knew I was going to have to put an end to... us. I thought it would die a natural death, since we'd be apart so much. Then you showed up tonight, and it was as though we'd never been separated." Her shoulders rose and fell in a forlorn gesture.

Boyd took one of her hands, kissed its palm and held it against his cheek. "Listen to me, hon, and believe what I say. I am not, repeat not, going to be governor of Arizona, much less President of the United States."

"I'm sure you mean that now, but I've seen the way your family operates. Your father calls the shots. If he wants you to be the governor... You once told me you do what he wants you to do."

"But that's because he's never asked me to do anything I didn't want to do. I do not want to run for public office, period. It's not my thing. Now, can you imagine a President who didn't want to be President?" He then gave her a smile that melted her insides. "Besides, even if I wanted it, I'd want you more."

For the first time during that highly emotional evening, Audrey felt tears welling. "Oh, Boyd... you say the nicest things."

"No more talk about putting an end to us, hear? We've just begun, Audrey, and it's going to be the stuff syrupy novels are made of."

"It... doesn't seem possible. I've been alone so long."

"But no more. Now you have me to bounce off of." He gave her a quick kiss, then looked at his watch. "It's still early. Call Betty."

Audrey grimaced. "I really hate to, you know. She's liable to tell me to mind my own business."

"I know, and if she does... well, then we'll decide our next move. But I'm afraid you'll never forgive yourself if you don't warn her."

"You're right, of course, but I'm not going to tell her anything I don't think I absolutely have to. Okay?"

"Sure." Boyd dialed the number and got his sister on the phone. He didn't waste time with small talk. He merely asked Betty to hold on, then handed the receiver to Audrey. "She sounds like she's been crying," he whispered.

"Betty?" Audrey asked anxiously.

"Hi, Audrey," Betty said dispiritedly.

"You sound awful."

"I've just had a big fight with Dad. That can ruin anyone's day."

"Betty, I hope I'm not being presumptuous, but...Boyd tells me you and Jesse are talking about getting married right away."

"Yeah." Betty made a sound of contempt. "Dad doesn't approve, of course. Now he's threatening to fire Jesse if I don't put this 'nonsense' out of my head. I tell you I've had it, Audrey! I'm plain fed up. Dad can disown me for all I care. I'm going to marry Jesse and that's that!"

Audrey took a deep breath and tried to interrupt, but Betty started raving. "Granddad left me a small trust fund, and Jesse has some money saved. Between the two of us we can afford a small parcel of land. I don't mind starting on a shoestring. Money doesn't mean all that much to me, and I don't give a flip for the prestige that goes with being a Benedict. As a matter of fact, it might be nice to be Betty Nobody for a change. All I want is to marry Jesse."

"Oh, Betty, I wish you would give that some thought. I think...no, I know you'll be making a dreadful mistake if you go against your father's wishes."

"Audrey, please, not you, too. I'm up to here with my father's wishes!"

"But I have something I need to tell you. You see, I..."

At that moment, however, something went pop inside Audrey's head. "Have you told Jesse this?"

"About defying Dad, you mean? No, I haven't. Unfortunately, Jesse seems to think he'll be welcomed into the fold with open arms. I just haven't had the heart to tell him it isn't so."

"I see." Audrey's mind whirled. "You know something, I think you should tell Jesse exactly what you just told me—the business about starting out on a shoestring and all. He might like knowing how you feel about money and being a Benedict. I think you should tell him everything."

"Really? Why?"

"I'll...ah, explain later. Will you do that? Right away?"

"Well...I don't understand, but...I guess so, if you think it's a good idea."

"Boyd and I will be there tomorrow."

"Hey, that's great!"

"Promise you won't do anything rash until we get there."

"Okay, Audrey. It's going to be good having you around again. I know you'll be on my side, and I damned sure could use a friendly face. Mom and Sara are no help at all."

That remark made Audrey cringe. For a moment she felt a little on the devious side herself, then quickly remembered she was doing it only for Betty's own good. "I'll see you tomorrow. Don't do anything until you talk to me." Hanging up, she turned to a puzzled Boyd.

"What was all that about?" he asked. "You didn't tell her a thing."

"I know, but maybe, just maybe... It would be so much better for Betty to find out for herself what a self-serving louse Jesse is."

"I don't understand."

"I know that, too. Let's just wait and see, okay? Betty's promised not to do a thing until we get there."

He shrugged and reached for her, drawing her into his arms. "I suspect that this is some sort of womanly reasoning that a dense male isn't even supposed to understand." He felt Audrey melt against him. "Tired?" he asked solicitously.

"Exhausted."

"Want to go to bed?"

"Um-hmm!"

Releasing her, Boyd bent and swept her off her feet. Audrey relaxed in the cradle of his arms as he carried her to bed. She had gotten a lot off her mind tonight, and the disburdening effect was wonderful, but in reality nothing concrete had been settled. There still was the problem of her past versus Buck B. Benedict. It wasn't realistic to hope Boyd's father would never hear about Jack Hamilton. Tomorrow when they got to the ranch, if Betty remained determined to marry Jesse, Audrey was going to have to tell her about the man, and there was no question in her mind what Jesse's next move would be. He would tell everyone within earshot about her father. As she well knew, Jesse was a man who liked getting his revenge.

But worrying about that could wait for tomorrow. She was so tired she was only dimly aware of Boyd setting her on her feet, slipping the robe off her shoulders and guiding her between the smooth sheets. Enough was enough for one day.

CHAPTER SEVENTEEN

THE FOLLOWING MORNING Boyd woke to an unfamiliar but decidedly pleasant sensation—the feel of Audrey's smooth, lithe body dovetailed into his. For long minutes he lay as still as a stone, not wanting to move for fear of disturbing her. She still slept soundly. Last night she had fallen asleep the minute her head hit the pillow, and she had hardly moved since. He knew that because his own sleep had been so fitful. Though he wouldn't have admitted it to Audrey, he was more than a little worried about what today held in store for them. If she was forced to reveal her past in order to save Betty from a disastrous mistake, things might get unpleasant. There was no need to wonder what Buck's reaction to the story would be.

Not that I give a damn, Boyd thought. But he knew Audrey would, and at the moment she was his only concern. No more pain and unhappiness for her. He wouldn't have believed it possible to love someone as much as he loved her. At last he had found a special woman who was more important than family or work, and nobody was going to come between them, least of all Buck Benedict.

But Boyd wasn't stupid. Saying he would openly defy his father if necessary and actually doing it were two entirely different things. Habits of a lifetime weren't easily broken. Plus, there was Audrey and her feelings to consider. He wouldn't dream of forcing her into a situation where she would feel unwanted and uncomfortable.

Well, wasn't he supposed to be the diplomat in the family? This might test his capabilities to the limit. Lying there, Boyd decided it was time to have a long talk with his father.

He probably should have done it before now. Buck was going to have to understand what Audrey meant to him, and while he was at it, he would forever lay to rest the absurd political ambitions his father had for him. All he wanted out of life was to continue doing what he was doing, only now with Audrey by his side.

She stirred beside him just then, and everything else was forgotten. He buried his face in her hair, sniffing its clean scent. "Good morning," he said.

"Good morning," she murmured drowsily. "Mmm, this is nice."

"This is the first time we've spent the night together. I could get used to it. Want to make it a habit?"

"Mmm."

"May I assume that means yes?"

"Mmm." Audrey was waking by slow degrees. She stretched luxuriously, slithering her body along the length of his in an unconsciously erotic maneuver. Boyd's responses stirred immediately. Tightening his hold on her, he showered light kisses across her shoulders and back. She shivered and uttered a little giggle. "Do you always sleep so soundly?" he asked.

"Just about. It comes from hard work, a clear conscience and all that."

Rolling her over, Boyd threw a leg across her stomach, effectively imprisoning her. "I've been awake off and on for hours. A time or two the urge to rouse you was strong. I was amazed at my own willpower, but you just looked too peaceful to be disturbed."

"Admirable of you."

"Are you good and awake now?"

"Um-hmm."

"Want to play house?"

"You're a sex maniac!"

"Nice, huh?"

Her arms slid up his chest and wound around his neck. "I really do have a lot to do before we get on the road."

He moved over her. "So let's make love and get the day off to a great start."

THOUGH AUDREY OFFERED to follow him to the ranch in her own car, Boyd refused, explaining that it would give him a good excuse to return to Phoenix with her for another night. Several hours later they were heading south out of Tucson toward the valley. It was a beautiful day. The sun was shining, the temperature was in the high sixties, and Audrey was sure she'd never seen Boyd in better spirits. It occurred to her that his sunny good mood might very well change before the day was over, but she quickly pushed the thought aside. She wasn't going to borrow trouble, and she was confident she and Boyd together could handle anything that came along.

So, in spite of a vague uneasiness, she was feeling pretty good herself. Loving and being loved in return did wonders for one's disposition, she was discovering. And as they neared the ranch, she was overcome by a sense of coming home again. Three weeks ago she had barely been aware of the valley's existence; now she was thinking how nice it would be to grow old here.

When they pulled up and stopped in front of the house, the dogs barked, as usual, and Jorge greeted them, also as usual. But inside the house things were strangely quiet. "I can't believe no one's watching a ball game on Saturday afternoon," Boyd said with a frown.

They wandered in and out of rooms, looking for someone, anyone, but they couldn't find a soul. Finally Maria appeared and explained that Buck, Elizabeth, Brent and Sara had decided to spend the weekend in Flagstaff. Audrey breathed a sigh of relief over that news. Whatever happened, at least Boyd's father wouldn't be in the center of it, not yet.

"Where's Betty?" Boyd asked the housekeeper.

Maria shrugged. "*No se*. I haven't seen her in . . . oh, in hours, not since breakfast."

"She wasn't here for lunch?"

"No. I'm sure she hasn't been back here since very early this morning."

Audrey shot an anxious glance in Boyd's direction. What if her little scheme had backfired? "Isn't that strange for Saturday?" she asked.

"Not really," he replied. "Any number of things could have come up. Maybe she just went into Agua Linda or to Tucson for shopping."

"But she knew we were coming."

Boyd turned back to Maria. "Has anything...er, unusual happened around here since I left yesterday?"

Maria fastened a blank stare on him. In the way of long-time servants, the woman was aware of just about everything that transpired in the household, yet she pretended to be aware of nothing. When the situation demanded, she also could conveniently forget English, which she spoke and understood as well as Boyd did. *"No comprendo, señor,"* she responded with a childlike innocence.

Boyd smiled. "All right, Maria. If you see Betty, tell her we're looking for her."

"Si," Maria nodded and scurried away.

"*'No comprendo,'*" Boyd explained to Audrey, "means 'I know but I'm not telling.' I'm betting there's been another blowup between Betty and Dad. She's either off somewhere licking her wounds or getting revenge. Let's just hope only hurt feelings are involved here. Maybe we should check her room."

Betty's room looked in order. At least there were no signs that she'd packed anything, which was mildly reassuring. "We're probably making a big deal out of nothing," Boyd said with a noticeable lack of conviction. "She'll show up before long. I'm going to get a beer. Want one?"

"No, thanks."

They went into the sun room. Boyd took a can of beer out of the refrigerator behind the bar and turned the television set on to a football game, while Audrey picked up a magazine and idly thumbed through it. An hour passed. Neither the game nor the magazine held much interest. Both of them glanced at their watches too often. Finally, Boyd got up, switched off the set and reached for his jacket. Audrey closed the magazine and stood up, too. "Where are you going?"

"Oh, no place in particular. I thought I'd wander around, check the horses or something. That was a lousy game."

She grabbed her own jacket. "I'll go with you."

THE FIRST THING Audrey noticed when they entered the barn was that the stall for Betty's horse was empty. That wasn't much cause for alarm, however. As Boyd had said, any number of things could have taken Betty away from the house.

"Let's see if we can find Jesse," he suggested when they left the barn.

Audrey nodded in agreement and stayed hard on his heels as he made his way to the bunkhouse.

They found Skeet Drummond sitting on his bunk, puffing on a cigarette and playing solitaire. The elderly cowboy was the only person around.

"Hi, Skeet," Boyd greeted.

"Howdy, Boyd." Then, seeing Audrey, Skeet scrambled to his feet. "Howdy, ma'am."

"Hello, Skeet. It's good to see you again. Please, don't get up."

But it wasn't in Skeet's nature to sit while a lady stood. "What can I do for you folks?"

"Seen Murdoch?" Boyd asked.

"Murdoch?" The old man squinted. "Jesse left."

"Left?"

"Yep. Drew his pay, collected his gear and jus' high-tailed it outta here. Said it was time for him to be movin' on. Right after breakfast, it was."

Boyd glanced at Audrey, who was thinking exactly what he was. Betty hadn't been seen since breakfast either. Anxiety tinged his voice as he turned back to Skeet. "Didn't happen to say where he was going, did he?"

"Nope, and nobody asked. He probably don't know where he's goin' hisself. Hell, Boyd—s'cuse me, ma'am—you know how the drifters are. Ain't one of 'em that don't have a bad case of itchy feet."

"Murdoch's been with us for some time now. He's no drifter," Boyd said.

Skeet cackled. "The hell he ain't . . . s'cuse me, ma'am. He's a cowpoke, ain't he?"

"Yeah, guess you're right. Tell me, Skeet, did he leave alone?"

"Reckon he did. At least, there wasn't nobody else around while he was packin'. Can't rightly say I actually *saw* him leave, though."

"Thanks, Skeet."

"Don't mention it. Nothing's wrong, is there?"

"I hope not."

Boyd took Audrey by the arm, and they left the bunkhouse. Outside they stopped and looked at each other worriedly. "Oh, Boyd, do you think they've gone off together?"

"The two of them on one horse?"

She shrugged and bit her bottom lip. "It's just such a coincidence, both of them disappearing right after breakfast."

"Yeah, I know."

"If she's gone off with that despicable man, I'll never forgive myself."

"None of this is your fault, Audrey."

"Yes, it is! I should have warned her about Jesse last night. I should have warned her about him when I first learned about their relationship, but I . . . I just kept telling myself it was none of my business. Actually, what I was doing was protecting *me*, and that's not right."

"No sense worrying about that now, hon. You do thrive on guilt, don't you? Come on, I've got some more checking to do."

First, Boyd ascertained that only one of the ranch's cars was missing—the Cadillac. His family wouldn't have driven all the way to Flagstaff for the weekend, so the Cadillac no doubt was parked at the airport in Tucson. Further investigation revealed that all of the horse trailers were on the premises. "Betty's definitely on horseback, and that means she can't have gone far," he told Audrey, clearly relieved.

Suddenly she turned to him with a start. "Betty's makeup," she exclaimed.

"What?"

"Her makeup was on her dresser. She doesn't use a lot of it, but she does use some, and it was sitting on her dresser. Women don't go off without their makeup, they just don't." The thought made her feel a little better.

Boyd pondered that a second, then said, "I have an idea. Let's take us a little ride around the ranch and see if we run into anything."

"What are you thinking?"

"Oh, I don't know. Maybe a rendezvous somewhere, like Summerfield camp. Go get in the pickup. I'll tell Maria we're leaving for a little while. I'll also tell her to keep Betty here if she shows up."

THEIR HOPES that Betty and Jesse might be at Summerfield camp were quickly dashed. The camp was deserted, and there were no signs that anyone had been near it since roundup. "There's only one other place on the ranch I can think of that she might be," Boyd speculated.

"Where's that?"

"My house. If she isn't there, and if she isn't at home, then we'll have to accept the fact that she's gone off somewhere. And there's a strong possibility she's with Jesse."

Audrey's heart sank. She felt so responsible for all this, and it was anything but a good feeling. "She promised me she wouldn't do anything until I got here."

"Yeah, but she's nutty about the guy. I'm afraid he could talk her into just about anything."

But as soon as the adobe house came into view a wave of relief swept through both of them. Betty's horse was tethered outside. "Thank heavens!" Audrey breathed.

That was encouraging, but when they parked the truck and got out, she hesitated. "Boyd, at least we know she hasn't left the ranch, but we don't know if Jesse's in there with her. Maybe we shouldn't barge in."

"Sorry, hon, but I've got to know what's going on."

Betty was alone. They found her in the bedroom sitting on the single bed, and she obviously had been crying. She was startled and none too pleased to see them. "What are you doing here?" she snapped at Boyd.

"Looking for you," he snapped back. "We were worried about you."

"Well, as you can see, I'm here and I'm fine."

"You don't look fine to me."

"Stop worrying and go back to the house. Obviously I want to be alone or I wouldn't be here."

Boyd ignored her. "How long have you been here?"

"Almost all day."

"Had anything to eat?"

Betty shook her head. "Not since breakfast, but I'm not hungry."

"You got to eat something."

"Leave me alone!"

Audrey stepped forward. "Boyd, why don't you go make us some coffee?"

He hesitated, looking first at one woman, then the other. Finally he shrugged. "Okay. Coffee it is."

When he'd left the room, Audrey closed the door and faced Betty. "Want to talk about it?"

"Not particularly."

"Maybe you should. Sometimes it helps."

Betty's mouth twisted wryly, and her chin trembled. "I followed your advice, Audrey. Last night I finally told Jesse how Dad felt about our relationship. I also told him I was willing to give up everything to marry him."

"And?" Audrey prodded, though she was sure she knew what had happened.

"I thought he'd be happy, but he acted so strangely. He kept saying there had to be a better solution. Naturally I supposed he just hated to see me on the outs with my father. I kept telling him I knew what I was doing." Betty laughed a dry, hollow laugh. "I guess it finally got through to him that I was dead serious. He said he'd see me in the morning and we'd talk about it. But this morning when I went to the bunkhouse after breakfast, I discovered he'd...gone. Just packed up and went away without a word."

"Oh, Betty..." Audrey went to sit beside her and put an arm around her shoulders. She'd never seen a sadder face, and her heart went out to the woman. "I'm so sorry...not that he left, since that's the best thing that could have happened to you. But I am sorry that you have to go through this."

"Can you beat it, Audrey? He just left. I'm having such a hard time believing any of it."

"I know, I know."

"He didn't want *me* at all. He wanted everything that came with me. How could I have been taken in by that kind of man? I thought I was a whole lot smarter than that."

"Lord, Betty, you're taking me back farther than I want to go."

Betty looked at her with a puzzled frown. "What?"

Audrey smiled ruefully. "What I'm saying is, I'll bet there aren't three dozen women in the world who don't have a Jesse somewhere in their past. Unfortunately, it seems to be carved in stone that we have to go through a Jesse as part of the education process."

Betty was struggling with her emotions. "It's just so...embarrassing."

"I know." *Someday,* Audrey thought, *I might tell her the whole story. Someday, but not now.*

"How do I explain?"

"You don't. Only a handful of people even know about you and Jesse, and no one's going to be thoughtless enough to ask any questions. I know it's hard, but try to be grateful that you found out about him before you married him.

Somehow I don't think that a man with avarice in his soul would make a very good husband.''

"Yeah.'' Betty sighed wearily. "This morning, once I realized he'd actually gone, I thought . . . I thought my heart was breaking. Now I think I'm just mad.''

"That's a good sign.''

"Trouble is, I don't know who I'm madder at . . . Jesse for being such a louse or me for being so stupid.''

Audrey was reliving the whole thing all over again. "I know exactly how you feel.''

Betty looked at her, feeling a rare kind of communion passing between them. "You really do understand, don't you? Was there a Jesse in your past, Audrey?''

"Oh, yes. You'll get over it, I promise. That's straight from the horse's mouth.''

Betty lapsed into thought for a minute. Then heaving another sigh, she got to her feet. "I guess I'll go back to the house before it gets dark.''

"Boyd always keeps food on hand. Don't you want something to eat?''

"Not really. I'll leave you and Boyd alone. I'm afraid I'm not very good company right now. I'll go home and find something to do. Enough of this sitting around feeling sorry for myself.''

Audrey stood and hugged Betty impulsively. "Tomorrow will be better, take my word for it.''

"Anything will be better than today. Thank God Dad won't be around tonight. I really don't think I could take him.'' Betty managed a small smile. "You know something, Audrey. I'll bet anything I'm not the first woman Jesse's pulled this stunt on.''

It was with a great deal of effort that Audrey kept a straight face. "You know something, I'll bet you're right.''

"I feel sorry for his next victim. He's bound to succeed one of these days.''

"Let's hope not.''

"Thanks for being such a good friend.''

"You're welcome.''

"I'll see you guys back at the house."

Audrey walked with her to the door and stood on the porch watching her ride off. Then she went into the kitchen looking for Boyd. He wasn't there, but the back door was open, so she went outside. He was sitting on the porch steps, staring off into the distance. When he heard the door open, he turned and eyed her quizzically.

"Betty went home," she told him. "I thought you were going to make coffee."

"I didn't figure you really wanted coffee. That was just an excuse to get me out of the room so you two could indulge in women talk."

Smiling, she sat down beside him. "How perceptive you are."

"How's Betty?"

"Older and wiser."

"And Jesse's really gone?"

"Right. Long gone." Audrey laid her head on his shoulder and slipped her arm through his. "Good ol' Jesse. It's hard to believe anyone could be such a thorough bastard. I think he's the only person I've ever known who doesn't have one redeeming quality. You just wonder what goes on in that head of his, how he can look at himself in the mirror."

"Is Betty taking it hard?"

"Yes, but she'll survive. We always seem to. She's beginning to get mad, so the healing process has already begun."

They sat together in companionable silence for a few minutes until Boyd said, "I'm thinking that any minute you're going to tell me what the hell's going on."

"That's right. You don't know, do you? Last night on the phone Betty was in a real snit. She said she didn't care if your father disowned her. She was going to run off with Jesse, and they were going to start out on a shoestring. I could imagine how Jesse would love hearing that, so I told her she ought to tell him exactly how she felt. She did."

"You figured he would split, right?"

"Of course. Leopards don't change their spots... or is it zebras their stripes? I feel sorry for Betty, but in time she'll come to see this as the best thing that could have happened to her.''

''And it's not too bad for you, for us, either.''

She pulled away slightly and looked at him. ''For us? How's that?''

''There's no need for anyone else to ever know about your father. Not my family, not anyone but you and me.''

Audrey pursed her lips, thinking, hoping, doubting. ''I don't know, Boyd. Is that honest?''

''It really isn't anyone else's business. It belongs in the past. Who needs to know?''

''But things have a way of getting out. What if someone from that past shows up one day, the way Jesse did? I could be an embarrassment for you and your family.''

A smile of pure adoration crossed Boyd's face. ''Audrey, I'm sure that you'll never be an embarrassment for me. And before long everyone in the family is going to love you so much they'll feel the same way I do.''

Her head went back to his shoulder. ''Oh, Boyd, maybe it's because things went so badly for me for so long, but... I'm almost afraid to believe everything has worked out this well.''

''Believe it, and enjoy it.''

Her gaze strayed across the grounds to the family cemetery in the distance. ''Wouldn't Bert be astonished to see what's happened to us because of that last-minute whim of his?''

''Yeah, probably. Astonished and pleased.''

''It so easily might not have happened. What if I hadn't stopped to talk to him that first day? He often said it was our little chats that brought him back again and again. If I hadn't taken the time to speak to him, he might never have come back to the hotel. You and I might never have met.''

''Audrey, I know deep down inside that wherever you were, whatever you'd been doing, you and I would somehow have met each other.''

''You believe in fate!'' she cried.

"I guess I do. What else could have kept me single so long? I had to be free for you."

"That's such a nice thought. It appeals to me."

"Love me?"

"Of course I do. Common sense tells me it really isn't reasonable for me to know that so soon, but I do."

"Are you going to marry me?"

"Probably."

"Only probably?"

Her eyes sparkled merrily. "Oh, I'm sure I'll marry you eventually, but I think you owe me something first."

"Hon, what in the devil are you talking about?"

"A courtship," she explained patiently. "Boyd, we've only known each other a few weeks. Admittedly, we've spent a lot of time together during those weeks, but nothing about this relationship has been exactly orthodox. We've never even had a bona fide date. A woman likes to be pursued a little. Now it seems that all you did was smile at me a couple of times, and I was in your arms."

"It didn't seem that easy to me."

"I'd like to see you have to work at it, have to rearrange your schedule in order to be in Phoenix, become frustrated with longing, that sort of thing."

"This is a fey side of you I haven't seen before." He grinned that irresistible grin. "You want to be wooed, huh?"

"Yes, is that so unusual?"

Boyd pretended to think about it seriously. "I hope you realize that a courtship won't tell you much about what kind of husband I'll be."

Audrey snuggled against him, so happy she thought she would explode. "Oh, I know what kind of husband you're going to be—thoughtful, considerate, devoted, loyal."

"You make me sound like a Boy Scout." His arm went around her, and he drew her closer. "All right, one courtship coming up. Trouble is, I'm not sure how one goes about conducting such a ritual. Any suggestions? What do I do?"

Raising her face, she kissed him soundly. "Surprise me."

CHAPTER EIGHTEEN

HE DID. In fact, he overwhelmed her. Boyd Benedict's courtship of Audrey Hamilton would remain the chief topic of gossip among the Greenspoint's staff for some time to come. It began in earnest on Monday morning when Audrey returned to work. She had left Boyd sleeping soundly at her apartment, yet she had been in her office less than half an hour when Marie Collier, the hotel's florist, showed up with a lavish bouquet of pink carnations. Naturally, they were from Boyd.

What a sweet gesture, Audrey thought, reaching for the phone to dial her number and thank him. There was no answer, which meant he was on his way back to the Triple B. She had to wait for his phone call that night. "The flowers are just lovely, Boyd. I wish you could see them. I can't even remember the last time someone sent me flowers."

She thought she heard him chuckle. "Audrey, you haven't seen anything yet."

The next morning she discovered what he meant. Another bouquet arrived, then another the following day, and that continued every day of the week.

"I'm running out of creative ideas," Marie complained. "How do you feel about green plants?"

"How long is this supposed to go on?" Audrey asked.

"The gentleman said I'm to bring you fresh flowers every day until he tells me to stop."

"Oh, I don't believe this!"

"Hey, enjoy it, Audrey. How many women ever have something this exciting happen to them? Besides, your generous boyfriend has sure done wonders for my business."

Peter walked into Audrey's office on the fourth day of the barrage, glanced around and asked, "Did someone die?" But Helen was enthralled. "This is absolutely the most romantic thing I ever heard of! I could cry."

When Boyd showed up at her apartment Friday night he was carrying red roses and wearing a tuxedo. In formal clothes he was something to behold, but Audrey couldn't hide her exasperation. "It's a good thing I don't have hay fever. You're crazy, you know that?"

"You're right. I'm crazy about you."

"Boyd, this is ridiculous! Please stop wasting your money."

"Hon, you wanted to be wooed. Please let me do it my own way. Go put on your finery. I'm taking you to a place that's so expensive there are tassels on the menus."

And so it went. Each gesture was more outrageous than the last. Frugal Audrey was appalled at the way he was spending money, but since Boyd obviously was having the time of his life, she suffered through weeks of the onslaught. She hated letting all the lovely flowers just wither on her desk, so she found a senior citizens' center where they were more than appreciated. It wasn't long before she was wearing a magnificent diamond ring on her left hand, and the weekends with Boyd were a delight. More than once she wondered how much of what was going on his family was aware of. Not much, she suspected, since she hadn't heard from Betty. Mostly, however, she just enjoyed the thrill of the pursuit. It would have been an exciting experience for anyone, but was especially so for a woman who had been alone such a long time.

Still, she remained adamant about not rushing into marriage. She felt they had all the time in the world. She didn't doubt that they would marry eventually, but she was convinced they would never regret moving slowly.

Actually, when she was being completely honest with herself, she admitted to some lingering doubts about how she would fit into the Benedict family structure. She had thought and thought about it but had yet to pinpoint a niche where she would fit comfortably. That was the only unsettling aspect of an idyll she would remember the rest of her life.

In the end, it was the singing telegram that stripped away the last vestiges of her resistance. For weeks Audrey had been aware of Boyd's growing impatience with the delay, and she had more or less braced herself for some new excessive gesture on his part. But when four fresh-faced young men in red-and-white striped jackets confronted her in the lobby late one afternoon to croon a saccharine love song, to the delight and merriment of all onlookers, she could only hide her flaming face with her hands and shake her head in disbelief. This was too much!

Audrey intended calling Boyd the minute she got home that evening, but the call wasn't necessary. He was waiting at her front door, grinning from ear to ear.

"It's only Thursday," she admonished.

"I know, but I came a day early. I wanted to find out if you got the telegram."

"Of course I got it. So did everyone else in the hotel. It was the highlight of the day. They're all holding their collective breath, waiting to see what preposterous thing you'll come up with next."

He stood aside while she opened the door, then followed her inside. "That was it, the pièce de résistance. I can't think of anything else to do."

"Good."

"Are you going to marry me?"

Audrey tossed her handbag onto the sofa and turned to slip her arms around his waist. "Yes, you win. No more of this nonsense. I accept your proposal." She looked at him, her eyes earnest. "But first we need to talk about something."

"Okay. Talk away."

"My future," she said solemnly.

Boyd didn't understand. "Your future? You're going to be my wife."

"Beyond that, I mean. It's something I've been thinking about a lot lately. Boyd, I simply can't live the way your mother and Sara do. I suppose there was a time when I thought my own life would be like theirs someday, but that was another time, another world. I've been working for years now, and I've changed. I'm going to have to do something more meaningful than attend teas and bridge luncheons for the wives of prominent men."

"Got any suggestions?"

"Well, I've been thinking.... I know I'm a little rusty, but with practice I could probably help Betty around the ranch."

"Okay, we'll give it some thought," Boyd said decisively. "Hon, I never had any intention of turning you into Susie Homemaker. The ranch will be home, but you'll have full rein to do whatever your inclinations dictate."

Audrey melted against him, holding him tightly. "I'm so relieved everything's settled. Now all we have to do is get married. Do you suppose we can just slip away quietly and do it?"

Boyd laughed. "I'm afraid not, hon, sorry. Mom will never let you get away with that."

OF COURSE he turned out to be correct. Weddings were right down Elizabeth's alley. Once Boyd had told his family of their plans to get married, his mother was in almost daily phone contact with Audrey. The arrangements became more and more elaborate, and soon Elizabeth's invitation list contained the names of three hundred of the Benedicts' "nearest and dearest." With resignation Audrey entered into the spirit of the occasion, juggling the preparations with her job.

It was decided that the actual ceremony would be held at the Greenspoint. The hotel staff were the only family Audrey had, and she conceded that only a banquet room would accommodate Elizabeth's crowd. By any standard, it was going to be a stunning affair, exactly the sort of wedding Audrey's mother would have insisted on. And despite the Benedicts' protests, she paid for the whole show herself out f her sizable inheritance. She thought Bert would have ked that.

On the day of the actual ceremony, she stood in the small oom off the banquet hall where she had dressed. Helen and etty had just left, and in the distance Audrey could hear e organ music. She hadn't expected to be nervous, but she as. Her stomach was executing flip-flops. Too late she de- ded she should have eaten breakfast.

There was a knock on the door. "Come in," she called nd turned, expecting to see Peter, who was walking her own the aisle. Instead, the commanding figure of Buck B. enedict strolled into the room. Attired in a three-piece avy-blue suit, Boyd's father presented an even more im- osing picture than usual.

Buck did nothing to still her stomach. Although she had een huddled with Elizabeth, Betty and even Sara for weeks, udrey had seen precious little of Buck. She doubted they ad exchanged more than half a dozen sentences since the gagement had been announced. She couldn't shake the otion that despite his overt politeness, Boyd's father wasn't ompletely pleased about the marriage.

"Mr. Benedict," she said quietly, though her pulses were ounding.

"Audrey, how lovely you look."

"Thank you."

"I hope you don't mind this intrusion."

"Of course not. It's no intrusion."

"I wanted to have a word alone with you. Things may get ctic later on."

"Of course."

"Boyd and I had a long talk last night. Is it true that ou're concerned over what your...er, official job will be ce you join the family?"

"Well, I...I'm not sure that *concerned* is the word...." Buck interrupted. "I understand that you're not the least terested in the social end of it, but that's fine. Sara and my fe handle that admirably. And, of course, Boyd and Betty anage to keep the ranch running smoothly."

Audrey felt her breath catch. Was he trying to tell her there really wasn't anything for her to do?

"Yet," Buck went on, "it's important that we all contribute to the common good, so I have a suggestion for you. How about this hotel?"

Audrey's eyes widened. "The . . . Greenspoint?"

"Yes. Boyd and I agree that it's time we took more of an active interest in the place. Unfortunately, not one of us knows a thing about hotel management. You, on the other hand, do. I like the idea of having one of the family show up here a couple of times a week to keep an eye on things and report back. Does that appeal to you, my dear?"

Appeal to her? Audrey couldn't believe it! She had assumed the Greenspoint would become part of the past. "Oh, it more than appeals to me. I'd *love* the job!"

"Good, good. Then it's settled." Buck reached out and patted her shoulder, then, in a surprising move, leaned forward and placed a kiss on her forehead. Audrey couldn't have been more astonished if he had slapped her. "Welcome to the family, Audrey."

For her it was a stunning moment. She was rendered almost speechless and felt dangerously close to tears. "Th. . . thank you."

Buck turned to leave, thought of something and faced her again. "You may be pleased to hear that my son let me know in no uncertain terms how he feels about my political plans for him. I won't say I'm not disappointed, but. . . When you get to be my age you better have learned to cope with disappointments. If you haven't, you're a fool . . . and I'm no fool." He shot her a smile. "I'll see you after you two are safely hitched."

He strode out, and a moment later Peter strode in. "What a beautiful bride you make, Audrey! Are you ready? The family's just been seated."

She picked up her bouquet and took Peter by the arm. "As ready as I'll ever be."

They reached the double doors just as Betty, as maid of honor, started down the aisle. Audrey and Peter stood or

he threshold for the brief moment before the "Wedding
March" began. Instinctively her eyes flew to the flower-
edecked altar and to the minister's left where Boyd and
Brent stood, looking stiff and uncomfortable in the elabo-
ate formal clothes. But the moment Boyd saw her, his face
roke into a wide smile, and he shot her a thumbs-up ges-
ure. At least half the wedding guests saw it and laughed.
Beside her, Peter laughed, too.

Only Boyd would do something like that, Audrey thought
s she began the long walk down the aisle. It was an auspi-
ious beginning.

EPILOGUE

AUDREY AND BOYD had been back from their honeymoon in Mexico less than a week. Boyd was spending the day at the family's offices in Tucson, and Audrey was alone in the adobe house, arranging the furniture that had been delivered that morning. All the new appliances had been hooked up, and that night she was going to prepare her first meal on the new gas range. Up until now, Boyd had had to do most of the cooking since the old wood cook stove had completely baffled her. She couldn't say she had been at all sorry to see the cast-iron monstrosity carted away.

Glancing around, she noted with satisfaction that the house was beginning to look as if someone actually lived in it, and tonight they were having company. Betty was coming to dinner and bringing a man named David Lindsey with her. David was a young Tucson attorney who had recently purchased some acreage in the valley and was venturing into the horse-raising business. His name had been popping up more and more frequently in Betty's conversation, so Audrey held out great hopes for the relationship. But even if nothing came of it, this was the first time her sister-in-law had shown the slightest interest in a man since Jesse's hasty departure.

It was midafternoon when Audrey heard a car pull to a stop in front of the house. Since it was far too early for Boyd to be getting home, she hurried to a window to look out. A well-dressed, middle-aged man was emerging from a blue sedan and starting up the walk. As he neared, she recognized him as one of the family's lawyers. She had met him once before, months ago when he'd officially notified her of

er inheritance, but his name escaped her completely. She
aited for his knock, then went to open the door.

"Good afternoon," she greeted.

"Hello, Audrey," the man said, extending his hand. "I'm
George Blackburn. Do you remember me?"

"Of course. It's nice to see you again."

"I stopped at the house, and Betty told me I could find
ou here. I was on vacation when your wedding took place.
Otherwise I would have gotten this to you before now." He
eached into his coat pocket and withdrew an envelope,
which he handed to her.

Audrey glanced down at the envelope. There was no
tamp, no letterhead, no return address on it. Only her
ame—Audrey Hamilton Benedict—was scrawled across it.

"It's from Bert," the lawyer explained.

Audrey's head came up with a jerk. "Bert?" she gasped.

George Blackburn nodded. "He gave it to me the day he
made the final revisions in his will. He said the letter was for
our eyes only. His instructions were to give it to you in
erson if you married Boyd. If either of you married any-
ne else, I was to destroy the letter unopened."

"Good Lord!" Audrey's heart began racing. A letter
rom Bert concerning Boyd and herself? How could that be?
The lawyer had to be mistaken. It didn't make any sense.
Then she remembered her manners. "I...ah, would you like
o come in for coffee, Mr. Blackburn?"

"No, thanks just the same. I imagine you're anxious to
ead the letter, and I really must be getting back to the city.
My apologies for the delay."

"That's quite all right. Thank you for coming all the way
ut here."

"Don't mention it. I'm sure I'll be seeing you again.
Please give Boyd my regards...and belated congratula-
ons."

The lawyer left, and Audrey hurried inside, alive with
uriosity. She sat cross-legged on the sofa, and her fingers
hook as she tore open the envelope. The letter had been

written in a bold, rather unsteady script. Her eyes widened as she began reading.

My dear Audrey,
If you're reading this, then my plans have worked out exactly as I envisioned. How gratifying! I've known for some time now that my days on this old planet are numbered, and I decided that getting you and Boyd together would be my last hurrah. It took me a while to figure out how to do it, though. I wish I could have seen the look on your face when you found out about the money. Was Boyd the one who gave you the news? I hope you went right out and did something frivolous and extravagant with it, but knowing you, I'll bet you didn't. I also wish I could have seen the look on Buck's face when the will was read, but that's another story entirely.

Back to you and Boyd. From the day I met you, I wanted the two of you to get together. Then as time went by and we became friends, I began planning to leave you a little stipend when I went to my reward. Gradually the two ideas melded into one. I reasoned that a modest sum would go unnoticed since I left a little money to a lot of people my family doesn't know. One day it dawned on me: I'd simply leave you enough to make everyone sit up and take notice. A hundred grand was bound to raise even a Benedict's eyebrows; at least it would make everyone curious about you. I figured Buck's curiosity would get the best of him, and if he ran true to form, he'd dispatch Boyd to the hotel to find out who in the devil you were. And once my grandson met you, I was sure my job would be done. I'm sure that's what happened, just as sure as if I were there to see it with my own eyes.

Why, you're probably asking yourself about now, if I wanted you and Boyd to meet, didn't I just drag him to the hotel and introduce you? A couple of reasons. One, I would have blown my cover, and I enjoyed the heck out of being anonymous. Two, Boyd's gotten a trifle touchy over my matchmaking attempts in the past. I didn't want to turn him off before you had a chance to turn him on.

So, my dear, I sign this with a great sense of personal satisfaction. You considerably brightened an old man's final days. I never made a million dollars that meant as much to me as the fifty bucks you loaned me. I trust you consider the debt repaid with interest. I hope you and Boyd reproduce like crazy and have a wonderful life together.

Affectionately,
Bert

P.S. Don't let anyone talk you into putting the money back in the family coffers. Take it and have a ball.

Audrey was crying so hard when she finished the letter at the print swam before her eyes. Setting it on the anking-new, glass-topped coffee table, she went in search a tissue, then slipped on a jacket and walked out the back oor. She knew there were at least a dozen things she could ve been doing in the house, but she was too overcome th emotion to concentrate on any of them.

Her misty eyes scanned the horizon. It was winter now, d the landscape was at its bleakest. Before they knew it, wever, spring branding season would be upon them. The rd would be turned out to pasture to feast on the grass at grew thick and lush during the summer rainy season, d the cycle would begin all over again. It wasn't too much hope that by the time next fall's roundup rolled around e would be too pregnant to be able to go along.

Without consciously realizing she was doing it, she ossed the expanse between the house and the cemetery, pped over the picket fence and went to stand in front of rt's grave.

"You conniving old darling," she sniffed. "I can't be- ve you did that, went to all that trouble! And to think it rked out exactly as you envisioned. Wait until I tell Boyd.

He's so fond of saying that fate brought us together, that h[e]
would have found me no matter where I was. I can hardl[y]
wait to tell him that 'fate' has another name, and it's Be[r]-
tram B. Benedict.''

Audrey didn't know how long she stood there, ha[lf]
laughing and half crying, but she thought it must have bee[n]
a long time. The air was becoming quite chilly, but sh[e]
seemed rooted to that spot, almost mesmerized. She was lo[st]
in a private reverie, oblivious to everything around he[r,]
when she heard her name being called. Turning, she sa[w]
Boyd standing on the back porch, waving one arm hig[h]
above his head.

"Hey!" he shouted.

"Hey, yourself!" she called back.

He motioned her toward the house. She waved to ind[i]-
cate she'd be right along, but first she turned to glance at th[e]
headstone again. "Boyd's home, so I've got to go no[w,]
Bert, but I'll be back...often. Thanks so much...for ev[-]
erything.''

She stepped over the fence again and ran to the house a[nd]
her future.